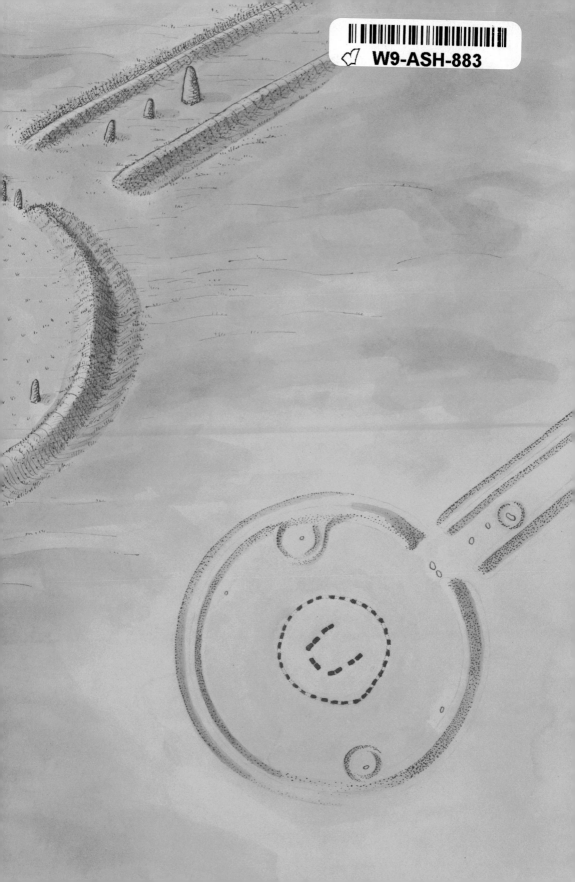

PILLAR
OF THE SKY

PILLAR OF THE SKY

A NOVEL BY

CECELIA HOLLAND

ALFRED A. KNOPF   NEW YORK   1985

THIS IS A BORZOI BOOK
PUBLISHED BY ALFRED A. KNOPF, INC.

Copyright © 1985 by Cecelia Holland

All rights reserved under International and Pan-American Copyright
Conventions. Published in the United States by Alfred A. Knopf, Inc.,
New York, and simultaneously in Canada by Random House of Canada
Limited, Toronto. Distributed by Random House, Inc., New York.

Library of Congress Cataloging in Publication Data

Holland, Cecelia, 1943–   Pillar of the sky.

1. Stonehenge (England)—History—Fiction.
2. Great Britain—History—To 55 B.C.—Fiction.   I. Title.
PS3558.0348P5   1985   813'.54   84-48659
ISBN 0-394-53538-3

Manufactured in the United States of America

FIRST EDITION

AUTHOR'S NOTE

For an object as old and as famous as Stonehenge is, surprisingly little is known about it. Certainly nothing is known of its meaning and value to the peoples who made it, over a period of a thousand years, first digging up the ground to build a circular embankment, then, in fits and starts, digging holes, into which they sometimes set stones. We have a good idea of where the stones stood; we know pretty much where they came from; we can explain how neolithic farmers, without the wheel, without beasts of burden, without practical metal tools, could do the work. Yet even in these simple physical facts there is much doubt.

So, scoured of meaning, Stonehenge takes whatever we bring to it and gives us back ourselves. Religious people take it for a temple; astronomers use it as an observatory. In the nineteenth century a railroad man even wanted to turn it into a train station. Being a storyteller, I see it as a piece of story, in an age when stories were the greatest power that people could bring to deal with the whirling universe around them, an era that is on us still.

I

AEL'S SON

The sun was rising. Mother of all things, she sent her foreguard on first, to light the sky, and make the earth ready, and at her first warm touch, all life awoke. The birds began to sing and twitter and cry in the high grass, in the trees scattered here and there over the sunken slopes and hollowed hillsides, in the gardens of the People, in the thatches of the longhouses. The little brown river mice darted out of their lairs along the bank, and the goats rose, bleating, from their beds of straw, and went to wait by the withy gate to be milked. The doors of the longhouses opened, and the People came out, to stretch and yawn in the blessed sunlight, and the great door of the round-house itself was thrown open, although mighty Ladon was not there; yet the roundhouse held enough of his power without his presence.

In the thickets along the river, the band of boys stirred; quicker than the grown-ups, because they had less to do, the boys scurried out over the world, looking for something to eat. While their mothers in the longhouses were still yawning over the morning fire, the boys ranged up through the People's gardens, looking for birds and snakes, and scattered along the edge of the forest to find wild berries.

Leader of the boys' band was Ladon's son, and he was tall and fair, his body handsomely smoothed and sleeked with a layer of fat, his clothes lovingly made by all the women of the People. He carried a big stick in his hand, and struck any boy with it who came too close to him, and shouted orders to them, and whatever they found, they brought him half.

As it was with his father, so it was with Ladon's son; each boy fought to bring him more than any other boy, and he hardly had to lift his hand to get what he wanted.

Now the sun was up. Her kind and giving light lay over the land of the People, the broad uneven ground that lay between the forest on the east and the broken hills to the west. This was female land, lying wide and rich under the grass, not flat, but given to swollen low hills rising gently into the sun, and swales and soft subsiding places where the sun reached only at midday. The pines and piney shrubs that had once covered all this ground now were giving way, as the climate grew drier, as the marshes filled in, to open grassland where the soil lay over stubborn chalk, to oaks and ash where the land was more hospitable to deep-rooted trees, but to the People these were changes so slow and friendly that they remarked them only in stories.

In the sunlight the women left the longhouses, and climbed up the slope toward the gardens. It was now midsummer, a little past the Great Gathering, and in the irregular patches that the women worked, the crops stood tall and green: barley, with heavy heads, and vetch that they staked up, so that the mice would not eat the developing pods, and onions bulging out of the soil. The women carried their tools with them, picks of deer antler, rakes of wood with flint teeth, hoes made of shell. The little children carried the baskets.

From the forest's edge, Ladon's son could look out and see all this industry, as if from above; he did not look for his mother among the bowing forms in the gardens. He was half a man already, and uninterested in low labor. Instead, he led his band in a straggle along the margin of the forest, looking half the while for berries, and the other half for Moloquin.

The other boys knew what to do. They charged here and there, to reach a clump of brambles first and pick the ripe fruit, and some even ventured a little into the forest, giving brave yells and stamping their feet on the ground, looking here and there for their enemy. Ladon's son strolled along eating a handful of fruit. It was past the time for the little red berries called mother's-kisses, too soon still for the fat purple thorny ones called bear-blood-drops, and he grimaced over the sour stuff he had been given and cast them down. The next boy who dared bring him green fruit he would thump with his stick.

Then: "Moloquin! Moloquin!"

He sprang high into the air at the shout. Ahead of him, where the oak trees pressed in upon the brow of a hill, the boys were racing toward a small spring marked by thickets, and as they ran, they yelled. Many of them brandished sticks. Ladon's son broke into a gallop after them.

He yelled with them; he waved his stick over his head. All converged on the thicket. Just before they reached it, a brown naked boy burst out of the cover and ran away from them.

The halloos and whistles of the boys' band doubled. Many of

them heaved their weapons at Moloquin before they were near enough to have a chance of hitting him, and untouched, the woods' orphan darted away into the high grass and suddenly vanished. Like the open-nesting bustards he could disappear at will. Ladon's son, panting, led the others in a broad range across the slope where he had seen Moloquin last.

They slowed to a walk, puzzled. Ladon's son poked with his stick at the ground, banged with his stick on a tuft of brambles, and looked up toward the forest looming above him to his right. The forest was dangerous, evil, and dark; part of the reason they all hated Moloquin was that he had come from the forest, and lived there still, when he was not haunting the places of the People. Ladon's son hated Moloquin for other reasons, too, and because his father had told him to hate Moloquin. Ladon's son did ever what his father told him. Now with his stick he went methodically along the curved uneven slope, prodding at hiding places, until abruptly the ground some paces before him seemed to explode, and the skinny brown boy sprang up from nowhere out of the grass and raced away, his tangle of black hair bouncing.

"Hiiyyaaah!"

The boys' band raced after him. Once again they threw sticks and stones after him, never hitting him. Moloquin led them off in a straight dash along the rising ground below the forest; here the grass was shorter and drier, and there was no place to hide, and the prey settled into a long hard run. Ladon's son with the rest of his band hung doggedly on the track. The stick grew heavy in his hand, but he dared not drop it: the stick meant his power to him. The breath in his lungs began to burn. Before him Moloquin ran always out of reach. When Ladon's son put on a burst of speed, Moloquin ran faster, as if he could see out of the back of his head; he never looked behind him, but ran with pumping arms and high-thrusting knees. When Ladon's son slowed down, tired, Moloquin too slowed, keeping the distance even between them.

They never caught Moloquin, however hard they chased him, and now, out of breath, his legs hurting, Ladon's son saw, ahead of them all, the ancient embankment and toppling stones of the dead place, and he stopped.

The boys stopped with him. No one wanted to go any closer to the place of the dead, and while Moloquin ran on toward it, they shouted and threw things and laughed at his folly.

"The spirits will suck his blood out," said Ladon's son, and the other boys clustered around him, loud with agreement, with new versions of this prediction.

"The spirits will eat his flesh!" "The spirits will gnaw on his bones!"

"Let's go home," said Ladon's son. "We should take the goats to grass, and maybe there will be some cheese for us." He laid his stick over his shoulder, feeling very jaunty at driving Moloquin away again. "He won't dare come near us any more." He strutted a few steps, although his legs were tired.

The boys fought to get close to him. The littlest, the newcomers to the band, were shoved away to the edge, and the biggest and strongest took up stations close by Ladon's son. In this pack they went down the sun-drenched slope, back toward the gardens where their mothers worked, to take the goats out to grass.

Young Moloquin knew no father. His mother had died of the bloody cough in the winter before he found the village. No one of the People cared for him, and Ladon hated him. All that they did not use themselves the People gave to Ladon; therefore Moloquin got nothing.

He stood at the top of the embankment and watched the boys' band go. They hated him, always chased him, occasionally got near enough to hurt him, but he longed for them; they gave him his only company. Today's chase had gone by too quickly for him. He stood on the embankment and yelled and waved his arms, but they ignored him, if they even saw him. He realized that he had come here too swiftly; they were afraid of this place, he was safe here, but alone here also.

He turned around and went down the inner wall of the bank. It was a vast circle of upthrown earth and chalk, not a complete ring, but broken to the northwest and to the east, as if to let people in, but the People almost never came in here. They came here only to leave their dead in the grass within the bank. Even now there were two bodies lying near the foot of the tall stone at the far side of the circle—one an old woman, the other a baby. The crows were picking on them, bold, careless of Moloquin's presence. He walked across the grass, going in between two of the standing stones, to his favorite place, the big rough stone at the north end; he slept in the hollow at its foot.

He loved this place. He felt none of the horror here that the People did. It was his own little world, round as the world was, bounded by the horizon of the top of the bank. There were no people, aside from the two dead ones, but there were the stones, several of them standing here and there, and a great many of them in a ring. The ring-stones were falling over and some lay buried in the grass. Above was only the brilliant, blazing sky.

He loved this place because his mother was here. She had died here. When he needed her he came here and she always answered him.

Sitting in the hollow at the foot of the big stone, he shut his eyes, thinking of his mother, and his heart grew soft and sore. Tall she had been, or seemed, to a child, her long hair hanging to her waist, her voice like a blast of the winter cold when she was angry, her arms like the warmth of the sun when she was kind to him. When she died he had been terrified, as if the world itself would end.

Blood burst from her lips whenever she coughed. They had been deep in the forest, far away from here. She said, "Take me as I tell you," and he had struggled to carry her weight, and she had leaned on sticks and against trees, and like that, bit by bit, they crept through the forest and came at last to the grassland's edge. Her body then so lean and bony he could see every rib. He wept as he half-carried her, half-dragged her along. Her voice drove him on, rasping and bubbling. "Keep going. Fail me, I'll kill you, boy, I will take you with me. Keep going, stupid weakling." At last he had pulled her into the circle of the bank, and there, exhausted, they both sank down into the high grass.

And there she died; he had seen the spirit pass away out of her, rise up from her like the dew rising in a vapor out of the grass when the sun shone on it. He clung to her, he called her back, he shook her. She would not come back to him. He dared not leave her. All his short life she had ruled him, fed him, taught him, beaten him when he was wrong, loved him when he was good; without her he knew nothing.

He chased the crows away from her; he sat by her for days, although his stomach grew taut and painful and his throat burned with thirst, he clung close to his mother. Then, one day, the first people he had ever seen other than her came into the circle.

There were six of them, carrying a seventh among them: another corpse. As they came they sang, and waved leafy branches around them, and one had a little pot of coals that gave off a sickly smoke. They entered the embankment through the northwestern opening and carried the body slowly into the center, laid it down, and put the leafy branches over it, all the while singing, and then they saw him.

And her. It was she who sent them screaming away. It was the sight of his mother who drove them with shrieks and howls away to the top of the bank, there to turn, to look again, and double their outcry. They ran away, and he followed them; they ran all the way down through the grassland, and he went after them, and there for the first time he saw Ladon's Village.

When he saw it he stopped in his tracks and stared, amazed, and joyous. Four great huts lay there, inside a fence of brush, huts much bigger than the one he and his mother had lived in, and the yards around them were full of people. Children like him, women like his mother, many many people, talking together, working, laughing, touching one another, breathing warm into one another's eyes, eyes meeting eyes, hugging one another, and his skin itched, longing for that, for closeness, protection, the welcome of his own kind. But when he went forward, gladly, toward them, his arms outstretched, hungry and wanting, they drove him away.

Now he lived along the edge of the village, shivering in the cold, stealing whatever he could find. In the summers he found fruit and roots and eggs to eat. Often he suckled the village goats while the goatherds were dozing in the sun.

In the winter he froze, sleeping in hollow logs, under drifts of leaves. He grew quick and lean, hollow-bellied, ready of hearing and sight, and hungry. Not merely for food. He watched the People every day, as often as he could, memorizing faces, overhearing words, drawing all he could from them in spite of their hate. They were his kind. Yet he was different; he was alone.

It was the Month of Low Water. In the village, the women carried water up from the river in their best baskets to give their plants to drink; the boys of the boys' band foraged up and down the river bank, looking for the chunks of flint that sometimes turned up in the chalk—these flints they took proudly to the roundhouse, to the men who worked stone. But these men were gone. With all the men of the People of Ladon's Village, they were used to spending this time along the northern river, fasting and sweating themselves and talking with the spirits whose world this really was.

Now they were returning, spilling down over the plain in a great disorderly swarm. In their midst, Ladon himself swept along in his litter, carried on the shoulders of a succession of lesser men. Wolftails hung from the rails of the litter, and bearskin covered it, black and glossy, as old as the lineage of the man who sat thereon, Ladon, the greatest chief of all the People.

He was a huge squat man, in the prime of his life, his belly rolled deep in fat. His hair was black as the bearskin. On his shoulders and chest the black hair grew thick as a pelt, an emblem of his splendor.

The other men fought to be close to him. They yearned for the favor of a single glance. If he spoke to them, they bragged to anyone who would listen of this sign of honor. If he frowned, they wilted like a plant that had been pulled up. Whenever the bearers of the litter tired, Ladon called for a change of hands, and then everybody fought for a place at the poles.

One alone did not. One alone was not a vessel for the mysterious power of the male, and she was fool enough not to care. Karella, headwoman of the kindred of the chief, had chosen to go with the men on their sacred way. She was the greatest of the storywomen of her people, and so made herself available to interpret the dreams and sickness and other encounters with the Overworld that the men might make in the course of their purification. Also as the headwoman of Ladon's kindred she considered it her duty to keep him under her eye.

She walked along by herself, off to one side of Ladon. Over her head and shoulders she wore a shawl, woven of the plucked wool of the goats, dyed brown and light brown and yellow with colors made of the skins of onions. She was a little, stooped woman, with a round face, her eyes merry, her voice sharp, her mouth habitually smiling. Her steps were short and quick, so that she seemed to scurry like a little brown mouse over the springing green of the world.

Although she and Ladon paid no outward heed to each other, there was between them a continual irritable awareness; they disliked each other. Ladon thought her too curious and too outspoken. Karella knew him to be a danger to all the People.

What that danger was had begun to press upon her through the

course of the purification rites. Over and over, she had seen how
Ladon spoke to the men of his son, and wrung promises from them
that his son should be the chief when Ladon died; over and over, the
men, under this pressure, and being often in the way of spirits, came
to her with dreams in which, disguised, she saw Ladon's ambition rise
to tower over the world.

Ladon was the chief. His power was great above all others in the
village; all that the People did, they brought to him, and he gave to
them whatever they needed, so that those who were old or orphaned
or weak or sick or stupid still managed. But he was chief by the will
of the headwomen, the old women who sat around the mill and knew
everything: they made the chief, and when Ladon died they would
make the next chief, not Ladon himself. If they did not—

She felt the past, the ways of the People, as a deep and well-
ordered space behind her; before her was an emptiness, a horror,
that must be formed and shaped like the past. If Ladon overturned
the ways of the People, everything might fly apart, the world
crumble.

It was more than that.

The power of the chief was a blood-power; it dwelled in his family, but it descended from layer to layer of the family not through the
fathers, whose seed was invisible, whose fecundity was ambiguous,
but through the women. They kept the gardens. They did the work.
They bore the babies. They and they alone conferred power: by elec-
tion to the chief, and through the chief's closest female relatives, to
the next generation of the family. When she saw this in her mind she
saw a passage of time and order so well knit together nothing could
pick it apart.

When she imagined that the power might jump from Ladon to
his son, she saw an abyss, and the power fell into the abyss and was
gone, and the People fell in after it and were gone as well. And now,
over the green rolling hills, here came Ladon's son himself.

The men all cheered his coming. All loved Ladon's son. Tall and
golden, he ran lightly toward his father with his arms upraised, and
after him came the band of boys, a stream of half-children, calling
and waving.

The whole great forward flow of the men stopped. Leaning
down from his litter, Ladon greeted his son with the gladness of a
man face to face with his immortality.

Karella went closer; the other men gave way to her, deferring to her, but Ladon saw her not. Ladon bent over the far side of the litter and wrung his son's hands and smiled into his face.

"Tell me what has happened, my dear boy."

"Nothing." Ladon's son shrugged, his face clear and open as the sky, and as empty of thoughts. "We have waited for you, Opa-Ladon."

"Are the fields growing? Are the women happy?"

"I suppose." The boy lifted one shoulder and let it sag again. All the interest in his leadership came from his father. He raised his smiling handsome face. "We chased Moloquin, nearly every day."

At that Ladon grunted. He straightened up in the litter, his face bound into a frown, and then he saw Karella and his gaze sharpened. He and the old storywoman stared at each other a moment. She drew her shawl closer around her, her eyes narrow. Finally, simultaneously, they looked away.

The procession began again, with Ladon's son walking along beside the litter, the men near him speaking to him fondly, ignoring their own sons who leapt and ran around them, noisy as crows. Karella drifted out to the edge of the swarm.

Ladon's son. They had tried to give him a name—all the boys had milk-names, of course, that their mothers gave them, but when they left their mothers and went to the boys' band, they got new names. But nothing had stuck to Ladon's son. They had tried several but no one had remembered them. When the People looked on this tall fair boy they saw only one thing, and that was what they called him.

When they saw that other one, they knew only one thing, and that was what they called him: Moloquin, the Unwanted One. But that had become a name, somehow; the accent fell on the first syllable, as in all men's names, not on the middle one, as it would have done had the phrase been simply a description of him. Moloquin had a name, however unkind it was.

Moloquin. She rolled it around in her mind, and as she considered it, the thought grew round and real to her: here was a way to deal with Ladon.

She hugged her shawl to herself. Casting an eye toward Heaven, she marked that there was still much daylight left—here in the deep of the summer, the sky held the light a long, long while after the sun withdrew—and she knew where to find Moloquin. She had time and knowledge, and no reason to fail. Quietly she slipped away from the horde of the men and went off toward the northeast.

Moloquin had spent the day ranging over the summery downlands, looking for something to eat, and had found nothing; he made a good cast of a stone at a bustard, but missed, as he usually did, and in the river he nearly caught a fish, diving down under the water and slowly, slowly creeping up on the grey shape hanging motionless in a pool under the bank, and then slipping his hands up, slowly, slowly, his lungs ready to burst, his lips shut against the tell-tale bubbles, but at the last instant with a flick of its tail the river-monster fled away. Now he went up over the rising land toward his place, and his body was tired and his heart was very low.

Halfway to his cold home, he passed close enough to the village to hear the singing and the drums and pipes, and to see the leaping fires. The men had come back, and the People rejoiced.

Locked out in the dark, he stood a moment and watched, and hated them, even as he longed for them; he saw how they touched one another, how they leaned together, body to body, and from some deep memory arose the feeling of being close to another, the shared warmth, the encircling arms, the safety. He hated them for denying him that, and he longed to have it again with them, that company, that value. Slowly he dragged himself on toward the cold stones.

When he trudged up over the embankment and looked down on the grassy circle he knew at once that someone else was there.

He did not see her at first. He did not smell or hear her. Yet he knew some other person occupied this place, his place, and the hairs on his back stood up, and his lips pulled back from his teeth in a growl. Crouched down a little, his hands fisted at his sides, he prowled in through the leaning stones.

"Here I am," said the calm voice, and he started up, his skin tingling; she was just to one side of him. In the failing light he had missed her utterly. He wheeled around, trying to look fierce.

She sat there at the foot of his stone, in the hollow he had made for himself, and she smiled at him. He knew her at once: Karella, storyteller, whom the little children ran after, begging for words.

"What are you doing here?" he cried. "This is my place. Go away."

He did not know all the right words, he made up some of them as he spoke. With his hands he swept at the air, to show her what he meant.

She did not move. She sat there cross-legged, as the women sat, her body formless in its enshrouding cloth, her hair the color of milkweed down. In the gathering dusk he could make out only the shape of her face. She raised one hand to him and said, "Come sit by me, and let us make a fire, I am very cold."

He frowned. He was not cold, and he seldom made fires, although his mother had taught him how. He stood uncertainly on the balls of his feet, ready to run or to leap on her. Storywoman. He had seen the others clustered tight around her while she talked, and although he had never been able to creep near enough to hear her voice, even from a distance the gestures of her hands and the look of her face in the firelight were compelling as an image. Now, abruptly, she leaned forward, and a spark glowed inside the round of her hands.

He sighed. The light spread up over her face, warming the old seamed skin, the deep eyes, and the curl of her mouth. Without any will of his own, he went forward, and sat down before her, sharing the light with her.

She nursed the sparks in the tinder, milking it gently with her hands to spread the fire through the tinder, and then she laid down the nursling in a little pile of twigs, and from beside her she took more wood and added that. He saw that she had gathered much wood, and made all ready for a fire; she must have waited here for a long while, and it came to him that she had waited here for him. That astonished him. He was used to spending his attention on the People; it was a new thing to have anyone pay him any witness in return.

The fire grew bolder and warmer, and sprang up through the peaked sticks she put together above it. In her eyes were tiny little fires. She said, "Are you hungry, boy?"

"I—"

He stopped, aware of how little he knew of words, and ashamed. His gaze fell to the flames. She reached behind her and brought forward a flat covered basket, with a rope for carrying over the shoulder, and opened it.

"Eat." She held out her hand, on it a piece of something.

An old memory twinged. He took the thing from her hand and

bit into it, and it was soft and flavorful. Once before he had eaten this. From his mother. Crouched by the fire with his feet under him, he ate it all.

She ate, her jaws moving contentedly, her gaze steadily on Moloquin. He wanted more, but he would not ask, and instead he locked his arms around his knees and watched her.

"Take another," she said, and he did, and ate it in a single gulp.

At that she smiled, and when she smiled her face was so lively and full of kindness that he had to smile too, and suddenly she was reaching across the fire, touching him, her hand warm on his arm. The touch was a shock; he jumped a little, and then was still, tensed, his arm burning where her hand rested on it. Seeing his discomfort, she drew back.

She said, "Boy, have you a name?"

"Moloquin," he said.

"No—the name your mother gave you."

"Moloquin," he said.

"No, no. Your mother, Ael, did she not call you something?"

"Ael," he said, catching the strange word.

"Ael, your mother."

All at once he realized what she meant, and the meaning of it broke on him, a flash like the lightning flash in his mind. He said, "My mother. Ael. That was her name. My mother was Ael."

He began to cry. Since her death he had not felt so near to her as he did now, when this stranger, this old woman, gave him what he had never had: his mother's name.

"Ael," he said, and threw his head back, his face raised toward Heaven, and he shouted, "Ael! Ael!"

The stones resounded; the vaulted sky itself boomed back his voice. He put his face into his hands and cried until he was empty.

At last he raised his head. She was watching him, the little old woman, magic in her eyes and in her mind, names and words and stories. He lunged across the fire at her and gripped her with both hands.

"My mother," he said, his throat thick. "My mother. My mother gone. Mother dead."

In his grip she was light as a husk. She laughed, half-smothered. "Moloquin," she said, "let me go." Her arms went around him, briefly, and tightened, and for a moment he was pressed against her, body to body, so close they were one body, warmth and life together. She said again, muffled, "Let me go," and he did.

He sat back. The cool air swept around him; he felt his skin all over, his boundary, his end, and was more lonely than he had ever been, even when his mother died. Once again he lowered his head and sobbed.

Karella said, "Moloquin, did she tell you anything? Your mother?"

"She told me—" he crept nearer the fire, and turned his gaze from Karella's face that scorched his inner eyes, turned his look to the blind and empty fire. "She told me, when I—she dead, I should go—that way." He waved toward the west. "Not go that way." He waved southward, toward the village of the People. Like bile in his throat there rose into his mind his first real understanding that she had meant him never to find the People. Maybe she had been right. He struggled with that; the words were not enough, the idea flittered away from him into the dark. He stared into the many-colored flames. "She hate me," he said, and covered his face with his hands. "She leave me."

"Moloquin," she said, and laid her fingers on his arm again. More used to the touch, he was at once calmed and steadied, and when she urged him closer to her he came to her, and she made him sit down by her. She said, "Did she tell you any stories?"

"Stories," he said, tentatively. His gaze searched her face. Her skin was wrinkled as an old apple.

She smiled at him. In a low, soft voice, she began, "In the beginning, everything was covered with ice, and nothing moved or breathed thereon. Then the Sun rose, and shone forth on the ice, and from the rising mist the first living being collected in the air, neither man nor woman, child nor adult, the creature of the Sun."

As she spoke, her hands moved, and she shaped out of the air that which inhabited the story; he saw the Sun rise, the mist climb up from the ice, and the first creature form from it; he forgot to breathe, or to wonder, but only listened.

"The Moon was jealous, because he could create nothing, and he slew the Sun's darling, and tore it into pieces. Then the Sun mourned her creature. She took up the body, and laid it out on the ground, and from the flesh made the world, of the bones the hills, of the hair the forests, of the blood the rivers. Looking on this world, the Sun rejoiced, and from the joy in her heart, she drew forth another being, as perfect as the first, unborn and undying, neither man nor woman, child or adult.

"Again the Moon grew jealous, and seized the feet of the Sun's new being, and the Sun held it by the arms, and they contested back and forth over it, until the being was pulled apart into two. And these two were the first man and the first woman, and they went forth into the world and made their home there."

He saw all this brought from nothing by the words she spoke, and by the forms her hands made. The words sank into him like drops of rain into dry earth.

"Now again the Moon grew jealous, and he waged a war against the Sun, and seized her and swallowed her whole. But the man and the woman saw what was happening to their divine mother, and they went up on a hilltop, very close to the Moon, and shouted and threw stones at him, until he disgorged the Sun, which rolled away safely across the sky once more. And the man and the woman rejoiced together, and the Sun shone on them, and they were blessed, and many were their children, and from each of their daughters came a kindred of the People, and so the whole world was inhabited."

Moloquin said, "The Moon and the Sun, I saw them together."

She nodded. "Yes, last winter. The Moon is evil. Sometimes he will try to devour the Sun, but she always escapes."

He said, "Where am I come from?"

Her face turned toward the fire, and her hands fell into her lap. It was as if she shut herself against him. The Moon swallowed her. She said, "I am not entirely sure I should tell you. What did your mother say to you?"

"She tell me what I tell you. Not to go that way. To go *that* way."

"No, I mean—about you. About her—why she—" she faced him again, her eyes wide. "She told you nothing."

His mouth moved; no sounds came out. He had run out of words. The story had filled him with new words, with space for the pictures of words, space for more stories. He tugged on her arm. "Tell me another."

She laughed. Raising her head, she looked up into the sky, and said, "To be truthful, boy, I am minded to spend the night here. It is very late, the moon is rising, it is a long, cold and fearful way to my own hearth." She put her hands down on the ground beside her, and she began to get up, carefully, bit by bit.

She was going. He flung out his hands toward her, terrified of losing her. "Stay here. Oh, please—" in a blind agony he went back to what he had done with his mother; he thrust out both hands to her and wept and cried, "Mama, Mama, please—"

She seized his wrists; she shook him roughly. "Now! Be still! Hah!" She shouted into his face and shook him hard and smacked him sharply on the cheek with her flattened hand. "Moloquin!"

He stopped, gasping, reassured; his mother had done exactly the same with him, whenever he cried.

She said, "Will you go down there with me?"

He leapt up, eager, delighted. "I go with you."

At that she laughed; she laughed like the bustard's high screechy cackle. They put the fire out and he took her basket for her and they went up out of that place and walked along toward the village, going down through a fold in the grassy slope. In the distance the fire in the center of the village was bright as blood.

Karella kept close by him; often she turned and cast her look all around her, peering sharply into the darkness like someone poking a stick into a hole. She came hardly to Moloquin's chin. As they walked he tried out the story again in his mind. Like food in his belly, the story made his mind fat. If all the People came from those first two, then was he one of the People? He had tried to ask Karella but she had turned away from him.

That was the bad part about having: it made not-having worse.

He wondered what it was that he had. Touching someone else, that made his skin hurt sometimes, sometimes thrilled him. Touching Karella. In the space inside that the story had made, there was room now for other stories, like: she came once, looking for me, she may come again. She came looking for me, why?

Why?

Of all words, that was the hammer, breaking everything open.

Beside him she was looking around her again, and now abruptly she lunged toward him, banging into him, clutching at his arm. He wheeled around. Her panic caught him a little; he was ready for an enemy, his hands fisted.

Nothing but the moon, just beginning to appear over a crest of the horizon. Karella caught hold of his arm and pulled him.

"Come. Run."

Obediently he broke into a trot beside her; she ran with blind feet, stumbling and tripping on the grass, and he grasped her arm and held her and kept her upright. The moon was mounting steadily into the sky, its body withered and blemished.

They reached the brush wall around the village and he stopped. The sounds of the People reached him. His skin prickled up as if ants crawled all over him.

"Come," Karella said, and tugged his arm.

He shook his head. "No. I go home. I go back."

She grunted. In the shelter of the village, she had forgotten her terror of the rising moon. She said, "Good-by, then. I will see you again soon."

She walked away. He almost started after her, but then a shout from within the high-mounded thorny barrier, higher than his head, and a wild thunder of drums reminded him of the band of boys, and of the other People, and he felt small and naked and helpless again. He turned and went back into the night.

Inside the brush fence of the village, there were four longhouses, built of withies and woven mats and poles; all their doorways faced the east wind. In the yard the women had a mill, for grinding their grain and nuts and beans into meal; it was a flat stone with a hole in the middle, and a stout stick stood up in the hole, and another flat stone fitted down onto the top of the stick. They poured the grain into a hole in the top stone, and turned it around and around, and the meal came out the edges.

The old women sat around the mill and turned it, and ground the grain into meal, and as they turned the mill they sang.

> *Sam-po, sam-po*
> *La li la la li li la*
> *With the sampo all the world is fed*

Karella went among them and sat down there among them, in the yard in the middle of the longhouses. The mill groaned as it turned. The women who sat around it were the elders, the headwomen, and their sisters. They turned the mill with their great broad dirt-colored feet. With their hands they did other work, making baskets, or plucking the wool of the goats, and they talked, and their talk was like the turning of the mill: they ground out everything that happened to the People into its meanings.

When Karella sat down into their midst, she cast a handful of grain into the mill, and she cast her words into the midst of the women.

"Oh, oh, my bones are aching, it will be a harsh winter certainly."

She had brought along a mat to sit on, and a frame of sticks with another mat to lean her back against. A little girl from her longhouse had carried them for her and now laid them out for her. Karella smiled, and the child went away. Karella settled herself down.

All around her sat the old women, with their busy hands. Karella had little to do with baskets, or the making of clay pots, or the tilling of soil; her craft had set her free from that. Still, she envied them their business. They sat so close together that they touched, and made a circle around the mill, all touching. Fat with age, their bodies massive and paunchy from bearing children, their hair powdery white and grey, they all seemed the same, closer than sisters. They shared their lives totally, from their first breath to the last, so that it was all the same life; there was no boundary between them.

In their midst, Karella was alone. Her craft set her apart. Her freedom set her apart. And cursed her, some said; she knew that. Married three times, yet she had borne no children, and now her womb was withered as her face, and when she died, while all the People would mourn, no daughter would remain in the world to connect her still with life.

She looked from face to face, and said, "I have been long in the company of men and now again I sit among my own, and I am grateful."

"Oh, Karella," said Tishka, who was the headwoman of the Oak Tree Kindred, and the most powerful woman in the village. "As sorely as you may have missed us, we missed you all the more. No stories! No stories at all, for the whole coming and going of the moon."

She shook her head, and all the others shook their heads too. Their hands flew back and forth, building up the rounds of reeds into baskets.

"Yet it was necessary," Karella said. "I have learned that which it makes me tremble to tell to you."

At that, many of the hands faltered, and the grey heads lifted,

and all eyes looked from Karella to Tishka. For a moment the Oak
Tree headwoman sat rigid, her face deeply graven and her eyes hard,
but then she worked her mouth into a laugh, loud and forced, and
around her all the other women laughed too.

"Karella, you are given to exaggeration. It is a secret of your art,
to give alarms."

"I give no alarms," Karella said, stiff. She disliked their unity
against her; she wanted to shake them all separately and say, "Listen
to me with your own ears, not Tishka's."

She said, "Oh? Then if I speak the name of Ladon, you will not
shiver?"

"Ladon. Ladon is our chief."

"Great is Ladon, Opa-Ladon," one of the women murmured,
and the others laughed, all touching.

"He is our chief," said Tishka, "and a great chief too. He forces
all the other chiefs to yield to him, and he makes us great among all
the People, and he divides up the harvest so that we all have what we
need. What is there to make us shiver about Ladon?"

Karella lowered her gaze to the mill, rumbling and groaning as
it turned, the meal slipping from the stones. A little silence fell, and
again the women sang the song of the mill.

> Sam-po, sam-po,
> Li la li la li li la
> All things flow from the Mill
> The Mill turns and turns
> Li la li la la la la la
> Nothing escapes, nothing is unfulfilled

"I am unfulfilled," said Karella, loudly.

"You!" Their faces turned on her like a dozen suns, wide with
astonishment. "You, who do exactly as you please!" One of them
snorted.

"Pagh," Karella said. "I know what you think—but for the virtue
of my sister, I should not be here at all."

Karella's older sister had been headwoman of the Red Deer
Kindred, while Karella went about doing as she wished; then her
sister died suddenly and Karella found herself raised up all at once
to be headwoman, to the astonishment of everyone.

She said, "I have no children. I have no one to pass my stories on to, and I am not long for this life, I know that. I need someone to give my stories to, or they will be lost."

A little ripple of excitement passed through the close-packed women. Tishka's sister, Grela, not even old yet, had the boldness to lean forward and say, "Karella, Ana-Karella, my oldest daughter is a fine talker—"

"Hush," Tishka said to her, in a harsh voice. "What would you do—would you thrust your brat on her? Do you think to make your child any greater than she is? What a nose you have! Keep it close to your face, Grela, or it will get caught in something."

The other women laughed heartily at that; they loved to see someone else chastised. Karella sat there with her hands in her lap, watching them. Her heart was full of black temper toward them. They sat here with their mill and their baskets and their full bellies, and gave no thought to larger things.

"In any case," she said, when the red-faced Grela had mumbled her apologies and accepted her humiliation and fit herself back into the close circle of the women—"in any case," Karella said, "I have found one I believe to be marked for my work."

"Ah," said Tishka, smiling. "And tell us now who she is."

"He," said Karella, steadily. "It is Moloquin."

"Moloquin!"

The name burst from them like an irresistible roar of laughter. They stared at her and their mouths opened and a flood of hilarity came out. Karella sat letting it rush over her. In her lap her hands twitched.

"Moloquin," Tishka said, her mirth subsiding. She lifted up the goats' wool she was working on; with a thorny stick she was combing the hairs straight, and the white wool glistened in the sun. "Karella, you cannot expect us to believe you."

"He is Ael's son," said another, Taella, the quietest of them, eldest daughter of the Salmon headwoman. "He is Ael's son, Karella."

Karella said nothing.

"You cannot mean us to accept Ael's son."

"I have no children of my own," Karella said.

Her gaze moved, leaving these infuriating women, looking away out of the village. Out there, outside the brush fence on the high ground by the river, was the roundhouse with its peaked roof of thatch, its walls of wood and mud-daub. Most of the men were there now, preparing for the ceremony of hunting the deer. Karella won-

dered with an acid humor why they did not actually go out and hunt
down the deer, instead of performing the three-day-long ceremony
that exhausted them all and brought nothing to the cooking fires,
but even she, who doubted everything, knew well how important
were these ceremonies, more important than mere food.

Food for the soul. The ceremonies connected the People with
the rest of life, the deer and the forest, and the ancestral spirits who
had taught the skills of hunting- and forest-lore to the People, and
who remained always in the same place where they had walked in life
and whose benevolence had to be maintained. She watched the mill
turn. The sun-warmed meal smelled deliciously of nuts. The women,
by their ceaseless drudgery in the fields, brought food into the village; the men, by their unwavering devotion to ceremony, maintained the eternal order of things.

Now Ladon wanted to disturb the order; his schemes and ambition would overturn everything. She lifted her head again, to face
Tishka.

"Ladon means his son to follow him to the high seat," she said.

Tishka grunted at her. Seventeen children had she borne; eight
of them still lived. Her hands were knotted and warped with her
years, and her eyes watered. At the center of this disintegration her
will was immovable.

"He cannot," she said. "Ladon's power ends with him. We shall
choose who follows him."

"The power would go to the son of his sister," said Karella. "But
he has no sister—not any more."

When she let drop those words, they fell into a silence that no
one chose to end. Tishka was staring at her. New lines appeared at
the corners of Tishka's mouth and in her forehead, and her eyes
were sharp and damp. She saw now where Karella was leading her.

Karella looked down at the mill; she put out her hand and
pushed the stone in its course.

> *Sam-po, sam-po*
> *Li la li li la la la li*
> *Turning, turning, ever turning*
> *All falls as it must*
> *Sam-po, sam-po*
> *World with no beginning*

World with no end
La li li la la li li la
Sam-po, sam-po

"How do you know what Ladon intends, Ana-Karella?" Tishka asked.

"Ana-Tishka," Karella said, and for emphasis she spun out all the terms of respect possible, "Ana-Tishka-el, great is she, great among the People! While we were at the river, while the men fasted and sweated themselves, I saw how Ladon went among them. He spoke to them ever of his son—how strong and fair the boy is—"

"He is very fair," one of the younger women murmured.

"He gathered up his ring-brothers and gave each of them a duty toward his son."

"He is permitted that. This is man's business, Karella—"

"Over and over, he bound them to his son, with promises and threats."

"The words of men are the chaff that the wind blows off the threshing floors," said Tishka in a harsh voice. "The deeds of men are the grain that falls to the earth and remains."

"They came to me, many of them, with dreams in which Ladon's son sat on the litter."

"And what did you tell them?"

"I told them nothing."

"Nothing! They must have liked that."

The women murmured to one another.

Karella said, "I told them nothing. I do not sully my craft with such things—I do not lower myself to the interpretation of false dreams."

Tishka smiled at her. Between the two headwomen there flowed a certain understanding.

In a low voice, Grela said, "You will choose the chief. The head-women. It is the way."

"Yes?" Karella said, impatiently; she resented having to lead them along one foot after the other through this. "And whom shall we choose? There is no sister-son among the People—Ladon saw to that."

"Ladon is not old, or weak, or dim of mind. It will be many many turnings of the mill before he falls."

"In that time Ladon will have planted this seed so well and tended it so well that it shall grow into a plant that overshadows us all."

Tishka said, "Ladon did not—remove his sister."

"Did he not? He drove her away!"

"Ael left," Tishka said, her voice rising, harsh and angry and fearful. "She went away as much as he drove her away—she was willful, and would not be ruled; she scorned us all, our ways, our hearths, her own People. Ladon did not drive her away—"

"Did he not?" Karella said; she lowered her voice, knowing the power of soft, soft words to grip all ears. "Yet it has worked well for him, has it not?"

Tishka licked her lips. With her crooked, dirt-brown fingers she wiped her eyes. She turned a little away, saying nothing. Nor would she speak again today on this subject. Karella sat back. In the silence, in Tishka's turning away, there was now an empty space among the People, like an unravelled place in the web: a good place for an unwanted one.

"Well," said Grela, with a twitch, as if she were wakening from a dream, "this is all wind still, is it not? Ladon will not die for some time. The choice need not be made now. By the time he lies among the stones, there will be other choices possible."

> Sam-po, sam-po
> La li la li la la la
> No one turns the sam-po
> The sampo turns itself

"Tell us a story, Ana-Karella. You burden our minds with this weighty stuff that may not even be real; now you must send our cares elsewhere with a story."

She nodded. Settling herself on her mat, she sat still a while, letting the words well up within her, letting the tale come as it would, while the mill rolled and rolled at the center of things.

Ladon's son went down to the roundhouse; with his head bowed in humility he passed through the gate in the wall around it, and crossed the yard. The men sat there in the sun, making ready their masks and cloaks, their leggings of deer-hide, their crowns of antlers, their magic arrows and their spears. Many who saw him spoke to him, and he answered with every gesture of respect and kept his eyes averted, out of deference to the manhood he had not yet attained.

The roundhouse was built of the trunks of trees, set spaced apart in circles one inside the next; the outermost supported the walls, and the inner circles, each one higher than the one outside it, raised up the roof toward its peak. Through gaps in the thatch the sunlight fell in shafts, and the trunks of the trees made a little forest. The floor was littered with the men's gear, thrown here and there without order; in the rafters, in baskets and sacks, were the hoarded goods of the People.

Ladon's son loved the roundhouse. In less than two years, he would come here to live, a novice in the tutelage of one of the masters; he loved to think ahead to that time, when he would be a man, full of power. As he passed he reached out his hands to touch the great trunks, polished of their bark, white in the sunlight. Ahead, in the light that fell through the hole at the peak of the roof, his father sat.

The chief wore only his loincloth. His great belly under its glossy black hair lay down on his thighs as he bent forward, his mask in his hands, cutting and shaping the hard wood. His son's steps slowed even more as he approached.

Ladon's fingers were long and shapely and he used the blade of flint with a deft precision, nicking away the wood, carving the mask with magical symbols that he had learned in his latest purification. The golden wood of the mask had been smoothed and oiled and worn into a deep mysterious luster. Bits of stones decorated it: flint teeth, agate in the nose and on the cheekbones. A row of amber beads studded the forehead. Ladon had first cut it from the living tree in the year he became a man; with every passing year he made it more complex, he worked more of his knowledge and power into it.

Now he said, without looking up, "Yes, little boy, you may come to your loving father."

His son went forward and knelt down beside him. His awed gaze remained on the mask. He longed to touch it, but the one time he had tried, when he was still a nursling, Ladon had beaten him senseless.

He said, "My father, you were long at the river."

"The work of the sacred way consumes the days, my son."

"While you were gone, I obeyed your words to me. I kept watch over the People, and I remember everything that I saw; you may ask me anything, and I shall know the answer."

Ladon turned now and smiled at him. "Really? Then you know who has worked well in her gardens, and who has not."

"Oh, they have all worked very well, Opa-Ladon-on."

"And you know who has given birth and who has not?"

"While you were gone, only the swine have given birth, Opa-Ladon-on."

"And you know who has brought me my due, and who has with-held it?"

The boy's eyes widened in surprise; rapidly he hurried through his memory, wondering what Ladon meant. "Surely no one dares to withhold from Ladon what is Ladon's due."

An explosive sound left his father's lips, half grunt and half laughter. Ladon looked down at the mask in his hands. With one forefinger he whisked away a splinter of wood from the surface. "Whoever has done so shall suffer, my son."

His son stood a while watching; Ladon seemed to do nothing, and yet he gave off a sort of radiance of strength, his thoughts so strong they threatened to become visible. Uncertainly the boy said, "We have chased Moloquin every day, my father."

"So you said, but you have not chased him away entirely, my son. I am not displeased with you over it, but I am not pleased, either."

"But, my father, he runs to the place of the dead, and I—I—the other boys will not go in, I cannot make them."

"The dead place!"

"The—" Ladon's son feared even the name; his lips stiffened so that he could barely pronounce it. "The Pillar of the Sky."

"What a fool. How does he live? Someone must be helping him. Who feeds him? Why does he not die?" Ladon glared at the boy beside him. "Who feeds him? Learn that for me, One-who-knows-everything."

"No one, Opa-Ladon. Sometimes he steals food, but no one—"

"Be quiet."

Ladon's son bit his lips, ashamed, his tongue an enemy in his mouth. His father rose, ponderous, frowning, and went out of the light a moment. When he came back his hands were empty, the mask gone. The frown was gone also, and Ladon faced his son with the same impassive looks he gave all the rest of the world.

He said, "Go, my son. Go do what boys do, and be glad, because when you are chief, all the cares and weighty woes of the People will fall on you, and you will have peace never again."

"Yes, Opa-Ladon-on." The boy made gestures of respect with his hands, and bowed his head, which let him linger; the boys' band was boring. He watched his father's face for some sign that he might stay, but Ladon was clearly going somewhere else and pushed at him with his hand.

"Go."

Ladon went away through the roundhouse, stopping at the edge of his central place to put on his bearskin coat, although the day was warm. It was always cool inside the roundhouse.

He had built this place himself—not with his own hands, but with the hands bestowed on him by his destiny. The trees were enormous, the biggest he could find, a tribute to the size and power of his People, and only the year before they had gone through it all and replaced some that were rotting away in the ground. As he walked through it he touched the trunks, and he was unsure whether he gave them of his affection for them or they supplied some of their strength to him.

In the yard, where many of the men sat readying themselves and their gear for the deer-hunt dances, he stopped and looked around him. As soon as they saw him the men raised their heads and stared at him; no more work was done; they waited with joyous faces for his command to fall on them. But the one whom Ladon sought was not here, and he went out of the yard and around the outside of the wall, down to the river.

Here the river turned a wide curve through the low rolling downlands; on the inside of the curve the land rose up a little, and on this height stood the roundhouse. The river cut down through the heavy soil and into the chalk below. The exposed chalk was a fine place to mine flint, and there many of the men were gathered, watching one of their number knock the edges off a new knife. But the one Ladon sought was not there either, and he went on.

Now he was running out of places to seek and he turned toward the village and his steps slowed. He disliked going among the women. He thought if they had favors to ask of him or pleasures to give him they should come to him. When he went down the little slope toward the four longhouses inside their fence of rolled brush he felt smaller and more ordinary than he knew himself to be. The fact that they could deny him was a canker in his heart.

Going toward the longhouses reminded him of his sister, Ael.

He stopped. She had gone away and he had thought her finished but somehow she had come back.

He had always hated his sister. Tall she had been, older than he, always better than he was. When he was a little boy she had struck him, taunted him, and outdone him—that was the worst of it, that was why they had all hated Ael, because she had outdone all of them. Women's work, men's pleasures, she had done them all, with the same arrogant condescending grace and ease. When they would not give her a bow, she went off into the forest and found wood and made one. When they would not let her play with the boys' band, she dashed in among them, stole the pig-skull they were playing with and carried it off at arm's length over her head, laughing, all the boys running at her heels like a pack of slaves, and she had hidden the trophy deep in the forest, where no one would find it.

When the women told her to weed the fields, she would not, but found her own plot, raised her own vetch and onions. Girls were supposed to wear only the brown colors of the earth. Ael had taken her garments out and found some berry, some root, some bark that dyed them red, brighter even than the orange-yellows allowed the headwomen of the kindreds.

And now, defying every hope and rule, she had brought forth a son, Moloquin, who was trampling on Ladon's dreams.

He remembered the horror that swept through the village on that day, when those mourning one of their dead had come flying back from the place of the dead, screaming that she was there. Then it had been easy; it had taken almost no sign from him at all, to set the whole People against the orphan. Somehow Moloquin survived. It was Ael, Ladon knew, Ael who guided him, Ael who protected him, Ael who went on ruining her brother's life.

He stopped, midway between the roundhouse and the longhouses, unwilling to go farther.

It was the old women who did this to him. His mind made the jump from Ael's wickedness to the general wickedness of all women, and the headwomen in particular.

They sat there, monstrous in their shapeless fat, their woven clothes, and said, "This is the way it has always been done." They had raised him, Ladon, to his high seat, and when he was dead, they would raise another. They gave him everything. All the great store of grain and beans and cheese that filled up the rafters of his round-house came from the work of the women, and this they gave to Ladon, and Ladon gave it to those who needed it, and so the People lived, but it was not Ladon who had the power; he might have been anyone, any fool, any beast with a male's anatomy. He was only the hands that lavished all that wealth on others. The real power was with the women.

He knew himself great, Ladon, knew himself remarkable beyond all men, deserving of power; but the power that he had mocked him.

It had not always been so. They pretended that it had been thus forever, but the men knew and he suspected that the women knew also that, long ago, in the first years, the men had ruled. Before the women learned to grub and hack at the earth, the men had been the true masters. The great hunting societies had provided the meat and the hides, the bone and antlers, the strength and ferocity, and the women had been properly humble and grateful and had done as they were told. (Perhaps, he thought, with the malice of impotence, that was why they were so good at grubbing the earth, because they had learned to submit.)

It was shameful and degrading to work as they did, to tear the dirt, to labor over seeds and seedlings, to thresh and winnow. No man would do it. It was low work but it fed them, and for the sake of their full bellies the People had turned from the true way, from the vault of Heaven and the honor of the trail, the lives of heroes.

Ladon meant to recapture that truth. He meant to seize power for his son and break the circle of the old women's endless custom. He meant to make them see that Ladon in himself was mighty, enough to pass on his power to his son.

Now, halfway between the roundhouse and the longhouses, he raised his fist toward the old women and swore to destroy them, Karella, Tishka, all of them. But he cared not to face them today, and he turned and on his heavy legs stumped back toward the round-house.

When he came in through the door, that man whom he had sought was there—Brant, the old master of the Green Bough Society. Ladon summoned him; and they went into the roundhouse together, the chief first, the old man trailing after.

Brant had taken Ladon on his knee as a boy, and Ladon remembered then that his hair had been white. He walked with a bent back, a stooped head, and knees bent, and in spite of his age, no one paid much heed to his words because he belonged to an unlucky society. Therefore, perhaps, Brant said nothing much to anybody.

Ladon took his place in the sunlight at the center of the roundhouse. The old man stood before him, in one hand still a flint knife and in the other a piece of wood.

"You have been lax, old man," Ladon said. "It is the responsibility of the Society of the Green Bough to keep the Pillar of the Sky, and even now it is defiled."

Brant shuffled the knife into the same hand that held the wood; with the hand thus freed, he wiped his nose. He said, "I wait for the words of Opa-Ladon-on."

"The woods-puppy, Moloquin, even now impudently lives in the place where only the dead may rest."

Brant said quietly, "I have heard that, Opa-Ladon-on."

"Then why have you done nothing about it?"

"I shall, Opa-Ladon-on."

"Go."

Brant turned and trudged away. Ladon's lips twisted in annoyance. There was no fire in the old man, no power at all; how would he serve against such as Ael? Ladon grunted; he got up and went into the back of the roundhouse, to find something to eat.

Karella was beginning to see unexpected problems in this. She walked along the path toward the place of the dead, her bundle on her back, and although she was tired she could not go slowly, because already the sun was lowering in the sky. She could not keep on walking out so far from the village every day; she was too old.

She hated that. Too old. She had spent her youth with a wild profligacy, confident that her vitality would always overflow, but now age was sinking its teeth into her, and she looked back on those wild days with a bitter longing: if she had that life again, she would do differently.

No you would not, she thought to herself. You did what you wanted.

At that she laughed. That was at the heart of herself, that she had always done what she wanted: and she was still doing it now, what she wanted, and so she defied age. Her steps came quicker, lighter over the grass.

But there were problems.

First of all, Moloquin was at the age—past the age, in fact— when his mother would have chased him away from her hearth and out of the longhouse, and he would have gone off to join the boys' band, living in the thickets by the river, fighting, running, learning who was leader and who was follower—making ready for his manhood. At the very time when Karella meant to take him in, she should by custom have been throwing him out.

That was easy. It was usual for mothers to keep their foolish children close to them, even past their maturity. Moloquin spoke so clumsily that the People would think him a fool—already, they considered him hopelessly backward—and by that reasoning Karella could keep him until he was a greybeard.

She knew he was no fool. She saw it in his looks, in his awkward questions—in the naked fact that he had lived so long alone, against the enmity of Ladon and the others.

Another problem: she had no clothes for him.

Had he been her own true son she would have gone to Ladon and asked for hides and been given hides, and then she would have made him a shirt and a coat, and he would have been dressed. But if she went to Ladon now, he would give her nothing. So she had taken her own clothes, the brown woven things she had worn before she became headwoman, and that was in the bundle that she carried on her back. If he wore woven clothes like a girl, it would only help the People's acceptance of him as a harmless fool.

But she could not go on climbing this slope every day. She had to bring him down into the village.

She reached the embankment and walked around the outer edge, on the lip of the ditch, until she reached an entry. Her legs were tired. Going into the grassy circle sheltered from the wind by the bank and made populous by the tilting stones, she let the bundle drop into the grass and looked around her.

He wasn't there. Disappointed, she roamed from one stone to the next, avoiding the bones strewn in the grass. But Moloquin was nowhere.

She sat down in the grass, drained of strength. The thought of the long way back now stood before her like an impossible task. As she settled down, the great flock of crows that always overhung this placed settled too, the fat black bodies dropping to the earth, the slippery flap of their wings and their ugly voices noisy in this place of stillness. There were no dead here now, nothing but bones. She watched a little crowd of the crows rush to Moloquin's usual place, under the North Watcher, to hunt for leavings.

They knew him, those great monstrous birds, knew him well.

She sat still, her hands in her lap, and thought over a story she was trying to remember. Her craft had come to her early—even as a little girl she had told stories, made up out of her own head, and ever since she had collected every tale she heard into her head, so that now it was a stuffed pack, like the bundle of rags she had brought for Moloquin. She thought she knew every story the People had ever told, and a few more perhaps. She knew stories she had never heard from any other; they rose in her brain like vapors from the swamps, that burst like small suns in the air. She thought she could remember everything, but once in a while, as if from deep deep down in some unfished pool, a sentence rose, a gesture, a name, and when she cast her attention upon it and drew it up, there followed after a long golden rush of a story, wonderful as a dream.

She sat with her eyes closed, and the stories came swiftly around her—the names of heroes, the deeds of people that unlocked the world's hidden places. To Karella nothing was more real than this, these presences summoned from her mind and this space between her and the world.

Abruptly the flock of crows, all cackling and stepping around her, gave out a racket that packed up her ears, and they rose in a black fluttering mass into the air. She stood up, expecting Moloquin.

It was not the boy. It was an old man who walked in through the opening in the bank, white-haired and bent, leaning on a walking staff. It was Brant, the Green Bough master.

Karella started back, away from him, toward the shelter of a half-fallen stone. He saw her; he raised his head.

"Ana-Karella," he said, and let go his staff and sat down. "What is this? What wakens here, after so long a sleep, that suddenly the dead place is a place for the living once again?" He shook his head; he looked exhausted. "This is too long a walk for me, Ana-Karella."

She went up to him and sat down by his side. "What brings you here, then?"

"I don't know."

"Surely Ladon sent you."

"Ladon."

The old man trembled, giving off some soft fluttery noise; alarmed, she leaned toward him, her hand on his back, thinking he might be ill, but then she saw that he was laughing.

"Ah, Brant," she said. "What amuses you? You old stick." Instead of stroking his back, she struck it and got up again. What would he say about Moloquin? She had to get him away before the boy came.

"Karella," he said, and looked at her. "Do you remember when we were little? You and I wore the grass ring, do you remember that?"

"You old stick," she said, affectionately. It was true; she had forgotten it, for all these years, that in their childhood she and this old fool had been sweethearts. She scanned the horizon for Moloquin.

"Why did Ladon send you here?"

"Because he is a fool." Brant lay down in the grass.

"Then why did you come?"

"I like it here."

"Ah, you old—" she sighed. Would Moloquin never come?

"He sent me to drive away this woods-pup," said Brant. "And I suspect, since I find you here, that you too take an interest in this homeless child, and I find that amusing. I am too old to find much interesting, you know."

"Why then don't you stay here, and die, and let the crows eat you?" She walked restlessly around in the grass, as if to prove that she had more life left in her than he did.

"Is it because of Ladon that you strive so?" the old man said. "Ladon strives, and so you see some danger, and you strive against him, is that it? You are both deluded."

"What do you mean?"

"I mean that Ladon's thoughts are large only to him. Nothing will come of them. If you strive against him, then you make his ambition larger yet, but if you let him go on, then all will fall away when he dies, fall away into nothing."

"Brant, you are mad."

He said no more; she looked, and saw that his eyes were closed. He was asleep in the grass. She stood a moment watching him, and then turned her eyes up, toward the great whirling cloud of crows suspended in the air above the Pillar of the Sky. They might think him dead, and drop down and eat him up, and no one would ever know the difference. Certainly not Brant.

She went away toward her bundle, intending to go back to the village; she would seek Moloquin here another time. But when she stooped to pick up the rags, a long low hiss reached her ears from off to her left, and she froze.

It was Moloquin. He sat beside the northernmost stone, where his home was, watching her.

She straightened, amazed. How long had he been there? She was sure he had not been there when she came. With the bundle in her hand she went to him and he moved aside and let her into the hollow at the foot of the stone.

"I surprise you," he said, and smiled at her.

"Yes," she said, and she smiled back. She felt a warm flush of affection for him. Ever since she had left him the night before, she had been thinking of him, but only in the large matter of her struggle against Ladon; now he was here, real again, a child, and all the rest seemed unimportant. She plunged her hand into her bundle and took out a bean cake, a little bowl of meal and a jug of goat's milk.

He took them, but not hungrily. He said, "I eat, just now. Before I come here."

"What could you find by yourself to eat?"

"Nuts. Berries." He shrugged one shoulder, his eyes wide. "I catched a bustard."

At that her eyes widened; she almost doubted him. The bustards were impossible even to approach. "How did you do that?"

"I maked a—" he formed something in the air. She watched his hands, intrigued; he seemed to have the storyteller's talent for gesture. "From grass. Put it over the nest. Wait. The bird comes, I close the—"

"Net," she said.

"Net," he said, and smiled. "Net net net net net."

She stared at him. What Brant had told her was seeping down into her mind. She thought, He does well enough outside the village. Am I wrong to want to bring him within? She thought, suddenly, Is Brant right? Will it all work out by itself, if I leave things alone? There flooded into her thoughts a sense of the power of reality, that fed on faith alone.

"I have no faith," she said aloud, and Moloquin's eyebrows went up. She said, "I want you to come and live with me, Moloquin."

"Live with you."

"In the village. In the longhouse, at my hearth."

He swallowed, his throat moving up and down, his gaze steady on her. He said nothing.

"I have no children," she said. She lowered her eyes. "I need—I want—"

He put out his hand and touched her, and her throat stopped up. Their eyes met. He laid his hands on her shoulders and awkwardly leaned toward her, embracing her, and she shut her eyes and put her head down on his shoulder.

He said, "Tell me a story."

"No. First, I—" she pulled apart from him; turning to her bundle, she spread it open. "You must have some clothes. I brought these, we shall make you some clothes from them." She shook out her old coat, full of holes, and ragged along the edges. She had brought an awl stuck into a piece of bark, and a ball of yarn. Moloquin fingered the cloth.

"What I need this for?"

"Because you must have clothes."

"Not here," he said.

"To live in the village."

"I not live in the village."

"But I want you to come and live with me."

"I not—"

He sprang up, so quickly that she shrank back in terror from the sudden movement; he wheeled around, dancing away from the stone. Karella put out her hand to him. "Wait!" But he was gone. A flash of legs, a torrent of black hair, he bounded away and was gone over the top of the bank.

Brant came toward her, leaning on his stick, his teeth showing in the midst of his sparse beard. He said, "Another lover, Ana-Karella."

Humiliated, furious, she sank down into the grass and glared at him. "You old fool, get away from me. Go away!"

"Ladon is right, he should not be here."

"Oh? Why not? Because of the dead? Because of the spirits? Then why have they not sickened him? Sent him foul dreams? Haunted him out of this place? He is safe here."

Brant said, "Come, we will walk back to the village together."

She remained still, her lips pressed firmly together; she was furious with him, the more so because Moloquin had refused her.

The old man moved away, leaning on his stick. "Come along,

Ana-Karella," he called, over his shoulder. "Come away, he will not be back. Not this day."

Slowly she got to her feet. The bundle lay there on the grass, opened and scattered, and she began to gather it up; then, impulsively, she collected the cloth and the awl and the yarn and stuffed it into the back of the hollow under the North Watcher. "Wait, Brant, you fool," she called. The sun was going down. Quickly she went after the old man, to walk back down to the village.

Karella did not come back. Moloquin found the bundle of cloth in the hollow under the stone, and he spread out each piece carefully and smoothed it with his hands, absorbed in the pattern of the crossing threads. It felt strange, too, not like animal hide: thinner, more flexible. Finally he rolled it all up into a ball once more and stuffed it back into the hollow.

He waited for a whole day by the stones, but still she did not come.

Something was wrong with him. Before he first met Karella he had been content to live as he did now, seeking food, sleeping under the stone, engaging in his daily contest with the boys' band, and that had seemed enough, or at least all he was likely to have. Then Karella had come, and told him stories, and now he was lonely all the time.

He wondered whether it was Karella he missed, or the stories. She touched him; no one else had touched him since his mother died. He remembered the feel of her hands on his skin, how warm and light, and the smell of her near him, and other things: over and over he thought of one time when he had glanced at her and seen her looking down, how the long grey hair had lain across her cheek, how soft and downy was the skin just below her half-closed eye. He could not say what it was, but the memory made his fingers tingle, longing to touch her, to be touched.

He told himself the stories she had told him, over and over, trying to repeat each word as she had, each gesture. It was not the same.

He lay on the grass between two leaning stones and stared up at the sky, figured with clouds. His mother had taught him how to make nets to catch fish and birds, how to choose good nuts from bad, how to make fires, how to skin rabbits. She had told him nothing of where

he had come from, or why, or what he should do, except to keep his
cutting stones sharp.

When he looked into a still pool, sometimes, on a bright day, the
water seemed impenetrable. All he saw was his own face and the
glare of the sun. If he moved, so that his body shaded the water from
the sun, then he could see down, below the surface, see the fish, the
deep water, the bottom of the river. The stories were like that for
him; they showed him what lay underneath.

It seemed to him that he had always known that what he saw was
only a surface; all that was important lay beneath.

Now Karella would not come, and without Karella he had no
stories, and as the day wore by without her he grew restless and unhappy to the point of tears. Abruptly, almost without being aware of
it, he was on his feet and running.

It was afternoon now. In the gardens of the village the women
were bent over their work, their hoes hacking at the earth. He ran
down toward them, keeping to the higher ground above the longhouses and far away from the roundhouse. His eyes searched the
world for signs of the boys' band, but they were nowhere in sight.
Then, at the edge of the worked land, he stopped.

Once this uneven hillside had been covered with trees; their
charred stumps still studded the gardens, and the women grew flowers around them, stored their tools in the hollows, sat on the flat tops.
Down there, in among all the stooped figures that bobbed and
swayed rhythmically in their work, one sat upon a stump, one whom
Moloquin could name at any distance: Karella, telling stories.

A swarm of smaller children sat around her; the women in their
gardens listened as they worked. Only Moloquin could not hear, Moloquin, stranded forever at the edge of the world.

A flash of hatred whitened his mind. She was giving his stories
to someone else, his stories.

He started down there, his feet leaving the tall rough grass for
the dust of the path. No one saw him. Karella sat on the stump with
her head bowed a little so that her long grey hair hung down, and
the wind lifted it; he saw her shape the air between her hands, bringing meaning from nothing. Each foot lower than the one before, he
went down the path toward her.

"Moloquin!"

He stopped in his tracks, every hair standing on end. The shout came from one of the women, and at that sound, everyone in the gardens turned and stared at him. He felt their looks like cold rain on his skin, but Karella was there, and she had seen him.

She stood up. With both arms she called him in, her mouth round with his name. All around her stood the hostile People, but she in their midst summoned him, and he took another step toward her. Thinking of stories, thinking of the warmth of her embrace. Another step followed the first. Then, abruptly, a stone flew through the air toward him.

He wheeled. The stone never came near him, but he was gone anyway, running for the woods, while behind him they screamed and whistled, they threw stones and clods of earth, they hooted and sneered at him, they raced slavering at his heels.

In the margin of the forest, under a poplar tree, he stopped and looked back.

They had not chased him; in fact, none of them even shouted, and he wondered if he had not heard them shout and whistle with the ears of memory that had heard it so often before. Now they simply watched him go, and in their midst, Karella jumped and waved her arms and yelled furiously around her.

Moloquin went away into the forest.

Karella settled down onto the stump again, out of breath, her eyes on the trees where Moloquin had gone. The crowd of little children at her feet goggled up at her, their mouths ajar; probably they had never seen her rage before. She wiped her rheumy eyes with her fingers.

The women had gone back to their work. None among them would confess to having thrown the stone at Moloquin, they all went on as if nothing had happened. Karella sank down, brooding, her chin on her chest; she stole another look at the forest.

He had tried to come to her. Now, perhaps, the People would know that Karella took an interest in him and they might leave him alone. Would he come back again?

She got to her feet, thinking of walking to the Pillar of the Sky again, but at the thought of the distance, her heart quaked. After the last time she had slept almost a whole day.

She was old. She had known that before, of course, but until now
it had not interfered with her. She had gone everywhere, walked to
the river with the men, done as she chose; now she could not, because she was old. Getting up off the stump, she went down the long
winding path, in between the ripening gardens, down toward the
longhouse.

The women and their children lived in the longhouses. Sometimes
the men lived there too, but usually the men preferred the roundhouse with its comradeship and Ladon's generosity. When the married men wished the experience of their wives, they went into the
longhouses, and there at the back, in the wall, was a little hole that
led into a small dark room, and there the men united with their
wives.

In the little room with her husband, Grela, the sister of Tishka,
said, "What do you make of Karella? Isn't it a scandal?"

Her husband lay on his back on the mats, sated. He muttered
something behind the arm he had flung over his face.

"She will regret it. He is a fool, a thief, a naked thing. And she
thinks to teach her stories to him!" Grela laughed. She was jealous of
Karella, who always seemed to get exactly what she wanted, and who
had gone from being the scandal of the village to headwoman of the
Red Deer without even talking it over with anyone. Grela talked to
everyone about everything that concerned her. Now she remembered, a little late, what Karella had told them around the sampo,
that she suspected Ladon of trying to steal power, and it occurred to
her that her sister, Tishka the Wise, would probably not want her to
tell all this to Fergolin, who being a man would be on Ladon's side.

He was a man, too, and she reached out and closed her hand
over his male part and squeezed, and he groaned. Grela laughed.

"Yesterday he tried to sit down with the other children while she
was telling stories in the fields, and when someone threw a stone at
him, Karella was furious, it was funny, you should have seen how she
jumped and shouted, her face got red as a berry."

Fergolin put his hand over hers, still soft on his softening penis,
and caressed himself with her palm; he rolled onto his side. "Grela,"
he said, "I understand nothing of this. What is this about Karella?"

"Oh, she's got this notion she will take Moloquin in."

"Moloquin. You mean that woods-sprite?"

"He's not a sprite, he's a dirty little naked fool." Still, what he had said struck some spark; she turned to him. "Do you think it is true what folk say, that Ael got pregnant by a spirit of the forest?"

"Ael," said Fergolin, yawning. "Who is Ael, now, river-tongued one? You know, Grela, you talk too much." But he was smiling at her.

"Ael, you know," she said, crossly; it often surprised her how different was a man's mind than a woman's. "Ladon's sister, the mother of Moloquin."

"She's dead, Grela." He sat up, drawing his knees up, his arms around them. "What is this about Moloquin and Karella? She wants to take in Moloquin? And Moloquin is the son of Ladon's sister?"

"She is only making him bolder and bolder. He would have sat right down with the other children! We shall have to drive him away again, before he steals everything."

Fergolin said nothing for a moment. Close beside her in the dimness he gave off the warmth and the warm mysterious odor of the male. She moved closer to him, snuggling into his shoulder, and he put his arm around her.

"Grela," he said, and put a kiss to her forehead. "You are a river, my wife, running fast and deep, but it takes a fine fisherman to draw forth much in the way of substance from you."

"Fergolin," she said, injured.

He was going. Getting his feet under him, he pulled on his long shirt and wrapped his belt around his middle. Crouched in the low room, he embraced her, reaching down between her thighs to give a painful and yet pleasureable tug to her woman's part. "Good-by, fat one."

She giggled, pleased at the compliment, and he went out. Grela stayed to neaten up the room.

Fergolin, Grela's husband, was of the Lineage of the Salmon and a master of the Bear Skull Society. Although he enjoyed being married to Grela, he passed his days at the roundhouse with the other men, where he could be of importance to Ladon; therefore he saw little of his wife, or indeed, of any woman. Except for the delightful uses of one another's bodies, he saw no way that men and women could share their lives, each being the opposite of the other, and he usually paid no attention to what he heard when he was with Grela, especially as she talked so much.

What she had let slip to him that morning, however, took a very forward place in his mind for the rest of the day. He was not a man of deep questions. When Moloquin had first appeared some few winters before, Fergolin had not wondered much where he had come from. Moloquin was not one of the People and therefore had no relationship to him except as an annoyance and a distraction.

Now he knew better. Moloquin was one of the People after all, the son of Ael, the sister-son of the chief.

He spoke of this to one or two of the other men, as they lingered in the yard outside the roundhouse door, waiting to be given some task to perform for their chief's sake.

"Ael," said one, blankly.

"I had forgotten that Ladon had a sister," said the other, who was Mishol, a member of the Bear Skull but not a master. "There is a bad story about her, I do not remember what it is."

At this moment Ladon's own son came out of the roundhouse, straightened after passing through the door, and stood blinking in the bright sunlight. Fergolin turned to him, smiling, and poked him affectionately in the ribs.

"Well, mighty hunter, are you going forth to slay the ring-tusked boar?"

The other men laughed, but there was some love in their mirth; they all liked Ladon's son. The boy blushed. His skin was so fair that the color showed all along his throat and cheeks, like a girl's.

"I know I shall never wield the short spear as well as you, Fergolin-on."

Fergolin barked with amusement; with all the other men, he hunted four times a year, but he slew nothing. Ladon's son, with many gestures of respect, was going away toward the gate and the men watched him go.

"He shall be a good chief," said Mishol.

Fergolin said nothing. He was one of Ladon's ring-brothers, and with the rest had sworn on oath in favor of Ladon's son, but he did not believe that the boy would ever be the chief. He spoke well, but too well, saying always what would flatter the listener; he looked well, but too well, seeking always for admiration and love. Fergolin looked down at his hands. If Moloquin was indeed Ael's son, then he saw trouble for Ladon and his schemes.

Mishol took a knife from his belt, shaved a splinter from a stick of wood, and used it to clean his teeth. He said, "If I were Ladon, I would slay this woods-puppy."

Fergolin's head jerked up; he felt a sudden stab of guilt, as if his inner thought had goaded Mishol to this remark. Sharply he said, "He is a child, and one of us."

"Don't be so upright, Fergolin," Mishol said roughly. "There is no one to protect him, and Ladon would smile on those who did it."

A few other men drifted closer, seeing them argue, and sat together in the sun; some were whittling, some picking through their hair and their friends' hair for lice and fleas. Mishol looked around at them, frowning—he was a big man, muscular and raw-throated.

"Well?" he said loudly. "Shall we do what is in our chief's heart?"

"Do what?" asked one who had not heard the whole conversation.

"He is a child," Fergolin said stubbornly. "And one of us. The Overworld looks down and will see what is done to one of the People—"

He caught a sudden, alarming, transcendent sense of himself as another person; he knew he was being watched. The souls of his ancestors watched him. Desperately he wanted to do that which would please them. He made a sign, surreptitiously, to summon their help. Mishol was still looking around him for support.

"I say, we should do what the chief would wish of us."

"Moloquin is just a thief," said another man. "He has no father and no mother, either, now—he is not one of the village. Perhaps Mishol is right. We could catch him and kill him, and Ladon would give us all greatly from his roundhouse."

"The chief's will is the will of Heaven," piped up little Sarbon and banged his thighs for emphasis.

Fergolin bit his lower lip; was that true, should he do as the others did—as the others spoke of doing? He glanced around him, looking for some answer in the faces of his fellows, but they showed him nothing; they sat there with dull looks, humming, or cracking lice, and the will of Heaven did not shine through their eyes. Old Brant came in, a little nearer Fergolin, and sat down.

"Who is this boy, anyway?" asked one at the back of the group.

"An enemy of our chief," Mishol bawled. "What else must you know?"

"He is Ael's son," said Fergolin. "The son of Ladon's sister."

That met a round of blank faces. "Ladon. Did he have a sister?" Sarbon, however, pulled on his lip, frowning.

"Ael? Oh, I remember her. That time, when we were playing with a pig's head, she stole it away, don't you remember?" He turned toward Fergolin who had joined the boys' band at the same time as he. "Don't you remember?"

Now Fergolin did remember; his mind leapt back into the past, when the most important thing in his life had been doing well in the sight of the other boys—vividly he saw before him a long, lithe figure, long black hair streaming, holding up in mockery a mangled bloody skull.

"He's just a woods-sprite," someone else muttered. "I don't believe he is even a real human being."

"Kill him," Mishol said. "Kill him, and Ladon will put us at the very front of the procession when we go to the Great Gathering."

Some of the men were nodding in agreement. Mishol got up onto his feet. "I will fetch a club," he said, and started around.

"Wait," Fergolin cried. He put out one hand to hold Mishol back. "What are you talking of? This is murder! The People do not raise their hands against one another."

"He is not one of us!"

"But he is. He is the son of the chief's sister. And that's why you want to kill him—" Fergolin leapt toward this knowledge as toward a safe landing—"Not because he isn't one of us, but because he is."

"Besides," said old Brant, who had been silent until now, "Karella has taken him under her wing."

At the mention of that name the men's faces cleared of their fierce resolve, and even Mishol, with a grunt, turned forward and settled down in his place. Fergolin wondered how Brant knew this, but it fitted with what Grela had told him—he saw again, as she had told it, Karella leaping and waving her fists and shouting at them for scaring her pet away. He laughed at the thought, and a few of the other men laughed too, not knowing why, but because Fergolin was respected.

"What Karella wishes, she will have," said someone in the back. "And I for one will not get in her way."

"Or into her stories," said another man, and made a quick gesture with his fingers, to ward off evil.

"Still, just because he is Ael's son—"

"He is nothing," said Mishol, loudly. "He shall never be other

than nothing, and I shall not trouble myself with nothing." He got
up and went into the roundhouse.

In the longhouses, each woman had her own hearth, a ring of stones
for her fire, a larger ring for her living space. Now, in the evening,
every hearth was noisy with children, warm with the cooking fire,
steamy with the smells of dinner.

Every hearth but Karella's, where she sat alone.

She put sticks into her fire. Near her was a pot of clay with a
broth ready to be heated, and a flat basket full of cakes made of
grain, but she could not bring herself to cook anything. It seemed
too much work just to feed one old woman. Even her hunger seemed
to belong to someone else.

She poked the fire with another stick. When she had married
the first time, she had thought she would bear many children, but
there had been none. Soon she quarreled with her husband and they
separated.

It was his fault, she had thought. His fault she bore no children.
So she married again.

That second one she had never loved, but he had a powerful
body, long strong legs, and whenever they had gone into the little
room together the whole longhouse quaked. No babies came of it.
Then she had not minded so much, because she was a storywoman,
and the stories were children enough, and anyhow she fought with
her husband whenever they were not in the little room together.
Even there they fought sometimes, even as their bodies thrust and
stroked together. When he died suddenly some people had said she
had killed him, working him into a story and causing his death first
in her mind and then in fact.

After that she had gone a long while without a man, and needing none, since any man she wanted she could lure to her and enjoy
for a moment and not have to worry about other times.

The women around the sampo buzzed about her; the men
watched her with an unhealthy intensity. All the People came to her
for stories; she could turn a whole crowd to stones, silent and still,
while she spun a new world around them in her words and gestures.

She still had that. Even now, especially now perhaps, as she sat
lonely by her hearth, if she lifted her head, and began to speak, and
put her hands before her in the air, then they would come and clus-

ter around her and listen, their eyes bright. Then they were her children.

When she was silent she had no one. Soon she would be silent forever, a spirit of the air, a creature of the Overworld, where all was known already and so there was no need for stories.

She poked at the fire, thinking of Moloquin, and she told herself she would go tomorrow, walk the long way up to the Pillar of the Sky, and tell him stories all day long.

She could go and live with him. Leave the People and live with him.

Once before she had done that. When she married for a third time, her husband was a man of another village, and she had told everyone here that she would go to his village to be with him because she was sick of them all. But they had not gone to his village; they had gone off and lived together, alone, in the west; he made a hut of withies and brush, she toiled dawn to dark in a garden, they slept together every night, they were enough for each other. Him she loved, and him she had only for that one season, because when the winter came he sickened and he died, her husband, and she had gone back to the People.

Thinking of him again, she lowered her chin to her chest, and tears filled her eyes. All her life seemed wasted, a dry leaf, after that one green season of love.

So, wrapped in her memories, Karella sat by the fire, the stick in her hand, and heard nothing of the bustle around her, the buoyant cries of the children, the laughter, the sounds of cooking and of eating, the crunch of feet and the crackle of the fire; she heard nothing at all, until suddenly there was nothing to hear: all the longhouse fell into an utter silence.

At that she lifted her head, surprised, and looked around.

In silence, in stillness, the People stood beside their hearths and stared. In silence, in stillness, there came down the middle of the longhouse a creature hidden in a mass of cloth.

It was Moloquin. Moloquin. He had taken the clothes she had brought and swaddled himself in them, only his long bare legs showing; even his head was covered up, his eyes peeping out through an opening. Slowly, fearfully, he was coming down the longhouse, looking for her.

She got up. Her heart swelled great as the longhouse; she could not keep her joy within, but opened her mouth and gave it off as a sigh. She stretched out her arms, and he ran into her embrace, a warm, living child, and she brought him tight against her breast, as close as her husbands had been, pressed her face to his wild earth-smelling hair. She led him to her hearth, and sat him down, and there, for the first time, she cooked food for him over her own fire.

Karella taught him how to wash himself in the morning, and what to eat and how. She said it was important not to shit anywhere inside the brush fence around the longhouses, and took him off to the ditch where all the People shit, but Moloquin could not bear the smell and went away a lot farther, to be by himself when he emptied his bowels. She told him how to put on clothes she gave him; she told him how to start a fire in the proper way, so that the spirits would agree to let it burn. All these things were very boring to Moloquin.

He sat by the fire in the longhouse and looked around him at the other people. They were nearly all women with their children. The spaces where they lived, each family to its own hearth, were divided from one another only by the air, a line of stones, and the knowledge of separation. Karella had told him not to stare, to keep his eyes downcast, but Moloquin disobeyed her.

He let his hair hang down over his face and he looked through it, so that no one would see him watching them.

He saw the women across the way make a loom of two pieces of wood and weave cloth on it, and he longed to go closer and watch the threads pass in and out of one another. The order in that pleased him. He liked also the colors that they used. A few of the children came up around him and called him names, but he ignored them. There were no boys in the longhouse that came near his size and age; the girls who were his age stayed close by their mothers; all the children who came to Moloquin were little things, their bellies still fat in front of them, their cheeks round and pink, and although they lisped insults at him he wanted to pick them up and squeeze them and make them laugh, as he saw them laugh with their mothers.

When he felt no one watching him, he got up and moved away around the longhouse, seeing everything. It was like stalking animals. When he saw that his presence and movement alarmed them, he stopped and sank down on his heels and was still, hardly even breathing, until they lost interest in him and looked elsewhere; then he got up and went off again.

In such a way he soon knew all the longhouse, even the little room at the end, with its delicious and provocative smells. Coming up the long side of the place once more, he happened on a lump of clay.

The wet mass of the clay was on a mat before a hearth where a low fire still burned; the woman had gone off somewhere. Moloquin squatted down by the clay. He had seen mud like this before. The People made pots of it. He had dug up such gooey mud himself out of the riverbank, and he knew how it felt. He knew also that he should leave this mud alone, but as he remembered how the mud felt, oozing through his fingers, and remembered also how he had seen other people shaping it, the temptation overwhelmed him and he reached out and took a handful.

The feel of it swiftly absorbed him. Sitting flat on his hams, he squeezed and rolled it between his palms. It would take any shape he could give it, and he began to form it into a ball, and twisted part away and saw a nose, a mouth, an ear—he gathered up more of the clay and patted it and pounded it, enjoying his power over it. The earthy smell reminded him of the riverbank and he tasted a little of it and thought of the river and wound and coiled the clay into a wild shape.

It was too easy, though: it made no resistance to him, and would be anything he wished; he found this disappointing.

Still he loved the handling of it, the sensation of the clay giving way to his strength. But while he sat there contentedly molding the clay, the woman who owned it came back.

She shrieked. Her shriek was his first warning that she had found him at this business, and he leapt up, ducking by instinct. She struck him like a bear-mother defending her cub, her hands open, her nails ripping at him. He backed up, trying to get away from her, and tripped over a stone and fell.

After that he merely rolled into a ball and let her beat him and scream at him. She did him no harm, but his soul sank into a cold despair; he would never like being with these people.

Now here came Karella to save him. He lowered his arms and got up, and Karella put her hand on his shoulder and gave him a little shake.

"Now see what you've done. Didn't I tell you to stay by the hearth and wait for me?"

Moloquin muttered under his breath. He let his hair hang down over his face, to hide his eyes, while he glared from Karella to the other woman, whose fury still glowed like a red blaze in her face. She struck at him again and missed. Karella led him away.

"You must never touch a woman's belongings like that," Karella said. "She meant that clay for some purpose, don't you understand? Now it is wasted."

"Wasted," he said, surprised. They had come back to her hearth; he sat down by the little fire, and saying the words she had told him he put new wood on it. "Why?" Looking over his shoulder he saw the woman taking the lump of clay away.

"It is woman's work," Karella said. "No man may be allowed to handle such things. The spirit of them is driven out by a man's hands."

"No spirit is in it," he said. He remembered how the clay had yielded unresisting to his hands. "There no soul in it at all."

"Moloquin, you must obey me, or you will be ruined."

"I want to go away, then," he said, and she slapped him.

"Never say that again."

He held his tongue. His anger seethed in him like water boiling in a pot; he wondered if the spirit of the hearth had somehow gotten into his belly and set his insides on fire. He pressed his hand to his belly. Everything he did, Karella told him, he had to do in certain ways, to avoid offending spirits, or to attract the benevolent aid of spirits; there seemed nothing he could do freely.

"You cannot live, except with us," Karella said to him. She gathered up the clutter of pots and baskets around her hearth, tipped out the garbage and thrust everything off to one side; although she acted very busy, he noticed, all she did was shuffle things from one place to another, and he laughed, his mood lifting.

"I live enough before," he said, forgetting the worst.

"Because some spirit protected you. Perhaps it was Ael, your mother. In any case, she has given you to me to care for, and you must obey me as if I were she."

He thought of going away, back to his place of stones, and lowered his head. She fussed around a while longer, making the space neat by shoving everything indiscriminately out to the edges. At last she said, "Now, come with me—I have work to do, and will need your help."

"Why?" Moloquin got to his feet.

"I am going to find wood."

He went after her down the longhouse to the door; all around him the hostile stares of the People were like walls of thorns. Karella led him outside, into the sun, and he breathed deep, his chest expanding, standing straight—as if, before, he could only stoop. In front of him his new mother stood, almost a head shorter than he, her face sharp, scanning the village.

"Now," she said, turning toward him, and put her hand on his arm. "Let us go and find wood for the fire."

At a little trot she took him away up the slope, toward the forest. He fell in beside her, needing only to walk fast to keep up with her. They made their way between the long winding strips of the gardens where the women were at work with their hoes and rakes, digging out the weeds from between their plants. Someone was singing nearby, and the others joined in sometimes, so that it was like question-and-answer; the voices fit smoothly together, filling all the song's spaces. As they passed the top edge of the worked ground, he saw some people off to his right a little way, digging up a hole in the ground.

"What are they doing over there?"

She hardly glanced that way. "We will harvest soon," she said. "They are digging a pit to thresh the grain in."

"Thresh."

Into his mind leapt the memory of his mother, gathering her sheaves of grain into bundles, shouting at him to thresh, to thresh—she had struck him, furious, when he dropped them. There had been no hole in the ground. He struggled to remember. All he remembered was the force of her blow, the knowledge that he had done wrong and drawn her anger. Craning his neck, he watched the people digging until he and Karella were into the close quarters of the forest.

Of course Karella was not used to gathering wood for herself. As the headwoman of the Red Deer Kindred, she had a dozen younger, stronger hands eager to do such work for her. But she wanted to give Moloquin a task; she knew that work would make him acceptable to the others, and that bringing wood into the village would put a value on him.

They followed a dusty path through the brambles of ripening berries at the edge of the forest, and wound a way back deeper into the trees. She stopped, unsure, here where the sun was so far away, and looked around her.

"What you want here?" Moloquin asked. "You want to burn?"

"Yes. Do you know where we can find some?"

He took her away through the oak trees. Now it was he who led. She followed close after him, her ears straining at the alien sounds of the wood, her eyes caught by swift little movements on either side. He took her to a great oak tree, clutching the earth in its knobbed roots, spreading its branches around it, driving off all other growth.

"Here," he said, and leapt up, and caught a low-hanging branch. As she watched, amazed, he swung himself nimbly up into the tree and climbed away into the leaves. As he disappeared among the green and brown tangles of the tree she imagined that he grew wings like a bird. She backed up a few steps, her head back, trying to make him out in the dense treetop but all she saw was the wild waving of a branch here and there as he stepped on it.

His voice came from the leaves. "Watch—be careful." With a rending crash a dead branch fell down through the lower levels, tearing off smaller twigs and limbs, and thudded to the earth a little way from Karella.

She approached it cautiously. The bark had all been worn away and the wood shone. Moloquin dropped to the ground beside her.

"Here," he said, and held out a little bird's nest to her.

"What do I want with that?" She shied from it, her temper short in this alien place.

For answer, he took the nest and plopped it onto her head, and burst out laughing.

Karella snarled at him; she snatched the nest out of her hair, watching him giggle and prance before her. She realized how she looked, and had to laugh also. She nodded to the branch.

"This is good wood, Moloquin, but it is too large."

He shrugged. "No care." He dragged the branch around until it rested with one end up against the oak trunk, and then he jumped on the middle. Nothing happened; the branch was very solid. He took up another branch off the ground and hit the first one, but the club was rotten and broke. Still he did not give up; Karella watched him, her hands at her sides, as he searched the area around him, found a large stone, and pried it out of the ground. He could barely lift it; groaning he hoisted it up over his head, and drove it down on the branch.

The wood cracked with a sharp report. Crowing, Moloquin pounced on it and tore the branch to pieces with his hands, banging the pieces on the stone when they would not yield to his strength.

"Now," he said, panting, "is some spirit needed to thank?"

Karella smiled at him. "I suppose there is. Tree-lore is not women's lore. The branch was dead already, the tree will not mind that we have taken it."

"My old mother," he said, "said no word of thanks."

"She was angry."

"Is that why she die?"

Karella's eyebrows rose; she smiled at him, pleased again with his quick wits. "Yes, probably. Yes."

"Give me—" he waved his hand at her.

She gave him the leather sling she had brought, and showed him how to put the wood into it. He went off again, to find more, and she sat by the sling, listening uneasily to the forest sounds, the twittering of the birds like free souls in the air, the unquiet rustle of the brush, and the wind sounds. Moloquin worked hard, finding good dead sound wood, breaking it up with stones or his hands, or slamming the limbs against the oak trunk, and soon the sling was full.

He put the sling up on his shoulders and they went back toward the village. As they walked, Moloquin began to sing.

It was not a true song, but a wordless undulating tone. Karella enjoyed it; she listened gratefully to it, ignoring the screeches and calls and whispers of the forest around her, and kept close by him. He had some power in him, she guessed, that let him move freely through a place so dense with spirits as this. That was why he had been able to take shelter in the Pillar of the Sky. She had been right to take him in. He was Ael's son, and had the favor of Heaven. She lifted her head, pleased with herself, keeping very close to Moloquin.

Moloquin went into the forest three more times that day, and brought out firewood on his back. The first three loads he stacked up in the longhouse, as Karella told him, but the last, she said, he was to take to the roundhouse.

"You go with me," he said.

"No, no," she said. "You go there. Take the wood in through the gate; you will see a great pile of wood inside the yard. Put your wood there."

"I no want to."

"Moloquin," she said, with the great air of patience she often assumed, "you are here, but you are not here, to many of the People. You must show them your worth."

"I bring wood here," he said. "Ladon there. Ladon hate me."

"Moloquin," she said, her patience something leaner, "if Ladon burns just one stick of wood you have brought, he will have accepted you and can no longer harm you. Now, do as I say; remember, I am your mother now."

What she said made some sense to him, and he knew, also, that like Ael she would only get angry with him if he defied her; he could not endure her anger. He loaded up a sling of wood onto his back and went down toward the roundhouse.

He had never been so close to Ladon's place before. On its high ground by the river it seemed to grow up from the heart of the earth. For a long while he stood outside the gate in the wall around it, gathering his courage, but in the end it was his curiosity that drove him through the gate.

The wall was made of tree trunks. Inside, the yard was wide and level, of pounded earth swept clean, and full of men, sitting on the ground, some busy with small tasks, others idle and talking. They all stared at him when he came in. He lowered his head a little and lugged his wood toward the heap against the inside of the wall.

The roundhouse also was made of great trees. Massive and up-thrusting, they supported other trees, split in half and laid down over the tops of the uprights. It was so wonderful to see this that he hesitated, gawking at it, the wood still balanced on his back, and all the stares of the men on him. The size and strength of the round-house reminded him of the forest. He stroked the huge trunks with his eyes, pleased with the symmetry of their structure.

Coming back to himself, he let the sling slip down, and began to stack up the wood he had brought. The wood already heaped there lay disorderly and he knew it would rot if left like that; he set his wood in neat rows and then began to stack the other wood also. Every few seconds he stole another glance at the roundhouse.

A shriek from behind him brought him wheeling around, his spine tingling. In the doorway of the roundhouse stood Ladon's son.

"Cur! Filth!" Ladon's son rushed forward, and Moloquin, warned, ran a few steps toward the gate in the wall; but the gate was closer to his enemy than it was to him, and when he saw Ladon's son stoop for a stone on the ground, Moloquin whirled and ran back toward the wood.

He thought to climb the wall; he was scrambling up over the heap of wood when the stone hit him in the head. All his sense left him for a moment. In a dizzy blackness he fell, and he felt that he fell down forever, struggling for his soul back.

He lay on the ground, panting, and heard other shouts, other feet pounding toward him. In a panic he fought to rise, but his body was in another power than his; nothing would obey him. Hands fell on him. He lashed out, sobbing between his teeth.

"Hold!"

Someone held him, but not with angry hands; someone held him close and wrapped arms around him to protect him. He kept still, tense.

"What are you doing?" shouted the man who held him. "What business is this?"

Moloquin pulled, and the grip on his arms eased; he backed away, his left eye full of blood. The man who had held him now got between him and Ladon's son and seized Ladon's son by the arm and shook him.

"What business is this? A true man does not set upon another like that, does not strike the first blow against one who is unarmed. I am amazed at you, chief's son—I thought you understood the bearing of a man of the People."

"Fergolin," Ladon's son cried. "He is not one of us."

Moloquin wiped his face. There was a swelling on the top of his forehead, and it dribbled blood down into his hair. The other men were gathering close around him. He lowered his head, feeling cramped. He could not breathe here without breathing of their air.

Fergolin was still shouting at Ladon's son, shaking him, and some of the other men joined him in the scolding; Ladon's son turned away, red-faced. Now Fergolin swung around, saw Moloquin again, and knelt beside him.

"Let me look at this." He touched Moloquin's head. "Can you hear me well? Is your vision clear?"

Moloquin recoiled from him. "Leave me alone!" He glared at

Fergolin as if he had thrown the stone. "I hate you. I hate all of you!"
He leapt up to his feet and sprinted out of the roundhouse yard.

Fergolin stood staring after Moloquin, who had disappeared out the
gate. Blood smeared the Bear Skull master's fingertips. Impulsively
he raised his hand to his lips and tasted of the blood, as if he might
find answers in that.

The other men stood close around him, their faces taut. Ladon's
son was still among them, but as Fergolin turned, seeking him, the
boy slipped out of the pack and ran away into the roundhouse.

"He will tell Ladon," said one of the other men.

"Let him," said Fergolin, surprised. "I have the right of it—you
saw. Ladon cannot do but what is right."

"But—Moloquin—"

They looked at one another, but no one spoke; they all felt this
to be a dangerous and subtle matter, and it was not getting any easier
as it went on. At last Fergolin said, "I think this will all come to a bad
end." He wondered where Moloquin had run to, probably to Karella,
who was protecting him. He was too old for the longhouses. At his
age boys were ready to enter a society and begin their lifetimes of
learning and study, obedience and memory.

Moloquin was supposed to be too stupid to have any capacity for
such things. He had not seemed stupid to Fergolin. It would have
been a relief if he had been stupid. Fergolin raised his fingertips
again, to sniff the drying blood.

"You disobeyed me!"

"Opa-Ladon-on—" his son quivered at the feet of the chief. "I
threw a stone at him. I have done it before—you told me to do it
before—"

Ladon struck him again, furious, raining several blows down on
his son's bowed trembling back. It was Karella who had done this,
and it was Karella he wished he could strike down.

Finally, with a kick at his son's bottom, the chief walked away
through the roundhouse. Many openings in the thatch let in the light
but it was still dim and shadowy below the roof. Each of the societies
had its own section; most of the men were gone now, off on their

daily rituals and duties. He wished Fergolin had been off somewhere when Moloquin came in.

With firewood. That was her doing, the serpent-hearted woman, sending the brat here with a load of firewood, making him important, forcing the men to see him, to accept him. Putting him out of Ladon's reach.

I am the chief, he thought. When one is hungry, he comes to me. When one is cold, he comes to me. I give everything to them, food, shelter, everything. Then why have I no power?

Why did she have such power? From the place of the dead, she reached back into his life and trifled with his plans, balked his resolution, made nothing of his dreams. She whom he had always hated: Ael, his sister.

It was Karella now, but somehow Ael had invaded Karella's mind and brought this from her. Always before, Karella had been an annoyance, with her keen understanding, her vast story-lore, her willingness to speak up at bad moments, but she had never done anything like this.

As if she stood before him he remembered Ael, as tall as he was, thin and hard from the grueling work of women, her black hair hanging down over her shoulders. She should have married. She should have married that first summer, when her body first bled, but she had refused. Untameable Ael. Walking in the woods with her bow, killing beasts for their meat and hide, growing a crop richer than any other, as if the plants sprang up from the drops of her sweat. She had done everything alone. She had mocked them all, and so they had all hated her, and when Ladon attacked her, they had done nothing. Turned their backs and not even watched her go.

He had thought he was finished with her, then, when she went away into the forest.

His stomach turned. She was here now, with him, mocking him again; he could almost smell the female odor of her body.

That frightened him, that smell, or the memory of that smell; it reminded him of what he and Ael had done, that one time. That was forbidden absolutely, and if the People ever learned of it—

Maybe that was why his sister was haunting him now. He put his hands over his face, sick with guilt.

Outside the men were talking, and he could hear Fergolin's voice, arguing perhaps: Fergolin questioned everything, not from the perverse delight of an Ael, but with the fearful concern of one who needed always to be right. Ladon drew nearer to the wall, to overhear what the men were saying, and realized that they knew that Moloquin was Ael's son, a piece of truth he had known was common among the women but not the men. Slowly Ladon's mind settled. He was still the chief, and if the women somehow managed to thwart him, they had been thwarting men from the beginning; it was no special weakness of his.

He gathered himself. Moloquin was a green boy, Karella old and held in dread rather than love; he would prevail over them. Lifting his shoulders, he expanded his chest with a deep breath and felt immediately more confident. He went out to the yard.

"Opa-Ladon-on!" The men had been squatting by the round-house wall, debating. They sprang up to their feet, spreading their open palms toward him in respect. "Mighty is he! Opa-Ladon-on!"

He raised his hand, palm out, to greet them, scanned them quickly, and with gestures and a few words he scattered them, sending this one here and that one there, until none remained but Fergolin. Then Ladon nodded to the Bear Skull master to follow him and went over to the outer wall, where the wood was piled in a disorderly heap.

Fergolin came up to his shoulder and stood there. At a gesture from Ladon, he set about straightening the heap of wood.

"My son was rude to you, I believe," Ladon said.

Fergolin stacked arm-length pieces of oak and ash. He straightened to speak to his chief, and met his eyes.

"The boy is young, Opa-on, and still unrestrained. I hope I did not trespass in showing him the proper way."

"No, I thank you for taking such a responsibility on yourself." Ladon indicated the wood with one hand. "Are we now to be supplied every day? This has been a problem all spring, the wood."

"I don't know, Opa-on. It was Moloquin who brought it here."

Ladon stooped to pick up a long chunk of the wood. It was sound, old oak and ash, well dried out, and broken into proper lengths. He had wanted to be disappointed. Now he had to say, "Yes, excellent, a well-done task. I shall see him when he returns."

"Opa-on? You mean Moloquin?"

"I mean Moloquin," said Ladon, and went back into the round-house.

. . .

Karella walked up the gentle slope, through the waist-high flowering grasses, the wind behind her, and before her, at the top of the long run of the world, the vast embankment and toppling stones of the Pillar of the Sky. She was looking for Moloquin. When the word had reached her that he had run away, she had immediately bent her steps here; she supposed he might have gone back to the forest, but if he had, she would never find him.

The story of his flight had come to her from mouth to mouth, girls and women, and she trusted none of what the last mouth had told her—that he had fought with Ladon's son and run away bleeding and defeated. Her stomach was queasy with uncertainty and bewilderment. What was happening now over Moloquin had begun with her, and she was eaten up with doubt of her deed.

The grass shivered in the wind; hordes of grasshoppers bounded out of her path, their arching leaps approaching flight; butterflies flitted off over the tops of the bending grass. Off to one side, a bustard suddenly sprang out of a hollow and raced away on its long legs, its heavy body balanced between its outstretched wings. The wind was rising, its roar merry in her ears, tangling up her legs in her own garment, and boiling up the sky with fat grey clouds.

She stopped, caught at the center of this: the joyous tumult of the Overworld. Raising her head, she let the wind bless her face with its cool caress. Everything was moving, the whole world, all in its harmony. She turned around, her arms out, whirling around and around, to make her own wind, to spin the mean human sense out of her head, and stopped, and with her mind a blur she felt all through herself the surging rhythm of the world-as-one.

The thrill faded. That was the flaw in being human: the need always to stop the flow and study it. She plodded on, tired now, her soul burdened with her questions of herself.

The place of humankind in the world was so small, so minor, that to fools it must seem that people could do as they wish, without harm to any but themselves. Karella knew better. A lifetime of stories had taught her that everything mattered. Now she imagined consequences to what she had done that could tear the world to tatters.

She should have left Moloquin as he was, and let Ladon spin his own destruction. Was it not said that all true crimes carried with them their own punishment? Yet she had meddled.

She reached the ditch outside the bank and stopped, tired, breathless, an old woman faced with more than she wanted to do.

The ditch was too deep, the bank too high. Slowly she began to walk around the other edge, toward the way in, but then a strange sound reached her that froze her in her steps.

A quavering low wail, it rose from within the dead place, a demon's voice. But she had heard it before. She forced her thumping heart to calm. It was Moloquin, singing.

She went to the opening in the bank and entered into the holy place. The day was fading away and the grassy bowl within the bank was nearly full of shadows. At first she could make out only the stones in their slow collapse, but the tuneless howl of the song went on, full of anger and sorrow, and following it she found Moloquin.

He sat beside the northernmost stone, called the North Watcher, his back to the rock, his legs tucked under him. He had cast off all his new clothes and pulled the orderly braids out of his hair. A streak of dried blood painted his cheek and jaw. Seeing Karella, he paid no heed to her and went on with his song. Karella sat down beside him and waited.

He sang a while longer, but the sound had changed, strained and false; with her there beside him he became aware of himself, and of the limits of himself. He fell still. His head sank down, his hair lying over his cheek. Karella said nothing.

The embankment shut out all the world. There seemed nothing of the earth but this small round, with its great stones to prop up the sky. Overhead the clouds raced by in the grip of the whistling air. By the ancient stone, the boy and the old woman sat together in silence.

Finally he turned to her and said, "Why did you come here? Why can you not leave me alone?"

"You are my son," she said.

"I am not your son! I am—I am Ael's son."

"Without me, you did not even know her name," she said.

He had no answer to that. She looked on him with sympathy, wishing she could put her arm around him, but she knew he would fight against her. She raised her face again toward the rushing sky. High above them, among the turbulent clouds, a dark speck moved, a bird, or an eye of the spirits, watching what happened here. She felt again the cold dread of this place, the aching memory, the promise of catastrophe.

He said, "I hate him, Karella. I want to kill him."

"What happened between you?"

"He throwed—threw a rock at me."

Karella waited; when he said no more, she asked, "And you?"

"I runned away. Or I killed him, Karella, as if he were a lizard or a fat frog."

She thought, He is not afraid then, and was pleased with him. Now she lifted her arm and put it around his shoulders, and he drew close to her, his skin cold. She leaned her cheek against his hair.

"You were happy before. I should have left you alone."

He said nothing for a moment, his face close to hers, his eyes shut. At last he said, "Tell me a story."

That pleased her; she tightened her grip on him, and looked around her, waiting for the proper tale to climb up to the surface of her mind. Almost at once the words reached her lips, and she let go of him, to have her hands free.

"Once Abadon went roaming, and he came into a strange country, and there he slew a white deer. But the deer was the pet of the wife of the North Star, and when Abadon slew it he fell at once under her spell, and could neither move nor speak without her will.

"The wife of the North Star took him to her longhouse, and there forced him to work for her. She made him hoe up her garden, and plant, but Abadon did not sow the seeds she gave him, but planted pebbles instead, and so nothing grew. She forced him to haul water, and send him with a bucket to the river, but at the river he drank up the water and pissed it into the bucket, and so the water was foul to her.

"Then she ordered him to make a great mill for her, and taught him spells to use, and lent him a magic hammer, and with her spells and her hammer and the commands she gave him, he fashioned a wonderful mill, so well made that it turned at the lightest touch, and the top stone was covered with a pattern of many lights, and the mill was the most beautiful of the works of men and spirits. It turned by night and day, and ground out plenty and peace, enough for the whole world.

"And when it was done the wife of the North Star set Abadon free, and she gave him the hammer for his payment, and sent him away.

"Abadon did not go. In the night when the North Star's wife was asleep he came back into her longhouse, and he stole the mill and bore it away.

"Now the North Star saw him go, and cast his beams on him, and Abadon was struck so sore that he stumbled, and he dropped the mill into the sea. And the mill broke. The cover of many lights fell off the center post and the bottom stone cracked. Now the mill grinds out nothing but salt and sand, that fills up the depths of the sea. But Abadon went on to his home and dwelt there."

She sat still, and the tears spilled down her cheeks. Moloquin put his finger to her face and traced the long wet fall.

"Why do you weep?"

"I weep for the breaking of the mill," she said, "that let evil into the world."

She wiped her cheeks with her hand. Moloquin was watching her steadily, his face no longer twisted by his own dissatisfactions, but clear and open, and the eyes deep-seeing. He said, "Why did you tell me that story?"

"Because we are here," she said.

"What is this place, Ana? Who made this place?"

"No one made this place." She shook her head, her gaze drawn upward again, following the invisible course of power from the center of the circle to the sky. "It has been here since the beginning, and will be here until the end. The lore is forbidden to any but the masters of the Green Bough, whose task it is to care for it, and I do believe that they themselves know very little. It is a place of great power, a gateway between worlds. And I can say no more than that."

Moloquin put out one hand toward the ring of stones. "How did these stones come to be here?"

She was still staring up at the sky. Tired, she said, "That is a mistake. Some few fathers' years ago, there was a Green Bough master who was chief also, and the village was then of a very great size; he thought to put a ring of stones here to rival the stones at Turnings-of-the-Year."

"Where is that?"

"You will see," she said, "when we all go there, at the Midsummer Gathering. Now I must go back, my child—will you go with me?"

"My mother," he said, and smiled at her; his eyes looked tired, like an old man's. "My mother, I stay here, I think a while here, and come back in morning-time."

"You will come back," she said, uneasy. "Won't you? Ladon's son will not hurt you."

"Ana," he said, "I fear nothing of Ladon's son. I fear me, that I may hurt him. Go. I come tomorrow again home."

Still she lingered, unwilling to go far from him, to lose sight of him; what he had said made no impression on her at first. Finally she rose up—night was coming, and she was afraid to be alone in the dark—and he stood and embraced her. Something in that reassured her, and she took heart to leave him.

Moloquin sat down again with his back to the stone and raised his head toward the sky. His head hurt a little but he ignored that.

The story of the broken mill, which drove Karella to tears, lifted him to a triumphant exultation. He knew at once what the story meant. The world was not meant to be as it was; therefore he saw no more need to compress himself into its ways. He could go if he wished, or he could stay if he wished, and he could do as he pleased.

Around him the quiet ground inside the bank was slowly filling up with shadows. He pressed his back to the stone, enjoying the solidarity and strength, and went through the story again in his mind.

It told him so much—why he loved it here, the still silent unchanging center of the whirl of all change. Here, for the last time, the world was whole.

He thought of his mother Ael, who had brought him here. There had been no still solid center with her—Ael with her wild moods, sometimes laughing and singing and leading him into a game that he, still chubby-legged, clump-fingered, could not help losing, and sometimes she had been sobbing and full of rage, driving him into a corner of their shelter, not speaking to him for days and days. He had adored her. He still loved her with a passion as strong as hunger or thirst.

He had thought, at first, that the People would be like her—that if he could only do the right things, their blows would change to caresses, they would take him in.

But they were less than Ael. They were mean and weak. She had left them because they were unworthy of her. She had left him for the same reason.

Karella was not like the others.

Maybe his mother had not abandoned him. Maybe she had given him to Karella to care for. Karella had found him here, where Ael had left him, and Karella told him stories, and the stories gave him what he had never had before: a way of knowing.

He told himself all her stories again, trying to repeat each word as she had: it gave him a feeling of power to bring them up out of his memory. He shut his eyes, to see the stories better, and he fell asleep.

He woke up wide-eyed, his whole body quivering, as if someone had shouted his name. The night lay over him. Raising his head, he looked up, and saw above him what he had seen a thousand thousand times, and never seen before: the slow-turning, everlasting mill, with its many lights, tilted steeply away from the earth, its edge a white blaze across the sky.

He lay down, his eyes turned toward the stars, and again he slept.

He dreamt of his mother, of Karella, of the whirling stars. He dreamt he stood on the open land, and before him was the embankment of the Pillar of the Sky, but instead of the sad untidy circle of stones, he saw within the circle of the bank a wonderful ring of great uprights, each twice as tall as a man, topped by flat lintels, like the trees of Ladon's roundhouse. Inside, rising above the outer ring, were five gates, the last higher than the two before, those two higher than the first two, rising up toward Heaven. He heard Karella's voice saying, "This is the gateway between worlds." Then from the center of the rings of stones a whirling light rose into Heaven, and around the light the mill of Heaven turned right again, and the world was as it was supposed to be, full of peace and plenty.

Then he saw that the whirling light was Moloquin himself, stretched tall as the space between Heaven and earth, and at his feet knelt Ladon's son, and begged for mercy. Moloquin himself would have been merciful, but all his power was gathered in the whirl of light. As he looked down, the stones became men, who seized Ladon's son and ground him to dust.

Then he woke up, and it was dawn.

He sat. The dream gripped him so that he trembled; he stared wildly around him, amazed, seeing the colossal gateways gone, the blazing stream of light no more. There was only the grass, waving a little in the breeze of the new day. The tired old stones hung in their sad decline, midway to the earth.

He cried out, disappointed, and covered his face with his hands and wept. It was cruel, to send him such a vision and then take it all away. His whole body rebelled against it. He hated Ael, for giving him life and for giving him dreams.

Karella would know what it meant. He set off at once at a run toward her longhouse.

. . .

When Moloquin stole into the longhouse, the women were all busy
at their morning tasks, feeding their children and getting ready to
go out to the fields, and in all the uproar of activity no one noticed
his arrival but the boy Grub, who had slept most of the night on the
threshold of the door and who still lingered there as the sun rose.

Moloquin stepped right over him; Grub shrank down, hoping
not to be noticed. When the other boy was past him, going down the
longhouse toward Karella's hearth, Grub sat up. Moloquin was much
older than Grub was and it was unfair that he could still come and
go as he wished to his mother's hearth, and Grub trailed after him a
little, envious, wondering how he kept his place here.

That took him to the edge of his own mother's hearth, and he
stood there a moment, looking in over the ring of the stones. His
mother sat by the fire, nursing the new baby in her arms. His oldest
sister hurried around trying to put shirts on the other two children;
their breakfast of cheese and grain and broth was strewn half-eaten
all around the place. Grub felt himself unnoticed in the middle of all
this bustle; he sank down on his hams, and reached one hand inside
the ring of stones, in toward a bit of the cheese, his eyes steadily on
his mother.

"Now, Grub."

She hardly raised her voice, but he felt the weight of her disapproval like a blow across his face. She frowned at him.

"Go away," she said. "Go find the other boys, and learn how to
do what they all do. This comes to all boys, my son, and now it's come
to you—be brave, go and master it. Get away, I cannot feed you any
more."

"Mama," he cried, his eyes filling up with tears, and stretched his
arms toward her.

"Mama, Mama," his sister said, jeering, and waggled her head at
him, and stuck out her tongue.

His mother slapped her. But her looks were no kinder toward
Grub, and she shook her head at him and shooed him off with her
free hand.

"Go away. How will you ever learn to be a man, hanging around
in the longhouse all day? Go on! Go on! I don't want to see you here
again."

At that moment the baby at her breast cried, and she turned to it with a finality, a whole attention, that locked him out; there was nothing for her now but the baby. He stood there a moment watching her. She was so beautiful, more beautiful than any other mother, more beautiful than the women in stories, and she did not love him any more. Once she had loved him as she loved the baby now, his little brother, but she did not love him any more. He turned and went away, dragging his feet, consumed with unhappiness.

Moloquin sat at Karella's hearth eating a bowl of meal and broth and talking; he talked even as he chewed, so that food sprayed out of his mouth. He was an idiot, as they all said, and that was why he could stay forever in the longhouse.

Grub went out the door. The sun was well up; all around him, the women spilled out of the longhouses and filled the yard inside the brush fence with their excitement, gathering their tools, talking with friends, stooping by the sampo to throw a lucky handful of grain into the hole in the top, and drawing the kindly looks of the fat old women there—today was threshing day; Grub had been out to the north fields to see the great floor of stones, set into the ground in the midst of the ripe grain. It was nothing to do with him.

Like a ghost, ignored or unseen altogether, he drifted through the midst of the excited women, out the gate in the brush fence, and away toward the river. He was hungry, and he knew nothing of finding food. Always before his mother had fed him. He waded through the high grass, still damp from the night dew, spooking mice and little birds ahead of him, but even the crickets were too fast for him to catch. Half in tears, he reached the bank of the river and sat down on it.

Here the river curled around, cutting deep down through the matted layers of grass, grass roots, dead grass, and dirt, down to the grey chalk underneath. On the far side was a broad stretch of flat ground, where once the women had planted gardens, but which was now overgrown with weeds, higher than a boy's head, nettles and thistles and brambles with thorns like knives. Threaded through this dense coarse green were the trails of the boys, burrows in the overgrowth like the tunnels of rabbits. Grub slipped down from this bank into the river and waded and swam across it.

All the paths on the far side led to one place. Here, deep inside the impenetrable jungle of weeds, was a clearing, and here the boys had struggled to raise up a shelter like their parents'; they had put up sticks, and tried to lash bundles of straw over them for a roof, but it was not so good a piece of work as the grown-ups did, and through the great gaping holes in the roof the sunlight streamed in, or the rain. Underneath was only the beaten ground, divided up naturally by the uparching roots and rotten stumps of an old wood.

When Grub came in, all the boys were gathered into the center of this shelter, where the fire burned. Ladon's son stood there on top of a stone, measuring out handfuls of grain to each of the boys by turn. He wore only a little squirrel-skin over his private parts and most of the other boys were similarly nearly naked. Grub went to the back of the waiting crowd.

Those nearest him hissed and pushed at him, crowding him off, making him stand last in line. He was the newest of them, the last one to leave his mother, and they never let him forget. "Mama's baby," one murmured, and giggled, and from the others rose up a little chorus of cries in falsetto: "Mama! Mama!" and some nasty laughter. He shivered, not from cold.

Up above everyone else, standing on his stone, Ladon's son went on giving out handfuls of milled grain from a pouch; at his feet, Grub knew, from the only previous time that he had managed to reach the front of the line, was a jug full of bean broth to mix into the meal, but to do that a boy had to have a vessel of some kind, and Grub had nothing. The older boys all had a dish, some had carved themselves bowls of wood, others used flat stones, and still others just used leaves, but Grub knew nothing yet of any of this, and none of the others would help him. He stood miserably in the line, thinking of his mother who had given him everything, everything he needed even before he asked for it, up until three days ago.

He had to eat. His stomach was throbbing with hunger; it felt flattened against his back, and he put his palm on it, expecting to feel the lumps of his spine through it; now at least he was drawing nearer to Ladon's son, and could overhear him talking.

"All the women shall be at the threshing," he was saying. "If we take the goats and the swine up to the edge of the forest there, we can go too."

"I'll take the swine," said one of the three big boys who were his best helpers.

"Good. Then I shall bring the goats, I and Kolon."

Grub was now only one boy away from the food, and his mouth

watered; he could smell the toasted barley, he could imagine the taste of the savory broth, thick with crushed beans and onion. Over his head they spoke to one another, just like grown-ups.

"Don't let the pigs get away this time."

"That wasn't I, that was some other. I know how to herd pigs, chief's son."

"Don't call me that," Ladon's son cried; Grub glanced at him, surprised. There was no one left to be fed save him, and he stood forward, holding out his hands, cupped together.

"Please," he said, and his stomach growled.

"Don't ever call me that again!" Ladon's son was shouting. He ignored the little boy before him; in his hand, the pouch of meal sagged, all but empty. "Call me Hawk-Feather, because I am above all of you." He swept his look around the boys' band. "Do you hear me?"

"Yes, yes," they shouted. "We hear you."

"Please," Grub whispered, holding out his hands.

Still Ladon's son paid him no heed at all. Still frowning, his chin thrust out, he scanned his followers with a look truly like a hawk's. Grub's belly was cramped with hunger and he reached out and touched the leader's arm.

Ladon's son struck disdainfully at him. "Leave me alone."

"I am hungry."

The son of the chief looked down, down at him, and his lip curled. "Have you brought me anything? I remember no gifts from you, no pieces of flint, no eggs or fledglings, no bright-colored feathers."

"I will bring you something," Grub cried.

"Pagh." The boy turned away. The other boys shouted to him, jubilant.

"Hawk-Feather! Hawk-Feather!"

"What about Moloquin?" asked one of the big boys.

At that a sort of hush fell, and the boys waited, intent on Ladon's son.

"I threw a stone at him yesterday," said Ladon's son. "He may not come back at all."

Grub leapt into the air. "I saw him! I saw him this morning!" He clapped his hands together, delighted.

Ladon's son jerked his gaze toward the little boy at his feet. "Saw him. Where?"

"At the hearth of Karella. He was eating. He looked so funny, he spat food when he talked." Grub laughed.

Ladon's son laughed also, and all the other boys laughed. Grub felt good suddenly; he looked around him, pleased to be in the middle, to have everyone know he had given Ladon's son a gift. And now he would receive food. Triumphant, he turned, his hands outstretched, cupped together.

The son of the chief was watching him, a small smile on his lips; slowly he put his hand into the pouch, and slowly drew it forth, heaped with meal. Grub's lips parted; he stepped closer, his hands rising. Then Ladon's son let the meal fall from a great height over Grub's hands, and the food showered down, some of it landing in the bowl of the boy's hands but most of it blown away.

Grub cried out. Ladon's son laughed, and all the other boys laughed. "Come on," said Hawk-Feather, and he went away, and the others all went with him in a great disorderly mass.

He had dropped the pouch, and the jug of bean broth was still there; Grub dropped to his knees beside them and plunged his hand into the pouch. There was nothing left but a few grains. He wet his fingers and picked up the last of the meal and licked it away. He turned the jug over his open mouth and a few drops fell on his tongue. Slowly, because even such a little amount of meal was too dry to eat easily, he swallowed the bit in his hand. He turned the jug over again and waited patiently until one final drop formed on the lip and fell, and then he went after the boys' band.

In the middle of the fields near the forest's edge, the People had dug a pit and set in it a floor of stones, to thresh their grain on. There were no stones in the ground around the village, so the stones were brought from another place and kept in the roundhouse from year to year. They were hard, flat, bright-colored stones like the ones of which the sampo was made, broken into chunks that could be handled, and set down edge to edge into the ground. The women built fires on the floor and fed them with oak wood; when the fires died down to coals and embers they swept off the ashes, leaving the stone floor clean and very hot.

The women had been harvesting their grain for several days, gathering the stalks and binding them into bundles. They surrounded the floor in a ring, each with her sheaf of grain, and her children waiting to bring her more, and beat the bundles of stalks on the stone floor.

This knocked the grain loose. Before long the floor was beginning to disappear under a layer of seeds, and the aroma went up of toasting grain, warm and dry and delicious. When the grains were toasted, the inedible chaff that encased them cracked and fell off by itself, and when the grain was winnowed the chaff blew away, and nothing was left but the sweet and nourishing seed, already cooked a little.

The women worked ceaselessly at the threshing; as they swayed and swung with their bundles of grain they seemed to be dancing, although women were generally forbidden to dance. The children ran back and forth between their mothers and the piles of harvest grain, taking away the emptied stalks and bringing new bundles, and the older girls now leaned in past their mothers and swept the toasted and threshed grain into baskets.

They could not all work at once, of course, and the crowds of women waiting for a chance to thresh their harvests gathered a little way away, and there Karella sat, and told stories.

Grela, the sister of the headwoman Tishka, worked with the first group of women over the floor, and she could see directly across the floor and beyond the other workers to where Karella sat. She worked as hard as she could to be done with it, so that she could join the others; she loved hearing Karella, who knew more stories of Abadon than anyone else.

Abadon was a favorite of Grela's, and had been since she was a little girl. Aware as she was of what was expected of her, she herself would never fall to the level of such tricks as Abadon was always playing, but it was a joy nonetheless to hear them done.

Grela swung the sheaves of wheat in great full strokes, dashing the heads of seeds on the floor, and a simple delight filled her: the rhythmic work satisfied her, and soon she would hear stories. There seemed room for little more happiness in her moment. She stepped back, to let her older daughter sweep a pile of grain into a basket; the inside of the basket was worked with the many-pointed star which was Grela's own sign. Waiting for room, the mother wiped her face on her forearm and looked across the floor toward Karella again, wondering what tale she was telling—besides her endless Abadon cycle, Karella had an abundance of stories of Rael the Birdwoman, and so many other stories that Grela knew no one who had heard them all. Then as she stood there she saw Moloquin coming.

He was carrying wood down from the forest, wood for the threshing floor; he was stooped under the weight of the sling on his back, and looked like a monstrous animal. Grela glanced to either side of her.

None other had noticed him. She hesitated, unsure what to do—after all, he came and went through the longhouses; why should he not be allowed here? But there were no other men here. She looked at him again, frowning, her mind struggling with this messiness.

It was woman's work, to thresh, and like all their works they preferred it done away from the men. But here was Moloquin, laying down the wood, and in truth the threshing floor would be cold by midafternoon, and would need to be fired again. Grela looked with piercing eyes to see that Moloquin was properly clothed—the first impression of many of the women was that he went about naked, and would leap on the girls. He wore a belt, a cloth drawn through it, down the back, between his legs, up over the front, all properly modest although only little boys wore woven cloth. He was piling the wood up, and no one else seemed to care that he was there. Now he was going away again. He was a fool, everyone said, and she remembered the strange child of old Riskel, with his funny misshapen little face and stubby fingers and stupid speech, whom everyone had loved, who had stayed with his mother until she died and then with her sister until he died, still a boy to them all, although he was full grown.

That was what Moloquin was. Pleased, Grela slipped him away into the same memory, there with Riskel's child, and now there was no confusion any more, everything belonged where it was. Everything had happened before. She took a sheaf of wheat from her elder daughter and turned to lash the stone floor with it.

Grub thought, It isn't fair.

He had meant to stay with the boys' band and avoid the women, but Ladon's son made that impossible. He got them to herd the swine and the goats together into the lush meadows at the lip of the forest, and then he himself, and all the older boys, stole away down to where Karella sat in the middle of a great mob. So all the other boys went too, and there Grub was again, in the middle of the women, looking for his mother.

He saw her at last, from a distance, and dared not go any closer. She was nursing his little brother again, cuddling him, crooning to him, allowing him the whole use of her breast. Grub turned away, his eyes scalded.

Then he saw Moloquin, coming down from the forest with his load of wood, and his resentment flared up. He thought, It isn't fair, and went after Moloquin, keeping his distance, staying out of range, but determined to follow him.

At first there was no place to go. Moloquin put down his wood, and instead of dumping it in a heap, he squatted down and stacked it neatly in crisscross rows. Grub drew a little nearer, watching his hands. Behind him, the crowd around Karella gave up a great shout of delight, and many whistled and pounded their hands together in applause.

Moloquin turned his head, looking that way; by chance his interest led him to look straight in Grub's direction, and for an instant their eyes met. Grub lowered his gaze at once, and his skin crawled uncomfortably. When he looked back, Moloquin was getting up, the sling over his shoulder, moving away toward the woods.

Grub went after him; he supposed he might find some berries to eat on the way, although everything this close to the threshing floor would long since have been eaten up. He kept his distance from Moloquin, but he kept him well within sight, because although he was a little afraid of Moloquin, he was much more afraid of the forest.

Moloquin was glad to be back in the forest. At the edge of the trees he broke into a run, and for a while he merely ran among the trees, leaping over fallen branches and brush and slapping the trunks of the oaks and lindens as he passed. He knew that one of the other boys was following him but he paid no heed to that. He ran down to the edge of the river, where the bank overhung the stream, and throwing aside the loincloth Karella had given him he leapt into the slow-moving water.

Diving down to the bottom, he groped through the stones and mud, chasing frogs off toward the green depths, and nearly caught

a wedge-shaped bug; he liked those for the way they crunched between his teeth, but this one escaped.

He slithered out onto the riverbank again and walked along the
river a little way, picking such berries that he found, eating lily shoots
and a few snails he broke out of their shells and washed—snails were
always full of dirt. While he lay on his back on the riverbank, he
noticed again that the other boy was nearby.

This was a little fair-haired boy, crouched down in the brush as
if he were hiding from Moloquin, and therefore Moloquin said nothing to him.

Karella had listened to his dream about the Pillar of the Sky and
had said nothing to him about it, but he could see by the flash of her
eyes and the little smile she gave him that the dream was important.
He liked to think about it whenever he could. The vision of the Pillar
of the Sky, completed, its great gateways open to the Sun and huger
than any man, gave him the same intense satisfaction as he got from
learning new things well. In his mind he saw the enormous stones,
he even felt them, their hardness and smoothness, and especially
their great weight and strength, that no man could move.

Nothing so clearly and exactly seen could exist only in his
dream. The great gateways were real somewhere, and somehow he
would make them be real in the place where they were meant to
stand: he, Moloquin.

Behind him the little boy coughed and rustled the brush and
sighed, and his stomach rumbled. He was hungry, with all this wealth
of food around him. Moloquin got up and went to his work, looking
for wood.

Grub saw, amazed, that Moloquin ate bits of the forest, and his neck
prickled up. He felt deeply uneasy just being beneath the trees,
where the sun reached him only in stray tendrils. The thorny and
impenetrable underbrush caught at him with its million fingers and
he knew that the rustlings and crunchings around him were the
sounds of ferocious beasts; he dared not even think about the demons and spirits giggling and chirruping behind every branch.

Moloquin belonged here. The forest fed him. The wild chaotic
brambles parted to let him through and then closed over to block
Grub's passage. The forest gave Moloquin wood as well; he went

straight to an oak tree and gathered up the smaller branches, breaking them to good lengths with chunks of wood.

He worked like a woman. Grub curled up at the foot of a bushy tree to watch and was amused. Moloquin never paused in his business. His stack of wood grew higher and rounder as the sun ascended. How did he imagine he would get all this back to the village? Grub would have laughed, but he was too hungry, and a little afraid of what Moloquin would do if he found him there.

When the sun reached the summit of the sky, so that her long fingers touched the floor of the forest, Moloquin stopped in his scurrying and rushing around; he came over toward Grub but seemed not to see him, and climbed up into the tree beside him, up to the high branches.

There he stayed a long time. Unable to see him now, Grub stopped thinking about Moloquin and instead thought of his mother.

He knew he should not want to stay with his mother. He knew he was supposed to go with the other boys, to follow Ladon's son in the boys' band, to learn the ways of men. In a few years he would enter one of the societies—the Bear Skull, he dearly wanted to be a novice of the Bear Skull, because that was the greatest of all—and carve his mask.

He should be thinking about that. He should be struggling with the other boys for a place in their midst, and not merely stand waiting at the edge, the last, always the last, always the least. But he wanted his mother. When he thought of his mother nothing else mattered except that he was far away from her, and tears welled into his eyes.

Something hard bounced off his knee. He looked around, startled, and something small and hard struck the tip of his nose and sailed away into the brush. He looked up.

There, high above his head, Moloquin sat among the green leaves of the tree, one knee crooked over a branch. Grub shivered, drawing back—surrounded by the sunlit green, Moloquin looked like a demon of the wood. As he stared upward, Moloquin put something small and red into his mouth and spat out another hard pit that fell down through the air and plopped into Grub's lap.

Grub leapt up, furious and ashamed. "I hate you," he shouted, and cast about him for stones to throw, but Moloquin was well out of reach of his arm. Coolly the boy in the treetop laughed down at him, picking the fruit from the top of the tree and eating it. Grub howled with rage. He bounced up and down below the tree, but Moloquin was not cowed at all.

The pile of firewood was still there in the clearing. Grub ran to it and threw the branches around, strewing them all over the open ground, but this also was useless against Moloquin, who laughed at him all the while. Grub ran away, back toward the village, furious.

As he neared the margin of the forest, his steps slowed. Out there the women were working, the other boys were herding the goats and swine, there was no place for him. He imagined the village as a great net, and through it he, Grub, fell like a little fish between the lines.

He was hungry. He wished he could do what Moloquin did and eat whatever he found. He kicked at the ground around him, turning over rotten sticks and tearing up bits of vine and brush, but he found nothing to eat, only a few green berries, a fat horrible worm, and some mushrooms.

At last he came on a plant that he had seen Moloquin eat. The thin white stalks were crunchy and sweet; they burned his tongue a little, but they felt good in his stomach. Feeling better, he went back into the forest to find Moloquin again, and see what else he ate.

In the afternoon Karella stopped telling stories; her throat was sore and her tongue stiff. The people clamored and begged and caught at her clothes to keep her there but she rose up out of their midst and went away, going toward the threshing floor; when she looked back, someone else had sat down on the stump where the storyteller sat and was trying to spin words.

Karella walked around a while, stretching her aging limbs. She stood by the threshing floor and watched as the women beat the sheaves of grain until the seeds flew; when they lay on the hot floor and the chaff cracked, the seeds sometimes bounced high, like grasshoppers. The smell was delicious. It was hard not to reach out and take a handful of the toasted seeds lying on the threshing floor. Karella sat down to watch a while longer. There was something comforting and fortifying in the sight of this work, done since time began, since the People began, since Rael the Birdwoman brought them knowledge of seeds. The mothers, whose gardens they were, stood tall and gracefully swaying all around the edge of the threshing floor, and when they bent to strike the grain on the stone they seemed like the growing grain itself, that bent and swayed in the wind. Between them their daughters pressed forward, their hands ready with baskets and with rakes and sweeps of wood to scoop the threshed grain away; when their mothers rose up, these girls pushed forward, and so there was an intense unceasing rhythm to their work, a completeness that left no room for trouble.

Karella drifted away, higher on the slope, toward the edge of the forest, and there she saw the boys' band which had brought out the swine from the village to forage under the oak trees; the boys sat in a row on the slope, looking down toward the village, a row of solemn little men. She feinted toward them, as if she would walk through their midst, and they shrank back from her; with a laugh she went on her way.

She was thinking of Moloquin's dream. He had told it to her in a rush of excited words, still troublesome to him although he learned how to speak better every day, and she had made him tell it twice, to be sure she heard everything, although she had said nothing to him about it. There was really nothing she could say. The dream of the stone gates was obvious in its potency and force. It was a message from the Overworld, first to him, to give him his destiny, but also to her, to Karella, because she had taken him in: the dream showed her what creature Moloquin was.

Not an ordinary child. Around him there appeared now, to her whose eyes had been schooled, showers of light, and images of greatness—trees, stars, and standing stones. She began to see details of his power, whenever she placed her mind in the service of the Overworld, and carefully she noted these, to give to him when the moment came.

The others knew nothing of this. To the women, he was still Ael's son, and they despised him for his mother's sake. To the men, she hoped, he was just another boy.

What he was to Ladon, she could only guess. She hoped he saw the boy as harmless; she hoped he would forget him. Her heart knew better than that. Her heart warned her ever against Ladon.

She saw her son coming through the forest, carrying firewood on his back, and she smiled, pleased with him. The work would degrade him in the eyes of the village but in Karella's eyes it made him stronger. Although now he was bent over double under the weight of the wood, yet she knew one day he would stand in the gateway between Heaven and earth. Now he carried firewood, but one day he would bear his People on his shoulders, and when he did, he would make dust of Ladon and his power.

She spoke of this to no one. Sometimes she herself, wakening at night or sitting by the fire, wondered if her expectations of him were not merely the wraiths of an old woman's declining soul. At such times she needed only to look at him to know better.

The other children crept closer to her hearth, sat around outside the ring of stones that marked the edge of her living space, and listened to her stories. She told how the red deer flew up close to the Sun and caught fire in its antlers to take to the People. But as the deer leapt toward the earth, a bit of the fire fell out of the bowl of its antlers and rolled down its back, and that was why on the back of the red deer there was a long black burn mark ever after.

She taught him all the old rites for dealing with fire, rites that the People no longer used very often, preferring to take a bit of fire from a living hearth to start a new one rather than cause the flame to be born of cold and death. He listened to her with his eyes wide, hearing everything. Sometimes she asked him to repeat a story to her, and he did so, reciting each word as she had told it to him, repeating the pitch and force of her voice, even the gestures of her hands.

Every day he gathered wood for the fires that heated the threshing floor, and he alone did this, all the others seeing that he did so well there was no need for any other to do the tedious work. Then on the eighteenth day, the threshing was done.

On the day following they had the ceremony of the Giving of the Power of Ladon.

For this rite all the women put on their best garments and dressed their children as gorgeously as they were able and lined them up by order of age. The men also put on their masks and their ceremonial clothes and took their drums, and all the People assembled together outside the roundhouse, and they took down some of the wall around the yard, removing the mats from the uprights of the wall, so that all the People could be in one crowd, together, facing Ladon.

There in the door of the roundhouse Ladon sat on his pile of bearskins and fox skins, and the men stood on either side of him with their drums. First the men danced, making three interconnecting rings that circled the roundhouse, and with the beating of their drums and their singing and their dance they evoked the whole of the Overworld to pay witness to what went on here.

Then the women came before him, beginning with the head-women, and set before him their harvest.

For this purpose the women made special baskets, which seemed deep and wide but were really worked in with withies to be shallow, and the woman spread a thin layer of unmilled grain on the top, so that it seemed the whole basket was full. She brought him beans as well in such baskets. She brought him jugs of honey, but the jugs were plugged just below the neck, so that a little honey would fill up many jugs, and seem a great deal; and she brought cheeses, in a great pile, but the top only was real cheese, and the bottom ones were of wood.

Thus each woman strove to bring before Ladon the greatest amount of all the People, but in truth what she could do in these ways was limited by the number of baskets and jugs she could make. When she had offered up so much show to Ladon, what was left over of her harvest went quietly into the roundhouse in ordinary baskets.

After each of the women had made her offering to Ladon, they prepared a great feast. The men in a hunting rite slaughtered some of the pigs, and these were roasted; the women milled grain, and formed it into flat cakes, and cooked them. There was also fruit gathered from the forest, and honey that had fermented, although that was known to be a favorite food of the spirits and was drunk only very sparingly by wise people, so that there would be enough for the ancestors.

And the ancestors came to the feast. All the food was piled up on a mat of bark on the step of the roundhouse, and all the People ate of it, and since no one with proper manners would take the last bite of anything, and there was so much food that everyone could eat his fill and still there would be more, the fact that when they were done all the food was gone proved that the spirits had come and eaten also, and had accepted the People, their harvest, and their feast. Thus Ladon, who was at the center of it all, acquired more power.

Also proof of the presence of spirits was the general levity of the crowd. No one would have drunk too much of the honey-liquor, and yet nearly all the men and most of the women seemed drunk, and danced and played like children with one another; some even went off into the quiet behind the roundhouse and coupled there, although they usually found, too late, that their quiet place concealed a number of small, loud children.

Karella told a few stories, but it was hard to tell stories to drunks, and after a little while she ceased and went around the place, amusing herself with other people's antics. Moloquin was nowhere to be found. She paused by the table of leaves where the roast pigs were laid out, and stooped and took a big piece of the crisp fat, and then when she rose she found herself face to face with Ladon.

Her back tingled. Like a deer in the forest coming face to face with a wolf she trembled with the urge to flight, but his fierce unfaltering gaze held her fast.

"Opa-Ladon-on," she said, her voice like a feather in her throat. "Mighty is he."

Unblinking, he fixed her with his gaze. He said, "You have given me much offense, woman."

After the ceremony, in the presence of the ancestors, he was full of power; he gave it off like a radiance. She raised her hand between them, as a shield.

"Ladon," she whispered, "let me go."

"Aaaah."

He crept nearer, massive, shimmering—capable, she knew, of destroying her with one hand, or with one word, if he knew that word. She felt his enmity like a pressure in her chest that would not let her breathe.

Then she found the word to use against him. The name that threatened him, the power that turned him human again.

"Ael, " she said.

He stopped in his slow serpentine advance.

"Ael, not I, is weaving your destiny together," Karella said; she took heart, and her force bloomed as his faded. "It is Ael, not old Karella, whom you must hate, Ladon-on."

His eyes were hot and bright now, but his strength was baffled. He moved in fits and jerks, the fluid strength gone from his limbs. Karella straightened, triumphant, her heart beating hard with the knowledge of victory, and she thrust her hand out toward him.

"Ael will destroy you, Ladon!"

"Ah!"

He seized hold of her hand. He tightened his grip until the small bones crunched and she cried out in pain. His face twisted with the effort of his grip. Then abruptly he let her go, turned and was gone.

She sank down where she was, her hand in her lap. The hand throbbed and ached all the way up to her elbow. She raised her head. Night was on them, night hovered all around them, driven up into the sky by the fires and the noise, but covering them all nonetheless. She shivered.

He was not beaten. She had brought Moloquin here, she had forced Ladon to accept his presence, she had put a stone into his belly, but she had not beaten him. He was only waiting.

That understanding filled her with a churning fear. Suddenly she had to see Moloquin, to know that he was well. Rising to her feet, she plunged away, into the dark turmoil of the celebration, looking for her son.

In this year the red traveller in the night sky began to course to the east, as it did often. The People believed that it turned its path because of anger and pride, and to protect themselves and to lure it back to the proper way, they performed ceremonies of worship and honor toward the red star. Because the circling of the traveller coincided with the passage of the sun into the star-gateway, where the two great stars Boy and Girl stood before the burning white scar that lay across the sky, the duty of leading the ceremonies fell to the masters of the Bear Skull Society.

Fergolin therefore was deeply involved in these mysteries. With his novices and his assistants he went away down the river until he was outside the village, and built a little hut of withies and made a fire inside, and sweated himself. On the way back to the village, a time when reality was so clear and exact it seemed to him he knew all things, he found a snakeskin hanging on a blade of grass, and he took this carefully and rolled it around his finger, to put into his amulet bag.

Then with his mask in both hands, his skin still shining and tender from the sweating so that the real world penetrated him through and through, he went before Ladon, to consult with him about the proper day for the ceremony. Standing before Ladon, he placed his mask over his chest so that the spirit to whom the mask gave a face could hear and see what went on.

Ladon stood before his fur-covered high seat, his mask before him, and listened to Fergolin recite the formal request for permission to conduct the ceremony.

"I hear and I will provide what my people require of me," Ladon said, in the ritual way. "I shall sit under the stars tonight and allow the holy radiance to descend on me. I shall have the wishes of the Overworld made known to me."

Fergolin thanked him with many bows, using words taught him in his boyhood, and backed away from the presence of the chief; but then he came up to Ladon again. Although the rituals had to be done exactly, with no variance of word or gesture, the actual performance of some of the details was done "under the straw," as the People said of things done privately. Therefore Fergolin came back with his head turned to one side and his hand over the face of his mask.

Ladon sat down again on his bearskin. His belly lapped his belt and rested on his knees. The sunlight coming in through the hole in the roof glistened blue-black highlights on the thick hair that covered Ladon's shoulders. He turned the face of his mask to the ground.

"Do it tomorrow," Ladon said. "If we start at dawn, it will be daylight enough."

"I hope so," Fergolin said. It was very bad to be caught in the middle of a ceremony when the sun went down. "It is very near the equinox." He seemed to hesitate.

Ladon looked beyond him. "Yes? What is it?"

Fergolin glanced over his shoulder; another man stood there, waiting to be acknowledged.

"Opa-Ladon, Moloquin is here."

"Hunh," Ladon said, as if the wind had been driven out of him by a sharp poke in the belly. He glanced at Fergolin who remained where he was, being hot with curiosity over this whole business.

"I'll see him later," Ladon said, and then shook himself, as if changing his mind meant changing all his body too. "No. Send him to me."

Fergolin drew off to one side. He saw that Ladon stooped for his mask and put it carefully away beside his high seat, but Fergolin turned his own mask so that it looked out at the world.

Moloquin came. His dense black hair was braided and he wore a piece of cloth wrapped around his body, imitating the clothes men wore, although those garments of course were of animal skins. Karella had been at work on him. Yet he still looked ragged and dirty somehow, as if the forest still claimed him; it seemed, to Fergolin, that he could as well have grown leaves on his head as hair.

And, Fergolin saw with great amazement, he looked like Ladon.

The chief spoke in his deep voice of power. "You are the boy Moloquin, who came out of the forest."

"I am the Unwanted One," said the boy.

"You are the son of Ana-Karella-el."

Fergolin stiffened, seeing what Ladon meant to do, and he turned toward Moloquin, expecting he knew not what—some insistence on his identity as Ael's son, the chief's sister's son—but the boy spoke without pause, and with no force.

He said, "I am Karella's son."

Fergolin breathed a long sigh, drawing both their looks, and Ladon smiled at him. "Go, Fergolin-on, my honored man."

Then Fergolin knew that what he had seen was to be talked over with the other men. He made gestures of respect to Ladon and went out of the roundhouse.

Once, halfway to the door, he paused and looked back; the sunlight coming down through the roof showered on the chief and the tall black-haired fosterling who faced him. They were not speaking, merely staring at each other. Fergolin thought, This will not go as Ladon wishes, and a cold feeling crept up his spine. More things to discuss with the other men. He went off to find company.

Ladon said, "You have been fetching wood for the village. Is that true?"

"Yes, Ladon," said the boy.

"Call me Opa-Ladon," said the chief sharply. "Opa-Ladon-on, mighty is he."

"Yes," said Moloquin.

The chief lolled on the side of his seat. He had expected more from Moloquin, defiance, threats, accusations; this bland obedient face before him could not be dangerous. He did not even look like Ael. And he had named Karella as his mother, there in front of Fergolin.

"You are a good gatherer of wood," Ladon said. "Therefore it is my wish that you go into the forest and gather wood, and fill up my woodlot with wood for the fires of the roundhouse. And when you have done all that, you will come to me again and I shall have more tasks for you."

He watched Moloquin's eyes as he spoke, expecting a betraying flash of anger, but Moloquin only nodded. "Yes, Opa-Ladon-on, mighty is he," and started away. A few steps off, he turned and looked back. "May I go now?"

"Go," said Ladon.

The boy left. Ladon watched him go, pleased with himself. There was nothing to fear from this one. He was stupid, even as the People thought, and knew nothing of power or truth, honor, pride and the fitness of things: would he have accepted such a mean and contemptible duty otherwise? He was dark and thin, no match for Ladon's son, with his splendid sunlit hair and handsome face. And Fergolin had heard him deny his mother. It was enough, once the others saw him doing work no man would touch. Ladon smiled to himself, victorious at last over both Ael and Karella.

At dawn the men put on their masks and took their feathered spears and made two long rows inside the roundhouse, each man standing beside the rooftree of his society, so that they formed two long living spirals under the roof. Then as the sun rose they went slowly forth from the roundhouse.

It was the work of the Salmon Kindred to make music, and so each man of that kindred carried a little drum on his belt, and as they danced they thumped the drum with their hands. The men of the Oak Tree Kindred chanted the rituals of honor to the red travelling star, whose other names were the Circling Star and the Left Eye.

They bent their steps, two long ropes of men, in ever-widening spirals through the village, through the abandoned fields of weeds and goats along the river, up through the newly harvested gardens where the stubble of the grain stood cropped and brown in the rows. Here the women stood among their crops and covered their faces with their hands, because this was men's doings. Even the children were silent, even the babies. The tump-tump of the drums was like the beating of the heart of the People.

The sun climbed into the sky as they danced and beat down on them with her long fierce arms; perhaps jealous of the honor shown the night travellers. The men kept their pace. They wound their way up through the highest fields, where still many trees grew, their bark stripped off all around the bottom; here one day the women would

grow grain and beans. At the very edge of the forest, the first pairs
of men turned and faced the village, and as the others climbed up
beside them, they spread out, until at last the chain of men circled
the whole village. Then at the height of the day they ate, and gave
food to the masks so that the spirits ate, and they sprinkled meal
around the edge of the village, and spoke the rituals of safe-keeping.

Down in the fields, the women bent to their work. There were
still beans to pick, and onions and other roots, and so, while the men
contended with the Overworld and made peace with the spirits, the
women worked like brutes as if nothing was happening.

At last the drums began again. In two long chains the men
danced down through the fields again, chanting and bowing. The
sun drifted downwards through the sky and the men followed the
prescribed spiralling path down toward the roundhouse. They
circled the longhouses and blessed them and one by one they went
into the roundhouse.

The sun set. Night came, and in the sky, among all the lights of
Heaven, the two eyes of the Overworld shone forth: the Right Eye,
blue-white and bright and true, above the western horizon, and the
Left Eye, red and sullen and false, circling back off its path, straying
away from its forward course, signalling error and pain and destruction to the earth below. The People slept, safe inside the spiralling
lines of the ritual, safe inside their houses.

Winter came. Nothing grew any more. The women sat in the longhouses when the weather was foul and made baskets and wove cloth
and listened to Karella's stories.

Moloquin went into the forest every day, to gather firewood; he
even went when the weather was evil, when the snow flew, when the
icy fogs hung from the trees, because he could not bear the heat and
the noise of the longhouse. He had always lived in the forest during
the winter. Now it was different; when he was hungry and could find
nothing else, he could go down the slope to his mother, and she fed
him. If he were lonely, too, he could go to her. And there was another, now, who made him less lonely.

The boy Grub, younger than Moloquin, slight and uncertain
and wretched, trailed after him wherever he went, around the village
and now into the woods. Now when the boys' band teased Moloquin,
they jeered at Grub also. Moloquin sometimes wished Grub would go

away, but there was no place for him. His mother refused him and the boys' band made him miserable. So Grub followed Moloquin everywhere, and whenever Moloquin found something in the forest to eat, he fed Grub, too.

Grub was afraid of everything in the forest; he saw demons in every tree, felt eyes watching him, screamed at every bird call. With his fingers he made signs against evil spirits. He would eat nothing without washing it first; he drank only from rushing streams. When he saw Moloquin doing none of this, he called him indignant names and with a solemn face threatened to tell Ladon's son.

When he saw that Moloquin still did none of it, and went around the forest as boldly as any beast, he himself did less. But he would not go ahead of Moloquin, not a single step; he always followed after him.

Moloquin had gathered up most of the good wood near the village, and every day he had to go deeper and deeper into the forest to find more. When he found a dead tree or a windfall, he stayed there until he had the wood all broken up, and then for a few days he and Grub travelled back and forth carrying the wood. Moloquin carried most of it, but he made Grub bring some, every time, although the little boy whined and complained.

With Grub walking on his heels, he went deep into the forest, following a faint deer trail down through stands of sycamore and maple. The ground was crusted with old snow, crystalline with age, and drilled through from the constant dripping from the branches overhead. At the foot of a slope darkened with pine trees they came out onto a meadow, waist-high in dead grass; once a grove of maples had stood here, but now all the trees were dead, standing white and naked in the stark winter sunlight.

This was strange enough to stop Moloquin in his tracks, and Grub pressed against him, saying, "Let's go back."

Moloquin pushed him away. Something stirred in him, some old memory, like a pull on him. He took a hesitant step forward, and Grub seized him again.

"Let's go back. I want to go back—"

"Ah, you always want to go back. Go by yourself." Moloquin pushed him away and ran off across the meadow, the grass bending and breaking away from him.

Straight ahead of him, a little stream ran along the edge of the meadow, turned below the foot of the hill and ran on, and he knew if he went around the turn, that he would find another meadow like this, beside the stream, and there, a sort of house—something—

But when he went around the hill the stream ran left, not right, and there was no meadow. He stopped again, hardly noticing Grub who panted up behind him, crying to go home. Moloquin moved away from him a little, looking around him.

Along this stream—somewhere—

His memory showed him flashes of it, like a salmon leaping. His old mother. She had peeled away the bark of the trees, she had lived here, somewhere.

But not here. Grub was pulling on him again. She was not here. When he realized that, it was with surprise he had ever thought she was. Grub was tugging on him, frantic. He looked around him again, longingly, at the trees, the stream that turned the wrong way, and saw again in his memory a broad sunny bench beside a stream near such a place as the dead grove, and a little house.

Not here. A nameless longing filled him, a numb hollow sense of loss. Grub's hand urged him away. He turned and let the little boy lead him back toward the living People.

In the deep of the winter, old Brant went up the long slope to the Pillar of the Sky. He was supposed to take his novices and apprentice masters, but none of them showed him any sign of interest in the holy place, and so he went alone.

He could see the place from far off, by the circling cloud of crows above it. His legs were tired; he stopped once or twice to rest, and each time his gaze went to the whirling black mass of the birds in the air.

They were alarmed. They wanted to settle down into the dead ground—there was flesh there, he knew of two deaths in the village since the end of summer—and yet whenever they descended, something below scared them and they whirled up again, the air noisy with their wings and cries. So there was someone there, or something.

He drove himself on. His duties today were necessary and important. And he had no enemies: he was afraid of nothing but the righteously angered spirits of his ancestors. It was curiosity that pushed him faster.

As he reached the bank, a cold rain began to fall, and he stopped and put down the bundle he carried, opened it up, and took out his long coat of deerskin. Now the crows were filling the sky with their din, the black blades of their wings, annoyed with him too. Safe inside his coat, he went through the bank.

It was Moloquin who kept the crows in the sky. Brant smiled to himself; he had suspected that.

Moloquin sat there by the North Watcher, his arms draped over his raised knees. He seemed unsurprised at Brant's appearance, and the old man went a few steps toward him, stopped, and turned, to give the place a long searching look.

The grass was dead and brown. At the far end of the sacred precinct, in between two of the tilting stones, lay the dead. The little boy, who had been his mother's delight, was covered over with cut boughs of a fir tree, and probably the old woman's body had been covered too, once, but the crows had been at it and the flesh was exposed and bloody and ragged. The great circle enclosed them all, dead and living, in its ring of power; even the rain, coming sharper and colder now, was a blessing here. Brant turned toward Moloquin again.

The boy rose up and came toward him. "Karella said you would be here," he said. "I will go if you wish."

Brant shook his head, smiling. "The rite is happier for the presence of the People." He laid his hand on the boy's shoulder and was surprised at the hard muscle he felt under Moloquin's thin woven coat. "Would you like to help me?"

At that Moloquin's face shone; he said nothing, but moved closer to Brant, and the old man again put out his hand and touched him. They went together around the place, walking in a circle around the outside of the standing stones.

As he walked, Brant let go a little of his knowledge, like the bird in the tale who dropped seeds from his beak to lead the People to safety. He said, "It is the circles that are great in all the places of standing stones, the circles are complete and hold the world inside them. Therefore if a master comes to a circle he may sit in the middle and yet see all the world. All the world that matters."

A few steps on, he said, "In the circles the ancestors have given us certain messages."

And yet a few steps on, he said, "The year also is a circle, and it is here that the circle of the year and the circle of the world may be seen together as one thing."

Moloquin said, "I don't understand."

Brant glanced sharply at him. He could not remember that he had ever spoken with Moloquin before; he had heard that the boy's use of speech was curt and undecorated, but to be addressed by one so young without the honorifices his age alone had earned made the old man a little angry. He pressed his lips together and kept walking. Moloquin kept pace with him. Brant looked up at the sky; he wondered if the setting of the sun would even be visible with this rain.

"If I cannot see what I must see tonight," he said, "I shall have to stay the night here."

"What must—"

Moloquin stopped, his eyes lowered, and Brant waited a moment for him to continue but he did not. Brant thought, He has learned not to annoy people. He touched Moloquin's arm again.

"I must see the sun set. I will show you where we will stand to watch. If we do not see it set then we must watch tomorrow morning for the sun to rise, and if that too cannot be seen we must stay another day. Are you ready for that?"

"I will stay until you say we have seen enough," said Moloquin.

"Good," Brant said. "Now, come here, I will tell you what we must do."

They went around to the eastern side of the circle, where there stood two more stones, set far apart, just inside the bank, the South and the East Watchers. Brant led the boy to the South Watcher and said, "Here. You must stand here, and look to the horizon, and tell me what you see."

Moloquin stood with his back to the stone and looked west, and he said, "I see nothing."

"Wait."

Brant went back to the East Watcher and stood before it, his back to it, and waited. The rain fell steadily, not hard, but cold and uncomfortable. Brant began to shiver inside his skin coat; he wondered how Moloquin did, wrapped in cloth. Nothing happened for a long while. He began to think it was impossible today, and he would have to spend the night here. With Moloquin to keep him company it would be pleasant to stay away from the village for a while. He had brought food with him, bean cakes, and a little jug of broth. There was nothing around here to build a fire with, but they would keep warm somehow. He remembered once seeing Moloquin asleep under the

North Watcher. That would be snug for two people, but warm enough.

He thought, with a certain grim enjoyment, that this waiting would be a true test of Moloquin; if he did belong to this place, then he would wait a lifetime. Perversely Brant hoped for a colder, harder rain, a longer wait, a true test.

The crows wheeled and dropped, circling lower and lower over their dinner; the rain suddenly became a deluge, a driving knife-edged downpour that blurred the shapes even of the faltering stones of the central ring. Brant sighed. Shutting his eyes, he let the rain sluice down his face. He was too old to do this. His bones hurt when it rained. He knew that sometime soon he himself would lie in the grass, his body imperfectly shielded from the assaults of the crows and his spirit whirling through the air with the rest of the People, the true People, the Overworld.

That was to be wished for, the culmination of life, to be accepted into the true and eternal world, and yet old Brant shrank from it. When he conceived of himself dead, and all the rest of life going on without him, it was such a sense of loss that his mind froze with fear; he could feel nothing but the sickening fear of not-being any more.

That was weakness. Sternly he told himself that all beings died and that death was the passageway into the real world, but in his mind that passageway was a dark twisting tunnel into nothing, and this world of life and change and sun and wind and tears and laughter was precious beyond any power.

Suddenly Moloquin cried, "Master!"

Brant jerked his head up, his eyes open—he thought for an instant he had been dozing, caught deep inside himself like that—and raised his face into the rain. The downpour was lessening. He straightened, turning his eyes to the west, and a low cry broke from his lips.

There, away to the west, he saw, first, the next stone, with Moloquin beside it; Brant was about to call to him to move in front of the stone again, when Moloquin suddenly turned, grasped the stone, which was nearly head and shoulders taller than he, and scrambled up onto the top of it. Brant choked off his words, his gaze going beyond the stone, beyond the bank whose upper edge coincided with the top of the stone, to the far horizon.

The storm was breaking. The rain was over. Above the world lay a roof of cloud, grey and heavy like slabs of stone laid from edge to edge of the world, but there in the west now the roof of cloud stood above the world a little, and the sun was falling beneath it. The sun slid down below the cloud slabs, and her lower edge touched the horizon, and her upper edge touched the cloud roof, and her light shone across the world, a blast of horizontal light that blazed across the whole wet world like a purifying ray. The stones glittered with it; the wild whirling crows shone black with it. Brant flung his arms up over his head and shouted for joy.

Slowly the sun sank down below the edge of the world. Moloquin sprang down from the stone and ran to the old man.

"What happened? Was it what you came to see?"

Brant nodded. The sun had set just to the right of the stone, which meant that a few days would see the end of the steady shortening of the days and lengthening of the nights that oppressed everyone during the failing of the year. He sat down on his hams and looked up at Moloquin and smiled.

"Yes," he said. "Yes, we have seen the mystery."

Moloquin sat down before him. "Will you tell me?"

Brant shrugged. He could tell the boy nothing he did not know already, it seemed to him. He said, "You know that as the summer wanes, the days grow shorter."

Moloquin nodded.

"From the first the People have known that. All beings know that, birds observe it in their travels, and even mice dig burrows to spend the winter in, when the light begins to fail. For a long while it was believed that the light would fail utterly, save for the actions of the People in calling forth the sun again, but now we know better. The light fails, and as it does, the point of the sunset moves along the edge of the world to the west, day by day. But when it reaches this point—" He nodded to the line of the two stones—"Then the sun turns, and goes back eastward again, and the light comes back again, every day. Not so fast at first."

Moloquin said nothing. His eyes were fixed on the old man's face.

"And this is the mystery," Brant said. Although the rain was beginning again, he was relaxed now, relaxed and happy, as after sex. He fingered the dead grass around him. The crows were dropping to the ground near the corpses, and he plucked up a small stone and threw it at them, to no effect: they were used to him now. He faced Moloquin again.

"This is the mystery, and it is a very plain one, Moloquin. It is that the world is orderly. It does everything in circles. When we know enough, and fit it all together, everything is a circle."

Moloquin stared at him a moment; Brant thought, disappointed, He does not see, but then the boy smiled at him.

"Yes," he said. "I like that. Yes."

Brant grunted at him. "I am overwhelmed that you are pleased, Moloquin. I am sure your opinion even now is the talk of the Overworld."

Still he smiled at Moloquin, who had proven himself today, although he probably did not know it. Brant got his feet under him.

"We shall go back now. I can tell Ladon now that we may have the Midwinter Feasting."

Moloquin stood, and the two went back together, going out through the gap in the bank directly opposite them. Brant walked side by side with the boy; in his mind he was sifting through what he had learned today. Moloquin was rough and untutored in the skills of men, but he belonged here, in this place. Brant had despaired of finding a true vessel into which to transfer his own mastery before he went on to the Overworld. Now he had one. Even Moloquin's strangeness worked for him here: the People expected a Green Bough master to be a little odd. Brant put his arm around the boy's shoulders. He pretended not to notice the half-smile that Moloquin gave him, the amusement in the boy's eyes. They went on down to the village.

The winter wore on, but as Brant had said, every day when the sun rose she lifted her head up a little to the east of where she had risen the day before, and she stayed in the sky a little longer each day. Soon the earth warmed to her caresses. At the equinox, there was a violent storm of snow and sleet and hail, as if the winter were loathe to give up his supremacy, but in the days following, the sky was blue and the wind warm, and the women knew it was time to go back to their gardens, to make them ready for the spring planting.

The men held a great ritual hunt, spending several days away from the village; they took many of the older boys with them, because soon these boys would be chosen into a society and the men wanted to look them over first. Moloquin did not go.

Steadily the sun climbed higher and higher into the sky, until she blazed forth as queen of Heaven, ruling all but a little corner of the night. Then a runner came from the village to the north, calling all the People to the Great Gathering at the place called Turnings-of-the-Year; and while he was in Ladon's roundhouse he let go another piece of news—that Mashod, the chief of the largest village to the north, had died during the winter, and his successor had been chosen: his sister's son, Rulon.

The People went away to the Great Gathering. From the long-houses the women set forth in disorderly crowds, talking amongst themselves, carrying their babies, their baskets of meal and dried beans and cheese, their strings of dried salmon and smoked salmon and smoked pig. With them, in no special place, walked the head-women of the People, looking the same as all the others, except for their bright clothes.

The men went off with great ceremony. They placed Ladon on his chair and bore him three times around the roundhouse, chanting the ritual song, and in long rows, each man in the proper order, they set their masks at their belts, and their drums and lances. Thus, as in everything, the men and women went separately, their paths crossing often, but never travelling together.

They walked up over the high arch of the downland, and into the hills to the north of them. Here the rolling land suddenly dropped off in steep cliffs down to a marshy stinking lowland, which they called the Dead River, although there was no river there. Away to the west, at the low end of the long narrow valley, was a pond; on top of the blunt hill above it appeared a round embankment with a standing stone, an ancient place, belonging to those who had lived in this place before the People came, which they called the Old Camp.

Here the valley was narrow, and the People chose this way across to the far side. The old paths, worn into the hillsides, were washed so slick and sheer with the winter storms that they had to make new paths to the top. From there, they had only a little way to go across open ground, following old trails between the slumping hills and sinks and treeless ridges, until they came to the Gathering.

Moloquin walked along beside Karella, with Grub just behind them, pretending to be by himself. As they approached the Gathering, the sun was going down and the air was dim; the fires of the People spread out across the plain before them like blossoms in the dark. There were so many fires that Moloquin drew closer to Karella and slipped his hand under her arm, and she looked quickly up at him and smiled.

Ladon's was not the only village of the People; here at the sacred place called Turnings-of-the-Year was another village, whose chief was Rulon, newly raised to the honor. His village lay on a broad flat plain where several springs burst forth, sending many little streams away to the east, to the river. All around Rulon's Village the People who had come to the Gathering laid out their camps under the sky, each staying with those of his own village, so that the hearths spread out in clumps around the village in the center.

This was a much smaller village than Ladon's, having but two longhouses; the roundhouse was tremendous.

Karella said, "Once this was the greatest village of the People, but things change."

"Where are their gardens?" Moloquin asked.

She shrugged. "Over there, perhaps." She waved vaguely to the south. "This village has been here a while; they must have to walk long to reach their work."

She led him to the camp where Ladon's People were making their hearths, and they chose a place to build a fire. Moloquin had been picking up wood as they walked up here from their own village, and he dumped it down in a big heap and went off to find stones for a hearth.

Karella sighed, glad to be done walking; her legs ached. She had brought half her home along on her back: mats for sitting and sleeping on, a basket and a pot to cook in, and a jug for water. She put down a mat to sit on and arranged another on a frame of sticks to lean her back against, and pointed to the jug.

"Grub," she said, "take that and fetch us some water."

The little boy's mouth fell open. "Me, Ana-Karella?"

"You," she said. "And be sure you go well upstream, so the water is clear."

Still he lingered, amazed she wanted him to work, and her ill temper burst and she flung a stick at him from Moloquin's pile. He bounded away like a rabbit, the jug in his hand, but she saw he did not go upstream, but went to the nearest place, where everybody else was, and the water was roiled to the color of the earth.

Moloquin came back, his arms full of stones. "Ana," he said, in a low voice, "there are too many people here." He squatted down and put the stones in a ring at Karella's feet.

"What is this, my brave boy, afraid of nothing?" She put out her hand to touch him, smiling, and he paused in his work to let her pick a bit of dead leaf out of his shaggy black hair. "Keep close by me. Pretend to be stupid and foolish, and then no one will mind if you act strangely and say strange things." She looked around for Grub, who was still by the river, and faced Moloquin again. "In fact, say nothing at all."

That was because he would not change his speech for them. He had learned to talk sensibly, in the year he had been with Karella, but he still spoke like a child to children, or like the women, in plain undecorated words. She thought it was because he spent so little time with men that he would not learn the speech of men.

She said, "Hold, now, here come strangers."

She meant that they were strangers to him; they were no strangers to her. She put out her hands, calling to them.

"Joba. Halla. Forgive me for not getting up to greet you, but my legs are still somewhere over the Dead River. Come sit down."

The newcomers took her hands and wrung them; Joba, hugely fat, her long loose hair streaked with grey and white like streaks of stars through the night sky, bent down to press a kiss to Karella's face.

"Heaven has taken pity on us, we are friends together again." She sat down on Karella's right hand and shook her head. "It has been an evil winter, my old sister."

"Now the summer is here," Karella said, and clutched tight the hand of Halla, younger than the other, with light brown hair, and a broad smile, who sat down on her left. "There is no evil in the world that does not pass away with the turnings of the year. I will have something to offer you in a moment, when my boy here has made the fire, and his lazy friend has brought the water."

In their midst, Moloquin was setting the sticks together for a fire; he did not look up. Grub came back with the jug.

Karella tasted of the water and spat it out. "The next time," she said, with a glare at Grub, "I shall send Moloquin. Go off now, I have no use for you if you will not obey me."

Grub drew away a little; she did not mark where he went, once he was out of her reach. Instead she fussed with her sitting mat and the backrest, trying to get comfortable. Moloquin had the fire going—they had brought a coal from the village—and now he came around behind her and, wordless, he helped her arrange herself.

The two strange women watched all this with eyes sharp as the eyes of a brown thrush hopping in a bush and looking out for snakes. Karella laid her hands in her lap.

"I hope you have many stories, Karella-el," said Joba.

Karella laughed. "With every moon another egg cracks open in my mind. But it is you, Joba-el, who needs our sympathy. Tell me how Mashod died."

"Oh, him." Joba discarded her dead brother with a scornful wave of her hand. "Let him lie. He turned grey and he died, just after the Feasting. No, no, it is Rulon who brings me sorrow now."

Rulon was her son. Karella murmured, "Fortunate the mother who sees her son grow to manhood."

"Yes—fortunate," said Joba sharply. "He is still a green boy, is my Rulon, still a little worm, but he thinks now he is a star in the sky. He remembers how Mashod was, and does not know that Mashod was mostly empty bluff. There will be trouble tomorrow, I am warning you."

Karella snorted, scratched her lip, and peered again into the jug, to see if the water had cleared. The fire leapt up bright and warm, and she was hungry. Moloquin squatted beside her in silence, watching everything from beneath his dark brows.

"Ladon will manage," Karella said. "He has been chief long enough to have learned the necessities of power, and if as you say Rulon is still trapped in his illusions—"

"He thinks he ought to walk first into the circle."

Halla, silent until now, gave a soft cackle. "I do not know which distresses her more," she said to Karella, "that Rulon should get his way, or that he should have his comeuppance. Who is this boy here?"

"He is a little fool whom I have taken into my care," Karella said. "Pay no heed to him."

Joba was prodding mournfully at the fire with a stick. "They say a woman gains peace with age, but it is not so. Be glad you have no children, Karella. My daughter also gives me no pleasure. It is a mournful life we have here, a well of sorrow."

Halla laughed at her. "Oh, let us all weep great tears for Joba, who suffers so much—weep, I say, weep all!"

Joba shot her an angry look and Karella joined in the gentle laughter of the other woman; Joba had ever been fond of lamenting. The fire was leaping brightly upward now, warm enough to push them all back a little, and Karella reached for the jug again.

"No," Moloquin said, and took it from her. "I shall fetch you

good water, my mother." He poured the water out on the ground
and went off upstream of the little river.

"Good," said Halla comfortably, folding her legs under her, and
her long skirt over her knees. "Now tell us who he really is, Karella."

"Who?"

"Karella! That boy. Who is he? He called you 'mother.' And fool
he is not, or I am no judge of faces."

Karella smiled at her. "He is Ael's son."

"Ael," said the two together, uncomprehending.

"Yes—Ael. The sister of Ladon, whom he drove away into the
forest, long ago, when she became pregnant with no husband. Don't
you remember?"

In the fiery glow Joba's face was round and flat like the moon;
her eyes widened round as the moon. Halla said, "I remember the
scandal, I think—I did not associate it with Ladon."

"It was before Ladon became the chief. The year before. You
did not know him then."

Joba said, "But then where did this one come from?"

"He came out of the forest," Karella said.

Joba rolled her eyes up toward Heaven. Halla sat back, staring
at Karella, and released another of her long ringing peals of laughter.

"Oh, oh. I see something deeper here than a pail of water." She
turned to Joba. "Set Ladon on Rulon, you see, and set this boy on
Ladon—that's how it works."

With a little private mutter, Joba leaned toward the fire, her eyes
half-shut. "You're a fool, Karella. You're better off without children,
mark me, they are nothing but toil and disappointment."

Moloquin came back; he had the jug full of clear water, and now
Karella busied herself making a broth for the women to drink. The
boy sat down quietly behind her and watched everything that went
on.

While the broth simmered, Halla said, "Harus Kum has come
back again."

"Harus Kum?" Karella bent her brows together, trying to remember the face that went with the outlandish name.

"The stranger," Joba said. "The bead-and-trouble-bringer."

"Oh." Karella saw, in her mind's eye, a tall man with a long face,
made longer by a curly beard. "How many folk has he with him?"

"Three or four."

"I see no harm in him. He has come before to the Gathering, he is favored of Ladon, who always gives him gifts."

Halla said, "His ways are strange. He carries a great long whip in his belt and I have seen him use it on his own folk. And he gives the chiefs very odd and potent gifts, full of magic, and the men go wild over them."

"I don't see why you worry," Karella said.

"What need have we for blue beads? And if there is no need, why should the men lust after them so much?"

At her choice of words the other two women began to laugh, and they poked Halla and made all the usual jokes about lust and the needs of men and the probability of blue beads ever rivalling women. Beside Karella Moloquin listened with a face that shone. He reached forward suddenly and put sticks into the fire, making a pattern of them in the flames, as Karella had taught him.

Then suddenly Joba's hand shot out and caught his wrist.

He startled from head to foot, like a tiny baby. Karella saw how he stiffened. Yet he did not draw back or try to free himself, but turned his head and stared into Joba's face, and for the space of two breaths the boy and the old woman gazed deeply into one another's eyes.

She let him go. She sat back, her head sinking into her rolls of chin and her eyes unblinking.

"Go," she said.

Silently the boy rose and went off. Joba did not move.

Halla and Karella waited a while, expecting some speech of her, but when she said nothing, Halla coughed and struck her knee with her hand.

"Now, now, Joba, can you not ride up on the top of life and not be continually sinking down into its depths? What is it now?"

"I don't know," Joba said and lifted her head, and to Karella's amazement there were tears gleaming in the seams and folds of the other woman's face. "He walked out of the forest, you say? Oh, Karella." She shook her head. With her forefinger she wiped off the drops of her tears from beneath her eyes. "Oh, Karella, tell us a story, tell us a long story, that we may forget ourselves in."

Over the plain to the north of Rulon's Village stood the stone circles called Turnings-of-the-Year. They were not true circles, but egg-shapes, one inside the other, and why they were made so was secret lore of the Bear Skull Society. Taller than any man, some of them twice as tall as the tallest man, the stones took two forms, alternating around the circle: one stone was straight up and down, and the next was pointed at the top and wider in the middle.

The unenlightened thought these shapes represented the male and the female, but this was not true. In the doings of the Bear Skull they used the one set of stones one year and the other set the next.

Within the larger of the two circles, but not inside the smaller, was a platform made of tree trunks, shaped like the litters in which chiefs travelled. Before the sun rose, on the first day of the Gathering, this upraised seat was covered over with bearskins and deerskins, and all around it stood feathered lances. The People had roused themselves in the night and come to stand all around the great bank outside the ring.

In the eastern end of it, they left a space, a walkway through their midst, where the rising sun could shine into the rings of the stones and spread her blessed rays over the platform and them who would sit on it.

They had not reached it yet, and it was the matter of who would go first to the platform that filled every mouth.

"Ladon!" some called, and the men beat their drums and waved their lances, and the women shook their hands above their heads. "Ladon!"

"Rulon!" others called. "Rulon!" And sent up a mighty drumming.

"Barlok! Barlok!"

"Mithom!"

"Ladon! Ladon!"

"Rulon!"

"Barlok!"

"Rulon! Rulon!"

Other voices called for other chiefs, but those were the smaller villages and their voices could not match the thunderous shouts of the People of Ladon and the People of Rulon, and one by one the other names were drowned out. And when their names sank into the shouts for Ladon and Rulon, the people of those other villages chose which of the two they would shout for, and added their voices to the combat.

Now the sun was coming up. The sky was absolutely cloudless, the air already warm and shimmering and the People full of vitality and hope. Their voices rang off the stones.

"Ladon! Ladon!"

"Rulon!"

Now here came the lesser chiefs, Barlok, an old man leaning on two younger men, his bearskin robe dragging in the dust at his heels. He came to the opening of the ring and drew back and stood to one side. Now here came Mithom also, to take up his place to one side of the way to the platform, and two other, lesser chiefs came down over the bank and down to the entry, and there each chose one side or the other and stood there waiting. All the while, the People shouted the two names, and there seemed no difference between them.

At last Rulon came over the bank.

He was young, and beautiful in his youth. His hair was braided and knotted and he wore a robe of bearskin and he carried a lance in one hand, trimmed with feathers dyed red and blue and yellow. In his right hand, held up aloft, he bore the club that was his village's special pride: it was said no man but a chief could lift it. Teeth of flint covered the round head of it, and in the long shaft were set bits of quartz and amber.

When the People saw him coming, his beauty overwhelmed them, and all of them opened their throats and let his name climb to the sky.

"Rulon! Rulon! Rulon!"

At that he seemed to stand even taller. At the very gateway to the throne he stood swollen with pride, his name surrounding him like a magic cloud and the great club held at arm's length over his head.

"Rulon! Rulon!"

There seemed no doubt. The throne was before him. He took a step toward it, and the crowd suddenly hushed.

"Rulon!"

That was one voice. One voice alone, that boomed over the Turnings-of-the-Year, and held Rulon fast in his tracks.

Now down the embankment Ladon came.

No one called his name. Many raised their hands before them, as if to shield themselves from a radiance. Even Rulon turned to face him. Huge he was, slow as a great bear in his steps, and if any marked the wooden wedges tied to his feet, which made his steps so slow and swaying, none thought any the less of his height. His robe was deco-

rated with feathers and bits of amber; in his hands he carried a lance
and a drum, and around his neck, in circles and circles that clinked
when he moved, he wore masses of blue beads.

He came slowly up before Rulon and stood there, towering over
the younger man, face to face in the gateway to the throne.

"Ladon!" the People roared.

Rulon lifted up the great club over his head as high as it would
go, and shook it.

"Rulon," the cry rose, and then like a thunder: "Ladon!"

Ladon did nothing. The rising sun struck the coils of beads that
covered his chest and showered him with light. Again Rulon raised
the club over his head, and again this drew his name from the crowd,
but that name seemed a whisper compared to the roar of Ladon's.

And now for a third time, Rulon put the club high up to the sky.
The crowd hushed. He held the club at arm's length, struggling visi-
bly with the weight; but the crowd was still, and no one called his
name. When at last he could bear the weight no more, he lowered
his arm, and then the voice of the crowd broke over him like a storm.

"Ladon! Ladon! Ladon!"

Rulon seemed to shrink. The club fell to his feet. His shoulders
slumped down. Ladon faced him a moment longer, drawing all the
savor from this victory, and turned, and in his swaying majestic walk
he crossed the flat grass to the platform, turned, and with his
upraised arms summoned his men out of the crowd. They rushed on
him; lifting him up bodily, they placed him on the bearskins, and all
the People bowed down before him. The rising sun shone full on
him. Raised above all others, he looked over the world, and he knew
that it was his.

Joba could not say what she had seen in the face of the strange boy
in Karella's camp, but it oppressed her.

She saw her son Rulon humiliated at the entry to the Turnings-
of-the-Year; that gave her a certain grim satisfaction, because no
chief was ever as great as Rulon had wanted to be from the moment
he first took the club into his hands. She was not close to her son and
she mistrusted all men anyway.

Still, her mood was very low. She sat by her hearth in the old
longhouse, knowing there was work to be done and unable to stir

herself to do it. Nearby her sat her daughter, Shateel, combing her hair, and the young woman's idleness stung Joba to bitter words.

"What! Is the store so much in the roundhouse that we need work no more? Get up, girl, and go to your work. Go!"

"Mother, it is the Gathering," Shateel said. "No one works at the Gathering."

She drew the wooden comb slowly through her long fair hair. Joba admitted to herself that her daughter was the most beautiful girl of all the People; she had the looks of a young doe, smooth and soft, unused and unproven, with all her life before her. Joba felt the weight of her past dragging on her like a stone that would haul her down into death. She knew her life was nearly over. Her soul was sick.

Out of this pit of unhappiness she turned on her daughter again.

"Can you not at least get up, so that I might make the hearth straight? If you will not help your poor old mother—"

At this she noticed a stranger coming down the length of the longhouse and she shut her mouth; it would not do to show rancor before someone of another village. Quickly she put her hearth in order, stepping past Shateel to do so.

The girl did not move to let her mother by. She held out a tress of her long hair to admire the sheen. If she saw the stranger coming she did not show it, even when he stopped before Joba's hearth.

At that, the older woman stood up and faced him, and made a broad gesture of welcome with both hands.

"Come into my hearth, stranger, and let me do honor to my ancestors and yours here: come in."

"Good greeting, Joba," said the stranger, smiling, "in the name of our common ancestors, because we are not utterly unknown to one another, although you do not remember your poor kinsman. I am Fergolin, of the Oak Tree and the Bear Skull."

"Fergolin," Joba said. "Shateel, bring a mat for our kinsman. Yes, enter, Opa-Fergolin-on, my great-grandmother's great-grandson."

He came inside the spacious circle of Joba's hearth; Shateel brought him one of the best mats to sit on, woven of reeds, with a design set into it of red and yellow. Before he sat, he stooped and put a bit of wood on the cold fire, and he took a handful of meal from a pouch on his belt and sprinkled it over the ground before the two women.

"Heaven protect and exalt you, Joba-el, greatest of women, daughter of the daughter of the daughter of my ancestor."

Joba's mood was much uplifted; she enjoyed nothing more than a discussion of genealogy, and to match her memory against a kinsman's. Besides, from the elaborate ceremony Fergolin was offering, he had important business with them. She arranged herself on a mat with due attention to the amenities, and sent Shateel to fetch clean water to share with their guest.

For once the girl was obedient; as she went off, supple of body and pliant of manner, Fergolin watched her keenly, and Joba knew that it was her daughter who had enticed this kinsman here.

She said, "Take a mother's blessing, Fergolin, for your first meat—long has it been since I heard news of the village of great Opa-Ladon."

"We have no news, Joba-el—all goes as it should among us. We heard of Mashod's dying with heavy hearts, and souls that wept."

"The earth trembles when a chief such as Mashod goes into the Overworld," Joba said. She had hated her brother, as everyone knew, but it was only prudent to speak well of one in a position to do mischief.

Shateel came back with fresh water, and the two women brewed a tea of herbs for Fergolin, and served him in a fine painted jug, and gave him cakes and nutmeats to eat, arranged in several baskets, to show off their handicraft. Fergolin put out a hand to take a bean cake from one of the shallow baskets, then withdrew his hand.

"What excellent work is this! I dare not touch it, for fear of disturbing the beauty."

Joba straightened, puffed up with pride, and glanced sideways at her daughter. "My child is a novice at the work of women's hands."

Shateel sat down behind her mother and a little to one side, and was still; Joba glanced at her once, hoping to see her interested, but the girl was staring off into the empty air, and curling a tress of her hair around her finger. Joba sniffed, annoyed.

Fergolin was saying, "Never have I tasted such an excellent cake, Joba-el, and the manner of serving it is a greater pleasure yet." He went on in the same way, making extravagant praises and tasting everything, while Joba sat enjoying the compliments; she knew where he was heading. She stole another look at Shateel but the girl was half-asleep.

"As women," Joba said, "we have only one wish, which is to serve men, Fergolin-on."

They bowed together over this falsehood, and Fergolin sat back, his hands on his stomach.

"You have made me replete, most excellent of mothers."

Joba spread her hands. "Forgive my poor resources—I can only hope that my delight in offering them makes up for their plain poverty."

"No other hearth among all the People rivals yours, Ana-Joba-el."

"Heaven takes pity on a poor old woman and her humble family."

"Heaven itself would delight at your hearth, most wonderful Joba-el."

"I am utterly beguiled by your kindness, Opa-Fergolin-on."

They went on this way for some time, each one trying to outdo the other in lavish compliments, while Shateel nodded in the shadows. Then at last, Fergolin put his hands down on his knees, and came to his point.

"Ana-Joba-el, who has everything, whose wealth is limitless, will you hear the plea of one who comes to ask a favor of you?"

"What poor possession of mine could I offer to a kinsman?"

"Not I, but one who fears even to come before you in person to ask."

"If my eye cannot see, yet my ear can hear."

"It is for Ladon that I speak first, Ana-Joba-el, and for his son, who comes of age this year and who is tall and strong as an oak tree, the joy of all his village, and who will enter into manhood alone, unless there is one who would deign take his hand and become his mate."

"Ah."

"Well is it known that at your hearth there is one whose beauty rivals that of Heaven in the glory of the stars, and whose accomplishments are the envy of all."

Joba sneaked another look at Shateel, and saw, pleased, that the girl was watching them with a new interest. She said, "I have indeed a daughter, Fergolin-on."

"A daughter!" Fergolin shook his head. He avoided looking at Shateel; rote praises tumbled from his lips. "Such plain words to describe one whose beauty and womanly skill already overwhelm the whole world!"

He went on like that for a while, and Joba smiled, delighting in the flow of compliments; beside her, Shateel crept a little closer, and leaned forward.

"As for Ladon's son," Fergolin said, "I have watched over him from his babyhood, and for fear of arousing the jealousy of the Overworld, I cannot praise him overmuch, but I make assurances to you that such a match as we propose will bring together two of equal lineage, equal beauty, and equal skill."

Also, Joba thought, she is the sister of the chief, and her son will be a chief. She smiled at Fergolin, but her simple pleasure in this was curdling a little. She remembered Karella's boy. There was more to this than a husband for her daughter; a little late now, she considered Ladon's place in this. For the first time, she turned and stared full at her daughter.

Fergolin said, "Let me take to him who waits with a pining heart the only words that can salve the ache of love."

Joba now regretted indulging herself in the warmth of his compliments; she wished she had kept a cool mind and wondered if she had gone too far to back out. But Shateel looked eager. She crept a little closer.

"Ladon's son? Is he not the tall boy, the fair-headed one?"

"As handsome as a red deer when the leaves turn," said Fergolin. "Manly beyond his years. He will enter the Bear Skull, and someday, perhaps, he himself will be a chief."

"What?" Joba said, blankly. "How can that be?"

Shateel murmured, "I saw him yesterday, with his father—he is very fine-looking."

Joba turned on Fergolin. "A chief! How can he become a chief?"

Fergolin colored up in his face, and a pleading look shone forth from his eyes. Certainly Ladon had told him what to say. He spoke in a low voice. "Who can tell the things to come? He is fit to sit above any village of the People."

"He is not—"

Joba stopped; she had been about to say, He is not the son of the chief's sister, but then she remembered who was the son of the chief's sister, and she saw suddenly how tangled this was becoming. She would have to talk to Karella. Her daughter plucked at her arm.

"Mother. I would like to be married, and he is very fair."

"The words of the daughter of Joba will ravish his heart, and bind them together forever," Fergolin said.

Joba pressed her lips together. She should not have let Fergolin get as far as this—among the People, if a proposal was even entertained to the point of being spoken, then the acceptance was all but certain—and she reproved herself for indulging in pretty speeches. Shateel was whispering to her, pushing her, urging her to agree. Still Joba held back. Fergolin smiled at her, not the ready, gentle smile of one wearing his own face, but a stiff-lipped grimace like the expression of a mask. Joba thought, They will use my daughter to make his son great.

It was too late now to say no. And they would live here, anyway, in Joba's village; she told herself that here they would be out of Ladon's reach. He was a handsome boy, she had seen him herself.

Even so, she could not bring herself to say yes. Instead, she said, "They are both young yet. Perhaps—if Ladon wills—we might wait a year."

Fergolin's smile was wooden. He did not like that. "I shall convey your answer to my chief and to him who waits with a wounded heart."

He gave them more compliments, all sounding the same, and with due addresses he left them. Joba sank down into a brooding posture, her hands in her lap.

"Mother!" Shateel pulled on her arm. "Mother, why did you not say yes? How can you do this? Now he will ask some other!"

"He will ask no other," said Joba, in a harsh voice. "What a fool, Shateel! It is you he must have."

At that the girl smiled and preened herself and seemed content now to wait a little. Joba turned her head away. She saw little hope for a match made for Ladon's purposes. Again and again her mind turned to Karella and Karella's strange new campfellow. What had she seen in the boy's face? She hardly remembered now; all that came to mind was the memory of his wide black eyes.

He came out of the forest. Ladon had got rid of him, but he had come back again, come out of the forest, and in those bold black eyes she had seen ruin.

All the more reason, perhaps, for Joba now to give Ladon power.

Shateel said softly, "I shall be married! Mother, let me go to my friends."

"Go," Joba said.

The girl went off, light-footed, knowing nothing. All she knew was her own will. Joba thought again of Rulon, struggling to hold the great ceremonial club aloft, while no one called his name. She trembled for her children.

They would live here, in her village; she would keep watch on them, and how could Ladon fulfill his plans when his son would be in another village entirely? Slowly she got up, collecting the baskets and jugs, crowding out her dark thoughts with the business of the day, but still, in a corner of her mind, she was afraid.

"The paints," said Harus Kum. "That's what they like, the bright colors. Give me lots of the paints."

The slave Tor came silently at his heels; they went through the enclosure the trader had made, when he came here, to keep his goods and his slaves separate from the savages. Inside the little fence of rolled brush, the other slaves squatted in the sun, waiting to be given work to do, and guarding the leather sacks and baskets in the center of the enclosure. When Harus Kum came in, the three slaves all shrank back, avoiding even his look.

The slave Tor, on his knees, opened the first of the bulging leather sacks and plunged his hand in, and took out some clay pots full of pigment. The clay pots were made with a plug on top of the stoppers and a matching recess in the bottom, so that several pots could be stacked up together, and Tor took apart one stack, opened each pot to see what color it held, and set it down on the ground beside him. Harus Kum paced up and down, looking around him, over the fence, toward the great sprawling camp of the savages.

In a few moments he would go down there and come face to face with the kings of these people, men who, he knew, would as soon trample him to death as let him go, men whose help would make his work here easier, men he dared not trust. He had been coming here every year now for three years, since he had learned of the Gathering, and he was beginning to understand the ways of these savages—at first, he had thought to come here and trade!—but he always felt in danger here, and that made him restless and bad-tempered.

He thumped Tor on the back with his fist, to hurry him up. "Get the cloth, too. Give them that."

The slave reached into the sack and pulled out a smaller sack. "What of this, master?"

"Not yet. Put them back." Those were for Ladon alone, if things went well.

The slave fumbled through the leather sacks, accumulating goods that Harus Kum could spread before the savage kings: dyes and cloth, tiny jars of sweet-smelling oil, beads and pins of shell-light, small things, easily carried over long distances. When he had it all together, it did not seem enough. He glanced at the leather sacks again, knowing what lay buried in their depths, tempted to give just a little away.

If they knew, would they not attack him? He was alone here, with only a handful of stupid cow-like slaves who would not even defend themselves. He turned away from the sacks with their hidden wonders. Tor was squatting down beside the array of gifts, doing nothing, and Harus Kum fetched him a kick on the bottom that knocked the slave face first into the dust.

"Put it in a basket." He tramped away, toward the little two-sided shelter at the back of the enclosure, to get his coat.

A few moments later, wearing his best clothes, his hair and beard combed and oiled, he and Tor left their little fort. Tor carried a basket with the gifts for the kings. Harus Kum walked ahead of him, his head high, his shoulders back, his chest thrust forward, each stride a strut. As he left the relative safety of his enclosure, he strutted all the more. All around the enclosure, in the grass, the savages waited in packs, huddling in the grass, staring at him, peering into his place. One good rush from the bunch of them would take it all, and Harus Kum knew himself in hideous danger. With high steps and an arrogant bearing he made his way down the slope and across the disorder of the camp, toward the stone circles.

Here in the center, the kings all sat on a wooden high seat piled up with furs. The wind whirled the feathers on the lances stuck in the earth all around them, the sun beat down on them, sitting there in an attitude of swinish pomp. As Harus Kum approached the place, whole masses of people began to close in around him, following him, moving ahead of him toward the throne, all faces turned toward him. When he came at last to the feet of the kings, the whole Gathering was there, they filled up the whole great space within the ring of stones.

There were too many of them, they made his skin crawl, the dirty brutes. He went to the edge of the platform, and said, "Hail to the kings of the People of the Stones!"

He spoke their language a little. Enough, anyway, to do what he had to do.

Before him in a semi-circle sat five or six men, hideously painted, dressed in skins and feathers. One was so old he dozed, the front of his coat dappled with drool. Others glanced at him incuriously, scratching themselves, yawning. In their midst, the greatest of them, Ladon the Mighty, leaned forward, his eyes fixed on Harus Kum.

"I, Opa-Ladon-on, welcome the outlander."

One of the other kings, a younger man, now leaned forward and stared at Harus Kum and turned to frown at Ladon. Harus Kum did not know him. The only one of these men whose name he knew was Ladon; he prided himself on his understanding of these savages, that he had swiftly realized that Ladon was pre-eminent among them, the only one worth dealing with. Even now, Harus Kum was pleased to see, he wore the coils of blue beads that Harus Kum had given him the year before.

The younger man was staring from Ladon to the trader, his face dark. Harus Kum said, "I have brought tokens of my respect and gratitude to the kings of the People of the Stones." With a gesture he brought Tor forward with the basket.

The kings all moved suddenly, leaning over to see—even the old man, knocked from his dozing. Tor held the basket, and one by one Harus Kum removed the small treasures and placed them on the thick furs at the kings' feet.

"Ah!"

At once, they reached for the goods; like children, if two of them seized the same thing, they struggled with each other for possession of it. Only Ladon sat motionless in their center, saying nothing, showing no interest in the pretties before him. The young man wrestled a pot of color away from another of the kings and turned the little jar over and over in his hands, even sniffing at it, trying to find the way in; when at last he pulled the stopper out, he had the jar upside down, and a shower of blue dye ran down over his lap.

The other kings laughed heartily at him, and the young man went red. He flung the jar down and brushed fitfully at the specks of blue on his clothes. Harus Kum watched the lovely color disappear into the dust; he remembered the hard work that had derived this tiny bit of blue from the rocks of the earth, which the wind now drifted away.

The young man twisted toward Ladon. "Opa-Ladon-on, mighty is he! Mighty before all the People! Mighty with the help of an outlander, who gives him blue beads, hah, Ladon, is that it? Is this where you got the blue beads?"

The other kings stirred, round-eyed, staring at the young man, and one reached out and laid a hand on the youth's shoulder as if to calm him, but the young man thrust him off. His gaze was fast on Ladon. "Tell us, Opa-Ladon-on, mighty, mighty, mighty. Tell us where you found the blue beads!"

Ladon ignored him. The other men glanced from one to the other of them and turned their attention to their prizes. The young man's words hung unanswered in the air, and like the flecks of blue, the wind wafted them away. Harus Kum bowed and spoke words of honor and praise to the kings, backing up, leaving them. As he left, however, he lingered there a moment by the gigantic stones, listening to the mutter of the crowd, and so he learned that Ladon's young rival was named Rulon.

Harus Kum was taller than any of the People, thin as a willow slip, with a brown beard that covered his chest. His clothes too were strange, a long shirt of woven stuff that reached to his knees, his legs wrapped in more cloth. Crouched just beyond the fence, Moloquin watched him roar and rant through his camp, shouting in his rattling harsh language at the others, and from the way these others scurried away from him and took the blows he dealt around him, Moloquin supposed much about the relationships among these strangers.

There were no women in Harus Kum's camp; the underlings did all the work, carrying wood and water, tending the fires, even cooking and cleaning up. To see them better, Moloquin pulled some of the brush out of the fence, but when he did this a slave came running at him, yelling, brandishing a stick, and Moloquin backed hastily away.

The brush fence was built around the top of a little hill. Halfway down the slope, Moloquin squatted down in the grass and went on watching.

Presently, behind him, he heard the grass rustle, and he knew Grub was there.

"Moloquin," said the little boy. "Have you anything to eat?"

Moloquin shook his head. "Go to Karella." Grub's constant

preoccupation with eating annoyed him. He fastened all his attention
on Harus Kum's camp.

The tall man was going somewhere. Yesterday he had taken gifts
to all the chiefs, which had become the main subject of discussion at
every camp in the Gathering. The little objects had gone from hand
to hand, admired and criticized; Karella had shown him some of the
cloth, smooth as worn bone to the touch, supple as the wind, before
she passed it on to Joba. Surely, all the people said, Harus Kum was
a magician to have such wonderful things, and it was a mark of the
power of the chiefs of the People that such a great magician should
bow to them and give them treasure.

Now Harus Kum was making himself ready again, putting on a
long tunic of red, smoothing his hair and beard with his fingers. The
balding man who had carried his basket of gifts to the chiefs in the
Turnings-of-the-Year was standing ready at the way out, carrying another basket.

Moloquin thought of the beads, the great strings of blue beads
that had taken Ladon first of all the chiefs into the stone circles.
There had been no beads among the gifts Harus Kum had offered
to the chiefs the day before, but the blue color, the blue that Rulon
had scattered into the dust, that was the same color as the beads, and
Moloquin, like Rulon, knew where Ladon had gotten his power.

Beside him, Grub whispered, "Are you going to the dancing tonight?"

"Dancing," Moloquin said blankly. Only the societies danced.

"Tonight." Grub edged closer to him; their arms touched. "The
girls dance. The men are all gone, or will be: tonight they go to the
High Hill, to dance the True Way of Seeking Honor."

"I don't know what you are talking about," Moloquin said, his
gaze returning to Harus Kum.

Grub sighed. "I can't go," he said. "I am too young." He put his
head down on his updrawn knees. "Ladon's son won't let me."

"He won't." Moloquin swivelled his attention toward the younger
boy. "Do you want to go?"

"Oh, yes! The girls will dance, and they say, if one of them likes
you, you can dance with her, and then afterward—"

He put his hand over his mouth, his eyes round. Moloquin
laughed.

"Then you shall go," he said. "I shall go with you."

"Oh," said Grub, pleased, and he moved up close to Moloquin, pressing his side to Moloquin's.

"Look at him," Moloquin said, nodding toward Harus Kum. "He is pretty as a horned buck. Will he dance?"

"Him," Grub said scornfully. "He is not one of the People. What can he know about the way of seeking honor?"

Moloquin settled his chin in his hands. Harus Kum was coming toward the opening in his enclosure, his underling behind him with a covered basket.

Grub tugged on his arm. "Come with me, we will go find something to eat, and then watch the Bear Skull masters line up the stars."

"I want to watch this. Besides, the sun is up; there are no stars."

"They do magic to call them forth, with the stones of the circles. Don't you want to be in the Bear Skull Society? You have to show them you are ready, or they will not choose you."

"They won't choose me," Moloquin said. "And I am not for them."

"What do you mean?" Grub leaned toward him, his eyes bright. "Have you already been chosen?"

Moloquin did not answer. He remembered the midwinter sunset, how he had watched the sun above the stones at the Pillar of the Sky; surely that meant something? Was he not now a member of the Green Bough, belonging to the Pillar of the Sky? Yet Brant had never spoken to him again since that evening.

He had shared some of the lore. He had given Moloquin the heart of the lore, the mystery, the promise of order.

"Aren't you hungry?" Grub asked, astonished. He was always hungry.

"I want to see—"

Now Harus Kum was finally emerging from his fort, the man behind him with the basket. He caught sight of Moloquin, sunk down there in the grass, and bellowed, and by the way he glared at the boys, Moloquin knew it was time to run. Even now more of the trader's men were rushing out the gate in the brush fence. Moloquin went swiftly away through the trampled grass.

Ladon was resting; before him lay a whole night's dancing, the most intricate and taxing dance of the whole year's cycle, and he had been sleeping nearly all day on the platform in the sun. But to meet Harus Kum he left the platform and the other chiefs, telling them he had matters to attend to in his own camp, and he went into the middle of his camp and had his men put feathered lances there to mark his high seat.

In the midst of the lances, with his men all around him, he waited for Harus Kum. When the trader came, he gestured to the men around him, and they all turned their backs, so that what Harus Kum and Ladon could say would be between the two of them alone.

Harus Kum had brought a big basket with him, and he set it down beside him when he sat on the ground before Ladon. Smiling, smooth, the outlander spoke words of greeting to him, but Ladon was impatient; he longed to come to the center of all this, and his fingers tapped on his thigh, his eyes shifted from side to side.

At last, Harus Kum opened his basket, and he drew forth strand after strand of the blue beads and laid them down before the chief. The blue was very pretty against the black of the bearskin. Ladon pushed at them with his foot.

"I want more," he said.

Had he been speaking with one of his own People he would have sheathed his remark in many words, but Harus Kum understood only the simplest of language.

The trader turned the basket over, and spilled all the beads in a mound onto the bearskin. Ladon kicked fretfully at them.

"I want more," he said again.

Harus Kum made a sound in his throat. At the corners of his mouth, small lines appeared. When he spoke it was in a louder voice than necessary.

"Great is mighty Ladon! Ladon, who has so much, whose wealth is the wonder of all the world—"

His words sounded like a chant, like words spoken to the beat of a drum. Ladon glanced at the blue beads. Heaps of beads like this had won him power over all the People, but Rulon now knew where they had come from; the power was chancy, always chancy, and he had to have more. Just to keep his place he had to have more and more. He raised his gaze to Harus Kum; the trader was like a blank stone, like a chunk of raw flint: if Ladon handled him the right way, would he not show the beauties hidden away within him?

He said, again, "I want more."

Abruptly Harus Kum thrust his face toward him, all the pretty phrases gone. "Then give me more!"

Ladon grunted. Now at least they had broken through the skin of the business. "What do you want of me, then, outlander?"

"I want grain," Harus Kum said. "Cheese. Honey. Onions." He did not add, *I need food to keep me and mine, so that we can use our strength and time for other things than finding food.*

The broad face of the chief showed nothing of his feelings. Only, he raised his head a little, looking down his nose at Harus Kum.

"What will you give me, if I give you what you wish?"

Harus Kum licked his lips. There was that in his packs that might serve, but he disliked giving such as that into the hands of these savages. He hemmed a little.

"I have excellent dyes, and much cloth. I can get much more cloth, too—"

"No!" Ladon slashed the air with his hand. "Cloth—colors—we have that. I want—I want—"

As he spoke, the high feeling seemed to swell him like a toad; Harus Kum felt himself threatened, and he slid backwards a little, away from the other man. He said, without thinking, "Perhaps Rulon will help me, for the sake of the beads."

At that, Ladon reared up. His face was dark with temper. His eyes glittered with malice. His great arms milled the air in furious slashes.

"Hear me, outlander. Even you should understand this. Rulon is nothing. What does he have? Two longhouses! He can give you nothing! Nothing! I—only I can give you what you want, and if you go to Rulon, I shall see you never leave this place at all! Do you understand me? Only I can help you!"

Harus Kum's head sank down between his shoulders; he regretted speaking of Rulon; he should have gone to Rulon behind Ladon's back.

"And I will help you," Ladon said, in a calmer voice. "But you must give me more than a few beads."

Harus Kum's heart jumped; at least Ladon was offering him what he needed. He thought again of the secrets in his packs, but again he shied from giving those things to mere savages.

He said, "I shall bring you more. Tomorrow." In the meantime, he would think of something else to offer.

"Good," Ladon said. His rage left him, and with it his noble bearing; he sank down again, his eyes half-shut. "Go. Tomorrow we shall speak again."

Harus Kum bubbled over with compliments and praises. With a gesture he got Tor to collect the basket and the rejected beads. Ladon now seemed asleep, his eyes drooping, his vast body slumped down on the bearskin. Bowing and murmuring, Harus Kum went away.

In the deep twilight, without a drum, without flutes, without a voice to summon them, the girls of the People gathered at the Turnings-of-the-Year.

No one knew how this had started. The elders of the People frowned on it and some tried to prevent it, keeping their daughters in, threatening and complaining. Still from the beginning of time the girls had come here, on this day, and gathered inside the rings, and danced.

Shateel had done it before. This time when she came into the ring and clasped hands with the other girls, it was different, because this was the last Midsummer's Night that she would be unmarried.

That thought blazed in her mind like a star. Soon she would be married, and her long fretful dissatisfying childhood would be over: she would be a woman, and have a woman's power and a woman's joys.

The other girls all knew. She wore her hair now in a long plait with flowers twined in it, and flowers wrapped together into a garland around her waist, and so everyone knew that soon she would be married. Therefore they said nothing to her. They belonged still to the green unfulfilled world of childhood, but Shateel stood on the threshold of her own life.

She clasped a hand on either side and swayed back and forth in the dance, smiling to herself. Soon she would be her mother's equal, no longer to be chided and scolded and ordered around; soon she would have a man of her own.

The girls swayed from side to side in their circle, broke the grip of hands to turn, swung back, and caught hands again. Some clapped and some sang. Slowly they found a rhythm, and their feet fell into step with it; here and there a bit of a song made itself felt, and their voices picked it up. Like the winddrift of thistledown that gathered in a sheltered place, so the bits and pieces of their ritual formed together by accident and chance.

Now the boys were coming.

Shateel kept her eyes shut. As she stepped from side to side, she let her body follow, curving, bending back and forth, and her knees bent with each step, dipping down. Her hair began to fall out of its plait; she felt the soft touch on her cheek, and her head fell forward a little and her hair swung around her. She swayed and twisted, stooped and straightened, turned and turned, and all the while she saw nothing but the promise of her wedding day to come.

But now the boys were there.

The boys gathered on the bank outside the rings of stone. They stood there watching the girls in their dance, and now and then one of them would slip down to the ditch, cross over, and try to join the circles of the girls. The girls would not accept them. Laughing, they slapped at the outstretched hands and pushed the boys away. Only, now and then, they pushed the boys forward, not back—into the circles, not away to the ditch, and then they danced around the boy in the center of the circle, laughing and kicking out at him.

So, slowly, as the night went on, more and more of the boys got inside. There they too made a ring, joining hands; they faced out, and the girls faced in. Shateel opened her eyes at last, and saw before her a strange boy's face.

She shivered. Somehow she had expected to see the face of her betrothed. She shut her eyes again, but the dance had left her behind; she had to look to see where she was. Opening her eyes, she found him there before her again, that same boy, dark as her betrothed was fair, thin and raw as he was sleek.

They danced face to face, step to step, while impatiently she waited for the rings to turn, to bring her to her beloved. The rings would not turn; still she was face to face with the strange dark boy, with his impudent stare. She kicked at him, and whirled away, putting her back to him.

Even so, for a long moment, she seemed to see his face in the dark air before her.

The dance turned her forward again, and to her relief, he was gone. The ring of boys was circling past her. She and the girls stepped sideways, bending, swaying, turning to their right, as the boys on the inside turned the other way, and they passed by her swiftly now, never looking at her. Then there he was, her betrothed,

Ladon's son, smiling at her. In his hair was the red feather, that meant he sought a wife.

They had not met yet. They were not supposed to meet until their hands were joined together before the chiefs. But she knew him, and he knew her, and she stretched her hands toward him, glad, and he took her hands in his own and they went away from the circles, out past the stones, out to the ditch.

"Shateel," he said, once, breathlessly.

She smiled at him. He was handsome with his yellow hair, his smooth body, and she wanted all the other girls to see her with him and envy her. She put her arms around him, to keep him close to her. Soon, soon, she thought, and then: why not now? They went over the ditch together, saying nothing to each other. With their hands clasped together there was nothing that needed to be said. Climbing up over the bank, they went down the far side, toward the protection of the trees along the little stream, and there, in the grass, she made her own ritual with Ladon's son, and passed by her own rites into womanhood.

Moloquin danced only one round, facing the girls, until the crowd inside the stone circle made him uneasy, and he went away, up over the bank, through the half-deserted camp to Karella's fire. The dancing made him tremble all over, even his insides seemed to tremble, to go on quivering long after his feet stopped dancing.

Karella said, "What did you see there?"

"Girls," he said, and was at once so ashamed that he buried his head in his arms. Karella touched his hair.

"My boy," she said, stroking him. "My silly boy. Will you marry soon, and leave me behind?"

"I will never leave you," Moloquin said, and put his arm around her waist and held her tight. When he shut his eyes and held her against him, some overpowering memory took new life from the touch, from the warmth and closeness of her body, a memory of belonging. He turned his face against her body, his eyes shut.

He said, "Tell me a story," and Karella told him a tale of Rael the Birdwoman, who learned the speech of animals and trees, and could understand the murmuring of streams and the cry of the wind. Moloquin sat within the circle of her arm, his gaze on the fire, longing for such an understanding as Rael's; in the red flames he thought he saw faces, eyes, and flowing hair, and into his mind leapt the memory of the girls at Turnings-of-the-Year, their hair, their faces, their shining eyes. His belly churned with a new hunger. Eat their eyes, their hair, their soft mouths. Soft against his cheek the arm of his mother Karella. He stroked his cheek against her arm, lazy, the story flowing into his ears. Beneath the whisper of her voice, he thought he heard the wind cry, as Rael heard it, full of words.

He startled, sitting up. There was a voice out there, screaming in the wind.

"Ana, do you hear that?"

"What?" Karella lifted her head; she had been lost in her story, she blinked and looked around her like one awakening from deep sleep.

"That." Moloquin sprang up, every hair on his body standing on end, as again the wind brought a thready screech of terror to his ears. "Someone—"

Karella gasped. She had heard it too. She scrambled to her feet and with a loud voice, a bellow that amazed him, she shouted to the women at the nearby fires.

"Come! Help—help—"

She started toward the screaming. Moloquin kept by her, his hand on her arm, uncertain, and she turned to him.

"Go—go quickly—some evil is there—"

He burst into a run, cutting between fires, in the direction of the screams, and she and the other women labored after him.

Now the screams came louder, more distant, and there were words in them. Out there someone—a woman—was shrieking for help. Moloquin lengthened his stride. At the edge of the camp was a line of willow trees, choking a little streambed, and he fought his way through this dense cover, splashed over the stream, and came into a grove of close-growing trees.

The women crashed through the brush after him. Before him, under the dark branches, bodies thrashed and wrestled on the ground.

"Help! Help me—"

She who screamed was tangled up with some others on the ground before him. He raced toward her, and as he approached, two men parted themselves from the thrashing close-clutched bodies and wheeled to run. Moloquin flung himself on the nearer of them and bore him down under him, and an instant later, the women ran into the glade.

They howled. The screaming that had drawn them disappeared into a general uproar. Moloquin got up, and the man he had dragged down scrambled to his feet and tried to run, but the women were on him at once. In the darkness Moloquin could see nothing clearly. He backed away, panting; he saw the man he had stopped vanish into a crowd of women, who set to beating him with their fists, kicking him as he fell. Then Karella came into the glade, and she had a torch in one hand.

The red-yellow light flickered across the grass, leapt and flashed over the trees that leaned down around them. In the center of the little glade, a woman knelt, sobbing, her hair disheveled and dirty, shiny streaks of tears striping her face. The other women bent over her, crooning to her.

"They took me!" The kneeling woman shrieked; she flung her arms out, pointing around her, pointing toward her attackers. "They used me for a wife! See—" She pulled up her clothes; before Moloquin turned his face away he saw, vivid in the torchlight, the white arches of her thighs, slimed and bloody. "They had me for a wife—"

At the sight of her abused body, the other women gave up their voices in a screech that turned Moloquin cold. He backed away, aware suddenly of being a man in a place where men had done evil, of having that between his legs that they would find evil, of having evil lust in him against all women; suddenly his heart was pounding enough to sicken him. He sidled swiftly away into the brush that clogged the streambanks, while in the glade the women closed on the two men they had caught.

Until now the men had been silent, but as the women laid their hands on them, their voices went up in a howl of terror. Moloquin cried out to hear it. His belly heaved. Turning, he clawed his way through the brush, desperate to get away. Behind him the hoarse cry of the men broke off abruptly, as if their throats were stopped. He struggled through the brush that held him fast, that kept him prisoner, within their reach. From the glade, there came only the grunts and triumphant roars of the women, the pounding of their feet on flesh, the crunch of bone. With the strength of terror, Moloquin broke free of the clinging underbrush and fled away.

. . .

The two men who had attacked the woman in the glade were from
Harus Kum's camp. As soon as they knew this, the women of the
People, with their headwomen leading them, went up to the place
where the outlander had his camp, and they sat themselves down all
around it, sat down so close no one could come in or out through the
wall of their bodies, and they faced Harus Kum, and they sent for
Ladon.

The women were pitched high as flutes, wild and unmanaged; some
sat weeping on the ground, with their sisters around them, and others sat in tight-gathered groups, talking earnestly one to the other,
and others strode back and forth glaring toward Harus Kum and
crying strange encouragements. Their babies caught their fever with
their milk, or through their skins from the very air, so that the whole
great swarm of women was overhung with mindless wails. In their
midst sat the headwomen, packed tightly together, a cluster of grey
heads.

Going toward them with Karella, Moloquin saw them massive as
stones, their action slow and irrevocable, their passion slow and malevolent; he imagined himself crushed beneath them, ground to
pieces in the mill of their rage.

He kept close by Karella. She picked a course through the stirring, noisy flock of the women, while Moloquin with her sitting mats
and a jug of water clung hard to her heels. The headwomen had
chosen a place directly below the gate into Harus Kum's enclosure,
on the flat ground, and had made a little fire, although in the high
sun of the day the flames were invisible, a mere flickering of the air.

At this fire, among the others, sat Joba, and when Karella came
into their midst, her words went first to Joba, and her voice was bitter.

"So you have made your bed with Ladon, have you? You will
soon regret marrying your daughter to his son, I promise you."

Joba lifted her head; in the tucks and creases and laps of her
face her eyes gleamed, small and full of malice. She glared past Karella at Moloquin.

"What is he doing here? Send him away, Karella—get rid of
him!"

Karella turned her eyes toward Moloquin, and without a word between them, he put down his armload of sticks and mats and went away. He walked up over the side of the hill, toward Harus Kum's enclosure; as he passed by, looking in, he saw the little huddled band of men there, ducked down behind the brush fence, each hand clutching an axe or a knife. He did not pause; he went on across the slope toward the open ground beyond, where he could see Grub sitting under a tree. Those men in there, clinging to their weapons, would not stand a moment against the women. He felt sorry for them, but he had to get away from here. There was Grub, waiting for him; for the first time, he saw himself and Grub as souls in common, united in their maleness. He went down over the shoulder of the hill, down to meet Grub, and escaped into the quiet of the wilderness.

Harus Kum kept up a steady monotone of curses. Crouching in the shelter of the brush fence, the remaining three slaves pressed close against him, he listened to the women's wild uproar and his skin turned cold. He had been mad to come here, mad to have anything to do with these savages.

He cursed the women; he cursed Ladon, for being chief over such women and not keeping them properly controlled; he cursed the two slaves who had stolen away from the safety of their fort and never come back again. He could guess at what they had done. It seemed fair enough to him—if these women insisted on going about so openly, how could a man be blamed for wanting them? But he himself would never want such women, fat, ugly, furious women, and as he thought that, from the mass of angry women that surrounded him a yell began, and grew louder and more undulating as he listened, until his hair stood on end.

He lifted his head cautiously until he could see over the brush fence, and a gusty sigh escaped him. "Ah! At last." He stood up, stooping a little, in case these madwomen should still attack, but down there, at the edge of the swarm, was Ladon's litter, swaying on the shoulders of many men, and a great crowd of other men paraded after it, in lines that reached away into the Gathering. Harus Kum watched the litter borne in through the midst of the women, going toward a spot at the foot of the slope directly below where Harus

Kum now stood peering out, and he straightened, relaxing, seeing a way to escape from this with his life.

Ladon was exhausted. He had danced all night at the High Hill, and then, lying on the ground this morning, his mask by his side, the women's message had come to him, and at first he had thought, Let them do it. He knew what they would do, if he did nothing. He had no such love for Harus Kum that he leapt up at once to go save him. It irked him, also, that the women should expect him to come running to do their will.

But as he lay there on the grass of the High Hill, his mask beside him, a witness, he considered that letting the women do as they would gave them some greatness, and that they took this greatness away from him. He roused himself, groaning, and called for his litter, and called all the men up from their fatigue and their emptiness after the great ritual, and slowly they went back to the west, back to the Gathering.

From a lifetime of dealing with them he knew what to expect, and so he was unsurprised when, coming among the headwomen, he was at once set upon and reviled and shouted at as if he had done the evil, not some strangers. He lay back in his litter, listening to all this, and waved to his men to set down the poles and stand back.

Joba and Tishka pressed on him from both sides. "You brought these outlanders here! You are responsible for what has been done!"

Ladon raised one hand, palm out. "I did nothing. I did not bring him—"

"You encouraged it! You and your blue beads—"

He collected himself. They were hysterical; the chief evidence of it was that they were speaking to him in the low tongue of women and children, not in the elevated language with which men and women were supposed to address one another, and now he raised himself up, squaring his shoulders, and gave them all such a lofty look of disapproval that they quieted.

They stood around him, a pack of old women, shapeless masses within their woven clothes, their hands broken and knotted from working the earth. From their midst, now, Karella stepped forward.

She spoke in a mocking voice, sharp as a bird's, using the most formal and elaborate phrases available to a mind overstocked with words.

She said, "Opa-Ladon-on, mighty, mighty, mighty! Let Heaven look down upon the great Son of the People! Let Heaven guide him ever in his judgment! Let someone guide him ever in his judgment, mighty one, mighty Ladon, whose judgment has been most false and most awful for the People! You let them stay here, Opa-Ladon-on, mighty is he, mighty above all men, you let them come here, and now they have seized one of us, they have tried to steal away her belly and plant their own seed therein, to make her a mere vessel for their continuance. Now what shall mighty, mighty, mighty Ladon do to redress this evil?"

The other women growled, and someone murmured, "She speaks with the tongue of Heaven itself!"

Ladon folded his arms over his chest and looked all around him, looking at each one of them; it helped him to confront them if he saw them each as a separate female and not as the great and terrifying crowd they could become. Finally he brought his gaze forward again, to Karella, to Joba and Tishka who stood on either hand, and said, "Bring me the wicked ones."

At once all the women pointed up the hill toward Harus Kum. "There he is!"

"Ah," Ladon said, "and you say that Harus Kum the outlander seized a woman and—"

Here he paused, and cleared his throat, because the high language had no words for the deed they claimed of Harus Kum and his men. He let the pause speak for him.

"Yes, yes," they said. "You brought them here, Opa-Ladon-on—"

"And how do you know that Harus Kum did this evil, this monstrous wickedness?"

"We saw it done," Joba said, and as she spoke, she swelled up with anger, her eyes glinting.

"And where are the men who did it?" Ladon asked.

"Ah!" Tishka smiled at him, her teeth showing. "Nowhere between Heaven and earth, I tell you that much."

"Then you have slain Harus Kum yourself?"

That bemused them. He smiled, knowing himself too clever for them, pleased with his cunning, until Karella stepped forward and began to speak to him.

"Ladon," she said, and she used the low tongue, the speech of women to children or one another, which no one had used toward

Ladon since he reached his manhood. "Ladon," she said, "give us no more dances, no more games. Go up there and get him away, forever and ever, or we shall do it ourselves."

He felt his face grow hot and red. His fists clenched. Small, she was, frail as a little bird; he could crush her with a blow, and yet she dared to speak to him with such contempt, she dared give orders to him.

Nor had he any choice save to obey. If he refused, they would do as she threatened; they would remove Harus Kum themselves, finally and horribly.

He turned to his litter. With a last, long, cold look at Karella, he sat down in the litter and called to his bearers, and they took him up on their shoulders, and went up the hill toward Harus Kum.

The trader sat on his heels, his back to the fence, his eyes hollow, his mouth set. He said, "I swear to you, Opa-Ladon, I swear on my balls." He put his hand down between his legs. "I did nothing."

Ladon swept his gaze around the enclosure. Certainly there were fewer men here than before. He relaxed; he slouched in his litter, fatigue heavy in his muscles, and stared at Harus Kum; he had just begun to realize that there was meat in this for him.

He said, "Where then are your other men, Harus Kum?"

"I don't know. They must have crept away—they have not come back. Maybe—maybe they ran away."

Ladon shook his head slowly from side to side, his eyes fixed on Harus Kum. "The women have dealt with them."

"Ah? Are they alive?"

"As they will deal with you," Ladon said, "if I do not save you from it."

"They are dead," Harus Kum said. He beat his fists on his knees. A swarm of words in his own tongue flew from his lips. He tramped around the little space, his hands thrashing the air. Ladon watched, patient, reclining in his litter as if on a bed.

Through the corner of his eye, he saw one of Harus Kum's men lick his lips; he guessed they were thirsty, with the women between them and water. He raised one hand, saying, "Fetch water for these sufferers," and behind him there was a bustle of several feet as his men fought to do his bidding.

He smiled at Harus Kum. He said, "So. We haggled before over peas and beans, Harus Kum, now will we haggle over blood and bones as well?"

The trader heaved up a sigh, the air slipping between his clenched teeth; his eyes shone. He nodded his head. "I shall give to mighty Ladon what is Ladon's due."

He went to the little round hut in the middle of the enclosure, and disappeared into it. Ladon's man came back with a tall two-mouthed jug of water. At a nod from Ladon, he gave the jug to the nearest of Harus Kum's men, who seized it with trembling hands and spilled half of it in drinking; the other men crowded around, their cupped palms catching a few drops of the overflow. Harus Kum came back.

He saw the men drinking and his steps hesitated an instant, but with a shrug he put aside such minor things as thirst and came to Ladon, and before Ladon he knelt down. In his hands he held a bundle of cloth. He spread this open on the dirt, and laid out on the cloth some objects.

While he arranged them his body shadowed them from the sun, but then he sat back, and the sunlight struck them. Behind Ladon, someone gasped. Ladon himself sat up straight, his gaze fastened to the blazing beauty before him.

"Aaaaah."

He stretched his hand forth and touched the nearest of the ornaments, a heavy curved band. It shone so in the sun he expected it to be warm, but the stuff was cold, hard and cold as stone.

"What is this?"

Harus Kum said, "Such jewels as great men use to decorate themselves." His voice was too casual. He took up the curved band, and slipped it onto his wrist. From the cloth he took another such, for the other wrist, and a long rope of oblong disks, linked together, he fastened around his neck, and the men cried out to see him dressed in flashing, gleaming shapes, like pieces of the sun.

Ladon rejoiced; he said, "Yet that is not enough, Harus Kum."

The trader stared at him, tight-jawed. One by one, he took off the pieces he wore and laid them down again on the cloth. He said, "There is more."

"Here?" Ladon asked, swiftly.

"No, no." Harus Kum worked his stiff lips into a smile. "Where I can put hands to them. But I must have other things in return."

"I offer you your life, Harus Kum."

"I need food. What I said to you the other day, that I need. Now I need men, also—two men, to help me get it all back to my home." The trader squatted down behind the wonderful ornaments. "Give me what I ask, and I shall give you such that you will not think yourself diminished by the bargain."

Ladon set his teeth together, his eyes on the little pieces of shining stuff. What was it? No stone he had ever seen could be shaped like that, or polished to such a shine. Surely some wonderful magic took this supple and amazing form. He told himself he had known all along that Harus Kum had some hidden power; had it been calling him, Ladon, its true master?

Even now it called him, the rest of the treasure, from within the little brush hut. He knew, as certainly as he knew his own thoughts, that the rest of Harus Kum's horde was right there, within easy reach, and if he let the women have these outlanders, then he, Ladon, could take it all.

He balanced that against the fact that if he let the women do violence to these men, the women would have much more than a treasure, the women would have awakened another power against which the shining pretties before him would be of no use at all.

And he could have them. Harus Kum was offering him all of it, in return for that which Ladon could very readily supply. The women wanted these men gone; Ladon would send them away. Harus Kum wanted food; Ladon would send him away to Ladon's own village, and there they could find plenty of food.

Harus Kum wanted men, and there were two young men Ladon wanted himself rid of.

This all fit together, like the egg inside its shell, so perfectly that Ladon lost himself a moment in contemplation of it. Harus Kum, waiting, turned at last to the jug of water, and holding it high drained the last few drops onto his tongue. Ladon raised one hand; from behind him a man sprang forward to take the jug and hurry away to fill it up again.

Ladon said, "The favor of Heaven, that makes all things possible, has fallen on both of us today, Harus Kum."

The trader blinked at him, perhaps not understanding; deep lines engraved his face, and he looked tired. Ladon smiled at him.

"Make ready to leave this place at once. I shall go find you a suitable guide, and prepare your way among the women."

Harus Kum's eyes shut. He bowed his head down, one hand on

his breast. "Mighty is Ladon, mighty." His voice quivered with weariness and relief. Ladon summoned his bearers with a nod and was
swiftly carried away.

Joba said, "You must stand still, Shateel, and let me put your hair up,
or you shall never be married."

The girl made a face at her. Joba held the long rope of her
daughter's hair in her hands, putting it up with pins of bone and
wood; around them the other women worked to weave flowers together into a garland for the young bride. Shateel would not be still.
Ever her feet moved; ever her head turned, looking away, looking
toward Ladon's camp. Joba struck her lightly with the flat of her
hand.

"Now be still, or—"

"How dare you!" Shateel cried, her face dark, and returned the
slap with a slap of her own, aimed fair at her mother's cheek.

Joba gasped; all the other women froze, staring. Joba straightened slowly to her feet. The girl stood there, ruddy-cheeked now,
her great eyes swimming with bad temper. Her mother's eyes met
hers for a long moment.

After a while, Shateel gave way; she looked down. Slowly, Joba
went back to her labors, but now her hands shook. She thought, She
has already left me.

Her hands were full of pins. For a moment, fussing with the
girl's hair, she could not remember exactly what she had been doing.
Her mind seethed, full of unfocussed alarms.

"Here comes the bride-leader," said one of the other women.

Joba looked up, surprised: he was early, the ceremony could not
take place until afternoon. Yet he had indeed come. Fergolin stood
near the entrance to Joba's hearth, smiling.

"Wait here," she said to Shateel, and got up, brushing off her
clothes. Circling the other women at their work, she went to Fergolin.

"What is the matter? We are still very busy, Fergolin-on."

"I came with this gift from the young husband."

He held out a piece of deerskin, folded over. She opened it up,
curious, and let out a low gasp. Inside, neatly rolled up, was a strand
of blue beads.

"Oh." Joba drew back. She had just seen Harus Kum and his
men taken by force out of the Gathering; now she was face to face

with him again, coiled like a serpent, insinuating himself into this marriage of her daughter. She put out her hand to push the beads away. Before she could touch them, her daughter reached her side.

"I shall take them." Shateel's hand closed over the beads; she gave her mother a long level stare.

Fergolin said, "Ana-Joba-el, most excellent mother of such a bride, you must know now that because of the difficulty this morning, there is some trouble with the wedding ceremony."

Joba's head rose. "What?" she said, harsh.

"Because of the matter of Harus Kum, great Opa-Ladon-on must make an unusual request of you."

"I am listening to it."

"Harus Kum was not easily dealt with, as you may imagine. Ladon, mighty is he, took the greatest care in dealing with him. To make certain that Harus Kum did indeed leave the Gathering, he put in escort of him his most trusted man, his own son, the bridegroom."

Shateel said, "Then where is he now?" Her voice was sharp.

Fergolin never looked at her; his gaze remained steadily on Joba's, as he said, "It is Ladon's wish that the wedding be done in his village, after the Gathering, when his son returns from his task."

"Is he in danger?" Shateel cried.

Joba was staring fixedly at Fergolin, her mind troubled. Her uneasiness was mounting. The marriage of her daughter had become a contest, somehow, a contest with Ladon, a struggle for control of her daughter. Suddenly she saw the wedding like a pit before her, a trap toward which they were dragging her. She turned and seized the blue beads from Shateel and flung them to the ground.

"No. I shall not agree. Once she goes there, will he let her come back here again? He will insist on staying there, and she will stay with him. No."

"Ana," Shateel cried. "I shall go wherever he wishes." She faced Fergolin; it was to Fergolin she offered her words, as if her mother no longer mattered.

Fergolin said, mildly, "It was your desire, among the others, that Harus Kum be removed, Ana-Joba-el. By your own deed, you have made the wedding impossible here, since the bridegroom is gone on a task of your devising."

Shateel wheeled toward her. "You made this happen!"

Joba seized her by the wrists. "You are a fool. Do not take Ladon's side against me. You are not married yet. Until he takes your hand, you are my child, and I shall bid you as I see fit."

Shateel hardly let her finish. The color high in her cheeks, her hair slipping out of its plaits, she faced Joba and struck at her mother with her words.

"I am no child any more, Ana. I have been with him who is my husband. We need no words of the elders. I shall go with him wherever he wishes, I am his wife now, and he is my husband."

With a wrench of her arms, she freed her wrists from her mother's grasp and turning her back on Joba, she stooped and took the string of blue beads from the ground and put them around her neck.

Joba stood there staring at her; there was nothing more to be said. Her mind flew back over the years, back to the baby Shateel had been, nuzzling at her breast, and she saw the little girl, learning to walk and to talk, secure under her mother's watchful gaze; she saw the older child, struggling for mastery of her crafts, her mother ever guiding, ever protecting, ever loving. Now her daughter stood with her back to her and said that she had broken away and was glad to be going. Joba lowered her head. All the others in the longhouse had witnessed her humiliation. Slowly she went back to her fire and sat down and pulled her shawl up over her head. And there she sat, for all the rest of the day.

Most of the People avoided Harus Kum's camp now that it was abandoned, but Karella insisted on going there, and so Moloquin took her. He watched her grope and poke around the little brush hut and the fence, pick a few threads of cloth from a bramble and straighten the fibers in her hand, sniff at a wet patch on the ground.

"What are you doing?" he said. "Why can I not go? I have wood to carry, and Grub and I found a place where we can swim."

She stood, crooked with her years, her face sharp. "I am wondering if Ladon did as he said he did with Harus Kum."

"How can you discover that by searching here?" Moloquin stirred, restless; the day was turning warm and sultry, and he looked away to the west, where the stream curled around. Out there, they had found a deep pool, delicious in the summer's heat. "Why can you not leave Ladon alone?"

"Bah." She whirled toward him, suddenly furious. "Listen to me, boy. You are the son of Ladon's sister, and therefore I dare not trust Ladon, ever."

"Karella—" he gave her a strange sideways look, and drew closer to her. "Can I not be only your son? Why must I always be set against Ladon?"

She glared at him, the heat of her temper rising like a blast against him. "Curse you! No!"

His eyes flashed. "You care nothing for me. You hate Ladon, and so you harbor me, for the sake of Ladon."

"Hah." She swung her arm around and smacked him on the face.

He took the blow without flinching, but his eyes were hot and dark with fury. He said nothing more to her but his gaze remained long on her, full of rage and warnings. She trembled; she wanted to throw her arms around him, to destroy the sudden breach between them, but her pride held her fast, and he would not yield to her without some sign. Abruptly he turned and ran out of Harus Kum's abandoned camp, down onto the flat ground, and she saw him turn to the west, toward the stream and the open ground, where Grub was waiting for him.

Karella let out her breath in a rush of wind. She felt old and stupid and empty. She sank down on her hams on the ground, her eyes full of tears.

She was a fool. He was right—she wanted to thwart Ladon, and so she placed this boy against him; yet now it was the boy who mattered to her. She lifted up her face toward the sky.

When he came back she would beg his forgiveness. When he came back, she would tell him that she loved him. She would call him her son. She would never again use him against Ladon, when he came back. She huddled down in the place of the outlanders, the smell and feel of the outlanders all around her, and longed for him to come back.

Ladon's son knew where Moloquin was. He had seen the other youth the day before, gathering wood along the stream; as Moloquin collected the wood, he left it in heaps to be taken back later, and so it was easy to follow him, going along the stream from one pile of wood to the next.

He wished it had been harder to find Moloquin. He wished his father had not set this task on him.

Harus Kum walked along just behind him, his arms swinging. The other three men followed close behind him. They had left their goods a little way to the south, on the way to Ladon's village, when they walked off from the Gathering; Ladon had told his son to take the men straight away, so that all who saw them leave would think they were going away at once, and forever. So Ladon's son had led them away, burdened down with their packs, the men groaning under the weight, going straight into the west, and only when he came into the rougher, hilly ground well west of the Gathering did Ladon's son swing around and move south, and turning eastward again cut the well-worn track that led south to Ladon's Village.

There they left the packs. Harus Kum gave orders to his men in their unpleasant language, and with coils of rope and clubs of wood they started north again.

Once or twice the trader tried to speak to Ladon's son, but he pretended not to understand. The trader smelled strange, and the evil business in the camp the night before had cast a sinister shadow over him in the eyes of Ladon's son, but even more than that, the young man was loathe to speak much about what they were doing. He tried not to think about it.

Instead he thought about Shateel, his new wife.

Since the night of the dancing, when he had lain between her legs, she had filled his mind. Every moment he was away from her he felt her slipping away from him, gone to some other man, doing that with some other man. Now they weren't even to be married until Ladon's People returned to their own village, and if her mother refused to let Shateel go there, would she ever be his wife? Yet she had given herself to him, that night; surely she had been his wife then.

He should be with her now, and not here, helping to destroy one of his own People.

He told himself he hated Moloquin. His father hated Moloquin. Everybody hated Moloquin.

They walked along the bank of the stream until the brush and low trees that sprouted there grew so thick together they could not pass, and then cut around to the outside, wading through thick grass. When they cleared the extremity of the copse of brush, he saw, away ahead of them, two figures, one running happily along before, the other bowed under a weight of wood, and his heart sank.

They were his own People, and he was giving them to Harus Kum.

His steps dragged. But now Harus Kum had seen them, and in a crisp voice was giving orders to his slaves. Ladon's son trudged along behind them now, as the three outlanders advanced in a rush, spreading apart to cut off the two boys' line of escape. Up there, ahead of them, Moloquin dropped the wood to the ground.

Ladon's son opened his mouth to shout a warning, but no words came. He thought of his father, who had ordered him to do this, and could think of no power high enough to countermand him. Instead he broke into a trot, to keep up with Harus Kum.

Up there, now, Moloquin was pushing Grub away, waving him off, shouting to him to run. He wore nothing but a loin cloth; he had used his shirt as a sling to carry wood. Harus Kum and his men closed swiftly on them, their arms out. Grub hesitated, unwilling to leave his friend, and Moloquin stooped and picked up a long branch.

Harus Kum roared. Snatching out his whip from his belt, he snaked it loose, stopped before the boy with his feet planted, and brandished the whip.

"Drop it," he shouted. "Drop it, now!"

Grub clung to Moloquin's back. "What do they want?"

Ladon's son reached the others, panting a little; the three slaves sidled around to hold Moloquin between them. The boy backed off, one hand on Grub behind him, the other raising up his club toward Harus Kum.

"What is this? What do you want?"

Harus Kum gave a flick of his wrist, and the whip undulated through the grass like a snake, and the tip licked up into the air once, only a step from Moloquin's foot.

"Your chief has sold you to me! Come now, or I will punish you."

Grub whined. He pressed ever closer to Moloquin who now circled his arm around him, protecting him like a mother. The club he still held, raised up between him and Harus Kum.

"I am not Ladon's thing, to give away," he said. "Nor is this boy— let him go, at least."

Harus Kum raised his arm, and the whip lashed out, coiling in the air. Moloquin flinched back, but he could not avoid the whip; it wrapped itself around and around him and Grub together, and the little boy cried out, and Moloquin dropped his club. Bound tight in the whip, he bit his lips together, his face dead white, and his eyes brimming with pain.

Harus Kum walked up to them, still bound tight in his whip, and ran his hands over them as if they were beasts.

"These two look no stronger than a few reeds lashed together. What promises Ladon makes!" He spat. "Well, they will have to do."

"Let Grub go," Moloquin said.

Harus Kum unwrapped the whip from around them, and the two slaves closed in on them with the rope, and bound them, hand to hand, and ankle to ankle. Moloquin stood still. Around his chest the whip-marks stood up from his skin in long red welts.

He said, "Let me say good-by to my mother."

Harus Kum struck him full in the face. "Keep silent, unless I speak to you! You have no mother, boy, you have no People, all you have is my whip and my hand over you."

At that Moloquin howled; he lunged forward, all wrapped in his bonds, flinging himself bodily forward, not at Harus Kum but at Ladon's son, behind him. The three slaves seized him. Ladon's son flung up his clenched fists, all his nerves prickling up.

"Let him go," he cried. "I shall fight him—"

"Coward," Moloquin cried. "Coward—"

Harus Kum stepped in between the two of them, raised the butt of his whip, and calmly struck Moloquin over the head, so that he fell down senseless. Ladon's son lowered his hands, his heart pounding.

"I am not a coward. I would have fought against him—"

Harus Kum grunted at him. "Come, let us bind him up, and then hurry. Ladon your father said that you would take us to his village, and there help us get the stores he promised us."

"Yes," said Ladon's son. "I know where everything is."

He could not take his eyes from Moloquin, lying half-dead on the ground; he thought, He need not have struck him down, I would have beaten him if we fought. He remembered all the other times he and Moloquin had fought, the stones thrown, the angry words; and had he not always come out the winner then? He made his feet move, circling the body on the ground. South lay Ladon's Village. South he led Harus Kum.

. . .

When the sun went down Moloquin still had not come back, and Karella got up and went off to find him. At first she looked among the hearths of the People, thinking in his anger he might have gone to another fire when the evening approached, but she found only the other women, giving their children the evening meal. Most of the People were making ready to leave the Gathering, and the great sprawl of the camp was a jumble of packed belongings and garbage. Everyone was distracted and tired and when she asked after her son she got curt, uninterested replies—no one had seen him or Grub.

She worked her way back through the disorder toward Rulon's Village. The sky was full of a rushing wind and the stars were appearing in the dusk. As she walked aimlessly along, she came on Fergolin, the Bear Skull master, sitting with a circle of young men before him—the new members of the society, whom he would be teaching the rudiments of star-lore. Around his neck Fergolin wore several strands of the beads that the foreigner Harus Kum had brought, and around his head was a band of painted leather.

"Have you seen my son Moloquin?" she asked.

"Moloquin," one of the boys murmured, and there was laughter. "She wants Moloquin."

Fergolin said, "I have not, Ana-Karella."

The boys were still giggling together, and with a glance he silenced them. Karella loitered, hearing something sinister in their laughter. She wondered if it were merely the joke, the play on Moloquin's name, that made them laugh, or if they knew some evil had fallen on him. Finally she went away.

She went to the edge of the camp, by the stream, and looked out across the plain. From here it rose toward the horizon, not evenly, but in rises and hollows, rumpled like the surface of a lake under the wind, and the wind curried the grass, blowing in waves away from her. The darkness crept over it, crowded with spirits and demons. Her fear of the dark, of being out there alone, held her still a moment, but her back was already to the camp, and she could see a heap of wood, out there, waiting to be gathered in. She knew he was out there.

Slowly she went forth onto the empty plain. The wind wrapped itself around her and howled joyously into her ears. Her feet padded over the grass. Out there a night bird was singing, its brilliant ringing song raising the hackles on her neck. She went forward along the stream's edge, following the stacks of wood he had made.

Once she paused and looked back, and there behind her she saw the yellow glow of the fires of the People, driving the darkness away, and the black arch of the sky overhead. Her skin was cold and tingling with alarm. Something plopped into the stream beside her and she jumped.

Moloquin, she thought, Moloquin, if I find you I shall never speak of Ladon again, I shall call you my son forever, Moloquin, let me find you.

From one stack of wood to the next she trudged on, and then, in the middle of the grass, a little way from the stream, she came on his shirt, half-covered with wood.

He had not stacked this pile. The shirt lay crumpled under it as if he had cast everything down at once. She drew the cloth free of the sticks. The grass here was all trampled. She knelt down, feeling the ground with her hands, and lowered her head down and sniffed the earth.

She could smell him. He had lain here. And now her fingers wiped something slimy from the grass, and a dampness that she lifted to her nose, and tasted on her tongue, and knew for Moloquin's blood.

She howled. She knew now something dreadful had happened to him. With the shirt clutched in her arms, she ran here and there in short dashes, looking for him, and gathering up her courage she stopped once or twice and called his name into the dark.

He was gone. Her ears knew it, in the silences that answered her, and her belly knew it, hollow with an emptiness that would never be filled up again. He was gone. She had lost him.

She sank down to the ground and put her face against his shirt and cried for him and for herself. The shirt smelled of him. She sniffed it all over, wiped her tears on it, and inspected it all over for signs of blood. There was no blood on the shirt, but when she went back to where she had found it, the moon rising behind her, she found the blood on the grass again.

She stood there, calling his name recklessly now, uncaring what demon might be drawn to her voice. She stumbled away to the west, shouting. One of her shoes came off and she did not turn to pick it up but hurried on, half-shod, her eyes hurting from poking their look into dark shadows and far-off places. Her head hurt. Exhausted, she stopped a while, his shirt on her lap, and was surprised into sleep. She dreamt she saw him, running through the sky, dressed like Abadon in stars, but he was going away from her and did not heed her call.

Waking, she went on again, in the deep night, going back toward the camp, calling and calling. Her feet throbbed and her throat was sore and painfully tight. At dawn, finally, she reached her hearth again.

Empty. The ashes cold, the wood half-burned. She spread out Moloquin's shirt on the ground. Her hands trembled. With handfuls of straw and clothing and other things from her camp, she filled out the shirt as if there were a man inside it and ran her hands over it, saying prayers, pleading with Heaven to keep him safe. When that was done, she picked herself up and walked heavily across the camp toward Ladon's platform.

The men were making ready to go. The litter waited there before the platform, all the men competing for a place nearest it, to be one of those who bore Ladon away. Karella pushed through them, jabbing them with her elbows, kicking out with her feet, and barged in under the platform.

There Ladon sat on his bed of furs, eating from a painted pot. She went up before him and stood there, planted on her feet.

"You took my son from me, Ladon."

He raised his head, his face bland as cream, his eyes unfocussed. "What do you mean, Ana-Karella-el?"

"I want my son back!"

"I know nothing of the unwanted one," said Ladon smoothly.

She began to weep. Her fingers twitched; she wanted to tear him into pieces, chew him to bits. "I want my son back!"

"He has many enemies. No one cares about him but you. I did nothing to him."

"You killed my son," she cried, and the tears ran down her face and splashed on the ground at his feet.

He tried to laugh. His cheeks above the glossy black of his beard were red as the red clay. His eyes slithered from side to side, seeking a way past her. Around the outside of the platform his men pressed close to listen and to watch. He said, "I know nothing of this, old woman. Go."

"You killed my son."

"Go," said Ladon, and stood up, throwing out his chest, and putting his hands on his hips.

She stared at him a while through the image-shattering film of her tears. "Yes," she said. "I will go. For now. But you, Ladon, you will suffer for this. I swear it to you. You killed my son and you will suffer."

She turned and went out of the shade of the platform. Behind her, she heard Ladon try to laugh, but the cracked sound fell into the silence like a stone. Karella went off by herself, to find her own way home.

Fergolin had a leather pouch full of small regularly shaped stones, which he used to teach his novices; he sat with them in the dust in the yard of Ladon's roundhouse and put the stones in circles in the shape of the Turnings-of-the-Year, and the young men crowded around him to see.

"From each of these stones," he said, pointing to the western edge of the ring, "we may look forth across one of these other stones—" he pointed to the eastern edge— "and then to the horizon, on Midsummer's Eve, and there see a certain star rising. A Bear Skull master knows every sighting line and every star, and if new things appear there, he remembers them and adds them to his knowledge."

This last Midsummer's Eve, the old traveller, called Father-of-Time, whose life from one beginning to the next was as long as a man's life, had risen with the great red star whose hearth the Midsummer's Eve horizon was, the fixed star named Seeds-of-Fire. What this portended made Fergolin uneasy. The old traveller was one of his special responsibilities. He had followed its course now since he had entered the society, and seen it travel exactly halfway across the sky. In its strange turnings and loops it encircled many of the most crucial of the fixed stars. When it rose side by side with the hot glare of Seeds-of-Fire it had spoken directly to Fergolin's heart, and the message made him tremble.

"My old master," he said, speaking to the boys, but also to himself, "gave me a priceless gift; he had seen the old traveller find its entire way through Heaven. He told me star by star how it passed. I hope one of you will prove worthy to have such knowledge of me."

The faces that watched him were slack and empty of understanding. The newness of their novitiate had faded and now they were faced with the long dull task of memorizing the groundwork of the Bear Skull lore. Fergolin knew none of them would be equal to the task. They had no fire in them, no passion for the stars; their

hearts were lumps of earth. Perhaps it was as well. In his own heart
the starry speck that fastened him to the sky now throbbed with a
warning message. His gaze fell to the tiny circles of stones in the dust
before him.

"There are five travellers," he said, watching the little stones.
"Two are hard to miss in the sky—the white traveller, that stands
forever in the pathway of the sun, either before or behind her, never
far from her, the Right Eye, the Blessed One, the Starmother, the
Womb-of-Heaven, she is one, and the other is the great traveller, so
bright that when he stands among the stars the eye is taken there as
if on wings. He is named the Drum of Heaven, White Rider, and the
Boat-of-Souls."

He did not look up to see the boredom in their faces. He loved
this lore. The names echoed up to him from the bottom of memory,
not merely his mere lifetime's memory, but that of the whole People.
When he rehearsed this knowledge, he was one with the first father,
and his unborn sons' sons' sons' sons were one with him. He could
not bear to see this gift offered to those who cared nothing for it.

"Two more of the travellers are easy to find—the red one—hot
and angry, the Left Eye, the Wicked One, the Breaker of Peace, the
Tears-of-Mothers, and the old traveller, Father-of-Time. The fifth is
rarely seen. It is a gift of the Overworld to their favorites—a gift and
a charge, a sign of benevolence and a call to great duty. This is the
swift one, Foot-of-the-Sun, who lives in her house, and never leaves,
save to stand at the door and look out, and tell her all he sees."

He stopped. The bored inattention of his pupils had become an
active distraction; they were all looking around behind him, craning
their necks to see. He turned.

Karella was coming into the roundhouse yard.

Fergolin straightened, peering closely at her, as she crossed the
roundhouse yard, set down her mat of reeds and her backrest of
withies and cloth, and took her place right beside the door into the
roundhouse, as if she meant to be there a long while. She faced him.
Her seamed, pouchy little squirrel's face was unreadable.

Fergolin gawked at her; the boys all gawked at her; everyone else
who was there stood silently watching her. When she knew that she
had them all waiting, she said, "I am here to tell a story."

Fergolin stood up, alarmed. "Ana-Karella-el, do—"

Her voice rose up over his, her words loud and clear and strong
with rage. "I am here to tell a story of a man who in his overreaching

pride struck at the center of the order of things, destroyed his sister, and killed her son, his own heir."

Fergolin lost his breath. This was going to be bad. Already the novices were inching away from him over toward Karella, and from the other parts of the yard more men were coming, curious, drawn, to sit down at her feet. Fergolin shuddered. In his heart the little speck of the star stabbed him with its pulsing warning pain. He went into the roundhouse to tell Ladon what was happening.

Karella sat in the heat of the sun, her voice cracked and dry from long use, and the story spun itself steadily forth, coming from the deeps, unwilled, driven up by the fury and cold grief in her heart. She had always been able to grip her listeners with her words, with the power of her voice and the grace of her gestures, and now as she sat in the midst of them and told one story after another, swaying a little as she spoke, her hands shaping and reshaping the air before her, the whole village gathered to hear, and no one moved, not even to turn his head away.

She was telling every story she knew that related to this crime of Ladon's. She told stories of the murder of sons, of brothers, and of nephews, stories of the enmity beween uncle and nephew, between sister and brother, between man and woman. She told every story she knew about the structure of the world, the relationships between the parts of it, women's duties and men's privileges, women's rule and men's envy, women's power and men's prestige. Some stories she told she had forgotten she knew, and others she had never told before, but they all came forth now, each word rising as she needed it.

Ladon's son and his new wife sat before her and listened and the young man wept. When his wife saw that, she turned away, her face twisted with disgust, but she was a stranger here, and had nowhere else to go, and so she sat there beside her husband, and her face was turned away, and his tears fell like poison between them.

Brant came and sat before her and listened, and raised up his face toward Heaven, and she saw there his anguish, his despair, that he had lost one who might have carried on the lore of the Pillar of the Sky.

Every mother with a son sat before her and as she spoke they lost their sons also, and mourned with her. And every man before her knew himself a son, who was lost, and whose mother mourned, and whose father had betrayed him and cut the link that bound him to the world.

Ladon did not come. Ladon never came.

When the night fell she stopped speaking, but she did not move, she was too exhausted to move. The People went away into their longhouses and the roundhouse and left her alone there, and she leaned back against her rest and watched the night close over her and waited for the light to come and loosen her tongue.

Then in the darkness from all around her came soft padding feet, and dishes of food for her, which they left at the edge of her mat, and bent down and touched their lips to her mat, and left. Then she knew that what she did was sacred.

There was no comfort in it for her, because Moloquin was no more. She ate only a little before her belly closed up against the food that she could not share with him. She drank only enough to moisten her lips before her throat refused to drink what he could not drink. When she slept, it was to dream of him.

In the morning she began again, and the People filled up the roundhouse yard to hear her. She told stories of Abadon, how he defied the order of things, and was invariably punished. Three times in a row she told the story of the breaking of the Mill of Heaven, whereby Abadon in his folly caused the whole world to fall into error and change.

Still Ladon did not come. She did not call for him by name. She merely told stories. Once, in the space between the stories, she began to chant the mill song.

> *Sam-po, sam-po*
> *La li la la li li la*
> *The Mill turns, the Mill grinds*
> *Nothing escapes the Mill of Heaven*
> *La li la la li li la*
> *Sam-po, sam-po*

The women all around the crowd lifted their voices and sang it with her, and their voices were harsh and cracked like the crows who ate the flesh of the dead, and all eyes turned toward the roundhouse. Yet Ladon remained invisible.

Karella was tired. Her throat hurt, and her chest hurt. She went on with her stories and the People listened to her, and when darkness fell Karella remained where she was, and they brought her food to sustain her. All night long, under the stars, she waited, and knew that inside the roundhouse, Ladon also waited, for the coming of the light, for the assault to begin again.

A few days after the return from the Gathering, the sickness began. It struck without pity, children, adults, old people, and carried them off in a few days, scorched with fever and crying from pain and delirium. It raged through the whole camp, taking away one or two from each hearth, and sometimes all those at a hearth, so that in the longhouses some places were cold and empty, and some tenanted only by the sick and dying.

There were some who said this was another gift of Harus Kum, that the trader had set a curse on them. The women especially spoke of the evil potency of the blue beads that Harus Kum had given to Ladon. But Ladon himself did not fall sick, and there were those who thought that meant he was proof against anything, even Karella's attacks.

They crowded together to hear her, and many of the sick and dying were carried close to her to hear her. Then she too was sick. Her voice wavered, the wonderful resonant power that formed pictures in the minds of her listeners, that wiped away the world and made it new again, and as she fell silent, they all saw that she was only an old, old woman now, light and frail as a dead leaf. All her power was gone.

So she died, there in front of them all, but before her life was gone, just at the same moment, she found her voice again. She put off the stories as, soon, her soul would put off her flesh, and she spoke to them directly. Poised there on the boundary between life and death, with the little cramped unhappy world of life behind her, and the infinite shining glory of the Overworld before, she turned her head to look back and she warned them that if a son of Ladon's ever reached the high seat, their whole world would go to ruin.

Then she was dead, and her body lay cast off on the mat in the yard of the roundhouse.

The women mourned her the most. They took her up, many hands to lift her, who would have been light enough in the arms of a single woman, and carried her away to the Pillar of the Sky. Already many of the People lay there, feeding the crows, so many that it was hard to find space for her within the circle of stones. There they put her down to rest.

She was the last to die of the sickness. There were those who said she had brought it all on them, that the Overworld protected Ladon from her, and that his power was greater than hers, and that he had beaten her.

There were others who said, however, that the struggle was not yet over.

II

THE FORGE

Harus Kum thought he had been cheated: Ladon had promised him two strong men and instead he got two boys, one no good at all. He wore his whip out on their backs, more from anger at Ladon than for any good it did—the boys could not draw as well as the men, and when he whipped them, the one cried, and the other stopped drawing altogether and railed at Harus Kum until he knocked the brat down, which made things worse, since they had to wait until the boy got his mind back.

After that, he put both boys on one sledge, the ropes laid over their shoulders and tied around their waists, and told them if they could not keep up with the rest they would draw all night to reach camp and get nothing to eat. Then the boys hauled together, and pulled the sledge with its baskets of beans and meal over the rough hillsides, and Harus Kum and his train went on back home.

At the end of the first day, he thought he would have to leave the little boy behind, he was so weak and worn, but the other boy seemed hale enough, even to thriving on the work. Harus Kum fed them both and let them sleep from dusk until dawn, and hitched them up again, and again they went off, following the river into the west.

They followed the trail they had taken to reach the land of the People of the Stones, and which was slowly wearing down under use into a path easier than the tangled ground on either side. The sledges skidded and bounced and banged over the rocky slopes. When the hillsides ran steeply down, Harus Kum put a man on the back of each sledge, while one pulled at the front, and let the sledge down carefully between them. On the second day of their travel the need for doing this often gave the boys a sound rest, and that evening the little boy seemed better, although he still fell asleep in his porridge, his nose in his cup.

The other boy sat there by the fire, looking around him. He was tall and thin, his skin dark as a cured hide, and his hair a wild black mass. Harus Kum went by him and nudged him with his foot, and the boy's head shot up, his dark eyes snapping with temper.

Harus Kum laughed. He liked breaking wild things.

"Don't you like that?" he asked, and kicked the boy harder, to inspire his temper.

To his surprise, the black-haired boy did not jump up at him, or shout, but merely sat there and glowered at him. Harus Kum wondered what would bring him on, and he kicked him again, and again the boy took the blow without either yielding or responding, but only stared at him.

"What is your name?" Harus Kum asked.

Now the boy did not answer for a while, and Harus Kum thought of taking his whip to him; an illogical rage kindled in him, that he could not stir the boy to any deed. But then the boy said, "My name is Moloquin."

"Oh, yes." He had heard that before, when the boys were taken. It was an odd name, meaning "the useless one," or something like that. "Well, we'll get some use out of you, won't we, will you or not." He laughed again. The boy merely stared at him. Harus Kum drew his foot back again, and the boy's lip curled. He turned his face away, as if he were bored with this, and Harus Kum began to feel like a fool. He did not want to look like a fool before his own slaves, and so he went away nearer the fire, feeling uneasy.

In the middle of the night, the rain began. The next day the rain fell continually, sometimes harder than other times, and the going was very bad. The trail led down over the hills, through a forest of pine trees, and the rain ran down over the path like a stream in its own bed; sometimes they were ankle deep in running water. Harus Kum himself put his shoulder to a sledge now and then, to hold it steady; when they came to a long slope, they wrapped their ropes around tree trunks and let the sledges down one by one over the slippery grass and the rocks.

One of the ropes broke, spilling the sledge and its cargo down into a marshy lowland, and they spent the rest of the afternoon gathering up what they could salvage and packing it away into the sledge again.

Thus they went, day after day. In the morning the sun warmed their backs and while they struggled and groaned and Harus Kum swung his whip back and forth the sun raced up over the sky and as if to mock them rolled away to the west, going where they struggled to go, and came up the next morning and burned their backs again. The countryside was rough and overgrown. A sledge broke and they stopped to cut new runners among the standing trees. They had to walk far off the path to find a suitable tree.

The boy Moloquin followed, watching everything with an all-absorbing attention. Harus Kum had brought the axe he had made of bronze, and he himself set to work with it to hew down the tree, but shortly the axe dulled, and he threw it down angrily and took another. Later in the day, as he stood watching the slaves split the felled trunk with wedges and mauls, he noticed Moloquin crouched nearby on the grass, running his fingers over the beautiful head of the dulled axe.

They went on. The rain fell again, and in the mud, on a precipitous short hillside, a rope broke, and the sledge roared down over the slippery ground and crushed one of the slaves under it. When they pried the sledge up off him he was dying. Harus Kum screamed and plied his whip like a madman but he could move none of the others back to their work; they stood in the driving rain, a circle around the dying man, and some wept. Finally, raging, the trader had to wait until they were ready—until their fellow had given up his life and lay still in the mud and the blood. Then at last they were willing to take up the ropes again, but as each one of them left the dead man behind him, he stooped and plucked some grass or a bough of green leaves and laid that over the body.

The sun dried them. Lacking one man, they had to bring the sledges on in two groups, taking the first set ahead a little, going back to bring the next one, dragging the first off again.

This gave the men a little leisure, which they spent singing and talking, like fools. The boy Moloquin caught a rabbit and two squirrels and found some bird's eggs, which he gave away to any who asked. He would not join in the singing and talking. The other boy followed him everywhere.

They dragged the four remaining sledges over a ridge, the ground underfoot loose and crumbling away under the weight of a foot, treacherous, sharp and spiky, and descended down the far side into the valley of the little stream that ran past home. The older slaves recognized it and rejoiced as if they sat already by their hearth.

Moloquin stood staring away into the west, looking down the

narrow gorge of the stream, the dark green pine trees all shrouded in a low clinging mist, and the clear sky blue above.

"What is that noise?" he asked.

Harus Kum did not know at first that the boy spoke to him; Moloquin had never addressed him before. Moloquin tugged on his arm.

"That sound? What is that sound?"

"Ah?" Harus Kum pricked up his ears. He heard sounds all around him, the twittering of birds in the brush, the slap and gurgle of the stream, and the wind sifting through the pine boughs. "Which sound?" He cuffed Moloquin for causing him to spend so much attention on him.

"That—the low one. The roar. It sounds as if the ground is roaring."

Harus Kum said, "You are mad, brat." He could hear nothing. He went away to the front of his train, away from this boy's ridiculous questions.

They hauled the sledges single-file down the gorge. The older slaves sang boisterously, as if soon their work would all be over—as if, once the sledges were dragged into the stockade, they did not then have to go to work in the mines. Moloquin stared always forward, even as he hauled the rope over his shoulder, looking for something; he sniffed the air, he cocked his ears. The wind was beating into their faces, coming up the stream, tasting of salt and rotting seaweed, the shore smell. Once in a while it brought with it the thunder of the surf, and halfway on, Harus Kum came to realize that that was the sound Moloquin had heard: the pounding of the sea. The ground itself roared. Harus Kum laughed, amused.

The others went singing by him, pulling on the ropes as if they were thistledown, and the sledges bounced away down the stream.

At last, in the evening, they hauled the sledges out of the narrow mouth of the gorge into the wide, flat, sandy valley where the stream ran into the sea. This was Harus Kum's home, although he had not been born here. It was an old place. Men from his home village on the far side of the sea had been coming here for a long while, generations, to mine the tin ore in the banks of the streambeds, and they had trampled down most of the green brush in this flat-bottomed wedge-shaped valley, and built a stockade of wood posts at the end near the sea. Mountains of grey-white and black slag were piled up on either side of the stream, so that the sledges had still to go single-file through them. As they approached, the great flock of gulls that picked over the midden heap rose like a dirty white cloud in the air.

Harus Kum busied himself getting the sledges into the stockade. The women came to the door of the big house to watch and greet them. He could smell beer brewing. It was good to be home. He released his breath in a sigh. Walking up and down through his stockade yard, the whip coiled over his shoulder, he shouted and kicked at the slaves who were hauling the baskets of meal into the storehouse. The women hurried to help and to see what they had brought. With yells and whoops, the men rushed toward the big house, their work done.

Moloquin did not go after them. Harus Kum, pulling the gate closed, saw the boy standing alone in the yard as the others ran by him; even the little boy had gone inside. Moloquin turned and started toward the gate.

"Where are you going?" Harus Kum blocked his way.

Moloquin said, "I want to see."

"See. See what?" Yet the full intensity of the boy's look was compelling. He stood back, holding the gate open. After all, where could he go? Moloquin went out; halfway across the threshold he broke into a run.

Harus Kum's back tingled. He told himself the boy was mad. His feet would not bear him into the comfort of his house, to his fire and his beer and the inviting warmth of the women. His feet took him after Moloquin.

When he walked out the gate, Moloquin was already halfway down to the shore, going at a dead run. Two of the half-wild cattle that provided Harus Kum with meat were browsing there on the salt grass; at the boy's approach they shied and galloped heavily away. Harus Kum followed him, his hand on his whip. He told himself, I am making sure he does not run away.

The boy ran down to meet the incoming waves, and there he stopped, the sea boiling up around his ankles. There was something of a beach here; because the stream's mouth gave some shelter from the pounding surf, a little irregular patch of sand had gathered here, behind the jagged black rocks. It always reminded Harus Kum of a woman's private part. Moloquin stood at the edge of the sand, his face turned into the wind, and the giant crashing boom of the surf around him. As Harus Kum came up behind him, the boy walked into the sea up to his waist.

The spray flew on the wind like whips of salt; Harus Kum could not hold his eyes open against it. He shouted, and the boy heard him and turned, and slowly waded out again, soaked.

He came up to Harus Kum, his eyes blazing, and said, "What is this?"

"This?" Harus Kum laughed, heavy with scorn, secure in his own knowledge. "The sea, you fool. It's the sea."

"Ah." The boy wheeled around again, facing the tumultuous surf. "Karella told me about the sea."

"Stupid fool. Go inside, you stupid fool, get out of the water."

He raised his hand to strike the boy, but Moloquin said, in a calm voice, "Do not hit me," and Harus Kum lowered his hand.

"Then get inside, you fool."

Instead, Moloquin turned and looked toward the sea again. He said, "What is beyond it?"

"Beyond it! The rest of the world, of course." Harus Kum laughed again. The wind snatched away his mirth. He tasted salt in his mouth. He wondered why he stood here answering this brat's questions.

"The rest of the broken millstone," Moloquin said. "Oh, she is wise, my mother. You—" he pointed at Harus Kum. "You came from beyond there?"

"I—yes. Yes."

Moloquin's face was beaded with the spray, his hair soggy, his eyelashes dripping. Harus Kum said, "Come inside," in another voice than he had used before, and did not call him a fool.

"No," Moloquin said. "You go—I will come in later."

He was dismissing Harus Kum out of his presence. The trader stiffened, angry, but the wind was cold. Inside the stockade there was a warm fire and a pot of beer to drink, and the women, from whom he had been gone so long. Slowly he went away.

At the gate he stopped and looked back. The sun was going down. The sky was streaked with low clouds, turning pale orange and darker orange and red. Moloquin had gone down into the surf again, and as Harus Kum watched, he dropped something from his arms into the water. He went back up the beach, stopped, and lifted a rock up, and another rock, and carried them into the surf and piled them one on top of the other. He was building a pillar of stones.

Harus Kum swallowed down his sudden anger, his taste of fear.

He had thought himself and this boy far from the land of the stone rings. But Moloquin had somehow brought them with him. Harus Kum turned and went into the shelter of the stockade.

The mines of Harus Kum, dug into the black pocked rocks that walled the stream's banks, produced a lumpy grey ore that was rich in tin. Harus Kum's slaves dug up the ores and carried them away to a stretch of flat ground outside the stockade. There, with great stones and mallets of wood, they crushed the rock until it was like meal; the master himself supervised this operation and every subsequent step, and the work was heavy and harsh, and the dust covered everything.

When the ores were smashed to grains no larger than grains of sand, Harus Kum had it hauled off to the furnaces inside the stockade. Here, within their own low wall of blackened craggy slag lumps, were three holes dug down into the ground and lined with rock. Here the ore was cooked.

Harus Kum himself set up the furnaces, piling in a thick layer of charcoal, sprinkling a layer of the ore dust on top, then another layer of charcoal, another thin sprinkle of the ore, until all the furnaces were filled up.

He lit the furnaces with a torch dipped in fresh fat, and then the men had to gather close to the fire, and put long thin tubes like reeds down close to the fire, and blow as hard as they could to get the fire hot. This was the hardest work of all, although no one had to run or jump or carry anything, and because a man blowing hard into the furnace was soon so exhausted and sick he would fall over, Harus Kum had them do it in groups of two, one group to each furnace, while the other men waited to take up the work as soon as one let go.

When the fire cooled, they dug the furnaces empty, and spread the insides out on the ground. What came out of the furnaces was a stew of ash and lumps of spongy black slag. Harus Kum himself smashed up these fist-sized chunks of cooked rock, and picked out the tiny bits of shining stuff inside, and poured these carefully into a leather pouch. It took the eighteen men of Harus Kum's crew more than half the month, from the digging of the ore out of the stream bank, until that thin trickle of beads of tin ran down into Harus Kum's pouch.

Moloquin and Grub worked with the others at this, hauling ores, pounding up the rock, and blowing into the furnaces. On the day after they had stood and watched the poor results of their work clink into Harus Kum's pouch, Grub said, "I hate this place." The next morning he was sick.

The two boys slept on the floor of the big house, against the wall; when Moloquin woke in the grey dawn, he knew at once that Grub was close to dying. He could feel the heat from the boy's body and on Grub's lips a yellowish foam was drying in flecks, and while Moloquin watched, propped up on his elbows, Grub began to cough. Moloquin wrapped him in the rag he had been sleeping on and sat there beside him, afraid.

Grub did not wake up. He lay there burning with a fever and coughing up gouts of green stuff. Moloquin took his hand and sat, waiting for something, he did not know what; waiting. The others were stirring awake; he could see them moving back and forth in the dark of the house. The younger of the two women knelt by the fire and raked over the coals, and the light spread over her face. Yawning and stretching, the other men moved closer to the hearth. Harus Kum, heavy-footed, loud-voiced, stamped in from the little room at the back where he slept.

He called the women to him and led them off to the storehouse, and they came back with pots and a basket of food. The men crowded around them and were fed. Moloquin crouched on his hams, one hand on Grub's hand, and watched.

Beside him Grub whimpered in his sleep. His skin was hot and dry and cracking at the corners of his mouth. If he died, Moloquin would be alone here, among people who did not speak his language and whose gutteral mumbling speech he was just beginning to accept as words.

"Grub," he said. "Don't die. Don't die." But he felt death in the boy's limp body, burning like a furnace.

Harus Kum tramped toward him. "What are you doing, lazy ones? Get up and put some food in you, you have work to do."

"He is sick," Moloquin said.

"Hunh." Harus Kum squatted down and touched Grub, felt his head and his limbs, and said, again, "Hunh." He stared at Grub a while, frowning, and finally tossed the blanket over him. "Go on, you. Get something to eat, you have to work."

"No," Moloquin cried, seized by a sudden panic; he knew if he left, he would find Grub dead when he came back. "No, I—"

Harus Kum struck him. "Go work. Now you've lost your chance

to eat, there isn't any left. Go to work on an empty stomach, it will teach you to stay nimble."

The tall man got up, turned to go, and looked back at Moloquin. The boy crouched down again beside Grub, determined not to leave him, the only creature of his own kind left to him. Harus Kum swung around toward him again, and his hand went to his belt.

"Come out and work, brat, or I will give your friend there a shorter way into the grave."

As he spoke, he took a little knife out of his belt, and the light jumped on the shining edge. It was made of the same stuff as the great axe. Moloquin licked his lips. He was afraid of losing Grub, and yet whenever he saw any of this magic stuff, his mind yearned toward it.

He turned toward Grub again; he knew Harus Kum would kill him without any care at all—to him Grub was only a set of hands, a back, and a pair of feet. If he would not work, he was useless, a broken tool. Moloquin got up and went out with the others to the mines.

They were digging ore out of the streambank a little way up from the stockade. Here a thick layer of the brittle, lumpy tin ore curled like a worm through the heavy clays of the stream's old bed. Conical heaps of the rock and dirt they had dug away to expose the vein stood all along the edge of the water. With mallets and wedges they hacked out lumps of the ore and piled them onto leather slings to carry away. Moloquin's job was to gather up the chunks of ore as the other men broke them free of the bank. He scurried in and out of the line of slaves as they slugged at the streambank, dodging the great swings of their mallets. The dust got into his nose and eyes and his mouth and he went down to the stream as often as he could, and plunged his head and shoulders into the swift flowing water. The racket of the work was easier to get used to.

At noon, the younger woman brought them meal and beer, and the men went across the stream to a little patch of grass and sat down and ate. Moloquin sat to one side of them, excluded from them. One of the women brought him a pot of the beer and a double handful of the meal; she was a young girl, broad across the cheekbones, flat down the nose, her eyes ever downcast. He thanked her in his language, knowing she did not understand him, and she gave no sign of hearing.

She would know how Grub did, but he had no way of asking her. Probably she did not care. No one here cared for him and Grub. He was far from the land where his ancestors had lived, far from the havens of their spirits: here he was nothing, unconnected to the world, a thing of winddrift, forgotten.

Around him sat the others, squatting like lumps on the grass, drinking beer, swilling up the meal with ther tongues, their bodies swollen with muscle, their skins grey with dust. The dust caked their hair and their eyelashes; they hardly seemed men at all. What did they know of the deep green forest, the open rolling downs, and the everchanging sky? They scrabbled at the dull earth, the marks of Harus Kum's whip crisscrossing their backs.

He poured some of the beer into the pot of meal and stirred it with his finger to a dense mush. It tasted much different than the food he was used to. All at once his soul was cast down as low as the ground under his feet.

Of all that had happened to him here, that only was familiar. He belonged to this feeling, of being utterly alone.

Now here came Harus Kum again, swinging his coiled whip. Hastily they leapt up and crossed through the stream to their work.

In the twilight, still miserable, now exhausted, Moloquin with the others carried the slings of ore back to the stockade. They bore the great burden as the men of the People bore Ladon, with poles across their shoulders. Moloquin wiped his face with his free hand. There was ore dust in his nostrils and in the corners of his eyes. The men around him chanted in tired, buoyant voices. They were going home.

But he was going away from home, to the not-home, to the deathbed.

He thought suddenly of his mother. But it was not Karella to whom his mind flew, like a bird going home to its nest. He thought for the first time in a long time of Ael.

He stiffened. He saw himself as she would have, had she been here—saw himself trudging along with the rest of the slaves, his eyes toward the ground, his shoulders round with another man's labor, and he straightened up. He breathed his body full of the wind. He was his mother's son. She had belonged to no one, to nothing, save to him, and now, around him, somehow, he sensed that she was with him still.

Now he heard the wind murmuring in the fir trees on the hillsides above him. Somewhere high over the tops of the trees, a hawk screamed its piercing sad whistle. Like a man who had been drowning, he raised his head up into the air and breathed life again.

Grub whimpered and sobbed, blazing with fever. The rug he was wrapped in was soggy with sweat. Moloquin lifted him up in his arms and carried him away, out of the house, into the stockade yard.

The sun had gone down and the stars were coming out; the air tasted of the sea brine. Moloquin's arms hurt. He carried Grub down to the wet sand and the lapping margin of the sea, and laid him down in the cool of the water.

"Grub," he said, "Grub, they are still here. The spirits are here somewhere, our souls' souls, and they will protect us, if we take heart."

He sat beside the dying boy and watched the stars slip down like tears over the sooty cheek of the sky. Over there somewhere was the rest of the world, other men, other ways of doing things. The millstone was broken, the order of things had fallen into disarray, but the truth of it was that all these apparently disparate things were actually one thing. The millstone should be whole. The people should all be one People. Therefore he was not alone, and he was always home.

The sea curled up and broke over his feet and swirled around him, foaming around his waist, chuckling on the black rocks scattered on the sand. Behind him, the sea gulls fought over garbage in the midden of Harus Kum's stockade. Moloquin thought of the stones he had tried to pile up into a pillar on this shore; he remembered how he had felt then, full of awe and amazement and delight, and how his hands had needed to raise up some monument to this new truth he had discovered. He got up and waded around in the surf, looking for the stones, but his pillar was gone. Only chunks of the lumpy black rock remained. The sea had broken up his column.

That challenged him. He went restlessly up and down the beach, now and then circling back to Grub, to touch him, to speak to him, to call forth the spirits of his ancestors to support him. Sometimes he stopped to watch the slow passage of the stars across the sky. Most of the night he spent searching for some matter to use, to shape with his hands, to make a sign that he had been there.

There were lots of rocks. The ones that he could move were too small; the ones that were large enough he could not move. He put his shoulder against a black mass and pushed with all his strength and felt the whole world pushing back. With a sigh, he gave up.

The night yielded to the first scattered sunlight and the stars vanished. The wind hushed. He lifted Grub up out of the cool water and carried him back toward the stockade. The gate was shut and barred, and he laid his friend down on the threshold, climbed over the wall, and opened the gate from the inside. He left both wings of the gate standing wide open, so that Harus Kum would surely know what he had done. Lifting Grub into his arms, he went back inside the house and laid the boy down on the sticky dirty rag against the wall.

The other people were stirring out of their brutish sleep. Moloquin made sure that Grub was comfortable and then he went out to the storeroom, where the women waited with their baskets and pots for Harus Kum to open the door and let them get the food out.

Moloquin went past them to the door. Under their astonished eyes, he tried the latch, and found it open: only Harus Kum's authority barred it from them. He went inside.

As he entered, the mice squeaked and rustled away from him through sacks of grain. A great cropped naked carcass hung from the rafter. Off to his right was the tub of beer. He found a pot on a shelf on the wall and dipped it down through the thick suds into the liquor, got a handful of meal from an open sack, and went out again.

Grub was awake when he reached him, his eyelids quivering with the effort of holding them open. Moloquin knelt beside him and held the beer so that he could drink. While he did this, bracing Grub on his hand and his knee, Harus Kum stormed into the house.

"Brat!" He rushed up to Moloquin and knocked the pot out of his hand. He held the whip, and he lashed Moloquin across the head with it, still coiled in his hand, the butt striking the boy's forehead hard enough to gash the skin.

"Stay out of my stores, brat—now get up, and leave him, and go to work."

Moloquin squatted there beside Grub; he raised his face, the blood running down either side of his nose.

"He has to be watched over. If he is cared for, maybe he will not die."

"I don't care about him! Get to work."

"I care about him," Moloquin said.

Harus Kum flung the whip down, and from his belt drew his knife with its short, tapering blade. "Then I shall get rid of him."

Grub whined, and put out his hand to Moloquin. Moloquin caught hold of his wrist and held him fast.

"If you kill him you must kill me too."

Harus Kum fingered the blade. "Perhaps that would be wise, ridding myself at once of a thief and a shirker."

"Moloquin," Grub whispered, clinging to his friend's hand.

Moloquin said, "Kill us if you want, Harus Kum, we cannot stop you, but if you do not kill us, I shall work for you, as hard as I can."

"Are you making a bargain with me, boy? A slave, making bargains with his master?"

The word he used was in his own language; Moloquin did not understand it. He repeated it awkwardly. "*Bargain.*"

Harus Kum kicked at him; when Moloquin shrank away, he kicked at Grub. "Why should I make trouble for myself, killing such as you? Let the fever kill you." He put the knife away in his belt. "But I am the master here!"

"Yes," Moloquin said, his breath suddenly short; he realized that Harus Kum was relenting.

"Say it."

"You are the master."

"Again."

"You are the master."

"Remember it." Harus Kum went away, strutting.

Moloquin wiped his bloody face. He had expected to die; he had thought himself ready to die rather than stay here in this strange place. Now, with his life restored, he tingled all over, the blood jumping in his veins, his skin shivering at the touch of the air, and he knew he would do anything to stay alive.

He looked down at Grub, lying beside him.

"You saved me," Grub whispered.

"No," Moloquin said. "Harus Kum saved you."

He wondered why Harus Kum had not killed them; surely he had meant to. Some spirit had influenced him, some power. The strange word somehow had invoked it. He no longer remembered the word; all he remembered was promising the trader that he would work if he lived.

It was not to Harus Kum he owed the work. It was to the spirit that had saved him. He bent down where he was, his hands on the floor, his face almost to the floor, and gave it thanks.

He lay beside Grub and slept; when he woke, the other men had all gone out. The two women were busy around the house, sweeping and cleaning. The young one sang in a sweet, high-pitched voice. Moloquin lay still, his head pillowed on his arm, and listened. His face hurt.

The women worked up to his end of the room; at the bench against the wall by his feet, the young one dipped beer from a big bowl into a small one. Then Harus Kum came in.

The women shrank away from him, the older one withdrawing into the shadows of the far wall. The tall man ignored them, going here and there around the place, looking for something. Whatever he sought he could not find, and he flung down what he did find with a run of harsh words. Then he tramped into the back of the room, near Moloquin and Grub, and took a pot of the beer from the bowl beside the younger woman and drank it down, as she cowered away from him, her head lowered.

In a loud yet mild voice he said something to her that Moloquin did not understand entirely—that nothing he did today was going as he wished—and poked her in the side. She gave a frightened titter, as if he had made a joke. He caught her around the waist and pulled her against him.

"No," she said. "No, please—not here—"

Harus Kum smacked her on the cheek. "Turn around."

"He is awake," the girl said, looking at Moloquin.

"Keep still." Harus Kum turned her around, her back to him, and with one hand on her back he bent her forward over the bench. She held the edge of the bench with her hands, her hair shielding her face, but Moloquin could see that she clenched her teeth. Harus Kum pulled up her heavy garments until her naked buttocks showed. Moloquin held his breath, watching. Harus Kum pulled open his clothes and took out his penis, and bending his knees slightly, he thrust it hard into the girl's body.

She stiffened, but she made no resistance, while the man humped and groaned over her; her head bobbed up and down with each thrust. Moloquin chewed his lips. He had never seen a man treat a woman with so little respect. It filled him with a physical excitement so powerful that his stomach churned and his guts knotted up and his own penis hardened like a staff. Even more thrilling was her submissiveness. His muscles twitched. He wanted to run over there, tear Harus Kum away from her and take her himself, pump his power into her flesh.

They parted, drawing away, their clothes slipping down over their nakedness. Harus Kum patted her on the backside and went away, but the girl stayed there a moment, bent over the tub, her head down. When she turned, her look went first to Moloquin.

She saw him watching, and her cheeks turned ruddy. She lowered her head until her hair veiled her, and she went away.

Moloquin rolled over, facing Grub and the wall, and put his hand on his male part. His hand wasn't good enough. His mind would not give up the image of her buttocks, like half moons, with the hard penis thrusting between them.

She had not wanted him but Harus Kum had taken her anyway. Half of Moloquin recoiled from that. Half of him rejoiced.

He lay there a while, listening to the women move around the room, bringing in wood for the fire, hauling water, and sweeping. The girl did not sing again. Even with his eyes shut he could make out the heavier steps of Harus Kum when the master came in again, looking for whatever it was he had come to find. At last the door shut on him, and the heavy feet sounded no more inside the house. Moloquin got up.

He went to the hearth, a raised round of stones in the center of the house; the cask of beer was there, with a pot to dip it up, and on the warm stones a little pot sat, full of grain soaking in water. The individual kernels were swelling and some had already burst, forming a thick milky pudding, and his mouth watered to see it. Harus Kum would be angry if he took it. He considered that a moment, considered also that his face hurt, and at last he sat down on the edge of the hearth and stirred up the pudding and ate it, even the hard kernels that hadn't burst open yet.

The girl came by him to dip up some beer and saw what he was doing, and she said something in her own tongue; she frowned at him and shook her head. Above the downturned mouth her eyes were sad. He thought, She cannot say no to him. At that, he determined to do as he pleased, no matter what Harus Kum did to him.

He went back to Grub again, felt of his face, and shifted the covers around. Grub was sleeping well, his skin cool, his breathing deep and even. He was getting well. Moloquin began to pull the rags of the blanket straighter, and the girl came over and knelt down beside him. By motions of her hands she told him to lift Grub up, and when he did so, she took the rags and shook them and laid them down again, spreading them out over the floor with her hands. Moloquin laid his friend down on the new-made bed and covered him.

The girl rose, turning to go. "Wait," Moloquin said. He caught her by the wrist and held her, stood up to face her, his lust rising again. She tried to push his hand away. A low whine escaped her; she lifted her face toward him, her eyes bright, her teeth in her lower lip.

He could do it to her—what Harus Kum had done. She would not stop him. The desperation shining in her eyes stopped him. Like him, she was at Harus Kum's mercy, and if she had not the will to fight, yet he would not be Harus Kum to her. He let her go.

She backed away, safe out of his reach, and they stared at each other a while. At last they lowered their gaze. Moloquin turned back to Grub, and the girl went away into the house. In a moment, she began to sing again, but her voice was lower than before, and the song was sad. Moloquin lay down to sleep.

Moloquin's face healed, leaving a long red scar, which Harus Kum used as a reminder to keep close watch on him. He expected more rebellion from him, especially when the little boy got well, but to his surprise Moloquin went willingly to his work. The little boy complained and shirked, and Moloquin got furious with him and shouted him to his labors; the other men hung back but Moloquin went at every task Harus Kum gave him as if he had some hidden purpose of his own.

He ate too much. He learned too fast—before the moon was full again, he could talk to the other men in their language, although they said little to him, and he said little to them. Between him and the other slaves there seemed a half-buried enmity. Harus Kum expected some fighting between them, and even looked forward to it— there was little other entertainment, on those few days when the summer rains kept them all indoors. On those days he watched eagerly as Moloquin, going here or there, went close by Tor and got a nasty warning snarl, and once or twice he even called out some encouragement to one or the other of them, hoping to see some action. Moloquin fought no one. Tor blustered and yelled, his pride af-

fronted, the pride of a slave with nothing of his own except the space
around him, and his authority with the other slaves. Moloquin went
where he would and did as he pleased.

Harus Kum wanted to break him; he knew there could be only
one master and all the others must be slaves, or the master was no
master at all. So he gave Moloquin more work than the others, sent
him into the hollows of the streambanks to hammer out the deeper
ores, ordered him here and there on errands. Moloquin did it all.
Harus Kum came to rely on him to do what the other slaves could
not. He began to need Moloquin.

One day, while the slaves sat listless in the blazing summer sun,
their noon meal devoured, their beer gone, and waited for the master to whip them back to work, Harus Kum saw Moloquin wading in
the stream. Before he could shout orders, the boy came to him, holding out his hand.

"See these—look."

In the cup of his hand he held several pebbles from the
streambed. Harus Kum frowned down at them, impatient, unwilling
to be lured into any lengthy discussions, but he saw that Moloquin
had not chosen the rocks at random but had gone out and found
interesting things. He held the boy's hand into the sunlight, to ex-
amine his finds.

"Hunh. This—" he picked out a little green-blue pebble. "This
is a sort of ore, if we could find enough of it, we would have much
more work to do. This—"

His forefinger rolled over a little bit of white stone. "This is only
quartz. I crush this and mix it with copper and soda to make those
blue beads your People love so well."

"But look." Moloquin turned it, and showed him a thin line of
some other stuff through it. "What is that?"

So they sat down together on the gravel bed of the stream and
talked over a handful of rocks. When Harus Kum at last returned to
his senses, he saw that the other slaves were still lounging on the
grass, and the sun was halfway down the sky. Moloquin had seduced
him into an afternoon's laziness. He roared. He got out his whip and
lashed around him, and they all went back to work.

Thereafter, Moloquin brought him new pebbles nearly every
day. Harus Kum struggled to remain uninterested, but he loved
rocks, he loved scrabbling around in streambeds for chunks of ores

and bits of quartz. More even than that, he loved showing off his knowledge, and when Moloquin sat at his feet and drank in every word he said, he could not stay aloof.

Moloquin never stopped working. As long as they were safely away from Harus Kum, and given whole days to spend in this soft little inland valley, Grub felt no inclination to work at all. He did every-thing slowly, and sat down often, smiling around him at the trees and open meadows that were so much like his old home, all ringing with the strokes of Moloquin's axe.

He did not call himself Grub any more, but Hems, the name the other slaves had given him, a name in the language of Harus Kum's people. With the other slaves he could talk freely now, having learned a good deal of their words, and even when he was alone with Molo-quin, he spoke that other language.

Still, the sight of the meadow filled him with a longing for his old home, and when he spoke now, it was in the old speech.

"Moloquin, why do you work so hard? Remember when we were in Ladon's Village, how we used to do nothing but play all day long?"

Behind him the rhythmic thud of the axe broke for a moment. "Grub," Moloquin said, "you have no memory."

"Don't call me Grub, please, Moloquin, I am Hems now."

A grunt was his answer. The strokes of the axe picked up again, heavy, booming blows, duller than the sharp crack of a hammer against stone. Grub—Hems—turned to watch. Moloquin was hew-ing down an oak; the tree stood at the very edge of the meadow, a gaunt grey skeleton in the midst of the lush green summery foliage. Something had eaten all the bark off the trunk from the ground up to about the height of Moloquin's shoulder, and that had killed the tree. Moloquin was hewing it down in the middle of the band of exposed wood.

Hems got up, stretched, and walked away across the flat floor of the narrow little valley in which they were camped. Their campsite was behind him, in a little cave at the bottom of the steep hill that marked the far margin of the valley. The stream curled away from him into the sunlight, chuckling over the stones of its bed.

Trees and brush grew thick along the far bank. It was the dying time of the year, and as Hems walked along, the leaves of the trees fluttered through the air on every gust of wind. He strolled along the streambank, trying to keep quiet, but he could hear the frogs leaping for the shelter of the water as he approached, and now, even as he stopped and tried to seem no more than a tree, a big old turtle that was sunning itself on a snag in the middle of the stream plodded forward a few heavy steps and dove into the green water. Hems gave up trying to catch anything. He dropped flat on his stomach on the bank and sucked up the water, his lips to the surface of the stream, until his belly was full and cold.

Anyhow, Moloquin would catch them dinner. Already Moloquin had built a little weir, damming off the stream just below a deep pool, and soon there would be a fat fish to lay open and sizzle up on the fire. Hems sighed. He lay in the sun, dreaming of fish.

After a while Moloquin called him. They dug a pit on the higher ground near their cave, where the earth was soft, a deep-piled midden of the debris of the trees that grew on the hillside. While Grub lined this pit with rocks, Moloquin felled another tree.

For two more days they worked, cutting up the trees into manageable lengths, and making the pit ready. Then they threw all the wood into the pit, covered it up, and built a big fire on top of it.

"Now will we catch some fish?" Hems asked. "I am tired of eating nothing but grain."

He had found a flat rock, which he scraped carefully clean and set into the ashes at the edge of the fire.

"Maybe," Moloquin said. He lay on his back in the grass, still for once, his face to the sky.

They had brought some meal and some beer with them, but that was now nearly gone. Hems poured a handful of it into his bowl and mixed a splash of beer into it. This was a thing he had learned from the other slaves.

"The salmon haven't begun to go upstream yet," Moloquin said. "There are fish in that pool but we have no nets. Maybe the turtle would be good to eat, but there is only one of him, that I can see, and I am loathe to kill him."

Hems poured the mixture of meal and beer onto the flat rock, where it hissed and bubbled and puffed up fat and light, a little cloud. Carefully, he turned it over with two sticks.

"Come on," Moloquin said, rolling to his feet. "Let's go down to the stream—we can find something to eat, and I can look for rocks."

"I am eating," said Hems. The cooked meal made a flat circle on the rock. With his fingers he rolled it quickly up, gasping at the heat.

"Ah—ah." He put the rolled-up mealcake down to cool and popped his fingers into his mouth.

"Eat while you walk." Moloquin came up behind Hems and urged him onto his feet, prodding him with one knee between the shoulderblades. "Let's go."

"Moloquin, why do you never stop moving around?"

"Grub. Why do you ever want to sit and do nothing? Come on!"

"Hems, Moloquin. Please call me Hems now? Wait! Wait for me—" he ran off after Moloquin down toward the stream.

They caught some of the fish in the pool, swimming slowly underwater to where the fish lay side by side in the deep hollows of the water; Moloquin especially was good at this, holding his breath as he stole closer to the fish, slipping his hands up around them as they slept. In the afternoon, as they sat by the fire cooking the fish, a light rain began to fall, which turned quickly into a deluge. They crept into the cave, and Moloquin dragged all the firewood in with them so there was hardly enough room to lie down. They kept the fire above the pit full of oak wood, and cooked the fish and sat in the cave. Hems told stories: he was good at stories, and had learned some of Karella's. Moloquin played with some stones in the soft dirt of the cave floor.

"What are you doing?" Hems asked him.

Moloquin was setting stones upright in rings, and trying with no success to put a little roofbeam across them. He said, "I had a dream once, about the Pillar of the Sky—that it looked like this."

"I hate that place," Hems said. "Although I would give much to see it again."

Moloquin took a stone in each hand and banged them together, trying to knock pieces off one with the other. Hems ate more of the fish. He watched the shadows the fire threw on the wall of the cave and the ceiling, pierced with trailing veils of roots.

"Hems, put more wood on the fire."

"You do it."

"I did it the last time, Hems."

"Oh, what if the fire does go out? I hate this work."

"You hate all work. If the fire goes out the wood will not cook, and if the wood isn't ready when Harus Kum gets here—"

Hems grunted at that; he imagined the anger of the master, and unwillingly he got to his feet and gathered up an armful of the firewood. They had cut up the branches of the two oak trees for firewood, and buried the pieces of the trunks to cook in the pit. He grumbled loudly about Harus Kum and how he wished he were home again, where no one made another work as hard as this. Moloquin paid him no heed. He was balancing a stone on top of two other stones, his head down close to the ground to see. Hems lugged the wood out to the rain and fed the fire, and hurried back out of the rain. The cave was much warmer than the open air.

"I wish you did not like Harus Kum so much."

Moloquin glanced briefly at him. "I hate Harus Kum."

"Hate him!" Hems blinked at him, surprised. "But—then—why are you doing all this? Why are you making his charcoal here? Why are we waiting for him to come and drag us back to his roundhouse and make us work even more? Why can we not merely go home again?"

He gasped at that thought, and in his imagination the hills and forests and sucking swamps that lay between him and his home shrank away to a mere ridge and a few trees. "Let's go now!"

Moloquin lifted his head and stared at him, his shadow lying on the little circles of stones. "We will go home. We shall be home again by midsummer. We shall go to the Turnings-of-the-Year and dance the midsummer dances, I swear."

"Why then? Why not now?"

"Because there is much here that I must learn. And I will learn it. Harus Kum is a wicked man who cares nothing for us, but he has a wonderful power."

He leapt up suddenly, his arms sweeping out around him, drawing the whole world in closer to him.

"Have you not wondered why we are doing all this? We dig up the earth and cook it and take tiny, tiny pieces from it, by such means that break our backs and consume our days until all we have to ourselves is sleep, and then Harus Kum takes the tiny bits carefully away into the storehouse! Why? What is it for? It cannot be eaten or drunk. No one makes baskets or jugs from it."

As he strode up and down in the small space of the cave, his arms moving, the fire cast his shadow hugely on the wall. Hems watched him thoughtfully. He loved this passion in Moloquin even as he loved the fire's heat.

"It is for making bronze," Moloquin said. "It has something to do with the bronze. The axe with the bronze head—the little knives, the bowls, even the beads and rings, the littlest things—they have some magic in them, yes, some key to power. Even Ladon knew that—you saw how he used the power in the beads to defeat the other chiefs, although Ladon knows nothing at all of how the beads are made."

He faced Hems, and his eyes were wild. By his feet, the little ring of stones had fallen over.

"Harus Kum knows. I mean to know. I mean to become a master of Harus Kum's magic."

Hems kept still a moment, impressed. He had never questioned why they did any of these things; it was merely work he hated, an obdurate fact of his life, like the sky above him.

"And then what?" he said at last. "Then we can go home?"

Moloquin nodded. He sank down on his hams and put his stones into their ring again. Abruptly he wheeled and strode out of the cave, to throw more wood on the fire. The rain fell popping and hissing into the flames. Hems watched him thoughtfully. He loved Moloquin but he was relieved not to be like him. Lifting a bit of the fish carefully from the ladder of the bones, he fed himself, although he was already full.

Harus Kum brought the rest of his slaves over the hill and through the forest and found the camp where Moloquin and Hems were cooking the oak wood into charcoal. They had made a good deal of it when he reached them, and he was pleased. Being in a hurry, he did not waste any time in praise of Moloquin, but with his whip and the whip of his tongue he got his men to load the charcoal up on their backs and carry it away down to the stockade.

He walked along behind them all, swinging his coiled whip in his hand. They went ahead of him in a single file, lugging their baskets of charcoal on their backs or balanced on their heads, a winding train of men, and he congratulated himself on having Moloquin.

Knowing Hems, he knew that the slave had done very little of the work. Moloquin must have done all the important parts, the cutting and the digging and the tending of the fire. It was a great delight to Harus Kum, who always before had had to come up here and supervise the charcoal burning himself, leaving the mines unworked. He wondered what Moloquin thought to gain by his labors; if he expected to wheedle his way into Harus Kum's favor, he was mistaken. So Harus Kum told himself.

Now Moloquin walked at the head of the line, where his long stride and tireless strength would bring a fair pace from the rest of them. He carried a great basket of charcoal on his back and another on his head. He was a savage. He was all muscle and bone, like a brute, and he fed on work as other men fed on meat and meal and beer.

A savage, a dirty savage.

Now they were twining down the path through the hills by the sea, and occasionally, through the gap ahead of them, the trader could see the flash of the sunlight on the water. The downhill walk was easy, especially since he carried nothing but his whip, and the brisk fresh sea wind braced him; he found himself smiling.

Maybe he would let Moloquin have one of the women, as a reward. After all, while the dirty savage was cutting and cooking the charcoal, Harus Kum had mined out a whole pouchful of the tin. He was not a boy any more, although Hems still seemed a boy. Let him take one of the women, just for a while, that would please him.

The men were singing. He had never known them to sing before, especially not while they were working. It was Moloquin who had started it. Harus Kum listened, his benevolence curdling, wondering what he should do about this.

There were no real words to the song, only some gibberish in Moloquin's tongue.

La li la la li li la
Sam-po, sam-po

The sounds fit the rhythm of their walk, and in fact now they seemed to be walking a little faster. Harus Kum thought of forbidding the song. At least Moloquin could sing in real words. Certainly he would not get a woman now. Anyway, the two women were of Harus Kum's people, from across the sea, and too fine for any dirty savage to possess.

Then, lifting his gaze beyond them all, back to the flash of sunlight on the sea, he saw that which swept all else from his mind.

"The boat!"

He leapt forward, brushing past the slaves, to a place where the trail wound down past a steep spire of rock. This tower he scaled like a lizard, on all fours. From the top he looked out over a wide swath of the coast, the wrinkled water, the path the sun made over the sea, and there, rocking and dipping in the grip of the waves, was the long brown shape of the boat.

Harus Kum let out another shout. He sprang down from the rock and ran up through the midst of his slaves, bumping into Hems on the way so that the boy almost fell. Reaching Moloquin, Harus Kum stopped and hastily put on his dignity again, staying the master.

"Bring them all down. Don't let any of them tarry, or I'll have it out of your back, do you hear? Move!" He slapped Moloquin on the shoulder with his whip; his buoyant excitement broke through the threats and commands in a broad smile. Moloquin's face was expressionless. Dumb brute, he knew nothing. Harus Kum raced away down the trail.

When he reached his stockade, the boat was just appearing around the point of land to the west, creeping up along the coast, battling the driving surf and the wind. Harus Kum climbed up onto a rock on the beach and waved his arms, and on the boat several arms shot up in answer. He could not make out any of the faces, they were still too far away, but their mere presence on the water got him dancing and leaping up and down.

The women had followed him down onto the beach, and he yelled at them to go back and make a feast ready.

Now the boat was wearing its way through the violent water where the stream poured out into the sea. The oars dipped and swayed and strained to drag the long black hull over the lashed foam and leaping waves. Harus Kum waved his arms again and shouted encouragement. He strained to see who sat in the bow.

It was a good-sized boat; there seemed eight men or more in it. The hull was made of hides stretched over a wooden frame, and it rode on the sea's back like a little pot, rocking back and forth. The thrust of the seaward stream drove it off, but then it rounded the surge, and the incoming waves bore it rapidly onto the shore, mocking the puny work of the oars.

"Watch out!" The onshore surf dashed the boat precipitously forward, toward the rocks. The men used their oars to fend off these perils. Harus Kum roared. It was his brother who stood on the bow. He ran into the foam, his arms outstretched.

His brother howled. Climbing up onto the bow of the boat, he balanced precariously a moment on bent legs, and sprang forward into the arms of Harus Kum.

"Hah! Hah!"

"In Hortha's name," his brother cried, "I did not think to see you, not now, or ever."

They embraced. Their arms around each other's shoulders, they walked up out of the surf while the other men bounded out of the boat and dragged it up through the last curling waves to the shore. The boat was piled up with sacks of goods; Harus Kum craned his neck to see.

"What have you brought me? I hope you have given me much food—I don't like relying on these natives for my supplies."

His brother straightened, smiling, shorter than he, barrel-chested. "You know, we cannot bring you grain, it takes too much space. Here are other things—cloth, copper. How has your harvest been?"

"Fair enough. I uncovered a new vein, very rich, you will take much wealth back with you, we shall be far-famous. Your travel was harsh, I gather."

His brother walked up and down, stretching his legs and his back. The wind blew salt against his cheek. "It was a terrible voyage. A storm blew us off the coast of home, and we were two whole days out of sight of land. I thought we would be swept away. Then we saw gulls, and followed them to the shore."

He sighed, caught in his net of memory, and turned with purpose toward the boat.

"Prayers to Hortha saved us. We must repay what she has given us."

He went to the boat, now lying half on its side, sleek and black as a huge water beetle. In the sharply beaked front hung a wooden image, and reverently Harus Kum's brother unfastened it, and called the others of his crew after him. They gathered around the image and kissed it, and lifting it up over his head the brother bore the image reverently up the shore and into the stockade.

Harus Kum followed. The women stood waiting at the door of the big house, and when they saw the newcomers smiles broke across their faces and they bowed and bent and waved, laughing. The boatsmen ignored them at first. They carried their wooden image into the house and set it down near the fire, and all knelt before it and thanked it for saving them from the terrors of the open sea. Harus

Kum himself got a little bowl of meal and brought it to the image, and his brother set the bowl down at the wooden feet.

"She is wonderful," his brother said. "When the storm came, I thought we should be overturned, but when I prayed to her she gave me new strength and confidence."

The others murmured in agreement. They crowded around the image, touching it, speaking to it, and Harus Kum laid his hand gratefully on the thing's head, glad to have his brother here, even if he had brought him no grain.

Now, relaxing, the boatsmen spread around the room, drinking the beer the women brought, and laughing and telling stories to one another about the voyage, reminding one another, now that they were safe, how perilous their journey had been—Harus Kum imagined how in the depths of their danger, they would have turned to one another and said that things were not so bad. He saw a few of them take the younger woman away into the back of the house. Drawing his brother nearer the fire, Harus Kum sat down with him on the hearth.

"How goes it, back home?"

"Oh, the same. The fishing has been very bad, all summer. You don't fish here."

"Not much."

"Maybe we should bring you some nets and a few hooks."

Harus Kum made such a face that his brother laughed. "You said you needed more food."

"I have food enough. I have the cattle for meat, and the savages inland of here grow grain and beans, and make cheeses from goats' milk, and that I have in plenty, because they are in awe of me. But they are a wicked lot, and I am unhappy dealing with them; the last time I barely escaped with my life."

"What is your suggestion, then?" his brother asked. "Is this place so rich that we should bring more people, and the tools and goods to make a life here for them?"

Harus Kum reached for his beer. The women had been malting the barley all afternoon and the room smelled richly of the steeping grain. He faced his brother again.

"Do you think the king would consider it?"

"I don't know. This has long been a place of profit for us, but, you know, people say the more you put into a mine, the less you take out. And you know, whenever he hears your name spoken, the king still gets angry."

"In Hortha's name," said Harus Kum, and stirred, restless. "How long must I suffer here? Am I to live out all my life in this place, surrounded only by slaves?"

At that, a shadow fell across the room, and he turned to see that the doorway was full of Moloquin, standing there, silent and waiting to be told what to do. Harus Kum jerked a thumb at him.

"Unload the charcoal into the storeroom. Do you know how to put it away?"

"I have done it," Moloquin said. He came forward half the way to the fire.

"Well then, take some of the slaves and unload the boat too. Take care that nothing gets wet."

"I will." Moloquin turned and went out.

"Who is that?" said Harus Kum's brother.

"One of my slaves," said Harus Kum.

"A slave!"

"Why do you seem so surprised? Is there any other here save me and the slaves?"

"He does not seem like a slave to me. The way he spoke to you, the way you spoke to him."

"Ah?" Harus Kum blinked, startled, into his brother's face. "Really? Yet he is certainly a slave, one of the savages I spoke of." He turned to look after Moloquin, but the young man was already gone. He resolved in the future to speak to Moloquin more as a master.

After three days of foul winds, the air turned fine again, and the brother of Harus Kum and his crew loaded up their boat with supplies for the voyage and with sacks of tin, tied their wooden image on in front, and rowed away. Harus Kum stood on the shore watching. The boat bucked over the surf, wallowed down into the trough behind the breaking wave, and struggled up the next slope. At the top, its stern rose high into the air and the boat slid down the far side of the wave and disappeared. A moment later it bobbed up again, farther away by one wave, the oars clawing at the water. Harus Kum stood there watching until his eyes burned from salt and the boat was long out of sight.

When he turned, his chest packed with rage and homesickness, he saw that Moloquin stood there also, squinting into the spray-laden wind. Harus Kum snarled at him, "Have you nothing to do? I shall give you work if you are idle."

Moloquin lowered his head submissively. He was nearly as tall now as Harus Kum.

"How many days must they travel?" he asked.

"That depends," said Harus Kum. "If the weather is fair and the seas run toward home—eight days, or ten. Then they come to a swampy coast, all eaten into with little rivers, where no people live. Our home is across the big bay to the south of that—our village is built on the seacliff, it is magnificent to see it, rising above the waters, as you sail in."

He shook his head, scuffing at the sand with his feet. "I would give up my soul to be back there."

"Why are you not, then?" asked Moloquin.

"Because I am here," Harus Kum said, furious suddenly. "Because someone must do this work, keep you stupid fools at work, and mine the tin. Someday, though, make no mistake, I shall go home again, and then I shall live like a rich man and have all that I wish, all that I desire, someday."

He strode away up the beach, winding a trail through the black sawtoothed outcroppings of rock that studded the sand. The tide was ebbing away, which would carry the little boat out to the safety of the open water, far from shoals and rocks. His heart yearned after it. Moloquin was still following him, and he wheeled, venting his bad temper in a burst.

"What, do you think because we have passed on all we mined that we shall mine no more? Get the others, we will go up the stream and bang the rocks around."

This time Moloquin obeyed him. Watching the young man's back as he walked with long strides up the beach, Harus Kum fought the urge to call him back—to walk beside him.

He told himself he was just lonely, now that his brother was gone.

Yet it was good to have Moloquin. He asked interesting questions, and he brought bits of rock for the master to inspect, and he learned everything Harus Kum tried to teach him—learned the way a piece of cloth absorbed a spill. He had a natural feel for this work. Once Harus Kum had loved the work. Being here, year after year,

driving slaves to it, bereft of his own kind and never knowing when
he might return to his home, he had grown dull and his interest had
lost its power, but Moloquin was bringing it back to him. He longed
now to open up the little hut at the back of the house, light the fires,
fill the bellows, and show this youth the real power in the rocks. Give
him something to admire in his master.

He glanced at the sky, cloudless and blue. There was no use in
wasting the good weather. Soon the winter storms would shut down
over them, and that would be the time to take Moloquin into the
forge. Harus Kum went into the storehouse for his whip.

They pounded the ore into rubble and lugged it back to the stockade, but before it could be cooked, the winter broke. One storm
chased another up across the western sea; each brought first a warm
furious wind, carrying the rain along in bursts and fits; then the
storm seemed to settle down and stopped blowing and rained hard
and steadily for days. Sometimes in the late day the rain would stop,
and the low-lying sun broke through and the rainbow appeared,
arched and glistening among the clouds.

After this had gone on for some time, Harus Kum came to Moloquin and said, "I need your help. Come with me."

Silently the youth rose and went after him. They left the big
house and walked around behind it to the little hut at the back, well
away from the other buildings. Harus Kum opened the door and led
Moloquin inside.

The rain was falling on the thatch overhead, rattling and rus-
tling like mice in the straw. Harus Kum opened a window at the far
side, and by that light found a big shell full of oil and dropped a wick
into it. Moloquin stood silently by the door, looking around him.

The hut was round, small, crowded with strange furniture. In
the center was a stone tub, waist high, with a long tube coming up
from halfway along its side. Next to this stood another huge chunk
of stone, worked roughly square, and set on a massive tree trunk.
Harus Kum went around the place, with his hands as much as his
eyes finding the tools laid out on a bench to one side, and stopping
to pick up a flat leather bag from the floor.

"Go fetch me a basket of charcoal," he said, as he passed Moloquin. When Moloquin went out, he looked over his shoulder and saw

Harus Kum fitting the leather bag to the tube in the side of the stone box.

Moloquin brought in the charcoal, and Harus Kum gave him further orders. He lit a fire in the stone box and put in the charcoal, gradually, until there was a thick layer of charcoal, burning well, in the stone tub. Meanwhile Harus Kum was fussing around in the semi-darkness. He went out once, and Moloquin heard him poking at the thatch; something grated, and looking up the young man saw a hole opening up in the roof directly over the tub of stone. A drop of rain blew in and hissed on the charcoal. Harus Kum returned.

"Today I will only sharpen knives," he said.

He laid out several knives on the edge of the stone tub, now glowing red with the charcoal fire. Moloquin said nothing. His hands were damp with excitement. He watched the master go to the bench and take up tools: a heavy mallet in his right hand, and a long flat stick in the other. Returning to the fire, he picked up one of the knives, fit it carefully into a hole in the stick, and laid the blade down on the hot coals.

"Now, this—"

He circled the tub to Moloquin's side. The leather bag hung between them, attached to the tube running into the firebox. Taking hold of the bag with both hands, Harus Kum pulled it open and squeezed it, and Moloquin heard the rush of the wind forced from the bag down the tube and into the charcoal, and the layer of orange coals bloomed a furious red and sizzled with the heat. "Pump," said Harus Kum, and gave the bag to Moloquin.

With Moloquin working the pump, Harus Kum went back to the far side of the firebox, pushed the knife blade into the coals a little, took it out, inspected it, put it back in again, and picked up his mallet. Now he stood midway between the firebox and the great stone square on its tree-trunk base, and his hand with the mallet was by the square stone. Taking the knife from the fire, he laid it on the stone, and struck it with the mallet.

The blade glowed, hot as the coals. Moloquin worked the pump with both hands, but his eyes were fixed on the red-hot blade. As the mallet struck it, he saw how the blade yielded, bent, and flattened, and with the next blow flattened still more.

He nearly cried out aloud. Hard as the stone when it was cold, somehow the metal got from stone turned malleable as clay when it was hot. When he saw this it was as if a new power sprang alive in his muscles. A new knowledge awoke in his mind. With a passionate energy he pumped and pumped on the leather bag, until the coals were white and shimmering, and Harus Kum gave a laugh and backed away, one hand up.

"Leave off a little, it is too hot."

"I'm sorry." Moloquin stepped back.

Harus Kum took the cooling blade and plunged it down into a bucket of water at his feet. There it hissed and darkened and a cloud of steam rose. Harus Kum fit another knife into the long stick and put it on the coals to heat. Moloquin watched every move of his hands. The deft, sure motions were full of beauty; each blow he struck was perfect. He hammered the dull blades until their edges gleamed, thin as fingernails, and plunged them into the water to cool. Done, he held one of the blades out for Moloquin to inspect.

It was sharp as a stone knife, and much finer to hold. Moloquin sighed. He stroked the flat of the blade with his thumb, lost in its smoothness and shine, and put it against his cheek. Harus Kum watched him with a little smile on his face.

"So. You see what it is all about, this work of ours."

Moloquin laid the blade down on the stone where it had been beaten. He thought of Ladon, pompous in his piles of blue beads, ignorant of that power in which he sheathed himself. Made foolish by his efforts to be wise.

He thought of Ladon's belly. Of this knife, piercing that fat belly.

"Now," said Harus Kum, his sharp voice breaking into Moloquin's thoughts. He laid down the mallet and the stick on the flat stone, and went into the back of the hut. When he came forth again, he had a stone bowl and one of the bricks of shining metal his brother had brought him.

"This is copper," he said. "There is some of it to be found here, but not enough to be mined—at least, none that I have found."

He put the stone bowl on the coals and dropped the brick of copper into it. All the while he talked.

"You find copper in ores that are green, or blue, very pretty. At first, I think, men used them for their prettiness, to paint pots with, and that was how they learned that cooking such ores will melt them, and then they run like water, and can be made into any shape."

Moloquin said, "Ah—" not from surprise, but from delight.

"But the copper is soft. It will not hold an edge, or stand up to hard work. So—"

He took a pouch of tin granules and poured them in on top of the copper. "Mix these two together, and they make bronze."

Already the copper was melting. Dark patches floated on the surface. The light cast subtle inflections of color on the shimmering melt. Harus Kum leaned over to see it and stirred it a little with his stick, and the soft reflected glow lit up his face like a mask.

"Keep the bellows going."

Moloquin worked the leather pump. Harus Kum went around the hut, laying out the cooled knives and sticking their handles back on; he hummed to himself as he did this, something Moloquin had never heard him do before, and in fact he seemed happier than Moloquin had ever seen him. In the stone bowl, the copper melted down to a shining soup. Moloquin watched it, absorbed. All his life he had strained against the world, and the world had packed itself around him and bound him tight in its own courses. Now, in the stone bowl, the earth itself was mere matter, to be shaped as he pleased. He smiled at the obedient copper.

When it was all melted, Harus Kum brought out a broad thick tray of pottery, which he set on the square anvil stone. Four long regular hollows indented the surface of the pottery. The master poured the hot bronze into the pottery tray and the molten metal ran into the hollows and lay there, still gently glowing.

"Now they will cool," Harus Kum said, and set down the little crucible on the side of the firebox. "Rake over the fire. Tomorrow we will fix the axe, and perhaps you can work a little on it."

Moloquin turned the fire over and they covered the box with a lid of stone. Harus Kum went around the forge again, fussing with his tools. The rain splashed in through the smokehole, hit the lid of the firebox, and jumped up, hissing, into the air. Moloquin, his hands empty, watched his master fiddle with his things. He guessed that Harus Kum was loathe to leave this place, and he knew why: there was a power here beyond anything any of the People had ever dreamed of. Moloquin filled his chest with air: a bellows for the fires of his brain. Harus Kum went past him to the door, and the two men left the forge.

Ap Min said, "Do you not think him fine to look at?"

The older woman grunted. She never said much; she did her work, her head bowed, and ate what Harus Kum gave to her and slept where he told her and rose in the morning to do more work. Today they were brewing the beer; first they had malted the barley that Harus Kum had brought from inland, spreading the grain out in shallow baskets and soaking it until it sprouted, and now they were cooking it in a great tub of water. Murky and bitter-smelling, it yielded slowly to Ap Min's paddle as she stirred, and gave off a soft murmur of its own, a low rippling music.

"Don't you think him good to look on?"

The older woman said, in her harsh, unused voice, "He is a man."

"He is kind to me."

"He wants something."

Ap Min shook her head. Moloquin wanted nothing of her. He noticed her only when she stood directly before him. Then he smiled, he spoke some soft, idle word to her, not to get anything, not to have his own way, but simply because she was there.

That was what amazed her. To the others she was there only as a thing to be used. Moloquin looked at her and met her eyes and smiled, the way men smiled at one another, to make friends one of the other.

She leaned on the side of the tub, stirring, and the beer sang to her.

The edge of the tub pressed against her belly; something hard and round in her belly pressed back. She had felt this way once before. Then Harus Kum had given her a potion stinking of penny-royal mint, and she fell very sick, and after three days of agony her body gave up a tiny withered corpse, hideous and ugly, that Harus Kum cast into the fire of the forge, saying it would bring good luck.

She dreaded the potion; she dreaded the horrible corpse. She gave her mind over instead to daydreaming of Moloquin.

"Do you think Harus Kum would let slaves marry?"

The older woman coughed and laughed at once, but she said nothing, she denied nothing. Ap Min swept the paddle in a broad arc through the young beer.

Hems came in, his hair wet from the rain, lugging a basket of malted barley on his shoulder, and went to the side of the tub and poured in the grain. Close to Ap Min, he moved sideways, pretending not to see her until he rubbed up against her, and then laughed. Looking down at her, he gave her a long smile, and his arm moved, nudging her breast.

"Go away," she said loftily, although she liked Hems; he smiled at her too. But he wanted something, and that was why he smiled.

"Come watch Moloquin chop wood in the rain," he said.

She straightened, letting go of the paddle, and the older woman caught the handle and laid the paddle up on the side of the tub. "Go," she said, and snorted.

Ap Min started toward the door, Hems beside her; he slid his arm around her waist and fondled her breast. She struck at his hand, not with any real intent of stopping him; it was play, part of the play between them, something as comforting in its own way as Moloquin's smile when he saw her. Hems caressed her whenever he could, but he never took her. She wondered if he really wanted her. Perhaps he only liked the play. She went out to the doorstep.

The rain was falling in a steady drenching downpour. The yard was half-lost under puddles, pocked with the rain falling, and there in the middle of the mud and the water was Moloquin, a chunk of wood at his feet and an axe in his hands.

He chopped at it, once, twice, three times, and straightened, the tool swinging down in his hand. "This will not work," he said, over his shoulder.

It was not to those in the doorway he spoke, but to Harus Kum, who stood in the shelter of the eave, just at the corner of the house, watching. He said, "Well, bring it back in, then, we shall try something else." His voice was flat with disappointment. Moloquin swung the axe up over his shoulder, a gesture so easy and full of lively grace that Ap Min sighed as he went away after the master toward the forge.

Hems clutched her. His voice in her ear said, "If you have no work, we could go somewhere together."

He said this often. She always had work, as he knew, and there was no place to go in any case. She thrust him off, laughing, annoyed, and went back to the beer.

With each blow of the mallet the tip of the bronze bar flattened out a little; he could flatten it less or more, by striking harder or softer. The metal wore the imprint of the hammer in a subtle mottling all over the work surface. He held the bar by a stick with a hole through it, and when he raised the mallet and brought it down, it was like making something whole again, like completing a circle. His body and the bar of bronze and the mallet formed a little world, an orbit of single purpose. He knew he loved the bronze.

Glum, Harus Kum said, "I did not think this would work."

He was stripping off the bronze sheath with which they had covered the axe. For most of the winter they had been trying to make an axe of bronze that would hold an edge, trying first one way, then another, always failing.

"What will we do now?" Moloquin asked.

"I have—something—"

The master got up, threw down the scraps of bronze, and stood the axe against the wall. "The bronze is beautiful," he said. "It makes beautiful things, and perhaps that is all it wishes. Maybe the demon resents being used for mean things. Maybe only stone is crude enough and simple enough for such low things as tools."

Moloquin put the bar of bronze back into the fire, and went to the bellows; he kept his head turned toward Harus Kum, to encourage the master to talk; he had learned much metal-lore listening to Harus Kum ramble. Now the master strolled around the forge, looking into the little shelves and wooden nooks on the walls.

He said, "I have some other ore here, somewhere, that may serve."

"More tin," Moloquin said.

"It is not so easy as that. I showed you, remember, what happens when you try to cast pure copper."

Moloquin nodded. They had melted a little copper and poured it out, but the metal would not flow evenly, and the castings, when they cooled, were full of holes and could not be worked at all without breaking.

"So we add the tin to it, and then it flows smoothly, it cools evenly and well, but the more tin you add to copper, the more brittle it becomes, and eventually it cannot be forged at all."

Moloquin flexed the bellows between his hands, watching the bronze bar glow. It was so beautiful, to take dull earth and turn it into something shining and hard, yielding gracefully to its master. Maybe that was enough, the whole virtue of it; maybe Harus Kum was right.

Yet as he faced the bronze, something hard and shining in himself arose and would not be defeated. He thought, I shall make an axe, and the axe shall lead me home again.

Now Harus Kum was back, a little leather pouch in his hand,

and he upended it and dumped some small rocks and dust onto the top of the anvil.

"Arsenic," he said. "Hard to come by. Hard to use. We shall add a little to the copper, and see what we shall see."

This new metal was soft and lustrous to look at. Moloquin put out his hand to touch it, and Harus Kum knocked his arm down.

"No. Handle it only as I show you. This is evil stuff, it can kill."

With a little flat stick he scooped the arsenic into a crucible of clay, and dumped in after it the pieces of copper with which they had sheathed the stone axe. With jointed sticks, they put the crucible into the fire, and Moloquin went to work the bellows.

Harus Kum said, "My brother told me that when the traders came from the east—they come in the spring—"

"Where do they come from?" Moloquin asked swiftly.

"Over the water. They come in the spring and buy our metals, but this time they spoke of another metal. They craved this metal more than the tin and the copper, almost as much as gold, which is so rare I myself have seen only a few things made of it. But we have none of that, not gold nor the other metal whose name I have forgotten."

In the crucible the metal flowed and ran, glowing red. Moloquin leaned over it, drawn by the shimmering colors. There was nothing more wonderful than this gift of the earth.

He said, dreamily, "The tree dulls the axe. Wood will dull a knife. But flesh—that yields, so soft—"

Harus Kum gave a harsh bark of laughter. "The bronze slays, again and again."

Moloquin smiled down into the crucible; he thought he saw the demon of the metal in the streams of molten copper.

"You want to kill Ladon, is that it?"

Moloquin could not bring himself to speak of this with Harus Kum. It was completely other than his life with Harus Kum. He watched the last cool shape of the metal disappear into the melt.

"Don't be a fool," Harus Kum said. "Forget Ladon. Forget those people. You are mine, now. This is where you belong. You have the hands and the soul for it, and I mean to teach you all I know of it. But you will be mine forever. You will never go back to your people."

Moloquin lifted his head, but he said nothing; with a sudden ache in his heart, as if his heart were cracking into two pieces, he saw that life before him, as Harus Kum had described it. He remembered Karella—what did she think of him, did she believe he was dead? Did she remember him? His thoughts rushed back to that moment when he had seen her last, when they were arguing. Harsh angry words, the last he had spoken to her. His heart was sore with longing for her. There were no stories here, as there was no bronze there. His heart was split in two. Grimly he lowered his gaze to the shining stuff in the crucible.

Moloquin awoke before dawn. He could hear the rain falling in the thatch, and the snores of the other slaves around him; the house was dark except by the fire, where a small red glow still shone. Quietly, without rousing Hems beside him, he rose up and went to the door.

Just as he reached it, the door opened. He stepped quickly back, his neck tingling, expecting Harus Kum, but it was Ap Min who came into the house, looking pale, her arms folded over the round bulge of her belly. She gave him a look of surprise and he moved aside to let her by, but instead she stood before him, blocking his way.

"Where are you going?"

"Out," he said.

"Don't go," she said, louder, and he glanced quickly behind him to see if she had wakened anyone else; his heart racing, he faced her again, where she stood in his way, and put his hand on her arm.

"I must go make water," he said, and with his arm he urged her gently out of his way.

"Moloquin," she said, "Moloquin, don't leave me here."

He gave her a startled look, wondering what she meant—wondering also how she knew what was on his mind—but he said nothing to her, and went out the door into the yard.

There, he did not piss. He went to the stockade fence and climbed up over it and walked away, to the east, up the gorge of the stream. Before he came to the mines, he veered off, climbed the steep crumbling bank, and went into the forest.

He did not know if he was going home or not. He had promised Hems to take him, when he left, but Hems had come to do well enough here, as well as he would do among his own People, or so Moloquin told himself as he put distance between himself and Hems.

Between himself and Harus Kum; between himself and the bronze.

He went on into the forest. The trees closed around him. The rain dripped and splashed around him, so that the whole forest shook. As usual, he ate whatever he came on as he walked, snails and grubs and lily bulbs, and his tongue told him what he feared to know, that the spring was wearing down toward summer, that soon the People would gather at the Turnings-of-the-Year.

He had promised Hems to take him there. Harus Kum, too, had business there, but Harus Kum, he guessed, would avoid the Gathering this year, after his experience there the year before. As he walked, the rain streaming down his naked shoulders and chest and matting his hair to his head, he played with the thought that he might go to the Gathering and do Harus Kum's work for him.

That would mean facing Ladon.

When he thought of Ladon his blood burned. His hands ached to grip that fat foolish neck.

He thought also of Karella, of her delight when he came back. He would have stories to tell her, for once. He would tell her he had seen the broken edge of the millstone. She knew of it already, the stories had given her that knowledge, although she had never seen it herself. That still impressed him, that mere words—noise and air— could carry such a burden, the whole world contained in a breath.

That was his choice. To the east, among his own People, were the words; to the west, with Harus Kum, was the bronze.

He longed to hold the hammer again, to beat the bar of bronze on the anvil. What a power that was! Even men who chipped stone into tools had no such power; a man working stone had to strike it at exactly the right spot, or the whole flint would shatter. The form was already there in the flint, the man merely released it with his blows. But the bronze would be whatever he wished of it; if he but used his strength and will and mind, he could dominate it wholly.

Around him the whole great dripping forest warmed with the coming of the sun. Birds chattered in the treetops, and he climbed a forked pine tree, split by lightning, and found a nest and ate the eggs. The pitch clung to his hands in black streaks. Crossing the stream, he knelt at the edge and tried to scrub his hands clean, but the pitch would not come off, although he ground his palms against the gritty sand of the streambed.

He stayed there by the stream, intermittently scrubbing at his hands, and let his mind bring him what thoughts it would. His choice tormented him. He told himself that if he crossed over this stream, he would go all the way back to Karella, but if he remained here on

this bank, he would go back to Harus Kum. The forest brightened
with daylight; as he sat there, hardly moving, the birds grew bolder
in the trees, leaping from branch to branch and screaming at one
another, and a squirrel ran down a trunk nearby him and began to
hunt for food in the deep mast of the forest floor.

The day wore on. Three times his resolution formed and he rose
to walk across the stream, and three times his feet would not carry
him over the water. The thought of Hems gnawed at him. If he went
home, he might never see Hems again, but his friend would not forget; his friend would go on knowing Moloquin had left him behind,
broken his promise and left him with Harus Kum, and Moloquin too
would know it. At the end of the afternoon, Moloquin rose up,
turned to the west, and walked back to Harus Kum's stockade.

The men were slaughtering one of the cattle; they had driven the
herd down into the gorge, all the slaves together yelling and waving
their arms, and there they separated a yearling from the others. Ap
Min stood in the gate of the stockade, watching them drag the calf
down the stream by a rope around its neck. The calf resisted, its four
legs braced, its hoofs tearing up the ground; behind it Harus Kum
walked, lashing it continually with his whip.

Hems left the other men and walked over to Ap Min in the gateway. "Has he come back?"

She shook her head. She could not bring herself to speak Moloquin's name.

Hems said, in a shaking voice, "He will come back."

He put his arm around her waist, and suddenly he laid his head
on her shoulder. She turned to him, her cheek against his hair. From
down the stream came a sudden high-pitched bleating of the calf.

She sat down, Hems beside her, and comforted him. Her arm
went around him, holding him fast—if Moloquin had gone, yet she
still had this one. She stroked his hair, murmuring to him.

As they sat there, his head on her shoulder, Harus Kum came
up from the lower valley; there was blood all over his hands and
sleeves. Ap Min rose to let him through the gate and he stopped and
frowned down at her.

"You are growing fat again, Ap Min." He put his hand roughly
on her belly. "I shall make you a potion for it, we shall have you thin
soon."

She froze. Suddenly everything around her, the stockade, even Hems seemed far, far away, and she alone with Harus Kum. She raised her face to him.

"No. Please."

"You will be no use to me if I do not cure you. Not now. You can do as you please for a while, I have to find the herbs."

He went off. She sank down as if her legs had lost their strength, turning her face to the wall of the stockade. Hems lifted his head to stare at her.

"He will kill my baby," she said. "And me too." Then she put her face into her hands.

Hems moved closer to her and laid his arm around her. She put her head on his shoulder and wept.

At sundown they all went inside. Even Ap Min, who had sat in the gateway of the fence all day long, looking for Moloquin, gave up her vigil. They had built a big fire in the hearth, and were roasting fresh meat over it, and the house was full of the delicious aromas of the meat. Harus Kum carved a chunk of it for himself and sat down to eat it, but the meat would not go past his teeth; it turned to ashes on his tongue.

He told himself he did not need Moloquin. He needed no one. Had he not stood against the king, when none other dared? And come here and lived by himself all these years, by himself, needing no one. Yet his mind turned over toward Moloquin, every step on the threshold brought his head around to see who entered, his ears strained for the voice of him who had gone. At last, furious, he rose up and went out of the house, though now it was after sundown, and went to the forge.

The smell of cold metal greeted him. The place was dank from the rain. He lit the lamp and stirred up the coals of the fire, and as he did so, the door opened and Moloquin came in.

Harus Kum wheeled toward him, ready to shout, to laugh, to welcome him, to chastise him, and unable to do all these things at once, he did nothing. Moloquin's head hung a little; he gave his master a sideways look and went by him to the bellows and took the handles in his hands.

"Is it too late to work now?"

Harus Kum shrugged. He struggled to keep the triumph from

his face. He had won something; he knew that now he had Moloquin forever. He crushed down his delight. Turning to the tools on the wall, he reached for the hammer, he reached for the tongs. He said, "Let us see what we can do with this piece of bronze." His voice shook. Avoiding Moloquin's gaze, fighting the smile on his lips, he bent to the task of his hands.

This time it was different.

They had mixed the copper and arsenic and tin together in the crucible, and poured the metal into a bar; when it cooled, they heated it up again in the forge, and began to beat it with the hammer. Harus Kum tried first, and before he had done three strokes he was shaking his head, backing away.

"It's too hard. It will not yield to me."

"Let me try," Moloquin said.

"It is too hard, I say. We must add more tin."

"Let me try it."

"Try it, then, fool, learn for yourself."

Moloquin took the hammer in his hand, and laid the bar on the anvil; he gathered himself up, and the hammer rose in his fist and struck down, and the whole forge rang with the blow. Harus Kum went to the bellows, to keep the fire hot and ready, and at the next stroke of the hammer, all his hair stood on end; he thought he could hear the metal sing in the stroke of the hammer.

In the house, the others slept the dull sleep of beasts. In the forge, the two men contested with the bronze.

"Is it coming?" Harus Kum cried.

"I feel it," Moloquin said, and he thrust the bronze into the fire.

Harus Kum pumped air into the firebox and leaned forward to see. The bronze lay in the coals, drew the heat and glow from them, and its shimmering color paled. Still blocky and awkward, yet it was finding a shape, a broad wedge, a flaring face, and already the line was so smooth, the curve so strong, that Harus Kum rejoiced to see it; he spat into the fire.

"We shall feed you flesh soon enough," he cried to the forge. "Go on, Moloquin, go on!"

Moloquin lifted up the glowing metal and laid it on the anvil, and he reared back with the hammer, and with all his strength he beat on the metal. Harus Kum watched, rapt. He saw something growing on the anvil, something more than merely an axe; he saw life and beauty there.

Yet the metal was strong, and one-minded; it would not yield easily. Even Moloquin's strength could not tame it wholly. As it cooled and turned dull again, and the man with the hammer stood panting over it, Harus Kum rejoiced also in the rebellion of the metal.

"Once more," Moloquin said, although he was clearly tired. He laid the bronze in the firebed, and Harus Kum lashed the coals to a white blaze.

He thought, This may be a masterwork, and if it is—

The king loved nothing more than great weapons.

Moloquin took up the bronze again and put it on the anvil, and he reached for the hammer. Harus Kum watched him closely. He saw how his pupil gripped the hammer, his fingers flexing again and again, dissatisfied with their grasp. He saw how Moloquin collected himself and raised up the hammer, and now Harus Kum flung himself forward and caught Moloquin by the arm.

"No! Leave off—you are too tired."

"I can do it," Moloquin said.

"Perhaps you can try, but you must not. If there is weakness in you when you form it, the axe will suffer. See—do you not see how it is?" Harus Kum took the tongs from him and moved the half-made axe over to the firebed. "There is that here we must not defile. We shall work on it again tomorrow."

Moloquin leaned on the anvil, his face older with fatigue. His gaze followed the axe from the anvil to the fire, from the fire to the tub of water where Harus Kum placed it. He said, "I cannot wait until tomorrow."

Harus Kum laughed. With a broad stroke of his arm he smacked his pupil on the shoulder. "Keep patience. Nothing good comes quickly. Let us go in and eat—there is fresh meat in plenty, and the others will be glad to know you are back."

At once he glanced at Moloquin, afraid, as if admitting that Moloquin had ever left would make it easier for him to do it again. The young man's head hung. He was exhausted. His curly black hair veiled his cheeks. Harus Kum thought, He could have left, but he came back. He is mine now, mine forever. Like a king leading away captives, he got Moloquin by the arm and took him in triumph off to the house.

. . .

In the morning, when Ap Min brought him beer, he saw again how advanced she was into her pregnancy, her belly grotesquely swollen, undesirable and ugly. Awakening as usual with an erection, he would have liked to possess her, but the old warnings of his people against coupling with a pregnant woman held him back, and he decided then to deal with this. He got up, put on his clothes, and went into the storehouse to find the pennyroyal.

When he had the brew steeped, he took it to her, where she knelt in the back of the house, milling grain in a little stone tub with a roller of stone.

"You should tell me these things as soon as you know," he said. "Then it can be got rid of quickly and easily; now you will suffer some more, as you did the last time. Now get up and drink this."

"I—"

She gawked at him, her face drawn long with new lines, and he saw the uneven color of her face and thought, How ugly she is, and he pushed at her impatiently with his foot. "Get up, Ap Min, you sluggard, get up."

She got up, all in a rush of energy, lighter than he would have supposed, but she did not do as he bade her. She ran forth toward the middle of the room, and when he shouted to her she put her hands over her ears. He went after her. There in the middle of the room, where all the men sat, she turned once around in a circle and dashed out the door.

"Ap Min!" Harus Kum roared. He resolved to beat her until she lost the baby; that would teach her to obey him. Long-striding, he plunged through the room after her, out the door into the yard.

The rain had ceased, although the earth and the sky still seemed soaked through; water dripped from all the eaves of the house. Ap Min was nowhere to be seen, but from around the corner came the steady thud and crack of an axe on wood, and Harus Kum went toward it.

In the lee of the house, where the stockade wall came close to it, Moloquin was cutting wood for the fire. At his feet Ap Min groveled.

Moloquin ignored her. He swung the axe in great, full strokes, throwing wood chips in showers high as his head. Harus Kum went toward his girl-slave, his hand out to snatch her away.

"No," she said. She clutched Moloquin's leg. "No. Help me. No. Please. Help me."

Moloquin stopped in his work. He faced Harus Kum, and the look on his face said he had no taste for this. He wiped the hair out of his eyes. Ap Min had her arms wrapped around his leg.

"What is this?" Moloquin asked.

"You can see for yourself," said Harus Kum. "She is heavy with child. She will be of no use to me when she is great or with a baby at the breast. I have a potion, it will get rid of the baby, everything will be as it should be."

He reached down to seize her, and she clung tighter to Moloquin and turned her face away. Moloquin did not move; he stared at Harus Kum, his black brows drawn down into a frown.

He said, "I have seen women working in their gardens until their moment comes on them, and they lie down and bear the baby, and get up again and take the hoe up and go back to work. I see no reason why she might not go on as she is."

As he spoke, he swung the axe down, resting the head beside his foot and leaning on the handle, and by coincidence, or some savage art, he had thereby made a sort of fence between Harus Kum and the cowering girl. The master roared.

"What is this, Moloquin? Do you suppose yourself the ruler here?"

Moloquin said nothing, but he did not give up the girl at his feet. Harus Kum stooped and took a chunk of wood and made as if to throw it at her.

"She is mine! You are all mine—you are my slaves, Moloquin—mine!"

"The child is yours, too," Moloquin said.

"What!"

"The child is yours! You take her whenever you wish—she never asks to lie under you, does she? And then when your pleasure of her bears some fruit, you would have her suffer for your doing."

"Moloquin," Harus Kum cried. "She is only a woman, and a slave at that. Give her to me."

Suddenly Ap Min herself took action. As the two men stared at each other, she sprang forward, and with a swipe of her hand she knocked the cup from Harus Kum's grasp, and the potion splashed to the ground.

Harus Kum struck at her with his foot. She scrambled away; ungainly, she ran off toward the house, leaving the two men alone.

Harus Kum grunted. "I shall mix another. I shall have my way, Moloquin. She is only a woman." Turning, he marched off after Ap Min.

Only a woman, Moloquin thought, and laughed.

He stared after Harus Kum; the strong smell of mint reached his nose. As weak and stupid and silly as Ap Min was, at one blow she had struck down all Harus Kum's designs; she was *only a woman,* but Harus Kum was only a man.

There was more to it than that. Moloquin turned back to the work of chopping the wood, but his thoughts winnowed through what had just happened here, and he grounded the axe again and leaned on it, his gaze going once more toward the big house.

Only a woman. Harus Kum rejoiced in the forge, in the power of the forge; yet he saw no value in the forge of her belly. Making great of his own power, he made nothing of hers. Yet what was his creature, compared to hers? Did his things of bronze breathe and think and run?

Now his mind leapt into the center of it; he saw suddenly that all this art of Harus Kum's was only an imitation of the real power, the only true power, which was to pass life on from soul to soul.

All morning, as he went about the small necessary tasks of the morning, he had been dreaming of the axe in the forge, the bronze glowing and ready in the forge, his hands longing to take hold of the hammer. Now that passion shrank in him. He saw himself at that work, not an omnipotent creator drawing forth being from nothing, but the same little boy who had sat on the ground in the longhouse, squeezing the clay through his fingers.

Yet he had some power in him, vigorous as any woman's, some passion that longed for a challenge great enough to prove itself. He thought, for the first time in a long while, and with a new and unquenchable lust, of the stones of the Pillar of the Sky.

In the afternoon he went into the forge, and while he waited for Harus Kum, he drew out the axe from the bucket of water where it had rested through the night, laid it on the anvil, and stared at it. With his forefinger he traced the wide smooth curve of the blade; at the end, where the curve was still blunt and unforged, he traced the shape into the air.

Harus Kum opened the door. "Come out. There is a storm coming, can you not sense it?"

"Come work the bellows." Moloquin reached for the hammer; a quick eager energy coursed through him.

"I will not," said Harus Kum. "I have seen lightning strike a forge, I helped to draw out the bodies, what was left of them."

"Then I shall do it alone," Moloquin said, and he went to the bellows and pumped them until their blast made the hot coals roar.

Without Harus Kum to help him, the work was slower. Before he had the bronze hot enough to work, the rain began to strike the thatch over his head, and the wind rose. All around him the air crackled, and his hair stood on end; he felt the attention of spirits on him, the whole great Overworld watching him, and when the first thunder rolled over the sky, he raised the hammer and beat on the bronze.

He had never felt such a strength in his arm as he felt now. With each blow the bronze axe sang, and as it sang it yielded to him, giving itself to him, a pure and holy power. The thunder rolled across the sky, and like the flickerings of some celestial forge the lightning flashed. He stopped and worked the bellows again and brought the bronze back to its season, and when he took the hammer again in his hand, his mouth opened and he began to sing, in tune with the thunder and the hammer that shaped the bronze.

He commanded the metal, and the metal obeyed him; the power of the heavens shaped it, the thunder and the lightning, forge of Heaven.

The storm was passing. The unnatural strength was leaving him, and the song left his lips. There on the anvil the axehead lay, beautiful and potent, ruddy as the rising sun, curved like the sun, and impulsively, before it cooled, he scratched a little rayed sun in the center of the blade.

Harus Kum came in. "You are lucky you are alive."

"I am finished," Moloquin said. He dropped the axehead into the bucket and hung up the hammer, and he went out of the forge.

Harus Kum waited until Moloquin left and leaned over the

bucket; the axe hissed quietly in the bottom of the water. With the tongs and a piece of cloth he lifted it out.

The king loved such things, and this was worthy of a king. The edge would never hew up a living tree, but it would cleave a skull, or lay open a chest, or take an arm off, as long as the man who carried it had the strength to lift it up.

He saw the crude little sun, and grunted, amused. His pupil had great skill, but he knew nothing of the craft of decoration. Harus Kum drew a larger sun with his finger on the flat of the blade. He would incise it and fill the cuts with wire, burnish the whole with a deer's legbone, buff the bronze until the glow seemed to begin deep within the metal. Take it across the sea. Lay it at the feet of the king, and be welcomed home forever more.

At that he could not but smile; he felt lighter, buoyant, half able to fly. He dropped the axe back into the bucket and went into the house.

In the night Moloquin awakened. He lay there a moment and let the sounds of the night reach his ears: the wind in the thatch, the low hiss of the fire, the snores of the other sleepers, the scurryings of the mice who sneaked in under the darkness to steal food. He let his mind wake up. Putting out one hand, he shook Hems beside him.

His friend woke with a grunt and a half-blurted question. In the dark Moloquin put one hand over Hems' mouth and leaned over and whispered in his ear, and Hems was at once silent and ready.

They put on such clothes as they had, and on stealthy feet they crossed the house toward the door. There Hems stayed, and Moloquin went off in another direction, around the edge of the room, stepping over the sleepers on the floor, until he came to the straw where Ap Min lay.

He knelt down beside her and touched her hand and her face, and she too woke, going rigid and fearful at his touch.

Leaning down, he spoke into her ear. She clutched his hand. For a long moment she made no answer. Then at last she whispered, "Yes," and she too rose up from her bed, put on her only garment, and followed him through the darkened house.

They opened the door and went out to the moonlight, pale and treacherous. Hems and Ap Min started toward the stockade gate, but Moloquin veered off and circled around to the back of the house.

The forge was locked up, to keep the slaves out. Moloquin tried the door, and when it would not open, he went around to the back, to the window. A piece of hide covered it. With two blows of his hands at the corners of the frame, Moloquin knocked the window free, and he leaned in, stretching his arm in through the opening, in past the racks of tools, past the low bench where Harus Kum sat when he worked small objects, down to the bucket at the foot of the anvil. Then he drew forth the great axe, dripping and shining in the moonlight. He put it under his shirt, against his chest, cold as it was, cold and wet, and he went after his friends.

The stockade gate was also locked, as usual, but with the edge of the axeblade Moloquin forced the latch. He and Hems pulled the gate open. With Ap Min between them, they went out, nor did they look back, but went on into the east, after the moon.

Shateel went early in the morning to the river and took up the reeds she had left to soak there overnight. As she walked back to the village the sun was just rising and the air was thick with the new light and the competing shadows. She held the reeds out to one side, so that they would not drip on her, and when she came to the yard in the middle of the longhouses, she went at once to her place, where her mat was, and sat down with her work.

The other women were just waking, just getting their children up, just beginning the day. Shateel knelt on her mat, her eyes downcast, and spread out the soaked reeds before her. With her fingernails she slit them into thin strips.

Now the doors of the longhouses opened, and out came the other women, their families bustling around them, into the sun.

They ignored her. After a year in the longhouses of Ladon's people, she was still a stranger. She worked at the reeds, keeping her gaze ever contained to the space of her mat, while the others clattered and hurried around her. When she had the reeds split, she chose the longest, and set about twining them together to form the spines of her basket. One by one, the other women set themselves to their day's tasks. Some of them got tools and baskets and water jugs, and went in a noisy herd up toward their gardens. Others sat down in a mass beside Shateel, and set to work with clay, or with reeds, or with their spinning, and with their tongues.

"Look! She is still doing it wrong."

"That is how those other people do it."

"But she is one of us now, and should make her baskets in our way. It is the proper way. Our baskets are better than those of the other people."

"Perhaps she is too stupid to learn our way."

"Perhaps she is."

Then they laughed. Shateel paid no outward heed to them and went on twining the reeds together, making the bottom of the basket as her mother had taught her. She thought that the other women knew she was listening and spoke as they did to draw her into defending herself against them.

She told herself it did not matter. Soon the Midsummer Gathering would begin, at the Turnings-of-the-Year, and there she would go to her mother and tell her that she wanted to come home again.

She had gathered the reeds carefully, choosing only sound long pieces, and soaked them well and split them properly, and the basket was making up swiftly and well as she worked. She finished the flat, tight bottom of the basket, and curved the spines upward for the sides, and wound the straw in through them, giving each third strand a half-twist to keep it flat through the curve of the basket. As she worked, a song welled up into her throat, but she did not give it voice. Here they sang no songs she knew. All they sang here was the Song of the Sampo.

Samp-po, sam-po,
Li la li la li li la la
Let what comes come
Let what goes go
Sam-po, sam-po
All will come again with time
Sam-po, sam-po
All will go again with time
La li la li la la la

Although she strove against it, she loved the sampo song; its wisdom had kept her patience for her, kept her head bowed and her eyes downcast for her all this long year, when she had thought she could endure no more.

She sat near the door to the longhouse, where the old women sat with the mill in their midst, and the younger women sat around them at their crafts. The gardens were all planted. Shateel had spent the whole spring at work in the soil her husband had given to her, when they brought her to this place. It was away up the slope, almost at the edge of the forest, where years before the trees had been girdled of their bark, and the year before she came they had been burned down. In this soil she worked until her back ached and her hands were ingrained with dirt; she turned the whole garden over, as well as she could, and put in seeds.

This work she had loved, although she knew, as they all knew, that in its baby year the garden would give her very little for her work. If she had stayed with her own people when she married, she would have had a piece of earth familiar to her, but just as young, and the tools she had brought with her from her mother's house were familiar to her, and the work was the same as she had done with her mother. With her baskets she had carried the water up from the river and watered the seeds, and she had even slept up there, stealing out of the longhouse after dark, and sleeping on the ground beside her garden, until the little green shoots pushed up through the soil and opened their leaves to the sun.

Now there was less to do. She would go up there in the afternoon and pull the weeds, take more water to the baby plants, and perhaps work the ground beyond her garden, as if she meant to plant there in the next year. But next year she would work the land her mother worked.

She folded the end of a straw down into the work and picked up another from her pile. The other women were gasping and sighing over a basket made by the fat woman Grela, whom they all believed was the best at making baskets. Shateel had seen many many better baskets among her own people; these people simply did not know what good baskets were. Unaccountably now her eyes were filling with tears.

"Shateel," said one of the women. "Here, girl, look."

Unwillingly, she raised her head. They were all smiling at her, their eyes sharp and bright, probing at her. Waiting for a weakness, to bring her down. One held out Grela's basket.

"Here, girl, see?"

"Yes," she said, making no move to take the basket into her own hands. "It is very fine."

"Here, girl, take it! Take it and look closely. See how tight the work is?"

"Yes," she said, not taking the basket, and she lowered her head and put her gaze back on her own hands and worked.

"See?" They murmured around her, their voices like the flutter of wings. "See? She does not care."

She cared. She loved her own home, her own people. She would go soon back to her own home, and let Ladon's son find another wife.

In the afternoon, Ladon's son went up from the roundhouse toward the longhouse where his wife lived. He brought a fox fur as a present for her. As he went, strutting a little, the people who saw him called out to him, and he raised his hand in answer.

Now that he was married everyone treated him very well. They still called him by his father's name, but Ladon was so mighty a man that perhaps that was only to be expected. He had been accepted into the Bear Skull Society, the most important of all societies, and spent most of each day memorizing the lore and learning his place in the dances and making his mask. When the Midsummer Gathering began, Ladon's son would dance with the men for the first time.

He was making the eyes of his mask out of quartz. He was very proud of it.

It was a long walk now from the roundhouse to the first of the longhouses. In the spring the women had moved all four of the longhouses closer to their gardens, the ground around the roundhouse being exhausted and choked with weeds. Paths wound through these abandoned gardens like braids, winding in and out, and the boys' band hunted mice and picked berries there. The nettles were high, where the ground was damp, and where the ground was drier the spiny burdock and thistles made an impenetrable mass of spikes and thorns. Ladon's son wondered why it was that nothing fit to eat would grow where the weeds grew so rampant.

Now ahead of him the four longhouses stood inside their fence of brush, their doors all facing east; they were narrower at that end than the other, the way trees grew shorter toward the wind.

When the women moved them, they merely detached the mats of straw and rushes from the piers of the walls, lifted off the roof, and carried it all away to the new site, singing loudly to lead the hearth-spirits after them. It had been a fine thing to see, the great thatches travelling off on many little legs toward higher ground.

His father had not thought it such a fine sight. Ladon had grumbled and argued with the women, and even spoken to some of the men about restraining them, but the other men would not consider it. The women grew the food. The men would do nothing that might induce the women to be tight with their produce. Therefore the longhouses went away from the river, up toward the forest, no matter what Ladon wanted.

Ladon was a fool to object, his son thought to himself. It was only a little way farther than before. If Ladon wished, he could give the order to move the roundhouse too, and then all would be together again. His son wondered why Ladon was so reluctant to move.

Maybe because he was getting so fat. Ladon's son giggled, thinking of that. His father had gotten old, somehow, very quickly, in the space of a single year, and while he was still a formidable man, his son was beginning to see the time coming when Ladon would be chief no more.

And then—

Some of the men thought that Karella had weakened Ladon, the old storywoman, with her curses and her charges against him. That was folly; it was Karella who had died.

Around the longhouses, the women bustled and talked and sang, and the children ran naked here and there doing chores and getting in trouble, and many people called out to Ladon's son in greeting. He answered every one of them. Everyone who spoke to him made him feel stronger and more admired. He stopped to see a new baby and spoke to the mother, and she smiled at him, her cheeks suddenly ruddy. He watched a goat being milked and accepted a drink of the fresh frothy food, and that seemed to him to be only his due.

The women loved him. They had always and would always; they would nurture him and coddle him and do as he said, as they did with every man.

Now he went into the longhouse where his wife lived. The holes in the thatch were still open, to let in the afternoon sun, but the air here was cooler than outside and the dim light was smoky with floating dust. Except for a few babies asleep with their mothers, the hearths were empty. He walked the length of the room, his feet loud on the packed earth of the floor.

The place had only stood here for a few months but it was already a midden of disorder. He wondered, as he walked, why the women could not keep their places as clean and neat as the men did. Here were clothes scattered everywhere, hung up everywhere, and pots and baskets lying all over the ground, and ashes from the fires, and pieces of wood, and mats and blankets; how did they know whose belongings these were? He could not remember well how he had lived here as a child. It was better for boys to leave their mothers early, he thought, and take up life among other men to learn order and discipline, before they had to apply these qualities to the work of men, the mastery of lore and the dance. He knew when he had a son he would encourage the boy to leave his mother's hearth as soon as he could run with the boys' band.

However it seemed unlikely that he would have a son soon, since he could not find his wife. She was never here when he came here. He wondered if she were avoiding him.

He stood before her cold hearth and fought his anger. The impulse filled him to scatter the stones of her hearth and pour ashes on the few things of hers that lay around it. Why did she have so little? He brought her something every time he came to her—a fur, a pot, a worked stone to use for a tool. Yet none of these things he had brought were visible to him as he stood looking into her hearth place. What did she do with them?

He knew what she did with most of them. She threw them away. She did not want them. She did not want him.

He looked through narrowed eyes from side to side, to see if anyone witnessed his humiliation. He dropped the fox fur on the cold hearth. Let her throw that away too. Then, thinking again, he stooped and picked it up and dusted the ashes off and went to find her.

He knew where she would be. Leaving the longhouse, he bent his steps higher up the slope, following the rutted paths that led to the women's gardens. A group of young girls was walking up ahead of him, carrying jugs of water on their shoulders; as he caught up with them, being longer of leg and less burdened than they, they stepped aside, laughing, and spoke to him in greeting. He smiled at them. Any one of them would have dropped her jug in her tracks and run after him if he had crooked his finger at her. Then why did Shateel hate him?

When he found her, he asked her that. "Why do you hate me?"

She was sitting beside her garden, eating wild strawberries from a little basket. At first she ignored him. He sank down on his heels, rubbing his hands together; his eyes strayed to the garden beside him. Its irregular shape filled up the space between two old stumps. Her new plants grew neatly in rows that curved to follow the outline of the plot, and at either end her hills of beans were already climbing up the stakes she had set into the ground to support them.

She said, at last, "I do not hate you, husband."

"Then why do you come here, and not stay in the longhouse when you know I am coming to you?"

"I wanted—" she spread out one hand toward her garden. "The deer will eat them, if I do not stay here to protect them."

As she spoke, she raised her face toward him. In her open guileless look he saw that she spoke the truth to him—that these tiny sprigs of green meant more to her than he did.

He sat down beside her and put the fox fur in her lap. "Here," he said. "You could make a lining for a basket out of this."

She smoothed down the lovely red fur. The hide was well tanned and supple as cloth. Suddenly she lifted it to her cheek and pressed her face to the softness.

"You could line a basket," he said, and put his hand on her thigh. "To put a baby in."

At that she sighed so deeply that he expected her to fall to weeping, but instead she turned to him, earnest and open, and said, "Husband, I do not hate you. It is nothing of your doing that makes me unhappy."

"Unhappy!" Startled, he stared into her face while his hand stroked her thigh. "Are you unhappy, Shateel?"

"I want to go back to my own people," she said.

"I—"

He stopped. He had been ready to leap forward, like a deer, to jump straight ahead thoughtlessly into telling her that they would go together to her people. That was the usual way, for a man to go to live with his wife's people. There was a Bear Skull Society among her people, and that was the life of a man—his lore, his dances, his society, and his chief. But now suddenly Ladon's son realized that if he went with her, he might not be here—would be most unlikely to be here—when Ladon died. And when Ladon died, the new chief would be chosen, and if he were not here—

"Don't be a fool," he said. His hand on her thigh reached up and up, across the tender skin, up to her secret place. "Don't be a fool," he said, and pressed her down backwards onto the ground.

"No," she said, muffled, but she did not try to hold him off.

"It will make your plants grow," he said and pulled her garments away and possessed her there on the grass. She spread open her legs for him, and put one arm around him, and seemed to want him, but all through it she held the fox fur against her cheek and she shut her eyes.

When the People all came together at the Turnings-of-the-Year, Shateel went to the nearby village of her brother, Rulon. She found her mother with the other women, sitting in the yard of their longhouses with their weaving and baskets. This was all much the same as it had been when she left this place to go off with her new husband; every face she saw was a face known since her babyhood.

It was so familiar to Shateel that she was half in tears when she reached her mother.

She came to her mother Joba with her arms out, expecting to be gathered in, and so she was; her mother took her well into her arms, and they pressed their cheeks together and wept a little together. But then her mother stepped back.

"Well, how do you do, my girl?" Joba patted Shateel's front. "No basket-belly yet, hah? Is Ladon's son so green he cannot make the sap run?"

Shateel blushed, embarrassed by this frank talk. Around her the other women—her aunts and cousins—raised their heads and laughed at her.

"Mother," she said, and her tongue caught. In the midst of so many listeners she could not speak properly, and she took her mother by the hand. "Come walk with me a little."

At that her mother's round glowing face lost its merriment. Her dark brows drew together over her nose, and her eyes glittered; Shateel had always feared this look in her mother. Nor did the older woman take the hand offered to her, but said only, "Walk, then, Shateel."

They went off a little way, across the yard to the gate in the fence.

Outside, they stopped. Before them lay the broad grassy stretch of ground where the People met for the Gathering; all was now covered with hearths and mats, men and women and children, dogs and goats, full of noise and bustle. Shateel led her mother away, around the outside of the brush fence, toward the embankment that surrounded the Turnings-of-the-Year.

Shateel lowered her head. She dared not look at her mother. The words came from her in a rush.

"I cannot bear it, Ana. I want to come home. I hate being among Ladon's people."

"Oh?" said her mother coldly.

"Everything there is different from here. They tease me and mock me—they say I do everything wrong—"

"Is Ladon's son cold or cruel to you?"

She watched her feet crush the grass down, wishing she could say that he was. Her mother would give her no help. The silence grew and grew, until at last she had to speak.

"No. He is kind. He is very good to me, he brings me presents often and gives me all I need. He is a good husband."

"All you need but a baby."

"Mother, I do not want a baby. I want to come home, and be with you again."

As she spoke she raised her eyes, hoping to find some smile there on her mother's face, some warmth and welcoming kindness, but Joba's face was harsh as a weathered stone. The older woman stopped still in the grass. She put her hands heavy on her daughter's shoulders and held her fast.

"Listen to me, Shateel. You are only a girl yet, and soft, and weak. You have gone off to be with your husband in a strange place, against my wishes, as you remember, and instead of growing up and becoming a woman, with a woman's work and a woman's pride, you meet your troubles by weeping and trying to run away. No. I will not allow you to come home to me, although once, as you remember, I begged you not to go. No. Stay with Ladon's son. Work your garden, raise your crops, make babies, keep your head up, and smile at the other women. When they tell you you are wrong, listen to them! Perhaps they are right."

At that, without any more, not even an embrace or a smile, Joba walked away, turning back toward the village. Shateel stood tear-ridden in the place where her mother had left her. For months the

girl had thought of nothing but coming here; she had soothed every
hurt and every loneliness with the promise of her mother's love. Now
she watched the older woman walk away, her great shapeless body
bundled in clothes the color of the dirt she tilled, her walk like the
rolling of a great stone over the grass. A surge of hatred rose
through her body. All her life she had depended on her mother and
now Joba had abandoned her. She sat down in the grass, determined
never to go back to any of them, ever again.

Shateel's mother went away fretful and did not go to her own fire,
but away to the hearths of Ladon's people.

There she found the old women sitting on their mats by the
hearth, passing around a newborn baby and oohing and aahing over
it. In their midst, the new mother glowed under their praises. When
Joba appeared, the women all looked up, and seeing it was she, they
all sighed.

"Well, Joba, sit down and tell us your troubles."

They made room for her in their midst, and the baby was returned to its mother and borne swiftly away.

Joba took her place beside Tishka and Grela and folded her legs
under her, rocking her bulk into comfort. She laid her hands on her
lap and stared into the little fire, its flames all but invisible in the
strong sunlight, and she shook her head.

"There is no joy in mothering a daughter," she said.

Beside her, Tishka grunted, patted Joba's arm, and said nothing.
On her other side, Grela said, "You should have brought that girl up
to respect her elders."

Some of the others murmured agreement. Joba kept her teeth
together; she saw no hope in fiery words and wounded pride. She
watched the fire springing up from its bed of twigs.

Now Tishka spoke, in a quiet grave voice. "She is just lonely and
hearthsick, Joba. We have tried to be kind, but she takes it all for ill
will."

Across the way, old Thyrella cackled. "It is the fault of Ladon's
son. If he would fill the pot—" she laughed and patted her own bulging belly, lumpy with age.

Grela said, "Maybe if they came to live with you, Joba, things
would work out better between them."

Joba sighed. She thought much of this was true, and yet it was small truth, having no power to shape the world. She said, "Would that Karella were here. She would have some story now, to comfort us, and make us see what will come of this matter."

Grela said, "Truly, since Karella died I have heard no stories. No one tells them as she did. She gave her craft to no one."

"No one except Moloquin," said Tishka.

These words fell on a silence that startled Joba; she raised her gaze from the fire and looked around her, seeing in the faces of these women some deep misgiving, some dread, beyond her knowing. Even fat Grela, who babbled constantly, said nothing; she sat with one leg extended, her weaving looped over her big toe to keep the work straight, and as the silence stretched on, Grela's weaving grew longer and longer. Joba suddenly shuddered all over. In that bit of weaving she thought she saw the fate of the world worked together.

She raised her voice, defending herself with words of her own power. "I spoke with my wicked daughter harshly, and have told her she cannot come home to me. So you may expect to find her walking back to your own village. Tell me, though, tell me how things fare with you."

They talked about the crops, the wet weather of the spring, and the moving of the longhouses.

"Did Ladon move his roundhouse?" Joba asked.

At that even Tishka laughed, and Grela clapped her thighs in amusement. "Oh, no. Do you think great Ladon would tag after a pack of mere women?"

At that they gave up a great roar of laughter. Beside Joba, Tishka sat with her head down, picking a burr from her skirt.

"He will travel farther yet, if he will not yield his pride."

They laughed again, nudging one another. The name Karella arose again in their speech; Karella, whom they had all envied and mistrusted in life, sounded in their speech now like a beloved talisman, their champion against Ladon. Joba heard all this with a growing unease. Early in her lifetime, she had seen her whole village moved; it was a devastating thing, when the people lifted up their roofs on their shoulders and walked away. Yet it was necessary, if the ground were turning sour. She saw much trouble for Ladon in this, if the women of his village had already moved their longhouses. If he moved as they bid him, he lost his supremacy, but if he stayed where he was, very soon he and the men would have no women, and the women in their longhouses would have no men. She began to wonder if she ought not to let her daughter come home after all.

Grela's fingers flew back and forth across her work, forming a pattern of birds. Opposite, old Thyrella watched as well, and her fingers worked in her lap, her knuckles swollen with arthritis. Joba said, "Well, if need be, you can come to us—our gardens are thriving. I have some seed—"

She took a pouch from her belt and gave it to Tishka. They spoke of the necessity of keeping bean plants staked up and well drained, and shared herb lore. Joba stretched herself, enjoying the genial conversation. The thought flitted through her mind that if many of Ladon's People did leave him, going off on their own, then not Ladon but her own son Rulon would be the greatest of the chiefs.

Grela looked up, past her, catching sight of something in the distance. Her gaze dropped again, and she turned across Joba toward Tishka. "Tell me how you would bind this off, Ana." She started to hand the woven work to her mother, but suddenly her head whipped around again, she stared away again, and her mouth fell open.

"Oh. Oh, what I see I do not believe." She scrambled up onto her feet, shading her eyes with her hand, and her weaving dropped unnoticed into the dust.

All the women twisted to look where she was looking, even old Thyrella. At first Joba made out nothing unusual; they were staring across the bustle and hurry of the camp, toward the west. The children were running and tumbling in the grass, the women bent over their fires to cook, or walked up with loads of wood, or milked goats; in the whole wild tumble Joba saw nothing to remark on, nothing—

Save the three people coming straight toward them down the far slope, a tall man, naked but for a loincloth, and a shorter man in a shirt, and a pregnant woman, coming last.

They were all strangers to Joba. But Grela remained on her feet, and now Tishka, too, was laboring to rise.

One of the other women said, evenly, "Yes. Yes, it is Moloquin."

"Moloquin," said Joba blankly. The name struck no spark of recollection from her memory. She looked again toward the three people walking up to them, and behind her, Grela spoke.

"Yes, Moloquin. It is Moloquin, Karella's son. Ael's son. Moloquin."

And now Joba did understand. She gathered her limbs in against her body and kept still.

He walked into their midst and squatted down by the fire and put out his hands over it, and his black eyes went from one woman to the next, with no respect, no reverence at all. He was so tall he looked thin but his body was laid over with smooth well-shaped muscle, his arms bulging hard between elbow and shoulder, and his neck fit down into a great roll of muscle like a cap across his shoulders. His hair was black and shaggy. In his belt he carried some tool, wrapped in deerskin, but he wore no ornaments at all. He was the barest man Joba had ever seen.

He said, "I want my mother. Where is Karella?"

Grela was still on her feet. In a low voice, she said, "Moloquin, we thought you were dead. Better for you at this moment perhaps that you were dead. Karella lives no more."

His mouth fell open a little. His eyes changed. Bright and hard before, now they glazed over, brighter yet, no longer hard.

He said, "What happened to her?"

"She died of the fevers." Grela now looked from one woman to the next, and faced him again. "Come with me, I shall tell it all to you, but we shall not inflict this again on these others, who loved Karella as well as you did."

"Never," he said, and his voice caught. "Never."

Grela walked away from the fire. "Come with me." She held out her hand to him, and his head swivelled, following her path, but he did not rise, not at once. She went on nonetheless, with measured steps, moving away from him, her arm still reaching back toward him and her head bowed down.

He turned to the two who had come with him. "Stay here," he said, and he got up all in a rush and hurried after Grela.

The two he left behind hesitated a moment. The man smiled diffidently at the women, and with several gestures of deference and respect he lowered himself down where Moloquin had been. The other women shifted away from him, and he called over to the strange woman and spoke to her in some outlandish gibberish, and she sat down close beside him. They all stared into the fire.

· · ·

Grela told Moloquin how Karella had died—how she had fought against Ladon with her stories, and how the fever took her away.

"Then we took her up to the Pillar of the Sky," Grela said. "When the crows had picked away her flesh, and freed her spirit, we put her bones into the tomb."

She stopped to face him. They had walked down by the stream, to be away from all the others. She had expected him to burst forth in grief, and had wanted some solitude to protect his dignity, but he said nothing. He looked down at her, much taller than she remembered, a man now, and one whose mere look made her hair stand on end.

He said, "Ladon killed her."

"Moloquin. Everyone must die. Not every death is someone's fault. In truth, though, when she thought you were dead, she lost her interest in living on."

"Oh. Oh—"

Now he seemed to mourn; he groaned, and his head swayed from side to side. His fists rose between them, and he thumped his thighs with them, and beat his chest. She put out her hand and pushed his hands gently to his side again. Where had he been? Time enough to learn that.

"Ladon killed her," he said.

"You should not have gone off and left her."

His gaze swung around toward her again. Hard again. The tears that had blurred his eyes now trickled down his cheeks.

"Ladon sold me. Sold me to the trader Harus Kum. Sold me to haul a sledge and pound rocks."

"Ah."

She glanced back over her shoulder, back toward the Gathering.

"Did you help her?" Moloquin asked. His voice was raw. "Did you sit with her, and confront Ladon over it? Did you do anything but watch? The lot of you! Did you do anything but stand and watch her die? Or was it as it was when he drove my mother Ael into the forest, and you stood and watched?"

"Moloquin," she said, startled; she had not thought of it before in this way.

"Where is Ladon now?" he said.

"He is—" seeing the risk in this, she paused, her eyes on him pensive. She wondered what Ladon would do against Moloquin.

"Where is he?"

"By the Turnings-of-the-Year," she said. "With the other chiefs."
Fergolin was there also, her husband, and all the other men. Surely
Moloquin would not challenge the whole manhood of the People.

For a moment he stood there looking down on her, and she wondered again what had happened to him. His hand went to his belt, to
the tool, wrapped in hide, whose ashwood handle jutted down past
his hip. Turning on his heel, he walked off, going back toward the
fire where he had left his companions.

Grela followed him at a little distance, unwilling to speak to him
any further. There was something unsettling about him, but there
had always been. He was different, alien, perhaps evil. He reached
the fire ahead of her and led his companions away, toward the embankment of the Turnings-of-the-Year. Grela went in among the
other women.

"Come quickly," she said.

"Where?" The younger and more spry among them were already getting to their feet.

"Moloquin is going to find Ladon," Grela said. "Come on, we
have to see what happens."

Now they were all hurrying. She walked away through the camp,
calling to the others.

Fergolin was standing inside the smaller of the rings of stones, surrounded in turn by a ring of boys: the novices of the Bear Skull. The
sun would not set for a long while yet, but he wanted these boys to
be ready when it did.

He said, "During the spring and fall, the sun's point of rising
and setting moves very quickly and obviously along the horizon.
But as Midsummer's Day approaches, that day on which she rises
and sets most to the north, the point of rising and setting moves
very slightly. It is very difficult to discern the difference from day to
day."

The boys were looking half-asleep. In the back, one nudged his
neighbor, and there were giggles. Fergolin ignored these.

"Therefore it is often necessary to count the days after the sun
passes a certain point until she returns again. Then take half that
number, to find the exact day of Midsummer."

He stopped. They were not listening to him; they were looking away, past him, straining to see. He turned.

A man was striding down the embankment from the direction of the women's camp—a tall, black-haired man who walked with the springy step of a hunter. In one hand he carried something wrapped in hide. Fergolin lost his breath. He blinked to clear his eyes, startled and amazed.

It was Moloquin. Or once he had been Moloquin, this man.

"What is it, master?" one of the boys said, and another said, "Who is that man?"

Fergolin ignored them. He leapt up onto his feet as Moloquin went past him, and as Moloquin went by, he pulled the deer hide cover from the tool he held in his hand, and like the sun coming out from behind a cloud, the massy red-gold head of the axe shone forth.

Fergolin saw where Moloquin was going. He followed after, keeping his distance, going toward the place at the far end of the larger of the rings, where Ladon and the other chiefs were sitting on the platform. After him the novices rushed, and from all sides others came to swell the crowd, all following after Moloquin.

Ladon was sitting on a great rug of hides stitched together, with the other chiefs around him. Their men hurried back and forth bringing them drink and food and sometimes just offering deference and respect, to give honor and receive it. Rulon sat there boasting of the industry of his women, who were raising up the greatest harvest ever grown in the whole world; two of the other men were tossing a pair of knucklebones, and the oldest of the chiefs had fallen asleep.

In truth Ladon had no wish to speak to any of them. He was pleased with himself.

Rulon had not challenged him this year. When the chiefs came to the Turnings-of-the-Year, all had given way to Ladon. All had cried his name aloud from the first moment; he was greatest of them all, and all accepted that.

He fingered the beads around his neck, the outward signs of his power, and smiled. Harus Kum had not arrived at the Gathering. If he never came again, then no one else would ever have these beads, or the wonderful anklets and bracelets and belt that Ladon also wore:

no one would ever attain such a power as he. And when he died, he would give these emblems to his son, and no one would stand against his son either.

He had achieved his greatest purpose. He sat on the platform, a man fulfilled in all things, greatest chief of his People, and the little problem of the village was nothing but the shadow of a bird's wing across the full radiant glory of the sun.

He had tried to keep the women from moving their longhouses, but they had not obeyed him. Maybe now they would listen, when they saw how great he was, or he could perhaps force them to bring the longhouses back where they belonged. He had no intention of moving his roundhouse.

He had never moved a village. His uncle had brought the People to their present place by the river when Ladon himself had been only a little boy named Twig, playing with a chestnut in the dust of the yard. He remembered nothing but the excitement of packing up, and the tiresome long walk to the new place.

He meant to stay where he was. His roundhouse was among the oldest of all the People's places, and all the while he had lived there he had done well. If he moved, then he opened himself to unpredictable dangers—the malice of spirits, the possibility of choosing an unlucky site. The women had cleared new gardens higher on the slope above the river, and although the extra work meant they had planted late, yet he had watched carefully to see that every ritual was properly performed, and the seed had all sprouted well.

His storerooms were nearly empty. He had given all his stores to Harus Kum, when the trader brought him the magic ornaments he wore now, the emblems of his power, and the last harvest that had not been good. That was another reason to be glad that Harus Kum was not here, because Ladon had nothing to give to him.

This year's harvest would fill up the storerooms again; he would be rich again, and no one would know how many of the baskets now were empty, how many of the jugs held only water.

"Ladon!" someone shouted.

He ignored that. People were always calling his name. He turned his mind to thoughts of Karella, whom he meant to revenge himself upon, now that his power was secure.

Her bones were laid in the round tomb east of the village. If he took them out and scattered them, then in little pieces would Karella walk around the Overworld, a mock for every other spirit.

"Ladon! Ladon!"

He raised his head, annoyed; his name should now be wreathed in compliments and expressions of respect, not offered bare as an old bone to the world. The press of the bodies around the platform loosened, and the level of noise dropped. Someone was coming toward him.

All around him people fell silent. Rulon left off his boasting, and the other men put aside their knucklebones. Ladon frowned. Before him, the crowd was pushing back to either side, leaving a long open space like an avenue, and at the far end of it stood someone tall and shaggy like an animal.

"Moloquin," Ladon said, and all through his body the nerves jumped and quivered.

"Ladon," Moloquin cried, and strode up toward him, and Ladon sat slumped on the platform and watched him come. With a lurch in his guts, he saw that all the bank around the standing stones was black with people watching. The whole of the People had come to witness this.

"Ladon," his sister's son cried again. "You killed my mother, Ladon, twice over. You are old and evil and powerless and doomed."

At that he raised his arm, and from all the watching crowd there went up a yell of amazement. In his hand Moloquin held a great axe, and the head was all of shining, magic stuff, like the matter of the sun.

"So," Ladon said, in a steady voice. "You have borrowed some stick of Harus Kum's and come to get your revenge, hah, Moloquin?"

"Revenge."

Moloquin lifted the axe and swung it, and the head whistled in the air. It struck the platform's edge and broke the wood down before it with a crunch. The chiefs yelled. Undignified as boys, they sprang down from the platform to the ground, leaving Ladon alone there.

"I need take no revenge on you, Ladon," Moloquin cried, and he raised up his axe again and with another great stroke he hewed at the center post supporting the platform. "Your doom is inevitable. You and everyone who stays with you—"

He struck the post again, and the wood gave way. The platform sagged. Ladon flung his arms out, determined not to be thrown down.

"Old and wicked and doomed!" Moloquin shouted. "The best of

you died when my mother Karella died! I, Moloquin, who made this—"

He turned in a circle, his arm uplifted, the axe extended high over his head into the blazing sunlight.

"I, Moloquin, have come to damn you all!"

He whirled around again and struck the post again, and the post broke entirely in half. The platform collapsed. Ladon slid forward, scrabbling with his hands for some hold to stop his fall, and he went down into the dust at Moloquin's feet.

He looked up, dazed and terrified. Above him the tall young man stood with his wonderful axe, and Ladon put up his hand to shield himself. Moloquin raised the axe above his head.

The crowd hushed. No one moved. No one came to help Ladon. As they had watched and waited while Karella died, so they watched and waited now for Ladon to die.

Moloquin lowered the axe. He said, "Live on, old man, as my gift."

Then he stepped by Ladon, and with the great axe he hewed down the platform of the chiefs, and left it a pile of rubble on the ground. In the middle of it, he turned.

"Now I will go and make my own village, where men and women can live in justice and honor. Any who wishes for life as it should be may come with me now, and the rest of you—"

He spat on Ladon, cowering at his feet.

"The rest of you can rot with Ladon!"

He spun around again, and again he struck with his axe at the pile of wood. Then he strode away, straight to the east, and those in his path stepped hurriedly out of his way. Behind him, unnoticed until now, went another man, and a woman well along with child. They walked away between two standing stones, away to the east.

Now from all over the crowd others broke free of the mass and plunged away after Moloquin. Not many: two or three at first, and then a few more, and then, to Ladon's surprise, old Brant, the Green Bough master. Then for a while, no one. In a dead silence the People stood and watched as Moloquin climbed the bank and went over the top and disappeared, and after him the little train of his followers, one by one, vanished also to the east.

Then: "Wait! Wait!"

From the pack of women on the bank one girl burst free. She

ran down through the stones, still calling after Moloquin to wait, and behind Ladon his own son gasped and started forward.

Ladon whirled and raised one hand, and the other men seized his son and held him fast.

"Shateel," cried his son. "Shateel—"

But she was gone, running up and over the bank, vanishing after Moloquin.

Moloquin walked a long way from the Turnings-of-the-Year before he turned and looked back. What he saw then surprised him, and he faced forward again and walked faster.

A whole band of people were following him, not merely Hems and Ap Min, but Brant, the Old Green Bough master, and some women, one with little children, and two young men. They were following him away from their hearths and their chiefs, and they would expect him to be their chief now; whenever they had need, they would come to him.

He had not intended this to happen when he spoke his proud words before Ladon. The words had come unbidden to his lips, as if some other spoke with his mouth.

Ael had spoken through him. Ael and Karella had used him to achieve their revenge, and now—

He walked at his best long-striding pace, as if he might leave them behind, and he went down over the Dead River, the deep-cleft valley, and found a twisting way up the scarp on the far side. Still all the people followed after him. At last in the evening, as the sun was going down, there ahead of him on the plain appeared, like a ring of teeth, the Pillar of the Sky.

When he saw it his heart leapt within his breast, and he broke into a run. He forgot the people coming after him and ran up the long slope, slippery with grass. A flock of bustards lumbered heavily out of his path. The crows fluttered up in a thick black cloud into the air. He ran over the embankment and walked down into his sacred place.

Entering it was like going back into his youth, back to the first time he had come here, when Ael had brought him here. She had leaned on him, coughing and falling, the blood running down her chin when she coughed; she had been so thin and frail—most of her body had already died—that at the end he had been able to lift her up and carry her in among the stones.

He stood in the middle of the circle and turned slowly around once. The wind bent the long grass down, sighing and whispering, and blew around the sad circle of collapsing stones, and over by the two taller stones that marked the northern edge a few fat crows settled down hungrily toward a half-picked body.

Here Karella had lain, at the last.

He knew she was here yet. He could feel her presence here, and Ael's presence, and if they remained, here where their bodies had dissolved, then all the rest remained also, all the generations of the People, incorporeal in their house of wind. Had he failed them already, when he led their children out of the safety of the villages?

He dropped to his knees, laying his axe down before him. The head was bent and battered from its work at Ladon's platform. They all thought it was wonderful, but he knew what it was, a man-made thing, and a failure. He put his face down into the grass, and from the great soreness and fear in his heart he spoke to Karella and Ael.

"Help me. Help me. Don't leave me. Help me, Mother."

His words did not rise unheard into the air. He knew that they heard him, and so he spoke in a rush of voice, asking them for help, telling them where he had been, and what Ladon had done to him, and why he had spoken as he had at the Turnings-of-the-Year. They had required it of him. He had felt some other being speak through him, when he defied Ladon. It had not been Moloquin's own doing, but he had been the tool of some other, and now he called to the other to help him.

The people who had followed Moloquin from the Turnings-of-the-Year watched him now from the bank of the Pillar of the Sky. Some of them had never been there before. Others were afraid of the place and picked grass to make charms against its power. The two children had fallen asleep in the shelter of their mother's body as she sat on the bank; an older woman drew closer and slid her arm around them, to share the warmth of her body.

Behind Shateel someone said, "What is he doing?"

Shateel hugged her arms together. She wished she had brought a blanket, now that the sun was gone down.

In the little silence after the question nobody said much, or even moved. Then Brant, oldest of them, shifted his feet and raised his head and looked around.

"He is speaking with the Old Ones. Now, listen to me: if any of you would go back, you must do it at once, because we shall make a camp, and whosoever sleeps in this camp tonight shall be Moloquin's forever."

Shateel did not like that; she was no man's, not now. But she was cold. She went off with the other women to find wood to make a fire. She had not been friends with either of the women before, but now they all kept close together and spoke like sisters to one another.

"What shall we eat?"

"I have some grain," said Wahela, the young mother. "I was grinding meal when the call came to me, and I took it all up. It is there in my basket."

She pointed behind them, up to where the embankment crowned the long slow slope. There the rest of their new people were gathered in the deepening twilight.

"There is no wood here," Shateel said. "We should go on, that way—" she pointed away to the east, where the forest began.

"We shall wait until the chief—until Moloquin tells us to go."

"Come this way," said the older woman, whose name was Taella. Her long hair was streaked with grey, and she had it in long braids that hung down over her shoulders. When she pointed, the braid slid over her arm. "There is a little stream over there, and I know there is brush and a few trees by it."

The three women set off together. The stars were coming out, but the wind that climbed the slope to meet them was damp and warm, and Shateel guessed that rain was coming. She thought of the warmth of her own hearth, the shelter of her longhouse, and thought, What a fool I am. Why did I come here?

"Why did you come?" she asked Wahela, walking on her left.

The other woman hugged her arms around herself as she walked. Her eyes searched the land around them for wood. "I don't know. I heard Moloquin's voice, and something told me to go with him, so I did."

She laughed at that, gay as a child.

Dissatisfied, Shateel turned from this explanation and spoke to Taella. "Why did you come?"

Taella brushed back her thick braids. She walked on several steps before she spoke. At last her voice came, heavier than Wahela's.

"Ladon is unlucky. Many things have happened since Karella died, all of them unlucky for Ladon, and not the least of it is that Moloquin came back. That is a sign, somehow, that he came back. Whatever luck there is, it goes with him."

"You think—"

"I think nothing," said Taella sharply. "It is the place of the chief to make decisions and do the thinking. There is the stream."

Ahead of them the land buckled into a deep crease, where a little water ran, no deeper than a finger's breadth. All around out, protected from the wind, grew brush and stunted trees. The women went into these thickets and collected dry twigs to start the fire and looked for bigger branches to keep it going. When they had all they could forage, they piled it up on the dry slope and Taella shook her head.

"Not enough."

They left their gatherings where they had piled them and went on, walking eastward. Shateel was tired, her legs sore from long walking. She was too tired to think much. Suddenly she had the feeling of floating along through the air, her legs aimlessly milling, while around her the wind was full of voices. She could not make out the words, but the voices comforted her. She knew she was cared for. She followed Taella over the crest of another low hill.

"There!"

Ahead of them, off to the east a little, was a tall old elm tree, all alone on the open plain. The three women hurried toward it; as they approached it, a host of small birds fluttered like a gust of wind out of the branches. Out of the company of other trees, the elm was dying; many of the higher branches rose up naked and skinned of their bark among the scattered leaves of the summer's growth. There was dry wood all over the ground around it. They gathered it all up, more than they could carry, and then in a little train they carried it: two of the women hauled the wood between them while the third rested. In this way, bearing more weight than they were able, they made their way back to the Pillar of the Sky.

Moloquin woke up in the dawn. He had slept all night in the shelter of the North Watcher. As soon as he woke he was stabbed with a sense of guilt. He got to his feet and looked around him.

Inside the embankment the grass stirred in the wind; the fat black crows lumbered around at the far end, and one flew up to sit on top of a stone and watch him. The first drops of rain touched his face and his hands, borne along on the breast of the wind like a scattering of seeds. He saw no sign of the people who had followed him from Ladon's camp.

He was relieved at that. He hoped they had all gone back to the People.

Picking up his axe, he put it into his belt and walked across the circle, going between two slowly falling stones, and climbed the bank. There they were, huddled together on the lee slope, and his heart sank to see them, unsheltered and unfed, waiting for him to do something.

Yet as he stood there watching them, he saw that the women were building a fire. Already the bright flames crackled in the midst of a heap of tinder, and another pile of wood waited beside it. He watched a while longer, seeing how they had made a camp here, spread out their few blankets and put their baskets around, rolled the high grass back into a little fence; somehow they had gotten some food, and were sharing it among them; he saw how the children had crept into the laps of the men for warmth and shelter from the wind, and how the men protected them with arms and curved backs, and his spirit bounded upward like the flames. He was not alone in this. The women would make their homes, whether under his leadership or Ladon's or Rulon's or any man's; they would lay out their hearths wherever they were. He could depend on the women. He went down among them to the warmth of the fire.

The rain fell all day long. Moloquin led his People away to the east, toward the forest.

When they came to the edge of the trees, his People faltered, and wanted to go back; they were afraid of the forest. Moloquin went on ahead of them, thinking they would follow him, but when he looked back, they were still standing in the open, in the late sunlight, watching him leave them. He broke into a run into the forest.

He had never understood why the People were so frightened of the woods. His baby-memories were of climbing trees and stealing eggs from the nests of birds. Now he ran through the forest, shouting and laughing, jumping over the brambles and stroking the great trees as he passed. His steps drew him even deeper into the woods. The oaks towered up over him, enormous placid beings, their branches chuckling and rasping in the light wind. Walking along at their feet, he felt safe again.

His People waited for him at the edge of the forest. His People would not come after him into his home.

Disconsolate and angry, he roamed through the woods for a while, thinking that he would leave them where they were. If they had no heart for it, let them go back to Ladon. But he could not draw his mind from them; he knew they were hungry, and they had left their homes for his sake, because of words he had spoken. So he went here and there, gathering nuts and berries, catching a turtle and a few lizards and a snake, and carried them back through the woods in a bowl of bark.

When he came out of the forest, they were still there. They had made another camp and sat huddled around it. When he appeared, they greeted him with dark looks, but he went in among them and spread out the tidbits he had found, and their faces opened with delight and gratitude. They cooked the turtle in its shell, and skinned the lizards and snakes; the children ate the berries, smearing their faces red.

He said, "You must not be afraid of the forest. Until we can plant, there is more to eat in the woods than on the plain, and the trees will shelter us."

"They are full of demons," said one of the two strange men who had followed him from the Gathering. "I can hear them talking even from here."

Even as he spoke, the wind rose, bringing to their ears the murmurs and cries of the forest. Moloquin said, "What is your name?"

"Bohodon, of the Salmon Leap Society."

"There are no societies here," Moloquin said. He looked at Brant, silent on the far side of the fire, and turned to Bohodon again. "What is your lore?"

Bohodon was a short, square-set young man with the beginnings of a scruffy black beard. His eyes were full of mistrust. He did not answer Moloquin's question until the stirrings and mutterings of the other People, and their harsh looks at him, forced him to open his mouth.

"I do not have much of the lore. I learned a little of stonecraft. I—"

His dark mistrustful look changed; suddenly he seemed much younger, a mere boy, and he dropped his gaze.

"I did not like it. That was why I left. I did not belong in the Red Salmon."

Brant said, mildly, "What of your mask?"

"I cut no mask," the youth muttered, and raised his face again, red to the ears. "I—I—I failed. The tree refused me. I could not cut on it. My tools broke."

Moloquin kept silent; he thought, All who could not do with Ladon and the other chiefs have come to me. All the failures. He turned away from Bohodon.

The third of the men among his new followers was watching him expectantly. Moloquin said, "Who are you?"

"My name is Kayon."

This was a youth of Bohodon's age, with rough brown hair. Moloquin said, "Did you belong to a society?"

"None would accept me."

Moloquin stared at him a moment, striving with his temper. He had called these people; he deserved what came to him. Again his gaze slipped sideways, toward Brant. Among Ladon's People, he knew, Brant was considered a dull fool, and yet Moloquin knew differently.

His attention shifted to all the men. There was Hems, who was no oak tree among men, but he did well enough. Maybe these other two would prove different from their first impressions. But he had no faith in that; they looked like lumps of earth to him. He sighed.

"I mean to go into the forest. I grew up there, and I know of a place—a good way from here, two days' walk with the children— where we will find a good place to live. There is water, wood, food, a place to plant. I am going there. Any who wishes may follow me."

Bohodon looked over his shoulder into the forest; Kayon drew his knees up to his chest and wrapped his arms around them. The old woman Taella leaned forward to look into Kayon's face.

"Do not be a silly boy. Falter, and you will fail again. Take heart, go forward, and perhaps you will find your way in life." She turned toward Moloquin. "I will go with you. I am only an old woman, but I have two hands to help and two feet to carry me and lore enough to make a new village."

Beside her, the two young women nodded together. "We shall go also."

The two little children sat nearest the fire, and the little boy, whose face was all sticky with the juice of the berries, said, "I shall go too, Moloquin."

Moloquin laughed. "Well, then I am happily followed." He glanced again at Bohodon and Kayon, thinking, If these two should give up, none will think it anything but the course of their lives, and he shrugged, as if some burden lightened on his shoulders. He got up, and with the help of the others he set some branches into the earth, to make a sort of shelter. There they slept the night, and in the morning they went on, into the forest.

They walked in a long line, Moloquin first, going a little way ahead to find the trail. He tried at first to mark the path with his axe, but its work against Ladon had destroyed its power, and instead he used bent twigs and small rocks. The People came willingly enough where he led them.

As he walked, he found things for them to eat—some lily bulbs, a few hazelnuts—and left them on the path for them who came after. They were travelling through stands of pine, drying marshes, and occasional patches of oak where the ground was crunchy with acorn mast. The rain was still coming down, and made a sort of music in the branches of the trees. He could hear the People exclaiming now and then, when they saw or heard something that alarmed them, but as the day wore on, their fears lessened, and they paid less attention to the quiverings and outcries of the forest. They learned quickly to recognize the food that Moloquin found, and to forage for themselves as they walked along. The children ran ahead at first, full of vigor, but in the afternoon they tired and the men took turns in carrying them on their backs.

In the evening, they stopped in a grove of old trees and made a shelter of branches and brush, and there they slept the night. Their makeshift dwelling did not keep the rain out, and by the coming of the sun they were all wet, downcast and very hungry, and there was no food. The children cried for food but there was nothing to give them. Moloquin led them off again, on through the woods, and they followed after, gnawing on sticks now, scrambling uselessly after squirrels, overturning logs for the grubs and snails. The rain dripped down steadily; they trudged dispirited through the mud and the brambles after Moloquin, deeper into the forest.

. . .

In the late morning they found a nut tree and the women gathered nuts in Wahela's basket. Shateel piled them up also in a tuck of her skirt. When they set off again, she ate as she walked, straining her legs to keep up with Moloquin.

She tried not to think about her home, her mother, the husband she had left, or her garden in Ladon's Village. The garden especially hurt her to remember, the tender green, the opening buds, which now the deer alone would eat, while her belly cramped and the children whined from hunger.

Did Moloquin know where he was going? Ahead of her was his straight, bare back, deeply grooved down the spine, leading her away from everything she had ever known. The forest oppressed her. Pressed thick and close around her, the trees obstructed her view; how could they find anything, if they could not see far? Once, pausing to drink at a little stream, she made a mark on a stone, pointing the way back the way they had come, in case she had to find her way home again by herself.

In the late afternoon they climbed up a steep slope and around through a stand of pines, and walking down an old deer trail they came into a ghost forest.

At the sight of the dead trees, white and gaunt in the midst of the exuberant summer foliage, all the women wailed. The grove covered the whole foot of the hillside; the grass and brush had grown up high as Shateel's waist in the sunlight. As they reached the edge of this meadow two red deer bounded away toward the living forest, crashing through the undergrowth.

The men chased them, shouting. Moloquin did not. Moloquin went into the grove of dead trees, went from one tree to the next, putting his hands on them, as if he knew them.

Shateel drifted nearer to him, wondering what he was doing. He was a strange man and she was a little afraid of him, certainly unwilling to talk to him, and now he was behaving very strangely, pawing the trees, leaning against them, and now, suddenly, giving off a yell that raised the hair on the back of her neck.

He ran up through the grove again, back toward his People, and now he brandished something at arm's length over his head. "I found it! She left it here—it was here all the time—"

Shateel looked at the two women beside her and found them

looking at her, wary of this madman. He ran into their midst and held out his hands. He held a stone axehead, crudely made. Shateel had seen axes as beautiful as flowers, the work of masters of stone-craft; whoever had made this axe had known very little of the work. Moloquin raised it to his lips suddenly and kissed it.

"The hut is here somewhere," he said, his voice trembling with intensity, and he whirled and ran off, down the slope, in among the dead trees.

Taella murmured, "This is very strange."

"He is mad," Shateel said. "Why did we come? He is mad, we shall all die here—"

Suddenly she felt herself suffocating in the forest, the dense growth all around her smothering her, stopping up the breath in her throat. Taella struck her firmly on the arm.

"Keep your wits, girl. This is not like other villages, no one here will take up your burdens if you let them fall." Throwing back her long grey braids, she started away down the slope after Moloquin.

Shateel struggled for breath. The others were passing her, going in a ragged file after their leader. She tamed herself. She had come along, after all, through her own choice; she had no one to blame but herself if things went ill for her. Abruptly she took some oblique pleasure from that, some reassurance. She followed the others down toward the low ground.

At the edge of the dead grove was a stream. Here the band turned, following the water downhill; as they went, the little boy, Wahela's son, stooped and groped through the pebbles of the streambed, chasing crawfish. Ahead, the stream curled around a high bank, topped by a huge old sycamore. The stream had under-cut the bank and the roots of the sycamore hung down like a veil over the path. Ducking, Shateel crawled in through the dirt-smelling mass of tendrils.

She came out onto a wide, flat, sunny stretch. The water ran along the low side of a broad gravelly bed; above the stream, the old bed sloped gradually up toward an ancient bank, twice as tall as a man. Between this bank and the stream the old gravel beds of the stream stood high in grass and weeds, yellow in the sun. The People walked out onto this meadow, Moloquin ahead of them.

He called out. Then he broke into a run toward the high bank, and reached it, and suddenly he disappeared into it.

Beside Shateel, the foreign woman let out a cry. All the People froze where they were, staring at the bank, at the great pile of wind-drift at its foot where he had vanished, and Shateel was swept again with fear; he was a woods demon, he had seduced them here to abandon them, they would die far from their own homes, from their ancestors, from the way to Heaven. Then he stuck his head out of the heap of brush at the foot of the bank.

"Come in here. There is room."

Hesitant, wary as the red deer, they picked a way through the fallen branches and the brambles, and he pushed back part of the brush and let them inside.

Shateel crept in on hands and knees, butting through the brush. Suddenly she was inside a room, or a cave. She could see nothing; she put out her hands and groped the empty air, smelling the raw earth around her; squatting, she scrambled forward, her hands out, until her fingers brushed the solid clay wall. She turned.

Now some light was coming in from the front, and she could see dimly around her. This was a low, round room, half dug into the clay bank, half built out with sticks and logs and branches; mounds of dirt and leaf mold and other trash choked the side of the room to her left. Taella scrambled in through the doorway.

"I can't see! Where are we?"

Shateel stretched her hand out toward her. Wahela pushed her way in, kicking trash away as she entered.

Taella's hand closed on Shateel's, a firm, warm grip. She crawled into the center of the room, peering around.

"It will do," she said. "Until we can make something better."

Wahela was calling her children into the hut. Shateel gathered the breath into her lungs. "I will find something to sweep with," she said, and went out to the sunlight again.

The rain fell harder. The women spread branches over the top of the shelter and wove other branches through them, but the rain still dripped through. They had plenty of firewood, and the fire burned brightly enough. They ate two turtles and a handful of crayfish, nettles boiled in the shell of the turtle, grubs toasted until they burst. There was not enough. When they had eaten it all, they crowded shoulder to shoulder into the warmth of the fire and a stillness fell on them, each one lost in his own separate sorrows.

Then Moloquin began to speak.

He told them the story of how the People had come to the place where they lived now. "Long ago," he said, using the same words in which Karella had told it to him, "long ago, the People lived in a fair, sunny land to the south, where the sun never failed, and it was always summer. There was food everywhere, fruit to be plucked from every tree, honey dripping from the rocks, water sweet and cold bubbling forth from the earth.

"But the People were discontent. There was enough for everyone, but some collected more than they needed and hid it away in caves, and the others broke into the caves and took the storage, and when that happened, the People began to fight among themselves, and some even killed others.

"Then out of the blood and the bones of the murdered people there grew a monster, and it grew up all in one night, between the darkness and the dawn, and it flew out over the soft and sunny land, and it slew men and women.

"Now among the People there was a man named Hradon, who thought himself too stupid to be cunning, and so did no evil, and there was a woman, named Rael, who was too wise to be shrewd, and so did no evil. They took their children and their brothers and sisters, and they set off away from the monster.

"All but Hradon wanted to go to the south, where the sun shone, but Hradon said, 'If we go there, the monster will see us by the light of the sun and pursue us, and we shall have no peace.' Because he was too stupid to be cunning, he did not believe he could outthink the beast. And therefore he led them away to the north, into the mists and the rain, until they came to the shore of the sea, and there they lived.

"They stayed there for twice two turnings of the sun. There was food to be had, for hard work, but enough for everyone, especially for those who were too stupid to think they could trick others into doing their work for them, and too wise to want to. And for two sun-years the People seemed to be well. But then again, there were some who were neither stupid nor wise. And they stole, and they did murders, and the monster grew up from the blood and bones of the dead, and set upon them again, until there was none left but Hradon and Rael, and their two children, a boy and a girl.

"Then Rael said, 'I shall make a basket, and put myself and my child into it, and we shall float away on the sea. Wherever the wind and the wave take us, there shall we live, even if it be at the bottom of the sea.' And she made a basket, and she climbed into it with her child, and the sea took them away.

"Now Hradon waited and waited, but they never came back again. And he said to himself, 'I am stupid, but Rael is wise, and I shall do as she did.' But he had no basket. So he took a deer's belly, and he blew it full of air and tied it closed, and setting his child on it, he floated away on the waves.

"The wind blew him up and down and the sea turned him around and around, but at last he was cast up on a rocky shore. There on the shore was Rael's basket, but she and her child were nowhere in sight.

"Then Hradon put his child on his shoulders, and said, 'What do you see?' and the child said, 'I see mist, and rain, but I do not see Rael.' They went on, leaving the shore behind, and came to a forest.

"Then Hradon put the child on his shoulders again and said, 'What do you see?'

"And the child said, 'I see pine trees and oak trees, but I do not see Rael.' So they went on and on.

"Then they came to a rolling plain, and Hradon put his son on his shoulders, and said, 'What do you see?' and the child said, 'I see grass and sun and sky, and I see a garden and a little house, and I see Rael and her child.'

"Then they joined Rael and her child, and Hradon put up a stone on the place where he had stood when the child first saw Rael, and there have the People lived since then."

When Moloquin's voice ended, the People all sighed, and shifted, rubbing against one another. They put their arms around one another for warmth, and they smiled on one another, and although the rain fell on them and they were hungry, they were content, at least for a while.

In the morning the rain had stopped. Hems went out along the stream, looking for something to eat, and the other men trailed after him, staying close together. Moloquin had gone off somewhere; they were alone, and now the forest around them seemed like an enemy.

The women busied themselves with the shelter, making a racket of their work. Hems sat down on a gravel bar of the stream and dipped his cupped hand into the water and drank a little, to ease the

gnawing of his stomach. The two young strangers, Bohodon and Kayon, dropped down beside him, and Brant wandered along a little
way away.

Bohodon said loudly, "I am hungry," and looked balefully
around him, as if he expected someone to walk out of the woods with
his breakfast.

Kayon drew closer to Hems. Softly, he said, "Where did he go?"

"Moloquin? I don't know." Hems shrugged. "He is always busy,
Moloquin."

"Have you been to this place before?"

"I? Never. Moloquin has, he lived here once, with his mother, or
so he told me."

He bent toward the stream again, and with his cupped hand
raised water to his lips, and Kayon watched him intently, absorbing
the minutest details of what he did, and then did the same thing.
Hems turned his head away, smiling.

Bohodon said, "I didn't leave my People just to come here and
starve. What are we supposed to eat? There is nothing here but
trees."

As he spoke, he raised his head to look around them at the forest, and at the same time he shrank down a little; he was afraid of
the trees, Hems saw, which relieved his own fear somewhat. Brant
was walking through the water downstream, peering down at his
feet, probably hunting for crayfish and turtles. The sun was pouring
in through the gap in the forest canopy; already it was hot.

Then Moloquin was striding toward them; it was as if he had
dropped from the sky; no one had seen him come into the clearing.
He came straight toward the men and squatted down beside Hems.

"There are a few things we must do at once," he said, speaking
to Hems, his voice loud enough to include the others. "We must find
a good supply of food, we must gather some firewood, and we must
make tools. I want you to go down the stream. Look for deer sign,
watch for birds, if there are deep pools see if there are fish in them.
Remember how I showed you how to catch fish?"

"Yes," Hems said. "But I—"

"Don't tell me *but*, Hems, go do it. Go down the stream as far as
you can, until noon, and then turn and come back."

"But if I—"

"Do as I say! When you come back, even if you are empty-
handed, I promise you you will eat." Moloquin put one hand on his

friend's shoulder and gave him a little shake. "Do as I say, and I will take care of you. Have faith in me."

His hand still on Hems' shoulder, he turned to Bohodon. "I want you to show me your stonecraft."

Bohodon scowled at him, not moving. "I am going nowhere without food."

"Then you will sit here a long while, there is no food, not yet. Come: I know something of stones, you must show me what sorts of stones are good for making tools."

Bohodon grunted, and turned his face away.

Moloquin's hand slipped away from Hems' shoulder; he squared himself around toward Bohodon, and his voice sharpened.

"Do as I say, Bohodon."

The young man glowered at him and mumbled something. Moloquin said, "What?"

"I said I don't know any stonecraft!" Bohodon shouted. His head sank down into his shoulders. "I never learned it well. I told you, I did not belong in the Red Salmon Society. I learned nothing."

Across Moloquin's face there washed a look of such contempt that Hems slid backward a little way, out of his friend's reach. But Moloquin directed himself still at Bohodon, and he contained his rage.

"You know nothing at all? Not even how to find the stone?"

Bohodon muttered under his breath. He picked at the earth by his feet.

"Bah." Moloquin dashed his hand against his thigh. "Well, then, go and pick up firewood."

Again Bohodon glowered at him. "I did not come away here to work like a woman."

Moloquin set his teeth together, and his eyes glittered. There was a stillness, during which the rattling of the women in the hut, their voices, the swish of their brooms was louder than the burble of the stream.

Finally, Moloquin said, "Then go back, Bohodon."

"Very well then, I will." Bohodon got stiffly up onto his feet. He glared at all the men, turned, and swept his gaze around him, over the clearing and the great murmurous forest beyond. He took a hesitant step away. Stopping, he turned.

"You must show me the way."

Moloquin still squatted on the gravel bar, picking at the stones before him. He did not raise his head. "Go. You are nothing of mine."

Bohodon looked around him again, his eyes wide and bright with fear. Hems saw that he was afraid of the forest, and certainly he did not know his way home; if he went off without a guide, he would get lost. He turned back to Moloquin.

"I can't! You brought me here, now you must show me the way home."

Moloquin stood up. "This is the only home I know, Bohodon."

The other man faced him, put his hands on his hips and threw his chest out. "You are no better than I am—you can't give me orders!"

Moloquin lunged at him. Bohodon dodged, expecting a blow, but Moloquin only caught him by the front of his shirt and held him fast.

"Listen to me," Moloquin said. "I am the chief here. You are mine, now, you must serve me or you are nothing. If you would eat, Bohodon, then you must work. You will do as I say! If you don't, then I will give you to the forest, Bohodon. Do you understand?"

Pale under his dirt, Bohodon gaped into Moloquin's face, and his lips moved.

Moloquin shook him.

"Louder!"

"I said I do!"

Moloquin pushed him down. "Louder still, Bohodon—who is master here?"

Bohodon staggered, trying to keep his feet. "I—"

With a sweep of his foot, Moloquin knocked the other man's legs out from under him, toppling him into the gravel and pushing him down on his face. "Who is master here, Bohodon?"

"You are!" Bohodon screamed. "You are!"

"Get up." Moloquin kicked him.

Bohodon sat up, dirt clinging to his shirt and his eyebrows. Moloquin turned toward the other men, looking from one to the next. Hems licked his lips. He had never seen Moloquin so fierce, and he did not like it: his friend reminded him of Harus Kum.

"You," Moloquin said, nodding to Kayon. "You go with Hems, look for something to eat. Hems—nut trees, lily bulbs, anything. Especially hazel trees, which the deer eat. Go." He faced Bohodon again. The square-set young man was picking the dirt out of his

teeth. "Gather firewood. As you do it, look for stone. Now get out."
He kicked at Bohodon, and the other man scurried away on all fours.
Hems got hastily up and went off down the stream, Kayon at his
heels; the rest of the day, as they followed the stream back and forth,
Kayon did exactly what Hems did, down to the least detail.

When the women had the little hut as well set up as they could, which
was not well at all, they went out to the meadow and began to look
around them.

The men were all gone. They had heard Moloquin shouting ear-
lier in the morning, and Shateel was relieved that he was nowhere to
be seen. She followed Taella out across the knee-deep grass of the
meadow, past flattened places where the deer had lain down for the
night, to the edge of the forest.

Some mushrooms were growing there, in the damp loam beneath the first trees, but Taella shook her head at them.

"They will make you sick to eat them."

Wahela's children ran out across the sunlit grass toward the trees
and their mother called them back. "Don't go near the trees! You
have no notion what may lurk in the forest—stay close to me."

The little girl pressed herself against her mother's leg. The boy
cast a fearful look around him. Shateel went forward, looking into
the dimness of the forest; the trees did not seem so terrible to her,
and she had noticed how Moloquin passed among these great beings
as if among beloved friends. She paused at the foot of an oak whose
heavy riven bark was covered over with green mosses. The enormous
height drew her eyes upward, upward, until she was staring straight
up into the sky, through masses of green leaves.

The wind rose. As she stood looking up, the tree's weighty head
began to move, swaying back and forth and tossing its leafy crown.
The voice of the wind came from all sides, an enormous sound like a
great breath, and raised the hackles on her neck. The trees seemed
to be bending closer, watching her.

Yet she did not feel afraid; they were not evil, nor even un-
friendly. She went on a little way, seeing tiny white flowers in the
mold and rot of the forest floor, and off to one side, suddenly, something scuttled away with a crash and a rustle into the brush.

That drove her back to the others in a hurry, her head twisted over her shoulder, her skin prickling. She never saw what it was that ran away from her.

The other women were walking through the meadow, looking doubtfully around them. The stranger who had come with Moloquin to the Gathering trailed after; Shateel had heard Hems and Moloquin call her Amin, or Abim, but she spoke almost no words that Shateel knew. Thus far Shateel had avoided her scrupulously.

She reached the other women, staying together in a pack in the sunlight and the open grass; the children had wandered off again, and now Wahela turned and called to them. The little boy jumped down from the top of the hut, where he had climbed. The little girl answered from somewhere unseen and Wahela called her impatiently to come.

Taella was shaking her head. "I see no sign that this land has ever been worked. Nothing grows here that I recognize. I know nothing here, I am as helpless and ignorant as a baby."

"Moloquin knows," said Shateel.

Taella frowned at her, shaking her head. "He knows how to feed himself. He cannot go gathering nuts for so many, every day."

Shateel began to be frightened; she looked around her at the high soft grass with its maturing flowers. This grass looked somewhat like the rye and barley that grew in the gardens of the People; she put out her hand to touch the flowers. Their beards were sharp like thorns.

Wahela turned again, her hands to her mouth, and bellowed her little girl's name. There was no answer at all. "Where is she?" Wahela asked, angrily, and went off with sweeping strides toward the hut.

"We shall have to move," Taella said, low-voiced. "There is no room here for us. The trees are everywhere." She put her hands over her eyes. "I wish—I wish—"

She would not say what it was she wished, as if to say it would be a betrayal. Shateel hugged her arms around her, fighting against tears.

Wahela had found her daughter; she dragged the child toward the other women, scolding her fiercely. The child wept all down her face. Impulsively Shateel knelt down to console her, and saw the chubby fists full of half-chewed green.

"What is this?" She gripped the baby's hand. "Taella, what has she been eating?" There leapt into her mind the fear that the little girl was poisoned.

Taella leaned down. Looking up into the round faces bending over her, the little girl raised her hands and opened them.

Shateel gasped. She looked up from Taella to Wahela and turned her gaze back to the child, whose hand now Wahela held, spreading the little fingers. There on the palm were the remains of an immature bean pod.

"Where did you find this?" Taella asked. "Child, tell us."

Shateel took a scrap of the green pod and sniffed it. It smelled delicious, familiar, like home. Quickly she followed the other women, who followed the child, who ran across the meadow to the far side.

Here the ancient streambank curved around to meet the water again. The bank was half-buried under what seemed at first to be merely dirt, overgrown with creepers and briars. A young tree grew up out of it, and around the bottom of the tree, wound around and around the trunk, was a great bean plant.

Wahela shouted. Taella flung up her arms and clambered up the soft heap of rubble and embraced the tree itself. Shateel went nearer, smiling. Even from here she could see the pink and white flowers, the young pods hanging among the great heart-shaped leaves.

How had they missed seeing it? Because they were afraid of the forest, afraid to go far from the hut. The child had found it, and they lifted her up and hugged her and kissed her until she began to cry.

The strange woman Ap Min went near the plant and put out her hand to pick a pod from it, and Taella caught her hand. "No," she said, and shook her head. She turned to the others. "Save it—for seed. We will let it mature."

She dropped on her knees then and began to tear away the thick layer of green vines and brambles over the ground, heedless that she scratched her hands on the sharp thorns. Shateel saw what she was doing and went to help, and Ap Min helped also. They dug away the screening vines from the top of the heap, down to the dirt, and there almost at once they found a piece of an old pot.

Taella sat back on her heels, laughing, and Shateel dug with furious energy into the soft earth. She broke her nails on the dirt and went to find a piece of bark to dig with. When she came back, Taella was passing the piece of broken pottery to Wahela and saying, "This was her midden. She threw everything here. Look around, perhaps we will find something else that is useful."

Shateel was still digging away at the pile; the earth was full of half-rotted nutshells. Whoever had left this here had done it long ago. It was startling that the beanstalk still grew here.

Taella said, "There has been a woman here, and she grew beans. She knew this place. She worked this land. Surely her spirit is here somewhere and will help us learn to do what we must to live here."

The women all drew together and hugged one another; it was as if, when they embraced, the unknown woman took form in their midst. A few moments later, digging, Shateel uncovered the butt end of a long stick; when she dug it out, Taella proclaimed that once it had been a rake handle.

The midden heap produced no new treasures. It had done enough. The women took courage; they went into the forest to find the wood to make tools, and as they did so found more things to eat. They divided up the meadow into gardens, one for each of them, and began to break down the grass with their feet and peel the bark off the low shrubs springing up everywhere in the meadow. They felt this place was theirs; they knew they belonged here, and it no longer frightened them, even though they were hungry.

Ap Min had never before been among women like this.

All her life she had been a slave. From her first years she had done what Harus Kum told her to do, dodging his blows and kicks and curses, and later enduring his use of her sex; she had taken for granted that she was a low, worthless creature, that only men had any power. In all her life she had known just two other women—her mother, who had died when she was young, and the other female slave at Harus Kum's stockade, both dull and exhausted from their brutal labors, stoop-shouldered and misused. It had never occurred to her that women walked upright, or laughed, or did as they pleased.

Now here were women who walked with their heads high, with light springy steps, who laughed and got angry and sang and argued, women who of their own will had left their families to follow Moloquin.

She knew she was one of them; had she not followed Moloquin too?

Of course she could not understand their language. She was trying, she knew some words already, and Hems was teaching her more. She followed them from place to place in the meadow, doing whatever they did, watching their lips move as they spoke, watching their hands as they worked, watching the quick flow of their passions over their faces. The first time one of them turned to her and touched her, Ap Min wept.

Mostly they ignored her. They could not speak to her either. They were busy with other things. The tallest, with her flashing dark eyes, was forever calling her children, scolding them or chasing them. Ap Min watched these children, amazed at their agility and their audacity. The little boy climbed trees and brought down a birds' nest, full of little squawking fledglings—his mother cruelly killed them at once, cooked them on a little fire, and fed her children with them. Ap Min put her hand on her belly, where her own baby moved.

She had not thought much of it. From the first moment she knew she was pregnant she had thought only that Harus Kum would make her drink the potion; it had not come much into her mind that she would bear a child, a little being, another life.

She wished Moloquin would come back, or Hems, so that she had someone to talk to.

She followed the fair-headed woman down to the stream, and washed her hands even as Shateel did. Shateel's hands were filthy from digging in the dirt where they had found the beanstalk. Ap Min's hands were clean, but she washed them anyway. The water was cold and clear; she could see down to the bottom, where the sand lay in ripples. She could see her face reflected in its surface. She sat leaning over the stream studying her face, lost in herself, for a long while, and did not notice that Shateel had gone.

When she saw that, she did not go off at once to find the others. She sat on the bank, feeling the baby move within her; she struggled to understand what was happening to her, but she could not. She had always known before what would happen; each day was the same, really, and each act had its warnings and its results—she had always known when Harus Kum would want her body, she could tell it almost by his footstep when he was lusty.

Now there were no reliable signs. What did it mean, that a leaf floated by her? What did it mean, that the wind blew? She looked across the stream, into the deep forest on the far side, swampy and dank, the trees coated with grey-green moss. A bird was singing somewhere, and another answered. Abruptly, from the water before her, something leapt into the air.

She sprang up. Her whole body began to tremble; she imagined monsters, although the stream went smoothly on before her. Whirling, she ran back to the hut and crawled inside, into its warm dark shelter.

Shateel walked along the stream, where in the shallows tall reeds grew; she thought she might be able to make baskets from them, and as she walked she gathered them by the armful. When she took them back to the hut, Moloquin was there, searching around the outside of the shelter.

Seeing her, he wheeled toward her, his face fretted with bad temper. "Did you and the others clean out the hut?"

"Yes," she said.

It made her uneasy to talk to him; she had trouble meeting his eyes. She busied herself laying the reeds down in heaps on the ground by the door.

"Did you find anything of use? There were tools here, when we lived here—we took nothing away, some may still be left. Are you listening to me?"

"Yes." She looked up, brushing back her hair with one hand. "No—we found nothing, not even a stone. Except—"

"What?" He seized her wrist and held her.

"We found a beanstalk. We found a midden heap, and there is a—"

"Where?"

She pointed to the far side of the meadow, and he strode off toward the midden. She sat down with the reeds and slit a few stems lengthwise with her thumbnail, to see how strong the fibers were.

In a few moments he was back. "How well did you clean the place? Did you not find anything—not a pot or an old basket?"

She shook her head. "Nothing. Maybe she had a storehouse."

He stared at her a moment, lifted his head and swept his gaze around the clearing. She watched him covertly as she sorted the reeds into two piles. Abruptly he plunged away through the door of the hut.

She got up and went after him, curious. Inside the hut, the air was dank and dim, and she stood for a moment just within the door, unable to make out much. Her eyes cleared a little, and she saw him prowling along the clay wall at the back, feeling over it with his hands.

He yelled as he pulled at the wall with his hands, and a great piece of it came free and fell forward to the floor of the hut, breaking into chunks of mud and reed mat. Where it had lain up against the bank there was now a large opening. Moloquin reached into it and drew forth a stick, which he threw behind him, and an old antler.

Shateel cried out and went forward to his side. "That is a pick. See—" she leaned forward to take the antler away from him. Brittle with age, the horn smelled of clay. A piece of wood still jutted from the butt end of it, the remnants of its handle.

Next Moloquin pulled a pile of trash out of the opening—rotten reeds and other fibers that collapsed to rubble when he touched them. Shateel watched him sift through the moldy garbage, crumbling it all between his fingers.

He gathered up a shapeless pile of debris, smelling of rot; a sliver of stone fell from it to the floor, and Shateel stooped for it. "An awl," she said. "And look!" She dove into the opening and pulled out a beaked pot of fired clay.

The stopper was still in place; the pot was half full of honey. As he tore into the mound of rubbish left in the opening in the wall, Shateel sniffed the pot and dipped her finger into the sweet stuff. It was strong enough to make her head whirl.

"Nothing of any use," Moloquin said. He got up, wiping his filthy hands on his thighs, and went out of the hut.

Shateel stayed where she was, kneeling in the midst of the rubble of the storeroom. She put out her hand and lifted a little of it and let it trickle away into dust. What had this been here, a basket? And there surely was the last rotten fibers of some sort of cloth. A woman had lived here, a woman by herself had lived here, and had worked, raised her son, alone, free, a world in herself. Shateel longed to know more about her. She longed suddenly to be more like her. Here in this place her presence shimmered in the air like a white radiance. Impulsively she knelt down and pressed her lips to the place where the stranger had walked.

Bohodon had gone straight off into the forest, intending to walk away from these fools and from Moloquin and never come back. They were no different than all the rest of the People; they wanted only to abuse him and force work out of him, caring nothing for his soul. He hated them all. Most of all he hated Moloquin.

He tramped off through the trees, moving aimlessly away, kicking at the wood and the leaves that covered the ground. The land turned abruptly marshy and he dragged his feet out of the black muck and climbed higher, hurting himself on buried stones and sticks; at the top of the ridge, he stumbled out through a row of birch trees into a patch of sunny meadow, and at the far end of it saw three deer.

They stood watching him, their heads turned over their shoulders; he froze where he was, his skin tingling with excitement, and thought to creep closer to them, but as soon as he moved his foot, they flung up their tails and bounded away.

He followed after them, but saw no more sign of them. Now he wandered away through the trees, his mind turned inward to survey his troubles. His belly grumbled. He was thirsty but he could not find the stream. Abruptly he realized he was lost.

At that, he panicked; he broke into a run back the way he had come and tripped and fell on his face. Lying on the ground he cast wild looks around him and saw nothing familiar. Slowly he got up, struggling with his fear which threatened to send him off again in a blind run. The trees around him leaned in closer, menacing and evil. He could hear something moving in the brush nearby. A rank smell reached his nostrils.

He stumbled away through the woods, striving to keep mastery over himself. If he walked straight ahead, surely he would come to some landmark he recognized, and he forced himself to walk straight, but after only a few strides he began to feel the heavy presence of the trees again, the unseen eyes around him, and the terror in his mind overcame him and drove him in a wild dash down a slope and into a swamp. He was in muck to his knees before he could stop.

He scrambled out of the swamp, stood on the edge, and put his face up to the sky. He made himself calm again, although his heart thundered. He made himself realize that nobody would care if he did not come back; no one would come looking for him. He had to save himself.

He had no idea how to do that. Grimly he trudged forward, trying to keep a straight course, and as he went he looked keenly around him, noticing for the first time how the trees grew, how the land was shaped, which way the wind came from, where the sun was, and at last, after what seemed a whole day's walk, he found a stream.

Was it the stream that flowed by the camp of his People? He flung himself down on his belly and drank from it until his empty belly was taut. Then, as he sat up, he heard the rhythmic crack and stroke of an axe cutting wood.

Relief washed over him, loosening every muscle; for an instant his quivering legs threatened to drop him to the ground. The sound of the axe came from downstream. He started that way, remembered he was supposed to be gathering wood, and picked up a few little twigs. At the next turning of the stream, he came into the upper end of the meadow, near the hut.

The women were all gathered at the center of the meadow, sitting in a circle, pounding something in their midst. Bohodon filled his lungs to call out, but at that moment he saw Hems and Kayon approaching from the other direction, and he saw how Kayon held triumphantly aloft a pair of stupid skinny squirrels.

They would make much of him for that. Bohodon drew back, his lips twisting in a grimace of distaste. He himself was bringing only a few sticks. He turned and went back into the forest, to gather a decent armload of wood.

The stone axe was old and clumsy and it needed a new edge. Moloquin went back across the stream, to the grove of dead oak trees, and he took up the work there where his mother had left it, felling the dead trees in the great clearing, so that there would be room for the women's gardens in the spring. Brant, the old Green Bough master, came to help him. It was Brant who first suggested to him that they build a roundhouse at the north end of the clearing, where the giant sycamore tree grew out of the bank.

"The lore of the Pillar of the Sky," he said, "that is building-lore."

He showed Moloquin how to choose the ground, how to lay out a circle on it, using a length of rope and a stake to mark the center, and he showed him how to use the rope also to find the perfect crossings of the circle's diameter. The circle thus divided into fours, Brant showed him how with ropes to divide it into twice-fours.

"This is big enough for now," Brant said. "There are only the four of us."

"There are the women," Moloquin said.

"The women," Brant said, surprised. "But they will have their longhouses."

Moloquin leaned on the axe. "No. I mean them to live with us. I don't want any of this separation between us and them."

Brant said, "The women have always lived in their longhouses. The men have always—"

"Brant," Moloquin said, "I mean to do this as I have told you. We shall all live together. We shall all be one People. The women shall live in the roundhouse with the rest of us."

The old man's face twisted with doubt. He looked around him, as if the roundhouse already stood here, and shook his head.

"The roundhouse is made for men. All the rituals and the lore belong to men. I cannot see how—"

"I can see it," Moloquin said, and would hear no more.

So they made the circle larger, and marked the positions of each of the great posts that would form the wall and hold up the roof; Brant went out to watch the night sky and made sure that everything was lined up properly. As the summer slid on, Moloquin found the proper trees to use for the posts and felled them with his axe and trimmed them, while all around him the others worked frantically to pile away a store of food against the coming of winter.

They had no grain, but the forest around them was bountiful with other things: nuts and roots, and game. Hems and his new follower Kayon fished and snared rabbits and squirrels. The women gathered acorns in the oak wood as Moloquin felled trees.

He could hear their voices; they teased Ap Min often about her enormous belly, as the girl grew slowly apt in the speech of the People, and told her how awful it was to bear children. Through the dusty sunlight he caught glimpses of them among the far-standing trees of the oak wood. Often he paused and rested a little between strokes of the axe, and sent his gaze after one or another of the women to watch.

They tormented him. He could not keep his mind from them, and his penis seemed constantly hard; he was ashamed that they might notice and tried to avoid them when he could, but always they were there, with their wonderful soft bodies, their smiles, their uninhibited laughter, their kindness to one another, their smells, their soft hair. He wanted to choose a wife from among them, but he could not decide which. He wanted them all, even Ap Min and old Taella, even Wahela's still-stumbling baby girl. Leading them here, caring for them every day, being so close to them had filled him with a possessive affection for them. Little by little he was coming to the notion that they belonged to him and he ought to have them all.

In the evenings, sitting by the fire with Brant, telling stories, he watched the other men. They too stole looks at the women, and stole caresses too. He knew they would begin to choose one another very soon.

Therefore one afternoon he sent Ap Min off into the forest to gather mushrooms and followed her. When they were far enough away from the others that no one would witness his humiliation if she refused him, he went up behind her and embraced her. She knew at once what he wanted. Saying nothing, she pulled up her ragged skirt, put her back to a wych elm's trunk, and let him in. It was unexpectedly difficult, because she was so pregnant. When he was done, he leaned against her, drained and shaking, and she stroked his hair and whispered something to him in her old language.

"Don't talk that way," he said. He sat down on the leaf-drift beside her. With a tug on her skirt he drew her down next to him.

She sat there a while, her head down, smiling. He knew her in a special way now, and yet she seemed even more secret to him; he would never possess her wholly. Absorbed in her, he studied her face, her profile to him. She had never seemed pretty to him before, but now the hollow of her cheek and the redness of her mouth were wonderful to him. He took her hand and pressed her palm to his face.

"Moloquin," she said, "what are you doing with me?"

"You wanted me to do it," he said. "You cannot say I forced you."

She smiled at him. She looked on him differently now. She looked him in the eyes now, with an easy, familiar gaze. Suddenly he realized that as he had possessed her, so now she possessed him: that was enough to make him move a little away from her.

She watched him calmly, her arms around her belly. She said, "No, you did not force me. But I have wanted you for a long time now, and you have never come to me before." She shook her head. "You need a wife, Moloquin, but I am not the woman for you."

She got up and went to find mushrooms, and Moloquin went back to the work with his axe. He thought all afternoon about what he had done.

The act itself was wonderful. To hold her, to fit together with her, filled him with a dizzying sense of space and room, as if with the ejaculation he burst beyond his skin and flooded into her and into worlds beyond her.

Now when he struck down the trees with his axe, with each blow he thought of sex; in the afterglow, everything he did seemed an extension of the act of sex.

But the glow faded, and next he sought out Wahela.

He did what he had done with Ap Min: he sent her away on an errand, going upstream to look for crayfish, and he made sure that her children were with the other women. Then he went after Wahela.

When he closed with her it was the same at first as it had been with Ap Min. She knew at once what he wanted, and by the sudden flush of her cheek and the bright flash of her eyes he knew she was willing, but she led him off on a chase through the trees, running in short dashes from tree to tree, shrieking in mock fear when he came close. She led him straight away from the others. When she finally sprawled down before him on the forest floor, he was hot as a fire.

From then on it bore little resemblance to sex with Ap Min. Wahela bounded and bucked together with him; she bit him and scratched his shoulders. When he held her down under him she writhed like a captive. When he was done, she came at him again, her lust barely diminished. He spent the whole afternoon with her under the trees, and hardly spoke to her at all.

When they were walking back to the clearing, she began to talk.

"Will you marry me, then?" she said.

He did not want to talk about that, or even think about it: there were two more women he wanted first. When he said nothing, she grew angry.

"So. You put me on my back and now you will not marry me, is that it?"

"Wahela," he said, "you'd have done the same for any man."

"What!" She flashed her magnificent dark eyes at him. "Well then, see if you have it again." With a flounce of her hips she ran past him and into the hut.

After that he set about having Shateel—Taella awed him some-how, with her grey hair and her shrewd looks; she reminded him of Karella. So he sent Shateel off next, and followed her. He found her sitting in the grass by the foot of a sycamore tree, peeling the fallen bark with her fingernails.

His success with the other women had made him bold. He went

straight to Shateel and put out his hands to her, expecting her to accept him at once, but instead he got a cold look from her.

"So," she said. "You think to have me too, like the others. I thought so, but I did not want to believe it."

He squatted down before her. Instantly he wanted her more than anything else in the world. Her hair was the color of flax, but her eyes were dark and wide, and her mouth was like a red flower, full of sweetness. He put his hand on her arm and she shook him off.

"Shateel," he said, "don't you want me at all?" It seemed amazing to him that anyone would refuse such a pleasure, when it could be had so simply and easily.

She said, "Leave me alone, Moloquin."

He seized hold of her, meaning to force himself on her and expecting her to fight him; instead she lay limply in his arms and turned her face away. She said, "I was the wife of Ladon's son, you know, and now I am carrying a child of his. What do you think of that?"

He let her go and sat back on his heels, staring at her: he saw no sign that she was pregnant. Finally he said, "Well, Ladon's son is not here, is he? You are not his wife any more."

"I am no man's wife now, Moloquin," she said. She got up and started away, back to the camp. He stayed where he was, thinking over what had happened; he was beginning to believe himself a fool in matters such as this.

Wahela sat with her children while they ate and talked to them and cleaned up after them; she had put down a little ring of stones around her part of the hut, to keep the others off, and she usually brought some coals in from the fire to warm the place while the children ate their supper and lay down for sleep. Her son fell asleep right away, but the little girl was fretful, wanted to be nursed and held, and kept Wahela there long after the others of the People had finished eating and begun their evening chores.

Moloquin came in last and sat down by the door. He always slept by the door, between his People and the night.

Wahela watched him from the corner of her eye. She had told him she would have no more to do with him, but whenever she saw him she longed to be close to him.

He wanted only sex. Men like that could not be trusted.

Now he sat there by the door, his shoulders slumped, his back bent, looking too tired even to lie down for sleep. Once, as she rocked and nursed and murmured to her daughter, Shateel came into the hut and had to ask him to move; when she spoke to him he got up and went out of the hut, and Shateel herself blushed and frowned and shook her head. Wahela knew at once that something had happened between them, and as she knew Shateel, she could guess what it was.

When he returned a few minutes later and took up his post again by the door, Wahela laid down her daughter in her bed and went to Moloquin.

"Here," she said, sitting down beside him. "You look tired."

She stroked his shoulders, pressing down with the palms of her hands, and he sighed and lifted his head. His muscles were knotty under her fingers. She loved touching him. His hair was matted with dried sweat and she began to comb it with her fingers.

"Wait," she said. "I will get my comb."

"If you want to," he said stiffly, and would not look at her.

She went back to her hearth and found the wooden comb. Sitting behind him again, she picked and combed his hair clean, cracking the lice between her fingernails. He said nothing to her, but when she glanced at his face, his eyes were closed, his mouth slack and sensuous. She did not look to see if Shateel was watching.

His beard was growing down over his chest, a mat of thick black curls, and she combed that also. Still he said nothing to her. She reminded herself that he had done much for her, that they all relied on him, and that a chief deserved to be cared for like this. When she was done, she took the comb and got up to go back to her hearth.

"Wahela," he said, and opened his eyes.

She paused. He put out his hand and tugged on her skirt, and she sat down in front of him, and there while all the People watched and murmured he combed her long dark hair until every strand lay straight. That night her children slept in the ring of her stones, but she and Moloquin lay in one another's arms by the door.

Moloquin felled the oak trees in the new clearing, cut up the branches for firewood and trimmed the trunks to make the posts for

the wall of his roundhouse. Brant showed him how to cut a knob in
the top of each post, to fit into a hole in the beam and so keep the
structure solid. Bohodon and Hems and Kayon dug the holes. Brant
used his rope to measure each trunk, and determined how deep each
hole should be so that all the posts were level along the top.

The summer was sweeping toward its climax. There was food
everywhere, the trees were heavy with fruit and nuts, the herbs and
roots of the edible plants were ready to pick and dry and store, the
forest teemed with game. Soon there would be nothing but cold and
snow. The People worked frantically to gather in all they could before the winter reached them. The leaves of the great sycamore were
already turning color; the wind at night was cold enough to make the
children cry.

Brant showed them how to raise each post into its position. They
looped rope around the huge grey trunk, and two men pulled and
two men pushed until the butt end slid down into its place with a
thud that shook the earth. While it swayed and tottered above them
they ran madly around it throwing everything they could find into
the hole to steady the trunk, and then filled it up with dirt and rocks
from the streambed. Twice, in the beginning, the posts simply fell
over.

Brant sat and watched them and made more rope, twisting the
heavy fibers of hemp plants until they kinked and then stretching
them from tree to tree. He said, "It is easier to do this out in the
open. There is chalk under the soil, and holes dug in chalk will hold
anything."

Moloquin sat beside him, exhausted. They had spent the day
raising two posts, one of which had fallen over. The other men had
gone down to the stream to wash. The roundhouse stood like a skeleton at the far end of the clearing; although only half-begun, with
three out of the eight posts in place, it already pleased Moloquin with
its shape, its suggestion of order.

He said, "Someday we will build something very like this at the
Pillar of the Sky."

To his surprise the old man frowned at him. "Nothing can be
built at the Pillar of the Sky!"

"I shall build something."

"I tell you, that is folly, that way is ruin, Moloquin. Nothing can
stand there."

Moloquin kept silent, but he was disappointed in the old man. He lowered his eyes. The roundhouse no longer pleased him. A cold evil tugged at his heart; he wondered for the first time if he would ever see what he had dreamed at the Pillar of the Sky.

The old man was watching him keenly, his fingers busy with the rope. Suddenly he said, "There is something I must ask of you, Moloquin."

"Ask," said Moloquin, his voice rasping; he was still angry at Brant, whom he had taken for his ally.

"I wish to marry," said Brant. "If you mean all of us to live together in the roundhouse, I for one do not intend to be that near to women and not have the comfort of one."

Moloquin said, "Marry, then." He smiled at the old man, grateful for this proof of the vigor of his People.

"It is Taella I wish to marry," Brant said. "I shall ask her." He rose, groaning as his knees straightened, and went off across the clearing toward where the women sat, storing away nuts in baskets made of bark and reeds.

Moloquin knew little of the rites of weddings. To marry Brant and Taella together, he took what he could remember from the few weddings he had seen and filled the spaces with other things, from stories and from his own heart. He braided together a rope of grass and filled a turtle shell with water and he made a little fire in the middle of the half-finished roundhouse.

Seven of the nine posts had been set now. The center post, taller than the others, and the four major points of the circle, north, south, east and west, had gone up first. He brought Taella and Brant together before the center post, which Brant called the North Star, and the rest of the People stood in a ring around them all. In their arms they held the last flowers of the summer, white day-star and yellow sundrops and red and blue fleetwood. The women sang in low voices, swaying from side to side, their eyes shining.

Moloquin took Taella's hand and Brant's and put them together, and he bound them together with the rope of grass.

"Now," he said, "you are married together, like the vine and the elm tree."

He made them walk past the fire, Taella on his left and Brant on his right, so that their bound hands passed above the flames, and he said, "Let nothing separate you; the fire that destroys all things shall not separate you."

He gave them the shell of water to drink from, Brant holding it to Taella's lips, and Taella holding it to Brant's, and Moloquin said, "You shall nourish each other in all ways, nor shall you deny one another anything."

Then he raised his hand over them. "You are married," and he backed away, leaving them standing there alone in the middle of the circle.

"Kiss! Kiss!" Wahela cried, boisterous, and flung a flower at them. Someone laughed, but Brant leaned forward and Taella put her hands to her new husband's shoulders and they kissed. Around them the others stretched out and caught hands with one another and began to dance. As they whirled around the new pairing, they flung flowers on them, and Wahela shouted, "Kiss! Kiss again! Brant, she is yours now, do as you wish with her! Taella—"

Brant stiffened, but Taella caught his clothes with both hands; a broad smile broke across her face. Flower petals lay on her long grey braids. As the People whirled and sang around them, Taella pulled and tugged on him, whispered to him, and drew him down on the ground. There in front of everybody they coupled, while the flowers pelted them and the People danced and laughed and sang and called advice and amazement at the prowess of an old man.

Moloquin moved away from them. He had not expected this but he saw that it was good: they had made the marriage, in their fornication, better than he had with his uncertain rites. But the sight of a man and a woman joining filled him with a lust so strong it made him sick. He backed away into the forest. The little fire was going out and evening was settling over the camp. In the blue twilight his People were only shapes that writhed and whirled like drifting smoke. He turned to go.

All the posts of the roundhouse had names, and some of them had more than one; each had other things about it that were important. Brant tried to explain this to the other men, but only Moloquin seemed to pay attention.

Brant said, "This one is Belly-of-the-Black-Wind," and laid his hand on the post at the north point of the circle. He said a few other names, savoring the music and the meaning. "Light-Bow, and The-

Way-Home. When someone dies in the roundhouse, we must open the wall here and take the body out this way, because this is the beginning of the path of the soul to Heaven."

They had raised all the posts now; they had come to the hardest part of the building. Brant said, "Now we must raise the beams. We could wait until next summer—we could put up sticks, to hold the roof for the winter."

Moloquin said, "We must finish it now—if we flinch from the work we shall never do it."

"We haven't enough men."

Moloquin watched him a moment, his face pensive. "What are you afraid of, Brant?"

"I don't think—I—" Brant drew a deep breath. "I don't know. Perhaps I am getting too old. Something about this place bothers me."

"Tell me what you feel."

Brant shook his head; he did not know what it was that he felt, he knew only that the thought of raising up the roof beams cast him down to the depths of his soul. He thought suddenly, I shall die here. He pressed his hands to his face.

"What is it?" Moloquin said. "Tell me! If you feel this place is unlucky, tell me now, it is senseless to keep working on it."

Brant looked around him; the posts around him stood up straight and true, their trunks, the bark peeled away, grey with weathering. Whatever he felt here, it was not that the place was unlucky, and he said so.

"Then we shall finish it," Moloquin said.

"I shall not see it finished," Brant said. "I—I—" then from the woods came a long screech of terror.

Both men leapt to their feet, wheeling toward the forest. Out of the deep of the trees came Wahela, her great black eyes wide and her hair streaming.

"Ap Min! Her baby is coming—"

From across the clearing, Shateel leapt up and ran into the forest, going back the way Wahela had come.

Wahela ran up to Moloquin and seized his hand. "Come—you must hurry—"

"Where is she?"

"In the forest, by the hazelnut grove. We were gathering nuts—"

"Isn't Taella with her?" Brant asked. "She ought to know something of midwifery."

"No—she says she doesn't know enough—the baby won't come, it is stuck." Wahela clutched at Moloquin's hand. "Please, you must come, hurry, please—"

From the stream the other men were coming, their bodies shining with wet; Hems reached the roundhouse first, flipping back his long damp hair with his hand. "What is it?"

Moloquin said, "Ap Min is bearing her baby, she is having some trouble with it. Come." He ran away into the forest with Wahela.

Ap Min lay on her side in the deep mast under the hazelnut tree. Her belly heaved in rhythmic convulsions. Shateel knelt beside her, pressing her hand between her two palms, while Ap Min screamed.

"I am dying—I am dying—"

Taella knelt between Ap Min's feet, forcing her knees apart, and stuck her fingers into the laboring woman's vagina. "I can feel something. I think it's the baby's foot."

"A foot," Shateel said blankly. "Then it's being born, it's all right, everything will be all right. Won't it?" Her voice cracked. She wanted to cry. Inside her own body, another baby churned and thrashed, ready to do this to her. Ap Min shrieked again, and from her vagina another gush of water and blood spurted, splashing Shateel's clothes. Shateel turned away, scrabbled off on all fours, and was sick into the crust of rotting nutshells.

"It's bad," Taella said, "when the foot comes first it's bad. Ap Min, you must try to push the baby out. Now, try."

"It hurts—oh!" Another great wave passed down the girl's body, and Ap Min twisted and heaved and grunted, lifting herself up off the ground on heels and shoulders, her face turning red, her eyes squeezed shut; she screamed and screamed until the forest rang with it.

Shateel said, "I can't bear this." She was weeping all down her cheeks.

"Be quiet," Taella said. "Nothing is happening to you. Hold her hand. Come on, we must help her, somehow—oh, I wish I had learned something of midwiving. My mother told me something once about this—"

Through the trees now came a man running; it was Hems, all

but naked, and after him came the other men in a stream. Hems flung himself down beside Ap Min and caught her hand. "Ah, look at her, how she suffers—" he thumped his fist on the ground. When the next wave of pain took her and she began to shriek, he lay face down beside her on the ground and shrieked too.

Taella struck him between the shoulderblades. "You fool! Get up—we must do something."

"Here comes Wahela," Shateel said. "And Moloquin."

When she saw Moloquin coming, her fluttering heart steadied; she wiped the tears quickly from her cheeks, so that he would not know she had been crying.

Moloquin knelt down in the dirt beside Ap Min and stooped over her to kiss her forehead. Even she seemed calmer now that he was there. He took her hand and held it against his cheek.

"Moloquin," she whispered. "I am dying—"

"No," he said. He swung his gaze toward the other women. "What's wrong?"

"It's backwards," Taella said. "The baby. It is coming out backwards, but it isn't moving, it's stuck."

"What is to be done?" He looked expectantly into each of their faces, and Shateel's face grew hot; she was ashamed of not being able to answer him. "Don't you know?" he cried. "How can you be women and not know?"

"I've seen babies born," Taella said. "It's not something I enjoy, I have never learned the craft. Most of the time nothing is necessary. I've never seen one born backwards."

She put her hand against Ap Min's oozing vagina again and poked her fingers inside, and when she did the poor creature writhed and shrieked, and Hems writhed and shrieked also beside her. Moloquin stroked her face absently with his hand, his eyes on Taella.

"That's a foot," Taella said. "I'm sure it's a foot."

"Pull it out," Moloquin said.

"You'll kill it."

Shateel gritted her teeth together. She remembered something she had heard once, long before—that Rulon her brother had been born backwards, that he had been drawn forth by the hand of a midwife. She said nothing, afraid of being called on to act. Moloquin was glaring at them all, as if they had caused this, and now suddenly he shoved Taella to one side and moved between Ap Min's knees.

"I will do it."

He leaned over Ap Min; there was a look of terror on the girl's face, and she whispered, "Don't hurt my baby."

He smiled at her. "Good. Don't think of yourself, think of the baby."

But when he slid his hand into her body she writhed and screamed, and he sat back.

"My hand is too big."

Shateel said, "Taella, do it."

"No. Not I."

Moloquin turned to Shateel. "You do it."

Shateel swallowed hard, remembering the story about her brother, and looked down at her hands. She did have small hands. She moved closer to Ap Min, and Moloquin shuffled out of her way.

Ap Min watched her over the huge mound of her belly; another pain seized her, and she stiffened all over, her head straining back, her body arching up off the ground.

"Ap Min!" Moloquin called. "Be calm." He touched Shateel's shoulder. "Do it."

Shateel bit her lip; she slid her fingers inside the slick red vagina. At first she could feel nothing but the wet walls of inside. Fearful, she pushed inward, harder, and touched something at the end of the passage.

But the moment was past; the pain was fading, and Ap Min's convulsive labor slowed. Hems crawled around behind her and held her head and shoulders against his chest.

Moloquin knelt behind Shateel. "Get ready. Here comes the next pain."

Ap Min was tensing all over, her body locked in a fierce combat with itself. Shateel slid her whole hand into the stretching slippery opening. Now she could feel the little object at the end of the passage well enough to pull it, and as Ap Min screamed and strained and thrashed she gave a gentle tug, and felt the tiny foot move.

"Pull," Moloquin cried.

Shateel drew on the baby's foot, and as Ap Min screamed and heaved it was as if some force pushed as Shateel pulled, and smooth and slippery the whole leg came down, the foot almost out of the vagina. Shateel gasped. Abruptly she was calm, intense, concentrated on this one moment and this one act. A wonderful power surged through her. She felt the life force trembling in her grasp. She reached up past the first leg, felt for another and could not find it, but without hesitation or doubt she grasped the little thigh, and waited. When Ap Min clenched and writhed again and screamed again, Shateel pulled, and again the unknown, unknowable power of life itself pushed the baby along after her drawing hand, and the whole leg came out into the world and part of the backside, tiny, ludicrously cloven, white as ash. Then everything stopped.

"Good," Moloquin cried, and stroked her shoulder roughly. "Here comes another."

Ap Min screamed; Shateel pulled, but the force was gone. The head was stuck and would not move. She clenched her jaws together. A trickle of cold fear invaded her confidence. For an instant she wanted to pull hard, although Ap Min was not ready yet, and she fought the impulse, her mind roiled and unsteady; she told herself, *Wait, wait*, and shut her eyes.

With her eyes shut, all her attention focussed on her hand, and she slid it up the channel, past the little body, and felt the shoulder. Now again Ap Min grunted and strained and shrieked, and Shateel felt the pushing against her fingers, and the little head slipped sideways. She guided it gently around and suddenly it slipped free and she felt the whole skull against her palm, and such a wild joyous power sprang down her arm from this touch that she opened her mouth and sang forth her overflowing feeling.

Moloquin struck her again on the shoulder in his strange caress and he sang also. Ap Min groaned. When the next pain came, she heaved and her body jerked and the baby slid out another few inches, and Shateel drew it slowly forth, singing, until the newborn one lay on her knees, still connected to its mother by its twisted blue and white cord, its body waxy and grey.

Then it opened its mouth and cried, and its whole body turned pink and rosy as a sunrise. Shateel turned it over in her lap and saw that it was cloven all the way.

"A girl," she said. "A girl, Ap Min, a daughter."

Ap Min began to laugh. With a grunt and a thrust of her body she expelled the rest of the twisted blue and white cord, and attached to the end, a great flapping mass of dark flesh, like an enormous clot of blood. Shateel stared at it.

"What's that?"

Wahela laughed. She bent down between Shateel and Ap Min's raised knee, took the cord up casually to her mouth and bit through it. A dribble of blood leaked from the end. "This is the moon's baby." She lifted the fleshy mass in her hands. "We have to bury it quickly, or the baby will sicken and die."

Ap Min was saying, "My baby, my baby," in a breathless tired voice full of exultation, and Shateel reluctantly laid the baby on her mother's breast. Everyone else was standing around staring at the newborn, and now Hems said suddenly, "It's cold," and reached out his hand to Moloquin. "Let me have your shirt."

Moloquin pulled off his shirt and gave it to him. Hems crouched by Ap Min and wrapped her and the baby in the garment, and stayed hovering near her, his arms around her, his cheek near her cheek. Ap Min, her face shining, helped the baby take the nipple, and cupped the tiny head in her palm, fingering its dark hair.

"Can I—might I name it Moloquin?"

Shateel sat down cross-legged, still amazed at what she herself had done; she wondered why nobody else seemed to think she had done anything wonderful.

Taella said, "It would be unlucky, to name her for someone who is already alive; his power would suck the life away from her. Anyway, his name means what it means, and you don't want to name her that, do you?"

"Oh." Ap Min looked down at the baby; suddenly she turned to Hems. "You name her. You know the names of the People."

Hems beamed at her and leaned protectively over her. Everyone else was crowding around the baby. Shateel got up. After all that she had done, Ap Min who had done nothing but scream now had everyone's eyes on her. Shateel told herself that it was enough to have felt that life force, she did not need the praises of the others. She got to her feet, and now she marked, surprised, that Moloquin had gone, although everyone else was still gathered around the baby. She went away through the forest to the stream to drink the cool clear water.

With all the posts of the roundhouse set into the ground and proven straight, they dressed the crosspieces. Bohodon, in his wood-gathering, had found a number of stones he thought would make good tools, and he sat with Brant and Moloquin by the streambank and tried to fashion a chisel out of flint, so that they could cut holes in the beams.

Brant sat quietly watching and never spoke, but Moloquin

leaned over Bohodon's shoulder, asking him questions, and as he worked and got nowhere, began to berate him and demand that he do better. Bohodon grew red in the face. Stubbornly he worked at the flint, trying to ignore Moloquin, trying to remember how the blows were struck that knocked clean chips off the edge of the stone.

"Oh," he said suddenly. "I need a piece of antler, that's what it is."

"What! All this while you have not even had the right tools?" Moloquin cried, and Bohodon sprang up and wheeled toward him.

"You do it, if you can do it better!" He flung the stone down and strode away across the clearing.

Moloquin shouted, "Go then—run away! You are useless, you are nothing!" He sat down on the stream's gravel bar and took the stone in his hand.

He bashed at it a few times with another stone, and the core broke uselessly in half. Brant laughed.

Moloquin twisted to glare at him. "Are you laughing at me?"

Brant looked the other way. He said, "Perhaps we can use the axe."

They went up to the clearing; as they passed by the place where the new gardens would be, where the women had begun to rake the cut brush into piles, Bohodon came past them, going in the other direction, his face black with bad temper. He said nothing to either of the other men, but walked straight back toward the stream. Moloquin cast a bitter look after him. He and Brant set to work with the axe, cutting holes in the ends of each beam to fit the knobs on the posts.

Bohodon sat all that day by the stream, banging rocks together. If he made anything of use, he did not show it to Moloquin.

The beams were trunks split lengthwise, so that one side was flat and the other curved. When the time came to lift them up onto the posts, everyone had to help, even Wahela's children.

They dragged each of the crossbeams into position on the ground just outside the two posts on which it would rest, and they put it on its round side, to make it easier to tip and roll it back and forth. Then with long sticks they pried one end up off the ground, and the women and children hurried to shove logs underneath. Rolling the trunk from side to side, they worked the logs well under the beam, adding more and more as they could, until at last they had gotten more than half the beam up onto a row of small logs. Then as many of the People as could get on leapt onto the high end of the beam, and the other end rocked up off the ground.

They put more logs under this end, and began the whole process over again, prying up one end, bracing it with logs, working the logs underneath until the beam could be tipped up horizontal, and building up the logs under that end.

As the beam rose into the air, supported on a cradle of logs many layers high, they tied ropes around it, and they prayed to it and cursed it, because the beam swayed and rolled treacherously, and several times it seemed ready to plunge off its mountings. As they learned the work and gained some confidence in the method, they worked faster.

When they had finally raised it to the level of the posts, they hooked more ropes around it, and again they cursed and prayed because the trunk would not move, it would not roll over, and they pulled the ropes and the trunk moved and fell crashing back down to the earth and lay there, almost exactly where it had been before they began.

The women all cried. The men stood staring at the ruins of their labors, and that day they worked no more.

The day after they began again. Twice more the beam fell before they got it up again to the level of the posts. When at last they had raised it up high enough, Moloquin went to the hut and brought back his bronze axe and laid it between the two posts, in the middle, so that it would be under the beam when it was in place. He called all the people together, and they threw ropes around the beam and used long poles to guide it, and slowly, fearfully, they began to move the beam over.

Moloquin began to sing as he worked; he sang the Song of the Sampo, and the women joined in.

> *Sam-po, sam-po*
> *La li la li la la li la*
> *The Mill turns, the Mill grinds*
> *The People come and go*
> *La li la la li li la*
> *Sam-po, sam-po*

Slowly the beam rolled up onto its edge, and it hung there, stiff against the poles, resisting the ropes; as they strained to move it, they sang, and now the men sang also.

>*Sam-po, sam-po*
>*La li la la li li la*
>*Into the Mill must all things fall*
>*Between Heaven and earth all things must lie*
>*La li la la li li la*

As they sang together, their strength worked together also, and the beam rolled over and landed on the posts with a thud.

On the next day they raised two more of the beams, and the day after that, three.

While they were working on the roundhouse, there was no one gathering food, and the season was turning; inexorably the Mill of Heaven was wheeling over them, and the year was sinking toward its close. Moloquin took the men off to hunt the fallow deer.

This was the time when the stags fought for the does, and the deer were bolder than usual. There was a small herd that ranged the whole area, although they had begun avoiding the places where the People lived and worked; when the People first arrived in the clearing Moloquin had seen the deer several times a day sometimes but now he saw them rarely, and only when he went looking for them. Moloquin led the other four men and Wahela's little boy, whom everybody called Laughter, away through the countryside, toward the ford where the deer often watered in the evening.

The forest was changing with the approach of winter. Now the sycamore trees and the lindens were dropping their leaves and letting in the pale sunlight like a rain; only the great oaks clung stubbornly to their foliage, the last to die. The racket of the birds and the chittering of insects had vanished into a stillness like the pause between breaths. The men walked beneath a sky tracked with clouds like the ripples in a stream, and the wind was sharp with the north cold. Here and there on the trees they passed were scraps of velvet from the horns of the stags, and once they heard the bellowing of two stags challenging one another.

Each of the men had brought some weapon. Moloquin took his

axe; Hems and Kayon had slings, which they had learned to use to bring down small game during the summer; Brant had a club that looked stronger than he was. The little boy had his hands full of stones, and Bohodon had cut himself a long thin spear of elm wood.

As they drew nearer the ford, the sounds of the competing stags rang out through the trees—the battering and clashing of their horns, and the thunder of their snorting breath. The little boy walked as close to Brant as he could, fearful, and the other men kept close together too. Moloquin went on before them all, crouching down, trying to pad his footfalls; he led them up into the top of the broad meadow by the ford.

From the hillside above he looked down, and there in the open he could see all the deer. The stags were fighting almost in the ford. Their enormous antlers were tangled together, and they leaned their heads into each other and wrenched back and forth, snorting great blasts from their nostrils and twisting their antlers, each trying to throw the other down. Up in the high grass between Moloquin and the stags were the does, grazing in the last of the sunlight.

Placidly, their tails switching, now and then stopping to eat a mouthful of grass, they watched the stags battle, and unlike the stags, they paid heed to the rest of the world also. Long before Moloquin wanted them to, the first doe spied the men in their cautious approach.

Moloquin hissed between his teeth and stood still; he was careful not to look straight at the deer, but stared away into the forest. He could hear Brant breathing, just behind him, and one of the other men moved, crunching a twig underfoot, but the whole band kept as still as they could. One after another, the does raised their heads and looked toward the men. There was a long moment when the stags paused in their clashing.

The little boy coughed. Instantly the does fled away into the trees.

"Now," Moloquin screamed, and he ran after them, bounding over the clumps of sumac and the brambles; as he ran, he shouted and waved his arms, driving the does on ahead of him. The stags struggled apart and bellowed, and one stood its ground a moment while the other charged away; after an instant's wild-eyed look, the second stag raced away also.

They all turned to go uphill, as Moloquin had known they would. He raced to cut them off, shouting his lungs raw, his men following in a noisy stream. Two of the does burst by them, their tails high, but most of the herd wheeled around and plunged back toward the ford, and there the dense underbrush and the close-packed trees stopped them.

Screaming, the men raced up almost on the heels of the panicking herd. Bohodon stopped, set himself, and hurled his spear; the little boy Laughter threw his stones. The deer wheeled and fled in all directions, crashing through the brush, the horns of the stags striking the trees. Then abruptly they were gone, the only remainder of them the fading sound of their flight through the forest, a rustle of brush, a crack of wood.

Baffled, the men milled around at the ford; they had killed nothing, nor even wounded one enough to be able to track it down. Moloquin waded into the stream up to his thighs and bent and splashed cold water onto his face and arms. Bohodon picked up his spear and examined the tip, as if he would find blood on it. He and the other men stared at Moloquin, frowning, wondering, Moloquin thought, if he were truly a chief after all. In silence, in a single file, he led them home again.

A few days later he tried again. He had seen Brant make the rope, stretching it between trees, and that had given him an idea; he took all Brant's rope, and he and the men spent much of a day running the rope from tree to tree along the ford, until the whole narrow space along the streambank was netted with rope. Then he spread out his band of men along the ford, each man hiding in the brush, and they waited.

All through the afternoon and into the evening they waited, but the deer did not come.

They came back the next day also and waited, hiding, keeping silent in the brush, their weapons by their hands, waiting, waiting. At last in the late evening, with the air heavy and grey and smoky with mist, the deer came to the ford. An old doe led them. Head down, feet light, she brought the herd slowly toward the water, and as she reached the water, Moloquin shouted and the men sprang up.

The deer wheeled around, their white tails flashing in the dusk, and bolted up the stream, into the nets of rope. The trees echoed with the shouts of the men. The deer hurtled through the brush ahead of them, bounding over fallen trees; when they hit the nets of rope, they floundered backwards, kicking and thrashing, and the men dashed in among them. Moloquin, in their midst, could see nothing but the blurred wild lashing of the trees and the close bodies of deer heaving around him. He struck with his axe and hit nothing. A deer bolted past him so close her shoulder struck him, her hoof grazed his thigh. He went down on his back in the water; when he rose, the wild racket was fading, and in the brush around him, none leapt and yelled and beat at the branches save his own men. The deer were gone.

Heavily he got to his feet. His thigh was bleeding where the deer had kicked him. His men stood around him with accusing faces in the twilight. His head bowed down, he went away toward the hut, hoping that they would follow him.

In the morning they went back to retrieve Brant's rope. None of the men spoke much to Moloquin, brooding on his failure. While they were coiling up the rope, Laughter found two sticks like the horns of deer, and holding them to his head, he made a playful run at old Brant.

The old man whooped. He caught up a stick from the ground and pretended to strike at the boy with his horns, and laughing they dashed up and down the meadow, the boy snorting and pawing the ground and waving his horns and the old man feigning the blows of a hunter.

Moloquin coiled the rope, pretending not to notice this, but the other men joined in. They took sticks from the ground and threw them at Laughter with his horns, and when the boy was hit, and cried, Hems took his stick-horns and put them on his head, and pretended to be the deer.

All the morning long, they did this. In the end, none played so hard as Bohodon, who cast his spear time after time at the deer, who never seemed to tire of it. When Hems left off at last, and lay down in the sun, Bohodon went off with his spear and threw it at trees and stones.

They carried the rope home again. Moloquin walked with his head down. They needed meat for the winter, meat to be dried and smoked; he had hoped to take several of the deer, but now he saw that some spirit protected the deer and would not suffer their deaths.

He thought of making some effort to speak to this spirit, but he knew no ritual for it. He went to Brant, and said, "Is there a dance for hunting the deer?"

Brant was sitting by the fire in the hut, young Laughter on his knee, picking through the child's hair. "There is a dance for the hunting of the red deer. I do not know what magic you might need for the fallow deer, like these."

Moloquin lowered his gaze to the fire. He felt his ignorance as a great void around him, into which all the People might fall, doomed by his failures. Outside, far off, a howl rose from the belly of the night, climbing higher and higher to a long lonely wail. The wolves also hunted. The wolves did better than he did. The wolves would survive. He put his head down on his knees, staring into the fire.

Bohodon cooked the tip of his spear in the fire, to make it harder, and went out into the forest and threw the spear at everything he saw that moved. He hit nothing, killed nothing. Then Moloquin came with his wild voice and furious looks and drove him away to find firewood.

As he searched for wood—he had to go farther and farther from the new village, the area immediately around it being cleared now of good wood—he searched for other things, for pieces of flint and for dropped antlers, to make a better spear.

In the evenings, when the rest of them sat like women with the women and wove mats of reeds for the walls of the roundhouse, Bohodon sat by the fire and smashed rocks together. Slowly he was recovering something of the craft that the masters of his society had tried to teach him. He had never been able to memorize even one of the many chants necessary to work magic into the stone, but he got the knack of striking the flint at exactly the right angle to knock chips off the edge, and finally he managed to make a stone tip for his spear.

He lashed it on with cords cut from a deerhide, but the first time he cast it into the woods at a rabbit, the tip fell off and he lost it.

So he began over again, making a new tip, although now the rains of autumn lashed the People, and it was cold and there was no game in the forest to hunt anyway. He made another spearhead, and this time he notched the end of his stick and stuck the butt end of the point down into it, bound it with strips of rawhide and soaked it good and long in the stream. When the hide dried out it shrank down around the tip so hard the hardest blow would not move it. He took the spear out to the woods and cast it at trees and shadows and the sky, and the spearpoint stayed fastened, and the spear itself felt good in his hand, light and strong and balanced, like part of his arm.

Moloquin came to him and said, "Put that down and come help us."

Bohodon faced him, his spear in his hands, and said, "No."

Moloquin smiled at him, not a pleasant smile, not the way he smiled at the women, and said, "Put that down and come help us."

"No," said Bohodon again, and raised his spear.

Moloquin raised his axe and struck, and the spear fell in two pieces. Moloquin smiled still. "Come help us," he said, in the same voice, and when Bohodon bent, aghast, for the pieces of his spear, Moloquin's foot was on them.

Hanging his head, he trudged away to join the others. His heart was cankered like a rotten walnut. He went back later to find his spear point but it was gone.

While the rain streamed down over them, and they struggled to raise the last crossbeam to the top of the roundhouse, he told himself that he would kill Moloquin for this.

This beam, being the last, was the hardest to put into place. The rain made everything slippery. Wahela's children sat near the great post North Star and cried, and some of the women cried, too, from effort and exhaustion and despair. They struggled the massive split trunk higher and higher on its cradle of logs, and halfway up the log structure broke and the crossbeam tumbled down.

Screaming, the People scattered away from it. In its fall the trunk like a live thing thrashed this way and that, bumping off other logs and teetering sideways and crashing at last to the ground. They crept in closer to look at it, the rain pouring down their faces.

Moloquin said, "Come, we must try it again."

The women wailed; Bohodon and the other men backed off, shaking their heads. Moloquin looked from one to the next, calm, his hair plastered to his head and his beard to his chest. His axe was in his belt but he did not draw it out to threaten them. Instead he spread out his arms and gathered them in together, close together where the warmth of their bodies surrounded them, and with his head down among their heads he told them a story.

He told them about Abadon, how he drank from a magic spring and was turned into an oak tree. He could neither move nor cry out, but the tree swayed and trembled with his suffering, and all its leaves shed like tears from the branches. Abadon could do nothing but endure this, until at last, in the spring, when the leaves grew again and the birds came and the sun warmed everything, Rael, the Birdwoman, heard the groans and sighs of the oak tree, and she cut down the tree and freed Abadon.

As they listened, they took heart, and they went back to the work again. They built another cradle of logs and lifted up the beam, and with ropes they pulled and tugged, and with poles they pushed and shoved, and at last the beam rolled onto its place.

One end of it would not fit down into the space, but lay up on the beam next to it. Moloquin climbed up on top of the structure and stood there, balanced on the back of the beam in the rain, and with his axe he hewed at the beam until it fit down into its place.

In haste they bound the mats to the walls and laid sticks from the outside to the top of the center post and stretched mats over that. They cut dry grass and branches and piled them onto the roof, crisscrossing the layers back and forth to make it strong against the snow and the rain. The rain soaked them; Brant fell sick and sat on the ground coughing and hanging his head, but no one had time for him. They were all working to make the roundhouse snug and dry and they paid no heed to Brant. Taella his wife brought him a few mats to lie on and a blanket to cover him, and she sat with him for a while, but the others called to her to help them and she left him to work with the others. They piled up leaves and grass against the outside of the roundhouse until the wall was thick as a man was tall; they cut branches to weave through the holes in the mats. When that was done, they hurried to the hut down by the stream, and began to move all their belongings into the new roundhouse, and at last, on the first day when the rain stopped, they went into the roundhouse and the women laid out their hearths, and the men poked smokeholes in the roof and made mats to cover them when the storms blew.

Taella went back to her husband and said, "Come inside, we shall make a fire and get you warm."

Brant lay on his back, his arms over his face, and coughed. Taella ran to find Moloquin.

When Moloquin came over to him, Shateel had joined Taella, and the two women had covered him with mats and hides until he looked like a little hill, but when Moloquin put his hand to the old man's face his skin was cold as a stone.

"Do not take me into the roundhouse," he said. "You will only have to break down the wall again, to get me out," and Moloquin understood what he meant.

Taella said, "We can make him a potion, he will get well." Her face was furrowed with worry; her gaze darted from Brant to Moloquin and back to Brant. She laid one hand to her husband's face. "When you are warm you will feel better."

Brant said, "I will never be warm." He looked at Moloquin beside him and said, "Tell me a story."

"What story?"

"Tell me—" Brant ran out of breath. There was blood on his lips.

Shateel came over to the two men, and she sank down on her knees. "Is he going to be well?" she asked, in a low voice.

Moloquin said nothing to her. He watched the old man's face, thinking that if Brant had stayed with Ladon's People, the old Green Bough master might not now be dying.

He thought of telling the story about Abadon's imprisonment in the oak tree, but instead a tale long unspoken rose to his lips.

"Once there was a child who loved the Sun more than a man loves a woman, or a woman loves her baby, or a chief loves his People. And the Child longed to go to her. Therefore one day he found a beam of sunlight and he began to climb.

"The sunbeam rose up through the branches of a tree. As the Child climbed, the tree said: 'Go back! Go back, little one, before you fall.'

"But the Child said, 'I shall not fall. My mother the Sun shall bear me on her light and I shall not fall.' He climbed higher, but that same day a man with an axe came and chopped down the tree, and the tree fell.

"And the Child climbed higher. And he came on a bird, floating in the air, and the bird said, 'Go back, little one, before you fall.'

"But the Child said, 'I shall not fall. The Sun my mother shall bear me up on her light and I shall not fall.' And he climbed higher.

"But that same day a man came by with a sling, and cast a stone at the bird and struck it, and the bird fell to the earth and was dead as a stone.

"The Child climbed higher still, and came to a cloud. The cloud said, 'Go back, little one, before you fall.'

"But the Child said, 'I shall not fall. The Sun my mother shall bear me up on her light, and I shall not fall.' And he climbed higher.

"And that same day, the cloud passed too near the earth, and the earth reached up and caught it, and drew down all its rain, and the cloud fell to the earth as rain, and was no more.

"And the Child climbed higher and higher. Now the Sun was going down, and she said, 'Child, I go to my rest. But I shall put you in the sky so that you will not fall, but shall share the sky with me.'

"And she took the Child up on her light, and she fixed him to the sky with a little bit of her light, and he shone there as a star forever more."

Moloquin fell still; he sat there a long while, his eyes unseeing. The two women waited, Shateel watching Moloquin, Taella stroking her husband's face.

After a certain time had passed, she said, "He is dead, Moloquin."

Moloquin turned his face toward her. For a long while he stared at her, unable to speak; beside him in a case of unliving flesh lay all the lore of the Pillar of the Sky, lost and gone forever more. At last he struggled back to the surface of time and he gathered the old man up in his arms.

"I will be gone a while," he said. "You must watch over the People."

Taella said, "I am going with you."

She followed him away into the forest. Shateel followed them for several steps.

"Where are you going?"

"To the Pillar of the Sky," said Moloquin, and he went off into the forest. Taella ran a few steps to catch up with him, and they disappeared among the trees.

Shateel stood watching them leave and shivered all over. Turning, she looked down at the bed where Brant had died, the poor pile of mats and little hides, and she fell to weeping. She gathered up the squirrel hides and pressed her face to them and wept.

Wahela came to her, her head twisted to watch where Moloquin had gone. "Where is he going? What is wrong with Brant?"

"Brant is dead," Shateel said. "While we were working, he fell sick, and no one cared for him, and now he is dead."

As she spoke, the horror of that overcame her; she felt that somehow they had abandoned Brant, that had they kept him in their attentions they might have drawn him along with them in the stream of life. Wahela took her hands, clutching the blankets.

"Come, girl, he was an old man, and old men die. Young men also."

Shateel wept the harder, thinking of the story of the Child that climbed to the Sun, and as she did so, inside her body she felt the first movement of her baby.

"Oh," she said. She laid her hand on her body.

Wahela laid her arm around her. "Come into the roundhouse. You will see how wonderful it is. We shall lay out your hearth."

Shateel allowed herself to be led along a few steps, then suddenly remembering what Moloquin had said to her, she stopped and raised her head.

"He went to the Pillar of the Sky."

"What?"

"He took Brant away to the Pillar of the Sky. He will be gone for days."

Wahela's eyes widened; she turned her head to look the way Moloquin had gone, and her arm tightened around Shateel. "I shall take care of you."

"No, you shall not," said Shateel. "He told me to watch over you."

Wahela faced her. Her encircling arm slipped down to her side. "You! You are only a green girl."

"He told me—"

"I for one will take care of myself!" Wahela marched away, up to the roundhouse.

Shateel followed slowly after her, wondering what Moloquin wished of her—she had no idea where to begin, and she knew that the People would not heed her anyway, that they would all be insulted, as Wahela had been. Instead of going into the roundhouse, she went out across the stream, to the new clearing, where in the spring they would plant gardens.

Moloquin had cut down all the dead trees, and the women had cleared the brush and raked it all up into heaps around the stumps. After the long rain there were puddles everywhere, but the sun was streaming in and drying out the ground. She thought, Should we not burn this? Is it dry enough yet?

At least if she did some work she would have something to show him when he came back. She went into the roundhouse, where the other women had taken up the space along the wall, to find a rake.

. . .

With Moloquin gone, Wahela saw no need to work hard. Anyway, it was a poor way to mourn Brant, to go out and work as if nothing had happened, and so she went back to her new hearth and sat down.

Kayon came in; he was making his hearth on the far side of the roundhouse, making space the way men did, just laying down the few things he owned and gouging a mark around them with his heel. Wahela started a fire and heated some rocks in it, to make a potion suitable for mourning. She sent her little boy for the water and rummaged through her stores for the herbs.

Drifting closer to her, Kayon said, "Where is Moloquin?"

"Brant is dead," she told him. "Moloquin took him away to the dead place."

"Dead." Kayon looked around him quickly, from side to side.

"Come sit down," Wahela said. "There is nothing to do anyway, we may as well share some tea."

Kayon came within her hearth and sat down. He was a skinny, tall youth, with reddish brown hair, who never said much. Wahela put a little cup of bark in front of him. When her son returned with the water, she filled his cup and her own, and dropped a hot rock into each, to heat the water.

"Dead," Kayon said again, and again he looked around him.

Ap Min was bustling around her hearth; overhearing what they said, she came closer. "Who is dead?"

"The old man. Brant."

"Ah." Ap Min lowered her head and covered her face with her hands.

"Come here," Wahela said. "Bring the baby, we will sit together and mourn." She brought another bark cup from the stack by the wall.

"Then where is Taella?" Ap Min asked. She brought her baby into Wahela's hearth, and Wahela took it at once and cuddled it and kissed the tiny forehead.

Kayon said, "I'm coming back," and got up and left the roundhouse.

The water was steaming, and Wahela sprinkled herbs into it and stirred it quickly with a twig. She cradled the baby comfortably against her. "Life begins and life ends," she said, and kissed the baby again. "The Mill grinds everything to dust, nothing grows younger."

Ap Min said, "He was a good old man."

"He never said much to me," Wahela said. "Here." She held out the cup of tea, and Ap Min took it.

Kayon came in, the other men behind him: Hems and Bohodon. They crowded into Wahela's hearth, and Hems said, "What is this about the old man?"

"He died," said Wahela. "Moloquin took him to the dead place. Taella followed. They will not be back for days."

She lifted the cup of tea, but Bohodon took it away. "What is this?" He snuffled at it, murmured, and gulped it down. Wahela laughed. They had just entered into a new house, after all; the time had come for a celebration. She sent her son for more water.

Shateel raked the garden slash over, trying to dry it out in the fresh sunlight; she noticed that the others had all gone inside the roundhouse, but she paid no heed to that, until a yell from inside brought her wheeling around.

From the roundhouse came a boisterous chanting. She went to the door and looked in.

There in the center of the roundhouse Bohodon and Kayon were dancing. Their flushed faces and quick jerky movements told her what they had been drinking, even before she smelled the sweet dry aroma in the air. Behind them, Wahela sat laughing in the midst of her hearth like a headwoman of old, surrounded by her children; she sat with her legs spread wide, her skirt looped down between them, and her hair wild as a nest of snakes. As Shateel came in, she raised up a cup and drained it down, and behind her, Hems whooped.

They were all drunk. Shateel went across the roundhouse, circling the two men in their dance.

"Come," she said. "Moloquin would not want you to be doing this."

They raised their faces toward her, their eyes shining, their looks unsteady and full of mirth. "Moloquin," said Wahela. "He will not be back for days. And Brant is dead." Saying that, she lay back comfortably on her elbow, and held out her cup to Shateel. "Come drink with us."

Shateel hesitated, wanting to join them, to be among them, but she remembered that Moloquin had told her to watch over them.

Still, what could she do? They would not obey her, a green girl, as Wahela had said. She went a little closer, and the other whooped.

"Here she comes! She is going to sit down with us, the mere people! This must be a special day." Wahela clapped her hands together. "Come, Shateel, you will see, being happy isn't so hard."

That offended Shateel. In a flash she saw how they looked on her, as someone who held herself apart and above them. Behind her the men were dancing in close circles, but as he passed her Bohodon put out his hand and stroked her backside.

At that she knew she did not belong here. She turned and went out, followed by the jeers and scornful shouts of the others; she went out to the bright sunlight and returned to her work. It was better to be alone, she told herself. She plied the rake savagely at the entangled brush. Better to be alone than with such as those.

Wahela made more tea, and even her children drank some; the little boy Laughter staggered around the roundhouse, throwing his chest out like a man, and strutting. He followed the men in their dancing, trying to imitate them, and fell down under their feet.

Ap Min sat there swaying slowly back and forth, her eyes empty, her lips moving, the baby asleep on her knees. Hems sank down beside her and put his lips to her ear and spoke to her.

The girl giggled. She put out her hand and pushed him, having no effect on him.

"What is it?" Wahela shuffled a little nearer. She was having trouble focussing her eyes; her tongue felt thick. "What does he want? Oh, I can guess!"

Ap Min giggled again, her head wobbling; suddenly she fell over sideways, and Hems caught her and lay down with her. Wahela retrieved the baby from between them. She had seen how Hems loved Ap Min; with approval she watched him pull the girl's clothes apart and fondle her, although Ap Min in a muffled laughing voice told him over and over again to stop. A woman needed a man, Wahela thought; her vision was wrapped in a golden smoky glow, her fingertips tingled, the slightest touch sent ripples of feeling through her. A woman needed a man, but her man was far away, and getting farther off with every step.

He hadn't even told her he was going. Worse, he had told Shateel to watch over his People.

She got up, balancing herself precariously on uncertain feet. In the middle of the roundhouse, the two men were still dancing, but their feet followed no order; their heads hung down, and they no longer tried to chant or beat time with their hands. She went in between them and hung her arms around their necks.

"No one has danced here before," she said. "You have made the roundhouse safe from the spirits, and I thank you."

First she kissed Kayon, but he was skinny and bony and resisted her a little, wide-eyed, perhaps afraid of Moloquin. Next she kissed Bohodon.

He answered with a fierce passion. His hands slipped down around her waist and he pulled her against him. Wahela laughed. She broke away from him, whirling around like a dancer.

"Come, we shall make more tea."

He followed hot behind her; she led him back to her hearth, where Hems and Ap Min lay entwined on the floor, and made him sit down. He got one hand inside her clothes, but she squirmed away from him, smiling over her shoulder at him, to keep him from becoming discouraged.

Kayon joined them all. He helped Wahela pour water into the cups, and dropped hot stones into them; they jiggled the cups to keep the stones from burning through the bark, and the sweet steam rose and made them all giddy. Abruptly Kayon began to sing, an old mourning song of the People, and everyone joined in with what they could remember. Nobody could remember much. The song trailed away into silence, and they sat shaking their heads and sighing.

"Poor old man," Wahela said. She draped one arm around Bohodon's neck and the other around Kayon's. "Even an old man ought to be mourned for, don't you think?"

She kissed them again. Bohodon slid his hands under the hem of her skirt and laid his palms on her thighs, and a delicious warmth spread through her body. Kayon turned his face away from her; he shifted around, so that his back was to her.

"What, are you afraid? Are you afraid of Moloquin?"

Kayon gave her a quick look but said nothing. Bohodon pressed against her, trying to push her down under him, his hands on her hips. "I am not afraid," he whispered into her ear. His fingers touched the curly pelt of her female place.

Wahela twisted away, laughing, her head cocked. "Now, have patience. The tea is almost ready."

A look of fury passed across his face, and she laughed again, delighted. She took the little bowl of herbs and sprinkled more of the dried leaves into the water, and the fragrance rose between them, almost palpable, making her head whirl.

Ap Min had gone to sleep. Hems gathered her up in his arms and carried her away to her own hearth; he came back in a moment and took the baby. His gaze avoided Wahela and Bohodon. He was afraid of Moloquin too. Wahela drank more of the tea. She was not afraid of Moloquin; Moloquin would do whatever she wanted, she had only to tease him and toy with him, as she did Bohodon.

Kayon still sat with his back to her. She leaned toward him, her lips against his ear.

"Come, what are you afraid of? Aren't you a man?" She reached around in front of him and plunged her hand down between his legs, and there, hard and straight, she found good evidence of his manhood; she crowed.

"Don't be afraid, Kayon. Don't be a baby. Let me show you how to be a man, Kayon."

Bohodon pulled her away from the other man. "Leave him alone—stay with me." He dragged her skirts up with one hand; with the other he pushed her down on her back.

"What are you doing?" Shateel cried.

Her voice came like a cold blast of wind into the foggy warmth of Wahela's drunkenness; she raised her wobbling head, unable to find Shateel with her eyes. Bohodon backed away from her, his hands sliding behind him; Kayon got up and walked unsteadily away.

Shateel came closer. Tall and slim, she stood before the hearth, shimmering all over in the veil of light the tea cast over everything. She said, "Is this how you mourn the good old man?"

"Shateel," Wahela said. "Go away."

"Moloquin told me to watch over you."

"We need no watching over." Wahela struggled to sit up. Her skirt was hiked up over her knees and she yanked it down again. "If any of us is the headwoman, it is me." Suddenly she was sick to her stomach.

"He told me!" Shateel said. "And well he did—look at you! What will he say when he learns of this?"

"Who will tell him? You?"

Shateel's mouth worked; she seemed far, far above Wahela, and it ached to keep her head cocked at this angle. Wahela got up on her knees. More tea would clear her mind. She reached for the water skin and the cup.

Shateel moved swiftly, batting the cup away from her. "Leave off!"

"Who are you to tell me what to do?" Wahela scrambled to her feet; her head spun, for a moment she could see nothing but a whirl of colors, and she steadied herself on widespread feet.

"He told me—"

"He can say what he chooses," Wahela cried, "but he sleeps with me!"

"Has he married you?" Shateel asked, in a nasty voice.

"In his heart he has married with me," Wahela said. She glared at Shateel, hating her.

The other woman looked pointedly around—at the drunken men, and the hearth littered with cups and clothes. Her gaze remained longest on Bohodon, glowering up at her from one side. Facing Wahela again, she said, "Have you married him?"

Wahela scowled at her. Swaying slightly, she stood in the midst of her revel and struggled with the understanding that Shateel was right. Finally she reached out her hand and pushed Bohodon away.

"Yes," she said. "I am his wife, and he is my husband." She turned, avoiding Bohodon's look of anger, avoiding Kayon's look. "Go away." She was tired, anyway. It would not have been much of a delight, she was too drunk. "Go away!" She wheeled, her fists lashing out, driving them all from her hearth, even her children, and she went into the back and lay down on her sleeping mat, covered herself with a mat of reeds, and went to sleep.

Shateel got the others to help her, and they raked up the dry brush that covered the garden into heaps and burned it, and they burned up the stumps of the oak trees too, as much as they could. When Moloquin and Taella returned, the whole garden was a bed of smoking grey ash.

He said to her, "Good, you have done well."

Shateel said, "The others all helped me."

Moloquin had his mother's axe over his shoulder; he looked at her a moment, and turned his head to survey the entire clearing. "Did you have any trouble?"

"No," Shateel said. "But we all mourned for Brant. The men danced."

Behind Moloquin, Taella raised her head. She had scratched her cheeks with her nails, in token of mourning; she looked tired. Shateel went past Moloquin to take the older woman's arm. "Come inside and sit, I will bring you something to eat."

Bohodon made himself another spear, and he crept away into the forest whenever he could and looked for something to kill with it. He saw a few rabbits, and once in the evening, as he stood dispirited by an elm tree, an owl slid by him like a shadow, but he missed every shot he took.

One night he fell asleep in the meadow above the ford where he and the other men had hunted the fallow deer, and he dreamt of a great deer that attacked him with its horns and felled him and would have slain him, had he not then wakened. When he opened his eyes the moon was high, but the meadow around him was strange, all blue and glistening, and he realized that a light snow was falling. There in the middle of it was a single deer, pawing up the snow to reach the grass. The snow that covered Bohodon had deadened his scent.

His spear lay beside him. He held his breath, for fear of warning the deer, and moved his hand slowly, patiently downward until he grasped the wooden shaft. He knew he should say some charm now, some chant, but all he could think of was Moloquin's name. He leapt up and cast the spear in a single motion.

The deer whirled away at the first motion, but it spun around into the path of the spear, and the stone point took it through the neck. The deer went down on its knees, the spear stuck fast in its white throat, and Bohodon bounded over the snow and fell on it. Seizing the haft of the spear, he drove it down into the ground, piercing the neck of the deer all through. It took all his strength to hold the spear while the animal thrashed and kicked and flopped, and then a gush of blood, black in the moonlight, erupted from its mouth, and its writhings grew feeble and it lay still at last.

Bohodon sank down beside it, panting after the struggle. The moon shone on the deer's wide dark eyes. He said to it, "I have killed you because I am hungry, and this shall feed me—me and my People. I, Bohodon, have killed you. You shall feed me and make me great with my People and I am grateful to you."

The beast gave a last shudder, and its legs stiffened out. He got up and felt at his belt for his knife, to dress it out.

The snow began to fall while Moloquin was chopping wood with his axe. He did not stop to look up but he felt the flakes that landed on his shoulders like blows, the warnings of the cold dead winter that was now on him.

When he was done, he carried a great load of the wood into the roundhouse, such a heavy load that it bent him over, and he went from one hearth to the next, giving each enough wood to keep them warm all night. What was left he took into the center of the round-house, to the foot of the post called North Star.

While he sat there, making his own fire, and listening to Ap Min's baby cry, first Taella and then Wahela came to him and gave him some of their food: a cake made of acorn meal, a soup of greens and bulbs in a turtle shell bowl that was Taella's proudest possession. Moloquin took this without speaking to the women. He ate fitfully, distracted; his head turned often toward the far side of the round-house, where Ap Min walked up and down, up and down, her baby yelling on her shoulder. The light of the several fires threw her shadow flickering against the wall and turned her hair the color of copper.

He thought, If the baby dies, all my People will die.

The baby's name was Elela, a name chosen after long debate, a name that meant Our First Woman. Moloquin had come to believe that this child, the first born to his People, was a talisman, and he watched her every day with delight or apprehension, according to the baby's ways.

Hems came in through the door and called, "It's snowing! Every-body, the snow is coming down."

Laughter and his sister ran to see, although it was dark, and Wahela crossed the roundhouse to call them in immediately. Molo-quin got up and looked patiently from hearth to hearth until he had seen everyone. Bohodon was not there, but Bohodon was gone often lately, and was of no use when he was here. Perhaps he was thinking of running away to join Ladon's People again.

Moloquin thought of Ladon's roundhouse, of the great piles of food in his storerooms. He raised his eyes, looking up into the rafters over his head, where the supplies of his own People were stored. There seemed so little. Now the winter had begun; there would be nothing to eat save what they had gathered. If that wasn't enough—

He thought, Ladon's People have much. If we run out of food, we can steal more from them.

If they had to steal from Ladon's People, then in truth they would still be Ladon's People. Moloquin sank down, his chin on his hand, his elbow on his knee. Brant was dead; his dream of building the Pillar of the Sky seemed dead also. All his life had closed down around him to one matter: that he should have food enough for his People through the winter.

And after that, if they lived until summer, what then? They would struggle to pack away enough food for the next winter. It was changeless, grim, inexorable. He could strive for years, do all things right for years and years, yet in the end one mistake would wipe them all out. For the first time he saw that the Mill would eventually destroy him.

Now, suddenly, that seemed something to be grateful for—a promise of rest, of deliverance from life. If he could not make his dream come true at the Pillar of the Sky, all else seemed the poor leavings of someone else's feast.

Late in the night a sound at the door brought him forth from sleep. He stood up, reaching for the bronze axe where it hung on the North Star post. In through the door came Bohodon, crouched down under the burden of a deer slung across his shoulders.

From behind Moloquin, Hems shouted, "Bohodon! Hi, hi, look what he has! Ap Min, wake up, we shall have fresh meat today."

The others woke too, their voices bubbling up in a sudden froth of sleepy sound. Exhausted, beaming widely, Bohodon trudged heavily into the center of the roundhouse and let his burden slip from his back.

"Aaaah," he said, straightening.

The others whooped. From all sides they rushed forth, and the little boy Laughter flung himself howling on the deer as if he himself

must kill it, and the women cried out Bohodon's name and the men
grunted and humphed and went to Bohodon and slapped him on
the back and admired his spear. Moloquin stood quietly by the tree
North Star, but he smiled on Bohodon, who had come back after all,
and brought meat with him.

Bohodon held out his spear for all to see; with many wide gestures and grimaces he showed them how he had struggled with the
deer and killed it. He danced a few steps of the Dance of Hunting
the Red Deer, and the men clapped their hands together to make a
drumbeat, and the women sang to him in triumph.

Wahela and Taella skinned out the deer and removed the tender
innards. The smell of blood filled up the roundhouse. Bohodon
raised his spear high and lunged down at the deer with it, and all the
men shouted; they surged around the close confines of the roundhouse, full of passion for the hunt.

At last Bohodon faced Moloquin, and their eyes met. The others
quieted, holding their breath, their faces bright with expectation.
Moloquin himself did not know what would happen next. His axe
hung on the tree behind him; had Bohodon chosen, he could have
driven his spear through Moloquin's chest.

Bohodon came forward a few steps, and then abruptly he bent
down and he laid his spear at Moloquin's feet.

The People gave up a roar of delight. The men closed around
Bohodon again, touching him, congratulating him, hoping for some
of his luck; the women went to build a fire, to cook the deer's lights.

Moloquin put his hands on Bohodon's shoulders and smiled into
his face, and the hunter went red and stammered something.

"You brought us fresh meat," Moloquin said, in a low voice.
"When the snow fell, and the earth was locked up against us, you
brought us food to eat. Therefore we shall not call you Bohodon
anymore, but Bahedyr, the Hero." He put his arm around the man
and embraced him.

"Bahedyr," Hems cried, and shook his fist above his head. "Bahedyr!"

The newly named one whirled around. He caught up his spear
and danced around the roundhouse; he danced with the swiftness
and leaps of the deer, and crouching low he danced the stalking of
the deer. The fire leapt high, lighting up the whole place, lighting
the faces of the People. The stew cooking in the belly of the deer
simmered and bubbled. Outside was snow and cold, but inside was

warmth and food, fire and friendship, and Moloquin, for a while anyway, could put off his longings and his dreams.

In the deep of the winter, Ladon's son came to Moloquin's Village.

He came with two other men of Ladon's People. They had gotten lost in the forest in their search for Moloquin, and had feared death, so when they finally found the tracks of their own kind in the snow, and followed them close enough to see the smoke of the fire, they were too relieved to maintain their dignity; they rushed forward into the village.

It was the middle of the day, and the sun was bright, hanging low in the sky, gilding the leafless tree branches. Moloquin's People were out of the roundhouse, enjoying the sunshine and the warmth; they had cleared away the snow from around the roundhouse and made a fire. On the frozen surface of the stream, down a little way from the roundhouse, the children were playing with the ribs of a deer tied to their feet, skidding back and forth over the ice. Shateel and Wahela, roasting chestnuts over the fire, saw the newcomers first.

Shateel recognized her husband at once, and stood up. She cast a quick look around her for Moloquin, but he was off chopping wood. She raised her hand, and Ladon's son and the others trudged up the little slope toward her. From inside the roundhouse, Taella called, "Who is there? Is someone coming?" and looked out.

Shateel put her hand on Wahela's shoulder. "Go find Moloquin."

Ladon's son came ahead of the others to the fire. Seeing Shateel, he smiled and reached out his hands to her. He was a grown man now, tall and slender like a birch tree, with long soft muscles in his arms and shoulders, and hair like the dry grass that stuck up through the snow; his skin, which even when he was a boy had always resisted the sun, was now as pale as the snow.

He held out his hands, but Shateel would not take them. She said, "Moloquin is coming, you must talk to him, whatever it is you have come here to say."

"Where is he?" said one of the other men, and she saw that it was Fergolin, the Bear Skull master, and she was amazed to see him, because he was gaunt as a stick.

Impulsively, she said, "Sit down and eat." Stooping, she took the chestnuts out of the fire and gestured to them to eat.

They struggled to keep their pride, but she saw how they fell on these few kernels of food, and her heart sickened; she knew that famine had struck Ladon's People. She went into the roundhouse, to find them more food. When she came out again, her hands full of nutcakes and dried deer meat, Moloquin was there.

He stood on the far side of the fire from Ladon's son. He stood straight and tall, with the axe over his shoulder, and before him Ladon's son seemed only a boy still.

He said, "What do you want to say to me?"

Ladon's son was leaning over the fire, trying to warm himself. He said, "Opa-Moloquin-on, my father is dying."

"I am not sorry to hear that," said Moloquin.

Now Fergolin stood, bringing himself up to his full height, and recovering the proud bearing of a Bear Skull master. He spoke in a low voice, and he spoke of hunger.

"There is hardly enough food for each of us to have a handful every day," he said. "The children cry without stopping, and their mothers are glad that they cry, for when they cease, it is from exhaustion and they die soon afterward. The men have no strength for dancing, and the spirits have crowded in on us; the longhouses are noisy with their murmurings; it is as much a village of the dead as of the living now."

"How did this happen to you?" Shateel asked.

"The weather was bad," said Fergolin. "And other things—I know little of such matters, women's matters—the fact is, I believe, that Ladon had given away all the stores, and so when this harvest failed, there was nothing to fall back on."

"Go to Rulon's People," Moloquin said. "We have enough here to feed ourselves, but we are only a small village. Go to Rulon."

"We have come to you," said Fergolin, "because the headwomen have chosen you to be our chief, now that Ladon is dying."

"Ah," said Moloquin.

"The headwomen say that only you can make things right again—that this has come upon us because Ladon tried to overturn the order of such things. You are his sister's son, and only you can save us."

Moloquin looked at Ladon's son. "What do you say to this?"

"They are right," said Ladon's son. "I will surely make no trouble for you. I could not bear it, to carry a whole People on my back."

"We have chosen you," said Fergolin. "Will you come to be our chief?"

All Moloquin's People had drawn near enough to hear this, and they hushed, listening for his answer; Shateel saw in each of their faces what she felt herself: that they were near to losing Moloquin, and without him they were nothing. Moloquin frowned. He faced the newcomers for a long time, his expression blank as the ice of the streambed, and as cold.

At last he said, "You drove out my mother Ael, and she died. You let my mother Karella die, although she warned you against Ladon. For these reasons you must suffer as you are. No, Fergolin, I shall not be your chief. Go back to Ladon's People and tell them to go to Rulon."

Fergolin bowed his head; Ladon's son pressed his fingers to his face. Moloquin looked around him for Shateel, and put out his hand to her.

"Will you speak to this man?"

She said, "I have nothing to say to him."

"What is that you are carrying?"

She held out her hands, full of food. "I thought to give this to them."

"Do it."

She went to the three men and put food into their hands, and saw with a sharp pang of sympathy how their hands were crooked and eaten with cold. Moloquin went into the roundhouse.

"How did you find us?" she asked.

Fergolin chewed the tough dried meat, swallowing the juices in his mouth. He said, "We noticed that Brant lay in the Pillar of the Sky, and so we knew you were not too far away—also, that you were still living, and still of the People, obeying the rituals. Then we came into the forest and searched."

She said, "I wish you had been spared the search. There is no hope for you here."

Ladon's son watched her steadily. Fergolin said, "Our only hope is here. If the spirits have not already determined that we should all die, they will soften Moloquin to us, and he will save us. It is in his hands now."

"That is a terrible burden to put on anyone," said Shateel.

"It is in his hands," Fergolin said again, and leaned closer to the fire.

. . .

Inside the roundhouse, Moloquin went to the tree North Star, and he took the bronze axe down from its peg, and he knelt before it. His mind was in a fury with itself, and his body shivered all over with the struggle within his heart.

He wanted to go to Ladon's People, to enter into his destiny, but he could not bear to go to that village and hear the wail of babies and see people suffering and starving when he could do nothing. He thought, *They must suffer for what they have done.* Yet he longed so to go there, and to see Ladon, before he died, that it was as if a hand pushed at him.

As he thought this, it became clear to him why he was in such turmoil, and what he must do. He picked up his axe and pressed his forehead to the flat of the blade, then put the weapon in his belt and went outside again.

The messengers stood around the fire, warming themselves. One by one the others of Moloquin's People had come closer to offer them something to eat—even the children responded to their suffering; Laughter brought them an acorn cake he had been given for his dinner, and the little girl crept nearer and offered up a handful of dead leaves to Fergolin.

The Bear Skull master took the leaves as if they were real food; he gathered the child into his arms and hugged her. Moloquin went forth, and Taella came to him, her face resolute.

"We have given up our day's food for them—all but the children's share."

He nodded to her. "You are my People, I know the great hearts of my People."

Fergolin looked up at him; he still held the little girl on his lap. Moloquin said, "I shall go with you, back to Ladon's Village, to see him before he dies."

Ladon's son raised his head, his eyes wide. "He spoke of that."

"Hah?"

"He said that he would not die without seeing you face to face."

Moloquin nodded, recognizing again the power that drew him toward that deathbed. They had been bound together, he and Ladon, all his life; it was fit that they should close out Ladon's life together. He said, "I shall get ready, we shall go soon."

He went into the roundhouse; as he went past Shateel, he gave her such a look that she went after him into the dark warmth of the dwelling. Inside, he took a coat that Wahela had made for him out of squirrel hides, and he filled a pouch with food for the journey. Sha-teel watched him, alarmed.

She said, "Will you come back?"

He swung toward her, wide-eyed, and put his hand on her arm. "Of course. Are you worried, little goose? How could I leave my People for very long?"

"Yet you could have Ladon's People, who are much greater than us."

His hand still lay on her arm; he looked deeply into her face and he tried to smile but could not. After a moment, he said, low, "You are my People. I will never desert you. While I am gone, you must care for everyone. There is a lot of wood already cut, get the boy to haul it in. Keep them from fighting."

"Why do you give this to me to do? Wahela was angry the last time, and would not obey me."

His eyebrows rose in round arches. "Yet you did well enough. Don't complain. Have you told Ladon's son about your baby?"

"Surely he must be able to see for himself."

Moloquin gave a little shake of his head. He cast his look around the roundhouse; finally his gaze returned to her.

"Take care of my People," he said, and gripped her arm so hard it hurt her. Taking the bronze axe, he went out the door.

Ladon's son had thought the journey through the forest to Molo-quin's Village was hard, but the way back was much worse—Molo-quin set such a pace that the others were forever breaking into a trot to keep up with him, and he chose a route that led over hills and across stretches of frozen marsh. Ladon's son slipped on the ice once and fell hard; when he rose, his back hurt.

He had always hated the forest. Even as a boy he had avoided the trees, loving the open grasslands, where he could see all around him for a long way. Now, plunging along in Moloquin's tracks, he saw the dim winter-gaunted woods around him as a cage, a construction of demons. Against the pallor of the snowy ground, the trees rose in thin black bars, and wraiths of mist drifted through them, rags of mist clinging like haunted women to the lower branches and rising in plumes from the patches of standing water, edged in crackling bubbly ice. Nothing lived here, yet he felt himself constantly watched and constantly despised.

At night they stopped and built a fire and huddled around it; Fergolin and Muron covered themselves with their coats and fell asleep, looking no more than rotted logs there beside the fire. Ladon's son shivered. His body was exhausted but his mind leapt and raced, frightened of the death-like stillness of sleep. He watched Moloquin poke the fire with a stick.

In spite of his new beard and his magic axe, Moloquin was no different, he told himself several times, as if repetition would make it true: he was still a skinny black-haired boy who said nothing. Still the outcast; still the Unwanted One. The irony of that name bore in on Ladon's son like the cold winter wind sweeping through the trees. They wanted him now. Even Ladon wanted him now. Ladon's son sank deeper into his coat, shivering, and his stomach growled for food.

"Here." Moloquin broke a seed-cake in half and held it out to him.

"No," said Ladon's son, stoutly, although his mouth watered at the sight of it.

"Don't be a fool. I will not carry you if you get too weak to walk. Eat." Moloquin tossed the piece of cake into his enemy's lap.

Ladon's son took it with fingers that trembled; he nibbled at it at first, but hunger seized him and he stuffed it all into his mouth and chewed a few times and swallowed the whole cake, barely softened. Then it was gone. He licked the sweet taste from his fingers until all he could taste was salt.

Moloquin was watching him, his face expressionless. He said, "What happened to you? How did such a numerous village fall into such a situation?"

Ladon's son licked his lips. He leaned toward the fire and put his hands out to it and laid his gaze on it, because he feared the scorn of Moloquin when he heard the truth.

"Ladon would not move the village. The women told him they needed it moved but he would not, because he would not do as they said, and because he was afraid that if he moved, then people would say he was afraid of you. I don't think he really was afraid of you, but he was afraid of seeming so."

Moloquin made a sound in his chest; Ladon's son stole a glance at him and saw Moloquin looking away, a smile on his lips.

"So we stayed. But the crops would not grow well, they grew thin and weak and bore no fruit, and then, just before the harvest, there was a storm that flattened everything into the mud. When the women managed to harvest there were only a few baskets from each of the gardens.

He passed his hand over his eyes, remembering how the women had wept in the middle of their fields. He himself had not understood. He had thought, as most of the People did, that in the rafters of the roundhouse was enough food to last them all for many winters.

"But there was nothing. There were only empty baskets, sacks stuffed with straw. He had given it all away to Harus Kum, to get the blue beads."

"What did the women do?"

"They cursed Ladon." Ladon's son sank his head down between his shoulders. "And me they cursed also. They did not know what part I had in it. Had they known—"

A surge of guilt rose in his throat and stopped his voice. He lifted his face toward Moloquin.

"You must save us. We have done evil, the spirits have condemned us. Only you can bring us back to the path of life again."

Moloquin turned his face away. "Sleep. We have far to go tomorrow." He pulled his coat around him. Ladon's son searched the features of the other man a long while, hoping for some sign that Moloquin would soften, but Moloquin's face was hard as stone. After a while, they both lay down and gave themselves to sleep.

When Moloquin came to the village of Ladon's People, it was like a village of the dead.

There were no dogs any more to bark. There were no pigs any more, nor any goats; all had been eaten. There were no songs any more, nor any dances, nor the busy sounds of work. In all the village the only noise was the whimpering and crying of the children.

The People sat in the sun and stared into the empty air; and some of those who sat there were already dead. The boys of the boys' band sat near their mothers; they did not run and chase one another and play their games in the old gardens by the river. The women sat with their children, their hands in their laps; they did not go any more to the gardens on the high ground, nor did they weave or make pots, or put wood on the dead fires in the hearths.

The men sat in the yard of the roundhouse; they did not dance, or work with their masks, or make tools. They sat where they were and did nothing, and their bodies were like the trees of the dead of winter that had no leaves on them, but only the gaunt and brittle branches.

Moloquin came through the village, looking around him with every step, and his heart quaked in his breast. It seemed to him that they were already enveloped in death, that they could not see him who was not of their company, who was alive. He felt that he moved invisibly through their midst.

He went by the circle of the old women, and there he saw the sampo, silent on its center post, and around it the old women sat like lumps of clay. They looked dead, except, when he looked closely at them, he saw in their eyes the last little flicker of life, trembling with weakness, and soon to go out.

He went on, and he came to the roundhouse.

When the men saw him there they struggled to rise. Some were strong enough to stand, and they stood up, and the others who could not stand stretched up their arms, and their brothers helped them stand to greet their new chief. At the sight of them Moloquin struggled to keep himself from weeping. He had seen them when they were his enemies, when they were strong and full of life, when they cursed him and stoned him, and he wished they were the same now as they had been, even if they should have been his enemies again.

He went into the roundhouse; he went through the roundhouse, until he came to the bed where Ladon lay, there at the center of the roundhouse, under the hole in the roof that let the light in, at the foot of the tree called North Star.

Moloquin went down on one knee beside the bed. Ladon lay there like a corpse; his body had shrunk down around him like a pile of dead leaves. Only, when Moloquin knelt down beside him, the dying man opened his eyes and saw him, and he opened his mouth and spoke.

"Moloquin," he said. "You have come."

"Yes," said Moloquin.

"I knew you would come," said Ladon, his voice barely above a whisper. "I have something to say to you before I die."

"Speak it," said Moloquin.

"The old women have named you the chief," said Ladon.

"Is that what you would say to me?"

"No. It is this: that Ael and I—"

The dying man sighed, and his eyes shut; Moloquin went stiff all through him, every muscle tensing. He forced himself still, to wait, and eventually Ladon opened his eyes again.

"Ael had many men," he whispered. "Or so I thought. But now that I am lying here and soon must go among those who went before me, I have been thinking, and I do not remember now that I knew certainly that she had many men. Perhaps I only thought that to excuse what I did with her."

Moloquin clenched his teeth. He clenched his fist on his knee. He said nothing.

"Maybe I was the only one who lay with her," Ladon whispered. "Maybe I am your father, Moloquin."

"No," Moloquin said.

"Maybe," said Ladon, and he smiled, and his eyes closed again; he lay there as if he were dead already.

Moloquin got up. He was trembling all over, and his mind boiled in a wild passion of feelings, of rage and shame and fear, and of blind hatred. He walked straight out through the old echoing roundhouse, with its rafters full of empty baskets and its shadows full of ghosts.

He went into the yard of the roundhouse where the men sat close around their fire, and he bent down and took a burning brand from the fire. He faced the men with their hollow faces and their sunken eyes and said, "Whatever you have inside that you want, you must get it out now."

Ladon's son came to him and said, "What are you going to do?"

Moloquin stared at him, hating him for his father's sake. He said, "This roundhouse is full of evil. It must be destroyed."

"My father—"

"Ladon is dead," Moloquin said, and turned his back on Ladon's son.

The other men obeyed him. They went into the roundhouse and came out again, each with his mask, a few tools, a blanket, a coat, some beads, some feathers, a flute, bits of rock. Some of them brought out the baskets that held what was left of their food—a few handfuls of meal, some roots, some herbs. None questioned Moloquin. Ladon's son himself went in and came out again with a bundle wrapped in a blanket. When they had all gotten what they wished out of the roundhouse, Moloquin lifted the burning torch in his hand and set the roof on fire.

The flames leapt quickly up across the whole roof and crept down the sides of the roundhouse; within a moment the whole building was blazing. Moloquin stepped back, and the other men all stepped back as well, their arms up to protect them against the heat. The women had come in from the longhouses, to see what was done, and they put out their hands and warmed themselves at the heat of the fire.

The baskets with what remained of their food stood by the fence, and some of the People crept to them. They bent over the baskets and put their hands into the meal and licked the raw meal from their fingers. When some dribbled into the dirt they bent to lick it up out of the dirt. The others hesitated only long enough to see that Moloquin was not stopping this, and then they too went to the food baskets and crowded in close to get as much as they could.

Moloquin stood watching them, his mind in black turmoil. Ladon's son came to him.

"They will eat it all," he said. "We shall all starve if they eat everything now, we shall be dead within days."

"Let them," Moloquin said, and he turned and walked away.

He went up across the plain to the Pillar of the Sky. Behind him the plume of smoke from the blazing roundhouse climbed into the pale clouds, carrying the stench of Ladon up to Heaven.

He walked into the Pillar of the Sky as if into the embrace of a lover. The grass was full of bones. When he climbed over the embankment, a great horde of crows flapped up into the air, so dense a cloud of them that they cast a deep shadow over the circle of collapsing stones. Moloquin walked down into the middle of the place, and he lay down and wept.

He had never wondered who his father was. In his loyalty to Ael he had needed no father. He had always assumed, deep in his mind, that, however she had come to be pregnant with him, she had been blameless. Now he knew she had done something foul, something worse than foul, to get him.

He wept until his eyes were empty; exhausted, he lay still. Then the air darkened; a deep shadow formed over him, and the crows dropped down into the grass, flopping and black, and waddled to the corpses lying in the grass, and drove their beaks like daggers into the raw flesh, tearing up chunks of the flesh of the dead.

Moloquin gave a hoarse cry. He sprang to his feet and ran forward, waving his arms, and before his onslaught the crows scattered up into the sky again, squawking and ugly.

He saw now how full the place was. Some of the bodies were sitting up, propped against stones; they had walked here, in their extremity, walked here to die, perhaps to save some of the food for others, perhaps merely to end their own suffering. Others, the little ones, the children, lay carefully covered up under piles of green boughs, yet still the carrion birds had reached them, torn out their eyes, pierced the skin with their beaks, and opened their bodies for the feast.

Thus Brant had passed from this world into the next one, and with him, all the ageless lore of the Pillar of the Sky, gone forever beyond the mind of man: a thousand generations of patient learning, gone.

Here Karella had lain, with her stories.

Soon they would all lie here; soon the last would walk up the long slope to take their places here, among the dead, at the gateway into the Overworld. When they were gone, there would be no more.

No more. Their laughter, their hopes, their quarrels, their hatreds: no more. Their lore, their stories, their skills, their understanding, all the meaning of their lives: no more.

Brant and Karella remained here still, alive in the memory of the People. Even Ael, the outcast, had come here in the end, to join her soul with the souls of her People, and even she they remembered, kept alive in their minds. Without the living People to sustain them, the spirits would vanish, scattered into the heartless depth of eternity.

Now, sitting there, while the crows hovered angrily above him, he saw how small his own passions were, how light and empty. Here was the real horror, that the strivings and learning of a whole People were about to be swept from the world; very soon it would be as if none of them had ever lived at all.

Around him the circular space murmured with the wind; surely all the spirits of the People crowded here today, gathering in the dead, and mourning the living. He turned, his eyes struggling to make them out in the air—to see Karella again, and Ael—and as he did, his heart grew strong, and his soul rebelled against their fate.

He would not let them die. Whatever they had done to him, they were his People. He would save them if he could, or go with them into oblivion. A trace of dark smoke still towered into the air above the village. He went out of the Pillar of the Sky and walked down toward that monument of smoke, to take up his destiny.

Ladon's son struggled along through dry grass to his waist, his breath short; there was a sharp pain under his ribs on the left side, and he pressed his hand to it. When he came at last to the top of the slope, he said, "This is useless, Moloquin—Rulon will give us nothing."

"They must have good food," said Moloquin, without pausing in his swinging stride. They went down the long rolling slope toward the river. For the best part of the day they had been following the river north, sometimes walking within sight of it and sometimes swerving over hilltops to avoid the marshes and the dense brush along the banks. Ladon's son was weak with hunger and often thought he could go no further.

Now he sank down onto his knees, the pain unbearable under his ribs, and called, "Leave me here. I must rest."

Moloquin came back to him through the whispering grass. "It is not so much farther now. Come along."

Ladon's son sat down, his legs folded under him, and leaned on one arm; he thought, looking down at the brown surface of the river, that it would not be so hard to sit here and to die quietly here in the open, with the river rolling by. His mother, dead many years now, had told him once that the river was one of the pathways to Heaven, and perhaps it was true. Moloquin took him by the arm.

"Come, get up, you are not dead yet. You ate well yesterday, didn't you?"

They had all eaten well yesterday, some had eaten until they were sick, and vomited the food on the ground, and lapped it up again like brutes, their tongues stroking the dust. Still, five more had died in the night, huddled on the ground near the ashes of the roundhouse.

"I cannot—I cannot—"

Moloquin pulled him onto his feet and held him there. "What a weakling you are. Keep going, or I will take my axe to you. What would Shateel think of you if she saw you crying like a baby?"

At that, Ladon's son stiffened his knees and tried to get himself upright again. His legs gave way. Moloquin grunted in his chest and effortlessly hoisted him up on to his shoulders.

"You are a baby," he said, and set out, walking lightly and easily under the weight of a grown man. "A fool, brother, and a weakling, and that is why you must do as I say and have no say of your own."

"Put me down," said Ladon's son, amazed. He hung over Moloquin's shoulder, his feet and his head bobbing at the level of Moloquin's waist. "Put me down—I will walk."

Abruptly he was swung around onto his feet again, and his head spun a little; now he wondered for an instant why Moloquin had called him brother, and wanted to ask but dared not. Already Moloquin was walking away, and Ladon's son followed him, trying to keep up, his hand to his side.

They went on, following the river north, and came to a place where the course of the stream bent a little to the east. There was an island in the middle of the stream and on it three old twisted willow trees dragged their branches in the water, like old women netting fish. Now Ladon's son stopped and turned west and pointed.

"There. That way is the High Hill—the Mount of Heaven, Abadon's High Seat. Rulon's roundhouse is just below it."

They went off along a well-worn path in the meadow grass, and as they came closer to the place where Rulon lived with his People, they crossed more paths, and saw some children playing in the lee of a long wedge-shaped hill. Coming down between that hill and another long lump of ground, they passed by a group of three standing stones, and then saw before them the High Hill.

It rose up from the flat plain, high and smooth, as evenly shaped as a woman's breast. On the top were three more standing stones, and all around the foot of the hill, set up against the base and lying in the grass, were stones, of the same deep-colored stuff as the stones at Turnings-of-the-Year, some two and three times as tall as a man.

This place throve, as Ladon's Village had once thrived. Here many people worked. There were strips of cleared ground around the foot of the hill, and in them women cut down brush and burned tree-stumps, to make ready for the spring planting, and on the slope of the hill a little flock of goats grazed, watched over by little boys. As Moloquin and Ladon's son came around the foot of the hill, they nearly walked on some cloth, spread out to bleach in the sun, and a woman shouted to them to change their course.

Moloquin paid no heed to any of this. With Ladon's son at his heels, he went around the foot of the High Hill, looking for Rulon's roundhouse.

At last they saw the brush fence, and above it, three thatched roofs. When they went into the village through the gap in the fence, the sun was going down. Ladon's son could smell meat broth cooking somewhere. He heard a sampo clattering and chattering at its work. They went in between the two longhouses, with their doors facing east, just as many of Rulon's People were crowding indoors, with armloads of firewood, with baskets and bowls, to begin the evening meal.

When Ladon's son saw this, all the things of the village—the women at their work, the men dressed in feathers and furs, the children fat and happy—his heart quaked, longing for this life again for himself. He hung his head, thinking of the evil that he and his People had done to bring ruin on them; in his heart he promised never to do wickedness again.

They reached the roundhouse, and standing before the door, Moloquin called out Rulon's name.

One of the men of the village came to the door. He scowled at Moloquin and Ladon's son and said, "What do you want, strangers?"

"We are not strangers," Moloquin said, "but of your own kind. We are of Ladon's Village, or that which once was Ladon's Village, and I have come to see Rulon."

The man squared himself in the doorway, his hands on his hips. His gaze went over Moloquin's shoulder to Ladon's son and back again. All around the yard now others of Rulon's People came to hear what was being said.

"I know that one," said the man in the doorway. "He is the son of Ladon, who could not keep Shateel happy and whose village is cursed now. You I do not know. Who are you, with your uncouth speech and your ugly looks?"

"I am Moloquin," said that one. "Ladon is dead now, and I am the chief of my People. I want to talk to Rulon."

"Moloquin," said the man in the doorway, in a jeering tone. "You are unwanted here, Unwanted One."

Ladon's son saw Moloquin put his hand to his belt, to the axe at his belt, and he sucked in his breath; but Moloquin's fingers only played along the ashwood handle of the weapon. The man in the doorway snarled at him.

"Your People are cursed. Great wrong you did, and now great wrong must fall on you, to repay you. That is what Rulon says."

"Let me hear that from Rulon," Moloquin said mildly.

From behind him now came the voices of the crowd. "Stone them! Drive them away—back to their hovels!" "Let them suffer!" "Go away, wicked ones—cursed ones." "They will pollute our village with their evil!"

But from the crowd came another, a woman, huge and shapeless as a mountain: Joba, the headwoman of her kindred, the mother of Rulon.

She said, "Is this how our village greets a chief of the People?"

At her voice all other voices fell silent. She advanced until she stood beside Moloquin, but she gave him no look; she stood there looking into the roundhouse, and she called for her son, she called for Rulon.

Now here Rulon came, stepping through the door into the sunlight.

He was no older than Ladon's son. His hair was oiled and braided and strung with painted feathers and his face was colored like a mask. Over his shoulders he wore a great black bearskin and he carried a club made of the root of a tree, studded with flint spikes. As he walked, he seemed tall as a young tree, and he teetered a little, swaying like a sapling in the wind; he walked on shoes with high soles, to make him bigger.

He said, "Who comes to make noise in my yard? Ah, it is Ladon's son, whom my sister spurned for a wild man out of the forest. And who is this you have brought with you?"

He peered at Moloquin, blinking, as if he did not see very well.

Moloquin said, "I am the wild man out of the forest. I have come to ask your help, Rulon."

From the crowd packed into the yard around them there went up a cry of scorn and anger, and Rulon straightened himself up, brandished his club, and bound his painted face into a mask of outrage. "Address me by my proper dignity, woods-child, or I shall drive you forth like a dog."

Moloquin looked around him again; beside him Joba stood with her chin up, her eyes directed straight forward, past her son, into the distance. Moloquin faced Rulon again.

"Yes, Opa-Rulon-on. You are the chief of a strong, fat People, and have much in your storerooms. My People are starving. We need food, and we have come to you to ask your help."

At that Rulon flung back his head and laughed, and all the crowd laughed too.

"Help! From me? For the People of Ladon, who lorded it over us for so long?"

The crowd was laughing too. Ladon's son hung his head, caught in the middle of this mockery, and wished he were far away.

Moloquin stepped forward, his hands out. "We have babies dying. The old people are dying every day. We have no more food. Ladon himself is dead, and with him the evil is dead also. We ask you only for what you can spare. We will honor you forever for it. In the Overworld your name shall be a glory forever."

Rulon threw out his chest and swung his club back and forth, and around him his People hooted and jeered. Someone called, "Stone them!"

Now Joba flung up her hands. "Stop," she cried. "Stop!"

Rulon came forward, stretching out his club before him. "It would be impious to help those whom the Overworld has condemned! Go, and endure your punishment, you have what you deserve."

"Ladon is dead," said Moloquin. "It was Ladon who brought down the wrath of Heaven on his People."

"You are all suffering," said Rulon. "Therefore you are all evil."

There was a yell of agreement from those packed into the yard behind Ladon's son, and he sighed and his head drooped; he saw that Moloquin would get nothing from these people. He put out his hand, to draw Moloquin away, but Moloquin struck his hand down.

"Rulon," he said, in a rough voice, "be grateful you have something to give. Someday perhaps you will have nothing also."

"Rulon," his mother cried, in a harsh voice, "will you damn us all? Give heed to him; he speaks with wisdom!"

Rulon smirked at them both. His hair was braided with strands of dyed flax, red and yellow and green; around his neck he wore beads of shell that clinked when he moved. He said, "You are rude and stupid, Moloquin. You dare to threaten me, when you ought to be begging and cringing at my feet. Yet my mother has asked me to help you, and for the sake of the womb that bore me I shall let you know my generosity."

Moloquin said, "Rulon is great; we shall honor him above all others."

In his voice Ladon's son, familiar with him now, heard a tight-gripped anger, and a deep suspicion.

"Yes," said Rulon smoothly. "You may take away from my stores all that you yourself can carry, Unwanted One. No man shall help you, and you must carry it all at once, and whatever you drop you must leave where it falls."

The People shouted, gratified by this; but Joba sat down where she was, and drew her shawl over her face.

Ladon's son said, "That will hardly give a mouthful to each of us."

"It is enough," Rulon said, "to gain me some honor, and teach you not to come begging. Do you accept?"

Moloquin stood still a moment, his back very straight. Unwillingly Ladon's son remembered the sleek, well-fed faces of the people at Moloquin's Forest Village. They had all they needed. Moloquin could turn and walk away from this insult, spurn Rulon, and go. Ladon's son bit his lips, wondering how much a single man could carry: not much. Moloquin stood there, his head flung back, glaring at Rulon, until the other chief began to frown and raised his club again.

"Take it, woods-child, or go."

"I will do it," Moloquin said. "Show me what I may have."

Rulon's face smoothed out, delighted, and he stepped back with a gesture. "Come."

Moloquin started forward, and Ladon's son with him. Rulon put out his hand to stop him. "You stay. Only this great and mighty chief will carry what I choose to give him. Come, great and mighty chief."

He went in through the door, and Moloquin followed. Ladon's son put his hand to his mouth, his gaze on the roundhouse door. His stomach churned. Almost against his will he thought that he and Moloquin at least would eat well this day. Behind him the crowd was stirring and shifting, and he glanced once over his shoulder and saw them ranging themselves along the way through the village, from the gate into the roundhouse yard out between the two longhouses. In their hands they had small stones and clods of dirt, and as he watched, they stooped to pick up more.

Ladon's son gritted his teeth. He knew what was about to happen.

After some time Moloquin came out of the roundhouse, bent double under a great burden of baskets. Even the waiting mob gasped at the sight of him, half-buried under his load; it seemed impossible for a man to walk so weighted down, so bent over. Ladon's son started forward, remembered he could not help, and stopped, his heart pounding.

Moloquin started out through the gate in the fence, and there before him the People stood, packed tightly together on either side of the way through the village. When Moloquin stepped out between these two mobs, his foot slipped in the mud, and his whole great burden swayed and tipped. The people on either side raised handfuls of stones and dirt and let fly at him.

Ladon's son ran forward, his hands out, trying to deflect the hail of rocks. A piece of stone struck him in the face and a dirt clod hit his mouth so that there was mud all over his tongue and earth between his teeth. He staggered, bowed over, trying to shield Moloquin with his body, struggling blindly through the pelting rain of stones and dirt.

He heard Moloquin gasp with pain, and twisting back he saw the chief's footsteps slow and his knees bend, weakening. Yet Moloquin let nothing fall. Bent over with his back level to the ground, his arms spread wide to support the towering load, he trudged away through the village.

Stones rattled off the baskets. Someone threw a stick that banged Moloquin behind the knee and nearly buckled his leg. Ladon's son went before him, to shield him from some of it, but Rulon's People merely waited until Moloquin was past them, and cast their stones at his back. Even so he kept on. He took each step deliberately and carefully, and when he reached the edge of the village, and the screaming mob and their stones were behind him, he had dropped nothing—not a root, not a bean—into the mud of Rulon's Village.

The hooting and the stones were behind them now. In the high grass at the edge of the village, Moloquin let go his burdens and let them slip to the ground and straightened with a sigh. He said, "It is not enough."

Ladon's son lifted one of the baskets; the weight startled him. "Enough for a while," he said. The basket was full of unmilled grain, and he plunged in one hand and took out a handful and was about to eat it when he thought of Moloquin and raised his head.

"Eat," said Moloquin, who was squatting now, the baskets in a circle around him, and staring out across the meadow toward the High Hill, where the goats of Rulon's People were grazing on the lower slopes.

"Someone is coming," said Ladon's son.

The other man twisted, looking over his shoulder. The village lay behind them, its edge marked in the low wall of debris and brush. From the village two women were walking, one several paces behind the other, carrying jars in their hands.

After them came another, and behind her yet another. They walked out to where Moloquin sat in the midst of Rulon's charity.

"I am sorry," said the first. "I threw no stones." She set down her jar at Moloquin's feet and went back again toward the village. One by one the others reached Moloquin, each with her token of food, and each the same words.

"I am sorry. I threw nothing."

They left their little gifts and went back again, and Moloquin stared after them a long while.

Ladon's son picked up the first jar and sniffed eagerly at it. "Oh, delicious. Oh, my tongue, my belly." It was meat, cooked with water and herbs, a rime of fat congealing on the surface as it cooled. He began to gobble it.

Moloquin said, "Be careful you don't make yourself sick." He got slowly up to his feet and began to lift baskets to his shoulders. Ladon's son could not stop pushing meat into his mouth, although his stomach already strained full. He watched Moloquin carry the baskets away toward the river; now, when he could choose, he carried only a few of the baskets at one time.

Carrying the charity of Rulon between them, they made their way back to the river, and then down along the bank toward their own village. Ladon's son was exhausted. Even the good food in his belly seemed like a poison to him now and weighed him down. He struggled to carry many baskets but his fingers stiffened and he dropped it all; under Moloquin's furious nagging he labored along under a lesser burden and soon was out of breath and had to rest.

Moloquin called him a fool, a weakling, a woman, and they had to leave some of the supply behind, carry the rest on ahead a way, and stop while Moloquin went back again and Ladon's son rested, and in this way they went back along the river, dragging the salvation of their People along with them.

They came up from the river past the Pillar of the Sky, and at the sight of the crows and their feastings, Ladon's son lost the last of his strength. He sank down under his burden and sat in the grass.

"Go on," he said. "Go on without me." He turned his eyes longingly on the place of the dead.

"No," Moloquin said. "Get up, it will take me all the longer without you. Get up. I need you. I need you, curse you!"

He struck Ladon's son full in the face as he said it, and the fair man recoiled. He flung up a fist between them.

"How dare you strike me!"

"Get up," said Moloquin, "or I will pound you harder yet."

Ladon's son lurched forward, his fist aimed at Moloquin, and he fell forward onto hands and knees. Then, looking past Moloquin, he saw someone ahead of them, coming across the plain.

"Who is that?"

Moloquin wheeled. Down the plain, there were figures running toward them, waving their arms. They were men from the village. Ladon's son cried out and raised his hand, and panting and cheering, they hurried up the long gradual slope toward Moloquin and Ladon's son.

When they saw all the food that Moloquin had won them, they gave a loud outcry of triumph. Each man seized as much as he could carry and hurried away toward the village. Ladon's son also, seized with a new energy, carried a basket along with them.

Moloquin followed after, his hands empty. He knew that what he had brought would keep them hardly long enough to get their strength back. Something else had to be done. He had won very little from Rulon, and at a great cost; soon he would have to go back again.

Walking back to the village, he let his mind work over some methods he could face Rulon with again and have what he wanted, and give Rulon a little back also.

The crowd of men who had taken the burden of the food were now almost lost in his sight. They had run on ahead of him, they had turned their backs to him; he could hear their voices, faint and distant, but that too was fading. Suddenly he felt alone in the whole world, as if the village had forgotten him. He walked along, tired and hungry, thinking of Rulon and paying little heed to anything, when a drumbeat reached his ears.

Surprised, he stopped and raised his head. The drums pounded closer. There ahead of him, coming up across the grey wintry plain, were his People, dancing and singing and clapping their hands together.

Startled, he stopped and watched them come. Slow, frail, they danced toward him in two columns, one of men and one of women. When they reached him, they surrounded him, singing to him. He stood motionless, unsure what to do, and said nothing; in their midst he was still not one of them. Then the men came close around him and lifted him on their backs and carried him away down to the village. The women sang and danced around them all, and they said his name, over and over, all adorned with words of respect and honor and awe; they called him Opa-Moloquin-on, and Ullahim-Moloquin, and Lemmanion-Moloquin, words he had never heard before, and they held up their little starving children to see him, and they spread their hands before him in tokens of honor and love. They set him down in the center of the village, they put him down to sit on a pile of animal skins, and they brought him food to eat in beautiful bowls and jars, and they all lay down before him and called him Moloquin, the Unwanted One, their chief.

In the morning Moloquin went to Ladon's son and told him, "Bring me all the men who are strong enough to travel and maybe fight."

At that Ladon's son lost his smile; his face smoothed into a look of worry. "Fight. Whom are we to fight?"

"Ah, you fool," Moloquin said to him. "Do you think what we have brought will last very long? Soon they will be starving again. Do as I say." And when Ladon's son did not move, he went on, "Am I not the chief?"

"Yes," said Ladon's son, and some of the worry left his face; he went and did as Moloquin told him.

Moloquin waited on the upland between the village and the forest where the old gardens lay, all tumbled with weeds and the shucks and husks of the ruined crop. He sat with his arms over his knees and looked around him and wondered if they dared to plant these fields again; he realized he knew nothing of such matters as the raising of plants, and he slapped his thigh with annoyance. He knew nothing at all; how could he be a chief? He had saved them for a moment from the abyss, but the abyss was still there, waiting.

It was always there. In the most prosperous times, they lived on the edge of extinction.

He pressed his fists together, thinking of the Pillar of the Sky. Thinking of the rounds of stones he meant to raise there. Thinking also of the stones that lay along the foot of the High Hill.

When I have raised my gateways at the Pillar of the Sky, he told himself, then something of the People will remain forever. Even if every soul dies, yet there will never really be an end to us.

Now, up the grassy frost-bitten slope came Ladon's son and the other men, nearly all the grown men and some of the older boys too, walking in files. They came up the slope from the longhouse toward Moloquin.

Here and there, in the hollows of the land, the snow lay deep and crusted. The sky was losing its color as the sun went down. To-night they would eat well, tell stories and dance, as in old times. Let them think the old times were still on them; Moloquin meant to change all that, now that he was chief.

In three files they came toward him, and sat down before him at a respectful distance. Moloquin took his axe from his belt; he pulled off the case of deerskin and laid the axe down on the crisped grass between him and the other men.

He said, "I want you to make ready to go with me to Rulon's Village. There I will face him and call him to judgment for the evil he did me and you, and you shall be there to help me if he is too foolish to regret what he did and make the proper amends."

At that all of them went pale, and some stammered, and some only looked down at the ground. Among them Fergolin, the Bear Skull master, said, "Do you mean to fight, Opa-Moloquin-on?"

"We do not fight against our own kind," said another man.

"Pagh," said Moloquin. "You grew up in the boys' band; I fought many times against the boys' band, and most of you gave blows then. I saw you fighting one another then. This is no different. Did Ladon's son tell you what happened to us in Rulon's Village? Do you think he gave me what I brought willingly and with words of peace and kindness?"

Now they were looking at Ladon's son, who shook his head. "Ru-lon refused us. He gave us a handful, as you throw a bone to a dog. He—" then his eyes met Moloquin's, and he stopped and looked down, flushing.

"He gave me all that I could carry on my back," said Moloquin to the men. "And when I carried it out, burdened down like a woman, they stoned me and made mock of me. All this I endured, for your sake, and now, for my sake, you will obey me."

That reached them; that drew them together and firmed their purpose. They sat straighter, and the looks they passed from man to man were burning and full of resolve. Still they seemed frightened, and he lowered his voice and shook his head.

"You are like rabbits. Believe me—you are too stupid and weak to know what to do. I know what to do. Do as I say, and all will be well."

He touched the bronze head of the axe, and they leaned forward to see it, and they murmured, amazed with it.

"I made this," he said. "I drew out the dust of the earth and warmed it until it became what you see here, and there is such a power in this stuff that you have never dreamed of. You saw how I brought Ladon and the chiefs down with it, at the Gathering, when I called my People forth. With this in my hand Rulon can do me no harm. Now hear me. We shall go into the forest and cut branches, and shape them, and those of you with stonecraft, can make us tips for spears and we shall make spears. When we are ready we shall go to Rulon and teach him how to treat his brothers."

The three young men directly before him let out a yell, and one called, "Teach us, Opa-Moloquin!"

Moloquin nodded, pleased. He looked from one to the next, and saw all the men ready to do his bidding.

"Between Heaven and earth there are no People like Moloquin's People. Good. Go get ready, and tonight when you dance you must think of fighting, and overcoming other men. Only, say nothing to the women, do you understand?"

"Yes, Opa-Moloquin," they said, and they got up and with many gestures of obeisance they left him. With one hand he held back La-don's son among them.

The fair man sank down beside him. Moloquin looked long at him, frowning, seeing nothing of Ladon in this soft, pale man.

He said, "You must go to my village in the forest. Tell them that

I am deep in this matter here. Tell Bahedyr to come and bring his spear. Tell Hems to come."

"May I talk to Shateel?" Ladon's son asked.

Moloquin gave him a pitying look. "You may talk. I cannot say she will listen." He put the cover on his axe.

Ladon's son went through the forest with the lightness and swiftness of a red deer, and the nearer he got to Shateel, the more eager was his soul to see her.

When he had come before, she had hardly looked at him, but then Moloquin had been there. This time Ladon's son would speak to her, and through her to the baby curled in her belly, and he knew he would bring her home again to him.

After two days' walking, he reached the little village where Moloquin's first roundhouse stood. He came from the forest into the clearing in the middle of the day, when the women were sitting in the sun, scraping a deerskin, and the two little children were skidding stones off the ice of the stream; the men were nowhere to be seen.

Shateel knelt in the circle of the women, but she did no work. In her arms she held a bundle wrapped in a rabbitskin, and while the other women saw Ladon's son immediately, Shateel did not, because her whole being seemed focussed on the bundle in the rabbitskin.

Ladon's son came out of the forest, and the oldest of the women stood up and faced him. Then Shateel saw him also.

Her face grew pale. She glanced around her at the others, and she raised the baby against her breast and gripped it tighter in her arms.

Ladon's son walked toward them, his hand out. He said, "Do I find a welcome at the fires of my People?"

"Your People," said Taella, skeptically. "When he left here, he was saying that he would never accept you."

Shateel said, "Where is Moloquin?"

At that the heart of Ladon's son sank a little. He drew nearer to the fire, and the women made him dutiful gestures of respect and welcome, and a robust red-cheeked woman he did not know got up and brought him a mat to sit on and a bowl of grain and broth. He busied himself with the food. Now that he was so near to Shateel, he could not raise his gaze to her face. He stirred up the hot broth until the grain swelled, and looked around him at the clearing, clean and orderly in the pale winter sunlight, the great pile of wood near the door into the roundhouse, the deerhides stretched on racks of bent willow branches hanging on the outside of the roundhouse.

"You are doing well here," he said.

"Moloquin brought us here," said Taella. "He knew what he was doing. He is our chief—have your People won him away from us?"

"He has not deserted you," said Ladon's son. He looked around again for the men. "I have messages for Bahedyr and Hems—he wants them to join him."

"Where?" Taella said.

"What is he doing?" said the red-cheeked woman, her eyes bright.

Now Ladon's son managed to slide a glance at Shateel, and found her staring at him; the heat rose in his neck and cheeks. He ate some of the porridge in his bowl. Remembering what Moloquin had told him, he gave himself over to the story of what had become of them in Rulon's Village.

They listened with glowing eyes. When Ladon's son spoke of Moloquin coming before Rulon as a suppliant and the honorable and excellent words he had spoken, they sighed and smiled to one another; when he told them Rulon's response, they gasped, and the red-cheeked woman thumped the ground with her fist.

Then he told them how Moloquin had gathered up on his own back all the food he could lift, as if he carried his whole People on his own poor back, and staggered out of Rulon's Village. The women leaned toward him, intent, their lips parted. He told them of the stoning, the insults, the humiliations that Moloquin had endured, and they cried out in rage.

Shateel shook her head; she raised the hem of her heavy coat over her face, and said, "I am ashamed of my brother. Rulon is no more my brother. I am ashamed, ashamed." When she lowered her garment, tears streaked her face.

Now Ladon's son told them how Moloquin had brought back his great burden of food, and how the People had come to meet him and borne him away to the village and named him their chief. The faces of the women were round with satisfaction, and they looked at one another and smiled and nodded. But when Ladon's son told them that Moloquin had taken the men into the forest to make weapons, all their looks stilled.

"I see evil in this," Taella said. "There is great evil waiting to be worked."

Then the fourth woman, a little brown creature Ladon's son had never seen before, and who had not yet spoken, raised her head, and said, "What Moloquin does cannot be evil. He wants my man to go with him, and I am glad that I have a man who will go and serve him well. Hems was the first to follow Moloquin, and I was the second, and we shall never turn our feet out of the path he has set for us."

Taella and the red-cheeked woman took hold of this brown creature's hands, and squeezed them, and smiled on her. Shateel alone still frowned.

"Has he spoken to you of all he intends? No. Moloquin will tell no one what he means. He will speak only of what he expects of each of us. Does no one dare to ask him what he means to do?"

"He suffered for our sake," said Ladon's son. It surprised him to find himself defending Moloquin.

"The kindreds of the People do not fight one another," said Shateel. "Not since the first man and the first woman came into this holy land have the kindreds risen up against one another and shed their common blood."

"We must have food to live. He will seize what is necessary for us to live. If they do not fight us—" Ladon's son saw now a way through this—"if they had done what is right, which is to feed us who are hungry, when they have so much, then no evil would fall on them."

"Better to starve," said Shateel flatly, and she got up, and with her baby in her arms she went into the roundhouse.

The other women stared after her. The red-cheeked woman muttered under her breath, "She is too serious in her new work, is Shateel."

"What is her new work?" Ladon's son asked.

Taella took the bowl out of his hands and filled it again from a pot on the fire. "Moloquin gave her the task of the chief while he is gone."

"Now she thinks she is better than we are," said the red-cheeked woman.

"She has always thought that," said Taella, and laughed.

The brown woman, the wife of Hems, said quietly, "She has done it well. I speak nothing against her, or any other work of Moloquin's."

"She is not Moloquin's," Ladon's son burst out. "She was my wife."

They goggled at him; they had forgotten that. Taella gave him back his bowl, but he put it down. His heart was beating violently. He got up and went after Shateel, into the roundhouse.

It was tiny, built on a single turning of posts; it would have fit entirely into that part of his father's roundhouse that Ladon had kept for himself. Just inside the door he met the warmth and darkness, pleasant after the cold outside, and he stood letting his eyes get used to the light and breathing in the warm smells of hearths and hides and people. Then Shateel's voice came from the gloom.

"I am here," she said, in a rough-edged voice. "You may come to me."

He went toward her voice, and found her at the back of the roundhouse, by a hearth of stones. She was kneeling on a straw mat, her baby before her on top of its rabbitskin, while she wiped up its mess.

It was a girl child. Ladon's son sat down hard beside Shateel, his breath going out of him as if he had been poked.

"Shateel," he said. "What is her name?"

"Dehra," Shateel said, proudly.

"She is very beautiful."

"Tell me of Moloquin," she said. "What does he mean to do to my brother and his People?"

"I don't want to talk about Moloquin. I want to ask you about coming back to me."

She bowed her head. With a handful of dry grass she swabbed the baby's tiny backside. The little thing let out a wail, small as itself, and the mother crooned to it, and Ladon's son suddenly had the feeling of being a world away from them, shut out.

He looked down at his hands, his heart breaking. He knew now she did not love him at all any more.

She dressed the baby up again, packing its loincloth with the white fluff of milkweed and thistles, and bundled it up again in the rabbitskin. Lifting her daughter in her arms, she faced Ladon's son.

"What did you want to say to me?"

He looked long into her face. She had never seemed so beautiful to him before. Above her large dark eyes the eyebrows were straight and thick; her chin was stubborn as a man's. He knew she was lost to him. He put out his hand to her.

"Let me help you stand."

She took his hand and he drew her up onto her feet. She said, "I am going with you."

"What!"

"I am going with you to Moloquin. He cannot bring such a terrible thing on the People, and perhaps I can change his mind. Or perhaps I can change Rulon's mind. Something must be done."

She threw the end of her coat up over her shoulder, covering the baby, and went out of the roundhouse. Calling to the little boy who played on the stream's ice, she sent him to find Hems and Bahedyr.

"There is no need to hurry," Ladon's son told her. "Moloquin will take time, to make weapons, to let the other men eat and regain their strength."

She hardly glanced at him. What he said seemed light as a moth-wing to her, and as of much interest. He put his hand on her arm.

"Do you love Moloquin?" he asked, in a low voice.

She faced him, her expression schooled to a smooth guilelessness. "Everyone loves Moloquin," she said. She walked away from him, very straight, back to the fire.

Shateel had last seen the village of Ladon's People when it was thriving and happy. When she came on it now, for the first time since she had left it at midsummer, it was so changed that she sat down where she was and stared at it.

The men who had come with her, Hems, Bahedyr with his spear, and Ladon's son, stopped and waited restlessly by her for a while. Wahela had come with her also; Wahela stood with her hand shading her eyes, looking all around them.

The baby Dehra cried, and Shateel gave it her breast, her eyes all the while on the plain where the village had been.

Once it had covered the ground between the edge of the forest, just behind her, and the river. The gardens had thronged with women at their work; the flat ground where the longhouses stood had been noisy with children, and by the river, the great roundhouse had stood vast and important under its peaked roof. Now the gardens were empty. Thistles and brambles covered the earth, brown skeletons of weeds with thorns like claws, and high brown grass. Of the four longhouses, one was gone completely, and one was collapsing, its walls broken and buckling, and its roof caved in. The round-house was a heap of blown ash.

The men went on, Wahela trailing after them, and after a few moments Shateel too rose and went on down into the dying village. Around the yard of the two remaining longhouses, people were sitting listlessly in the sun. They were thin as dead leaves that had lost all their substance and were now only twigs and veins, and they seemed to have no will anymore, no motion of their own. Shateel could not look them in the eyes, not while her fat and lively baby kicked within her arms, not while she herself was fat and lively. Then, as she stood in the dust of the yard, she heard the voice of the sampo.

It came from the yard of the other longhouse. She went around the corner, and there she saw the old women sitting around the mill which clattered and turned happily as ever, although now it ground nothing but the words of the old women. Shateel went closer, and sat down behind them, and listened.

> *Sam-po, sam-po,*
> *La li la la li li la*
> *The Mill turns, the Mill grinds*
> *La li la la li li la*
> *When the sampo stops, the world ends.*
> *La li la la la*

The old women, who had seemed to her as changeless as mountains, had suffered much. Tishka was gone; now Grela sat in her place. Fat she once had been, but now Grela's skin hung empty and slack from her bones. Next to her sat one who had been robust when Shateel left, and who now dozed, exhausted, her chin on her chest, and the other women around the sampo were no better than this. They seemed not to have seen Shateel, but when they spoke, they spoke of those things which she was most anxious to know.

"Where is Moloquin? Why has he been gone so long? We are nearly out of food again."

"Where did he take the men?"

"He fed us. He put food into the mouths of our children. Whatever he does I will accept."

"I like this very little. Perhaps it would be better if we did all die."

"He is Ael's son, our rightful chief. We shall do as he tells us, as he wishes of us, as long as he is our chief."

"But where has he taken the men?"

La li la li la la la
Sam-po, sam-po
The Mill turns, the Mill grinds
La li la li la li li
The hardest nut, the softest grain
Sam-po, sam-po
The sampo grinds them all the same

Shateel crept closer; she leaned forward, and she cast her words into their midst.

"Where is Moloquin? How did he save you?"

"He brought us food from Rulon's Village. Some say he bore it away on his back, the whole of Rulon's store, by magic. Some say he stole the whole of Rulon's store by magic."

"And now where has he gone?"

"Into the forest, to make magic."

"What does he intend?"

"We do not know. He saved us once; he will save us again, if we have faith. Yet he is Ael's son. He is our chief, but he is Ael's son, and like Ael he cares nothing for our ways."

"We must have faith in him. Karella—"

At that name, all voices died; all the women looked at one another, and they bowed their heads at last.

"What of Karella?" asked Shateel.

Sam-po, sam-po
La li la la li li la
What is living may fall silent
What is dead may sometimes speak
La li la la li li la
Sam-po, sam-po

"Karella said that he would save us. Karella said that he would be our chief."

Grela raised her head; the loose skin of her face hung down like a collar over her neck.

"In dreams we saw Karella and heard her words. She told us to seek out Moloquin. We did so, and he brought us food. He has great power, great magic, and we must give ourselves into his hands."

"Yet he has taken away the men," Shateel said. "And you are full of fears, anyone can see that, full of dread."

"We are weak. Moloquin is strong. We must submit to him."

"Submit," Shateel cried. "What word is this for the headwomen of the People?"

Now for the first time they faced her, and they did so all at once, as if they were one creature. Their faces had shrunk beneath the skin, and they seemed to look out from deep inside. They said nothing to her, but in their faces she saw that they had already yielded themselves to Moloquin.

Then Dehra cried, inside Shateel's coat, and the women in one breath cooed and sighed, and they reached out and drew Shateel into their midst. She uncovered the baby and showed her to them, and they bent over Dehra and crooned to her, and passed her from one set of great sagging starving arms to the next, and their faces warmed with smiles. Shateel sat among them, seeing the lively joy of the baby, and the death creeping over the women: their hair falling out, their teeth rotting, their skin scaling and flaking. They bent over the baby, with all her future before her, and their voices were gentle and soft. Shateel put out her hand and turned the mill around once more.

> *Sam-po, sam-po*
> *The People plan, the People dream*
> *La li la la li li la*
> *The sampo only turns and turns*
> *La li la la li li la*
> *The People's plans and dreams are dust*
> *The sampo turns and turns*
> *La li la li la la la*
> *Sam-po, sam-po*

. . .

Bahedyr spoke to one of the boys of the village, and learned something of where Moloquin had gone; with Hems he walked off toward the forest, and Wahela followed.

She was glad she had come. When Shateel announced, back in the Forest Village, that she was coming, the other women had cried out, dismayed; but Wahela had known at once that if Shateel went, she would go also. She had no notion of what was going on, but she knew it was exciting and she wanted to see Moloquin.

Now she followed the two men away down through the trees, down toward the river. They ignored her; she made no effort to catch up with them. When Moloquin saw she was here, he might be angry with her—this was men's business, after all—but everything she had seen thus far of what was going on here stirred her blood and made her keen and eager as a she-wolf.

The men went down along the bank of the river where it curled through the forest and reached a broad meadow, and there she saw a crowd of men. Some sat on the ground around a fire, working at something in their laps; some were casting sticks at a tree near the edge of the meadow; some merely strutted around, waving sticks over their heads.

Bahedyr and Hems went down among them, and from among them, Moloquin rose.

At the sight of him, Wahela could no longer hold back. She broke into a run and went down into the meadow, and called his name.

He turned. He saw her, and he looked to either side. She paused, a little way from him, uncertain: would he drive her away? But he came toward her with his arms out to her, and she rushed into his embrace, laughing.

"What are you doing here?" he said, into her ear. He hugged her tight, rubbing his body against hers.

"I came to help you," she said.

He burst into a smile; turning, he looked all around him at the other men, and facing her again, he said, "Such spirit as yours ought to dwell in the body of a man, Wahela. You see all these others, who seem to be men—all this while, they have wondered and doubted, and even now I am not sure they will do as I ask—surely they are the women, and you are the man."

He said this in a loud voice, so that all would hear, and he gathered her again into his embrace, and they kissed. Wahela held him tight, wanting all to see how he loved her. When he let her go again, she stood with her hands on his arms, unwilling to part from him.

"What are you doing?"

He said, "I am making teeth and claws to rend my enemies."

"Where are your enemies?"

"In Rulon's Village. Come, we are all but finished, soon we shall start on our journey to find justice."

Then he took her by the arm, and they walked around the meadow, and he looked at the weapons the other men had made— clubs, and spears of wood, the tips cooked hard in the fire. Moloquin carried his axe in his belt, and his hand rested often on it; she saw the eagerness in his face, and it heated up her blood. She took him by the hand.

"Come with me," she said. "We have not been together for a long time."

He smiled down at her. "I am ready for you."

"I see you are ready for anything," she said. "Come."

He followed her away into the forest, and out of sight of the other men they lay down on the ground together and got their fill of one another.

When they were done, though, he said, "What of Shateel?"

Wahela darkened like a stormcloud. She sat up straight and pulled her clothes around her. "Shateel! Why do you speak of Shateel?"

He watched her with sharp eyes. "What—are you jealous? How does she fare? I left her in my place in the village, after all."

"I wish you would not do that. She thinks she is above us all as it is."

He caught her chin in his hand. "Are you afraid I will take her instead of you? What a fool, Wahela. She is cold as ice, and you—" he caught her to him again, pressing her against him. "And you are warm as my own soul, Wahela."

Mollified, she stroked him, and they shared tender caresses for a while, until again he said, "Tell me about Shateel."

"Why are you so eager to know of her? She bore her baby."

"She did!"

"A girl. When Ladon's son came, he talked to her, but she refused him again. You are right, she is nothing but a snow-woman."

Moloquin laughed; he turned his face away. "And the others?"
"They are well."

From the meadow now came a sudden roar. Moloquin sprang to
his feet, and catching Wahela's hand he pulled her up beside him.
They went back through the trees.

There in the meadow, Bahedyr stood in the midst of the other
men; he raised his spear in his hand, and cast it with all his strength.
The men yelled, amazed. The spear flew in a long flat arc through
the air and struck a tree at the far end of the meadow and stuck
there, quivering, and all the men shouted. Swiftly they fought for
place, to be the next one to throw his spear.

Moloquin said, under his breath, "Let them be so eager when it
is men they cast at."

"What are you going to do?" Wahela asked.

"I am going to make a new chief for Rulon's People," he said.

"How can you do that?"

He smiled at her. "Wait and you will see, my Wahela." From behind him came another roar from the men with their spears.

Near sundown, a boy ran into the dying village, shouting, "Moloquin
is coming! Moloquin! Moloquin!"

The women raised their heads. Among them Shateel hastily
wrapped up her baby in her coat and got to her feet, and with all the
others she walked out to see Moloquin and the men come back from
the forest.

The sun was going down; low flat clouds covered the sky, and
the rays of the sun slipped beneath them and stretched across the
world like spears of light. Beneath this enormous sky the little band
of men walking up through the waving grass seemed tiny and insig-
nificant. Yet all the women could see that they carried spears and
clubs.

The baby squirmed in Shateel's arms. She covered it carefully
with her shawl against the night wind that swooped over the plain.
The spears in the hands of the men jabbed at the belly of the sky. A
shudder passed through her. She thought, He will assault Heaven
itself.

She saw Wahela, walking beside him, and knew how the other
woman's passions would fit in with Moloquin's. She stood straight,

leaning a little forward, as if to keep her balance against a blasting wind.

Now Moloquin had seen her, and he put out one hand to stop Wahela and came on by himself, coming toward her ahead of the others. She stepped away from the villagers, and he walked up face to face with her.

"Did I not leave my People in your care?" he asked. "What are you doing here?"

"Are you displeased to see me, Moloquin? Perhaps you are right—I came because I heard that which tears my heart."

"Rulon is your brother," he said.

"Rulon is nothing to me," she said. "It is not Rulon I have come here to protect, but all the People."

"I am here to lead my People," he said.

"You are here to have your way by force," she said.

"And you think that is a mistake?"

"You will tear the People into pieces," she said.

"Then go to Rulon," he said, "and tell him. Because it is Rulon's doing. All that befalls us now began with Rulon, who would not help his People."

"Better to die," she said, "than to kill one another."

As she said this, the baby Dehra inside her coat squirmed and let out a mewling hungry cry.

Moloquin's eyes widened. "Let me see," he said, and put out his hands.

The baby was hungry. Shateel opened her clothes, showing him the child, meaning to put her to the breast, but before she could, Moloquin snatched the baby from her.

"Now," he cried, "we shall test your words, Shateel!"

She cried out. "Give her to me!" Lunging toward him, she stretched out her hands for the baby.

He dodged. He held the baby at arm's length and danced back away from Shateel as she struggled to reach her child. With his free hand he pulled the great bronze axe from his belt and flung it down on the ground between them.

"Now, Shateel! Tell me she should die!"

Shateel gasped. The baby was howling, and each cry pierced her mother like a spear thrown. She flung out her arms toward her child. "Give her to me!"

Moloquin bounded away. The baby thrashed and wriggled and

he nearly dropped her. Shateel let out a wail of rage. Stooping, she caught up the bronze axe in both hands and ran at Moloquin with it, meaning to hew him down.

"Give me my baby!"

She swung the axe up over her shoulder; it was much heavier than she expected, top-heavy, and it gave off a radiance of power like a chill. The baby shrieked. She rushed forward, swinging the axe in a great whistling arc at Moloquin's body.

"Ho! Ho!"

He caught the haft of the axe with his free hand. Turning, he slipped the baby neatly from his grasp into the arms of her mother, and stepped back.

Shateel sobbed. She clutched the baby tight, lifted it, pressed her face to it, and finally laid her to her swollen leaking breast and sat down to nurse.

The People gathered around her and Moloquin; they were laughing. His little show had pleased them. Ashamed, Shateel bent over the baby. She had let him make a game out of her, and she had not done well with her indignation. Now he was ordering them all to the village, to make a feast out of the last of the food that they had. They would be even more his creatures now. And he had changed, somehow—to threaten the baby, even in a game. She rocked the baby, half in tears again at the mere memory of the danger. The baby sucked happily, her hand on her mother's breast.

The People went off, singing, some dancing, the men proud under their upraised spears. Night was coming. Shateel drew her shawl around her, cold.

Something heavier, warmer, swept around her: Moloquin's coat. He squatted down beside her, sheltering her in his outstretched arm.

"You are angry with me," he said. "That pleases me, Shateel."

"Pleases you." She looked at him, surprised.

"I am tired of all these people who fawn on me," he said. "I want someone who will stand against me now and then."

"Moloquin," she said, "you are assuming much."

"Yes," he said. "Will you go to your brother?"

"Do you wish it?"

"Yes. I want no more trouble than necessary. But I will get what I want. Tell him that. Tell him he can yield, or he can endure the consequences. Tell him I have many men, and a power such as he has never laid his hands to in his whole life, and I shall cut him down as I cut down the chiefs at the Gathering if he defies me again."

She remembered that they had stoned him, and her face heated; now her rage turned on her brother who was stupid and cruel, and she said, "You have saved your People. That is your power, Moloquin, not your axe and the spears of your men."

"We shall see about that," he said.

He got up. The People had gone on back toward the village, all but one, who waited a little way off: Wahela, the wind blowing her hair. Moloquin went to her and took her hand, and they walked back toward the village together. Shateel bowed her head over her baby.

Rulon carried the club of the chief; he wore the painted feathers of the chief, and the chief's shoes, that made him greater than other men. He sat in the middle of his roundhouse, and his people brought him whatever he wished, and soon, he told himself, at the next Gathering, he would walk first into the Turnings-of-the-Year, and all would know who was the greatest chief of all the People.

Now he sat on his bearskin and ate the cakes he had been brought for his breakfast, and he heard an uproar outside the roundhouse but he paid it no heed. Then one of his men came to him.

"Opa-Rulon-on," he said, and bowed down before his chief. "Greatest of all, there is one outside who would ask a favor of you."

"Let him approach me," said Rulon, who never gave anyone favors.

"Opa-Rulon-on, mighty is he, it is your sister, Ana-Shateel-el, who stands before the roundhouse."

"Shateel," Rulon said, amazed. "Where has she come from?"

The man kneeling before him said nothing. Rulon put down his bowl and got up.

He put on his bearskin cloak, and he put on his necklace of painted feathers, and he put on his wooden shoes that made him tower over everyone, and he took his club in his hand, and he went forth to the door of the roundhouse. And there he stopped.

It was Shateel. Ordinary as any woman, her clothes brown with dust, she stood before the door of his roundhouse, and a whole crowd of his People was pushing through the gate to watch. Rulon drew himself up as tall as he could.

"What do you wish of me, woman?"

She said, "I have come to ask you to do your duty, Rulon."

"My duty!" He looked her over; surely she was of no conse-
quence—she wore no beautiful clothes or beads, she carried no emblems of power. "Did Moloquin send you here? Did Ladon's son send
you?"

"Moloquin sent me," she said.

"And you would ask me for a favor?" Rulon smiled. "Kneel
down, woman."

She knelt down before him in the dust, her head bowed. She
had come a long way and her long fine hair in its bindings was dusty
and her face was dirty as a little child's. He remembered all the times
she had slighted him when they were children—how he had always
had to step aside for her: Rulon, who would be chief. But she was
Shateel, mother of chiefs, and now she knelt before him.

She said, "I beg you, my brother, to give up all you can to feed
the starvelings."

From the crowd encircling them, voices rose, clamoring, conflict-
ing.

"Drive her away! We gave enough!"

"Feed them, Rulon—feed them—"

"Let them eat the grass—"

Rulon smiled, looking down on his sister's head, and thought
what sort of man this Moloquin was, who begged for food, who let
himself be stoned and humiliated, and now was so cowardly that he
sent a woman to do his work. Rulon wanted to be great, and he
wanted a great thing to do now, and so he rose up, took his sister by
the hand, and lifted her.

"Shateel," he said, in a voice of false tenderness. "Come back to
your true People, and we shall all be happy. Leave these others who
are accursed and doomed."

She tipped her face up to him. She looked older now, and worn,
not the beautiful child she had always been, beautiful and willful.
Behind her stood her mother, Joba, with a new baby in her arms.
Shateel clung to her brother's hand, but she did not rise; she pulled
on him as if to draw him down with her.

"Rulon, Rulon," she said. "I beg you. If you do not do what is
right, there will be terrible consequences. Do what is right, Rulon.
Save your brothers."

"They are not my brothers. Ladon spurned me before all the
People. No one then stood up for me and spoke to him of right and

wrong and grave consequences. No!" He jerked his hand out of her grasp. "I have spoken. I am the chief of my People, and we shall keep what is ours!"

Shateel groaned; she turned toward her mother, and said, "Can you not persuade him?" Her voice was lost in the shouting of the People; most of them supported Rulon and would not feed Ladon's People, who had incurred the wrath of Heaven. Rulon stood straight and tall and folded his arms over his chest, as if to say the matter was done. He knew himself a giant among these others. By his side his great club leaned up against the wall of the roundhouse, and around him his People shouted his name: what could a fatherless beggar do to him?

He said, "Stay with us, Shateel. These others are doomed." Turning, he started back into the roundhouse.

"Stop!"

That voice raised the hackles on the back of his neck; against his will, he paused, and slowly he turned to face him who shouted. The People stilled. They were turning to look behind them, even his mother; only Shateel still faced him, with such an expression of sorrow that his heart clenched. Then, through the crowd, Moloquin came.

No feathers, no paint, no great bearskin made Moloquin wonderful. In spite of the cold, he was almost naked, dressed only in a loincloth, his long black hair shaggy over his shoulders and chest. He walked with a springy stride like an animal. In his hand he carried his axe.

Rulon reached for his club, which so many chiefs had carried, and which was also full of magic. He said, "So, beggar, you have come to beg once more?"

Moloquin stopped before him. "I have come," he said, "to call this People to their destiny."

At that such a shout went up from the gathered throng that Rulon's ears rang, and for a long moment, while the thunderous crowd gave tongue, he and Moloquin could only face one another. Rulon's back tingled. These were his People, and no one could call them to any duty, any grace or any power save him, their chief. His fingers tightened around the club.

"What a fool," he cried, but the deafening uproar of the crowd had not slackened enough for his voice to be heard, and he had to say it again, in a high piping voice, "What a fool!"

"Not I," Moloquin said. "Look around you, Rulon. Look well, Rulon's People!"

He wheeled around, swinging his axe out in a broad sweep through the air; the sun glanced on the great head. All the People twisted to see behind them. Rulon stood tall to see over them. For an instant there was nothing at all, only the wall of the roundhouse, and the blank blue sky, and then abruptly above the wall a man climbed, brandishing a long stick, and another man appeared beside him, and another, and another. The People cried out. Packed into the yard of the roundhouse, surrounded by men with spears, they wheeled around toward Rulon and cried out to him. "Rulon— Rulon—"

"I am here," Moloquin roared, in a voice that carried over the whole village, "I am here to punish evil, and to do justice, and let him who dares stand against me!"

Rulon said, "You mean to steal our stores."

"No," Moloquin said. "I mean to see that those who are hungry are fed, and that those who have more than they need give to those who have nothing. You ought to have done so, but you have failed. You are the chief here no more. I shall be chief over all the People."

Rulon's mother pushed forward, the baby in her arms. "You cannot choose yourself, Moloquin—we choose our chiefs here—"

"You have chosen me," Moloquin said, "by your acts, Joba. When Rulon refused me, who came to me and tried to make it right as well as she could? You did, and the other women. You knew then how he had failed. So be it! There is good, and there is evil, and a man must fit in with the good or he is doomed. I am chief here, and you have no choice."

The People were all shouting again, their voices hoarse with distress, and a baby wailed—Shateel's baby. She still faced Rulon, standing to one side of him, and now tears ran down her face. Rulon tore his gaze from her. All his life he had known exactly what to do, and who he was, and what he could expect of everyone else: the whole pattern of his life was known. Now the pattern was broken.

Moloquin had broken it. Moloquin had violated the faith of the People.

Rulon drew in a deep breath; his fingers tightened around the haft of the club, so long and heavy he needed two hands to lift it, painted and studded with stones, passed from chief down to chief and never bloodied. The uproar of the People was like a storm in the distance, thunder and lightning in the sky, while he and Moloquin faced each other.

He said, "Come inside, Moloquin, we shall talk of this. Inside."

The clamor of the People died away into a breathless silence. The two women in the center of the circle exchanged a look; Shateel's face was wet with tears, and her mother's mouth was grim. Then Moloquin said, "I will go inside and talk with you, Rulon."

Rulon coughed out the sudden dryness in his throat. "Come," he said, and turned and went into the roundhouse.

Shateel watched him go. She knew at once what he intended, and knew also that Moloquin understood. Now Moloquin stepped forward, to follow her brother through the dark cave of the roundhouse door, and Shateel opened her mouth to call a warning, but she knew not which one to warn, whether to preserve the old way, flawed and failing though it was, or to take sides with a new way, whose risks seemed terrible. While she hesitated, Moloquin went into the roundhouse after Rulon.

She turned to look again into her mother's face, and from behind her, from the roundhouse, came a loud shout of surprise and pain, and the thud of a blow.

The crowd of people in the yard all shouted at once. Shateel fell to her knees, facing the roundhouse; she knew one of them would come out the door, but she dreaded either one.

Through that door the future of her People would come, and she and her People had lost their power to determine who that would be. Their fate lay now in the swing of a club and the answering blow of an axe, in the treachery of a chief and the courage of an outcast.

Moloquin came out the door. In his hand he held his great bronze axe, and the metal was smeared all over with blood.

"He turned on me in the dark," he said to Shateel, and showed her the blade of the axe. "Speak to your mother. Tell her that she and the other headwomen will divide up all of Rulon's stores, so that everyone shall have what he needs. I will talk to the masters of the societies in a little while, by the foot of the High Hill."

She put out her hand and touched the blood drying on the metal; absently she brought her fingers to her lips. Moloquin went on past her, into the silent crowd.

. . ..

In the evening, with the masters of the societies of Rulon's People, Moloquin walked along the foot of the High Hill, and he spoke of the gateways he meant to build at the Pillar of the Sky.

"The Green Bough Society has no living master."

"I am the Green Bough master," Moloquin said, and no one dared to challenge this.

He paused before a great stone lying in the grass. "This one. Bring this one."

"You mean us to haul these stones to the Pillar of the Sky? It is impossible."

"There are stones there."

"Small pieces—nothing as large as these."

"These stones are here. They did not fall out of the sky here—they were dragged."

"It is impossible."

"Yet you will find the way," Moloquin said.

He turned; the little group of men moved closer together to face him. He walked in among them, forcing them apart so that he could walk between one man and the next, and he looked each one in the eyes as he passed.

He said, "When the People starved, there were many more than just Rulon who would have been happy enough to see us all die. Will any of you admit to it?"

He walked back and forth through their midst, while none of them said a word.

"Then," he said, "since you will not admit to it, you must know how evil it was. Therefore you know how great a deed you must do to make up for the evil you almost did."

They were looking at one another, if they could not look at him. He went away, toward the stones lying by the path up to the top of the High Hill. His hands were trembling.

He loathed these people. They had stoned him and berated him, and they had scorned Shateel when she humbled herself to save them; above all, they had served Rulon. Even now, when he thought of that moment in the dark roundhouse when Rulon had turned and struck, his soul flared to a white heat; his fists clenched.

If such a man as that could be the chief, what could the People themselves be like? He went back to them, and his voice struck them like the lashings of a whip.

"I will have as many stones as I choose brought to the Pillar of the Sky. Move them the way you move large trees for roundhouses—roll them over logs, drag them with ropes—take them down to the river and float them there. If you do not do it—"

He stopped and shook his head. "Do it," he said.

"We shall try," said the oldest of them, the Salmon Leap master.

"You shall do it," said Moloquin. "Now, go."

They left him. He walked along by the High Hill a while, admiring the stones.

These would not fail him. If he set these stones in well-dug holes, they would stand forever. *Chalk will hold anything,* the old man had said. Moloquin stopped and sat down on a stone lying beneath a little green tree.

Someone was coming toward him, walking up from Rulon's Village. It was twilight, and the last of the sunshine was slowly fading into a dusky mist, and the figure coming toward him seemed to form out of the mist. Then he saw that it was Shateel.

He stood up. She came at once toward him; she had left the baby behind, and her arms swung free at her sides.

"It has been done," she said. "There is enough for all. No one shall hunger, not for a while."

He took hold of her hand. "Sit down here with me. I have something I want to tell you."

She sat down beside him on the stone. He could not find a way to begin with her; instead, he stared down at his hands, and the silence grew long and uncomfortable between them.

At last she turned to him and said, "My brother struck at you?"

He nodded. "He was unused to the work. Otherwise he would have killed me at once."

"There are many who are saying you gave him no chance."

"I don't care what they say."

"What have you done here? Have you thought of that yet? Do you mean to rule all the People in both these villages and in ours too?"

He faced her. "You think I cannot do it?"

"I don't see why you would want to."

"Shateel." He took hold of her hand. "Do you never wonder about the world—why it is as it is? Once it must have been perfect—no one hungered, no one suffered—you can see the perfection still in the pieces of it. Yet now see how it lies in ruins around us! Everywhere, people strive and die, suffer and die, and there is no justice, no order—"

She frowned at him, her face vivid with her argument. "I see an order in everything, from the tree's green life to my own baby. What do you mean?"

"I mean to make it right. Here, at least, I mean to see justice done among people. Yes, I will rule them all, and more besides, if the chance comes to me. Who can do it better?"

"I think you tempt the Overworld with your pride, Moloquin."

He still held her hand, and she made no effort to free it; now he tightened his grip.

"I mean to marry you. It will make it easier for Rulon's People to accept me."

"Yes," she said, "I can see that. Do you mean it to be a marriage merely for the sake of their sense of things? I have no interest in a sham."

"No," he said. "I have always wanted you. And that will be no obstacle to you, you are too young to give up your life yet, to live like a grey widow. You have the heart to rule, married with me you shall rule as much as I." He gripped her hand hard. "Marry me, Shateel. Together we will make the world right again."

"What about Wahela?"

At that, he let her go. "I will not give up Wahela. But she is different from you. Between her and me there is something else, we will keep it so."

"We shall see how that goes," said Shateel.

She leaned toward him, her hand on his arm; chaste as the stones, they kissed, and he put his arm around her shoulders.

"You are too potent to fade away into the corner, Shateel." He leaned toward her, speaking into her ear, his voice quick with his visions. "I need you. I have work enough for fifty of us. I mean to make of all the villages one People, as once there must have been only one People. You can see it, can't you—in the stars at night, in the stories, in the dances and the lore—once there was one People, and they knew one Truth, and so what they did was great. Oh, Shateel—I mean to make us great again—"

She put her fingers over his mouth. "Moloquin. Be quiet, now, do not put so much into the world, but look and see what you might take out of it."

He caught her by the wrist. "Pagh. I cannot imagine what it is like, to look at the world and not want to change it. Well then, come along, wife. I am eager for the marriage bed."

She followed him, ready for him, for his smaller, human hungers.

III

THE GATEWAY

III

THE GATEWAY

The People of Rulon's Village cut logs, and they pried up the first of the great stones by the High Hill, digging it out of the grass where it had lain so long, and worked the rollers under it. They made rope, and with the rope, and with men pushing, they moved the stone over the land to the river, and it took them well into the spring simply to reach the river with the first stone.

At the river's edge, they built a frame of wood for the stone. They sewed up the skins of pigs and goats and filled them with water and thrust them under the frame, so that the stone floated up off the bottom of the river, and wading along beside it, and pulling with ropes on either bank, they brought the first great stone down the river to the place it came nearest to the Pillar of the Sky.

There, they brought the huge stone onto the bank, and worked the rollers under it again, and with ropes and pushing and groaning and saying many prayers, and giving much to the spirits to make them strong also, they hauled the stone up across the plain to the Pillar of the Sky. Altogether it took them from the time Moloquin laid the task on them until the Midsummer Gathering to bring the first stone to the Pillar of the Sky.

Moloquin did not go to the Gathering. Most of the People went but Moloquin stayed at the Pillar of the Sky, where he was digging up the old ring of stones, and many of those who loved him stayed with him.

He had ordered the People of Ladon's Village to move their longhouses up to a site on the far side of the Pillar of the Sky, and there they raised their new roundhouse, and built a fence around the village; there they cut down the brush and the trees, burned them, and dug up the ground to make new gardens. From these gardens he charged them to keep all those fed who worked at the Pillar of the Sky.

At the place of work itself, outside the embankment, he and the men of the Forest Village built another roundhouse, and there at night they ate and told stories and slept; but everything they ate, and all their goods, came from the other villages. All they did at this place was work to build Moloquin's gateways.

Toward the time of the equinox, another of the great stones arrived from Rulon's Village, the men groaning and complaining. These were the two largest stones that Moloquin had chosen; he had made them bring them first because in his heart he was afraid that if they had brought smaller stones first, and learned how hard the work was, they would refuse even to try to move the bigger stones. These stones were so huge that with all the men of the village working at them they only travelled a few paces a day over the land, and they left a trail behind them in the grass, a track of mud and pulped green, like a great scar, visible from all around. Now they lay side by side in the high grass of the Pillar of the Sky.

The harvest began. Moloquin went from one village to the next, to see the harvest brought in, to see that all would be enough. He took his family with him, walking from the Forest Village, where Wahela had raised her garden and borne him a son, up to the New Village, where Ladon's son stood in Moloquin's place and did the chief's business when Moloquin was not there, and from there to Rulon's Village, where Shateel lived and kept things as Moloquin wanted them.

While he was there, the men of this village all came to him, and they told him they were tired of dragging stones around.

He sat in front of the roundhouse and listened to them, his face impassive. The men lined up in orderly rows, as if they were dancing, and Shateel came and heard what they said, standing a little to one side of them all.

"You cannot make us do this work," said the leader of the men, the old Salmon Leap master, whose name was Ruak, the Speaker. "We must do our own tasks, those given us by our ancestors, the dances that preserve the village and the study of the ancient lore. We have no time for hauling stones around."

Moloquin said, "What you are doing with the stones is more important than the dances."

Ruak said, "You are our chief, or so you have said, and we have tried to accept you. But you do not live in our village. You do not lead the dances. You do not come to the Gathering and make us proud when we see you among the other chiefs. We might as well be a leaderless People as have you for our chief."

Moloquin said, "I am leading you to do what will overshadow all the other things you have ever done."

"We see nothing but what is before us, and we are ashamed."

Now Moloquin stared at Ruak a moment, his face bland and smooth as a baby's. He turned toward Shateel and beckoned to her to come forward.

"Wife," he said, "why are my people unhappy? Is there food enough for them to eat?"

"There was a very great harvest this year," said Shateel, "as you know well, husband."

"Are they set upon by wolves or demons?"

"No, they are safe in the village."

"Then why do they complain to me?"

She went closer yet; her eyes shone. He had come into the village late the night before, and she had joined him in the roundhouse, and they had enjoyed each other all night long.

She said, "They are only ordinary men, husband. They do not see what you see at the Pillar of the Sky, only work, and work that means nothing."

He faced the men again; he said, "Once before you denied me, and you know what happened then. Have you no faith in me still? Now listen to me, I shall keep my patience, because you are my People and I love you. But my patience is short, and the Pillar of the Sky is very dear to me. You have taken the two biggest stones. Those you must haul next are smaller, and I shall gather up all the men out of the New Village and send them to you, to make it easier."

An outcry rose from the men, and they all shouted at once. Moloquin raised his hand and they went on shouting, and he took the bronze axe from his belt and held it up, and they stilled.

He said, "You will do as I say, or I shall go to the New Village, where people even now remember that when they were hungry you denied them, and I shall gather up all the men there and bring them here and lay waste to your whole village."

At that they stilled utterly. They looked from one to the next, and all looked at Ruak, but the old man simply turned and walked out of the roundhouse yard. The rest followed him, their heads down.

Shateel came to her husband and put her hand on his shoulder. "You are so harsh with them, they will never learn to love you."

"They are stupid," he said. "They will not do it willingly, they force me to threaten them."

"They will mutter against you when you are gone."

"They will haul my stones to the Pillar of the Sky, he said, "which is all that matters to me."

Still she looked down at him, her face troubled and her hand stroking slowly at his shoulder. He watched her a moment, thinking of the night before. She had no such wild passion as Wahela, but they made a good mating. She was exciting in other ways. He always knew what went on in Wahela's mind, and usually he cared very little, but with Shateel he could only guess, and all she thought amazed him.

Now he said, "What disturbs you, wife?"

"There is much that is different from the old ways," she said. "We can pretend that it is the same, but all has changed, and it makes everyone tremble a little. No one knows how it will turn out."

"Do they love you here?"

"They love me here," she said. "At first for my mother's sake. Now for my own. I have been a good headwoman. You saw how great the harvest was."

He took her wrist and pulled her down beside him, and they sat together on the threshold of the roundhouse. Little by little, the men were coming back, avoiding Moloquin with their looks. They went in and out of the roundhouse, and the pair by the door made room for them. Some of the men came out to the yard with stones to work, and others brought their masks and worked at them, and still others sat talking and doing nothing.

It offended Moloquin that they did nothing. He kept his teeth together, he reminded himself to be patient, but he meant to show these people what work was.

He turned to Shateel. "I shall need much of your harvest to feed the people at the Pillar of the Sky."

"There is enough," she said.

"I want you to tell me exactly how much there is," he said. "I want you to take a long stick, and for each basket of grain, cut a notch in the stick. Make sure all the baskets are the same size. When you have numbered all the grain, number the beans and the vegetables in the same way. Then hang the sticks on the rafter of the roundhouse, and we shall see how much there will be left over, when all the people here have what they need to eat through the winter."

"I will do it," she said. "They will not like it."

"I do not care if they like it." He moved closer to her, he put his arm around her, and there in the full sight of all the men he kissed her. This too was against the old ways; but he meant to overturn the old ways. "Come inside," he said. "I want a child of you."

She laughed. "Moloquin. Do you expect us all to work as hard as you do?" But she got up and went into the roundhouse ahead of him.

That winter, with the harvests in, all the men of the three villages went up with Moloquin at their head to the High Hill, and they chose another stone from the stones collected there. They slid rollers under it and pushed it away to the river, floated it down the river, and hauled it over the plain to the Pillar of the Sky.

After that, they went back up to the High Hill and brought another stone down. When the bad weather struck them, Moloquin would not let them stop. The stone crept along, but Moloquin seemed to fly; he was everywhere, shouting and nagging the men with the ropes, urging on the men who pushed at the back of the stone, bullying the boys who moved the rollers. The rain lashed them; the snow fell on them, so that their hands froze and the ends of their fingers split open against the stone and bled into the muck, but Moloquin was always at their backs, always driving them on.

At night they made campfires and huddled shivering around them, and Moloquin himself passed out the food. There was always plenty to eat, and he himself did not eat until the littlest boy had gotten his fill—this they noticed, grudgingly, and grudgingly admired, along with his strength and his will and his tirelessness. When his back was turned, they cursed him under their breath and daydreamed of killing him.

In the midwinter, the bad weather broke for a while. The second stone was just arriving at the Pillar of the Sky; the sudden warmth and sunshine filled them all with new life, and that night, after they had eaten, all the men gathered together inside the embankment and danced.

There were no dances connected with the Pillar of the Sky; most of them, dreading the place, had never spent more than a few moments there, leaving the bodies of their dead. Now the site had become a sort of home to them, a place of joy, since reaching it meant they could stop working. They formed rings in the middle and danced as their feet took them, and that seemed right enough: a new dance for a new People.

Moloquin went up to watch them. The drumbeat floated to him on the soft thawing wind. They had lit fires along the top of the embankment and their bodies moved like shadows through the orange light. He and the men of the New Village had pulled up the old stones in the first winter of his rule, and these stones were thrown carelessly around at the southern end of the place; he climbed up on top of them and stood watching the men dance in the Pillar of the Sky.

He wanted to stop them. Always before, this had been his place. Their dread of it had been his protection; he had felt safe here. Now, too late, he saw that what he had begun here would change everything for him too.

He sat down on the stone, thinking of Karella, and a sudden longing swept over him. The old woman had known everything. She had had a story for everything. Now he looked into the future and saw only a grey blank. She would have given him a story to put there, something to move into.

He thought of his mother Ael, and tore his mind away. He hated Ael. He never thought of her any more.

That left him lonely. In the dark, alone, he watched his People dancing in the only home he had and knew he had lost something, somehow, that he had never imagined could be separated from him.

"Moloquin."

He turned toward the voice. She stood there, behind him in the shadows, the warm wind billowing out her skirts. She held out a hand to him. "Moloquin," she called.

He stood; he cast one last look toward the Pillar of the Sky, and turned and went into the darkness with Wahela.

Now he set about laying out the circles on which he would raise the stones, and now for the first time he realized that within his design there were demons waiting to trap him.

He had not given thought to it before. When Brant made the rope and laid out the circles for the roundhouse, he had not asked how Brant knew that the rope must be a certain length, but he saw now that he would have to know even before he cut the rope how his stones would stand, how far apart, and therefore, how long the stone beams of the gateways would be.

The other men were there, waiting to work, or doing work: the Salmon Leap Society, which knew much stone-lore, was beginning to shape the stones they had brought down. Moloquin, with the demons in his mind, went to watch.

These stones were hard. He had seen flint worked, and that was easy: a blow struck in the right place knocked off exactly the size and shape of chip that the master wanted, and shrewd hands could fashion a rough core into a tool in a matter of a few blows. Harus Kum himself had taught Moloquin much stone-lore, but from another way of thinking; he had crushed stones in the mines, and he had seen some that went to dust at a mere touch, and some that resisted, but none that ignored the hand of man as these stones did.

The Salmon Leap master, Ruak, led his society at the work. He used a maul made of stone, and with all his strength he bashed at the edge of one of the building-stones, and nothing happened. He slugged at the stone with all his strength, until at last a little trickle of dust blew away, and then the others could see that what Ruak did had some effect, but the effect was very small.

Now Moloquin went up, and he took the maul from Ruak and began to smash at the stone with it—Ruak, with swift gestures, showed him where to hit. The maul was heavy, taking all his power to lift, and he drove it at the building-stone with his whole might. At first he seemed to do nothing, but then gradually he saw that his work was wearing the great stone smooth and straight along its edge.

At that he let out a roar. He flung down the maul, whirled, and raised his fist to the others, sharing his triumph with them; but all he had from them were puzzled looks. Disgusted, he turned to Ruak.

"Keep at the work. It can be done, if we but keep faith with the stone."

"Keep faith with the stone," Ruak said, disbelieving. "How can you speak of it that way—the stone refuses, it will not obey—what faith are we to have in it?"

"This," said Moloquin. "You may have this faith: that if we are men enough, the stone will yield to us, and then we shall have been masters of something worth mastering. Now—go finish what we have begun, because if we leave off, there will be such a hole in the world here that all the demons ever hatched will come rushing in and devour all of us."

Ruak gave him a white look of suspicion, but he went to the men and gathered them together and spoke with them, and when Moloquin walked back into the embankment to study his problem of the circles, he could hear the men bashing at the stone again with their mauls.

He sat on his haunches and looked at the Pillar of the Sky. With the failed circle of stones now taken away, it was smooth and pure as a virgin; the only stones that remained were the four ancient uprights, the Watchers, where Brant had been used to observe the setting and rising of the midwinter sun and the midsummer sun, the stones at the major entrance through the bank, at the northwestern end, and the misshapen corrupted stone some paces beyond, which from the center of the circle pointed toward the midsummer sunrise. The circle was so clean it seemed almost wicked to put anything on it. He tried to imagine his gateways standing on it, but the wholeness of it resisted him; his mind could not see it complete.

He went outside the embankment and cleared away a space in the dust, and with his forefinger traced his circles in the dust. At first he could not find a way into it, but he realized right away that he could see it best from above it, and drew two rings in the dust, and saw everything. The size of the circle depended upon the length of the beams; if he chose beams of a certain length, the circle would have to be exactly as long as all the beams laid end to end, or they would not fit.

The shorter the beam, also, the easier it would be to lift it to its place on top of the gate. He went to where the great stones lay waiting in the grass, and he took his rope and measured their width, each stone, where each was narrowest. Clearly if they were all to look the same, none could be wider than the narrowest of them, and the work of the stonesmiths would wear off more of their width. To find the space between, he measured his own shoulders. The width of this beam he marked with a piece of chalk on the shortest of the stones in the grass.

Then he stretched his rope from the North Watcher to the South Watcher, and marked its place, and marked the line also from the East to the West Watcher, and where these two lines crossed was the center of the circle. With the rope and the stakes he found the perpendicular through the center and marked that with stones.

Now he took the rope and he measured the beam ten times, since he could keep track of that on his fingers. Even without experiment he could see that that length would make too small a circle, and he measured the beam ten more times and called the other men in.

They came gladly from their labor. They were coated with dust and sweat, and their hands were bashed bloody; as soon as they came inside the bank they dropped down on their backsides on the ground. Moloquin counted twenty of them and made these get up again, and he tied the rope together into a circle and made the men hold it out in a ring.

Ruak sat on the grass with the others, and when he saw how small the ring of men was, he turned to the fellow next to him and said, "At least he does not mean to rival Turnings-of-the-Year."

Moloquin swung toward him; Ruak and the others had no notion yet that he intended to raise a beam of stone across the tops of the uprights. He said, "Then come and we shall make it bigger. Ten more."

He widened the circle by ten more men. Ruak sneered at him. "Turnings-of-the-Year is bigger yet than this."

"I am a humble man," said Moloquin. He marked the ring with stones and gathered in his rope again. "I shall be content with this."

Ruak was obviously enjoying his condescension. "I shall not complain any more, since I see I am asked to do nothing that other men have not done before me." He strutted back toward the bank, and the other men trailed after him, their spirits uplifted. Moloquin took his rope and laid out another circle, halfway between the first one and the center.

That done, he went back outside the embankment, to the place where he had drawn his rings on the ground, and he squatted down and stared at the image for a while. Finally he set in the other marks of the Pillar of the Sky: the four Watchers, the two entry stones, and the stone beyond that.

Now the design began to satisfy him; it seemed complete, somehow, full. As he watched it, however, a discontent with it arose in his mind, because to see it his eyes had to move constantly, from one place to another; there did not seem to be a one-ness to it, a single looking at it. The two rings in the center seemed unrelated, and he began to draw the smaller one again, shrinking and expanding it, and moving the center up and down the line of the midsummer sunrise. In his mind he saw the two rings of uprights, connected at the top by the smooth circle of the beams. He had always intended to make the inner ring higher than the outer, climbing up toward Heaven, and now suddenly it occurred to him to make the inner ring not a ring at all, but a circle of five free-standing gateways. As soon as he saw that in his mind, his hand went out and opened up the end of the inner ring that faced the midsummer sunrise, accepting in the flood of light, and at once the design filled him with a profound delight, everything seemed part of one order, steadily more intense from the bank inward to the central space, with its smooth curve, and its east-extended, indrawing arms.

As he squatted there, looking down at the sketch in the dirt, the power of the place worked on him again. Again he saw before him the finished building. The smooth lines, the hugeness of the stones, the difficulty of doing it, and above all the flow of the light of the sunrise through it delighted him like the ecstasy of sex. For a while, contemplating the Pillar of the Sky, he saw everything whole; he understood all things.

Nearby, not within his sight but within his hearing, the men of Shateel's People were hammering away at the stones. Whatever Ruak had said, they complained and cursed as they worked, and their curses were aimed at Moloquin; they called for demons to eat his flesh, and for the rot and ruin of his whole kindred, and for the extinction of his People, and he heard all this and cared nothing for it. With his fingertip he traced again the shapes in the dust. Before him in the dirt lay the key to Heaven, and Moloquin wanted nothing more.

When Shateel came back to live in her mother's village, everyone waited to see what she meant to do, now that she was Moloquin's wife.

With the death of Rulon, the village had no chief. Moloquin claimed to be their chief but he was far away and showed no interest in them. Yet because of his claim there would be some obvious risk in naming another chief, and anyway there was no man of that family old enough, with Rulon dead, to take his place. Therefore some people were glad that Shateel came back to live with them, with her daughter, without her husband.

Joba was not pleased. She was headwoman of her kindred, and when she spoke around the sampo, the others listened to her with respect. Now that Shateel would sit among them, Joba knew her daughter would challenge her, as she had always challenged her.

So she waited with the other women around the sampo for Shateel to come among them and for Shateel to speak forth and expect to be heeded because she was Moloquin's wife.

Shateel did not come. For the first few months she lived again among the People she had grown up with, she did nothing at all to claim any rank or authority. She made a hearth in the longhouse, close by Joba's, giving a fine basket and a blanket to another woman to secure the place. She went out to the fallow ground lying at the edge of the village and she dug up the ground to make a garden.

She had no seed, Joba knew, and waited for her daughter to come and ask her for seed. But Shateel did not. Shateel seemed not to know her mother was there, although she had given a fine basket and a good blanket to be nearby her hearth, and instead when a runner went off to the Pillar of the Sky, to Moloquin, she gave him a message for her husband, and when he came back he had a pouch full of seed for her.

Now Shateel came to her mother's hearth, with Dehra in her arms. She came in through the opening in the front of the wall of stones that separated Joba's home from the rest, and knelt down there, right in front of the hearthplace, and she put out before her a round basket and a jug of glazed clay with two spouts and a cured deerskin, and finally she put down a little flat wooden bowl, and on it a handful of seed. Then with bowed head she sat there and waited for her gifts to be accepted or rejected.

Joba sat where she was, saying nothing. The whole of her daughter's deed charmed her; she recognized it as an admission that Shateel knew she had been wrong before in her relations with her mother, and for a long while Joba could not bring herself to speak, her feelings brimmed so near to overflow. Then Shateel raised her head, and the two women leaned together and embraced.

Joba's tongue was now freed from restraint, and she said at once, "How do you mean to live here?"

"As I am doing," Shateel said. She held the baby on her lap; the child woke, mewled loudly, and Joba's daughter opened her clothes and gave the baby the breast. Now Joba's breast also seemed to draw with milk. Shateel stroked the baby's cheek. She lifted her gaze again to her mother's.

"You do not understand," she said to Joba. "When I left the Gathering to follow Moloquin, he took us away to a place where there was nothing at all, no village, no older people, no hearth—nothing but the forest and the earth, and we began from nothing, and for a long while we had nothing. To live here, to be among so many other people, to have so much—I am very content just to be here again, and to know what I have here. I want nothing else."

Joba said, "What does Moloquin wish of you?"

"I don't know," said Shateel. "His mind is like a wild bird, it touches the common earth only now and then, and very lightly. I do not know what Moloquin wishes of any of us."

Joba stroked her chin. She saw that Shateel held Moloquin in some awe. She herself saw him more clearly, she thought.

She said, "He has little regard for our ways. Yet before Rulon, he spoke in a voice that moved me. I cannot believe he means us to be doing as we wish."

"Then he shall have to come here himself," Shateel said. "I do not mean to do anything other than what I am doing now."

Joba smiled at her. "Then why did you marry him?"

Shateel opened her mouth but no reply came out, and slowly she flushed. She lowered her eyes and said nothing. Joba did not press her. They spoke of other things, especially the baby, who resembled Joba slightly.

With the men gone off to haul stones to the Pillar of the Sky the village was peaceful. The old Bear Skull master who kept the village's year brought the news from Turnings-of-the-Year that the sun was coming to her midsummer ascendency, and the women made ready for the Gathering. Shateel sent a runner to the other villages, to the north and to the south, that the Gathering would soon begin.

She did this without seeming to notice that in doing it she set herself apart from the others. It was the chief's duty to send the runner off. Joba saw how her daughter managed this, quietly and without calling any attention to herself, and wondered how long Shateel would remain blind to her own power. Around the sampo, when the other women asked her how her daughter did, Joba only shrugged.

"You should come sit down around the sampo," she said to Shateel. "You might hear things of interest to you."

"I cannot now," said Shateel. "My garden is growing too quickly. I was too ambitious, I planted too much, I must work from dawn until dark, my back breaks every day."

They all went to the Gathering. Moloquin did not come; it was the principal subject of conversation throughout the camps, and the people of the northern villages indulged themselves in sneers and laughter at the others, called them Unwanted People, making jokes on Moloquin's name.

The men had all come from the Pillar of the Sky to the Gathering, and when they heard the northern villagers' taunts, there were mutters and arguments and angry talk around all the hearthfires. The men danced every night until they dropped, and none danced longer, leapt higher, played the drums faster than the men of Shateel's Village, who had no chief to lead them.

Still the northern villagers made mock; that was the way of the People, when things happened they did not understand.

The Gathering ended. The men of Shateel's Village all came home again, to pry up another stone from the tumble by the High Hill and haul it away to Moloquin's dead place. They grumbled about the work; they were in no hurry to do it at all, and they lay around the roundhouse yard most of the day working on their masks and taking turns in the sweathouse. Then one day a bear appeared on the village midden.

The boys' band saw it first, early one morning when they were coming up from the stream, and they ran at once to the village, shouting the news.

When the women of the village heard of the danger, they gathered up their children, sat down in the longhouses, and refused to go out. They turned their eyes expectantly toward the roundhouse, toward the chief who was not there.

Joba, with the rest of the old women, went to the roundhouse yard, and there they found the men lazing around. Shateel was with the women, but she stood in their midst, not at their head, and she said nothing.

Joba it was who spoke. Joba advanced into the yard, glared around her, and said in a loud voice, "Now there is a bear on the midden, and no one can go out of the village, the gardens will fail, we shall all starve, and here you sit, doing nothing."

The men stared insolently back at her. Among them were many young men, Bear Skull novices, makers of stones, watchers of stars, and now haulers of stones; they stared insolently at the headwoman, and slowly, with elaborate carelessness, they got up, took their masks, and went out the roundhouse gate.

They went forth, with their drums and their masks and their flutes, and the whole village gathered to see what they would do. They went out the gate in the roundhouse fence by twos, because the gate was narrow, but they remained in pairs as they walked through the village, and by the time they reached the gate in the brush fence that was nearest to the midden, they were dancing.

Shateel went after them, in among the women. She had not yet seen the bear.

The midden lay to the southeast of the village, outside the brush fence. Between it and the path from the village was a wide flat meadow, trampled to dust. Here the men danced, in pairs, their feet striking the earth in the rhythm of the drums; they put their masks on. With the rest of the villagers in a tight pack behind them, they advanced on the midden, shaking their arms and wagging their heads back and forth. At first no one saw the bear.

The midden was old, and piled high with refuse. There the women daily took the sweepings of their hearths; there they cast out offal and garbage, the innards of slaughtered pigs and goats, the chaff of their grain. It lay in a hollow at the far edge of the flat grass, at the foot of a steep rise crowned with little trees. As the men danced slowly forward toward it, there seemed nothing more formidable before them than a line of saplings.

Then from the top of the midden a great black head thrust up, and the men faltered in their dance—now, instead of going forward, they spread out sideways, forming a wide curved line of dancers before the midden. The head rose above the midden and sniffed. Its muzzle was brown. Its eyes were tiny and red, like a pig's.

The men shouted and kicked high in their dance, and the black head tossed. It grunted. With a lurch, the rest of the bear heaved up into view, vast and strong, and wholly unafraid.

The women all screamed. The bear lumbered forward a few steps, tossed its head again, and let out a roar that sent the bravest of the boys' band scuttling toward their mothers.

The men beat furiously on their drums. All up and down the line many faltered, many would have given ground before the bear, but others stepped forward. Here and there young men with gaudy masks stepped forward waving their arms, daring the bear's attack.

The women stayed back with the children, and had to crane their necks to see. Around Shateel they murmured to one another. "What can they do, with no chief to lead them?" A few shook their heads. "Look at them! What fools—they have no chief, no power, the bear will kill them." Some others began to speculate on the bear's power: if it were a demon, or just a beast from the forest.

Shateel moved a little closer, trying to see what was happening. The bear prowled along the edge of the midden, sniffing, and then abruptly it stood up on its hind legs and roared again.

Now nearly all the men shrank away. The rhythm of the dance fell apart, the drums stilled, most of them, and stark in the sudden quiet were the voices of those few men who still had the heart for this.

There were several of them. They surged forward when the others fell back. They shouted taunts and insults at the bear; they leapt high in their dance, they shook their arms in furious gestures, competing with one another for ferocity, gaining strength somehow from the bear.

Shateel saw this; she saw also that among these men one would soon stand out alone, and if this one man drove away the bear, or killed it, then he would have a claim to the roundhouse, a claim that Moloquin, far away, would have to struggle to deny.

A claim that could only be a mortal danger to her. Dehra lay in her arms, and Joba stood beside her. She thrust the child into her mother's grasp and moved forward, leaving the other women.

She passed between two silenced retreating dancers, going up among the other men, the challengers. She saw herself as only one of them, a rival for the power in the bear. Now suddenly she wondered if the bear might not think she was a man, if she assumed the aspect of one.

She pulled herself up as straight and tall as she could. She threw her chest out, and strutted, lifting up her legs in high ground-seizing strides, and she shouted in a deep harsh voice. Waving her arms over her head, she went slowly toward the bear.

The great beast, on all fours, watched her come. Blasts of air snorted from its nostrils. Bits of the garbage of the midden clung to its glossy black fur. Shateel danced harder. She shook her arms and waggled her head from side to side, and she lifted her legs high, knees bent, and worked her face into hideous grimaces, sticking out her tongue and rolling her eyes to simulate a mask. Behind her, the drums picked up again. A flute began to pierce the air with its ringing voice.

The bear stood up again, stretching its forelegs to offer its murderous embrace. She sprang into the air and shouted, throwing her limbs wide; coming down again, she leapt up once more, and all the drums beat furiously.

The bear grunted. Turning, it ambled slowly away down the other side of the midden, and a moment later they saw it scale the steep rise just beyond and vanish among the trees. Shateel sank down, trembling.

The People went running past her, scrambling over the midden, as if they could wipe away the bear's presence by trampling its tracks. Shateel went back into the village. Joba followed her; they came together just inside the brush fence.

"What did I do?" Shateel asked her. "What did I do?"

Joba gave her back her daughter. "What you meant to do, Shateel." She went on back to the sampo, leaving Shateel behind, more unsettled now than when she had faced the bear.

After that the whole village waited for Shateel to take her place at the sampo. Instead, she went to her garden every day and worked among the plants; she tended her child, and lived as quietly as any other woman.

Now around the sampo the old women spoke of times when there had been no chief, when the chief had died suddenly with no boy of the proper mother old enough to follow him, that in such times the women had chosen one among them to be first. They spoke also of Rael the Birdwoman, who had the power to assume the shape of birds and trees, and who lived so quietly among her green growing things that no one noticed her, taking her instead for a blade of grass, or a thrush, and yet in every harvest was her handiwork.

Now Joba had given Shateel the wool from one of her goats, and Shateel used a round of wood and a long stick to make a spindle, but to spin the wool she had to sit up high off the ground, so that she could keep the spindle turning with her feet. Therefore, not long after the bear had gone, she went to the roundhouse, found some of the men idling there, and told them to bring her a stump from the fields. This they did, and set it before the door of the longhouse, across the yard from the sampo. After that, all through the summer, Shateel sat up on the stump and spun the wool of the goat into yarn, and from her high vantage point she looked out over the whole village, and the others got very used to seeing her there.

Not all the men complained about the work at Pillar of the Sky. Fergolin enjoyed it.

With Ruak he shaped the first of the great uprights; they stood on opposite sides of the stone and smashed the edges straight and even, using a piece of rope to keep the line, and while Ruak grumbled and cursed Moloquin under his breath, Fergolin watched the stone give way to his strength and knew what Moloquin had said was true: if they had faith in the stone, they would become its master.

As he worked, bit by bit he found the craft. He had made tools all his life, but this was different: not merely the hardness of the stone, but the size and the result all made this something other than his tool-making skill. But it was an easy thing to learn: all it took was strength and resolution. They bashed and crushed the long edge of the stone until a hollow appeared in the surface, then they worked the hollow across the width of the stone and turned at the far edge and went back the other way. Between each hollow a ridge formed; these they wore off quickly, striking from both sides.

Inside the embankment, Moloquin and another bank of men were digging the first hole. They cleared away the grass and the topsoil, reached the chalk layer beneath, and with antler picks they pried up chunks of the chalk. Moloquin came with his rope and measured the stone Ruak and Fergolin were working, went to the next longest stone, which lay nearby in the grass, rude as a wild beast's tooth compared to the shape slowly emerging from the stone between Ruak and Fergolin, and measured that one, and then he went back to his place just outside the bank where he had cleared away the grass and he drew in the dust with his finger.

Ruak said, "He is mad. Where did you come from? Why did you choose him to be your chief?"

Fergolin straightened, his back sore. His hands throbbed from the many small collisions with the stone. Turning, he sought out Moloquin with his eyes.

"The women chose him. We had fallen into terrible times, we needed someone with great power."

"What power does he have? All he does is sit in the dirt!"

Fergolin smiled at him, and Ruak with an oath stooped down for his maul and attacked the stone again, furiously, as if he did it for his own sake and not Moloquin's.

When the sides of the stone were smoothly shaped, Moloquin came to them, and measured out the stone again with his rope. He laid his hand on one end and said, "This is the top of it. On the top, here, make a knob."

Ruak grunted at him, gave a shake of his head, and said, "What?"

Moloquin stroked his hand over the top of the stone. With the rope he made two or three brisk measurements. "Here," he said. "Knock off the top part on either side, make a knob in the middle, as you might do if you were making a roundhouse post."

"Why?" said Ruak. The other men drifted closer to hear.

Moloquin said calmly, "Because I mean to lift a beam onto the top of it, and the knob will hold it steady."

Ruak and the other men crowded tight around him. "What are you going to do?"

Moloquin said again, "When the uprights are in place, we will put a beam across the top. Therefore—"

The rest of his explanation was lost in the shouting and arguments of the other men. Fergolin stepped aside from the others; he went slowly to the gap in the embankment and looked in.

The place was clean and empty. Without the old ring of stones it looked somehow wilder, more pure and more holy. He tried to see Moloquin's stones in place here and could not. But his back tingled. In his mind he could see the thing, two stone uprights, a stone beam across them, and he knew how high it would stand by the throbs and pains and soreness in his back and hands—by the work he had done on the upright. When he imagined it all the hair tingled up on the back of his neck. He went slowly away to where Moloquin stood in the center of the crowd, with Ruak shouting into his face.

Ruak was saying, "It is impossible. Impossible! We cannot lift one of these stones high enough from the ground to slip a finger underneath."

"If we cannot do this first one," Moloquin said, "we will stop utterly. If I fail now I will not try again."

That silenced Ruak. Moloquin looked around him, at the men staring at him, their faces long with disbelief and dislike. His curly black hair and beard wreathed his head. He wore only his loincloth. Years of hard work had sleeked his body smooth and hard. His face was impassive as the stones; only the glint in his eyes revealed the passion in his soul.

He said, "If I cannot do what I intend, then you can go home, I will trouble you no more. But you must give me all you have. I warn you, if you shirk, there are such powers gathered here that will canker up your heart and eat your mind, and tear the whole of the People apart." He looked around him, staring into their faces. "Now we must begin. Ruak, do as I bade you, make the knob."

Ruak ground his teeth together; he flung a fiery look at Moloquin. A twist of cloth around his forehead kept his long grey hair in place, and now in a sudden fierce notion he tore it off, untied it, wrapped it tight again around his brow, and fastened it. With the same energy he seized his maul and set upon the stone, and Fergolin went up to help him.

"Here and here." Ruak's hand stroked quickly over the butt end of the stone. Side by side, the men began to smash down the surface.

On a cold rainy day they set about raising the first stone. With ropes and rollers they hauled the stone in through the gap in the embankment; while they were grunting and straining, the word got down to the New Village that they were putting up the stone, and the women and children drifted up to watch. By the time they hauled the foot of the stone up over its hole, the bank was crowded with the curious.

Moloquin jumped down into the hole, and with his rope he measured everything. The other men stood around with their hands on their hips. Fergolin had never seen a stone raised and was impatient to begin, but the other men sat down or sprawled on the stone and groaned loudly of their fatigue.

"Up. Up." Moloquin burst out of the hole and strode around the stone, driving the men to their work, and they scattered before him like chaff before a gust of wind. He sent half of them to fetch the logs stacked in the lee of the embankment and gave the other half rope and showed them how to loop the rope around the stone, to hold it fast.

The stone was going nowhere. Fergolin had raised the uprights of roundhouses, and thought that hard work; now he strove with all his strength and all the strength of a mass of other men and they could not budge the stone. Moloquin jumped down into the hole again.

Ruak said, under his breath, "Push it in on top of him," and the men near enough to hear all laughed and pretended to heave at the stone.

Moloquin called out for help. Fergolin and some few others went cautiously forward. Moloquin stood in the hole, looking up past them. He said, "Bring some picks and shovels. Quick!"

From the embankment came some of the women, who had been working in their gardens and had brought their tools with them here. Fergolin got a pick and took a shovel and went back to the hole.

Moloquin seized the pick. Still standing in the hole, under the butt end of the stone, he began to attack the wall of the hole under the stone, wedging the tip of the antler pick into the chalk, and heaving and wrenching at it until a great block of the chalk fell out. He stepped aside, gesturing to Fergolin to get in beside him and shovel the chalk out.

Fergolin climbed down into the hole and busied himself a few moments shovelling out the debris before he straightened and turned to look at the stone.

When he did, his heart contracted. The stone seemed poised above him. When it came down into this hole it would fill the whole space; it would crush all that lay beneath it. Now, with Moloquin, he was digging out the ground under it, to make it fall. He nearly leapt up out of the pit. His hands trembled. Bending his back, he forced his attention down to the ground and worked, but his back knew the stone was there; his back itched and crawled with expectation of the fall.

Moloquin hacked and wrenched at the hole, filling it up with rubble which Fergolin shoveled away; at last they had dug out almost the whole side of the hole under the stone. Moloquin struck Fergolin's shoulder. "Go up," he said, and Fergolin flew out of the hole, lightly as a little bird. Moloquin climbed out the other side.

A light rain was beginning to fall. The other men stood around with their heads lowered, their eyes glaring, and Ruak came forward, his mouth open. Moloquin raised one hand to quiet him. "Now, we have to raise the other end. We shall need sticks, poles—be ready to stick the rollers underneath."

The men raised up such a groan that the watchers on the bank burst into laughter. Moloquin made each one take a tool, and they gathered around the top end of the stone, where the knob was.

Again it was as Ruak had predicted. They could not budge the stone, not even a little. They laid the ends of their sticks under it and pried and cursed and hung their weight on it; they did this separately and all together, but the stone would not rise up.

Then from the bank the women came, one by one, casting down their gardening tools, and they added their weight and strength to the strength of the men, and they hauled and hauled. The rain fell all around them, trickling down off the smooth surface of the stone and pebbling the faces of the workers.

They tried once, and failed. Many slumped down to sit on the grass, dispirited, but Moloquin went around and urged them up again, and again they strove, and again they failed.

More and more people were appearing from the New Village, and as they came they joined the workmen. The rain was coming down more heavily, and their feet slipped in the grass. Moloquin stood watching from one side as they struggled, and when they had failed again, he went in among them, took the poles they used, and arranged the men so that there were the same number on each of the poles. Under the center of each pole he put chunks of chalk and bits of broken logs, so that the tip of the pole was beneath the stone, and the end where the men worked thrust high into the air, and the center of the pole rested on the piles of debris, and then he stood back and called to them all to pull down together.

They hauled down on the poles, and from behind Moloquin a little boy cried out, "It moved! It moved!"

The People began to laugh and shout; they dropped the poles and ran around laughing, leaping on the stone and banging it with their fists. When Moloquin shouted to them to get back to the work, they fell on the poles like wolves on a dying deer, and heaved.

The stone did move. It moved only a little, just enough for the children to wedge logs underneath, but when they strained again at the poles, it moved another little bit, and again they could push logs and earth under it, to keep the space they had won. With the rain sluicing down their faces, they lifted the stone up steadily, bit by bit, until at nightfall, when they had to stop, the great stone hung with its foot over the hole, its head as high above the ground as a child's, its body braced up with earth and sticks and chalk.

Singing, the women and the children marched away toward the village, and most of the men followed them. The men of Shateel's Village wandered off toward their roundhouse, on the far side of the Pillar of the Sky. Fergolin could smell food cooking, and his belly was flat with hunger; he went around in the deepening twilight, gathering up tools and stacking them against the bank.

He thought he was alone. But when he came around the bank, he came on Moloquin, squatting in the mud, tracing in the mud with his finger.

Fergolin almost spoke to him. He gathered words in his mind to say, ordinary words such as one man might say to another merely to narrow the space between them, but in the end he said nothing. Moloquin was busy, drawing in the mud; whatever Fergolin said to him would be only an annoyance to him. Fergolin went away, toward the New Village, toward the society of men he knew.

In the morning, in the rain, they went to work again. The women did not go to their gardens, nor the boys to the games and errands of the boys' band; the littlest children ran to help in the raising of the stone.

All morning they struggled and strove with their poles and logs and baskets of earth, fighting the stone up a little higher, a little higher, until it seemed poised above the hole, ready to slip down the sloping side. Moloquin was everywhere, running all around the stone, shouting orders, racing to help where he thought they could not hold. The rain eased a little. Near noon, as they braced up the stone, now high as a man above the ground, the monster slipped a little.

"It goes! It goes!" Screaming, flinging their tools aside, the whole crew dodged back away from the stone.

It hung there, precarious on its broad footing of dirt and wood, its head stuck up into the air, its foot reaching down into the hole, and everyone thought he could see it wobble. Moloquin dashed to the bank and ran back with coils of rope.

"Fergolin! Ruak, Hems, Bahedyr—" he flung a heavy mass of rope into Ruak's arms, and they swung the ends up and over the stone, one rope to the right, one to the left. As they did so, the stone slipped again.

All the People screamed. The men on the ropes strained back to hold the great stone still, while it wobbled back and forth on its wedge of earth, and Moloquin, still running, gathered up the poles and pressed them into the hands of those people standing idle, and running to the stone he put the tip of a pole against it and pushed. As he did so, all of a sudden, the sun came out.

In the warmth and light the people sighed, lifted their faces and

spread out their arms to the sun. Moloquin shouted to them to push
the stone. He gathered up as many men as he could, and got them
three and four to a pole, put the tips of the poles against the stone
and heaved, and the stone slipped again, crunching on the earth,
and stopped. The men on the ropes leaned away, yelling in their
excitement, hardly knowing what they were doing; the men with the
poles flung their weight against them and thrust, but the stone
seemed to have reached its balance, and it would not do as they
wished. Then all at once, it roared downward, skidding over the
sloping edge of its hole, slamming butt first into the bottom of the
hole with a thud that shook the ground, and swayed upright, the
ropes whipping out of the hands of the men.

Slow-bending like a great old tree in the wind, the stone swayed
solemnly back and forth, and Moloquin howled. Snatching up a
shovel, he dashed forward, into the shadow of the stone as it wobbled
and tipped, and began to scoop the clumped dirt into the hole.

Only the chalk close around its foot held the stone upright. As
Moloquin piled the dirt in around it the stone swayed above him,
leaning over him, ready to crush him. On the grass around him, Fergolin started forward to help, and the shadow of the stone fell on
him and he shrank back. Moloquin cried, "Help me!" His arms
worked in a frantic rhythm. Fergolin plunged forward to his side,
dropped to his knees, and with his hands began to shove the heaped
earth into the hole.

As if they wakened suddenly from a daze, now the other men
rushed in around the foot of the stone. They flung all they could
find into the hole, to steady the stone, and the great swaying upright
slowly found its roots and was still. They backed away from it, looking up at it, and a shout left their throats. Turning to one another,
they banged each other on the backs, shouted their own praises,
flung out their chests, and marched around the stone in triumph.
Moloquin went away a little, alone, and stood there looking at it.

Fergolin went up to him, and said, "It is magnificent."

"It is only the first, Fergolin-on," Moloquin said. "And the hard
part is yet to come."

He clapped Fergolin on the shoulder, half a blow, half a caress,
and went down toward the gap in the embankment. The other men
were dancing around the stone they had raised; they had forgotten
how they had cursed the stone and Moloquin together while the
great brute still lay in the grass. Fergolin smiled to himself. The men

were malleable and soft, much softer than the stone. Under the maul of Moloquin's will, what could they not do? And praise themselves full well afterwards. Fergolin went after Moloquin, out to the next stone, and taking up his tool he set to work to smooth it into shape.

In the late spring, while the men were digging the hole for the next stone and the women were tending their gardens, a boy went to play in the ashes of Ladon's roundhouse, down by the river.

Usually the People avoided this place, because they felt Ladon's malevolent spirit lingered there; although Ladon's son had dug the bones out of the ruins and taken them away to one of the old tombs on the far side of the river, everyone remembered that Ladon's body had not been brought to rest in the Pillar of the Sky, where his spirit might be lifted up at once to join the rest of the dead, and so they suspected their dead chief might remain where he had died, waiting for a chance at revenge.

The boys of the boys' band shunned the place also, because their parents did, but one boy was adventuresome, and at the height of the day, in the full blast of the sun, he went down to the great scar on the riverbank, the place of ashes and char, and began to turn over the lumps of half-burned wood. At once he found some small bowls of clay, shrunken and cracked and hard from the heat, and that spurred him on; he circled around and around the immense flat bed of fire-ruin, and found a stone knife.

Excited, he ran back up the slope, to where the boys' band was herding the goats of the New Village to pasture, and he showed the other boys what he had found. The leader of the boys' band was Grela's son, whose boy's-name was Sickle because he was so thin his bones looked sharp enough to cut, and he led the others in a wild rush down to the old burned-out roundhouse.

Some of the trunks that had held up the roof had not burned down all the way, and their stumps jutted up from the black blowing ash. There were holes hidden under the debris, and bits of wood that caught the boys' feet and tripped them. As the boys prowled around, the wind suddenly lifted up a whirl of grey ash and carried it away toward the river, and the little boys screamed that Ladon was walking the ruin, and they fled. At that, many of the older boys lost their enthusiasm and announced loudly that there was nothing here anyway and they too drifted off.

The boy who had found the stone knife remained; Sickle remained, and a few others. They crisscrossed the blackened circle, kicking at the ground and turning over lumps of rain-soaked ash. Then the boy who had found the stone knife saw something gleaming in the dirt.

He stooped and pried it loose: a lump of shining stuff, like a rock. Not a rock. Looking around him, he saw the other boys distracted, heeding only their own searching, and he hid the shining thing in the pouch on his belt and turned over the ashes with his hands, and quickly he uncovered more of the same stuff. Some the fire had warped. Some kept its shape: links of sleek red-yellow disks and curved forms.

He tried to put it all into his little pouch and could not. He thought of hiding it there and coming back again, but the whirling column of ash had frightened him too, and he was loathe to return here again, once he had gone. He folded the treasure he had found into the front of his loincloth and tried to walk casually away, as if he had lost interest in the place.

Sickle saw him at once and trailed suspiciously after him a few steps; the littler boy panicked and burst into a run, and as he ran, he dropped the shining treasure behind him. Sickle let out a yell and gathered up all he could. He knew immediately what they were; he sat down where he was and put the curved bracelets on his ankles and on his wrists, and he hung the belt around his middle, and strutting and flinging his arms around he went to find the rest of the boys' band and show off his delights.

Wahela's son Laughter ran with the boys' band, although they were cautious with him and often excluded him because his mother was not really of their village. When he saw what they had found in the burned-out roundhouse, he went straight to the New Village where his mother sat in the midst of other women.

She had not planted this year, not at the Forest Village, nor here at the New Village; she had decided that Moloquin would take care of her, and so she had no need to work. Therefore she had nothing to do all day but sit in the sun and play with her children. Some of the younger women usually joined her with their weaving and their wool-plucking, but the older women, sitting around the sampo, refused her company and would not let her sit with them.

Chief among these rivals was Grela. Tishka had died in the Famine, and Grela had become headwoman in her place, which had brought a great change on her. Before, she had been talkative and light-minded, but now she felt the weight of the whole People on her back, and everything she did she examined closely to be sure that it was a good example for the others to follow. Wahela was her special enemy. Wahela did nothing that Grela wanted others to imitate. No one knew exactly how she stood with Moloquin, except what was obvious—that they slept together and she had borne him a little boy, yet it was Shateel who was his wife. Also, he fed Wahela, instead of the other way around, which all the women considered a great scandal.

So Wahela sat with her circle, the young women who resented the power of their elders, and Grela sat around the sampo with the elders, and they made gossip like wicked nets to throw at one another, and throughout the whole village the overriding question was who sat with Wahela and who sat with Grela.

Now Wahela sat in the sun, with her hands idle in her lap; her baby son played in the dirt nearby with a pile of little bones, threading them on and off a cord. The other young women were busy with their crafts. As they worked they talked of how ugly and old the headwomen were, but Wahela was tired of that; words had lost their power to amuse her. Then her son Laughter came to her.

He said, "Ana-el, Sickle and the other boys have found something in the old roundhouse."

"What were they doing there?" One of the other women raised her head. "Ladon walks there—he will eat them certainly."

Wahela took her son by the arms and made him stand before her; restlessly she fussed with him, dusting him off, straightening his loincloth, patting his tangled hair flat. Done with her grooming, she reached up under his loincloth and gave his male part a tug, and he yelped and clutched his groin. The other women laughed at him.

"Ana," he said again, "they found something wonderful."

Wahela turned to the other women. "What could be wonderful about that place? It is a place of shame."

They nodded, agreeing with her, smiling at her—Wahela expected immediate agreement in all things from her circle. The little boy shrugged his shoulders.

"I think I will go and tell Moloquin then," he said, loudly.

At that Wahela straightened up, her black brows flattening into an angry frown. "What is this? There is nothing you can tell Moloquin you cannot tell to me."

"I told you," her boy said, swinging his linked hands back and forth; his voice was a taunting singsong. "You would not listen to me."

"Tell me again."

"I told you." Laughter twisted his whole body back and forth, enjoying the attention of his mother.

"Tell me again, little worm, or I will turn your hide to stripes."

The other women giggled. Laughter sidled away.

"I think I will go and tell Moloquin!"

Wahela lunged at him and got him by the ankle. "Come here, and let me warm my hand on your backside, impudent one."

"No," he cried, as she dragged him in toward her lap. "No, no, I will tell."

She pulled him bodily into her lap, as if he were a baby, and held him tight. She put a loud kiss on his forehead. "Then tell me. Sishka, give me some of that honey-cake for my boy here."

Sishka gave her a sticky hard cake of honey and ground nuts, and she broke it in half and gave one half to Laughter on her lap. The other half she gave to the little boy who sat in the dust behind her, threading goat's bones onto a cord.

"Now," she said, comfortably, "tell me."

"Shining things," Laughter said, his mouth stuffed. "Sickle has them now. He wears them, there is a belt, and some bracelets and anklets."

"Pooh," said Wahela. "Just some men's pretties."

"No," Laughter cried. "It is magic—it is the same as Moloquin's great axe—that stuff!"

At that Wahela lost her easy ways. She turned on her son as if he were a little bird and she a hunting snake, and she fixed him with her eyes. "What did you say?"

Laughter swallowed the last of the cake. "I said—Sickle and the other boys found some things in the old roundhouse, things made of the magic stuff, like Moloquin's axe."

"Hah." Wahela sat still, her head turned, her gaze directed nowhere.

"It's true!"

"I believe you," she said, absently.

She remembered, now, that at the Great Gathering where Moloquin chopped down the chiefs' platform and called his People away into the forest, Ladon had worn wonderful ornaments. Until now she had not connected the beauty and mystery of these ornaments with the great axe with which Moloquin destroyed the power of the chiefs. They must have lain hidden away in the roundhouse, all this time, waiting. She got to her feet.

"Where are you going?" the other women asked her.

She waved to them; she waved away Laughter when he would have followed her, and she went down through the village, toward the sampo.

The New Village was shaped much the same as the old one had been. It stood on a rise close by the Pillar of the Sky, with the gardens all on the well-drained slopes with their light soils; there was a little pond in a hollow of the hillside, that the People used for water. The village faced east, as all villages did; where before there had been four longhouses, now there were only two, because so many people had died in the Famine.

The roundhouse was small, only two turnings of posts, and had no yard; the men were always busy with the Pillar of the Sky, and Moloquin was never at this roundhouse. Ladon's son lived there, and they stored food in it, but it was not the same as the roundhouses of other villages; it had no air of power and beauty about it, it was only a little round building where they kept tools and food, and where the women could go when they wanted to talk to Ladon's son.

The real center of the New Village was the sampo, which the women had dragged reverently up the long slope from the old village and set down between the two doors of the longhouses. There the headwomen sat, grinding the day's grain, and grinding out the news of the village. There Wahela bent her steps, her mind full of what her son had told her.

The old women saw her coming and raised their heads, one by one—grizzled heads, ugly old faces, unfit for power, and yet they had so much power. Wahela went in among them and sank down on her knees.

She turned to Grela; without any preliminary, she said, "I want that which your son has found, in the ashes of the old roundhouse."

Grela's face widened with surprise. She looked from the woman on her left to the one on her right and faced Wahela again.

She said, "Go away, foolish woman. Nothing you say means much to us, you are full of wind."

Wahela said, "I see you are ignorant of everything as usual. Now, heed me. Your son found something in the old roundhouse—something of such a power that it will burn his bones to black dust and curdle up his soul unless he puts it into the hands of one whose power is capable of the charm. Now, I charge you with this, old woman—find those charms for me, and bring them to me, or else all evil will fall on you and I shall do nothing to turn it aside from you."

She remained where she was a moment, glaring around at the old women; at last she got up, and straight and slim as a birch tree, she walked away through the village.

Grela watched her go. Grela lowered her head, her gaze on the sampo, and put out her hand to turn the wheel around.

> Sam-po, sam-po
> La li la la li li la
> All must rise and all must fall
> La li la la la la li la
> Sam-po, sam-po

"What is this?" asked one of the other women.

Grela shrugged. She watched the mill turn around and around, the meal dribbling from its edges, and wished she had a knife, and the courage to thrust it into Wahela's heart.

She said, "The Mill turns, that's all. I must go and find my son."

"Grela! You will not do that woman's bidding?"

Struggling up to her feet, the headwoman turned and scowled around her at her companions around the mill. She said, "Do not be fools! Let the idle catch themselves in their own nets. I shall come back."

Moloquin stroked his hand over the stone, warm from the sun, and kneeling down he looked along the edge. Ruak and Fergolin watched him impatiently, and when he straightened and nodded they broke into wide smiles, warm as the sun.

"You must put the knob on this end," Moloquin said. "The other end is uneven."

He stood a moment with his hand on the stone, but his gaze went to the other stone, standing just beyond the embankment, its head raised to the sky. He itched to throw this stone up beside it, to begin the crucial work of raising the beam up to the top of the gateway; it was maddening that everything went so slowly. Here these two men stood smiling at him because he had said this stone was ready to raise up into its place, as if their work ended with that, when it had just begun, and the days were slipping by—the days went by like the clouds that scudded past the top of the standing stone, the time bleeding away.

He said, "The hole isn't quite dug out yet. Come, let us see how deep it is."

Ruak said, "I will wait here." He sat down on the end of the stone in the grass.

"Come," Moloquin said, and walked away through the gap in the embankment, Fergolin on his heels.

The other men were digging up the chalk, clearing out the hole and piling the rubble beside it. Moloquin carried his rope on his shoulder and now he took it down again, leaned down over the edge of the hole, and lowered the end of the rope to the bottom.

Ruak came up, grumbling, slapping his palms on his thighs. He looked up into the sky, squinting at the bright sunlight.

"Soon will be the Great Gathering. I have a lust to be there, I cannot wait until the sun rises over the stone."

Moloquin, kneeling by the hole, said, "We have much to do here."

"Yet I mean to go to the Gathering," said Ruak.

Moloquin straightened, holding the rope bunched in his fist. He said, "How can you want to go to that place, where all the stones had been raised for generations, when you can be raising this one? Here."

He went back to the new stone, lying in the high grass outside the bank. The other stones were waiting a little way away, still rough and unworked; like a shadow beside this stone a patch of crushed grass and muck showed where it had lain before they rolled it over to work the other side. Moloquin measured it off again with his rope. He did this many times a day; the other men always smiled to see it, and he knew they thought him mad, but the exact sizes of the stones had begun to obsess him. At night sometimes he dreamt of measuring the stones. Now he took a piece of charcoal from his belt and made a mark on the stone.

"This much of it will go into the hole. This line here—" with the charcoal he drew a line all the way across the stone—"this marks where the stone will rise above the earth, and this—"

He measured with his rope and drew another line, one hand's breadth from the top. "This is where the top of the stone must be.

When you chop away the stone to make the knob, chop it down to this line."

Ruak grunted. "What difference does it make?"

Moloquin ignored him. He had gotten used to Ruak's challenging everything he did.

With his maul, Fergolin set to work at the end of the stone, shaping the knob, and Ruak fell in beside him. Moloquin went off to his favorite place, just outside the embankment, where he could draw in the dust. But when he came there, Wahela was there.

She sat cross-legged in the grass, her back to the embankment, and she seemed almost asleep, her limbs splayed comfortably in the sunlight, her head back and her hair loose around her all warmed with the sunlight, but he saw the glint of her eyes when he approached, and knew she was awake, alert as a wild bird, and wanted something. He sat down beside her and she turned to face him.

"I have told you many times that Grela is wicked, and now perhaps you will believe me."

He snorted. "I wish you would not bring me these little quarrels of yours. I have much to do here."

He leaned forward and traced circles in the dust and drew lines through them, this way and that, examining the way the lines met at the center. Wahela leaned forward and with her hand wiped the dust blank again.

"Will you not listen to me? Moloquin, sometimes I think this place has robbed you of your wits."

He smoothed the dust with his palm. "Tell me, then."

"Grela hates us. She wants us destroyed, and now she has the power to do so."

At that Moloquin threw his head back and laughed, and his laughter boomed up toward Heaven; all the men turned to see what drew forth this unaccustomed mirth from him. He faced Wahela again, his hand protecting the dust from her—as he turned, he put his body between her and the place in the dust where he drew.

"Now," he said, "tell me more, Wahela."

"She has some magic, I am telling you, magic like your axe. Her boy found it in the old roundhouse. She will use it to bring demons on us, because she hates us."

As she spoke, her eyes shone; she lifted her hands and tossed her hair back. She was beautiful, he loved to look at her with her passionate beauty, and every look reminded him of the times when she gave her beauty to him to enjoy; looking at her always made him lusty. Now she leaned toward him, her gaze fixed on his, as if she could draw forth his soul through his eyes, and she said, "I want that magic, Moloquin. Make her give it to me."

He laughed; he put his hands on her arms and pulled her toward him, smelling the sun in her hair and on her skin, feeling the soft glide of her skin against his.

She thrust at him with both hands. "Are you listening to me?"

"Oh, yes," he said. "You say that Grela has found the ornaments that Harus Kum gave to Ladon."

"I want them," she cried, and beat with her fists on her thighs. "They should be mine—as you have your axe, and I am your woman, so I ought to have the things that Grela has!"

He sat watching her, his hands still on her, smiling at her passion. She flung back her long black hair with one hand, and her eyes flashed at him.

"They ought to be mine!"

"They brought Ladon no good," Moloquin said. "They brought no good to anyone. If you wish Grela such ill, then leave them with her, they will surely bring her unhappiness." He did not tell her that the ornaments were the price of the two boys Harus Kum had dragged away into slavery.

"Moloquin." She leaned toward him, hissing between her teeth. "I want them. Make her give them to me, or I will go back to the forest."

He smiled at her, enjoying her wild temper. "Are you threatening me? Go, then—go, never come to me again, Wahela."

She scowled at him, her face flaming, and he laughed at her; he knew as well as she that without him she had nothing, not even a garden. He took her by the arms and drew her close to him, and he kissed her mouth.

"Tonight," he said softly, "we shall lie together, you and I, and you can have your temper out of me then. Now, listen to me—the things that Grela has will bring her no good. Leave off quarrelling with her over them. Let things work as they will."

Bitterly she said, "You care nothing for me. I have given you my whole life, and you will not even grant me this one small wish."

"No," he said, "I will not. Now, go and let me do my work."

She spat at him. Getting up, she walked away toward the New

Village, her back very straight, and her skirts gathered up in her hands. Moloquin watched her go; he told himself that by nightfall she would forget that she was angry with him. He told himself he was right not to marry her. Bending over the dust, he drew his circles in the dirt with his forefinger.

Moloquin went down from the Pillar of the Sky in the late afternoon, when the day was fat and full and warm; he went into the New Village, to the sampo, and there he squatted down on his heels behind the circle of old women.

At first they paid no heed to them. No chief had ever come to them before; always in the past they had been summoned here and there, to answer a chief's questions and to receive his orders and his anger at their failures. Moloquin was unlike other chiefs. There were times when Grela thought he was no chief at all, and as she sat there, turning the millwheel, talking over the gossip of the village (there had been a birth in the night, the new child's ancestry had to be fully discussed, to make her name, her connections and her duties known), she became angry with him for his ambiguities.

She knew why he was there. The night before, she had taken from her son Sickle a great heap of glossy red-yellow ornaments, beautiful and glowing, and she had hidden them away outside the village, afraid to bring such potent stuff inside the fence. She would have liked to talk this over with the other women but she was afraid even to mention the treasure, afraid of its magic, afraid of those who wanted its magic. Now, her thoughts knotted, she turned angrily toward Moloquin and said, "Well? What have you to say to us?"

He squatted there like a boy from the boys' band, his quick dark eyes like beams of light. He studied her a moment, and she did not look away; but she felt his power, and that too irritated her.

At last he said, "Do you think I am here to speak to you, Ana-Grela-el? What knowledge can I offer you who sits at the foot of the Mill all day long? I am here to listen."

The women turned toward him; they turned their backs to the sampo to face him; they drew up their shawls over their heads and faced him, seven old women, each so like the next that they could have been one creature. Then Grela said, "What are we to say to one as potent as you, Opa-Moloquin-on, who will not bow even to Heaven?"

He said, "I am waiting to hear it."

"Pah! Go listen to your woman, Wahela!"

"I have listened to Wahela. Now I have come to listen to you, Ana-Grela."

"Hah." Grela frowned at him. The thought of the treasure pressed on her mind, yet she could not free her tongue to speak of it, especially to him. He was a man, and a chief, set apart from women; she had no common ground with him. Still, she remembered how he had sat beside Karella when the old storywoman joined the circle at the sampo, and how he had listened then. He had not changed; he still spoke more like a child among women than a chief among men, and this understanding loosened her tongue, although even now she could not speak of the treasure.

"It is Wahela," she cried, and flung back her shawl. Her anger spilled from her like water overflowing a jar. "She comes among us as if she had some formidable power, and yet what has she? Is she not merely a woman like the rest of us? And you! It is your doing that she is as she is. You have taken her to wife and yet not to wife, none knows who she is to you save you yourself."

He said, "Abadon has many lovers, and marries none."

"What! Do you dare compare yourself to Abadon, who walks among the stars?"

"I compare Abadon with me, who walks in the world. Have you seen my stones at the Pillar of the Sky?"

Grela was still mulling over the mention of Abadon, who did seem in many ways like Moloquin. Reluctantly, she said, "I have seen your work, Opa-Moloquin-on."

"That is my answer. Let any who doubt my devotion go there and see: no man is more reverent than I toward the order of Heaven and earth." He cast his gaze around the circle of the old women, their faces pouched and seamed and riven with age. "I care for you above all things. At the Pillar of the Sky I am raising you to glory. If I fail you in small ways, fix your minds on the greater."

Now Grela said, "What of the treasure the boys found in Ladon's house?"

He shook his head. "The treasure matters nothing to me."

That impressed her. She studied his face a while longer and turned her eyes toward the women around her and found them all watching her, waiting for her to go on.

Cautiously she said, "The boys found it in Ladon's house."

He nodded his head once. He did not seem much interested in the matter, and that emboldened her; she knew he would tell her the truth.

"It brought much evil on us," she said. "It is full of magic."

Moloquin shook his head. "It has no power of its own. Whoever understands the lore, he has the power, and none here has the lore save me." He got to his feet, and with one hand he saluted them. "Keep faith with me," he said, "and I will keep faith with you." Saying no more, he walked away through the village, and all heads turned to watch him go.

Grela sank down in her place. The other women bubbled over with quick talk, excited, exclaiming over the minutest details of his appearance and the lightest inflection of his words. By day's end, the whole village would have witness of Moloquin's sitting among the women. Grela drew her shawl around her and turned her gaze inward.

The treasure lay only a few paces away from where she sat, outside the brush fence in a hole in the ground, covered with grass. What Moloquin had said lightened her mind somewhat. For all the glossy beauty of the stuff, the rings and belt were only charms, decorations, vessels of power, not important in themselves.

If they had been magical, surely he would have wanted them.

Wahela wanted them. Grela drew her shawl closer around her, thinking with anger of Wahela. Moloquin had shunted aside her complaints, he had made light of Grela's own power, which was to keep the order of things among the women.

Smooth and sleek and glowing, the treasure of Ladon. Even now, buried away in the grass outside the village, it fascinated her; her feet itched to carry her there, her fingers yearned to touch, to lift, to wear the charms on her own body.

Then it did have a power of its own. He was lying to her.

She gnawed her lip. She wanted to believe him—that was his gift; when he spoke to her, she believed whatever he said. She watched the sampo turn, her thoughts inward and full of doubt. When she had been only Tishka's sister, the work of the headwomen had seemed so easy—they sat here, they heard all things, they conformed all things to the rule of Heaven. Now that she sat here, the rule of Heaven itself was veiled in mysteries. What was she supposed to do?

Evil, the treasure, evil and potent, whatever Moloquin said.

Yet that made no sense to her, because if the treasure had so much value, then he would want it for himself, and he seemed indifferent to it. What had he said?—that the charms themselves were empty—that the power lay in him who had the lore.

Only Moloquin had the lore.

She sat there, rocking back and forth as she thought, turning the mill with her hand. The other women had threshed out all their opinions about Moloquin. Their speech now turned to other things—to babies, to gardens, to weaving, to the thousand small crafts that bound the world in its course. Yet Grela still crouched inside her shawl and could not free her mind of the treasure.

> *Sam-po, sam-po*
> *La li la li la la li la*
> *The Mill turns forward, never backward*
> *The Mill returns ever where it was before*
> *La li la la li li la*
> *Sam-po, sam-po*

Grela covered her face with her shawl.

In the afternoon the runner came from Turnings-of-the-Year, to bid them all come to the Great Gathering. The women of the village had been expecting it—their gardens kept time for them as well as the heavens kept time for the men—and they went at once into the longhouses, to make ready for the journey.

Wahela also went into the longhouse, and there she packed up her blankets, her clothes, and the things her children would need. The women of her circle helped her, fluttering around her like butterflies around a blossom, and when everything was packed up and ready, she took her little son Twig, who was Moloquin's son, and she walked away to the Pillar of the Sky.

The men were all there, working fast, because Moloquin wanted to raise the second stone before they left for the Gathering. They had the stone with its foot over the hole and its head tipped up into the air and its body supported on mounds of earth steadied with logs. On the far side of the hole, they had raised three tall wooden posts, tipped so that their heads all came together in a cross, and over this joint they cast more ropes, so that ropes hung around the great stone like the flying-strings of spiders. When Wahela came, the men were bracing up the stone with their poles, hauling up the stone with the ropes over the posts, trying to force more earth beneath it; Moloquin stood almost in the hole itself, looking up at the work.

She called him. He would not come; he gestured toward her behind his back to wait for him. She stamped her foot. The stone would always be there, and she wanted to speak with him, just a few words. In her arms, Twig squirmed to be put down.

"No," she said. "It is too dangerous here—do you want the stone to fall on you?"

He looked up at her; he had the wide black eyes of his father, and when he looked at her, solemn and intent, she often had to struggle away the belief that he was Moloquin himself, somehow, locked in a baby's body. Sometimes she spoke to him at length of things that would have bewildered even Moloquin.

He pointed to the stone. "Opa," he said.

"Yes, there is your father."

"Down." He wiggled again, his fat legs banging against hers. "Down!"

At that moment, suddenly, the stone slipped. The men shouted, loud enough that Twig clutched his mother's clothes and pressed himself tight against her breast, and she crouched, instinctively bending her body over him. The men flung themselves at the stone in a fury of activity, flinging ropes around it, heaving their weight against the poles that forced its head up.

The stone had moved only a little. Its foot still hung over the hole where it would stand, and now, strive as they would, they could not budge it a finger's breadth. Wahela straightened, smiling. It amused her that the stones sometimes moved of their own will, when they would not move at Moloquin's.

"Down!" Twig cried, and he slithered free of his mother's grasp, landed on his feet, and ran across the beaten grass of the holy place toward his father.

Moloquin was shouting at the other men; with waves of his arms, he directed the men with the ropes to stand wide to either side of the stone, and he himself joined the swarm around the poles. Halfway to them, Twig stopped. Wahela waited, ready to pounce on him and drag him back if he went closer. The men strained at the poles, but the stone resisted, lying there in the cradle of ropes and earth; strive as they would, the men could not budge it, and they gave up. They fell back, away from the poles, and let the ropes slack, and Moloquin wiped his face on his forearm and walked around the stone once, looking up at it.

"Wait," he called, and went to the tools tilted up against the other stone. He took a shovel and jumped into the hole.

Wahela shrieked. He had leapt down beneath the foot of the stone, and in her mind she saw him crushed, and she started forward, and Twig ran forward also. Twig ran forward to the very edge of the hole, and then the stone began to move.

The men let out a roar; they leapt to the ropes, to guide the stone. Moloquin bounded up out of the hole, flinging the shovel aside, and the great stone slid down past him into the hole and tipped up on end.

The ropes snapped tight. The men flung their weight against them. Caught in the net of the ropes, the great stone wobbled back and forth, its shadow swaying over the ground. Moloquin and the others rushed around it, shoveling heaps of earth into the hole— some of the men even leaned against the stone, as if their weight might somehow hold it upright.

In their midst, at the brink of the hole, Twig stood, looking up at the monster whose shadow swung back and forth over him.

Slowly the stone settled. The men clustered tight around its foot, beating the earth down, freeing the ropes; their voices rose in an excited triumphant babble. Wahela went forward toward her son.

Moloquin turned. For the first time he saw the little boy there, and he scooped him up. "What are you doing here?"

Twig flung up his arm toward the stone. "Mine," he cried, and Moloquin burst out laughing.

"Yours, hah? Yours?" He tossed the little boy into the air. The other men turned, laughing, and watched. The little boy grew red in the face; he fell into his father's arms and struggled to be put down; he pointed to the stone again.

"Mine!"

Moloquin put him down and went toward Wahela. When he reached her, he put his arm around her, but he turned to look at the stone again, not at her.

She said, "I am going to the Gathering."

"Ah?" He let his arm slip away from her. "I am not."

"That is why I am going," she said, and flounced away from him, tossing her head. "Perhaps when I am gone you will come to know how much I am to you." She reached Twig and lifted him up, protesting, into her arms.

Moloquin set his hands on his hips. "Perhaps," he said, and smiled at her. He made no move to stop her; nor did he try to make amends to her by offering her the treasure. She stuck her son on her hip and walked angrily away, back toward the New Village.

Moloquin sat on the ground between the two upright stones, and one by one those who loved him best came to say good-by to him.

First Wahela said good-by, in her own way, and took her children off to the Gathering. Next came Bahedyr, who also was going to the Gathering, and who came to ask Moloquin's opinion on the matter of marriage: Bahedyr intended to find a wife at the Turnings-of-the-Year, and needed his chief's advice.

Moloquin said, "Pick an ugly one. She will be grateful to you, and more reasonable about what she wants." He was thinking of Wahela, beautiful as a thunderstorm.

Bahedyr laughed, thinking he meant a joke, and Moloquin smiled at him and struck him lightly on the arm. "You will know which one to take," he said. "You need nothing from me to do that."

Bahedyr saluted him and went off, a bundle on his shoulder, his spear in his hand. Next came Hems, squatting down before his friend.

"I am going back to the Forest Village," he said. "To see Ap Min."

"Be well," Moloquin said. "Tell her I will see her soon, I hope."

As he spoke, he thought of the Forest Village, and his heart grew sore; he wanted that quiet, that peace. Hems touched him with his hand and left.

Then came a host of others who did not matter much to him, save that they were his People, and they came and told him they were going and some asked his advice on small matters and one by one they left.

He sat there alone, in the late morning, with the stones behind him, and his thoughts went to his work here. Now, looking back on his first ideas about the Pillar of the Sky, he saw what a foolish boy he had been, knowing nothing of the practical matter, thinking all things might be accomplished simply by wanting them. It had taken him two full years to raise two stones here. The People constantly complained and shirked and would not do as he wished; their enthusiasm bloomed in the flush of each triumph and withered away in the first challenge of their strength and will. He was afraid now that he would never finish the building; when he saw them walking away from him, away from the work, his heart grew hard and tight within him, and a weight of doom pressed on his mind, like a shadow cast over him.

Someone was walking up the slope toward him. He raised his head.

It was Grela, alone. Her shawl covered her head; in her arms she carried a basket. She reached him and knelt down before him, laid the basket down before him, and pulled back the lid.

Inside the basket lay the price that Harus Kum had paid Ladon, long before, for two boys, a pile of grain, and the People's future. Moloquin put out his hand and lifted the belt with its oblong links and let it drop.

"This is yours," Grela said. "You alone have the power of it, and so I am bringing it to you."

"Thank you," Moloquin said.

She rose, adjusting her shawl over her head. "I want the basket."

He tipped the treasure into the grass and held out the basket to her, and she took it away, going off down the slope, not back to the New Village: to join the others, on their way to the Gathering. Moloquin sat there a long while, watching the sun shine on the bronze in the grass.

The platform in the center of the Turnings-of-the-Year had been rebuilt closer to the ground, so that the fall would be lighter if Moloquin came and chopped it down again. Shateel stood with her People and watched as the chiefs of the three northern villages paraded to the entry; she saw Wahela, in a crowd of her followers, standing a little higher on the embankment, and turned her back.

Moloquin was not here. Moloquin made trouble for her constantly, simply by not being where he was supposed to be, by not doing what was expected of him, and that Wahela had chosen to be here only made things worse. Glumly Shateel watched as Barlok, so old he drooled, staggered on the arms of his underlings to the way into the ring.

His People raised their voices in shouts of his name, but Shateel's People were silent, the People of the New Village were silent, the

People of the Forest Village weren't there at all, and so as Barlok
hobbled to the rings, his name rose feebly as a little breeze up toward
Heaven.

Now here came Mithom, striding along like a bear, his body
decked with feathers and bits of quartz and amber, his arms banded
with rings of leather sewn with colored beads made of porcupine
quill; in his right hand he carried a painted club, and in his left a
round basket, with a loop in the center to hold it: these were the
emblems of his power.

As he approached his People cheered his name, but once again
their voices rose up timidly, and most of the People kept silent.

Now here came the twin brothers, Eilik and Muon, decked with
their painted emblems, their black hair studded with red feathers,
their bodies painted with blue and red and green, in their hands the
ceremonial spears and arrows, and at the gate into the ring they
joined the other chiefs, and like the faint wafting of a little wind
through the branches of the trees there rose up the voices of their
People, but for the rest, there was silence.

The chiefs stood there, looking at one another, waiting for the
People to make their choice, waiting for the People to proclaim one
of them the first, and all they heard was silence.

Then out of the crowd a woman came, and she wore only a woman's long dress of woven stuff, and she carried no emblems at all, and
she went up among the chiefs, and from all the crowd along the
embankment her name rose, bellowed forth from the throats of her
People: "Shateel! Shateel! Shateel!"

Now from the People of the New Village who knew her not at
all, but knew Moloquin and knew that she was Moloquin's wife, there
rose the roar of many voices: "Shateel! Shateel! Shateel!"

She stood there, looking around her, amazed. She had meant
only to ask them to enter into the ring together, and now she stood
before the four chiefs, magnificent in their panoply, gorgeous in
their manhood, and all around her the People raised her name.

She turned her back on the chiefs, her heart pounding, and
wondered what to do. Her name thundered to the skies. Before her
the platform stood, stubby and awkward in the center of the ring of
stones, and she thought to walk to it, she thought to lead the other
men there, but abruptly the shout changed that urged her on.

"Shateel," they cried with one breath, and in the next, they bellowed, "Moloquin! Moloquin! Moloquin!"

Now she understood. She turned away from the platform, from the Turnings-of-the-Year, and she faced the northern chiefs.

"Go," she said. "They call for one who is not here; therefore, let the platform stand empty."

She walked by them, going back up the embankment, travelling through waves of noise, the cheers of Moloquin's name. As she walked through their midst, the People turned to watch her and showered her with Moloquin's name.

At the top of the bank, she paused and looked back. All the People had turned toward her, turned their backs on the stones and the lesser chiefs. But down there at the entry, Mithom suddenly strode forward into the ring of stones.

The two brothers rushed in after him, and Barlok's underlings carried the old man swiftly after. On the embankment, the People clapped and chanted. Moloquin's name sank slowly down into the rhythms and sounds of other songs and the crowd dissolved into a mass of little crowds, all doing something different. None paid heed at all to the chiefs, who in the center of the Turnings-of-the-Year had reached the platform and there were fighting over who should sit down first upon it. Shateel went away, back to her hearth.

Wahela had taken Bahedyr into her company, and learning that he sought a wife, she took on herself the task of finding one for him. Because he was of the Salmon Leap Kindred, he had to marry a woman of the Oak Tree Lineage, and Wahela went away to Shateel's People among whom were many of the Oak Tree.

Also she wanted to face Shateel and try her power against the other woman's; it seemed to her foolish and dangerous that a man should have for wife one woman, who never came to him, and for lover another woman, whom he would not name his wife.

She walked through the Gathering, a pack of her followers on her heels: young women, restless and uncertain, wanting to try the borders of the elders' world. As she passed, all the People looked up, and her name went on before her, and they crowded close to see her, and with every step she held herself straighter and taller, feeding on their attentions.

In the camps of Shateel's People, fewer came to see. Some of the looks cast at her were dark and full of anger. She felt here that a cold

wind blew in her face, and when she sat down at the hearth where
Shateel sat, combing her daughter's hair, Wahela knew what belly the
black wind blew out of.

She sat down across the fire from Shateel and tucked her hands
into her lap. Behind her stood her own daughter, a gawky half-
grown girl, holding Twig on her hip.

"I bring you greetings, Shateel," Wahela said. "It has been long
since we saw your face around our fires."

"I have been doing as Moloquin bade me," Shateel said. In her
long hand the comb was like a row of teeth that she stabbed into the
child's hair.

Wahela said, "You must be doing his work very well, since I see
your People are fat and joyful, and they called your name with the
fervor of those who love their chief."

"I am not their chief," Shateel said, and the comb jerked through
the child's long fair hair.

"Well," Wahela said, "strange things are happening to all of us. I
am here because a man of my People, who is of the Salmon Leap
Kindred, desires a wife."

"Oh? Who? Bahedyr?" Shateel began to laugh—when she
laughed, she looked much younger and her eyes sparkled. Wahela
wanted her solemn at once.

"This is no occasion for merriment, surely? Have you knowledge
of marriageable girls of the proper kindred among your People?"

"Oh, yes, many," said Shateel. "I shall speak to their mothers.
Bahedyr must make himself beautiful, and appear often at the Turnings-of-the-Year, and wear the red feather very prominently. Let the
girls and their mothers see him, and we shall await their decision.
Tell me about Moloquin."

Caught off her guard, Wahela had no time for anything but the
truth. "He spends every day at the Pillar of the Sky, he cares for
nothing but the stones."

Shateel said calmly, "He has never cared much for people."

Now Wahela cast her lure into the stream, to see if the fish
jumped. "Perhaps if you would come to see him more, he would
warm to the pleasures of marriage."

"I understand you give him the pleasures of marriage very well
already. Is that his child? Let me see."

Now she was stretching forth her arms toward Twig. Wahela

nodded, and her daughter let the little boy down to the ground, but he was reluctant to go to a stranger. Instead he went up to his mother and wormed his way into the circle of her arm.

Leaning around to look into her face, he babbled a long string of nonsense, and his mother laughed at him.

"See—he does not know you." She gathered the little boy up, cooing to him. "See, Twig, this is your father's wife."

He pressed himself against his mother and favored Shateel with a disapproving look. Shateel laughed.

"Ah, he is much like his father."

She turned her head away as she spoke; Wahela knew she wanted a child of Moloquin. Wahela said, "Small wonder your marriage is barren, since you never see each other—do you think babies come on the spring breeze?"

Twig turned toward her again, and again he babbled out his nonsense. Wahela shushed him with her hand over his mouth.

Shateel was frowning. "What is that he said—something of a stone falling?"

Wahela made the child sit down in her lap; it occurred to her, a little late, that Twig's insistent babble did have something to do with a stone—with the great stone he had seen raised at the Pillar of the Sky; he had not stopped talking of it since then. It annoyed her that Shateel had understood this while she, his mother, had not.

"Have his stones fallen?" Shateel asked.

"Moloquin has raised two stones only," said Wahela, and sniffed. "It is an arduous and painful work and there seems no point to it. No, neither of them has fallen. The child saw one stone put into the hole, and his head is full of it now."

"Wise child," Shateel murmured, and stretched her arms out. "Twig, come to me, I am your mother too, in a way."

Twig squirmed around and pressed his face to his mother's shoulder. Wahela laughed. "You have no craft with children, Shateel."

Shateel shrugged, her face bland, and returned to combing her daughter's hair. Satisfied, Wahela made her farewells and went back to her own camp.

In the light, all the People cheered Moloquin, but in the dark, their voices changed.

Shateel sat on the embankment in the darkness of the late twilight, and around her she heard her People murmuring.

"Why is he not here? There is none to lead the dances, none to command the readings of the stars."

"They read the stars anyway. The dances—"

"We have no chief to give praise and homage to, no chief to show off our greatness. The northern villages are laughing at us."

"Yet things go well for us. The harvest will be fat this year again."

"That is Shateel's doing. We have not seen Moloquin in over a year."

"See how his woman goes about the place, handsome as a chief! We are being ruled over by women."

And the People of the northern villages came among Shateel's People and taunted them, saying, "You are a village of women! Where have your men been, all year long?"

"They work at the Pillar of the Sky, with Moloquin."

"Where is your chief?"

"At the Pillar of the Sky."

"Pssst! You are a village of nothing but women."

Now Shateel imagined that the world was a tight-woven basket, formed of the interlocking lives of the People; but Moloquin stood alone. He had opened a hole in the basket, through which the whole world could dribble away. She had avoided the New Village, because Wahela was often there; she had expected that Moloquin would come to her when he wished. Now she knew that he would never leave the Pillar of the Sky. She would have to go to him. Returning to her hearth where her daughter slept inside her blankets, Shateel made ready to go over the plain to her husband.

While the People were at the Gathering, Moloquin slept in the Pillar of the Sky, in the hollow under the North Watcher. He woke in the dawn light and went down to the New Village and washed himself in the pond and ate in the door of the roundhouse. The days were long and empty. Sometimes he went onto the downs and hunted for the bustards, whose nestlings were now learning to fly, but he found himself no longer lithe and quick enough to catch them, even with nets, and he got his food out of the roundhouse, like any other man of the People.

Most of the day he spent at the Pillar of the Sky, digging a hole for the next upright, although the work before him now was to raise up the beam to the top of the two stones that already stood there. In his mind he performed the task over and over, and in his mind it was easy, yet when he was done, the stone lay on the ground, the two uprights held nothing into the sky.

He was digging the new hole when the first of the People came back from the Gathering: Ruak, grumbling as usual, and some of his followers from the Salmon Leap Society. He tramped through the Pillar of the Sky, grunted a welcome to his chief, and passed on to the roundhouse just beyond the embankment to stow away his belongings. After him came the others in a steady trickle.

It was almost sundown when the People came back, too late to begin any work. When they had put away their things they all came together in the middle of the village, built a fire, and welcomed themselves home with a feast. Afterward, the men danced, and the women shared gossip, sitting in the fireglow, their children sleeping in their laps.

Moloquin went into the roundhouse, and Wahela followed him.

She said, "You should have come to the Gathering. There were things said there you ought to have heard."

"Ah? What?"

She shrugged, coy, her dark eyes pretending to look elsewhere, and her hips swaying. "Had you been there, no one would have dared speak them."

"Wahela," he said, "this is a riddle. Come sit down beside me and let me make you welcome."

He was sitting on a pile of fur at the center of the roundhouse, his back to the post North Star; by his feet a turtle shell of pig's fat, burning at a little twisted wick, cast its light all around him. Wahela, her hips swaying, her eyes elsewhere, moved slowly around him, circling him without approaching him, and her voice was languid and idle.

She said, "They whispered against you. The northern villages especially do not love you, Moloquin. They spoke in the ears of the others that they should cast you out."

Her words struck him like thrown stones; he started to his feet, and made himself sit down again. In the light of the lamp her face was indefinite of expression, her long eyes enigmatic, and the smooth gestures of her hands told him more than anything she said.

She said, "If you came to the Gathering, and dressed yourself and all those around you in the treasure—"

At the mention of the treasure he could not keep still. He got up and walked away through the roundhouse, to the door. Wahela followed him, murmuring, her skirts hissing together like a garment of snakes. In the door to the roundhouse, he stood with his back to her, and looked out through the little yard to the center of the village, where the men were dancing.

"Who spoke against me?"

"The northern villages. They say we are ruled by women! They never see you. If you walked among them, with all your power, with the treasure gleaming around you—"

"Who else?"

"Shateel's People have no love for you."

He nodded once, believing that. They hated him for Rulon's sake, or so he thought, having no real knowledge of how they regarded him. Now here came someone, walking up from the great fire, a tall, stooped man with feathers in his hair.

It was Ladon's son. He greeted Moloquin with a smile, and Moloquin put out his hands to him, glad for one who would not burn him with his tongue.

"Welcome home, brother," he said, and took Ladon's son by the hands.

"I am glad to be home," said Ladon's son. "Perhaps next year I shall make my Gathering with you, Moloquin-on. It is too far to the Turnings-of-the-Year, and nothing of importance happens there."

The two men sat down together on the ground just outside the roundhouse. Although the summer was at its height, the air was chill and damp; a mist drove by above their heads, above the tops of the roundhouse posts, showing mainly as a blankness of the night sky. Wahela lingered in the doorway.

Ladon's son said, "What has she told you?"

"That the People speak against me," Moloquin said.

"They do," Ladon's son said. "Those who know you not. Glad I am that I am no chief, Moloquin-on."

"It would be worse," Moloquin said, with a laugh, "if those who know me spoke against me."

"Many more there are who do not know you. I would fear their ignorance rather than trust in the knowledge of the rest of us."

Moloquin laughed again, but it was a false sound, and he hunched his shoulders against the cold. He turned his mind from the unquiet of his People. "Tomorrow we shall begin to raise the beam."

Ladon's son nodded. He picked at the ground between his feet. "Ruak came back?"

"Yes, and his novices."

"That's good. He might as well have gone home to his own village."

A cold tide of foreboding swept over Moloquin; he saw how the whispers and murmurs of the People could take the Pillar of the Sky from him, and the urge swelled in him to go there, to begin the work now, at once, in the dark, while the men were still here. He caught himself; it was foolish to give himself to panic. Then up toward the roundhouse came Bahedyr.

"Did Bahedyr find a wife?"

Wahela laughed. "Several," she said, and flung up her arm and greeted the hero. "When will you marry, Bahedyr-on?"

The man grunted at her, obviously tired and a little drunk, and went straight into the roundhouse, not noticing Moloquin there. Moloquin watched him go, relieved. The People might grumble and murmur, but surely they would not rush to marry off their daughters to Bahedyr if they hated Bahedyr's chief.

"If you would bring forth the treasure," Wahela began again, and he wheeled toward her.

"Wahela, hold your tongue. I have had quiet here, these past few days, and have learned to like it."

Her eyes glittered at him. She said, "If you would give less of yourself to the Pillar of the Sky, and more to me—"

He surged to his feet; she recognized his mood and backed away, but he pursued her, walking straight at her, so that she had to scurry away from him in a rush. Whirling, she ran away toward the fires.

Moloquin turned back to Ladon's son. "Did anything else occur that I should know about?"

Ladon's son got up and stretched. "We watched the stars. Fergolin can tell you that better than I."

"Are you not of the Bear Skull?"

"I am, but I have never mastered it. They say—Fergolin told me that some close passage of star to star portends—something." He shrugged, smiling, apologetic, a soft pale man. "Ask Fergolin."

Moloquin turned toward the fires; down there, they were dancing again. He thought of Wahela among them, dancing. Fergolin was
probably there, and he started his feet in that direction, but instead
of joining his People, he turned aside, and climbed up the slope to
the Pillar of the Sky.

Shateel had walked across the downs to the Pillar of the Sky, not with
the general flood of Moloquin's People but by herself. When she
came to the edge of the village and saw the fire burning and heard
the drums and the pipes and saw that the men were dancing, she
stopped and could not bring herself to go in. Instead she went up
the slope, to where the embankment of the Pillar of the Sky rose up
into the darkness, and the mist curled around the two new stones.

The stones amazed her. They were bigger than anything at the
Turnings-of-the-Year, and unlike the Turnings-of-the-Year, this place
had been much different the last time she saw it, so the newness of
the stones and the face of their placement was a marvel to her. It was
easy to believe that the Turnings-of-the-Year had always been there,
but this place certainly had been made by men, and by the ordinary
men she knew.

There were two corpses lying in the grass at the center of the
circle, and she avoided them. She stood between the two new stones
and looked up at their tops; the night mist dragged over them, curling around the stone edges like smoke. The stones were perfectly
alike. She laid her hand on one, stroking it, feeling the great strength
in it.

"Shateel."

The voice came from behind her, so suddenly that she jumped.
It was Moloquin; he came up beside her and looked into her face.

"What are you doing here? Have you come to tell me evil news?"

She faced him, her hands still trembling from the fright of his
voice coming suddenly out of the darkness.

"Evil news? Is that how you think of me, husband? Is that why
you never come to me?"

He said, "I have heard from Ladon's son and—others—that the
People spoke against me at the Gathering."

She lifted her face toward the top of the two stones, bathed in
the mist. It was cold here, and she shivered.

"Yes—they made noises of discontent. I think they always do. It is the way of people to be discontented with the chiefs, that way they seem to themselves like chiefs. At the Turnings-of-the-Year, when the other chiefs appeared, it was not Mithom's name the People shouted, nor Barlok's, it was yours."

"Mine," he said, surprised.

She wrapped her arms around her against the cold. "They shouted for you—had you been there, none would have walked before you. That is something, isn't it?"

He said, "Are you cold?"

"You should come to the Gathering," she said. "You should honor the ways of your People, if you wish them to honor you. This is what I have come here to tell you, Moloquin."

He put his arm around her and drew her close to him, into the warmth of his body. "Come here—there is a place here where you will be warm."

She let him guide her across the great flat grassy circle of the holy place; he did not avoid the bodies rotting in the grass, but stepped right past them, and took her into the shelter of the North Watcher. There, down out of the wind, a little hollow accepted them both, and he kept his arm about her, and she was warm again.

She said, "The stones are wonderful." She was sleepy suddenly, after the long walk. She laid her head against his shoulder.

He said in a low voice, "They shall be greater than any other."

"Did Ruak come back?"

"Yes."

"Then you should not worry about the loyalty of the People to you."

He turned to her, drawing her closer against him, and his hands passed in rough caresses over her body and her face. He said, "I want more than loyalty, Shateel." He pressed his face into the hollow of her throat.

They lay down together, in the hollow under the North Watcher. She was ready for him, after more than a year without him; they made the first dance together under the stone; as she held him and groaned and raised her hips to meet him, she looked up and saw the stone, and she imagined that it was this stone that thrust and worked within her body; when they shouted together, their juices mingling, their voices rang off the stone.

They could not cling together forever. The heat past, they fell apart into separate beings again. The cool air swept in around her.

Sad, she turned her face toward the rough dark surface of the stone behind her.

He said, "Here Karella told me the first stories I ever heard."

His voice trembled. She turned her face toward him again.

"Tell me a story," she said.

He opened his mouth, and the tales poured forth, one after another. He told her first the Beginning, how the world was all ice, and the Sun with her warmth raised up the world from cold and death, and how the Moon struggled over it. He told her how Abadon stole the Mill of Heaven and broke it. He told her how Rael the Bird-woman made a pact with the red deer, that she would give the deer a soul if the deer would steal some of the fire of Heaven and bring it to the People.

As he spoke, all that he told her appeared before her in the dark air; it was as if she had never heard these stories before. She drew nearer to him, and he put his arm around her, and his voice murmured into her ear.

He told her, "It was here that Brant told me that the world is orderly."

That was no story, and yet it meant what a story meant to Moloquin. She could see nothing of his face in the dark. His voice came to her across the darkness, as if from the other side of the world.

He said, "Karella lay here, and Brant lay here, and Ael also lay here, and would that Ladon had lain here also, because then he might have gone on to Heaven. Would that I had never slain him. Now he keeps me company, he presses himself against me like a lover, he dwells ever in the corners of my mind, ready to leap out. Oh, that I had let him die, and let them bring him here, to find his way to Heaven."

She held her tongue, although the idea that he had killed Ladon made her shiver all over with horror. As if from the far side of the world, his voice came to her, a rush of words, a torrent from his mind.

"I will never be free of him now. He haunts me now, forever. I see him in me whenever I see my weakness, whenever I see that I may fail here, I see Ladon in me, swollen fat with ambitions he had not the power to fulfill, an ordinary little man caught in a web of dreams."

He had his arms around her, and now she circled him with her arms, put her face against his throat and kissed him. Still she said nothing; she thought that any words from her would stop up this flood of demons pouring forth from him.

"Already two full years have gone by," he said, "two years, and all I have raised up are these two stones. My life is falling away; I shall never do it all, time fights against me, and my People fight against me, and other things—the treasure—all these things steal my mind from my work."

"What treasure?"

He moved against her, his skin sliding against hers. He turned and crushed her against him, and hungrily he mouthed her cheek, her ear, her throat and her breast, and again, there under the stone, they performed the magic that made life from life.

He slept. She lay in the warmth of his body, her head against him, and sensed around them the unquiet spirits of those he had spoken of—the old storywoman, Karella, whom Shateel remembered only as a huddled figure in Ladon's dooryard, dying as she spoke, every word a figure of power. Ladon himself, whose soul had wrapped itself around the cords and fibers of Moloquin's heart. Ael, the woman alone.

He would not speak of her. She had marked that, before, that Ael had come to occupy a place in his mind that he dared not enter any more. Yet in Shateel's mind she grew more alive every time she thought of her: Ael, who had gone into the forest, and lived by herself, and needed neither man nor woman.

So it was she slept; and in her sleep she saw Ael, taller than the stones, standing in the grass and mist of the Pillar of the Sky, the People small and humble around her feet, her hair the floating clouds of Heaven.

In the morning they went to the New Village and sat around the fire by the roundhouse and ate. The men were coming to and from the roundhouse, noisy with their business, and each who came greeted Moloquin as he passed. Wahela was nowhere to be seen. Shateel sat by the fire eating honey cakes and drinking a broth of herbs; she saw how the men came to Moloquin and how he sent them off on this errand and that, but told each one to come to the Pillar of the Sky as soon as everything else was done.

She saw how he itched to go back to his work, how he turned his eyes constantly in that direction.

She said, "Moloquin, I have spoken with the women of my village about the baskets—you said they must bring their harvest to me
in baskets all of the same size, and they will not do it."

He squatted by the fire, eating the last of a handful of seeds.
"The harvest baskets are a trick, an empty rivalry. Why do they cling
to such things?" He rinsed his mouth with a sip of the broth and spat
it out. "We cannot measure the grain if they bring it in different baskets."

"Yet it is their way. Our way. It is a woman's pride, to make splendid baskets for the harvest, and they will not give it up."

He frowned at her. Bahedyr came up to him and went down on
one knee beside him, and before Moloquin spoke again to Shateel he
turned to Bahedyr and said, "We shall need all the new rope—bring
it out of the roundhouse. Get the younger men to help you. See they
keep it in coils."

"Yes, Moloquin." Bahedyr went swiftly off.

Her husband turned to Shateel again. "Then let them keep their
baskets—only, when they bring you the harvest, have your own baskets, each the same as the others, and empty theirs into yours."

"They will not like that either."

"They like nothing I do, it seems to me. Do it in the roundhouse,
where none can see."

"Am I to deceive them? This is troublesome to me."

"They will never know, if you do it in secret."

"They will know, and almost at once."

He smiled at her. "All the better."

In the smile was something she disliked, something sly and ugly.
Something, she thought, much like Ladon.

She rose, shaking out her skirts. "I must go back to my People."

"Come here," he said.

He took her into the roundhouse. In the dim space under the
rafters, as they walked toward the shaft of light at the center, he said,
"I shall come to your village at midwinter, and let them come to me
then with all their complaints and I shall thresh them all out."

"What of your work here?" she said, because she had marked
how loath he was to go even as far as the New Village from the Pillar
of the Sky.

"I have told Ruak that if we cannot raise the stones as I want
them, then I shall give up the whole enterprise. By this fall I shall be
the fool of the People, or I shall need more stones."

They went into the center of the roundhouse where there was a pile of furs, where his axe hung on the tree North Star, where other emblems of his power marked the place as his even if he was so seldom there. He pulled the fur back and pulled out a basket, and beckoning to Shateel to stoop beside him as he lifted the lid on the basket.

"Ah!"

Before her in the basket lay a heap of glowing red-yellow objects. She stretched forth her hand to touch the smooth cold surfaces. Moloquin took hold of her forearm; he chose a wristlet from the mass of ornaments and slipped it over her hand.

"Let this be a token," he said, "of my power and yours. I will be there at midwinter."

He put the lid back on the basket, pulled the furs over everything and rose. Without waiting for her, he went out of the roundhouse, and she could hear him calling to the men outside, bringing them together to go to the Pillar of the Sky. She did not move. Long she remained there, the wristlet heavy on her arm, her thoughts churning; at last she lifted the wristlet to her face and pressed the cold metal to her cheek.

The stone that Moloquin intended to raise up onto the top of the first gateway was roughly shaped. Ruak soaked wood shavings and small twigs in pig fat, and laid the stinking mess in a line along the side of the stone, and set it on fire.

At the whoosh of the flames all the men stepped back, their arms raised over their faces. Moloquin paced up and down, watching. He had never seen this done; he chafed at his ignorance, at his dependence on Ruak. The Salmon Leap master watched the flames calmly from the side. Behind him he had lined up several of the boys, each with a jug of cold water, and as the flames began to die down, he urged them forward with sweeps of his arms and they dashed the cold water onto the rock.

Nothing happened. They pushed aside the slop from the fire, the soaked char and floating ash, and the men pounded with their stone mauls along the line the fire had drawn on the rock. As usual the tools made almost no impression on the stone. Moloquin walked up and down, up and down.

In the middle of the day, Ruak again piled his fat-soaked tinder onto the line where he wished the stone to break, and again he set it on fire. The fat popped and snapped as it burned, and a thick black smoke climbed a little into the sky and was blown off in a ragged streamer toward the east. The boys with their jugs rushed forward and dashed the cold water onto the fire, and again there was no result that Moloquin could see.

He could not bear to watch the long, slow, fruitless labor. He walked away from the work, away toward the North Watcher; the air smelled rankly of the smoke. In the grass before him lay a tangle of bones. His mind turned to Shateel, and what he had told her, the night before, as they lay together beneath the stone—he would have told that to no one else. He wondered at himself, that he had told it even to her.

He could not have spoken so to Wahela. If he showed any weakness to Wahela she would despise him, and the whole village would know of it—if not from her lips, from her attitudes. He knew that Shateel would tell no one.

Yet he was relieved that she was gone. He had shown his soul to her and he was afraid now if he looked into her eyes he would see himself mirrored there. He would see the truth about himself in Shateel's eyes, and so he was glad she had gone away.

Behind him, now, the fire sprang up with its thousand tongues, its roaring voice, and he turned and walked back that way. The boys ran forward with their jugs and poured the water down the line of the rock, and the smoke rolled up in a thick rank plume, and the stone cracked.

The sound raised the hairs on the back of his neck. Like a stick breaking, the stone split and popped all its length, and the men shouted and whooped. Moloquin went closer; with Ruak he bent over the stone and pushed away the debris of the fire, stinking and oily, and the two men bent together over the stone saw the long crack in it, the fresh rock below gleaming in a dozen colors, new to the sun and the air as a new baby. They raised their heads and smiled at each other.

Ruak bawled to his men and they jumped forward with their mauls to begin the work of shaping the beam. The Salmon Leap master backed away, his hands on his hips, smiling. He looked up at Moloquin beside him.

"You thought it would not work."

Moloquin shrugged. "You proved me wrong again, Ruak-on."

Ruak said, "Let you prove me wrong when we go to lift it up, Moloquin-on."

Moloquin looked quickly at him, surprised; he had thought Ruak wanted him to fail, so that they could all go home. The Salmon Leap master, squat and square as a trimmed stone, stood watching his novices pound away at the beam. His hands and arms and face were streaked with oily black. Moloquin went to fetch his measuring rope.

For many days they worked the stone into shape, pounding away the edges and beating hollows into it to fit the knobs on top of the uprights. Those who did not work the stone made rope and cut logs. The summer sun rose hot and dry and beat on them as they beat on the stone. By midday the men who had begun the work at dawn were too exhausted to continue; they went to the bank and sat in the shade, and ate the food the women had brought from the New Village.

Fergolin sat there in the grass; his eyes stung with sweat and stone dust, and he had broken a finger which swelled up and turned black and hurt him every time he moved. Lying in the grass, looking up at the two stones they had already raised, he was certain that they would never achieve what Moloquin wanted. To his fatigued mind the whole idea seemed ridiculous—to float stones in the air! He shut his aching eyes.

With his vision sealed off, he found the small sounds around him grew larger and more precise. The ceaseless pounding of the stone mauls on the beam faded to a background; nearer he heard the sighs and groans of the men who rested in the shade of the bank, and he heard their jaws champing at their food, and the slosh of the broth in the pots. He heard a woman laugh, just beyond the bank, and he heard also a child's little tuneless song.

"A-stone-a, a-stone-a-a-a-a—"

Fergolin looked around him; it was Twig, Wahela's son, who climbed on the bank and sang his little song. The boy walked along the top of the bank, lost his footing and rolled down the grassy slope, in among the men.

They laughed; in spite of their exhaustion, they scooped him up and tossed him about, and the boy shrieked with pleasure and when he was let go he tumbled by himself in the grass, rolling over and over. Fergolin rose and caught him up and kissed him.

"What do you do, little boy?"

"Measuring the stones!" Twig bounced down from Fergolin's arms and darted away toward the nearer of the outlying stones, standing inside its own little ditch in the curve of the embankment.

Fergolin strolled after the child. His thoughts leapt up lively again. At the Turnings-of-the-Year, where he had watched the stars, seen the sun and the moon rise, and shaped all this into his memory, the idea had come to him that probably the stones at the Pillar of the Sky were star-pointers also. Moloquin had thrown down the circle of stones but he had left standing the old four that stood at the sides of the space. Fergolin went to the nearest, the one that Twig was playing by, and leaned against it, and looked toward the horizon.

These two stones were a pair, certainly: when he stood here on the mound, and looked across the top of the second stone to the west, his line of sight passed neatly through a gap in the bank, framing a section of the horizon. He smiled to himself, pleased; he had a sense of recovering something.

What was it? The child gamboled around him, singing his child's song.

"A-stone-a, a-stone-a-a-a-a-a—"

Fergolin walked on down to the other of this pair of stones, turned and looked back. Raised up on its mound, the stone he had just left cleared the top of the embankment and laid its point against the sky.

He knew he would see nothing if he looked today. Surely the stones were meant to be used at some particular day, probably midsummer and midwinter. Brant had known all this.

Brant knew it. The stones knew it also.

As he stood there, thinking of this, a strange excitement came to him. There was knowledge locked in the stones, and if he found the way to free it—

Long-striding, he crossed the broad grassy circle to the far side, where the second pair of stones stood. Here it was the western stone that stood on a mound, a ditch around it, and he stood with his back to the stone and looked across the eastern stone, and to his deep delight he saw that the top of the eastern stone now lay exactly within a notch in the distant hills.

What star rose there? What light-beacon shone there, on some certain day, that would throw its beams of light through the notch in the hills, across the eastern stone, and strike the eye of him who stood in this place? A hand tugged at his shirt.

Twig stood there beside him. "Opa, what are you doing?"

"I am—" Fergolin stooped and picked the boy up. "I am with my ancestors, child. And with my sons' sons' sons." He kissed the boy on the forehead.

"What do you mean?"

Fergolin shook his head. There was no sense in speaking much to a tiny boy. The pleasure he took in his discovery was something he could not communicate. He felt himself suddenly sliding into place, a part of the universe; everything fit, everything mattered. He sauntered off around the circle again.

Just inside the bank the ground was clogged with chunks of chalk; the grass grew unevenly over it and in places would not grow at all, and as he walked he realized that there were such chalk marks, evenly spaced, all around the whole circle. Had Brant known also what these chalk studs knew? He came to the North Watcher, at the mouth of the gap in the bank. It was tipped over to one side; under it was a deep hollow, like a cave. He had seen Moloquin here, any number of times, sleeping here, or just sitting in the hollow.

What did Moloquin know? Could he read the stones?

Fergolin thought not: Moloquin had no men's lore. As he stood there, the strangeness and wonder of that came to him for the first time. Here was a chief of the People, and a great one, master of several villages, who neither danced nor made a mask, and who had no lore, and yet was bringing the People to this place to raise up something no one had ever heard of before: a stone roundhouse.

That was what it was that Moloquin was building here: a stone roundhouse, a dwelling of spirits. Fergolin stroked his hands together, excited. His body jumped with new energy. Quickly he went back to the stone, to begin his work again.

When the stone beam was shaped, they pried the end up and forced the rollers underneath it and shoved it up through the bank to the foot of the two upright stones. Now the impossible task began.

They did with this beam as they had with so many others; they levered up one end, shoved logs under, and levered up the other, and shoved logs under that one. Half the men grunted and groaned at the levers, and the other half ran in with the logs and thrust them into place. With the weight of the stone on them, the logs sank down into the soft earth, so the stone rose hardly at all.

They forced the levers under the end again and strained and heaved to pry it up, and forced more logs beneath.

When they tried to lift the other end, a log rolled suddenly, and another splintered and cracked; the beam slid sideways. The men scattered back away from it, afraid of the weight, and Ruak and Moloquin together, shouting and furious, had to drive them back to the work with threats. But when they struggled the stone up enough to jam another log in, more wood crunched, and the stone tipped sideways.

Moloquin backed away, squatted on his heels and stared at the stone. In a knot the workmen gathered to murmur in low voices that the end of their labors was near.

Ruak paced up and down, his hands on his hips. "Well? What shall we do now?"

Moloquin stood up. "Get the boys here. Where are they?"

The boys' band was lingering outside the embankment, playing games and watching the men. They came into the circle, wiggling and shy, and stood before Moloquin.

"Go to the village," he said, "and fetch all the baskets you can find, and fill them with dirt and stones, and bring them here."

"My mother will give me no baskets," said the leader of the boys' band, Grela's son Sickle.

"I said nothing about asking her," said Moloquin. "Go and steal them, if she will not give them up. Now go!"

They raced away, streaming away through the gaps in the embankment; Twig scuttled after them on his round legs. Ruak grinned at Moloquin.

"The women will turn their tongues on you, Opa-Moloquin."

He shrugged. "Then I shall tell them that they must make more baskets."

They went back to the stone lying on its heap of crushed wood, and all the rest of the day they spent dragging out the ruined wood and letting the stone back down again to the earth. In the evening, the boys came back, burdened down with baskets full of dirt and rocks; and that night, even the boys of the boys' band slept in the roundhouse beside the Pillar of the Sky.

In the morning they began again. They levered up one end of

the stone, and thrust oaken logs under it, and raised the other, and shoved the logs under. Now Moloquin got coils of rope, and they lashed the stone to the logs, to make a cradle for it.

"Now, raise it all up," he said, and he brought the boys forward, each with his basket, and made them ready, and when the men heaved at the poles, and the stone crept monstrously into the air, he shouted the boys forward with their baskets.

The stone hung there, inches above the earth, the men on the levers crying out with their effort. Moloquin's voice rang forth with a wild urgency. On his hands and knees, he thrust the baskets of earth under the stone. The boys understood; without his orders they hurried to imitate him, and they packed the space under the stone with earth, so that when the men on the levers let down the giant, it rested not on the wood but on the earth itself.

The baskets gave way, but the dirt and rocks did not; they packed down a little, but they held the stone up, like a child in the lap of its mother, and when they saw that this would work, all the men cheered until the sky boomed.

Now the baskets were used up. Moloquin gathered the boys around him.

"You must bring me more baskets."

"Opa-Moloquin-on," said Sickle, "if I take more of my mother's baskets, she will cast stones at me and there will be none to gather up the harvest."

Moloquin was still. He saw that what the boy said was true, and yet the thing had worked; he had to strive to keep himself from declaring that the harvest did not matter.

He fastened his gaze on Sickle. "Then bring me earth and rocks. I don't care how you bring it, but I must have earth and rocks here, as quickly as you can."

The boy gathered in his breath, and his feelings walked across his face, doubt and wonder, indecision and resolution, his face like a sky over which the clouds blew.

"I will," he said. He yelled to the band, and they ran after him through the gap in the embankment.

Moloquin went back to the stone; the men were standing there, watching him. They could do nothing more with the beam. He set them all to digging more holes, and all the earth he collected carefully in piles.

In the morning the boys came back. They had made slings of

cloth and sticks, and they hauled earth in them; they brought earth in sacks made of their clothes, and they had more baskets full of earth and stones, and the little boys carried stones in their arms. While the men heaved the stone up off the ground, the boys rammed the earth under it, using shovels and antler sweeps. Moloquin knelt beside him, his face as dirty as theirs, and thrust his arms under the stone, deep under the weight of the stone, packing the earth in. The little boys crawled beneath the stone to obey him, and the stone wobbled over their heads as the men groaned and cried at the levers. But when they let down the stone, it was a little higher than before, lying safe on its cradle of earth.

But then the women came.

Grela led them. All her fat quaked when she walked. Her face was dark with bad temper, and when she saw Moloquin she marched straight up to him, and she said, "You have set the boys to stealing our baskets."

He said, "I need them. You see my work here."

She swatted the air with her arm. "I see nothing here but dirt and stones! I need my baskets for the harvest and for my daily work."

"Then make new ones. And make me new ones too."

"They stole cloth also."

"Make new cloth," he said.

She glowered around her; she glowered at him and at the stone. "You will never raise it up," she said. "It belongs in the earth and there it will stay."

"It is on the earth still," he said. "The earth itself helps me lift it."

"Pagh! Fool!"

He said, "You did not call me a fool when I put food into your mouth, Ana-Grela-el."

Her face slackened; she wore her outrage like a mask, while behind it her feelings moved. At last, she said, "You have done what you have done."

"Yes."

She looked away; when her face was revealed to him again, all her rage was wiped away. She said, "I shall do as you wish." Ponderous as a stone, she walked away across the circle; she hardly glanced at the men's work, but passed through the gap in the embankment and was gone, and the other women followed after.

All but Wahela. Her hips swaying, she walked across the embankment to Moloquin. "Well, you have stirred up the women now;

if you think you have trouble with the stones, you shall have real trouble now."

Moloquin put his hands on his hips. "Are you going to help me?"

"Help you!" She laughed, her eyes flashing. "What help can I be to you, keeper of treasures!"

His temper flared. He seized hold of her with both hands, and when she twisted away, squealing, he got hold of her skirt and ripped it free, all around her waist.

She screamed. Half-naked before all the men, she staggered back away from Moloquin, crouched to hide herself, turned red and ran, bare as a baby, after the other women. The men shouted and whistled after her. Moloquin watched her go, her skirt in his hand.

"Here." He tossed the skirt to the boy Sickle. "You can make another sling from this."

All that day they heaved at the stone; they pried it up a finger's breadth and braced it with earth and rocks, took the levers to the other end, and did the same thing there. By nightfall the stone was level with Moloquin's knee.

The men went down to the roundhouse. Moloquin remained beside the stone; he had come to recognize the places where the demons lurked in his task, and now he foresaw another. The men braced their poles on logs, to pry up the stone, but the log had to be placed higher than the bottom of the stone for the levers to work. Soon that would be impossible.

He sat there, studying the problem, and behind him there were certain small sounds that he recognized; he paid little heed to them, since he had expected them, and before long Wahela sat down beside him.

"You humiliated me before the men."

He said, "You ought not to challenge me, Wahela."

"How can you treat me this way? When I have loved you so long."

She hung her arms around his neck; she pressed her kisses to his face. He studied the stone, submitting absently to her caresses, but when he did not respond to her, she turned on him and struck him.

He recoiled from her. "Why did you do that?"

"Pay heed to me!"

"I shall pay heed to you—" he drew his hand back and slapped her.

She fell down at his feet; without pause she got up again and came at him, scratching and weeping. Moloquin wrapped his arms around her and held her, pinning her arms to her sides, and when she tried to bite him he wrestled her around backwards to him. She strove with her feet to kick him and he gathered her legs up and held her like a baby.

"Let me go," she cried, and he dropped her.

He went away a little, and sat down again in the dark, facing the stone. His heart hammered. Fighting with her had awakened his lust for her. He had lain with Shateel only recently, but his hunger for Shateel was only a little flicker of his appetite compared to the way he craved Wahela, and when he fought with her he craved her more.

She had crept away; she sat on the grass a certain distance from him, and he could hear her loud sobs. He knew she cried for his sake. She was hard as a stone; everything he did to her rebounded from her, leaving no impression. Was that why he lusted so for her, because she was impossible to master?

She wept loudly into her hands. His heart sank. Before him were the stones; he could lift stones into the air, but he could not bring himself to comfort the woman he loved. For the sake of his stones he had taken the baskets of the women, and for the sake of his stones he would take everything else his People had.

He knew himself the fool Grela had called him. He strove and strained to do that which was impossible, and which would bring him no happiness; while that which would bring him happiness was within the power of any man, and yet he could not do it.

Was this not Ladon in him? Did he not hear Ladon, even now, laughing in his ears? Ladon, whom he had burned, and whose soul now hovered in the space behind his eyes. Ladon, his father.

He almost rose up. The power swelled in him to stand, to turn his back on the stones and go to Wahela and lift her into his arms and swear never to treat her ill again. They would go down to the roundhouse, and live together in peace, and he would come no more to the Pillar of the Sky.

But it was too late. Before he could yield, she had yielded. She came to him over the grass, crying, and sank down beside him, and leaned against him; she turned her face toward the stones and he did not have to choose between her and the stones. He put his arm around her shoulders. He faced the stones, and the great problem of the stones, and she pressed against his side, and with her there beside him, his regrets and even his care for her slipped away into the background of his mind, while the stones stood there before him, as they always had, huge and real, the only thing that mattered.

In the morning, when the workmen gathered at the Pillar of the Sky, Moloquin set half of them to the task of prying up the beam, one end at a time, and ramming earth and chalk beneath it. The other half of the men he got to work at building a wooden platform, next to the beam on the opposite side of the upright stones.

He himself chose the wood for the platform, going over each log carefully with his hands to find any cracks or holes that would weaken it, and he watched ceaselessly as the men dragged the logs into position and lashed them tight to one another, crisscrossing the logs back and forth, to make the structure strong enough to hold the stone. And this work took them many days.

Ruak was overseeing the other work, the levering up of the beam. One day while Moloquin stood watching a layer of logs bound tight to the logs under them, Ruak came to him and said, "We cannot lift this stone any higher."

Moloquin nodded absently. "Leave it for now."

Ruak stood there watching him a while; Moloquin ignored him. At last Ruak went away and took his workmen off to the river, to swim in the cool water.

The summer was climbing to its height. The heat of the sun cooked the world, turning the beans fat and creamy inside their furry coats of green, ripening the grains of rye and barley in their bearded heads; the sun's heat boiled up the clouds and stirred them to a dark and violent temper. The men cowered down in the ditch outside the bank and watched the storm roll over them. The rain battered them, streamed down the sides of the bank into the ditch and made pools around their feet, but it was from the voice of the storm that they hid, from the howl of the wind and the crash of the clouds, and from the long forked hands of the clouds, that reached down to pluck away the souls of men.

Now the workmen began to ask themselves if the storm were not a warning, that Moloquin was climbing too high—that Heaven frowned on the thing he was building here, this monster, this stone that would hang in the air. When the rain had passed, and the sun came out again, he had to drive them back to the work with the lightning of his tongue and the thunder of his rage.

He stood with Ruak before the stone, now lifted up on a bed of dirt and chalk and rubble, and he showed Ruak how he intended the stone to be placed on the wooden platform beside it. Ruak shook his head.

"You should have told me this before, Opa-Moloquin-on." The workman put his hand on the beam, with the holes worked deep into either end, to fit over the knobs on the tops of the uprights. "Now the ground holes will be on the wrong side."

"Make new holes," Moloquin said.

Ruak flung his arms up. "You say things as if it were as easy to do them as it is to say them."

They gathered up all the men, and once more they dug two holes in the ground, and fit two tall logs into them, bound together at the top, so that the ropes could be thrown over this cross. With this structure and the one still standing on the far side of the uprights, and with levers, they tipped the stone slowly up onto its side and rolled it tenderly as a new baby over onto the top of the platform.

The wood groaned, but it held fast. Moloquin walked restlessly around the whole structure, looking for cracks and signs of collapse, while Ruak and Fergolin, their stone mauls in their hands, climbed up onto the platform and bashed new holes in the ends.

Now the work began again. The platform was large enough that the men could work entirely on top of it, levering up one end of the beam, sliding logs beneath, and levering up the other, but the task was very low, because they had to build up the platform also as they went along. Before they had gotten the beam up as high as Moloquin's head, they ran out of wood, and he had to lead them all to the forest to find more wood to use.

Here again he encountered the fear most of the People held for the forest; most of the workmen refused even to set their feet beneath the trees. Therefore, he sent to the Forest Village, where Hems and Bahedyr were with the women, and ordered them to cut wood for the Pillar of the Sky.

At this time also, he gave them word that they should come to the New Village at the end of the summer, when the berries ripened. He did not tell them why. The reasons he had for this, and for want-

ing the first gateway to be finished before the equinox, he told to no
one.

They found more wood, and built the platform high and wide,
and the beam rose, a little at a time. As the platform got higher it
began to shake and sway, and Moloquin got his men to dig holes all
around it and put in heavy posts like the trees that supported the
roundhouse, and they lashed the platform to the posts.

One night one of Ruak's novices dreamt that the stones reached
to the sky, and the platform reached almost to the sky, and that he
was at work on it and fell and lay on the ground dying. The dream
was so real to him that when he woke up in a sweat, and shaking, he
lay on the ground inside the roundhouse and cried out to his friends
not to leave him there alone in the place of the dead. And thereafter
none of the men would climb the platform; only Ruak and Fergolin
and Moloquin would climb to the top of it.

Moloquin threw ropes around the ends of the levers so that the
men could work them from the ground. He climbed over and
around the beam as it rose into the air; he sat on it and let it carry
him higher into the air; he seemed to see nothing but the beam.

Now he ordered them all to dig away the mound of earth on
which they had first raised the beam and which lay between it and
the upright stones, and when they had done this he made them build
another platform closer to the stones. From the Forest Village came
the wood, dragged in on sledges and borne on the shoulders of men
and women; Wahela came up from the Forest Village, with her son
Twig.

They hauled and lifted the beam along the platform, until it was
so close to the upright stones that only a finger could slip between
the edge of the beam and the stones. The work was so slow and so
arduous that no one came to watch any more. It was late in the summer and the women were in the fields, protecting their crops against
deer and mice. At night, the skies were clear and full of stars. Fergolin sat on the bank at night with Twig in his lap, and pointed out
the stars to him, and told him their names and their powers, and the
time came when the boy could find the night travellers and name
them and name also the places where they were, as well as any novice
of the Bear Skull.

They raised the beam up level with the uprights, and again they
coiled rope around it, slung the ropes over the great posts that now
stood all around the place. Moloquin brought every man up from

the New Village; when people came to him from Shateel's Village, he
brought them to the work also, although they protested—they had
come only to tell him that the equinox was near, not to work. With so
many hands on the ropes, and so many backs working the levers,
they moved the beam as slowly and carefully as a mother with her
new baby. They rolled it up and over onto the tops of the upright
stones, and there it rested.

Still there was much to do. Moloquin would not let them stop to
enjoy what they had done. He drove them to the work of dismantling
the platform, stacking the wood carefully by the bank and digging
up the posts and filling in the holes with rammed chalk rubble. The
day was hot and the work tedious, and the men grumbled as they did
it. They bent to their work, their eyes on the ground, like women,
and never looked up again. Fergolin with Twig at his heels hauled
baskets of chalk rubble to fill holes, and his back ached, and his hands
were sore. When they were done, although the sun was still up in the
sky, he was exhausted.

Moloquin looked on them and saw they were tired and let them
go. The sun was low on the horizon anyway. Stooped with fatigue,
worn and hungry, the mass of the workmen started away down the
slope toward the roundhouse. Then Fergolin happened to look back.

He looked back, and what he saw froze him in his place. He let
out a low cry of amazement, and the others all turned.

They all turned, and they looked back where they had been, and
there they saw what they had done. For the first time, they stood
looking up at the great Gateway, poised against the sky, with the sunlight shining through it. No one spoke or moved. They stood with
their mouths hanging open, astonished at what they had done, and
slowly the burden of their weariness left them. They straightened up,
and their eyes brightened. They turned to look at one another and
they laughed, and they smote one another on the shoulders and
laughed, and then suddenly they were whirling around in a vast
dance, hugging one another, and laughing, and they ran up toward
the Gateway and stood around it, and they roared with pleasure at
what they had done: to raise stones up, to hang a stone in the air.

That night no one left the Pillar of the Sky. The women came from
the New Village, and when they saw what stood there on the plain
they gathered their children, and they brought food for all the

People, and they all sat down around the place and ate their dinner and admired their work. They did not dance. The men were too tired for that. They made fires and told stories, and when Moloquin walked through their midst, they lowered their voices to a hush and followed him with awe and love in their eyes.

Fergolin sat on the bank and stared at the Gateway before him, and with each beat of his heart he saw the thing new and was amazed all over again. There it was, the stone hanging in the air, although he knew that was impossible. He remembered how they had done it, he and the other men, but now that all the wood and earth was gone the memory was a pale dream compared to the solid fact of the stones before him.

Moloquin had told them how, but Fergolin himself had done it, he and all the other men, the ordinary, little men.

Moloquin was a man of great power, certainly greater than any power Fergolin himself had known. Yet the stone had not risen into the air by any magic. Moloquin's gift had been to move ordinary men to do what was impossible.

Sitting before the Gateway, Fergolin saw that the whole world had changed. Everything had become new with the rising of the stones. Nothing was impossible to him any more. If ordinary men could do this, they could do anything, the only limit to what they could do was their power to imagine it.

In the first instant he knew this, he rejoiced. In the next, he was cast into despair. Through that Gateway lay their freedom, and through that Gateway lay their doom.

Yet he would not hold back. The Gateway led to a world wider and greater and more dangerous than this one, and Fergolin rose up, and he walked forward, and he passed through the Gateway that Moloquin had raised, there on the plain at the Pillar of the Sky.

IV

THE HOUSE OF HEAVEN

The people who had come from Shateel's Village to tell Moloquin of the equinox went back to their hearths, and took with them word of the wonderful Gateway that had appeared on the plain at the Pillar of the Sky. Many came down to see it for themselves, and when they saw it they were amazed, and envious also of those who had raised it and who now went about strutting and boastful. All those who had once laughed at the workmen for their trouble now craved a place among them.

Moloquin had something else to do, but he could not ignore so many willing workers. Therefore he set Ruak and Fergolin, who knew the whole business, to gather up all the eager hands, shape the next set of uprights, and set them into the holes.

There were only two more stones at the Pillar of the Sky anyway. When these two were raised up, they would need all the hands they could find, to drag new ones down from the High Hill.

He marked where the holes were to go; he gave his rope to Fergolin, to keep the measurements, and told him how high the next gateway was to stand. Then he took his axe. He took Bahedyr and Hems, and Kayon, and Ladon's son, those men who had been his, heart and soul, longer than any other, and without a word to anyone he led them away to the west.

At the equinox, Moloquin remembered, the boat had come from over the sea to Harus Kum's mine.

He had his axe. Bahedyr, as usual, had brought his spear. As the men travelled through the hilly overgrown slopes west of the Pillar of the Sky, Moloquin bade the others find weapons for themselves, but he would not tell them where they were going.

Hems knew. Moloquin could see it in his face, as they went west; Hems recognized the trail they followed, and now and again he turned his eyes toward Moloquin, questioning, but he said nothing. Only at night, when they made a fire and roasted the small animals that they caught as they travelled, Hems would ask Moloquin to tell them stories.

"Tell us about Abadon," he would say. "Tell us about heroes."

Moloquin told them how Abadon went down to the Country-Where-There-Are-No-Men. The women in this place were as strong and fierce as men; they wore their hair bound up in knots at the base of their skulls, to keep it out of their way, and carried knives in their belts, and when they spoke their voices boomed like the wind blowing up from the deep caves. They did battle with bears and wolves, and wore skins like men, and when their babies were born, they nicked the skin of their breasts, above the nipple, and gave the child to suck there, so that the first food the baby would taste was blood, not milk. But they only allowed their girl children to live. They left their boy children in the forest, for the wolves and the bears.

Now Abadon came in among these women, and he stole their goats. The women called for their headwoman, whose name was Essa, and she challenged Abadon to a combat.

They came together for their combat on a great plain, and all the women gathered around in a close circle, and Abadon could see that even if he overcame their leader, they meant to slay him. Now, he was bigger than any one of the women, but not bigger than two of them. He was stronger than any one of the women, but he was not stronger than two of them. Therefore he knew he would be slain unless he was clever.

He took up his spear, which was of ashwood, the male tree, and hardened in the fire, which is also male, and he flung it at Essa. But she had a shield made of elm, which is female, and she held it up, and the spear passed through it, but in doing so it fell into the magic of the shield, and from the shield sprang three new spears, and Essa took them up and cast them back at Abadon, and wounded him in the foot and in the hand and in the face.

Abadon took up his sling, which was made of the hide of the leg of a male bear, and he put into it a sharp stone, and he flung it at Essa. But Essa had a basket made of the rushes of the stream, and when the stone fell into the basket, three round stones appeared, and she took them up and threw them at Abadon, and she wounded him in the hip and the thigh and the breast.

Now Abadon began to see that he would not survive unless he did things differently. And he had his flute, which was magic, given him by Rael the Birdwoman when they lay together beside the spring where all the water in the world wells up. Now Abadon sat down, and very softly he began to play his flute.

The women drew closer to hear him, but as they came nearer, Abadon played still more softly. And Essa could not hear him at all, and she came nearer yet, and lay down with her head in his lap, and heard the music.

Then Abadon lay with her, and she brought forth three children by him, who were all male. These children she did not give to the wolves and bears, but raised as her own, and thereafter there were men also among these People, and they were as other People, except that before they lay together to bear children, the men always played upon the flute.

Hems heard this story and shook his head. "This is not a good story for where we are going."

"Where are we going?" asked Bahedyr, but Hems would not answer him; Moloquin would not answer him.

They went away into the west, and every night as they sat by the fire Moloquin told stories. He told them all the stories he knew in which men fought and struggled with other beings and overcame them. As they walked along the old trail, which was dimly imprinted on the grass and wild brush of the country they were crossing, the men found clubs, and made slings and threw stones with them, and cast their new spears at the trees, and so they knew they were making ready for some great battle. But Moloquin would not tell them who they were to fight.

In the dawn of a cold, rainy day, they came down from the tree-covered hills into the bed of the stream, and walked along it, past where Harus Kum's men had dug out the banks, past the raw piles of broken rock, the husks of the ore, that Harus Kum's men had left behind. In the rain and the cold wind they went up into the narrow valley at the mouth of the stream, where Harus Kum's stockade huddled on the sand among the black rocks, with the wind blasting off the sea.

There was smoke coming from the chimney of the big house; even outside the stockade, Hems could hear the sounds of the people inside, waking, getting ready for the day's work, and it made him colder than the wind to hear Harus Kum's voice again. He trembled to be in this place again. With both hands he held his club, and he trembled all over.

Moloquin laid his hand on Hems' shoulder. "Are you afraid?" he said.

Hems had only to look at him to give him his answer. Moloquin grasped his shoulder and gave him a gentle shake.

"Think of your wife. Think of the evil that was done to her here. Now we shall repay all that was done to us here. Now, keep heart. I want you to climb up over the stockade wall and unlatch the gate, and let us all in."

Hems nodded. He thought of Ap Min, his dear wife, and knew what Moloquin had said was true: now he could avenge that which had befallen him here, and he laid down his club and scaled up over the wall of logs, dropped down on the far side, and went to the gate.

As he opened the gate, he could hear Harus Kum shouting, inside the big house. He pulled the latch up, and the gate opened and his friends and Moloquin came in, one at a time. Kayon gave him his club, and with his weapon in his hands, Hems walked toward the big house.

Around the corner, a woman came, carrying a basket; she had come out of the storehouse. Her head was down, to keep her face out of the rain, and the newcomers were stealthy, so that she saw and heard nothing of them until she reached the corner of the big house, and was almost in their midst.

She saw them; at once Kayon sprang on her and struck her down with his club. Moloquin swept his arm forward, and the little band rushed at the door and crashed it inward and swarmed into the warm, smoky, shadowy room beyond.

The slaves were gathered by the fire, eating, and when the door burst open and the cold wind blasted through it and Moloquin and his men poured in like creatures of the cold wind, the slaves cried out and huddled against the hearth, their hands raised. By the far doorway, Harus Kum wheeled around.

Hems faced him, his club raised. In his memory Harus Kum was immensely tall, with a beard like a pine forest and a voice like the surf, and Hems strode toward him with his club held up over his shoulder.

"Wait," Harus Kum cried, and thrust his hand out.

Hems paused. His heart was hammering in his chest. He had

expected Harus Kum to attack him, to fight with him, and now here before him stood a man no bigger than he was himself, with a little matted, greying beard, and a voice that shook as he said, "Wait!"

Moloquin came forward. "Harus Kum," he said, "I have come back again."

Harus Kum lowered his hands. His gaze swept the room, taking in everything: his slaves cowering by the hearth, and Moloquin's men spread out around them, their weapons raised. Hems could see the trader sorting things out in his mind, and now Harus Kum raised his hands again, his palms up, friendly.

"Moloquin," he said. "The child of my heart has returned."

Moloquin said nothing.

"Moloquin," said Harum Kum. "Come by the fire, let me warm you at my hearth. Are you hungry? We shall feed you. Lead your companions to the fire, and we shall give you a feast of welcome."

Hems licked his lips, puzzled; he had not expected this. His eyes turned toward Moloquin, standing there nearby him, his axe in his hands. Face to face, Moloquin and Harus Kum measured each other, and neither of them spoke for a while.

Then like a mask Harus Kum put on a smile, and spread out his arms, and said, "Come, sit in the warmth of the fire. We shall give you beer, and meat. Come."

"We shall," said Moloquin gravely, but his eyes glittered. He gestured to his men, and they went to the fire to warm themselves; they stretched out their hands to the fire, and laid down their weapons, and Harus Kum shouted to his women to bring them food to eat and beer to drink, and he sent someone off to close the door.

After the long walk, after the first excitement of breaking into the house, Moloquin and his men sank into the warmth and comfort of Harus Kum's society and relaxed. The slaves brought them blankets to dry themselves, and heaped wood on the fire; the women—the girl they had struck down outside came in, looking dazed, and was at once hustled off to wait on them—the women brought them bowls of meat and grain, and cups of the new beer.

The men drank much, not used to the beer, and soon they were half-asleep. Then Harus Kum collected his slaves together, and said in a loud voice, "We shall go off to the mines. When we are home again we shall feast once more, make yourselves comfortable here, do as you wish, I shall be gone all the rest of the day," and with much noise and purpose he and his slaves went out.

Moloquin sat by the hearth, his men around him. They were nodding; Hems already slept, his head in his arm, a cup of the beer half-finished in his slack fingers. Kayon rose and went across the room to the door, and as he went out the door he was yawning. He pissed, and came inside again. He lay down on the floor and went to sleep, and Moloquin saw all this and said nothing and did nothing.

One by one, his men went to sleep in the warmth, with the beer in their bellies, and Moloquin also lay down among them, his axe beside him, and shut his eyes; but Moloquin did not sleep.

And now, after only a little while, with his ear pressed to the ground, he heard the faint thud of footsteps.

He shut his eyes and lay still, but his hand curled around the haft of his axe. He heard the door glide open. In his ear, pressed against the ground, the slow padding footsteps were like heartbeats.

Still he waited, listening, his hand around the haft of his axe, until he heard the light cautious footsteps creep in among his sleeping men, until he heard, directly over him, the soft hiss of a breath sucked in, as a man gathered himself for a great effort.

At that sound Moloquin leapt up. He shouted, and his axe swung, level with his waist, a great sweep of the blade through the air. Before that blade, Harus Kum flinched back, and the great club in his hands missed Moloquin's head and slammed into the floor.

Moloquin shouted again, and all his men leapt up. They were surrounded by Harus Kum's slaves, but when they sprang to their feet, the slaves gave way, and Bahedyr with a roar plunged forward and threw his spear.

A slave screamed. Staggering backward, the spear lodged in his chest, he collapsed onto the floor. At that, the other slaves flung themselves down on their faces and screamed for mercy.

Harus Kum did not. Harus Kum still held the club, which was a mallet for crushing ore, and while everyone was gawking at Bahedyr and the slave with the spear in his chest, Harus Kum stepped forward and swung his weapon full at Moloquin.

Moloquin shrank back, and the mallet swung past his belly. Harum Kum roared. He wheeled the mallet up for another blow, and then from behind him, from either side, Moloquin's men came on him. They used no weapons but their bodies, and they seized him with their bare hands. Their weight bore him down on the ground before Moloquin.

"Preserve me," Harus Kum said, and panted for breath. "Preserve me, and I shall do whatever you wish."

"Until I turn my back again," Moloquin said. "I gave you my trust once, Harus Kum, and you betrayed it. Now you shall suffer for it." Lifting his axe, he struck Harus Kum on the head, so that his skull cracked, and he died.

He sagged in the arms of Moloquin's men, and they let him go. They backed away, leaving him there on the floor, and now slowly the slaves stole forward, peering at their master. When they saw that he was dead, they rejoiced, and they fell down on their knees before Moloquin and his men, and thanked them.

Moloquin drew one of them aside and asked him if the boat had come yet. The slave shook his head.

"Good," Moloquin said. "Now, go and eat all you wish, and rest all you wish."

"Will you take us away from here?"

"I don't know," Moloquin said. "We shall see about that," and he went away to the side of the house, where Harus Kum lay.

The master was dead. His head had cracked, and blood oozed out, and grey brain matter, caking his hair. Moloquin knelt down beside him. Already Harus Kum was stiffening and cold. He touched the man's hands, that had so much craft now gone with him, and he wondered if he ought to have let Harus Kum live.

He remembered the treachery with which Harus Kum had greeted them, and the stealth with which Harus Kum had come back to murder them, and he was glad the man was dead. He called for some of the others to help him, and they took the body out to the yard.

The slave Bahedyr had struck with his spear was also dead. Moloquin had both the bodies taken outside the gate, near the stream, and there stretched them on the ground and covered them with stones. Moloquin had no wish for Harus Kum's spirit to linger around him, as the spirit of Ladon did, and he did everything he could to make certain that Harus Kum's soul would find its way to Heaven: he turned his face to the west, and in the dirt around his grave Moloquin traced a circle, opening toward the west, and made a little lane in the dirt leading west so that the spirit would know which way to go. He put a bit of grain in with the body, to nourish the spirit, and he put a bowl of beer with it. But just to be safe, he also pried open the mouth of the corpse and stuffed it full of mud, so that if Harus Kum's soul chose to stay behind and force itself on Moloquin, the soul would have no voice.

The dead slave they buried in the same way. When this was done, Moloquin and his men rested, but he set one of them to watch by the shore for the boat. And so they sat down in Harus Kum's stockade, waiting, and did nothing for a time.

Buras Ram had been at sea for more days than he could count on his fingers; when he first saw the pointed hilltop that marked the site of his brother's mine, he nearly wept from relief. With the rest of his crew, he bent to the oars, hauling the little skin boat through the water, his head twisted constantly around to look over his shoulder, to guide them toward the land.

The boat slid sideways with each gust of wind, each contrary wave. Its round hull skidded over the water even when weighed down, and sometimes it lay over suddenly and dug its gunwale into the wave, slopping the sea into the boat. Numberless times only the presence of the goddess kept them from sinking, and while Buras Ram pulled on his oar and turned to look to the shore, the other men, pulling their oars, prayed without pausing to Hortha, coursing the seas of the cosmos in her boat of shell.

The sea resisted; the sea craved them, wanted to keep them, wanted to eat them, and so the boat labored in the calmest water. The sea held them back from land, even with the land so close as this, and Buras Ram cursed the sea under his breath—softly, because the sea too was a god, and could hear, and resent. After all, for every ill the sea gave a thousand favors. Buras Ram ended his curse with a fervent prayer to Hortha, to bring them safe to land.

He looked back over his shoulder. The rough, black puzzle of the coastline looked no closer than it had before.

All the rest of the day, he and his crew strained at their oars, striving against a crosswise wind and a fierce current to drag their craft in to shore. They had been rowing for many days; their hands were tough, their backs strong. This time the sea did not keep them prisoner; this time, reluctantly, the sea loosened its grasp, and let them creep up on the flank of the land, in the little sandy cove where Harus Kum had his stockade and his mine.

Usually Harus Kum was there to greet the boat. This time there was no one on the sand waiting.

Buras Ram thought little of that. He leapt into the foaming surf and pulled the boat in between the toothed rocks to the safety of the sand, and there with the help of the other crewmen they pulled the boat entirely out of the water. Still no one came to welcome them.

The sun was sinking. Buras Ram looked around him, stamping his feet and stretching his legs, grateful for the space to move after the long cramping confines of the boat, and saw no sign of any human being. The other boatmen were walking up and down, exclaiming over their safe voyage. One went reverently to Hortha in the bow of the boat and began to free her from the thongs that held her fast there. Buras Ram walked up the shore.

The stockade stood inland a little, not quite within sight of the beach, but as he climbed, as the bare sand gave way to sawgrass and twining vines and scrub, he saw the stockade as he expected to. Nothing seemed wrong. He went toward the gate, thinking at any moment to hear his brother shout, or at least to see a slave he could send to tell his brother they had come, but there was no one. A few cattle grazed at the top of the slope behind the stockade, but there were no people anywhere at all.

The place was deserted. No smoke drifted up from the roof of the house. A shiver of foreboding passed down Buras Ram's spine, a message from a god: something was wrong. Cautiously he pushed at the stockade gate, and it swung open, unlatched, untended.

Had they all died of some sickness? Buras Ram put his head through, looked all around, saw no one. Yet something was wrong here. He turned, his mouth open to call to his crew, but before he could give voice, something large and heavy leapt down on him from the top of the stockade and wrapped an arm around his face.

He shouted, but the arm around him muffled his cry; he struggled, but the man behind him held him fast. Now suddenly a great curve-bladed axe of bronze appeared before him, held in a brown hand, aimed at his throat.

In his ear, a voice in his own language said, "Keep still until I bid you."

Buras Ram shut his teeth. His heart pounded; he saw the axe blade gleaming by his throat. Slowly the arms around him slackened.

"Good," said the man behind him. "Now, call them up, a few at a time."

"Who are you?"

The axe poked at him. "Call your men. A few at a time."

Still Buras Ram hesitated, unwilling to lure his own people into a trap; also, it seemed that there were fewer of the strangers than there were of him and his men, and if he could somehow get all his crew here at once—

The hand on his arm whirled him around; he faced a tall man with a curly black beard and gleaming black eyes, a man he had seen before, once, somewhere, obviously here. This man said, "You are Harus Kum's brother?"

Buras Ram nodded his head once, struggling with his memory.

"I am Moloquin," said the man before him.

"Ah," said Buras Ram.

"Your brother is dead," Moloquin said. "I came here to deal with him honestly, and he tried to kill me by stealth, and so I had to kill him."

Buras Ram said nothing. His palms were sweating and his back itched; he wondered if he were going to live through this, and had his doubts. He made a little silent prayer to Hortha, although the goddess had never shown an inclination to help people on dry land.

"Call your men," said Moloquin.

"I remember you," Buras Ram said. "I warned my brother about you once, when you were younger."

"Maybe you did," said Moloquin, and smiled, a nasty smile, perfectly humorless. "Maybe that means you are cleverer than he was."

"What do you intend to do with us?"

"I will make an honest agreement with you, as I meant to do with your brother, if you are just with me. If you fail me I shall kill you all and burn this place down. Now, call your men, or I shall begin with that."

Buras Ram turned slowly to the gate. His skin crawled all over him. He faced the decision with a jittery heart and a mind that seethed with contradictions. By the blood-law he was bound to avenge his brother, and yet if Harus Kum had done evil, and his punishment was just, there was no need for vengeance. What sort of agreement did this Moloquin want with him? His crew was safer on the beach where they were all together and could escape into the sea.

Behind him, Moloquin said, "You need tin. If you want tin, you will have to deal with me. Now, do it."

That was true. In all the whirling uncertainty of this, that at least was solid and true: the tin was here, and he needed it. If he reached his home again without it, he would be ruined. His whole family would be ruined. He went to the gate in the stockade wall and shouted to some of his men to come in.

As he spoke, Moloquin raised his arm, and from the back of the big house came several men, running, each armed with a spear and a knife, and they took up places on either side of the gate. Buras Ram waited, his stomach churning. He knew his crew would hate him for this. He regretted it now, but it was too late. The first two men came in, bearing Hortha between them, and Moloquin's men set upon them and subdued them at once, easily, and tied their hands with rope.

Buras Ram lowered his eyes. His boatmen glared at him, but there were knives held to their throats, and they made no effort to warn the others, who came tamely as lambs up through the gate and were made prisoner. All were bound except Buras Ram, but Moloquin kept Buras Ram ever before him, and Moloquin's hand never strayed far from the great bronze axe at his belt.

When all the boat's crew were captive, Moloquin led them into the big house. His men obeyed him almost without words. They seemed to know his mind; they moved as if they were one creature, with Moloquin at the center, a spider in a web of being. Buras Ram sat down by the hearth, the little wooden goddess by his side, and glanced at her. She should be fed, she should be honored, she would resent this careless treatment after the long difficult journey. But he was afraid to move without Moloquin's permission.

The tall man stalked restlessly around the room. There were many more people here than simply his men and Buras Ram's; they had to be Harus Kum's slaves, and Buras Ram watched them for any sign that they would help him against this stranger. The slaves paid no heed to him. They rushed to do anything Moloquin told them, they fell at Moloquin's feet as he passed. Buras Ram turned his head away, back to the image beside him.

One of the women brought him food. Although he was ravenously hungry, especially for cooked food, he laid his portion down before the goddess. He needed her now more than ever, and he was afraid she would desert him if he ignored her honor.

When Moloquin saw this, he came up to Buras Ram and said, "Are you not hungry?"

"The goddess is hungry," said Buras Ram.

Moloquin studied him a moment, turned his head and called to one of the slaves to bring more food for Buras Ram. The seaman took it gratefully. Moloquin stood there watching him eat.

At last, his belly full, Buras Ram set his bowl aside and looked up at the man who had killed his brother. "What do you intend to do to us?"

"Come with me," said Moloquin.

Buras Ram got up and followed him, and Moloquin took him out of the big house. Night had fallen. A mist was rising up out of the sea, shrouding half the sky, but the other half glittered with stars. The wind was warm and moist, a promise of rain tingling in its fullness and humidity. Buras Ram followed Moloquin around the big house to the storeroom.

The tall man opened the door and stood aside, so that Buras Ram could see into the storeroom. It was dark; all Buras Ram could see was a butchered carcass hanging from the rafter and the bundled shapes of stored goods, but Moloquin stooped and picked up a leather sack from the floor and held it out to him.

It was heavy enough that Buras Ram grunted when he took it; he could tell by the feel of the pellets through the leather that it was full of tin.

Moloquin said, "You need tin. I want copper, bronze—whatever metal you can bring me. I want metalcraft and metal-lore. You come here and mine the tin and every year give me copper and bronze and I shall let you stay here in peace, but if you do not, I will come here and kill everybody and burn the place down."

Buras Ram hefted the leather sack of tin in his arms. There was copper in his boat. He thought of his brother and shrugged. Harus Kum had betrayed this man's trust and deserved to die. He would speak to the elders of his family, when he returned to his village, and have their opinions on it. They would know what offerings could be made to make up for any failure of duty to Harus Kum. In the meantime he wanted this great heavy sack of tin.

He said, "That seems good to me."

Moloquin said, "Harus Kum is gone. You must bring someone here who knows the work. None here does."

Buras Ram nodded, licking his lips, his mind racing ahead through the difficulties in that, another sea voyage. "We shall do that." He himself could stay, at least until the weather improved.

"I have a friend, a man like a younger brother to me. He speaks your language, he has a wife of your people, I will leave him here with you, and you are to teach him the craft, so that he can come back to my people and do the work there."

"Some cannot learn it."

"If he fails I will send another."

"You had the craft."

"Some of it. Now my work is elsewhere."

"I will do as you say."

Moloquin stood watching him; in the darkness Buras Ram could distinguish nothing of his expression, and became restless under the intense look. Then Moloquin took him by the arm and led him away, into the open.

He took the knife from his belt—it was a knife of bronze, one Harus Kum had made, Buras Ram saw now—and he held it out to Buras Ram and said, "Cut me." He offered his left forearm to the blade.

Buras Ram held the knife between them. "What?" He looked around them, wondering if this were a trap.

"Cut me," said Moloquin. "Your brother's soul will seek revenge, and although he brought on himself what happened to him, yet I do not love the thought that his spirit will hunger for my blood. Therefore, you must cut me, and give of my blood to the spirit, and that perhaps will satisfy it."

Buras Ram gripped the knife. His heart pounded. The stupid savage had given him another chance; in an instant he could drive the knife into Moloquin's chest, and so free them all from this unlooked-for trouble, and avenge his brother at the same time.

As he thought that, he turned the knife in his hand, and he saw Moloquin's eyes follow the little move of the blade, and all along Moloquin's arm, the muscles tightened and swelled. Suddenly, as if some god spoke in his ear, Buras Ram saw the trap. Moloquin wished to discover if he were treacherous; if he struck at Moloquin now, the savage would deal with him as he had with Harus Kum. Buras Ram let out his breath with a sigh, like a man who has just turned aside from disaster.

He lifted the knife; he nicked his own thumb, and let the blood run. He said, "So be it," and held out the knife to Moloquin. "Let my blood serve, not yours."

In spite of what he said, he did not do this for Harus Kum, but to honor the god who had just saved him.

The savage chieftain broke into a wide smile. He took the knife, and taking it he clasped Buras Ram's arm with his free hand. He said, "Let us go inside, it is going to rain," and together the two men went back into the big house.

At midwinter, Moloquin went north to Shateel's Village, to keep his promise to the people there, that he would sit among them and hear their complaints.

He went north from the Pillar of the Sky, and with him went the men who had raised the first Gateway, and who had also raised up the next two upright stones. They had no more stones at the Pillar of the Sky, and wanted more. The raising of the first Gateway had filled them all with a lust for the work. They no longer complained that it was impossible. Now they strove at it with a confidence and a pride that made the work much faster, and as they went north with Moloquin, they sang.

Each of them wore a strand of blue beads around his neck; Ruak himself wore several. As they entered into Shateel's Village, they strutted and preened and threw their chests out, displaying their ornaments, and all the women came running to stare at them and whistle and gasp in awe at their beauty.

Shateel was waiting at the gate into the roundhouse yard. When her husband appeared, she stepped aside to let him into the place of honor, but he stopped before her, and did not go in. Behind him all his People gathered in a great mob, calling his name and clapping and laughing. Some of the men were already trying to dance, but the thick press of people was too close for dancing.

Moloquin stood before Shateel. "I have come," he said.

"Yes," she said. "Come into the roundhouse, we shall make you welcome as befits a chief."

He shook his head. "I must go out to the High Hill, to choose stones. Will you come with me?"

"You should rest," she said. "You should sit in the roundhouse and let people get used to the notion that you are here."

"I have to find stones," he said, and took a step away. "Come with me."

"I will come," she said.

She went after him, back through the village. The men were parading up and down, showing off their beauty to the women, and making the place theirs again with wild shrieks and leaps into the air. The women were gathered around the longhouses to watch, and some were preparing a great feast of welcome. The dogs barked in a steady racket, and little children ran everywhere, screaming and laughing.

Some of the men would have followed Moloquin, but he waved them off. As he and Shateel reached the brush fence around the village, a child ran up to them.

"Ana, Ana, let me go with you."

Moloquin frowned down at the child. "Who is this?"

"Dehra." Shateel stooped and hugged the little girl, whose tangled hair was full of dead leaves and who scowled at Moloquin past her mother's arm. "No, no," Shateel told the child. "We are going to the High Hill, you must stay here. See, there will be feasting and dancing."

She kissed Dehra, who paid no heed to her, but stared angrily at Moloquin. Moloquin started off along the worn path to the High Hill, and Shateel followed him.

They went a long way in silence, Shateel stretching her steps to keep pace with him, and after a time he reached out and took hold of her hand. They had come far from the village. He looked around them and stopped, and they embraced.

"Husband," Shateel said. "You have been gone too long."

"Maybe that is true," he said. "I thought after the last time we were together that I would hear soon afterward you were with child."

She shook her head. She turned a little away from him. "I am sorry."

"We shall make a child this time."

She turned back to him and he bent to kiss her; she began to shut her eyes, to surrender to his caresses, when suddenly with a yell something ran in on them.

It was Dehra. She danced and leapt around them, shouting and waving her arms, and although she laughed she looked more angry than happy. Moloquin let Shateel go and backed away from her.

"Go away, demon," he said, and swatted at Dehra with his hand. The child shrieked. "He hit me! He hit me!"

Shateel stooped down and caught the girl in her arms. "I told you to stay in the village, little one. Now, go do as I say."

"No! I want to be with you!"

Moloquin stood impassively, waiting; Shateel could see that he was angry. She took hold of Dehra's arms and shook her hard.

"Now, hear me, little one—go back, find your grandmother, and help her prepare the feast. Go!"

"I won't," Dehra cried, and flung another furious stare at Moloquin. "I want to stay with you."

Moloquin said, "Good-by, Shateel." He turned and walked away, going to the High Hill.

Shateel watched him go; her eyes filled with tears. She squatted down before her daughter and thrust her nose up close to Dehra's.

"Do as I say! Go back to the village, or I shall strike you."

Dehra was not watching her at all, but was staring away at Moloquin, now half-vanished into the brush. "I don't like him," she said. "I hate him."

Shateel lifted her hand and slapped the child hard across the face. "Go!"

Dehra gasped; she put her hand to her flaming cheek. "Ana," she said, whimpering, and again, "Ana," and flung herself forward, weeping, into Shateel's arms.

"Now, there." Shateel held her, murmuring to her. She had never struck the child before, and now suddenly she too began to weep. She looked longingly after Moloquin, who had vanished into the brush and trees. In her arms Dehra shivered and cried, a warm, wet, imponderable bundle. Shateel stood up and lifted her, and she carried the child back to the village.

Ruak and his novices, festooned with strings of blue beads, danced all night long, showing the People how they had shaped the stones and raised them. All the People saw now that those who had worked at the Pillar of the Sky had attained some special virtue. They spoke familiarly to the chief, who was not a man anyone could approach easily, and they wore the special signs of his friendship, and they had a new power, a new sense of their own power, that shone forth from them.

Thereafter all the People went to Moloquin and asked to help work at the Pillar of the Sky.

He lived in the roundhouse all that winter. He sat every day in the roundhouse yard, with Shateel at his side, and listened to the complaints and problems of the People. He danced none of the dances, and he had no mask.

The old women, who also had no masks, said that he derived his power not from his ancestors, whose spirits would have been let into the world through the mask, but from the bronze axe he always carried. It was the axe that was his emblem. Before he got the axe, they told one another, he had had no power at all; the People had even thought him half-witted enough to stay with his mother, Karella, long after most women would have driven him away. Then he received the axe, somehow, and now he stood before them, and there was nothing he could not do.

Except, said the malicious, get Shateel with child.

Everyone marked how much they were together. They knew Shateel now, well enough that every gesture she made, every lowered eyelid, every half-smile betrayed her deepest thoughts and feelings to them, and they knew she was open to him. Yet there was no child between them.

There was Dehra.

Joba especially marked it, that Dehra followed her mother everywhere and did all she could to keep her and Moloquin apart. Dehra had poisoned this marriage, or so Joba thought.

She kept her suspicions to herself for a long while, nearly the whole winter, but on the day when all the People went forth to the High Hill, to help drag the stone away, Joba opened her mouth at last to her daughter.

She said, first, "You have been much with your husband lately."

Shateel stood beside her, near the flank of the High Hill. There before them, the flat ground swarmed with people. Ruak and his novices and several other men had built a sledge to carry the stone; another of the societies, the Ox-Horn, had spent the winter finding and cutting logs for rollers and bringing them here, and still another society, the Blade of Grass, had made rope, and all these groups were ready now to put their preparations to use. The Blade of Grass waited to one side with their rope; the Ox-Horn stood to the other side, proudly, beside their great heap of logs.

The stone they wanted lay tipped up against the flank of the High Hill. Ruak and his men had laid the sledge up against it, and now at a gesture from Moloquin the Blade of Grass hurried forward to lash the stone fast to the wooden frame. Drums beat and many people clapped in time, so that the whole area resounded with that rhythm. Moloquin hurried all around the place, making sure that everything was exactly as he wanted it.

Joba said, "You have been much with your husband, yet you bear no fruit of it."

Shateel turned to her mother, angry, and said, "Why is everyone so concerned about that? He has many children." Only that winter a runner had come from the Forest Village, announcing that Wahela had borne a healthy daughter.

"You have only Dehra," said Joba, unperturbed; she could see that Shateel was angry only because she herself worried.

Shateel turned toward the work again. The banging of the drums filled her ears. She looked in vain for Dehra among the flights of children circling and circling the field.

"From your womb must the chieftain spring," said Joba. "If you bear no sons, we shall have no chief, when Moloquin dies."

"There is time yet to make a son for him, if that really matters so much to you," said Shateel.

"Something stands between your womb and his power," Joba said. "Something must be done first about Dehra."

Shateel wheeled toward her. "What? What should I do with my child?"

Joba looked surprised; her eyes opened wide and her mouth pursed. At last, she said, "I thought only that you might send her to my hearth, perhaps, or to another's. I meant no ill to her, Shateel."

Shateel jerked herself around to face the work again. Her eyes stung. She put her hands to her wrist, where she wore the bronze bracelet.

He had given her this bracelet, and he had given her the power over this village; he would give her the power of life as well, if it all went as everyone else thought it should. She stared at the work below, the men prying at the stone with poles, the men grunting and leaning on ropes, but she saw nothing of it.

What was her power? In every being, surely, there was some center, some kernel from which all its desires and abilities flowed: where was hers? It could not be merely that she was the niece of a chief. It could not be merely that she was the wife of a chief, or the mother of a chief: where was her power, then?

She raised her eyes again to the circling stream of children, looking for Dehra, but saw no sign of her. She knew it was true. For Dehra's sake, Shateel often stayed with her daughter instead of going to Moloquin. For Dehra's sake, her womb had closed itself against the possibility of a rival. For Dehra's sake. What was to be done for Shateel's?

Her unseeing eyes were fixed now on the great stone cradled in its wooden frame, that the men strove to free from the grasp of the High Hill. She saw none of them; she saw only shadows, that moved and shifted through the light of the world. She saw only that the world lay before her, and that she was powerless to enter it.

Then suddenly the Hill gave up its prize, and the stone reared up.

The People roared. The men scattered and ran back, and the stone stood up on end, poised a moment there, and fell over backwards with a thud that shook the world. Shateel herself, deep as she was in her own thoughts, let out a cry of surprise and wonder, and the rest of the People, who had watched everything with attention, now broke from their ranks and ran forward to surround the stone.

They buried the stone in themselves. They swarmed over it, stroking it, heaving at it, testing it with themselves. Moloquin waited nearby, knowing that in their frenzy they would not hear him, waiting until their passions cleared. Shateel shook herself. She was alone on the hillside, alone, looking down at the stone and at the People who struggled now to master the stone. Now, suddenly, Dehra appeared beside her.

"Ana, what is it?"

Shateel said nothing. She put out her arm and gathered the child to her; her fingers closed on a fistful of the little girl's hair. Pressing the child tight against her, she watched the work below.

With levers now they were prying up the front end of the stone and struggling to force a roller under it. Already they had tied ropes to the front of the sledge, and the People were fighting for a place at the ropes. Their voices rose, ebullient, crackling like flames, a fire leaping toward Heaven. They stretched out in lines, each line clinging to a rope, and the lines of the People stretched away into the distance, so far away that she had to squint to see the end. Then, with a wave of Moloquin's hand, the drums began to beat again, and an old man blew upon a horn made of a goat's horn, and the People leaned into the ropes.

The stone resisted. It had lain so long in this place it had roots here. It wanted only to stay where it was. The People strained at the ropes. The drums beat furiously and the horn blew again and again. Moloquin walked around and around the stone, stroking it with his hands. The People heaved against the ropes. Even Joba had gone among them; even Joba leaned her weight against the weight of the stone.

They screamed, they shouted, and the drums beat, and the horns blew. The stone heard them and it answered them, slowly, yielding its grip of the earth, creeping forward toward its new home. As it gave way to them the People gave tongue to one tremendous cry. Their faces had been turned backward toward the stone, to plead with it, to call it after them, but now they faced forward, they stooped to the work, and they stepped forward, driving steadily forward. The stone followed obediently along in their wake.

The boys' band leapt and danced at the edge of the flat ground. Now Moloquin waved to them, and they ran up to the nether end of the stone, which was just now leaving behind the last of the rollers. Two boys at each end lifted the roller, and two more bore the middle of it. They ran around to the front of the stone, wove their way in through the many ropes, and laid the roller down, and as the stone moved slowly forward it crept up onto that roller, and left another behind, and that one also they ran to bring to the front.

Shateel stood there, watching this, and it seemed to her that the whole world wore away while this stone was moving a distance no longer than a man's hand.

She touched the bracelet again. That was power: to cause other people to do as Moloquin wished. That was Moloquin's power. She turned her back; she wanted something else, but what it was she had no notion of. She walked away, Dehra beside her, away over the flank of the High Hill.

The work at the Pillar of the Sky belonged to Moloquin no longer. It was the work of the People now, and they went to it with hearts as full and hot as a lover's. All that year, they dragged the stones away from the High Hill to the Pillar of the Sky, and all the next year they did so, until there were ten more stones lying outside the embankment, and they went to the work then of raising them up.

Moloquin measured everything, and told them what to do, and with each stone some new problem presented itself: either one of the uprights was too short, and had to be shaped with a great knob at its base to keep it in its hole, or when they got the beam up there, the holes did not fit the knobs on the tops of the uprights, and had to be cut again. Yet each problem seemed to vanish before the will of the People. In the year after they got the stones to the Pillar of the Sky, they raised up the third Gateway, and in the year after that, the fourth.

All the People said that the place was lucky for them. Everyone who worked at the task was a talisman, and those who could not work, the women, who had to keep the gardens, the old and the sick and the young, envied the others and would go to them for luck, for counsel, for some cast-off glory. Many of them travelled across the country to see the Pillar of the Sky, even if they could not work on it, and all could see now what a magnificent thing it was.

The great Gateway stood at the foot of the place. On either flank, shorter than the center one but exactly even with one another, stood another pair of gates; now, on the northwestern side, the first of another pair rose up in its place. When the sun shone on them, and cast their shadows on the ground, the People often danced in and out of the shadows, rejoicing.

They still took their dead to the place, but they left the bodies at the very edge of the circle, where the two entry stones were. After the flesh was gone, rather than take the bones away to one of the many old tombs nearby, some of the families burned the bones inside a pot of clay and buried them there at the Pillar of the Sky.

There were holes along the outer edge of the place, just within the embankment, holes full of old chalk, and the People took to digging out the chalk and sticking the burned bones and ashes into these holes and ramming the chalk in on top. That way, they reasoned, in the end, the spirits of the ancestors would stand around the place in a protective circle, like the circles of stones, like the circle of the horizon that enclosed the world.

In the next summer, they went to raise the last of the gateways, the fifth.

Ruak knew the work now better than anyone except Moloquin.

He and Moloquin measured the stones, and they oversaw the digging of the holes. They had come to see the value of shoring up the inner edge of the hole with wood, so that when the uprights thundered down into the holes there was something inside to brace them up, and now they dug the ramps down into the hole when they dug the hole itself, not waiting until the stone lay ready to go in.

The summer was hot and rainy. Moloquin had to go away to the Forest Village, where Hems, returned from his apprenticeship with Baras Ram, was building himself a forge. While Moloquin was gone, Ruak did the work, glad of the chance to show that he, Ruak, was potent in himself.

None of the People of the New Village, none of the workmen from Shateel's Village, none of the People of the Forest Village went to the Midsummer Gathering at the Turnings-of-the-Year. Not even Fergolin went, the Bear Skull master. He had found ways of observing the stars and their passing at the Pillar of the Sky, and he had his own novice now, Twig, the son of Wahela, who learned everything Fergolin could teach him and was hungry for more. Instead of going to the Gathering, the People stayed at the Pillar of the Sky, and there they danced and feasted, and told stories and sang, made marriages and gave tokens.

At the end of the summer, with the two uprights for the fifth Gateway in the ground, and the beam dressed and ready to go up on top of them, Moloquin was away at the Forest Village, welcoming Hems, building the forge. And Ruak set about raising up the beam.

When he left Buras Ram's mine, Hems had brought with him a box made of a cedar tree, full of the copper that Buras Ram had promised Moloquin, but he was a little unwilling to bring it forth. He had looked into it and knew what it contained; he thought Moloquin would be displeased.

First, therefore, he showed Moloquin his prize, the last and finest work he had made, while he learned the craft in the old forge at Harus Kum's mine. It was a collar made of links of copper wire from which hung bronze plaques, incised with decorations and studded with pieces of polished stone. When Moloquin saw it, he took it into both hands and stared at it a while, smiling.

Then Hems brought out the chest of copper, and when Moloquin saw it, he lost his smile. With a grunt, he reached into the chest and lifted out some of the bracelets and necklaces and armbands and rings that filled it. "They are throwing out their garbage."

Hems poked at the chest full of castings and broken pieces of jewelry. Buras Ram had made as if he were giving Hems a great treasure to take home to his chief, but in fact he was throwing out flawed and worthless work, fit only to be melted down for the copper, itself impure, and much less than it seemed in this form, filling up the chest.

Hems said, "I am sorry. I have failed you."

"No," Moloquin said, and his gaze shifted sideways, to the collar lying on the mat beside him. "This is excellent. I am very pleased with you. We shall make a forge here, there are better things to do with this than rings and pins."

They went out of the roundhouse, into the broad clearing by the stream, the site of Moloquin's first village. The roundhouse behind them had grown too small, now that Hems had children, and Bahedyr had his wife and children, and Kayon also was married, and the men had raised a second roundhouse at the far end of the clearing. Between these two, Hems and Moloquin built a forge.

First they built the firebox, out of stones and mud from the river, and they dragged in a stump of a tree and set it down flat into the ground, to make an anvil. In this, and in the rest of the work, Hems knew more than Moloquin, and was the leader, the first time he could remember when he had not followed Moloquin but had seen Moloquin follow him, obeying him, performing faithfully whatever Hems asked of him.

It was the bronze and his mastery of it that had won him this new position. It had given him strength and pride, a new manhood for the boy the other boys had always taunted. As he struggled with Moloquin to raise up the corner posts of the forge, he promised himself never to yield this hard-won place again, not to anyone.

At night, their work done, they sat in the roundhouse, and Ap Min brought them food and beer which now she brewed herself, here in this village, with barley from the gardens of the New Village, and yeast that Buras Ram had given Hems.

Hems grunted at her. "This is cold," he said, and thrust the dish of meat back at her. She took it and hurried away to bring him something better, and Hems turned and smiled at Moloquin.

"She is very glad to see me, she does everything I say."

Moloquin broke a seed cake in half. "She did whatever Harus Kum said, also."

Hems scowled at him. "What do you mean?"

Moloquin shrugged. "I would be very happy if my women did as I told them. It seems to be a gift of the men of those people."

"It comes from the bronze," Hems said, loudly. Ap Min came back and put down food at his feet, and hovered around him, waiting to make sure that he was pleased.

"Perhaps it is," Moloquin said.

"They are not such a bad people," said Hems. "When I was a slave, I hated them, but this time I was one of them and not a slave, and they treated me very well."

Ap Min brought them both more beer; when her husband caught her skirt and pulled her down against him, she giggled. Hems hugged her. He liked this life very well. He was master here, in this village; even Moloquin knew it, deferring to him, and he had a wife who would obey him, coddle him, and never leave him. All this came from the bronze, from the hammer and the anvil, from the force of the blow.

He said, "Those other people, they say there is a spirit who watches over men, a spirit who is a —"

His voice trailed off. He struggled again with the notion that Buras Ram had given him, that the bronze contained a demon that responded to the work of a virtuous man but not an evil one. Actually Buras Ram had never said the demon was in the bronze, but that the demon worked the bronze, somehow, like a man, in a spiritual forge, somewhere in the sky, and his hammer strokes made the lightning, and the ringing of his metal made the thunder.

It was a fine story, but Buras Ram had meant it for more than a story. Hems shook his head.

"He said we should have a mask and make offerings to it, for the sake of the bronze."

Moloquin said, "Those are their demons. They have nothing to do with us. How could they? They are not our ancestors, this isn't even their land. Pay less heed to Buras Ram when he speaks of such things, he is deluded."

Ap Min went out, and returned with a tall jug full of the beer, but as she came in the door, after her came another.

He was a stranger to this village but not to Moloquin, who seeing him stood up at once and said, "What is it?"

The stranger stumbled on into the middle of the roundhouse. He was exhausted, filthy from his travels, and he dropped down to his hands and knees in the warmth of the roundhouse, and Ap Min at a nod from her husband brought him food and drink.

Moloquin said, in a harsh voice, "This is one of my workmen from the Pillar of the Sky. Why have you come here? What has happened?"

The man shook his head. "Awful. Terrible. You must go back." Worn to nothing with fatigue, he leaned sideways on his outstretched arm and hung his head. Ap Min knelt beside him with a cup of the beer and gently urged him to drink.

Moloquin rose; he went into the back of the roundhouse and got his bearskin coat. To Hems he said, "Keep well. Go on here as you will, I trust you here." He put the bronze axe into his belt.

"Wait," Hems cried, and leapt up. He crossed the roundhouse in three long strides to the place where he kept his goods, and came back with the magnificent collar he had made.

"This is for you," he said, and held it out to Moloquin, and all his new pride and his long-enduring love shone in his eyes. "I made this for you."

Moloquin took it, smiling, and clasped Hems by the hand. "Make me something every year," he said. "Something fine." He coiled up the collar and slipped it into the pouch at his belt, and whirling he went away out the door.

Twig said, "Master, if they raise more of the gateways, they shall block our lines of sight."

Alarmed, Fergolin was walking around and around the North Watcher, which was sagging over to one side. The rains had weakened it, he thought, or perhaps all the digging under it that Moloquin had done, as a boy, when he had made his caves under the stones. Soon the stone would collapse. He went to find a log, to brace it up, although part of his mind told him that no piece of wood would keep the stone in place. Yet it comforted him to do something.

He said, "When Moloquin comes back, we must talk to him about this."

Twig said, "Master, did you hear me? Look how the gateways will block our line of sight."

Fergolin straightened. The center of the space, around the gateways, was filled with men. Out of them, rising up from the midst of their bodies as if it grew from their bodies, the platform stood that held the fifth Gateway's beam, and that too was swarmed over with workmen, crawling on the wood, straining at the ropes, prying with the levers, hurrying to get the beam up into the air before Moloquin came home.

Those men who did not have work to do now sat around the place, telling stories, eating, and drinking beer. Many of them said the beer gave them dreams, visions, and insights into the will of Heaven, but Fergolin did not like the sour taste. He remembered now what Twig had been saying, and he looked at the gateways and shook his head.

"I don't understand you. The lines of sight are clear. The building is in the middle, the lines of sight are along the edge."

"Master." Twig came closer, as if they had a secret between them he feared to let the others know. Tall and scrawny as his name suggested, his hair shaggy and black as his father's, and his eyes like his father's intense and black, he was like a wandering river, into which all knowledge poured, while Moloquin was the blasting of the wind, that strove ever to break down whatever stood before it.

"Master," said Twig now, and laid his hand on Fergolin's shoulder. "Remember? We are going to see what we might see, if we look from that stone to that one, next midwinter."

He pointed out the diagonal between the North and the South Watchers. Fergolin shrugged. Unless they did something soon the northern stone would fall before the next Midwinter's Day came.

He said, "My boy, you said that, not I. For I have looked across them, and on the horizon there is nothing that might serve as another sighting point. Therefore it is not intended to be used so."

"But you said that I could try."

"We shall try." Fergolin nodded, absently. He turned toward the gateways, frowning: would they indeed interfere with any sighting lines?

On the platform, Ruak, his grey hair bound back in a twist of rope, was climbing across the beam, measuring it with rope, measuring it with himself. They had it nearly up to the top now; perhaps tomorrow, or the day after, they would put it in place.

Then what? Would Moloquin be satisfied? Fergolin looked around him, remembering the place as it had been before. It was so different he had to struggle to recall it, the falling stones, the emptiness.

He did not think Moloquin would end here. He knew Moloquin now; he doubted Moloquin would stop wanting more until the day came when he lay here on his back, with the crows pecking out his eyes.

He turned to Twig again. "We shall stand on top of the stone, if we have to. If we have to, we shall get your father to build a platform that we can stand on."

Twig laughed at that, as Fergolin had meant him to, but his eyes were dreamy. He loved this lore. Fergolin put out his arm and drew the boy close to him.

Ruak was calling, "Now! Up—up—" his voice rang out, a thin high call in the middle of the general jumble of talk. Fergolin started in that direction, to see what he might do to help. Twig left him, going back to the sighting stones. Then suddenly there was a rending crack of wood, and the snap of a log breaking.

The men let up a loud moan, recognizing the sound of failure and more work, and all stood up to see. The crossbeam was sagging down at the end. The platform had broken under it. Ruak scrambled around on the top of it, roaring curses, and beating at the stones with his fists.

"Here! Quickly—bring more wood—here!"

The men got to their feet, casual, and some of them went to the heap of wood; some others drifted closer to the platform, where the crew who had been at work on it were climbing down and circling around to inspect the damage. Still Ruak perched on top of the stone, shouting at them to move faster. Fergolin went wide around the bottom of the stone, to see what had happened.

Before he could make anything out of the tangle of crushed wood, there was another explosive crack, and the whole platform leaned over.

Fergolin shouted, "Ruak!" He rushed forward, his arms out. On top of the stone, Ruak bounded sideways, trying to get out of the way of the falling beam, and for an instant, poised above the collapsing platform, the sliding, tumbling beam, it seemed he would leap free. His foot caught, on a rope, on the wood, on the stone itself. The platform caved in. The beam rolled sideways, gathering speed as it fell, and slid off the end of the platform and smashed to the ground, bringing Ruak down with it.

A great gasp went up from the men. They rushed forward, packing together so tight none of them could reach Ruak. Fergolin fought his way through them. Just as he came to the front of the crowd, there was a scream from the few between him and the stone, and the whole mob surged backward. Ruak was dead.

Fergolin stood where he was. The men backed away and left him alone there, alone with Ruak, who lay on the ground between the stone and the platform. His head was crushed. He had pitched forward onto the stone as he fell; in the side of his head was a deep dent, from which blood and brain was oozing.

From the men behind Fergolin, now, a cry went up that seemed to come from deeper than their lungs. They whirled, and they ran away, out of the place of the dead, out past the embankment, out across the open plain.

Fergolin alone did not move, although he trembled in the presence of death. He stood looking down at the dead man, and even now in his ears he thought he heard Ruak's voice calling orders, calling for help. It was impossible that a power strong as Ruak's life had been swept away so quickly.

Yet it was. Kneeling cautiously by the body, Fergolin touched Ruak's hand, and felt the cold, flaccid texture of the flesh. The spirit was gone utterly. Perhaps, here at the foot of the way to Heaven, it had vanished into the Overworld at the instant that its body failed.

Fergolin shrank back. In a sudden intense passage of thought, he saw that this had been inevitable. The Pillar of the Sky had been waiting here, all its power disarranged, all its formidable might trampled over by little men, until at last they had tripped, and the place had closed around them, crushing Ruak in the very instant he had thought himself the master here. It was a warning, and a message. Only a fool would deny that message. Fergolin turned and ran away, ran as fast as he could, down through the gap in the embankment, away through the high grass, away after the other men, already small figures in the distance.

Later, much later, Fergolin came back.

He left Twig behind. The boy begged and argued and finally

shouted at him in fury, wanting to come, but Fergolin in his terror would not expose the youth he loved to any danger, and with an uncharacteristic harshness he commanded Twig to stay where he was. Alone, Fergolin walked up the long gradual slope to the Pillar of the Sky.

He brought his mask. He knew in his soul that the mask would not protect him against the crushing power of the Pillar of the Sky but he needed courage, and the mask with its ways of access to his ancestors gave him courage. When he came to the edge of the embankment, he stopped and put it on.

Trembling, he invaded the sacred precinct.

Nothing had changed. There at the center the gateways stood, massive, enormous, rising above the detritus of their building like some supernatural being bursting from its shell. He stood a long moment looking up at them. Even in his fear, he raised his eyes to the stones against the sky and was proud.

He thought, even as he was proud, that it was the builders' pride that had brought on them the blows of Heaven. When the first Gateway appeared, had he, Fergolin, not then imagined that men were free forever, to do whatever they pleased? The Pillar of the Sky had struck them down for their impudence.

He moved wide around the gateways. It was not the enormous gateways that drew him here. It was the leaning pointer stone that had called him back into this place of death.

Facing this one stone, his back to the pile at the center, he could control his mind. He knelt down before the stone and in a quiet voice explained that he meant to help it—in time he hoped to set it erect again. He took off his mask and laid it down before the stone, and he went back to the litter around the gateways to find wood to support the falling weight.

As soon as he faced the gateways again his fear returned, his sense of imminent disaster. He had to force his legs to move. As he trudged closer, a great mass of flapping black crows suddenly hurtled up into the air with a raucous cawing and croaking that sent him to his hands and knees and turned his skin to a cold rough shell.

Ruak. He got up and went closer, trembling.

The master of the stones still lay where he had fallen, one arm splayed across the beam that had killed him. The crows had been at him. Much of his flesh was gone, the bones exposed. When Fergolin saw him, their common work, their days together, the words spoken each to the other all flooded back into his mind; he forgot about the malevolent power standing all around him, and went forward to Ruak and wept over him. He gathered up whatever green things he could find, mostly grass, and spread it over Ruak's body.

When he had done what he could, he became suddenly aware of another presence behind him. He shivered and twisted to see over his shoulder.

It was Moloquin who stood there, watching him.

"Ho." Fergolin stood up, his stomach queasy. He had not heard of the chief's return from the Forest Village. He made a gesture of respect and bowed his head.

Moloquin stepped forward. Obviously he had just returned from his journey; probably in the village they had babbled out the news to him, and he had come straight here, to his real home. Over his shoulders he wore a bearskin coat and he carried his bronze axe in his belt. He reached the poor thinly veiled corpse and knelt down, brushed the grass away, and touched the crow-eaten face of Ruak with his hand.

"Old man," he murmured, "old man, you should have waited for me." With his fingers he restored the covering of grass to the ruined flesh.

Fergolin said, "What is to be done now, Opa-Moloquin?"

Moloquin stood up, raising his head, and looked calmly all around him. He never answered Fergolin's question. He said, "What are you doing here, Opa-Fergolin? Are you not as frightened as the rest? They tell me they will never come here again."

"I would not, Opa-Moloquin-on, because I am very frightened, but the stone there—" he pointed to the leaning stone on the edge of the precinct. "It must be set right again."

As he said that, he realized suddenly that the collapse of the North Watcher had been a warning, a sign they should all have read, that the swirling forces at the center of this place were gathering to strike. He put his hands to his face, overwhelmed.

Moloquin said, "Come show me."

Fergolin stumbled after him across the trampled grass. "Perhaps we ought not to touch it. Perhaps we ought never to come near this place again. Opa-Moloquin, I feel we are at the edge of something men ought never to go near. The Mill is turning—"

"The Mill is always turning," Moloquin said. He reached the tilting stone and pushed on it, as if he might heave it back upright by himself. "Come, let us dig out the hole a little more, and let it come down entirely; then we can set it up again."

Fergolin licked his lips. "I—you and I alone?"

"We have some help," Moloquin said, and shouted, "Twig!"

At the shout, the boy came bounding up over the earthworks and down into the Pillar of the Sky, his limbs as smooth and supple as the stones were unyielding. Fergolin wheeled toward Moloquin.

"Why did you bring him? He ought not to be here!"

Moloquin smiled at him; there was something cold and ugly in the smile. "Is he not my son, Fergolin?" He knelt down before the toppling stone, digging away at its foot. "His heart is here. He belongs here."

Fergolin could not move for a moment; his mind seethed with cross-flowing feelings. He loved Twig; and Moloquin had never seemed to notice him. Now as lightly as the passing moment Moloquin had claimed him away from the one who cherished him. And Twig accepted it. Flinging himself down beside his father, digging with much energy at the ground, he poured his excited talk into Moloquin's ear even as before he would have given his mind to Fergolin.

The Bear Skull master said, unnecessarily loudly, "I will get some wood." On legs like slabs of wood, he walked back into the center of the place, to pick up logs, to rest the stone upon.

All that day, Moloquin and Fergolin and the boy Twig worked at the Watcher, digging out the earth around its foot until they reached the chalk below. No one came from the village to help them. The workmen who lived in the roundhouse just beyond the embankment had returned, but only long enough to pack up their belongings. They were going home, to Shateel's Village.

With an antler pick, Moloquin broke away the chalk at the foot of the North Watcher and the stone tipped even more. They threw rope around it, pried at it with sticks, and eventually managed to push the stone over completely onto its side.

Fergolin sat down beside it, his hands on it. He kept his back ever to the gateways at the center of the place. Moloquin watched him closely. Fergolin was at the root of his plans; if Fergolin's heart had dried up, then there was no hope of ever finishing the work at the Pillar of the Sky. But it seemed to Moloquin that Fergolin's passion still flowed; only his fear turned it away from the real work, away to this other stone, to this Watcher.

Now Fergolin said, "It is rough, this stone. I will make it smoother." He rose, and with his head bowed a little, so that he did not have to see the upthrusting gateways, he went in among the piles of stone and wood and tools to find a maul.

Twig got up from the ground where he had been inspecting the hole, and stood beside Moloquin. "Will he let me help him?"

Moloquin nodded once.

"How will we raise it again, if the other men will not come back?"

Moloquin said, "I don't know, little one."

"I'm not little any more," Twig said.

Moloquin had been watching Fergolin, but now he turned toward the boy beside him. "Will you run away, too," he said, "when the place shows its true nature once again?"

"I won't," said Twig, and stood up straight. "I promise."

Moloquin smiled at him; he could hear, beyond the embankment, the men of Shateel's Village leaving for their homes. He touched the boy's shoulder.

"Help Fergolin," he said, and stayed there long enough to see the two of them at work on the stone, pounding and pounding at the surface to smooth it. Then Moloquin went down to the New Village.

Moloquin had thought that Ladon was long since left behind, but now he heard that voice in his ear again, that laughter in his ear.

You are my son. See how you have failed, just as I did? You are my son, my woefully begotten, cast-off, unwanted son!

In the New Village, where the men sat in little groups talking, holding their masks before them, he went from one to the next, listening to them more than he himself spoke. They poured their fears out, they spoke of seeing Ruak fall, even those who could not have seen anything now believed that they had seen Ruak fall, that the Pillar of the Sky had quaked beneath him and brought him down. They said there had been a giant voice, like thunder, from the sky, speaking in words they had not understood. They said they would never go back again.

Moloquin squatted before them, listening, his eyes on their masks. They held the masks before them as they spoke, as if their voices could be made larger in the mouth of the mask, and when they had done talking to him they set the masks down and gave them a little food to eat. By this he knew how frightened they were.

That night, he sat in the center of the roundhouse and heard them murmuring in the darkness, heard the rustle of their movements in the darkness, and his mind was downcast and bitter, and the voice of Ladon spoke ever in his ear.

Wahela came to him. She sat behind him and preened him, combing his hair, and stroking his shoulders and his ears.

She said, "Will we go to the Gathering, now?"

"The Gathering," he said. He had given no thought at all to anything except the Pillar of the Sky; the Gathering seemed of no importance at all.

"You should go to the Gathering," she said. She touched his cheek with her hand, drawing his hair back, twining her fingers in the curls. He loved to be touched, and she knew it; as she caressed him her voice fell to a soft and tender murmur.

"You should go to the Gathering. All those people have mocked you, now you must go and make them submit. Now that—"

She stopped, wise enough now, after many encounters, not to tell him he had failed at the Pillar of the Sky. He leaned his head back against her shoulder, listening to her, and in this new quiet of his mind something unlooked-for stirred.

"The northern villages have never given you the respect you deserve," she said. "Go to the Gathering, show yourself, make them kneel down to you, Moloquin. If you are the chief, be chief of all the People."

He said nothing, but in the stirring of his mind an idea formed.

Her hands brushed the sides of his face. "I hate those northern people. You should hear how they talk about us—they laugh at us. It's time they learned to respect us. You have to make them respect us, Moloquin."

He turned his head toward her, his face against her breast. She had borne him another son in the spring, but the baby had died after only a few days; since then she had seemed hungry, unsatisfied, her sexual passion more a longing than a lusting. He pressed his face against her breast and shut his eyes.

"Moloquin," she murmured. Her hands moved down over his body. He turned to her, his arms out, and gathered her in.

In the morning he went out to the yard of the roundhouse where the men were sitting, and he went from one group to the next.

He said, "We must finish the Gateway where Ruak died. We cannot leave it open like that—the hole in the place will let through evil
enough to sweep us all away."

"If we go near it again, it will devour us," they said.

He said, patiently, "If we fix it, make it whole and one, the power
there will protect us."

"We are afraid. We will stay here. Find someone else."

He used the old argument, that had worked before: "When you
were starving, I fed you. I did not ask then for any help. I carried
you all on my back. Now I need your help."

They said, "We are not hungry now, Opa-Moloquin-on."

He looked into their faces and saw nothing there, no interest, no
passion, not even any anger, only the stupid fear of panicked animals, and he knew he would not get them back this way. And he went
on to the next group.

Bahedyr had come up from the Forest Village, where he lived
with his wife and children, and was staying in the roundhouse. Moloquin found him with several other men, throwing a sheep's bone
for sips of beer. When Moloquin said, "We must finish the Gateway.
I need help to finish the Gateway," all the other men shook their
heads and crept away, but Bahedyr said, "I shall help you, Moloquin."

Like all those who had followed Moloquin into the forest, that
Midsummer's Day long before, he called Moloquin ever by his simple
name, undecorated.

Moloquin went back into the roundhouse, to collect his things to
go to the Pillar of the Sky, and now Ladon's son came to him.

Tall and pale, the enemy of his youth came before him with gestures of respect, and said, "I am sorry I was gone, Moloquin—I spent
the night with my wife in her longhouse."

Having lost Shateel, he had married again the next spring.

Moloquin said, "I do not need you." His voice was harsh.

Ladon's son spread his hands and bowed his head. "I heard that
you went to the other men and asked their help."

"They refused me. They are frightened fools."

"They are surely frightened," said Ladon's son. "They are not
fools. I will help you."

"You."

Moloquin laughed. The rage he felt toward all of them bubbled
up in him now. "You have never worked at the Pillar of the Sky. What
use would you be to me?"

Ladon's son lifted his head a little, surprise shining in his eyes. "Perhaps I am not offering much, but it is something—"

"Not enough," Moloquin said. "I do not need you, brother. You have failed at everything, but I do not mean to fail. Go." When Ladon's son still hesitated, his cheeks red with shame, Moloquin said, harshly, "Go!"

Ladon's son turned and walked away, his shoulders stiff. Moloquin watched him, trembling with anger, and as his mind cooled he wondered if his voice had spoken so to Ladon's son, or Ladon's own.

Therefore only Moloquin, and Bahedyr, and Fergolin and Twig went to the Pillar of the Sky. There was work for them—the shaping of the North Watcher; the clearing away of the broken platform where Ruak had died. As they worked, Moloquin saw, the others lost some of their fear, although Fergolin, most pious of all of them, would not look at the gateways if he could avoid it. Moloquin did the work inside the gateways, he and Bahedyr together, moving Ruak's decomposing body and dragging off the crushed and jagged logs of the platform.

As he worked, Moloquin thought about what he must do.

He could not leave this place. Even now, when many thought it was nearly finished, he knew it was barely begun. And his time was failing him. His youth was already gone; he knew himself a man on the edge of decline, even as he lifted up logs and hauled and shoved them here and there, he knew his strength was mortal. He saw forward to his death, and he saw forward to the finishing of the Pillar of the Sky and he knew that his death would come first.

Therefore he began to pay more heed to his son, Twig.

"Barakal," he called him now, whenever he saw Twig. Barakal, the Promise. Everybody thought it was a sort of joke, because when Moloquin had asked if he would not flee the Pillar of the Sky, Twig had said, "I promise." It ran deeper than a joke for Moloquin.

The boy was very young, but already he showed himself his father's child. He did not run with the boys' band, but stayed with Fergolin, and studied the Pillar of the Sky. In the few years they had been working here, Fergolin and Twig had recovered much of the lore that had died with Brant. They had used the Watchers to find the point of the midsummer sunrise, so that no longer had the New Village to rely on the Turnings-of-the-Year to keep their time; now, in the evenings, when the four workers rested, Twig sat with Fergolin and listened to the Bear Skull master talk about the stars.

Moloquin listened also; his mind was full of the pieces of something that he was struggling to fit together, something dark and furious, something even he was afraid of, and as he worked with his thoughts, he felt in the blazing night sky above him the mirror of himself.

Fergolin said, "There, see? The White Wanderer stands high in the sky, as high as I have ever seen her."

There in the west, where the sun had just gone down, the blue-white star hung in the clear vault, pure and holy, the beauty that stirred the heart.

"She stands near the Gate of Heaven," Fergolin said. "Perhaps she is waiting for some great chief to enter, or perhaps some crowd of lesser souls. She does not often signal terrible things. She is a quiet, welcoming star."

And Twig said, "Which signals evil, Opa-on?"

"The Red Wanderer, and the Old Wanderer when he enters into certain circles of the sky, especially when he goes backward to reach them, these are grave portents. But now, look, the moon is rising."

At that, both the man and the boy leapt up and went running across the Pillar of the Sky. Bahedyr and Moloquin watched them, startled, as Twig went to the West Watcher, and Fergolin to the easternmost of the four great old stones.

Twig scaled the West Watcher like a squirrel going up a tree. Bahedyr laughed to see it done. Turning to Moloquin, he said, "We are broken sticks compared to that one, Moloquin."

"The fire is bright in him," Moloquin said.

Fergolin was out of their sight. Moloquin got up and walked around the outside of the circle of the sacred precinct until he could see both Twig, on top of the western stone, and Fergolin, standing by the East Watcher.

The moon was just appearing, a pale glow in the east. As Twig stood there, poised on top of the stone, Moloquin saw why he had climbed it; now he could see across the gateways to the tip of the other stone, where Fergolin stood, and could use the two points as a line of sight to the horizon. Moloquin turned to watch what they saw.

Above the distant skyline, a fat pale blob had appeared: the upper limb of the moon. Its point of rising was far to the north of the line of sight of the two Watchers, and Twig and Fergolin left their positions at once, and came together at the edge of the circle and stood talking. Moloquin went to them.

"You must have the line of sight wrong."

Twig looked up at him and smiled, reassuring, or condescending to the ignorant. Fergolin shook his head.

"No—it is useful. First, this is not the full moon, but its older brother, and it is the rising of the full moon that most concerns us."

"Then why watch this one at all?"

Fergolin's eyes widened a little; he looked mildly surprised. "As I said, they are brothers." He smiled, his eyes narrowing, as if at some secret joke. "And we must look, if we would see."

At that he shrugged, and raised his eyes to the night sky; the mist was creeping up the horizon from the south, a pale breath of vapors. He turned and pointed to the west.

"See, the White Wanderer goes to her rest."

Indeed, the blazing pure glory was lower in the sky than before, following the sun away.

Twig stood by his father's elbow. "Tomorrow she will not climb so high, and the next day even less, and soon she will be gone utterly."

He spoke with pride and authority, giving knowledge to the un-knowing. Moloquin laid his hand on the boy's shoulder, pleased with him, proud of him. Then into his mind leapt the memory of Ladon, who had stood thus before his other son, glowing with pride.

Moloquin pulled his hand away; he turned his back on Barakal. With a last glance up at the sky, now fading into the blank mist, he went away.

The spring grew warm and rainy. In the fields the women dug and hoed, put in their seeds and watched them sprout; many of them slept in their gardens, to protect the seedlings from deer and birds.

Ladon's son took the men of the New Village away to the river, where they built a sweathouse and sweated themselves.

In the dark and stifling heat of the sweathouse, Ladon's son struggled with his soul. Around him were the men of his village, men who had been boys when he was a boy, men who did as he told them, as if he were the chief. But he was not the chief.

Could he not be the chief? Moloquin had failed. The Pillar of the Sky had mocked them all, destroyed him who strove to conquer it—was Moloquin not proven false, a fool, and dangerous?

He knew the other men would follow him. He could go among them now, and tell them that he meant to be the chief, and they would follow him; they would cast Moloquin out, and Ladon's son would at last become what Ladon had intended.

He thought of the women. The women belonged to Moloquin.

Or Moloquin belonged to the women, it was unclear to Ladon's son where that circle began. They had raised him to his place, and they were loyal to him as they had never been to Ladon, stirred up as they had been by the suspicions of Karella and Tishka; but these women, the women of the New Village, with Grela at their head, did whatever Moloquin told them.

He sat in the hut with his skin flowing like a river, all the impurities of his body rising to the surface, and the impurity of his mind rose like a froth to the surface.

The men around him spoke of Moloquin and of the Pillar of the Sky, and some were angry that Moloquin had brought them to such a turn, and some despised themselves for their weakness and cowardice. In the darkness of the sweathouse they spoke freely, whatever thought came first to the tongue, and a man who one moment cursed Moloquin for an evil sorcerer spoke in the next moment of the shame of failing his chief.

Ladon's son went out of the sweathouse and plunged into the river to cleanse his skin. On the bank of the river, with the other men, he ate ritual herbs and seeds and drank a bitter tea. The sun was still high, but the tea made him sleep.

The tea made him dream, and it was a horrible dream.

He found himself again in the old village, during the famine, when his father lay dying. He walked through the middle of the village and saw the People dying, all around him were the dead, so starved their bones thrust up through the skin. They stretched their arms toward him, the dead and the dying alike, and begged him for food. They seized him as he passed through their midst, they dragged him down into their tangle of bones, and they gnawed on his flesh, they consumed him, they devoured him, and he grew weaker, but they grew no stronger; they were dead, and just before the dream ended, he was dead too.

When he woke, he knew he would not be the chief.

He got up from his place. The other men were sprawled around him, some in the middle of dreams, twitching and murmuring, and others merely sleeping, their souls elsewhere. Ladon's son went back to the sweathouse, where his mask, with the others, sat in a circle.

He knelt down before his mask. He had carved it from a living tree, and put eyes of quartz into it, and painted the lips with red ochre; when Moloquin had given him a string of blue beads, he took the string apart and fixed the beads to the mask like blue hair.

Now he knelt down before it, and he told it, and through it told his ancestors, that he understood. He had been tested. They had sent him a temptation, a lure, to test him, and he had nearly fallen victim to the trap, but they had also sent him a dream, to help him understand how to be, and he had taken heed. He gave the mask a handful of seeds to eat. Then he went back to the men, and as they woke he talked to them of his dream, his revelation of the right way.

"We cannot do it by ourselves," Fergolin said.

They had cleared away all the debris from around the gateways. They had laid the North Watcher down on its side and with mauls smoothed it and worked it to a symmetry and polish like the uprights of the gateways. Now there was no more work to do save that which they could not do without the help of others.

"We can try," Moloquin said.

They dug holes for posts, set the posts, crossed them together at the top, and hung ropes over them; they looped the ropes around the stone, and while two men pulled, the other two rammed poles under the stone and struggled to pry it up. The stone refused. It lay there without moving and would not obey them.

All four of them pulled at once on the ropes, with no success, and all four of them pried at the stone with levers, with no success.

Bahedyr said, "I must go back to my village, Moloquin. If there is nothing to be done here—"

Moloquin gave him a sharp look, but when he spoke it was not of the struggle here at the Pillar of the Sky.

He said, "The Gathering will be soon. Fergolin: when?"

"Within the waxing of the moon," said Fergolin.

Bahedyr grunted. Like most of Moloquin's People he seldom went to the Gathering. He put his hands on his hips. "My wife will bear before the end of the summer. I would be with her when she labors."

Moloquin fixed him with a look. "I want you with me at the Gathering."

"*You* are going to the Gathering?"

Moloquin said, "We are all going."

"Why?"

Moloquin smiled at him, saying nothing, his eyes unblinking. Bahedyr scrubbed his face with his hand.

"I still must go to the Forest Village."

"That fits in very well with me. There is something there I need, and you can bring it back with you. And bring your spear, also."

"I will."

"Good," Moloquin said, and went away, back to the work they could not do.

With a sharp stone and a mallet, Fergolin was pecking a design into the face of the North Watcher. Moloquin sat on the ground nearby watching him, but his thoughts whirled.

He was beginning to understand what the Pillar of the Sky demanded: the heart and soul of the whole People. When he had raised the first upright, all the people, even the children, had come to help, and they had succeeded, but now those who shirked were bringing everything to ruin, failing everybody, the living and the dead.

He had to bring them together, draw them to this one purpose, save them from their weakness and stupidity.

And they were weak and stupid. Nothing in their ordinary little lives could matter as much as the Pillar of the Sky; what they resisted was their own greatness. Anything he did was justified, if it brought them to the task.

So his thoughts ran, as he sat in the shadow of the Great Gateway, yet his mind would not rest. He had been thinking through this now for a long while, ever since he came back from the Forest Village and found Ruak dead and the rest of them scattered, but still he himself shrank from the work before him. In what he planned, he saw more than Ruak crushed beneath the Pillar of the Sky.

He would make enemies. There were some among those closest to him, on whom he most relied, who would turn against him.

Bahedyr he could trust, not because of the quality of the man so much as the quality of the work, which would suit him. Most of the other men would follow where they were led. Wahela would go with him anywhere. Grela would support him. But there were others. He was unsure now of Ladon's son. Shateel—

They belonged to him. They were his people, he alone saw the thing whole, while they were lost in their little, daily lives. He would do what he had to do.

Karella, with her stories, her hatred of Ladon, her contempt for rigid custom, she would know that this was necessary, this thing he had to do. Ladon himself would cheer it. Ael—

He no longer cared about Ael. He gave her no thoughts at all, no reverence, nothing of his life to sustain her dead spirit. He hated Ael.

The steady measure of Fergolin's mallet ticked in his ears. The sun was moving, turning the shadow of the Gateway, so that now Moloquin sat in the light again. He raised his eyes to Heaven. They were stupid, his people, they were useless, meaningless, without him to guide them. Whatever he did was justified. He was the heart and soul of his People. He shut his eyes, struggling with the voices that told him otherwise.

In the evening, when the four men sat around a fire in the work-men's roundhouse, Wahela came with several other women and brought them food to eat. Wahela sat watching Moloquin eat; she said, almost idly, "Ladon's son has brought the men back from the river."

"Good," said Moloquin.

"I see no good in it, if they will not obey you."

Moloquin scraped the bowl clean with his fingers and set it down beside him. "We shall go to the Gathering within a few days, you should get ready, you and the other women."

She brightened like the sun rising. "We are going to the Gathering?"

Behind him, Fergolin and Barakal raised their heads and turned to listen.

"We shall all go," Moloquin said. "You must take whatever you have that is wonderful—your best clothes, your hair combs of shell, and the beads I gave you."

"Oh, I shall," said Wahela, delighted, and she leapt up and went out of the roundhouse and was away at once to the New Village, full of her news.

Fergolin drew closer to Moloquin. "You are all going to the Gathering?"

Moloquin swung his head toward him, made no answer, but only stared.

"We would prefer to stay here," Fergolin said. "Twig and I."

"Ah?"

"The full moon will rise while you are at the Gathering."

"Oh. Yes." Moloquin nodded. He leaned toward Bahedyr, who was drinking beer from a tall jug, and the spear-bearer gave him the jug. Ap Min made the beer, down in the Forest Village; there was little of it left. Moloquin drank. He nodded again to Fergolin.

"Yes. You two stay here."

"Thank you." Fergolin turned and with a smile shared his pleasure with Barakal.

Moloquin watched them a moment longer, pleased. He saw their ardor and their success at the Pillar of the Sky as signs that what he did was right. Brant had died, but everything Brant had known was kept somehow at the Pillar of the Sky, and so in a way Brant had not died at all. Like the green plant in the springtime that was reborn, he was reborn at the Pillar of the Sky.

For another reason he was relieved that Fergolin and Barakal would not be at the Gathering. He knew Fergolin's mind; Fergolin would not like what Moloquin intended to do among the People. And he wanted Barakal kept free of it. Everything was going very well now. He turned to Bahedyr again, and putting out his hand he asked for another sip of the beer.

In the morning, the four of them went out again to the Pillar of the Sky, to the gigantic work they were unequal to.

The sun was rising. The great gateways stood there on the grass, reaching toward Heaven. Moloquin walked among them, leaned against them, pressed his hands to them; he thought again and again of Karella, and of the story of the Broken Mill.

Someone walked up over the embankment and came down into the sacred precinct.

Fergolin called out, and the newcomer swerved toward the North Watcher. It was a man of the New Village, a son of Grela's, whose boy's name had been Sickle; now he was a tall dish-faced man, whom Moloquin had hardly noticed before. He went to Fergolin and said, "I will help you, Opa-on."

Moloquin overheard him; he went up beside the youth, while Fergolin smiled at the son of his wife.

"You will! Well, there is little we can do in such numbers."

Moloquin said, "Why did you change your mind?"

The young man turned, his head bowed. "I had a dream," he said. "I will help." As if to prove it, he went to the Watcher, which lay on the ground with the ropes veiling it and the levers stuck under its head, and he heaved by himself at the stone.

Fergolin said, under his breath, "My People are a great People. Let Heaven see this!" His eyes were shining.

Moloquin stood silent. One more would do no good, but if one had changed his mind, others might also. He turned to Fergolin.

"Go down to the New Village and see—"

"Wait," Fergolin said, and put his hand on Moloquin's arm.

He was looking away, over Moloquin's shoulder, and Moloquin turned to see what he saw.

There were more coming. One by one, two by two, they were coming up from the direction of the New Village. They hung their heads as they entered the holy place. They muttered their greetings to their chief; they would not raise their heads to look at the gateways. Their fear hung on them like a snake's half-shed skin. Yet they came.

That day and the next, with all the men there to help, they set the North Watcher in its place. The day after that, Moloquin took them all down to the New Village, to make ready for the Gathering.

Wahela was delighted with the prospect of the Gathering. She gave no thought to Moloquin's decision, except to congratulate herself on talking him into it.

She made ready her dress of red and blue and yellow, woven of the wool of yearling goats, with its long fluttering sleeves and its skirt that swept the grass as she walked. She made ready her hair combs of wood and shell. She made ready her long strands of blue beads to wear to the Gathering.

On the day before they were to leave, Moloquin came, and he called all the People together at the roundhouse. Then he went into the roundhouse, and he came out with a box made of a section of a cedar log, hollowed out, covered with a lid of bark.

He took the lid off and he turned the box over on top of a hide, and out of the box fell a shower of such brightness and beauty that all the People gasped.

There were anklets and bracelets, necklaces and pins, made of fine worked copper and bronze and decorated with pieces of shell and blue beads. There were belts of links of copper; there were strands and strands of beads; there was a great collar of beads and copper. With this treasure at his feet, Moloquin went among his People, and he put ornaments on all of them.

He gave the women pins—he gave to old Grela a necklace—and he put beads around the necks of the children, and he gave the boys of the boys' band necklaces of copper. He brought the men before him, one by one, and he covered them with anklets and bracelets and belts. Then he himself put on the collar of beads and copper, and he took his bronze axe in his hand.

He stood before his People, and they all gazed on him, with the sun shining over him, and they felt the weight of the treasure on them, and they rejoiced.

"Opa-Moloquin-on," they cried, "who has made us great!"

He let them sing and rejoice, he let them praise him, and when they were still again, he raised his hands.

He said, "We go now to the Gathering, where there are many who have despised us. Now we shall show them that they have been wrong, blind, and foolish. We shall go among them, and they shall fall down on their faces before us, and if they do not—"

He bit off his words, and his gaze passed slowly from one to the next of the People, and although he spoke no more, each one heard what he intended. They put their hands to their new beauty, and stroked it, and the magic of the ornaments flowed into the People. They felt themselves strong; they knew themselves invulnerable. Strutting with their knowledge, filled up to brimming with their power, they went away to the Gathering, and Moloquin walked at their head, his axe in his belt.

The people of the northern villages kept herds of oxen, and they used the hides for their clothes, and the horns of the oxen were a special emblem for them, which was why the chiefs of their villages all wore masks with horns. They made music with the horns some-times also, and when they reached the Gathering, the blasting of the horns could be heard all over the plain, all over the Turnings-of-the-Year.

Shateel heard them, and came out to watch them. Dehra came

with her. They went down from their village and across the circles of
stones, and stood on top of the embankment and looked across the
Gathering and saw the People of Mithom and Barlok and the twin
brothers Eilik and Muon entering the Gathering in a great array,
with the blasting of horns.

Dehra covered her ears with her hands. A scrawny, sharp-eyed
girl, she had already gotten a name for being too quick to speak.

She said, "The noise hurts my ears, Ana-el."

Shateel laughed. "It is their way, to make a great noise and raise
the dust and do nothing."

In long parades the men of the largest northern village entered
the Gathering. They wore their masks and their horns, and carried
drums and staffs. They danced as they came into the Gathering. All
around, the people who were already there—the People of Shateel's
Village—stood and watched, and some clapped their hands in
rhythm, and some called out to the newcomers.

Shateel said, "Come, we shall go make ready to bring our hearth
here." She turned to go.

"Ana-el," Dehra said. "Look!"

Shateel cast another glance into the broad scene before her: the
fires, the scattered People, the twining ropes of dancers. "Come," she
said, "I shall need your help."

"No, no, Ana-el, look! Look there!"

Shateel turned again, impatient, and saw only the Gathering as
it had been before, although now the dancers had come to the place
where they would make a camp, and were settling in little circles
around it. She opened her mouth to speak to Dehra again, and a
flash of the sun caught her eye.

She looked at the far edge of the Gathering, and her voice stuck
in her throat.

Dehra said, "Ana-el, look!"

All around the Gathering, others had seen what Dehra had
seen; others were turning, and as they turned and saw, they hushed,
they stilled, they stood as they were and watched. Now down from
the horizon came rows of a People, walking together in ranks.

The sun shone on them as if on her most favored children. The
sun struck them from such beams of light that it hurt to look on
them. They chimed as they walked. There were many of them, rank
on rank, that came up over the top of the slope and walked down

toward the Gathering, all gleaming and glowing with the fire of the sun, and at their head walked one on whom the sun shone brightest of all.

Now from the Gathering there went up a single cry, a shout of amazement and awe, and the cry took the sound of power and of magic. They shouted, "Moloquin!"

"Ana-el," said Dehra. "It is Moloquin. He has come to the Gathering! His People have come to the Gathering!"

"Yes," said Shateel, and she was amazed.

She knew what had happened at the Pillar of the Sky; when the men of her village came back, the word of Ruak's death had passed through the whole place like a cold wind. She had known then that Moloquin would face this challenge too, as he had all the others. This she had not foreseen.

She touched Dehra's arm. "Go to the village, make our hearth ready."

"Ana-el!"

"Do as I say," said Shateel.

Sickle had walked to the Gathering with his mother, Grela, carrying her camp goods for her. She was annoyed with him; she wanted the long walk to harangue him, because although he was well grown, of an age to marry, he had not yet entered a society. All the way up to the Turnings-of-the-Year, she told him of the necessity of becoming at least a novice, preferably a Bear Skull novice, so that he would have a high place among the men.

He said, "Moloquin is not a master."

"Moloquin is the Green Bough master. Join the Green Bough Society, then."

"What Green Bough Society? There is none, they do no dances, they have no place in the roundhouse—"

She said, furious, "Then join another!"

"Why?"

"You must have a place among the men!" She struck at him. "I am the headwoman of my kindred, and I will not have the other women laughing at me behind my back because my son is a wastrel."

"I am not a wastrel. I have been helping raise the stones at the Pillar of the Sky. That is my society."

"That is something else," she said, and would hear no more of his notion that because he had the Pillar of the Sky, and Moloquin for his master, he did not need a society.

Yet he had said it to her, and in saying it, he gave words to something he had felt for a long while. As they entered the Gathering, all shining with their copper, and he among the others strutted and showed off his excellence, he said that over and over in his mind: I am of the Green Bough, and Moloquin is my master.

With one or two of his friends, he paraded up through the Gathering, waving his arms to display the copper bracelets he wore. Walking in among the scattered fires of the People, he drew the long envious looks of many of those he passed. Other young men joined him. It felt good to be among so many others, to be one of those who wore copper, and the young men joined arms and swaggered along through the Gathering. As they came up toward the western flank of the embankment around the Turnings-of-the-Year, they encountered some youths of one of the northern villages, sitting in a circle with their masks.

"Ho, ho," Sickle shouted. "See the cattle-boys playing with their wooden faces!"

He made a face of his own at them. The boy on his left dug an elbow into his ribs and hissed into his ear.

"Don't say things like that! You'll offend his ancestors, who may be yours too, you know."

Sickle grunted. He puffed his chest out. "I wear the emblems of my people—Moloquin's People! Let lowlings make their emblems of wood—" he waggled his arm, shining with its copper bracelet.

The young men from the north hooted and jeered, and the two groups faced one another, shouting insults. Off in the direction of the Gathering some girls were passing, and stopped to watch. Sickle jumped forward, where they could see him, and paced up and down, waving his arms with the copper bracelets so that they caught the light.

"Cattle-boys! Horned ones! Make your fires out of dung!"

"Go haul stone," one of the northern boys cried, and his friends joined in, a sudden clamor of whining voices. "You don't even have a mask! What society are you in, anyway?"

"The Green Bough," Sickle cried, and swelled with pride. "Moloquin is my master!"

"Moloquin is a fool," one of the other boys cried, and Sickle stooped down, picked up a stone, and threw it.

At once all the others were throwing stones. The girls screamed and cheered, urging them on, while moving back so that no stones would strike them. Sickle scurried up the embankment, scrabbling in the grass for things to throw. Straightening on the height, his hands full of stones, he looked around and saw a swarm of women, coming purposefully toward the fighting below him. Whirling, he ran away, down the bank, across the ditch, and off through the Turnings-of-the-Year.

Hems had made a new point for Bahedyr's spear at the forge at the Forest Village, a point of shining bronze. It was softer than a stone point, and would not take an edge, but Hems had worked it into a splendid three-forked shape, and it shone.

Bahedyr carried it with him as he walked through the Gathering, and everyone turned to see.

He wore also the anklets and bracelets that Moloquin had given him, over the years, rewards for the deeds Bahedyr had done in his chief's behalf, and he wore a long coat of woven stuff, and as he walked, he drew all eyes.

Some admired him—the women, especially, he thought, admired him very much. Others, the men, the men of other villages who did not know his strength and ferocity, were envious, and they looked insults at him, and murmured to one another about him. He actually heard no insults; he saw them in the way a man looked at him, or even in the way a man did not look at him.

Moloquin said to him, "They do not know you. If they did, would they dare to treat you like an ordinary man? You should show them what you really are."

Moloquin was at the Turnings-of-the-Year, where he had entered first of all the chiefs to an acclaim that shook the clouds. He had refused to sit on the platform with the other chiefs and instead had caused his People to make a separate place for him, a roof of cloth, supported on four slender poles, and held fast with cords staked to the ground at the corners. Then, because there Moloquin sat upon the ground, he would not let the other chiefs sit on the platform at all.

Instead, the other chiefs sat under the platform, and Moloquin sat under his roof of cloth that rose and fell on the wind like a piece of the sky, and all those who came there to ask favors and to give reverence went to Moloquin on their hands and knees.

This did not sit well with many of the People, especially the Peoples of the northern villages, and they clustered together around their fires and talked about it, and the more they talked, the more they decided that Moloquin had gone too far.

They said, "He came that year and chopped the platform down and said he was going away forever, didn't he? Why is he back here now, then?"

Moloquin's People paraded in their bronze and their beads. Shateel's People, seeing them, said, "We are Moloquin's People also." All the men who had worked at the Pillar of the Sky knew the New Villagers well, and so had friends among them, and before the first day of the Gathering was out, most of Shateel's People were staying around the hearths of Moloquin's People.

Shateel saw this, and she saw also that Moloquin himself did not come out from beneath his roof of cloth. No one ever saw him except the few who went back and forth from the roof of cloth, and yet everybody in the whole Gathering talked of no one else.

That night, when the men came together to dance at the Turnings-of-the-Year, there were several fights between the men of the northern villages and the men of Moloquin's People, and in the morning, hearing of this, Shateel went to Moloquin.

He sat at the center of the great ring of standing stones, under the soft flutter of the cloth; Wahela had come and tied tassels of wool and feathers to the edge of it, so that the wind turned it all constantly. In the shade of it, Moloquin sat on piles of furs and woven cloth, his back against a backprop such as storytellers used. Behind him was Bahedyr and another man with a spear.

Shateel went in under the roof of cloth and stood before him. "Husband," she said, "you are lax in your favor to me. Have I done you some ill, that you do not come to me?"

He said, "You are the most excellent of wives, Shateel."

"Yet you are not pleased to see me," she said, and she sat down before him. She raised her eyes to Bahedyr, standing at her husband's shoulder, and she said, "Go, now, and watch that Wahela does not disturb us."

The other spearman looked startled, his eyes pale with surprise in the shadow, and Bahedyr did not move. Moloquin's eyes never left Shateel's face. He said, "My wife has spoken to you, Bahedyr."

At once the two men left. Shateel sighed; there was in Moloquin's way something that gave her confidence, and she thought, *I
will make him see what he is doing, and he will stop.*

She said, "You did not dance, last night."

"I do not dance at all, wife," he said, and smiled at her.

"Perhaps you should! Perhaps you should do many more of the
things a chief is supposed to do."

"Pagh," he said, and spat to his left. "What does a chief do? He
struts and poses, he wears his beads and feathers. The doings of little
men, gone within a day. What I am doing now at the Pillar of the Sky
will stand forever. Those who are my People know this, they have
seen the signs, they have been tested and have passed the test. I am
leading them to Heaven. The wise ones know it. They know these
other fools are only envious of us."

As he spoke, he shifted his weight, he seemed ever about to rise,
but there was no room for him to rise here. She saw how this space
cramped and confined him, how he longed to move around, as he
did usually, restless and active, and yet he stayed here; and this more
than his words struck to her heart. She saw now that he meant everything he did here.

She said, "Why did you not come to me, when you arrived? I
waited for you half the night."

He looked away. A shadow fell across his face. "I was—I had—
other work."

"Also, you know I will not keep silent if I see wrong done."

He rounded on her, his eyes fierce. His words came at her like
bolts of fire. "I cannot do wrong, Shateel! I am the soul of my People.
They have no power save to do that which I wish of them."

"Yet I say that you do wrong!"

His steady stare cooled. He looked down at her as if from a great
distance.

"Why have you become my enemy, wife? Has standing in my
place in this village given you a man's belly?" With one hand he
waved at her. "Go."

"Moloquin," she said, amazed. "You must hear me, at least."

"I will hear nothing from an enemy. Go." He turned his head
aside.

"I am not your enemy," she said.

"Go!"

She lingered a moment longer, and a gnawing doubt crept into her soul. Was he right—had she gotten beyond herself, doing a man's work in the village? Perhaps he was right. She turned and crept away, out from beneath his roof of cloth and tassels, out to the sunlight again.

Eilik, who with his twin brother was chief of the most northern village, went with the other men of the Bear Skull Society to the Turnings-of-the-Year, and there they watched the sun rise in her appointed place. He raised his voice with the others in greeting to the sun, but his mind was elsewhere.

Like the others of the northern peoples he had paid little heed to Moloquin, except to mock the strangeness of his ways. He had kept his herds and ordered his People, listened to his headwomen, performed the obediences of the calendar; what some other chief did somewhere else had mattered nothing to him. The Mill would take care of Moloquin.

Now he came here and found the whole place overturned. The platform where the chiefs had once sat at the center of the world and looked out over everything was now a laughingstock, and no one led the dances; worst of all, Moloquin's People went everywhere in such an array of wealth that Eilik himself was miserable with envy.

His uncle had been chief when Ladon was chief of the southern village, and Eilik remembered how Ladon's few strings of blue beads had made him first among them all—a few strings of beads! Now the least of Moloquin's men wore ornaments as potent as any chief's. No one knew where they had all come from. There was some rumor that Moloquin found them in the womb of the earth, but Eilik did not believe that. Nor did he believe what others said, that the metal came in thunderbolts from the sky, because he had seen many thunderbolts, but he had never seen any metal before.

At Turnings-of-the-Year, with all the others of the Bear Skull around him, he said the sacred words. He put on his mask, with the great horns of the oxen crowning it, and with the mask on he ate and drank, and so his ancestors witnessed the lives of the People; so the People continued on, from the distant beginning to the unknowable end. In his mask, carrying the three red-feathered arrows that were the emblems of his power, he walked to the High Hill and climbed the path, his feet stepping where the feet of every man before him stepped, making the earth new again, bringing the past alive again.

Yet it all seemed nothing, without beads and ornaments of shining bronze.

His brother Muon said, "Leave it alone. Soon we shall go back home, and take the herds away to the summer pastures, and you can forget about Moloquin."

Eilik grunted at him, angry. Everything that happened these days made him angry.

He went with a crowd of his men through the Gathering, and as he walked his men beat their drums and waved their arms to call attention to his passage. Everyone turned and looked, and some bent low to give him respect. Not enough gave him respect. He lifted his feet high, and held his shoulders back, his chin in the air, the ox horns waving in the air, and drew all eyes, but in their looks he saw less than he wanted. He thought their eyes said, If you are great, why have you no beads, no copper, no bronze?

Then before him he saw a man who did have beads and copper ornaments, and this man was not even a chief.

He stopped. He had been crossing the main part of the Gathering, the low ground, where the hearth-fires were thick, and the children ran here and there and the women sat in knots talking. Ahead of him was an old stump. On it sat a man of Moloquin's People, eating from a bowl of glazed clay.

On his arms he wore rings of metal, and on his ankles; around his neck he wore loops and loops of beads. Beside him, tipped up against the stump, was a spear with a three-pronged tip of bronze.

Eilik went slowly forward, his head lowered, his teeth clenched. The man on the stump saw him but ignored him. Instead of giving Eilik the respect he deserved, this man went on eating.

Before the stump, Eilik paused. He said loudly, "I see here one who has no propriety."

The man on the stump glanced at him. "I see there a man who has no wealth." With a grin, he dipped his fingers into the bowl and scooped up a gob of meal.

Eilik gave a yell. Backing up two steps, he turned to the men on either side of him and said, "Put this impudent fool on his face before me."

His men sprang forward. The man on the stump leapt to his feet, snatching his spear into his hand as he rose; Eilik's men seized him by the clothes to drag him down, but Moloquin's man roared and struck out with the butt end of his spear, fending off their hands.

All around them, a cry went up, and people came running. Eilik shouted to his men, "Bring him down! Kill him! Kill him!" He leapt into the air and beat the air with his fists. His men were struggling to reach Moloquin's man, perched up on the stump, but from this high point the man with the spear could hold off all who came at him. Then Eilik stooped and took a stone from the ground, and he threw it at the man on the stump.

The stone caught the other man square in the face, and he staggered, and in an instant Eilik's men had brought him down off the stump. Eilik shouted, triumphant. A moment later a rush of bodies from behind him knocked him flat.

He shouted, but he was flat on the ground, and above him the crowd closed like a pool of water above a drowning man. He struggled to rise. Someone was standing on his thigh. A blow glanced off his head and his horns fell into the dirt. He got to his hands and feet, buffeted on all sides, and took an elbow in the chin.

"Stop! Stop!"

A woman's voice. Used from infancy to heeding women's voices, he fell still, shying back, and so did all the other men. For a moment, across a stretch of dust, he faced the man with the spear, the blood a bright streak down his face, but then a dozen women forced themselves in between them.

"Stop!" First among the women, the headwoman Shateel ran forward, her arms out. "What are you doing? Opa-Eilik-on—" she paused before him, stooped, and lifted up his horned cap. "What demon has infected you? What work is this for a chief?"

"That fool there, that misfit outcast would not bow to me, Ana-Shateel-el."

"Shateel," the spearman shouted, hoarsely. "He struck me, Shateel—he drew my blood!"

He charged forward, his arms milling, and the women closed on him, held him back, as he roared and brandished his spear, and by weight of their numbers made him helpless.

"Eilik," he shouted, over their heads, as their arms bound him. "I will come for you tonight—Eilik—run and hide—Eilik—"

More women were crowding in between the two bands of men, forcing them apart. Eilik bellowed, "I will be ready, impudent one!" Shateel gave him a single white-eyed glare, but the surge of bodies was carrying her away from him. He could explain nothing to her. His back itched. His jaw hurt where the elbow had struck him. Since his boyhood in the boy's band no one had struck him. He was a chief, the center of his People. He had no bronze, no beads. With the horns in his hand, he turned and went away, his head down, surrounded by the men of his village.

With the other women Shateel stayed by the stump until all the men had gone off elsewhere, until there was no more chance of fighting.

The sun had gone behind clouds. The day was cool and the wind was blowing hard from the east; soon it would rain. In the evening the stargazers would see nothing but the angry face of the night. Even now a few drops sailed upon the wind.

Around her, the other women talked in low voices of the fighting; Joba came to her and took her by the arm.

"This is very bad," said the old woman. "We should all go home, before it comes to worse."

"How could it be worse?" Shateel asked, a little wildly.

Joba shook her head. "I remember once, when I was a young girl, when two chiefs wanted the same wife, they fought all through the Gathering and there was blood spilled and thereafter one of the villages would not even come to the Gathering until the other chief died. Do you want that here?"

"What must we do, then?"

Joba said, "We must talk to Grela. If she calls her People away, the Gathering will end, all this will end, too, I hope." Joba sighed. She had been ill often lately and looked worn and tired today. "You must talk to her. She may heed you."

"Grela has never liked me."

"It is not liking you that will move her, but the truth of your words, Shateel. There, good, they are by the sampo. There we can talk openly."

They walked across the low flat ground of the Gathering, weaving a path around the hearths on the ground, speaking to everyone they saw, because everyone they saw was friend or kindred in some way. At last they came to the hearths of Moloquin's People. The old women had brought their sampo to the Gathering, to grind their grain, and there before it sat Grela, and some other women, their fingers busy with their weaving, their mouths busy with their talk.

Shateel and her mother sat down among them; Grela turned to

her. "So. Here you are; I have expected you for some while now, surely you are come to make glum talk of all this quarrelling among the men."

Shateel looked into Grela's face, seeing the broad cheeks, the small shrewd eyes, the merry mouth of one who thought she dealt with ordinary trouble. Leaning forward, the younger woman gave a turn to the mill.

"It is all doings of Moloquin," she said.

"Moloquin," said several of the women, Grela among them. "It was not Moloquin who attacked Bahedyr."

"The other people are jealous of us," Grela said. "That is no problem of ours. I do not see why we should suffer for their failures."

"I say we should all go home," another woman said. "Right now, and wait until next year, for the next Gathering, then everyone shall have forgotten their problems."

"Ah," Shateel said, "will you not heed me? This is not a tangle of threads, blown here by the wind—this is a whole cloth, and we are the loom, and Moloquin is the weaver!"

Grela turned on her. "Why do you accuse him, who is your own husband? He is our chief, and he has been a great chief. It is the northern chief—Eilik! He is to blame!"

Joba put out her hand and gripped Shateel by the arm, and Shateel kept still, although her cheeks burned. Now Grela leaned toward the other women, and said, "It is Eilik who makes the trouble." She turned the sampo around, calling the Mill to witness.

Another woman cried, "Yet it is only man's trouble—why make so much of it? Let them bang themselves on the heads now and then, if they wish. What has that to do with us?"

Many of the others began to talk in the same way; they shared stories of the quarrelling among the men, funny stories, some of them, how a group of boys from the New Village had wound a strand of blue beads around a pig's neck and paraded it on a rope through the Gathering, declaring even their pigs finer than the northern chiefs; that did not end as a funny story, since all the boys had been beaten bloody. In their midst the sampo chattered and turned in its endless song. Shateel listened with her head down, wondering why they saw only these small bits of the piece and not the whole design.

Then she sensed someone behind her, and she raised her head, and turning she looked behind her.

There squatting on his heels behind her was Moloquin, listening to what the women said. His axe was in his belt, but he wore no other ornaments or signs of power.

Shateel said, "What are you doing here? You have no business here."

At the sound of her voice, all the other women hushed; they turned toward him, and many gasped to see him there. He gave Shateel a long cold look, but when he spoke his voice was warm with praises, and given to Grela.

"Ana-Grela-el, mighty is she! Her mind is deep, she keeps well the memory of how I have served my People—how when they were starving, I gave myself to feed them, I saved them from death."

Shateel stiffened. She had never before heard him speak in the elevated language used among men and between men and women. She swung to face the other women, and her words rang out.

"You hear Moloquin. Now I shall speak to you, but I shall use the simple tongue of women and children, not the language of indirections, misunderstandings, and lies. He is a man. He does not belong here, shadowing our minds and swaying our decisions. Send him away, that we may deal with the troubles he has brought on us."

The other women leaned together, a solid wall of their bodies, in their center the turning, turning mill. Beside Shateel, her mother put out her hand again to take hold of her wrist, but it was to Grela that Joba looked, and to Grela that Shateel also looked, and all the other women too.

Grela said, "Moloquin has sat at the mill before, when he was with Karella. There is nothing wrong in that. Let him be here, if he wishes. I have no quarrel with him. Only you, Shateel, have a quarrel with him, as the whole People knows, so great a quarrel that in all your years of marriage you have never made a child together."

The other women murmured, and among them some laughed, covering their mouths with their hands, their eyes bright. Shateel lowered her eyes, her face hot with shame. She could not bring herself to argue further with Grela. When she raised her head at last, Moloquin was gone.

Wahela said, "It is raining. They will not dance long tonight, I think."

She turned from the front of the shelter, smiling; when the sun went down, she had to withdraw from the Gathering, and so she was glad that the rain would keep all others under cover also. If she could not be the center of whatever went on she wanted nothing to happen at all. She moved away from the front of the lean-to, where the air was chilly and damp, back toward the fire.

Moloquin had caused this building to be put up so that he would have some place to go to, away from the eyes of the crowd, when the sun went down; it stood on the far side of the Gathering from the High Hill, away on the slowly rising slope that led to the west, and it had some special meaning for him because he himself had chosen it—he had gone looking for some low place in the ground, a little away from the stream, and had commanded his People to build his shelter there. The shelter itself was nothing but a wall of mats and poles, tipped at an angle, the sides filled in with brush and leafy boughs.

All around it those men stood who were Moloquin's trusted followers, Bahedyr and Ladon's son chief among them, those men who had proven they would do anything their chief asked of them. They stood with their spears, a circle of men like the circles of standing stones, and at their center Moloquin paced up and down, his head ducked to keep from striking the sloping roof of his shelter.

He said, "Let them dance all they wish. Let Eilik dance, if he wishes."

Bahedyr grunted. "I would put my spear through his chest, let him dance that way."

The other men all rumbled forth their agreement, and they shifted and moved in the darkness, staying close together in a pack. Moloquin said, "Eilik will step wrong soon enough. Keep careful. There is that rising here that could crush the whole herd of you, if you let yourselves be lulled."

He moved constantly through the little space under the lean-to, stooping, straightening, bending, his hands out to touch the walls; it was his own dance, Wahela thought, the greater dance. She went to him; it delighted her to go to him, before all these men who quaked at his least displeasure, and lay hands on him as she did now, stroking his hair and beard, and picking imaginary flecks of dust from his shirt. She let her hands rest at last on his arms and looked up into his face.

"Sit down, let us eat. I myself shall serve you."

He smiled at her. "I am flattered, Most High One."

She tossed her head at him. "Does it displease you that I take pride in myself?"

"Serve me then, Wahela." He went into the back of the lean-to where it was warmest, and sat down.

Wahela did not intend to serve him with her own hands, of course. She went out to the front of the shelter, out to the rain, and called to the women out there.

Several of them had made their hearths near Moloquin's shelter. They huddled in the steady rain, unprotected from the skies, like animals with their tails to the wind, like lumps of earth in the twilit downpour. At her beckon, the nearest to her rose and brought in bowls and baskets and Wahela gave them commands, to go here and there, to set this dish down and to move that one, while Moloquin sat at the back of the shelter, his head lowered, and said nothing.

Only he lifted his head once toward the men with their spears, and at his nod they all left.

When the women had served them, Wahela sat down beside him, and they ate together. Wahela talked to him about the Gathering, giving him scraps of news from the hearths she had visited. If he heeded her she saw no sign of it, but she knew if she did not speak, there would be silence between them. He ate everything she fed him—now and then, she lifted a morsel to his lips with her own fingers—but he was thinking deeply; as she talked, she thought her words bounced off him as the rain bounced off the top of the lean-to.

She said, "No one in all the Gathering has a dress such as mine. Ap Min is very clever with dyes."

He reached for a cup, and she handed it to him. "We should teach the other villages to make beer," she said.

The wind came up suddenly, and the whole lean-to roared with it; the roof bellied up off its poles and frame and the wind boomed in the hollow above their heads. Moloquin licked his fingers clean. He slid back, away from the food.

"Put some wood on the fire," he said.

She turned, and called someone from outside the lean-to to bring wood and feed the fire, and from the dusk someone came.

Wahela said, "Tonight the girls will dance in the Turnings-of-the-Year. I can remember, when I was a girl, the dances made my blood race."

He said nothing.

"Do you think that ugly child of Shateel's is old enough to marry yet? I am sure Shateel will keep her in tonight."

He said nothing.

"I would, if I had a daughter of that age. I would let no daughter of mine go to the Turnings-of-the-Year tonight, I promise you."

He said nothing.

"When our daughters are old enough, they shall already have many marriage offers, we shall have to choose carefully. And keep them away from all dances."

He said nothing. Far off, through the clatter and hiss of the rain, a shout of many voices sounded, and he lifted his head.

"What are you listening for?" she asked.

He sighed. Putting down his cup, he turned to her and put out his arms to her. "Wahela," he said, "I have need of you."

She went to him, and they lay down together on the furs and mats at the back of the lean-to. Usually he let her kiss him, baby-like, and would caress her with his hands and lips, but tonight he wanted only to possess her, and he handled her so roughly that she cried out, more in surprise than in pain. His head burrowed down beside hers; he held her hard against him, pinning her down with his weight.

Then at the moment of his climax, there was another distant shout, and he jerked his head up, looked around, and listened, and under her hands the tension passed through all his muscles like the wind rippling a field of high grass.

"What is it?" she said. "What are you listening for?"

He did not answer her. Instead he bent down over her again, and thrust so hard at her she bit her lip, and for a moment, helpless in his arms, she was afraid.

That night, no one danced. The girls did not appear in the circles, and the men kept their masks covered by the hearths. The women huddled by the hearths in the rain with their children, and the men walked the windy darkness, prowling in packs from fire to fire, stopping a few moments, slouching off again. The night was full of spirits that whistled and gibbered in the dark, and no one wanted to be alone.

Toward the dead of the night the rain slackened and the air grew sharply cold. Bahedyr and his friends crowded together for warmth; they stopped at a hearth where several other men were already piling wood on the coals and stood around the leaping flames warming their hands. Bahedyr lifted his face toward the sky.

"No moon. It will be dark tonight, dark as the first night, before the sun was made."

Beside him, a toothy little man, one of Shateel's People, grinned up at him. "You would like finding Eilik by himself on such a night, wouldn't you?"

"If I did—" Bahedyr held up his spear. "There would be holes in him to fit his own horns into, I tell you that."

The wind was rising, cold at their backs. From somewhere away to the southeast, toward the Turnings-of-the-Year, there was a sharp, short yell. Bahedyr wheeled.

"What was that?"

"Everybody in the Gathering is moving around tonight, it feels very strange."

"Eilik's out there somewhere," said the toothy man beside Bahedyr. "Looking for us."

"For us," Bahedyr said, surprised. "You are not one of us."

"I am Moloquin's man," said the toothy man. "As much as you are."

Bahedyr put one hand on the other man's chest and pushed him. "You're just from Shateel's Village."

"Stop," Ladon's son said suddenly, and walked in between Bahedyr and the toothy man. "Stop, and keep counsel. Bahedyr, don't be a fool. He is one of us, he worked at the Pillar of the Sky, and he will stand at your back when Eilik is cutting at your front, you can be sure of that."

"Until I die!" said the toothy man, and around him many others nodded: Shateel's men, wanting to be Moloquin's. Bahedyr grunted.

"Well, then—"

From off in the darkness came another yell, this time many voices, and the quick pattering of feet. Everyone by the fire wheeled toward the sounds. There was nothing to be seen; the night swallowed the fading noises, and they were left with silence again, silence and darkness.

Bahedyr caught his spear by the haft. "Come," he said.

"Where are we going?" asked Kayon.

"To find Eilik before he finds us," Bahedyr said, and led them away from the fire.

. . .

Ladon's son followed after the others, trailing his spear behind him. He had never gotten the use of the spear perfectly, and it felt awkward and alien in his hand. Tonight everything he did felt awkward and alien. He had never been so miserable, not even when his People were starving and his wife had deserted him.

In the darkness around him the other men moved like shadows. Like spirits they drifted along from place to place and their voices were shrill and their words made no sense. He thought, *Why are we trying to kill each other? Has no one asked?* But he himself did not dare ask.

Around his neck hung chains of blue beads. On his wrists he wore bronze rings, and his wife wore clothes decorated with little circles of the metal, so that she chimed when she walked. Yet here where he was supposed to join other men in great dances, no one danced; here where all the People were supposed to come together, all the People were hunting one another.

He did not dare ask himself what place Moloquin had in this.

Moloquin had done nothing. So they all said—that Moloquin all the while had been sitting quietly by his fire, while Eilik and the lesser men made the trouble: Moloquin was not to blame. To suggest that Moloquin was at the root of this was impossible. Even to think of it was impossible. It was Eilik who had started it all. Eilik, with his jealousy and his silly pride.

Ladon's son told himself never to doubt Moloquin. Moloquin had never failed; Moloquin had the favor of Heaven—he knew that, from dreams and signs. If he doubted Moloquin, he would open such a hole in his understanding that the whole world would fall through it.

So he walked along after Bahedyr, dragging his spear after him, following the sounds of his own party through the night. He had faith in Moloquin. Whatever happened, Moloquin would guide them through it. Moloquin would make it right. He lowered his head and plunged blind through the demon-ridden night.

The night seemed endless, a warning from Heaven. No moon rose to show the passage of the time, nor did any stars appear in the sky. In packs the men went from fire to fire, peering over their shoulders,

throwing stones into the dark. When Bahedyr and his band saw another band they stopped and shouted, until they knew who it was
they faced; then, if the others were Moloquin's men also, they joined
Bahedyr's pack, gladly fitting themselves into the warmth and numbers, and again the prowling and stalking began.

If the men they encountered were not Moloquin's, they fled
away.

In the bowels of the night, when the day seemed forever lost,
Bahedyr at the head of an uncountable number reached the Turnings-of-the-Year. He was tired, his head throbbing, his thoughts slow
and morose; only the men at his back drove him on, he had forgotten
what he was looking for. When he stumbled down the inside of the
bank at Turnings-of-the-Year and walked across the ditch to the first
of the stones, he wanted only to sleep.

Then, as he passed between two stones, something set on him.

He screamed like a woman. The shape flew at him from the air,
it seemed to him, a piece ripped out of the night sky, a smothering
black mass. His spear arm was free, and he stabbed and stabbed at
the body struggling with him, banging at it with the haft of the spear
because it was too close to use the point, and went down hard with
the fighting form on top of him. All around him he heard the thud
and rumble of feet, and men were shouting. Something pressed itself
down over his face and he bit, and the being on him shrieked.

That gave him courage; he lost the spear, but he fought with
both hands, scratching and striking, and he bit again, and the vile
thing that clutched him let go. He heaved it away and stood up.

At once another body struck him and knocked him down again.
The whole of the Turnings-of-the-Year seemed full of whirling,
shouting men. Bahedyr crawled to the nearest stone and in its shelter
he stood up.

He could see no one he knew; he could make out nothing in the
dark but the surge and struggle of the fighting. He shouted, "Moloquin! Moloquin!" From the violent crowd before him the cry came
back, breathless, furious. He went out away from his sheltering
stone, looking for his spear, and found it, and lying beside it, unconscious, a man in a long coat. Bahedyr picked up the spear; the feel
of the weapon in his hands gave him a sudden burst of courage
which made the memory of his fear intolerable. He lifted the spear
and drove it down into the body before him.

When he pulled it out, the blood followed in a leaping burst. He staggered backwards, frightened again. The blood had gotten on his shirt. He was marked, tainted. He swiped at it with his hand. Around him no one fought any more; nearby, two men sat on the ground breathing hard, and a few others stood dazed and slumped by the stone ring. Down at the far end of the ring there was still shouting and the bang and thud of blows, but then suddenly, as Bahedyr stood trying to wipe away the blood, there was a shriek like a woman's.

"Eilik! Eilik, where are you?"

Bahedyr whirled. He caught the arm of the man nearest him, one of Moloquin's, and hurried him away between the stones. The others followed. "Come—come—" they called it over their shoulders as they ran, and all around the great space men turned and followed, running through the place where men and girls had danced, between the standing stones, across the ditch, up over the bank, and were gone.

In the morning there were three men lying dead in the Turnings-of-the-Year.

Shateel heard it, and did not believe it. She went out from her village where she had gone when the rain began, needing also to think, and she walked over the hill and down to the sacred place. All the People were there, gathered in tight masses according to their village, talking in low voices, and many of them wept. On the ground between the stones lay the dead.

Seeing this, Shateel did not stop to talk to anyone but went off at once across the Gathering, away into the wilderness, where Moloquin had made his shelter.

His lean-to stood in a hollow of the land, with a line of old sycamore trees rising to the west. When she came into the camp, she found all her husband's spearmen sitting around a fire, dazed and exhausted, and she went slowly through their midst, looking keenly into their faces, seeing the marks of fighting. Just before she came to the lean-to, she found Ladon's son, slumped on the ground, his spear beside him.

She said, "Well then, did you dance last night, my friend?"

He raised his head and looked at her as if she were mad. She sat down beside him, curious, knowing him well enough to guess he had no belly for fighting, and seeing on him no marks of battle, no bruises, no blood. He lowered his head again; his eyes looked bruised, but that was fatigue only.

He said, "Heaven keep me from such a night as that again, Shateel."

She said, "Why did you do it, then?"

"What else could I have done?"

"It was wicked. Evil, horrible. Could you not have refused?"

"Refused what? They hunted us—was I to let them kill me?"

"But—"

He turned his face away from her, and she grew silent. His words were like a thicket of brambles, fencing her out, while his soul crouched like a little rabbit at the center. Her heart sank. There was no place left to go save to Moloquin, and she got to her feet and went to the lean-to.

He was there. He was preparing to go to the Turnings-of-the-Year. On his chest and shoulders he wore a great bronze collar of links and little circles, joined with blue beads; on his wrists he wore broad cuffs of bronze, and in his belt he carried his axe, the emblem of his power. He stood just inside his shelter, in the center of a host of men, and all those men wore ornaments of bronze, and they carried spears and spoke in booming voices. But when Shateel came into their midst they quieted.

She came in among them, small among them, and went straight to Moloquin.

"Ho, wife," he said; she saw that he was not surprised to see her. She wondered if anything surprised him any more. He seemed huge, as if the aura of his power had taken solid flesh around him, his hair and beard flowing together into a curly black mane.

She lost her tongue before him, and her resolution shrank. She cast down her gaze, wondering what pride had brought her here, what demon influence.

He said, "Are you still my enemy, Shateel?"

That woke her to her purpose. She raised her face toward him, all her insides quailing, and she said, "I am your enemy, husband. Three men lie dead today because of you."

"Because of me! I have done nothing."

"You have done great evil to your People," she said. "You must turn aside now from this path you have chosen."

He looked down at her as if from a great height; now, suddenly, for the first time, she saw in the luxuriant mass of his beard a streak of grey. He said, "I mourn for my wife, who is my enemy now," and his head·rose, his gaze went beyond her, and he said, "Take this woman and make her prisoner."

She stiffened, too amazed even to protest; before she could summon words, the men had closed around her. Their hands grasped her arms. They were drawing her away, moving her as if she had no will of her own. Behind Moloquin, Wahela appeared, smiling.

Shateel cried, "Moloquin, are you leading your People, or are you having your revenge on us? I beg you, have mercy on us, this will destroy us all, and you also." The men lifted her up like a bundle and took her off.

Wahela stood on the embankment with the other women and watched Moloquin enter the Turnings-of-the-Year.

No one cheered now. The turmoil of the night before lay too heavily on their minds. They came together to watch the chieftains and the women held their children close, and the lesser men swarmed to join the ranks of men who followed after Moloquin. None wanted to seem slow to follow Moloquin.

When he appeared, it was as if the sun itself came down to roll along the earth, so magnificent was he. The People sighed to see him. Wahela held out her arms toward him, shining in his reflection. Beside her, Grela sighed.

"He is the child of Heaven," Grela said, and around her all the other women murmured, agreeing.

Now Moloquin entered into the Turnings-of-the-Year, and his men around him made a lane of their bodies for him to pass along to his shelter of cloth, but before he began his walk, Eilik came.

Eilik came with his horns and his plumed arrows, and his brother Muon slower behind him, and as many of their men as they could muster. They came up through the gap in the embankment and through the Turnings-of-the-Year, and there they came face to face with Moloquin.

"Go no farther," Eilik cried, and raised his sacred arrows. "I have come to demand you punish the men who slew my men last night."

Moloquin frowned at him. "You make demands of me!"

Eilik held out the bunch of arrows between them. "Take the spears of your men and break them. Make no more weapons! Slay no more of us, Moloquin!"

All around them the People murmured, and Moloquin looked around him, his look calm, his great head cocked from one side to the other to see them, before he brought his gaze again to Eilik.

"It amazes me," he said, and his voice carried over the whole Gathering, "that you dare come here at all, Eilik. Yesterday you set upon my man Bahedyr and stoned him, so that he barely escaped with his life. Last night while my People trembled in the darkness, your men went in search of more blood, and when my People tried to defend themselves, you struck and killed. Of the dead, Eilik, one was yours, but two were men of mine, and now they are dead, lost to me and to the People forever, their spirits driven away in the dark. Now you want me to break the spears of my men! Why, so they will be helpless before you?"

Eilik heard these words and he went red with rage. His brother held out his hands, trying to restrain him, but Eilik plunged forward, shaking his feathered arrows in Moloquin's face.

"I say, Get gone from here, Unwanted One! You came from nowhere, go to nowhere again and leave us as we were! Go!"

Moloquin reared his head, the points of the arrows in his face, and took a step backward. Eilik pressed on, shouting. On the bank, Wahela forgot to smile. She had never seen Moloquin give way before, and now again he was yielding to Eilik. The People whispered, their voices like the low buzz of the bees in a linden tree, and she heard their bewilderment that Moloquin should give ground.

Behind Eilik, his brother reached out to stop him. But Eilik saw only that the man he hated was backing away before him, and he flung himself forward, more furious as he grew more confident, the sacred arrows jabbing at Moloquin's nose, and then suddenly, in a surge of passion, he lifted the arrows and struck Moloquin full in the face with them.

The People screamed. From all around Moloquin the spearmen surged forward, packing tight around their chief, and before Eilik could draw back they had pierced him through and through with their spears.

Wahela clutched her fist to her chest; Moloquin stood there, blood on his face, still as a stone, while the lesser men surged back and forth around him. The People screamed and cried out, and many of the children began to cry. Moloquin raised one hand, and the uproar quieted a little.

Muon had seized his brother. Calling for help, he drew Eilik back away from Moloquin and laid the dead man on the ground, and kneeling beside his brother he looked up at Moloquin and the spearmen.

"All the People saw," Moloquin shouted, "that I struck no blow. Eilik struck the blow, and he has suffered for it."

Muon sprang up. "He did as you wished of him, Moloquin," he cried, and he flung himself forward at the man with the bronze axe.

At once all his men rushed after him, armed with knives and clubs. Moloquin shouted something, Wahela could not hear the words, and the spearmen closed on Muon and his followers. There was a short struggle, but there were far more of the spearmen than there were of Muon's People, and swiftly they fell into the power of Bahedyr and the others; swiftly they were forced down to their knees at Moloquin's feet.

Now Moloquin began to speak, and he sent his words out to all the People; as he spoke, he walked up and down through the Turnings-of-the-Year and swept the crowds on the embankment with his gaze, so that all would feel the weight of what he was saying.

He said, "Eilik and Muon are chiefs no more! Henceforth, you shall all be my People—you shall all be one People again, as it was meant to be. Only wretched ignorance and sin has driven you apart. Now I am calling you to be one again, to be as Heaven meant you, to be as the ancestors were: One People. Will you answer me? Will you do what is right, my People, and save yourselves? I weep to see you throw away your lives, wasting your lives in sin and error. All I want for you is that you be what you are meant to be. Now, on the plain at the Pillar of the Sky, I am raising up a House of Heaven, and therein shall we all dwell, all our spirits forever more, if you will only help me."

The crowd fell still and silent, listening, save for the wails of a few babies; the wind blew over them, and Moloquin's words reached them like a call on the wind. Wahela looked around her, but she saw only her own People, who had followed him almost from the beginning; they were eager enough. She looked out to see the others, the strangers, to whom he really spoke.

He said, "I need you. To raise up my stones, I need every hand, every soul. Let there be no weakness in the People! If there is weakness in the People, then the stones themselves cannot stand. I need you to be what you have almost forgotten you can be. Remember the old stories? In them are men foolish and frightened—are men weaklings, who strive against one another with bundles of feathers? Be as you were then! Be strong, and upright, like the stones! Come to the Pillar of the Sky and there we shall live forever!"

He raised his hands, and on the embankment, all around Wahela, people flung their arms up and cried out, "Forever!" They looked keenly around them, to see who did not shout. "Forever!" All along the embankment, more and more arms shot up toward the sky, and more throats opened. "Forever!"

Now before Moloquin, kneeling in the trampled grass, Muon raised his head; Bahedyr had put the tip of his spear at Muon's throat, and at the motion he stepped forward. Muon ignored him and stared up at Moloquin, who was looming over him, and Muon raised one arm and called, "Forever!"

With that, it seemed, the clouds themselves gave voice. All the People shouted in one breath.

"Forever! Forever! Forever!"

Packed tight around Muon, the men who had followed him and his brother flung up their arms and shouted louder than any other. At Moloquin's feet, Muon lowered his head to the dust.

That night all the men danced at the Turnings-of-the-Year, all the men save Moloquin.

The People built fires along the top of the bank, so that the whole place was filled with a leaping, crackling light. The women gathered to watch, holding their sleeping children, and as the night wore on, many of the women began to clap their hands together and sing. They ate and drank well, and laughed and made games, and the memory of the night before dimmed and lost its power to frighten them.

Moloquin himself sat under his roof of cloth at the center of the Turnings-of-the-Year, where everybody could see him. Wahela sat beside him. In their wonderful ornaments they were magnificent, and the People went up to the edge of the shelter just to see them and be amazed. None dared talk to them. Moloquin sat in silence, his head turned a little. Wahela was up and down often and called to her friends and demanded food and drink, but Moloquin kept silent.

Then Dehra came.

She was still only a girl, thin as a stick, with lank pale hair and a face sharp as a willow switch. She wore clothes as carelessly as the last leaves hanging on an oak tree in the autumn. She walked with no grace, but with long strides like a man's, and her eyes were full of fury.

She came walking down through the noise and tumult of the dancing, brushing against people as she passed, as if she did not see them; her gaze was fixed ever on Moloquin, there beneath his roof of cloth. She strode in between the stones and went straight up before him, and her voice rose in a cracked cry, like the voice of a bird.

"Moloquin," she cried, "what have you done with my mother?"

Around her, those who heard stopped what they were doing and turned to look, and seeing it was she, and hearing what she came to say, most people thought it better to pretend they did not hear. They turned their backs on her; they left her to Moloquin.

Under his roof of cloth, he stared back at Dehra, and he said nothing. She came a step closer, and again her voice rose.

"Moloquin, what have you done with my mother?"

Beside the chief, Wahela stood up. "Go, you unlucky, undeserving—" Moloquin put out his hand and stopped her.

He said nothing to Dehra. He merely stared at her, as if from a long distance, with a faint curiosity on his face.

Dehra came to the very edge of the shelter, and again she raised her cry.

"Moloquin! What have you done with my mother?"

He gave her no answer. He stared at her without speaking any word at all. Beside him, Wahela sat rigid, twitching her head from side to side, to look first at him and then at Dehra; her fists were clenched in her lap.

Dehra turned and walked away; Moloquin's gaze followed her. Wahela heaved a sigh, and lowered her eyes.

He had succeeded. The whole People belonged to him now, the whole People would come to the Pillar of the Sky. Everything was one now, everything round and full, complete.

In his mind he saw the broken millstone mended, the nether millstone, world of living men.

Some had died. He had foreseen that, and made some provision for it—he himself had killed no one, he had done nothing himself. In the Overworld, it was Eilik who would receive blame, as it should be, because Eilik had resisted the truth. Moloquin had done nothing save follow the right way.

They all knew it. They had all come to him, finally, even Muon and the others of the northern villages, bowed down to him, submitted to his vision. Only one, in all the People, had defied him.

Only one. He told himself, over and over, that one alone could make no difference.

She had stood before him as if he were an ordinary man, and chided him like a child, scolded him like a mother. But she was the only one. All the others had come to him. All the others were his.

She who had listened to his deep thoughts. She who knew his soul.

But she was the only one, and she was wrong; all the others knew she was wrong, all the others had come to him, and only one—

He had done what he knew to be necessary. He had forged the People together, he had shaped them to his purpose. If she had resisted the tempering, she was unworthy of it, she deserved to be thrown aside.

Yet when he thought of her cast aside, he saw, in his mind, something else cast aside. With her she took something of Moloquin.

She was unworthy. In the testing she had proven herself flawed. That part of him that he had sent away with her—

He would find another to listen to him as she had. He had sent her away and he could easily bring another to her place, he was master here, all around him did as he bid them. If they did not, he would crush them, as the stones had crushed Ruak. He did not need Shateel.

He laughed to think of that. He was chief of all the People, master of the bronze, master of the Pillar of the Sky, whose power stretched from the sea to the forest. He drew forth matter from the belly of the earth, and shaped it to his wishes; he raised stones no other man had ever dreamed of lifting, and suspended them in the air. No longer had he to walk, like an ordinary man; his People carried him wherever he wished to go. He was the center of their world; they brought him what they made, and he gave them what they needed. There was no flaw in this circle, nothing missing, no room for anything else. What could one woman matter? He put away his longing for Shateel.

V

THE MILL OF HEAVEN

"Can you see them yet?" Fergolin asked.

Barakal shook his head. He shaded his eyes with his hand. "Only the dust." He peered keenly away to the northeast, over the rolling country, trying to make out what lay between the brown haze of dust boiling into the air and the earth below it. Beside him, Fergolin sat on the ground, breathing hard.

They had come out here to see the stone hauled up from the river. It was a long walk for Fergolin, who was sick again, coughing blood now, and Barakal had at first refused to go, but the old man had insisted. He loved the stones, and their procession over the earth moved him unutterably, and, he said, if he were to die one day sooner because he had come here, yet he would come here whenever he could, to see the stones brought to the Pillar of the Sky.

"I see them," Barakal cried.

There beneath the spreading cloud of dust and the brown earth, small dark figures moved. Fergolin turned and stood, the young man's hand on his arm.

"Shall we go nearer?" Barakal asked.

"No," said Fergolin.

So they waited where they were. Here the open rolling plain sloped away to the river; except for a few isolated trees, nothing grew here but grass. The sun had just risen. It shone with a hot bright glow on the cloud of dust, a bronze overlay of the blue sky, and the promise of the day's heat crackled in the air. Barakal had brought a jug of beer and he gave it to Fergolin and made the old man sit down again. The stone would be many days yet passing by this place.

Barakal said, "Only three more days to the full moon, Opa-on."

Fergolin smiled at him. "Are you eager, my boy?"

"My blood leaps even to think of it."

"And if we are proven wrong?"

Barakal shrugged one shoulder. He did not see how they could

be wrong. They had been watching the full moon rise at the Pillar of
the Sky for years. He knew every motion that the light made; he had
learned to stand in the Pillar of the Sky in full daylight and point to
the horizon and say, There he will appear tonight, and when the
moon rose, if there were no mist and no rain and no cloud, he appeared where Barakal had foreseen.

He had learned that this point of rising moved up and down the
horizon, north to south and back again, in the course of each month;
more, he had seen that the point of rising of the full moon shifted
steadily along the horizon also. In the month previous to this, the full
moon had risen exactly in line with the West and the East Watchers,
a line running diagonally across the Pillar of the Sky. Tonight, when
the full moon rose again, Barakal knew it would have shifted back to
the north again.

He did not know why he knew this. He thought the Pillar of the
Sky had spoken to him, perhaps in a dream. Yet he was certain of it.
The Four Watchers marked not only the point of rising of the midsummer and the midwinter sun, but also the extremes of the rising
of the full moon.

When he thought about this, which was nearly all the time now,
his soul grew light and joyous. His pleasure in the simple elegance of
this design was without words. It was perfect, and it proved what
Moloquin himself could only guess at, that the world was one, a
single turning of the wheel, and the one-ness began here at the Pillar
of the Sky.

Now, against the drifting bronze cloud of dust, he could make
out the figures of men, creeping toward them over the plain.

Fergolin was dozing. Barakal took the jug of beer and drank
some of it, enjoying the warmth of the sun and his own idleness. It
was a good thing, over all, to be Moloquin's son; it meant he did not
have to drag stones around, he had all day long to think, to sit in the
sun, to sleep, so that at night he could watch stars rise.

Far down the plain now more of the figures were creeping into
view. There were several lines of them, strung out along lengths of
rope, each man bent to the rope over his shoulder, their legs bent to
thrust against the ground, their heads bent. Every little while, the
men at the back of the line would run up to the front, and the men
at the front would move back; otherwise, the dust of their own passage would overcome them. Once, when Moloquin had had many
fewer men than this at his command, it had taken them a whole sea-

son to move a single stone. Now the entire People labored, and it was as if the whole earth moved.

Barakal stood up. There was respect due these men, these faceless wordless choiceless men who hauled the stones.

All the rest of the day they came on. Fergolin woke coughing and spitting blood, and Barakal half-carried him away to the roundhouse at the Pillar of the Sky, and then returned to the slope to watch.

Now the sun was sinking, blood-red in the dusty sky. Like a brown mist the clouds of the earth billowed up on the slow summer wind. Between the sky and the earth, lines of men crawled along on their ropes, stretching from horizon to horizon, and still the stone was not in sight. Barakal stood and watched them. Below him the men strained for each step, their bodies curled around the ropes, their bodies covered with the dust. With each step they gave up a sigh like the earth exhaling.

The sun was dropping toward the horizon. Soon the moon would rise. He turned his back on the People at their filthy brutal work. He turned his back on the forward-creeping stone. He went up to the Pillar of the Sky, to watch the full moon rise, to see the perfection of the universe fulfilled.

Moloquin caused the People of the northern villages, with their great herds of oxen, to cull their herds and drive as many as they could spare to the Pillar of the Sky.

He also sent a few men away to the north, and to the east, and they went as far as the mountains in the north, and as far as the sea to the east, and there they found other people. But these people lived in huts of sod and wood, and fished in the sea, and made no pots, and used no metal, nor did they raise up stones; they had nothing that Moloquin wanted, and so he forgot them.

He himself went nowhere. He stayed always at the Pillar of the Sky, watching every stone put up, and around him he kept all those whom he needed for his comfort: Wahela, and his children, and a host of other people who cooked for him and wove cloth for him, made his pots and hauled his wood and water, so that at the Pillar of the Sky a sort of village appeared.

It was different from the other villages of the People. There Moloquin caused a forge to be built, like the forge in the Forest Village, and also a kiln, for firing pots. Before this, the women had been used to waiting until they had several pots to fire, and then they had merely dug a hole in the ground for the fire and put the pots on top, covered over with a roof of stones and clay, but now they had a stout little dome-shaped kiln of bricks.

There also, he built a sampo. Moloquin remembered how, at the Bloody Gathering, Shateel, sitting at the sampo, had nearly turned the women against him; he knew where in his new village words could collect against him. Therefore he made his sampo too big to be turned by old women sitting in a circle around it, singing an old song. This sampo was too great for that. It had wooden spokes that stuck out of the sides, and men walked in circles and pushed at the spokes, and so turned the sampo, and no one sang.

In the fall after the Bloody Gathering, Grela was threshing grain as usual, when she fell down against the threshing floor. She could not rise by herself, but had to be helped back to her longhouse, where she lay moaning in pain.

For a few days it seemed she would get well, but then the pain worsened, and the flesh of her leg began to turn black.

Knowing she was dying, she called all her daughters together, and her son, Sickle, and she said good-by to each of them, and gave each of them some of her goods. She berated her son again for his failure to join a society, told him no good would ever come of him, and sent them all away except Fergolin, her husband.

Fergolin came and sat down beside her, and they were silent a little while, which was not usual with Grela. At last she sighed and turned to him.

"Fergolin," she said, "you have been the best of husbands."

"Ah, Grela," he said, and wrung her hand.

"The best of husbands," she said. "But you have failed me."

"Ah? How so?"

"You have induced me to trust men, thinking all men like you, and so I trusted Moloquin."

Having said that, she allowed him to enclose her in his arms, and with her head on his shoulder, she died.

Not long afterwards the women of the New Village gathered around the sampo, to talk over who should become headwoman in

Grela's place, and while they sat there Moloquin came and squatted down behind them, and listened. With him there, they could not loosen their tongues, and so they named no headwoman.

He told them: "You do not need this sampo. Come to my village, I have there a great mill, more wonderful than this one, and I shall grind your grain for you there."

So the women carried their grain up over the slope, past the Pillar of the Sky, to Moloquin's Village, and there they ground it up. But Moloquin took the two stones of the sampo and he carried them to the river, and broke the stones, and threw them into the river, and the water rushed over them and they were gone.

After the Bloody Gathering, when her mother disappeared, Dehra had walked to the northern villages and looked among the People there, but Shateel was not among them. Then she went back to her own village, where her mother had been headwoman. Moloquin had given this village into Bahedyr's keeping and Bahedyr was hostile to her, but while Joba lived, Dehra was safe in the village.

Joba did not live long. Day to day she grew weaker, as if parts of her departed for Heaven long before the whole gave way. One night she called Dehra to her as she lay by her hearth in the longhouse, and asked the girl to hold her hand.

"Grandmother," Dehra said, "let me cook you a broth."

"I need no broth," said Joba. "You cannot pour a broth over a pile of old bones."

"Grandmother," Dehra said, because she was afraid, "you must fight for your life."

"Hah," Joba said, and gave a feeble laugh. "Fight for what? I have no life here. My life was lived in another place, I have no understanding of this place. The whole world has changed, and I do not belong here any more."

That night she died. In the morning Dehra packed her blanket, her pots, her knives of stone, her second dress into a leather sack, slung the sack over her shoulder and went away to find her mother.

She did not hope to find her. She thought Moloquin had killed her.

She went down from her own village, down across the valley, and climbed up the other side and went over the hills to the Pillar of the

Sky. There she found Moloquin's Village spread out along the eastern slope below the sacred precinct, and she circled around it, looking for the longhouses.

There were no longhouses. Instead of longhouses there were many little dome-shaped huts, some in groups and some separate from the others. There was a sort of a fence around the village, made of rolled brush like the fence around her home village, but it formed no continuous line and the edge of the village was hard to locate.

Confused, she went into the village and walked through the twisting spaces between the huts. It was midafternoon, and the screams and shrieks of little children burst through the air like flights of birds: a whole flock of children was playing on the midden, throwing stones at one another. She went by a tall hut made of stones, that gave off a heat so intense it wrinkled the air. The woman waiting by it gave her a look of suspicion, and she hurried away.

She could find no center to this place, no circle of women to welcome her, to give her a place here. Once she heard the rhythmic grinding of the sampo, and with a glad heart she ran toward the sound, but when she rounded a little hut and saw it, she was astonished. She had never seen such a thing. It was huge, sunken down in a pit in the ground, and two men trudged endlessly around and around to move it, leaning on spokes of wood set into the lips of the top stone. There were no women here at all.

Now she became afraid; she thought, *This place is under a spell*, and she began to steal along, peering anxiously around her, and taking care not to leave too many tracks or to step on shadows or throw her own shadow over anything else.

She came to the roundhouse, squatting in the center of all things, and there at last she heard the voices of women.

"Can you do nothing right? Bah! I shall send you all up to work on the stones. Do it properly!"

"Yes, Ana-Wahela-el."

Dehra crept to the door and peered in, and saw there in the roundhouse yard a great loom set up, such as her mother had used, and many women struggling to weave on it, while another sat perched to one side, a willow withy in her hand. Dehra shrank back, recognizing the woman with the switch from long ago, although she did not know her name.

She stood just outside the roundhouse and looked around her and thought again, *There is a spell on this place*. Nothing here was as it should be, and she could find no place in it for her. If her mother was here, Dehra had no way of finding her.

She went out of the village; she went up toward the Pillar of the Sky.

As she reached it, the sun was sinking, and the workmen were leaving. They stacked up their tools by the bank, and in groups and files they drifted away toward the village, talking. Dehra walked along the outside of the bank, crouching in the ditch sometimes to avoid being seen, until she came to an opening in the bank.

Two great stones stood on either side of the opening. She peered around them to look into the holy place. What she saw amazed her, and she drew a little closer, although there were still many people about; she stood between the two stones to look at the Pillar of the Sky.

It was smaller than Turnings-of-the-Year. Tighter, packed together, the stones fit closely together. It rose up before her in one intense thrust: she looked straight into the center of it, in through the first set of gateways, past the second, higher set, to the great central gate, her gaze carried steadily upward to the tremendous stone hanging there like a threshold of Heaven.

Around it, the men were raising another circle. They had put up nearly all the upright stones, smooth and shaped like great teeth, their surfaces rising cleanly to a level far above her head; and off to her left, by some feat of magic, they had lifted up more stones to the top of the uprights, making a sort of narrow roof that ran around the upper edge of the building.

She hung back, although she longed to go closer, to see more. The men were leaving. She told herself that in a moment they would all go and she could walk freely around this place and see it all.

Magic. There was power at work here, to raise those stones so high. She had sensed it in the village, but this was the center of it. From this place the magic spread like overflowing water, distorting and changing all that it touched. That was why the village had grown so cankered, because it lay so near this point of power.

She leaned against the stone at the entrance, watching the last of the men go. Her eyes travelled over the building again. The lintels that topped the uprights of the circle, away to her left, were so perfectly shaped that no gap appeared between them; each stone fit exactly against its neighbor. They followed the curve of the circle, every edge even, smooth, and precise.

What man could have done this? Surely it was the work of magic.

She went into the place. She no longer cared if any of the men were left. The magic had overwhelmed her. She had to go closer to it, to touch it, and so she walked forward, into the midst of the stones.

The sun had warmed them. She laid her hand on one smooth surface, seeing, from this close, the subtle mix of colors in the stone. She went on, until she stood before the great Gateway, until she stood at the center of the place.

She had expected to sense some great rush of power, a whirling of forces, but instead as she stood there she felt nothing. Silence: stillness. The Gateway rose up before her, leading her gaze toward the sky. She tipped her head back to look straight up. Then suddenly all the force took her, sweeping up from below through her up toward the center of Heaven, and she understood, although she had no words for it, where she was.

She flung her arms out, to keep from falling, and as she swayed and lost her balance, she called on names her mother had given her, names of power.

"Rael, Birdwoman! Help me! Mother—Shateel—" another name, lost in the deeps of her memory. "Ael! Ael!"

"Ho!" a voice shouted, nearby.

Dehra fell. Feet ran toward her. Frantic, she started to rise, to flee, but she tripped herself up and fell again.

"Are you hurt?" A young man dropped to one knee beside her. "Who are you?"

She gaped up into his face; she had never seen him before. A smooth, pale face, with wide eyes. She said, "I am not hurt. My name is Dehra."

"Barakal," another man called, breathless, the voice failing. "Barakal, do you need me?"

The young man turned to call over his shoulder. "All is well, Opa-on." He smiled down at Dehra. "You should be going home, girl—the sun is down."

"I have no home," she said.

She stood. The young man smiled at her again, but he was going, returning to his friend. Uncertain, she stood where she was, watching him join an old man, who hobbled, crook-backed, in between two of the stones, and sat down heavily on the ground.

"I am done, Barakal," this old man said, and he began to cough, and from his lips a torrent of blood burst.

Dehra gasped. She took two steps nearer.

Barakal said, "Rest, Opa-On—you hurt yourself when you do this. Here is some water. I have the blanket and the bear robe—" he raced away, back outside the stone ring.

Dehra went a little closer, watching the old man. The blood had dribbled down the front of his shirt. Like a baby, he could not keep himself clean. The course of life had come full round in him: like the baby just coming into the world, he was feeble and helpless as he went out of it. Yet he looked at her with a cheerful gaze.

He said, "Girl, what do you do here?"

"I am looking for my mother," she said.

"Your mother! There are no women here, at the Pillar of the Sky—this is a man's place, girl."

"I am sorry," she said. "I meant no harm. It is wonderful here."

"Yes," said the old man, and then the young man appeared again, carrying a blanket and a bearskin robe, and fussy as a mother he covered up the old man, tucked the blanket around him, gave him water in a jug to drink, and sat down beside him.

"Opa-on," he said, "you have chosen a clear night to die in."

The old man chuckled under his breath. "I am a stupid one, my boy. I need a straight path to Heaven."

Then again he erupted into his bloody coughing, and the youth Barakal bent over him, tender and kind. Dehra went up beside him and squatted down, her arms around her knees; she longed for such gentleness as these two used toward one another.

The old man's fit eased. He laid his hand on Barakal's arm.

"She is looking for her mother."

Barakal looked at her, his eyebrows rounded. "Her mother. Who is she?"

"My mother's name is Shateel."

At that, both of the men looked sharply up, and the old man gave a low choked cry that spattered blood on Dehra's hands. He wiped his lips. "Shateel!" he said, and peered at her. "Shateel's child!"

"Did you know my mother?"

Barakal shook his head. "By name only."

The old man said, "I knew her once. Not well. Is she alive still?"

"She disappeared," Dehra said. "After the Bloody Gathering."

The old man lowered his head slightly. Barakal curved his arm around his shoulders, but he spoke to Dehra.

"You must ask Moloquin. He knows."

Dehra shook her head. "I dare not ask Moloquin."

"Then I shall ask him for you."

"No, no!" Dehra drew closer, putting out her hand to him, as if he might leap up at once and run to Moloquin. "Do not, I beg you. Do not let him know I am—that I am seeking her."

Barakal stared at her, his brow furrowed, his mouth pursed. Then beside him the old man began to cough again, and the youth turned to him, bending over him, murmuring, and thereafter Dehra was of no interest to him. She went away a little, to look at the stones.

Fergolin leaned his back against a stone. He had moved so that he was facing the northwestern part of the building, the part that was finished. Barakal covered him with a blanket and gave him water to drink, but Fergolin wanted nothing any more.

The world was fading away. As the light died and the stars began to burn and the canopy of Heaven grew brighter and more vivid above him, so he felt the dross of life falling from him, leaving behind the pure and infinite soul. He had come to the foot of the pathway home.

Around him Barakal moved, doing this, doing that, a heavy shadow. Even an annoyance, now, the beloved boy: left behind.

The girl, too, annoyed him, ruffling the serenity of his passing, making him worried. Shateel's daughter! What had happened to Shateel? What had happened to all of them? He remembered how, when he heard of the Bloody Gathering, he had looked up at the sky, wondering why no star had warned him of this catastrophe.

Before him the white radiance shone, drawing him closer; yet now, disturbed by these annoyances, he struggled a little, resisting it. He thought again of the girl, of Barakal, of Shateel who had vanished, of the People whose lives had been overturned, of the stars that had not warned him. His flesh was heavy and dull around him, opaque to the truth. His flesh connected him to the troubles of the People. And why had the stars not given him a sign?

Barakal came again, with water. He tried to turn aside, but he was weak, and to allow the youth his moment of seeming to help, he let a few drops into his throat. Now all his flesh quaked, dissolving in the radiance, and the blood burst from its channels and flowed forth in a river from him.

Barakal sat beside him, and encircled him with his arms, and leaned his young head on Fergolin's shoulder, and wept. He held only the old man's flesh. Only the cage. The soul was freeing itself, bit by bit; the soul was spreading out its wings; the soul was trembling on the brink of flight.

Now he knew why the stars had not told him that Moloquin would overthrow the whole order of things. As he stood poised on the beginning of the pathway, he saw that Moloquin changed nothing. There was no catastrophe. Whatever Moloquin did might cause loud noises and small calamities for a while, but in the end, all would be as it had to be, as it had been before. There was no real change. The corruption of order that seemed like change, the evil of change, would always fail.

Understanding that, he saw the blazing light before him grow brighter yet, swallowing up all his vision, the summoning voice of Heaven. His flesh was dying, falling away from him, and he was leaving it behind. Leaving behind with it the illusion of freedom. Leaving also the illusion of being separate. The illusion of being—

Barakal held the old man all through the night, although Fergolin was dead before the moon rose.

For a while, the girl moved around the Pillar of the Sky, and then she found some place to shelter and she too was still. The night rolled over them.

With Fergolin in his arms, he sat there, staring blindly into the face of Heaven, and struggled with his soul. He held the old man tight, as if he could keep him from the pathway; his soul struggled to follow, as if feet of flesh and blood and bone could tread that sacred road of light.

Why? His mind hammered at the thing with words, and yet the thing would not become words. Would not dissolve into ideas. *Why are we given life, given youth and strength and understanding, just to have it all seep away?* Like a stone, the thing. Like a stone that he battered with his mind and could not wear at all, not so much as a trickle of dust. He put his face against the dead flesh and wept.

The moon rose, horned with envy, its face corrupted with its fierce desires. It passed away overhead. He could not sleep. When his mind quieted, the thoughts rose again, irresistible, thrusting up above the surface: *Why? Why did Fergolin have to leave me? Why must I die too?* Then all his mind was a tossing, seething tumult, all his feelings loosed, pain and rage, terror and love and reverence, set free to struggle together, and he could not sleep at all, his mind and body at the mercy of his passions.

So when the sun appeared again, Barakal was awake, and his mind was worn down from the long struggle, worn so smooth no passion could fix itself to its surface. Then, when the sun rose, he was like a still pool of water, that gave back exactly what it saw.

The sun came up behind him. He felt its warmth and saw the first light streaking up through the sky, and he crept away from Fergolin's empty and horrible body and turned. The Great Gateway was between him and the brightest part of the horizon, and he moved until the Gateway framed it. There was thick fog all along the horizon. The light streamed up into the sky, but the sun herself was only a pale disk through the grey.

She reached the thinning edge of the fog, and suddenly the light brightened, her full power burst through, and he flinched back, throwing his arm across his face. Before his eyes, the disk shone a moment longer, a perfect circle.

Straightening, his arm falling to his sides, he cast his eyes around him and saw the circle of the uprights, with the lintel-beams closing their tops, and that too he saw was a perfect circle.

Yet it was not finished. He saw the shape although it was not even there before him, because the circle showed itself in every part; it was there complete in every part. Because he saw part of the curve, he saw it all.

At once he saw that this was true of all circles.

He had lived here all his life, seen every stone rise, known his place all his life, and yet he had never wondered deeply about it. He walked forward into the center of the building, wondering how Moloquin had known where to put the stones.

He did then what he had seen Moloquin do, long ago. He sank down on his haunches and drew a circle with his finger in the dust.

With his finger he had merely to trace the outline, but Moloquin could not have done that. Moloquin had to do something else, because the circle of Pillar of the Sky was so large. Yet it was in all other ways like the circle that Barakal had drawn in the dust. Then Barakal saw that the circles both began the same, with a point at the center, and grew larger by expanding steadily in all directions, and he knew that a man might measure a circle by knowing how far it was from the center to any point on the edge.

He stood up, shaking. He had been given some knowledge,

some understanding: the Pillar of the Sky had spoken to him, as it had before. It seemed small, useless knowledge, but he was shaking from head to foot; he knew this was power, somehow, this lore. Why had he been given this powerful understanding? He raised his eyes from the circle at the dust of his feet, looked long at the stone curve suspended in the sky, and turned his gaze to the horizon.

That was the circle. That was the curve that Moloquin had represented in the Pillar of the Sky.

His hands were trembling. He followed the horizon with his eyes, sweeping the circle of the building. Here Moloquin had raised up his own world in stones.

That was why the stones aligned to show the motion of the stars; any circle would have worked as well.

Yet there was another thing to do. A man could strive for mastery over the world, as Moloquin did. Or a man could strive for understanding. They were opposite things: to master the world, a man had to be within it, part of it; but to understand, a man could take himself out of it, see with a quiet mind, as if from afar, and thus survive.

With a piece of rope and a wooden stake, a man could measure out the whole world. Measure the sun, too, which was a circle. Measure all things. Perhaps, in the end, come to measure himself.

Bahedyr no longer carried his own spear; he had a boy, one of his sons, to carry it for him, the haft sheathed in bronze and worked in cunning designs. He himself wore cuffs and a collar of bronze. When he came into Moloquin's Village, there by the Pillar of the Sky, he had his men go on ahead of him with horns and flutes and drums to draw the People together and turn their heads toward him, and when he walked through their midst, they cheered him until the skies rang with it.

This made him smile, and he puffed himself up, taking great pride in the acclaim, taking some comfort too, because he had that to tell Moloquin which Moloquin would not like to hear.

With his son before him holding aloft his spear, he walked slowly in through the uproar and activity of Moloquin's Village. The people here no longer lived in longhouses, and only Moloquin himself lived in the roundhouse; all the others lived in huts, men and women together in couples, with their children. So the place was disorderly.

Instead of one great yard there were many, and instead of one place where the people worked, there were many. They all did Moloquin's bidding, and at the center of it Moloquin sat and watched and gave orders and did nothing himself.

Knowing this, knowing also that Moloquin would be angry when he heard what Bahedyr had come to tell him, Bahedyr walked slowly and let the shouted praises of the people fall on him like the nourishing rain. He went on a winding path among the little round huts, and the children came running after him, laughing and cheering him. The women looked up from their spinning and weaving and called his name. The men, just back from the day's work at the Pillar of the Sky, resting in their doorways, raised their hands to him.

Bahedyr spoke to those he knew, who were many, and so, although the sun had been high in the sky when he came into the village, the light had set when he reached the roundhouse.

There he found Moloquin sitting on the ground outside his door, while his women made the evening meal ready; the smell of roasting meat perfumed the air, and there was also the tang of beer brewing. Wahela's voice rose strident with orders above the bustle of the other women—Wahela herself did nothing, but walked up and down, clapping her hands together, giving reproof to the lazy and stupid.

Bahedyr came before the chieftain and at a nod from Moloquin he sat down cross-legged opposite him. His boy with the spear stood behind him, and the others of Bahedyr's men formed a crescent shape around him.

Bahedyr was glad of their presence; he felt stronger for their presence; he quaked to think what Moloquin would say to him, when he had to tell him his news.

First there were other things.

"The harvest is going well," he said. "The women have gotten in the beans and dried them, and soon they will cut and thresh the grain. There will be enough to feed us all and also add several baskets to the stores."

Moloquin nodded. He was leaning against a backrest, his shoulders propped up, which made him look fat and slack. Wahela brought him a cup of beer and he drank some and put it down, and nodded to her to serve Bahedyr also.

They talked about the gardens around Bahedyr's Village; Moloquin believed the time was coming when the village would have to be moved, but Bahedyr insisted the ground was still fruitful. They talked about fishing for salmon; Moloquin wanted Bahedyr to take some of his men away to the streams to the north and catch fish out of the autumn run, but Bahedyr was loathe to do so, since the weather was always bad.

Moloquin chuckled at him. "The fish are clever, Bahedyr. The People are lazy and soft. They go out to fish when the sun is warm and the air is light, and when the rain comes they go home and fish no more, but the fish run when the rain comes and the water runs cold."

"We do not need to fish," Bahedyr said.

He knew many of the men who surrounded him did so because he got them out of working. If he told them to work, he feared many would go elsewhere.

"The fish are there," Moloquin said. "You and your People must be like fish, loving the cold and the wet, to catch them. Get men of the Salmon Leap Society. I have many stones now, there is no need to haul any more for a while, and therefore I need fewer men here to build."

That brought them face to face with Bahedyr's unpleasant news. Bahedyr gulped, and in his face Moloquin read the evil; his eyes sharpened, and he leaned forward.

"What is it?"

Loudly, Bahedyr said, "I shall talk to the Salmon Leap masters, they—"

"Bahedyr," Moloquin said. "Tell me the truth."

The spearman met his chieftain's gaze, and for a long moment there was a kind of struggle between them; Bahedyr wanted to forget what it was he knew but Moloquin would not let him turn aside from it, and so, in the end, reluctantly, Bahedyr gave up his knowledge.

"You said you had many stones now. Are there enough?"

"Enough?" Moloquin said. "What do you mean? Enough to finish the Pillar of the Sky? Not at all."

Bahedyr cleared his throat. Moloquin's hard stare dragged the words from him. "There have to be. There are no more stones at the High Hill large enough for your purposes."

Moloquin stared at him; there seemed no change in his expression. At last he said, "They need not be so large. Not all of them. The beams are much smaller than the uprights."

"There are no more stones long enough for uprights," said Bahedyr.

"I only need a few more uprights." Moloquin stood up; he turned to look toward his holy place, standing tall as if he could see it over the swarm and babble of his village. "Only a handful more, I think."

"The only stones left at the High Hill are shorter even than I am," said Bahedyr.

Moloquin swung toward him. The slack, fat man who had greeted Bahedyr was gone now, and in his place stood the old Moloquin, harsh and hard, moving ever, restlessly moving around the fire, back and forth, his gaze like a flight of arrows.

"I must have stones. There are stones elsewhere."

"On the northern downs," said Bahedyr slowly. "There are some stones there, still lying in the earth."

"Then bring those."

Bahedyr licked his lips. He glanced back over his shoulder at the men clustered tight behind him, and saw in their faces the dread he himself felt. He confronted Moloquin again.

"I went there. The People have been pulling up those stones for generations, and they are nearly all gone also. There are a few cracked, weak stones, that no one has wanted."

Moloquin wheeled away from him. He strode off across his yard, the women scurrying out of his way, his children dodging out of his way, and spun around and walked back toward Bahedyr, and his face was black with rage, and his arms swung like clubs, his hands fists. He strode up to Bahedyr.

"Find me stones!"

"Opa-Moloquin-on, there are no more stones anywhere. We cannot make stones where none exist—"

"Bah!" Moloquin put his hand on Bahedyr's chest and thrust him backward, wobbling, two long steps, and he himself took two steps after, so that he crowded Bahedyr even further, pushing him back into the pack of his men. "Find me those stones, Bahedyr—"

"But there are none!"

"Don't lie to me!"

Again he drove the flat of his hand into Bahedyr's chest and again Bahedyr staggered backward, scattering his men away behind him, while his chief leaned hard at his front. Moloquin shouted, "I know where there are more stones, Bahedyr! You do also! Bring me the stones, Bahedyr!"

Bahedyr goggled at him. "Where?"

"At the Turnings-of-the-Year!"

Now all the men gasped, and Bahedyr straightened, resisting Moloquin's push. "What are you talking about?"

"There are great enough stones at the Turnings-of-the-Year," Moloquin said. "Bring them to me."

"You cannot do that," Bahedyr said. "Those stones are sacred. They belong only where they are."

Moloquin let him finish, let the other men murmur in agreement, lifted his eyes to scan them, brought his gaze back to Bahedyr, and said, "Bring me those stones, Bahedyr. I have made you what you are, and I will unmake you if you do not serve me. Go."

He turned his back. Amazed, Bahedyr saw that he would listen no more to arguments against his orders. The spearman stood gawking into space; he gave a sudden shiver from his head to his feet, as if a magic spell settled over him. Behind him his men were whispering to one another. None dared speak to Moloquin, who was sitting down again where he had been when Bahedyr first came to him— sitting down on his mat, his back to his backrest, sitting down into a fat, aging, ordinary man. Bahedyr turned and went away.

In the morning, Wahela sat in the yard of the roundhouse, ordering the lesser women around; they were spreading out the blankets in the sun, to air them and make them smell fresh. Wahela sat on a pile of rush mats, a cup of beer beside her and her youngest daughter in her lap, and watched for the women to catch them if they made mistakes.

As she sat there, feeding the child bits of honey and seeds, Bahedyr came into the yard.

He looked all around him, and he came to her. Wahela frowned to see this; she knew that Moloquin had argued with Bahedyr about something, and now Moloquin was sunk into a foul temper that nothing seemed to pierce. Bahedyr came and sat beside her, laying his spear down on his far side from her, and for a moment he sat there without saying anything.

Wahela would not say anything; she knew he was here to get something from her.

At last he turned to her. "Wahela," he said, "we have come a long way from the hut by the stream."

Wahela gave him a deep look. Lifting up her daughter, she kissed her and sent her away to the roundhouse. Then she faced Bahedyr.

"A long way? It's not such a long way, we could walk there in two days."

"Wahela, you know what I mean."

She tossed her head, looking elsewhere—really, she was keeping watch out for Moloquin. "I know nothing. I am a mere woman."

"Wahela—" he crept a little closer to her. "I need your help."

"Ah?"

"He has asked me to do that which may destroy us all, Wahela."

She grunted at him. Turning to face him, she said, "*Ask* you. I have not seen him *ask* anything of anyone for many years now, Bahedyr. He gave you orders."

Bahedyr frowned at her. Her gaze lingered on him; she saw now how drawn his face was, how weary and tormented, and she thought, *He is indeed much distressed.*

"What is it, Bahedyr?"

"Wahela, he wants us to take stones from Turnings-of-the-Year to build the Pillar of the Sky."

"What?"

"That's what he wants."

Her mouth formed a round, soundless sigh. Her gaze moved around the yard again, toward the roundhouse, seeking for Moloquin. "That is mad," she said. She thought of the Turnings-of-the-Year, the stones that had stood there since the beginning, and a sudden burst of rage warmed her: how did he dare uproot those holy old stones?

At the same moment, she knew she would do nothing to prevent it.

She faced Bahedyr again. "Now, what do you want of me, hah? You want me to stand up to him which you dare not do, is that it?"

"You are his wife, Wahela."

"No! I am not his wife. His wife is—was—Shateel. She told him he did evil, at the Bloody Gathering. Where is she now, Bahedyr? No. I will do nothing."

"Wahela." He leaned toward her, he even put his hand on her arm, and his eyes shone with desperation. "I cannot force my people to do this thing."

"Leave here, Bahedyr."

"If he persists in this—"

At these words, she saw a motion in the roundhouse, just inside the door, and swiftly she moved away from Bahedyr, dragging her mats after her, putting room between her and him. "No!" she said, furious, and threw a fierce look at him.

He had not seen Moloquin standing there. His desperate panic still gripped him; he came on hands and knees after her, saying, "Wahela, you must help me!"

She thrust out her hand to ward him off. She lifted her gaze and there saw Moloquin, standing in the roundhouse door.

He was staring at them. He had seen them. All her nerves tingling, she put her hand in her lap and looked away. At her look, Bahedyr twisted, and he too saw the chieftain, and with a sigh he rose and went to greet him.

"Welcome, Opa-Moloquin-on!"

In his fear he used the words of one greeting a visitor; his voice boomed with false confidence. Moloquin nodded to him.

"Very welcome, Bahedyr. I have a task for you today."

"I live to serve my chief."

Moloquin's mouth stretched into a smile. "Very good, Bahedyr. Now, I charge you with this: take your men with their spears and their ornaments, and go out to the west a little way, not far, and go to the high point, there by the old sycamore, and watch for people coming."

Wahela got up and went to him; she wanted to show Bahedyr that she was not really afraid of Moloquin after all, and she leaned against him and stroked his beard.

"Who is coming, Moloquin?"

"Buras Ram," Moloquin said. "The trader from the west, from the mines. Bahedyr, you have your task, now go."

The spearman bowed down. Round, empty words spilled from his lips. He took his spear and went away.

Wahela still leaned on her lover's chest. She said, "The trader will have metal for us."

Moloquin said, "What did you say to Bahedyr?"

"Nothing. We spoke of the old days, in the Forest Village."

"Oh? Is that all?"

"Certainly." She tossed her head, giving him a long look through the corners of her eyes. "What else would I have to talk about with Bahedyr?"

"Who knows?" said Moloquin. "Now come with me, I have work for you also, before Buras Ram comes."

Buras Ram had begun to think he would never find Moloquin's country. With six slaves and two freemen of his people, he had left the mines by the coast several days before and travelled steadily to the east, through shrub forest, through swamps and over stony ridges, and with each day the land seemed wilder and the path they followed was harder to trace. He could hardly believe that his brother Harus Kum had brought heavily laden sledges down these brush-choked slopes and packed stands of trees.

With each sundown, his band complained the more. They wanted to go home again. In this strange place there seemed to be demons everywhere, waiting to fall on the unwary. The water tasted strange in the streams and ponds where they drank; they had no luck in hunting the game.

"There is a god here who hates us," said his people. "Some god here means us evil. We want to go home."

Buras Ram said, "One more day. If we do not find them in one more day, we shall turn around and go back."

When the next sundown came, there was still no sign of Moloquin and his People.

"Are we going home now? Shall we go home now?" they asked him.

"One more day," he said, and they howled and wept and threatened to go back by themselves.

"Go back, then," he said. "I am going that way," and he pointed to the east. "One more day."

They grumbled; they cursed him under their tongues, but without him to lead them they were afraid to go anywhere, even back home. The next dawn found them all trudging away to the east.

They had left behind the tangled brushy forest and the rough hills. Now they travelled over a desolate rolling country, where the few trees stood up like guardsmen, and the wind keened like a harp in the grass. Grey clouds crowded the sky. In the evenings, a sinister vapor rose from every hollow, every low ground, and the wind drifted it off across the wide expanses of the grass, as if to hide away this land from the strangers travelling into it.

Near sundown, as he walked along at the head of his train, he realized with a start that someone was watching him.

He spun around, stopping in his tracks, and scanned the low featureless slopes around him. There seemed no one but he himself and his servants, nothing at all showing above the wind-blown grass but an old half-killed tree on the ridge to his left, but as he stood there with his tongue thick with fear, a man with a spear stood up beside the tree.

Buras Ram's people all screamed. They ran together into a little pack, terrified. By the tree, the man with the spear waved his weapon over his head, and from all around him, standing up out of the grass as if they had grown there like grass, other men appeared.

Buras Ram said, "Steady—steady—they are friends."

He held out one hand, palm forward, in the gesture of friendship, but his knees were banging together and his heart thumped. He hoped they were friends. If they were not, there was no chance for him and his men. He stood watching the line of spearmen walk down toward him.

"They are Moloquin's," he said, with a burst of relief; he saw the copper ornaments on their wrists and around their necks, and abruptly his throat loosened. He began to laugh, turned to his men to reassure them with a look, and raised his hand in a merry wave to the spearmen. Now he could even recognize one of them, the leader, magnificent in a breastplate of beads and little copper links. Smiling, he waited to be taken to Moloquin.

When Bahedyr brought the trader and his band to the village the sun was still high, and therefore Moloquin was at the Pillar of the Sky. Bahedyr led Buras Ram there.

He had grown used to the place, after so many years around it; he led the foreigner up the little slope and through the gap in the embankment, and when he heard the trader gasp, he thought it was from the sight of Moloquin who sat on a covered litter at the center of the place, supervising the work. But when he turned, he saw that Buras Ram was gazing up at the Pillar of the Sky itself, his mouth open.

"What work of the gods is this?"

Bahedyr smiled; his chest expanded, he felt himself growing larger, large as the stones. Buras Ram looked around them with eyes wide and awed as a little child's. He peered up at the tremendous gateways, and walked away a little to see how the men were raising up a lintel to the outer circle—the wooden frame was already half-way high enough, the stone resting on top in its cradle of logs; as Bahedyr and the trader stood there, the workmen bent to the levers, a hoarse voice called, "Heave!" and with a slow desperate gathering of their strength the lever-men pried the stone up a finger's breadth, and the others rushed to fit more logs under it. Buras Ram sighed.

The face he turned toward Bahedyr was still marked with his astonishment. He said, "To what god do you raise this monument?"

Bahedyr had no answer for that. Buras Ram spoke his language badly, and used many of his own words in it, and Bahedyr had no understanding of what he had said. He took the trader by the arm and led him to Moloquin.

The chieftain sat in his litter, under a broad roof of cloth that shaded him from the sun. Wahela had decorated the litter with braids and streamers and piled it up with furs and blankets, so that it seemed snug as a cave. Moloquin sat leaning forward, drawing circles with his finger on a piece of hide; the youth Barakal squatted before him; they were talking together about whatever it was they drew on the hide, but since they used their fingers, no one else could see what it was.

As Buras Ram approached, the youth drew back, turning, and Moloquin straightened. He nodded to Barakal to go.

"Buras Ram," he said. From his tongue the alien language came easily, and Bahedyr backed off a little.

The trader bowed down before Moloquin. "Great is the chieftain of the People of the Stones!"

Bahedyr stood watching as the two men exchanged greetings. He saw how Buras Ram bowed and lowered himself; Bahedyr turned and looked around him again at the Pillar of the Sky, and tried to see it as this stranger had. It was so familiar to him that it seemed almost ordinary now. Yet this stranger, with his mysterious powers and wide knowledge, had stood in awe before it—even now, he debased himself to Moloquin because of it.

He thought, *Perhaps it is such a thing as Moloquin says. Perhaps it is worth the stealing of stones from Turnings-of-the-Year.*

But when he thought of that, and thought of his people and how they would hear such words, and thought also of the spirits that clustered thick around the Turnings-of-the-Year, investing the stones, the earth itself, with their resounding presence, he knew that to take any of those stones would be to shake the whole world. Again the dread swept over him. His choice was impossible: he could refuse Moloquin, or he could betray the Turnings-of-the-Year. He went away, full of trouble.

Buras Ram said, "This is magnificent."

He sat in the shade of the litter, facing Moloquin; on the black bearskin between them lay several bits of work from Hems' forge in the Forest Village. "Did you make these?"

Moloquin shook his head. The trader was inspecting a small bowl, smooth and shining, the edge worked in a zigzag design. "The man you taught came back and built a forge, and he has taught others."

"The work is excellent." Buras Ram tapped the edge of the bowl with his finger. "Nothing we do in our own forges is superior to this."

Moloquin said nothing. Part of him wanted to believe this praise, but the ruling part of his mind knew that Buras Ram was here to get something from him, and so everything he said was suspect.

"I have brought gifts for you," Buras Ram said, "although I fear they shall not find favor with one surrounded by such wonderful things as you are."

Now Moloquin was sure he was being flattered, and he leaned back, his eyes narrow. He looked out from the litter, out to the Pillar of the Sky; as he lifted his head, the men raising the next lintel cried out, "Ho, ho, ho!" and heaved up the stone another fraction of the way. Beyond, outside the circle, other men were smoothing and shaping a stone, and the continual thud of their mauls sounded like a drumbeat behind all the other noise.

He said, "You admire the Pillar of the Sky."

"Is that what it is called?"

"Among other things."

"It will be a splendid temple, fit for the most mighty of the gods. What god do you worship here?"

Moloquin blinked at him. He had thought he knew this language but now Buras Ram was using words that meant nothing to him; he had to struggle to keep his lofty look. Needing some answer, he turned to point behind him, out between the two lower gateways, out toward the entry stones and the gap in the bank, and said, "There the sun rises, on the day she is greatest."

Buras Ram nodded, his face smooth with understanding, although what it was he understood Moloquin did not know. Watching the foreigner, he had the sudden sense of being the whole world away from him, as if Buras Ram sat on the horizon, and Moloquin on the far horizon.

"I hesitate to present my poor tokens of our love and friendship to one whose wealth is so enormous." Buras Ram turned to take his pack, which lay behind him, and pulled it around in front. Untying the strings, he folded back the flap and removed, first, two bars of copper.

Moloquin said nothing. After they had tried to buy him off with the chest full of trash, he had told them he wanted five bars of copper. He wondered if the trader's fawning was the start of trying to deny him his due.

"And we have this," said Buras Ram, and took another bar of metal from his sack.

At first Moloquin thought this too was copper, but he saw how it caught the sunlight, and he bent forward and took the bar, which was only half as large as the copper bars, and turned to let the sunlight fall on it. At once his heart lusted for it. Smooth and glowing, this metal was the very color of the sun. He pressed his fingernail against the surface and it dented. Soft and fine, it would take the most sinuous shape, the most delicate form.

He said, "What is this?"

Buras Ram was smiling at him. "It comes from a mine on another island, west of here. It is the royal metal, fit for one who commands Heaven and earth."

More flattery. Yet he could not bring himself to give up the shining bar. He turned again to place it in the sun.

"Have you more?"

"No more. This is hard to find, hard to mine. Only a little of it exists."

Moloquin's gaze remained on the glowing metal. He knew that Buras Ram would want something in return, but he knew already that whatever it was the trader wanted, Moloquin would give it to him, for the sake of this shining stuff. Buras Ram was talking again.

He said, "This gold does not darken with age. Nothing destroys it. It is perfect as the body of a god. From the east come many traders seeking it, all men want it, it is the emblem of the greatest men everywhere."

"Ah."

"It is yours. You alone are worthy of it."

"Ah."

"In return, we ask only that you help us. We need your gracious help, to keep our mines working, to support our colony."

"Ah?"

"We need food. We cannot raise enough food to feed all our workers."

Moloquin lifted his gaze from the gold and fastened his attention on Buras Ram. In his guts, a knot formed, twisting tighter and tighter, and an old voice woke in his brain and began to feed words into his ears. He said, "You have your cattle."

"We want to bring more people here. To open up more mines. The land there will not support too many, there is no place for adequate gardens and grazing land for the cattle."

"You can hunt."

"Not for the numbers we mean to bring here. In my brother's time, another chief of your people supplied him with grain and beans."

Ladon's voice said, *You are my son.*

"My people work hard to grow enough to feed us," Moloquin said.

"Your people are rich."

"We are rich sometimes, but sometimes, when the harvest is bad—"

Take the gold, give up the grain. You are my son. The harvest will be great again this year. You can take the risk. You are my son.

Buras Ram said, "The more people we bring to the mines, the more tribute we can give to you, our overlord."

Moloquin gathered in his breath; he raised his eyes, struggling with himself, but the gold lay close to his hand, warm in the sun, glowing with the sun's own power, and the word that Buras Ram had used—the admission he had made—that Moloquin was their *overlord*—

He said, "I shall think on it, Buras Ram."

"The king of the People of the Stones is most great."

From outside the litter came another shout: "Ho, ho, ho!" Both men turned and stooped to see the lintel pried up another tiny bit. Buras Ram swung back to Moloquin.

"Let me walk through your temple. I must see for myself what a wonder you are making here, with the help and mercy of the gods."

"As you wish," said Moloquin.

The trader backed away on hands and knees, bowing and murmuring compliments, and went away. Moloquin sat in the litter, slumped down, his eyes on empty space.

He did not struggle with himself. His struggle was over. He would give Buras Ram whatever he wanted. Like Ladon, he would give away the safeguards of his people for the symbols of power. He despised himself for it, yet he could not do otherwise. All the rest of the day he sat slumped in the litter, and not once did he lift his gaze to see the Pillar of the Sky.

As soon as Moloquin came back, Wahela saw that he was in a black mood.

She sent their children away to another part of the roundhouse; she called to the women who served her to bring beer and meat for him, and she herself arranged his backrest and his bearskins and blankets so that he could sit down comfortably. Still his temper did not lighten. He prowled around the roundhouse, moving from the light at the center, where the lamp burned, out to the darkness, and back again, and he would not meet her eyes.

He had brought a heavy sack with him, which he had left beside his place at the center of the roundhouse. While he was off somewhere else, she knelt down quickly beside it and slid her hand in, and she felt the bars of metal inside.

The trader had brought him the copper then. She wondered why he was so angry.

He came back; she served him herself, sending away all the others. He ate only a little. He drank more beer than he did usually, and a raw flush came into his cheeks; his eyes glittered.

Abruptly, with no warning, he turned to her and said, "What did you say to Bahedyr this morning?"

"To Bahedyr!" she had to struggle to remember. "Nothing. He was only being friendly to me."

Moloquin leaned toward her. "Don't lie to me, Wahela!"

"I am not lying. I—"

He struck her in the face. She fell; her face hurt, and a hot rush of terror began in her guts and spread up through her body. She cried, "Moloquin, Moloquin, I did nothing wrong!"

He was coming at her, his face bound up with fury, and she flung up one arm to protect herself. "Moloquin, please—"

His fist descended on her. She gulped, dazed, all the sense knocked whirling in her head. Blurry-eyed, she felt herself pulled to her feet, and she threw out her hands, trying to catch her balance, and by accident she hit him.

He roared. His blows came hard and fast around her head. She screamed; she wept, struggling to protect herself, but he beat down her arms, he knocked her down and yanked her up again, his hands pounding on her. She screamed again. No one came. No one could help her. Another blow dashed the awareness from her. She sank down senseless to the ground.

Even when she lay unconscious at his feet, he had to struggle to keep from hitting her.

He went down on one knee beside her. Already there were bruises forming on the side of her face. He took her limp hand and pressed it to his mouth, to his cheek.

It was her fault. She should never have talked to Bahedyr like that. Letting him touch her. She was Moloquin's; she belonged to him. He could do what he wanted with her.

Still his heart sickened to see what he had done to her.

She breathed; her heart beat strongly. He gathered her into his arms and laid her down tenderly on the bed they shared, the pile of bearskin robes, the mats and blankets where they made one body of their two bodies, where they made other bodies with their two bodies. Holding her hand, watching her face swell and grow misshapen from his savage blows, he lifted her limp hand and struck himself across the cheek.

That did no good.

She stirred a little, her lips parting, and murmured. He leaned close to her; he whispered, "It was not I, it was Ladon." Suddenly his eyes burned. He longed for tears, for the freedom of tears, but he was too old a man to cry, too old, too corrupt, and too sad.

He lay down beside her; he gathered her into his arms. The

smell of her blood reached his nostrils. When she woke, he would show her the bar of gold, he would promise her ornaments made of it. He would cover her bruised flesh with new flesh of metal. He promised her this. With his eyes closed, he promised her never to hurt her again. With his eyes closed, so that he could not see what he had done to her. What Ladon had done to her. He hated Ladon. He held Wahela tight, to keep Ladon from her.

In the dark, Wahela awoke.

The lamp had gone out. She could smell the stink of the oil and knew that the wick had been allowed to burn out, and the first thing she knew, as she woke, was a vague irritation that no one had snuffed the light.

After that, she felt the pain in her face.

That brought her memory back. She remembered him hitting her, and the pain burst through the side of her face, the bone, the teeth, her eye, her forehead.

He lay next to her. She could feel him there, all along her side, his warmth, his body there next to her, as if he had done nothing at all. Lying there like a lover who had done nothing but love. Rigid as a piece of stone, she lay there aware of him beside her, hating him.

But she had no one except him. All she had depended on him.

Stiff, she lay there, thinking she might kill him, remembering where the knife was, or his axe: that would be the choicest revenge, to slaughter him with his own axe. As she lay there thinking of his death, he moved a little, there next to her, and she knew he was coming awake.

She moved sharply away from him, putting empty space between them, and lay still.

In the darkness, he said, "Wahela."

"Leave me alone," she said, and sobbed, half in fury, half in grief.

"Wahela." His voice was soft with pleading, and his hand touched her arm.

"Leave me alone!"

They lay there a while longer, and she thought of murder, and she thought of living without Moloquin—without his power, without his prestige and wealth. Her body relaxed somewhat, and she sighed.

At that, he touched her again, and spoke words of love to her, begging her forgiveness, promising her whatever she wanted. She listened and did not push his hand away. Her face hurt, but she would make him regret it, in small ways, over and over. She would relish that. She turned toward him, and he kissed her, his lips tender, his hands gentle.

She told herself there was no other who could deal with him. She let him caress her, thinking that none but she could tame him like this. If she hurt, yet she could hurt him, too. She was his, but he was hers, and even the bruises on her face proved it. He belonged to her; he was all she had. She slid her arms around him, holding him fast.

Since the death of Fergolin, Barakal had made himself his own little hut, close by the Pillar of the Sky, on the far side of it from his father's village. He did not live alone there. He took into his shelter the girl Dehra, who had no other home.

She needed him; she needed his kindness. He needed her also. With Fergolin gone, he had a feeling of being loose, of drifting in the wind like the fluff of a thistle. He loved the stars, and he lived for the Pillar of the Sky, but neither could tie him fast to the earth: for that he had to have another soul, another body, another human voice, and he took Dehra into his life, grateful to have her.

Day by day they lived together, talking long and deeply sometimes, as he explained to her how the whirling of Heaven was the fundamental order of things; that she seemed not to care about, but she loved to hear him tell her the names of the stars.

She cooked their food, cleaned the hut, foraged for nuts and berries and fruit. The winter was coming and the last burst of the summer made the land rich for a while.

He said, "I shall ask Moloquin where your mother is."

"It will be of no use," she said.

He looked long at her. "Why do you say that? Has he ever shown himself your enemy?"

"He killed my mother."

"I do not believe that. I shall go to him and speak to him of it."

Therefore, although she protested and grew angry and threw things at him, he went to the roundhouse, to ask his father about Shateel.

He went in the late afternoon, some days after the arrival of the trader from the west. They had seated a lintel on top of the outer circle that day, and the whole village was rejoicing. The men were gathered in the roundhouse yard with their drums and masks, making ready to dance, and the women hurried around bringing food for a feast. Barakal went in through their midst to the roundhouse.

Taller than most of them, he moved through them like an alien being, as strange in his own way as the trader. He was long and slim, with muscles flat and soft, because he did no arduous work. His days were spent sleeping, his nights watching the stars; he was pale where all the others were tanned brown as the earth that sustained them. Many who saw him bowed as he passed, although he did not notice.

He came into the center of the roundhouse, and there he found his father and the trader Buras Ram.

Around them stood piles of baskets and leather sacks filled to the top and sewn shut. Barakal hung back, watching the two men, wondering, and slowly he came to see that Moloquin was giving all these goods away to the trader.

He looked hard at the goods; unskilled at such things, yet he saw that all these baskets and sacks were filled with the harvest of the gardens. His stomach tightened with alarm. He, who did not work, depended utterly on the produce of the gardens. In another moment he realized that they all depended on it, that this was their true wealth, and here Moloquin was giving it away.

As he stood there, his mother came up beside him.

"Ana-Wahela," he said, and turned to her, and his breath caught in his throat. "Ana!"

Her face was bruised black all along the left side. Her eye was swollen shut. He laid his hands on her, his mouth ajar.

"What happened to you?"

Her swollen lips moved; her voice was too low for him to hear, and she had to repeat it.

"I fell," she said.

He knew she was lying. He turned toward Moloquin again, and his mind brimmed with indignant anger.

He stepped forward, long-striding, breaking away from his mother. He marched up to Moloquin and in a voice that reached out through the whole roundhouse, he said, "Opa-Moloquin, why are you giving away all the wealth of the People for the sake of a few rocks?"

Moloquin straightened, facing him; Buras Ram gawked at him. Moloquin met his son's eyes. For a long time they stared at each other, while all around them was the intense silence of many listening ears. Then Moloquin turned away.

"Go, Barakal."

"Opa-on—"

The chief whirled, his eyes gleaming. "Go!"

Barakal stood where he was, forming more words, but his mother caught his arm. "Come. Come away, please."

"Ana, he—"

"Oh, Barakal, come—" her face was white with fear. She cast a look of terror in Moloquin's direction. "Come away!"

Now others whispered to him from the darkness. "Go—go, before he is angered—go—" their hands caught him. They were pulling him away. He had not asked yet about Shateel. They were removing him before he could ask. He thought of the sacks and sacks of food, the harvest of the women, the patient labor of the women, gone to feed strangers. He had not asked about Dehra's mother. His shoulders slumped. He let them take him away.

When he reached his little hut again, she said, "Did he tell you anything?"

"No." He sat down heavily in the darkness of his hut, brooding on what he had seen in his father's house.

"I told you," she said. "He is a wicked man, there is no use in dealing with him."

"He is not," Barakal said, but his words were mere breath. He remembered his mother's bruised face. He remembered the voices in the roundhouse, whispering to him to flee. He thought, *I have been like a baby, sheltered in the womb, here at the Pillar of the Sky.*

It was that time of the year when the sun was in decline, when the dark and the cold grew every day more intense and dominant. Buras Ram left, his slaves groaning under their burden of the People's goods. Several days later, in the morning, some of the People fell sick.

They died before nightfall. A fever parched them, their bowels opened, and they could neither eat nor drink without vomiting. Their kindred took their bodies to the Pillar of the Sky, and the next day many more were sick.

The men worked no more at the Pillar of the Sky. Bahedyr and his men left in a hurry for the north. The first to die were a man and a woman of Moloquin's Village, but in the New Village, only a short distance away, the people were soon falling sick as well, and dying as quickly.

Ladon's son fell sick.

When word came of this to Moloquin, he went out of his own village and over the hill to the New Village. He came in his litter, all jingling and shining with copper ornament, carried on the shoulders of a dozen men. He proceeded down through the middle of the New Village to the roundhouse, and all who saw him followed after.

In the yard of the roundhouse Moloquin ordered the litter set down, and on foot and alone he went into the roundhouse.

As he walked in through the semi-darkness toward the light at the center, he shed his heavy bearskin cloak, and he stripped off the copper wristbands and armbands that he wore, and he let them drop to the ground as he passed. When he came to Ladon's son he wore nothing but his loincloth.

Ladon's son lay on a bed of straw mats and heavy blankets. The center hole in the roundhouse roof was above him, but not directly above: he lay behind the shaft of light that pierced down to the floor of the roundhouse. He was awake. When he saw Moloquin he strove to raise his hand in greeting.

"I knew you would come," he said.

Moloquin squatted down beside him. "How does it go with you, my brother?" he said.

"Moloquin, I am dying," whispered the other man.

That seemed likely from his looks. His body was drying and cracking like a lump of clay in the blaze of the fever; the bones of his face showed through the skin. All around him was a stench that turned the stomach.

"Perhaps there is something to be done," Moloquin said.

"I am dying, and soon. But, my brother, there is this I must tell you, and there is something I must ask of you."

"Do it," Moloquin said.

Ladon's son fastened his gaze on him. "When my father was the chief, he struggled with Karella, you know, and in the strife between them she died. But before she died she said that if a son of Ladon's should ever rule the People then the world would surely come to an end."

His breath failed him; he shut his eyes. Moloquin lowered his

head. He could not bear to look on this man who had been so handsome and who now was shrivelled and black as a rotting walnut, and
the name of Karella was like a rock in his belly.

Ladon's son spoke again. "Now I have this to ask you, my
brother: Are you that man?"

Moloquin raised his eyes to the face of the dying man; he looked
deep into the face of Ladon's son, the flesh already appearing to rot,
and a shudder passed through him. For a moment he thought it was
Karella herself who spoke to him from the world beyond death, and
a terrible yearning overcame him, a longing for these people he had
lost.

He said, "Karella knew much, my brother. More even than she
supposed. But what will become of us no one knows."

Ladon's son sighed, and he lay still a while. Moloquin was sunk
down in gloomy memory, but presently he stirred himself, found a
jug of water, and bathed the dying man's face. The heat from his
body was horrible to feel. Moloquin pressed the damp cloth to his
brother's lips. He could feel the flutter of the soul there, waiting
there, ready.

"Shall I take you to the Pillar of the Sky?" Moloquin asked.

"That is where I belong."

Moloquin lifted him up, and he was light as an old bone. He
bore him away out of the roundhouse and laid him in the litter, and
the chieftain himself walked before the litter that carried Ladon's son
away to the Pillar of the Sky.

All the people of the New Village who could still walk were gathered at the gate into the roundhouse yard. When they saw that Ladon's son was leaving them, they cried out in one voice, mourning
and frightened, and many burst into tears. Moloquin led the litter in
through their midst.

They stepped aside for him, making room for him: all but one.
One blocked his way, although those around her tried to pull her
away.

"Moloquin," she cried. "Moloquin, this is your doing! You have
brought this down on us—"

Before she could say more, a great outcry rose from the crowd.
"Who is that?" "Silence!" "Get her out of the way!" From behind
Moloquin someone threw a stone at her. "Get away!"

Dehra raised one hand; her face was white, and she looked
frightened suddenly. From either side of her came volleys of stones

and clods of earth, striking the ground around her, glancing off her shoulder and her thigh.

Moloquin strode forward; she shrank back from him, but he got her by the arm and held her close to him, and the People cried out and no one threw stones. He glared around him at them, and their voices faded away and they seemed to crouch down under his stare, making themselves smaller, inoffensive, tame.

He said, "I am going to the Pillar of the Sky." Letting go of Dehra, he pushed her away to one side and led the litter out of the village, up the hill, toward the place of the dead.

Ladon's son died as the sun went down. Moloquin was with him. When he knew that the soul had gone, he went off to the ditch where tall grasses grew and plucked up handfuls of the grass, and returning to the body he covered it with the straw, because there was nothing green left.

He sat there a long while afterward, his head hunched down between his shoulders, his mind inward.

Around him the crows clucked and chuckled happily over their feast. The bodies of the People lay mostly in the finished part of the Pillar of the Sky; Ladon's son had died sitting up against an upright of the Great Gateway, and Moloquin moved away from him, to let the crows at him. The night settled down around him. He felt the tremendous stones around him like two jaws closing on him.

Through the grass came the wind, winnowing through the long blades, sniffing like a beast around the stones and the bodies of the dead. A mist drifted across the tops of the stones, burying the crossbeam of the Great Gateway, hanging like moss from the lintels of the outer circle.

There seemed others here too, close invisible swarms, the ancestors, come to welcome the newly dead. Moloquin lifted his head.

I did this for you, he thought. *I meant no evil. I meant to preserve the People, dead and alive, for ever and ever.*

The death of Ladon's son had reached deep into his belly and uprooted half his past. His life had been bound up with the life of Ladon's son for so long, the dark and the pale, the favored and the unfavored, the power and the denial of power; it seemed impossible that Ladon's son could die and Moloquin still live.

He heard a voice, and for a moment thought he heard the spirits around him speaking with a real tongue, but then he saw that it was Barakal.

The young man came up through the place, carrying a staff which he used in the dark to find his way. Walking in through the western gap in the embankment, he paused before each body as he passed and peered closely at it, murmured some charm, and went on. He had not seen Moloquin there, and, thinking of Dehra whom he knew to be Barakal's friend, Moloquin was unwilling to speak to him. He watched the youth go past the outer circle, toward the East Watcher.

What would he see there? No stars tonight, no light of the moon would pierce through the fog that pressed closer and denser around the stones of the Pillar of the Sky. Or perhaps he came here merely from habit, the way a dog did, when she who fed it had moved her hearth, and yet the dog went still to the old hearth.

That, too, was Moloquin's doing. When Brant died, none knew the old lore, but the lore had been somewhat preserved in this place, and because Moloquin had brought them here, Fergolin and now Barakal had recovered it.

That deed astonished Moloquin more than any other, and as he thought over it, the power that it suggested, his burden of grief and guilt eased. He raised his head, feeling stronger.

Someone else was coming. The crows cawed and cackled and fluttered away. Moloquin gathered himself, readying himself to deal with living people, and in through the unfinished side of the circle came Bahedyr.

"Ho," Moloquin said, surprised. He stood up. Bahedyr carried a torch in one hand, his spear in the other; three or four of his men trailed after him.

Bahedyr walked up to him, smiling. "I greet you, Opa-Moloquin-on." He held his hand out, palm up.

Moloquin mouthed some words to him, his eyes sharp. "What do you here?"

"I have brought you good news," Bahedyr said. His voice was strange, high, piercing, jovial, a false note somewhere in it. "We have found another stone, big enough for the upright circle."

"Ah," said Moloquin. "Where? Bring it."

"You must come and see it. There is a crack in it, perhaps you will not want it."

"Bring it," Moloquin said. "If it does not break in the passage, it will stand."

"You must come and tell me if it is worthy," Bahedyr said stubbornly.

Moloquin gazed at him a while, sorting through this in his mind; if there were a crack in the stone, there was a crack also in this smooth insistence of Bahedyr's, and he was wary.

"Where is this stone?"

"At the Old Camp."

"Hunh." Moloquin grunted, half-turning away. He knew that stone; huge, unworked and ugly, it belonged, like the Old Camp, to a time before the People came. "Why should we take that one, but not the stones from Turnings-of-the-Year?"

At that, Bahedyr's face clouded and he struggled with thought. Moloquin grew more wary of this when he saw that Bahedyr had no ready answer, but then the spearman brightened. He said, "Because it is closer."

Moloquin raised his eyebrows. "I shall go see it, then."

"When?" Bahedyr asked.

The chieftain looked long on him before he answered. At last he said, "When the sickness has passed. I will not leave my People while this evil still devours them."

Bahedyr nodded, accepting that. "We shall go. There is no sickness in our villages, only here."

Moloquin grunted at him, angry, hearing something that he did not want to hear. "Now go, I am here because my brother has died. Go. I will go to the Old Camp when the time comes."

Bahedyr bowed very low, sweeping the ground with his spear in the one hand, his torch in the other, and backed away. Moloquin heard him murmur to the others as they walked out of the Pillar of the Sky. The chieftain turned away, his mood dark.

In the morning, Moloquin sent the men of his village and those of the New Village also to sweat themselves, and when they were purified, he bade them dance for three days and three nights around the two villages, to frighten away the sickness that was eating up the People. He himself went every day from one hearth to the next, talking to the living, seeing who had died, and making sure that the bodies were carried away to the Pillar of the Sky. The People saw him and took heart from his courage.

They saw also that he himself never fell sick, although he walked through the midst of the evil. Therefore they knew that Dehra had been wrong, and Moloquin was not the cause of their suffering.

After the dancing, the sickness began to pass; it gave up its grip on the young and the old, and many who fell sick recovered. When at last there were no more of his People in the power of the disease, Moloquin prepared to go to the Old Camp, to see the stone that Bahedyr had found.

He was still suspicious of this and so he did not send to tell Bahedyr that he was going there; he did not want the spearman to know. Also he gathered up a large number of his men and told them to follow after him at a little distance, and to wait for him at the foot of the lofty hill where the Old Camp was. Then he got into his litter, and he took Wahela in beside him, and on the shoulders of as many men as could crowd around the litter and carry it, he proceeded west over the wintry slopes to the Old Camp.

The Old Camp stood on top of a steep-sided treeless hill at the narrow end of the valley where the Dead River lay. Moloquin reached it at sundown. Because the trail was so steep, he dismounted from the litter, and let the men carry Wahela up by herself. He walked along in front of them, out of breath, his legs aching: he thought to himself, *I am an old man,* and he knew he would take this stone, however cracked and ugly it was. By the time he reached the top of the hill, his sides were bursting with his burning breath, and his legs and back throbbed.

He walked out across the top of the hill, and saw that on the far side was a gentler way down; they could ease the stone down that way. The Old Camp itself was just an embankment with a deep ditch inside. The stone stood near one end of it.

He went close to it. The sun was sinking, but from this height the red blaze still hung above the horizon. He stopped and looked out over the valley below, swooping away from him in an opening wedge, its floor massed full of brush and low trees, the swampy pond at the far end glistening in the last light of the day.

From here he could see back almost as far as the Pillar of the

Sky. The view held him a moment, drew him out of himself, and he stood there, empty, and let the sight flow into him.

Wahela called, "Are we to spend the night here, Moloquin?"

He turned toward her, where she sat in the litter. "Yes. You can get down." He went toward the standing stone.

Big enough, and ugly. It was the same kind of stone that he had been using all along, the surface dimmed by lichens and mosses. A deep crack ran down one face of it, crossing from one top corner to the other side, about half the way down. He laid one hand on it. It was surprisingly warm.

They made a fire inside the embankment, ate what they had brought, and went to sleep. Wahela slept in the litter, but Moloquin was restless and could not lose himself, and he got up and walked around the Old Camp a little, looking out through the darkness over the valley. As he walked back toward his fire and his woman, he heard noises coming from the side of the hill, from the easier trail.

He drew closer. The hairs on his shoulders and back stood up. Many men were creeping up the trail from the bottom.

He whirled. His litter-bearers slept by the fire, in the lee of the bank, their heads buried in their blankets. He ran in among them, stooped, shook them awake, whispered, "Get up! Get up—we are being attacked," and ran on, toward the steep trail down to the foot of the hill where the great band of men waited. Before he could shout, Bahedyr and his men burst up over the far side of the hill.

They made no outcry, gave no warning; they rushed in on Moloquin's camp with their spears thrusting, and while Moloquin's litter-bearers were still groping for their senses, still caught in their blankets, they struck and slew them. Moloquin shouted; furious, he roared at them. His axe was in his belt, and he drew it out, and as they came at him, crouching, their spears aimed at his belly, he rushed at them with a cry of rage that drove them back like children.

"On, on," Bahedyr shrieked. "Kill him—" He himself cocked back his arm and let his spear fly.

Moloquin saw the weapon hurled; he crouched down, and the spear passed over him. He lashed out around him with his axe. In the dark he dared not pause even to see who it was he struck. He felt more than saw the bodies whirling around him. In swift lunges he fought his way across the Old Camp; they fled before him, but they struck at him from behind, and he took wounds as he went, his legs slashed, his back torn, until he reached the old standing stone.

There he put his back to the stone, and he faced his attackers, and as they came at him he struck blow for blow with them. A spear came flying toward him and he dodged it and the stone shattered it. Bahedyr shouted, "All at once! Go at him all at once!"

Then from behind them all, the great mass of men that Moloquin had brought and hidden at the foot of the hill came charging up onto the Old Camp. They fell on Bahedyr and his men from the rear, and swiftly they subdued them.

Moloquin lowered his hands. He saw that the attack was over, that Bahedyr himself was captured and most of his men dead or dying. Now suddenly Moloquin felt the pain in his back and his legs, the throbbing in his lungs and the pounding of his heart, and now also, for the first time, he thought of Wahela.

He cried her name. He dropped his axe. Running from the stone, he went in through the crowd, pushing men out of his way, careless of them all, until he came to the litter.

In it Wahela lay, as she had lain when he left her, wrapped in her blankets, her head to one side, her eyes closed. She had never wakened. When he put his hand on her body he felt the wet sticky warmth of the blood that soaked her blanket. She was dead.

Barakal stooped and dug away the earth and grass at his feet; beneath was a round plaque of chalk.

He had noticed these before. Fergolin had pointed them out to him. Someone had dug a hole here and filled it up again with chalk, so that when the dirt and grass were cleared away, a disk of chalk showed against the darker ground around it. He rose, paced off five steps farther, knelt down, and dug around in the dirt, and found another of the chalk-filled holes.

Evenly spaced, the holes ran in a circle all around the Pillar of the Sky, just inside the bank. He had walked the whole ring now, found all the holes, even the ones that lay in the ditches and the rubble around the Four Watchers, whose positions the ring of holes intersected. Slowly he walked once more around the circle, his head lowered, trying to force answers from this symmetry.

He ignored the extraneous sounds of the world around him: nothing mattered to him but the world in his mind, peopled with chalk-filled holes and upright stones and wandering stars.

Then Dehra burst into the Pillar of the Sky.

She came at a run, gasping for breath. Seeing him, she rushed toward him, jarring him out of his concentration, and he turned on her with a frown.

"What is it now?"

"Your mother." She gripped his hand. "Your mother is dead, Barakal."

"My mother," he said. His fingers closed on Dehra's; he looked around him. "My mother is dead? Where is she? What happened to her?"

Dehra led him forward, toward the two entry stones. As they approached, he could see out through the gap in the bank, down the plain a little way, and now he could hear the wailing of pipes and the pounding of the drums, and he went faster, brushing past Dehra. He swallowed hard.

There on the plain a great swarm of people were dancing toward the Pillar of the Sky. They came in no real order, but singly and in masses, spread out across the irregular plain toward the west and north. The wind broke up their voices, so that sometimes their wails battered his ears, and sometimes he could hear nothing at all.

First of them all was Moloquin.

He carried his axe in one hand. Around his shoulders he wore his bearskin coat, and the wild rumpled curls of his hair and beard flowed over the animal's hide so that he himself seemed a great black bear. After him the litter swayed along, borne on the backs of many men, like a little boat on a stormy water.

In that litter Wahela lay. Barakal let out a low cry. He plunged forward, running down out of the Pillar of the Sky, running to his mother.

The litter-bearers shifted away to let him near. One hand on the side-pole of the furniture, he went along with it, leaning into it, and saw in it his mother, and she was dead, and he saw the blood that covered her.

"What happened to her? Why did she die?"

The men around the litter murmured; one said, "See there?" and Barakal looked where he pointed.

After the litter came a tight swarm of men, all bearing spears or clubs or slings. In their midst, held fast in their midst, Bahedyr walked, with his arms bound and a rope around his neck, his head bowed, and as he walked, the men with him struck him, spat on him, and cursed him.

Barakal wheeled; he ran on past the litter, ahead of it, and came to Moloquin.

"Opa-on," he said. "What happened?"

Moloquin's head swiveled toward him. All around his face, through the curly black hair of his head and beard, the grey wound in streaks and swirls. His eyes blazed.

"Boy," he said, "trust no one. Have faith in no one. Make no one great. Give no one power. Watch ever, ever at your back."

Barakal's jaw fell open; he saw the tears glittering in his father's eyes, and heard the rasp of terror and grief in his father's voice. He stopped where he was. Moloquin walked on past him. Past him they bore the litter where his mother lay. Past him Bahedyr was led, and his men. Slowly Barakal followed after them, into the Pillar of the Sky.

They laid Wahela down before the Great Gateway, and they covered her with grass and branches, but when the crows descended in a swarm to do their work, Moloquin rushed at them and drove them away.

He raged up and down through the Pillar of the Sky. His People drew back to the bank, and many left to go to their homes, but many more stayed. They sat down on the bank, close together for the comfort and the warmth, and watched Moloquin.

He was exhausted, but his fury would not let him rest. Whenever he moved away from Wahela, the great fluttering mass of the crows would swoop down, and he came back, shouting, waving his arms, to drive them up again into the air. They hovered overhead, darkening the sun, waiting. Beneath them, Moloquin wept and raged.

As he strode up and down here, as he passed through the stones, he saw the places where Fergolin had lain, and Ruak, where Grela and Ladon's son had lain, he thought of Karella who had lain here, and of that other whose name he no longer allowed himself to think, who had lain here, whose coming here to die had brought him to the People, and it seemed to him that this whole place was filled with the spirits of those he trusted, and who had gone from him. When he raised his eyes to the living who surrounded him he saw nothing but strangers and enemies. All those he had loved had passed through the Pillar of the Sky into the heart of the universe. Now Wahela would follow them, but he could not bear to let her go.

He saw Dehra, standing by the East Watcher, and he lunged at her, savage.

"Do you blame me for this, too? Am I the cause of her death also? Go! Go from me! Your mother is in the Forest Village, little fool. Go to her, before I send you on with Wahela!"

Dehra's eyes widened, white all around; she glanced away from him to Barakal, and whirled and ran.

Barakal was next; Moloquin strode to him, and shouted, "What have your stars and your circles to tell you of this? If all is made of perfect circles as you say, what turning brought this on me? Why did you not read the stars and warn me?"

The youth lowered his eyes. Moloquin rushed away, because the crows were descending again, and at his approach they clattered up again into the air, beating the air with their wings, a dirty black cloud hovering in the sky over Wahela.

He went down on his knees. The passions that drove him could not overcome the weakness and fatigue of his body. Like a fire that had burned high and was now exhausted he sank down to the ground, and when next the great swarm of the crows settled down toward their due and necessary feast, Moloquin let them have her.

Shateel said, "Ap Min, I shall do it."

Ap Min gave her a grateful look and held out the baby to her. Beside her, her eldest daughter, Elela, tossed her head and pouted and shrugged one shoulder.

"She should do it anyway, Ana—is she not our servant?"

Ap Min ignored her. Like most of the people of the Forest Village she let Elela do as the girl pleased. Stooping, the older woman settled herself before the lump of clay she was about to shape, and Shateel, sitting down on the far side of the wheel from her, cradled the baby in her lap and used both hands to turn the round of wood on which the clay rested.

As she did so, she raised her eyes toward Elela, still standing behind her mother, and said, "I am not your servant. I am no one's servant."

Ap Min gave her a quick glance. Dipping her hands into a bronze bowl of water, she leaned over the clay and smoothed its surface as it turned into an even rotundity.

Elela looked away, watching Shateel from the corner of her eye.

The girl was fat as an old woman; Hems adored her, and would allow no unpleasantness to fall on her; he called her the Root of the Village. Therefore she did whatever came into her mind, which usually was nothing, and considered all others beneath her.

Now she said, "It is true, though, that you were sent here for disobeying Moloquin."

"No, that is not true," Shateel said evenly.

"You lie," Elela said.

Shateel held her tongue. Deep in her belly a hot anger began to burn, but she kept herself still. It did no good to answer Elela, who was forever seeking arguments with her. She lowered her gaze to the hands of Ap Min, now drawing the clay upward, one thumb inside the lip to hollow it out. As with one hand Ap Min formed the vessel she slid the other down into the wet soft lips of the clay, to open up the inside, and Shateel remembered how she had slipped her own hand inside Ap Min's vagina, to draw forth the baby who had grown up to be Elela, and she turned her head away.

They sat doing this in the sun outside the roundhouse, where Hems lived with his wife and his many children. The other families of the Forest Village lived in a second roundhouse, across the clearing, past the forge. The winter had stripped the trees and the sun flooded down around them, too feeble to warm them. Hems himself was in his forge, off to one side of the roundhouse. Shateel wondered what he was doing: he had ceased hammering some time before, all was silence now from that place.

Shateel herself had no hearth. On Moloquin's orders, she was allowed no place of her own to live, but had to go from one family to the next, asking for shelter and food, doing whatever work they asked of her in return.

Elela snorted at her. Languid, bearing her great belly and enormous hams like marks of pride, she strolled away through the meadow, a fat, useless, arrogant girl. Ap Min sighed.

"I cannot guess what will become of her when she marries."

Shateel turned the wheel. The baby lying in her lap thrust up his tiny fists and gurgled, and she shifted him a little, his head resting on her knee, his legs across her other thigh. She did not think Elela would ever marry. Already she was well beyond the age of marriage, and none of the youths here had put on the red feather for her; nor did the Forest People go to the other villages where husbands might be found for her. She hoped Elela did not marry.

She said, mildly, "You should take her in hand, Ap Min."

Ap Min laughed. "Oh, no. Hems would never allow it."

"Hems is not her mother."

Shateel did not add: *nor her father, either*.

Ap Min shrugged. Her face was clear and round as a full moon. Her eyes rested on the clay she shaped. "Hems is master here." She said that to any suggestion that she herself ought to do what was right; she left such things to Hems, and Hems did what was easy for him.

Ap Min's hands with the clay were deft and swift. One pot after another she made, and set on a slab of wood beside her. The baby whimpered to be fed, and the two women left their task. Ap Min opened her clothes and gave the child the breast, and Shateel carried the pots away to the far side of the village, where they had made a little kiln of bricks.

This little hut-shaped oven was another of the things Hems had brought back with him from the tin mines. Shateel set the pots down before the kiln, knelt at the opening into the bottom, and pulled out the bricks that shut it up. There was a stack of wood waiting by the kiln and she filled up the lower level with branches and twigs and went to the nearest house to beg some coals.

When she came back to the kiln, the coals in a little pot in her hand, there was a hail from the forest. She turned to see who was coming, and from the house behind her one of the men stepped, to see also, and Ap Min by the door of the roundhouse turned, and so when the girl walked out of the forest it was into the attention of many.

The girl came down the path from the north. She wore a long coat of woven stuff, but it was all tattered, and she wore no shoes and carried only a sack on her shoulder. Shateel took a step toward her, frowning, drawn to her even before she saw who it was, and then suddenly she knew who it was, and she dropped the pot of coals.

"Dehra."

She went forward, her arms out. The girl hesitated, blinking in the sunlight, her gaze moving slowly from the roundhouse on her right through the rest of the village; at last her gaze fell on Shateel, and she came forward with a rush into her mother's arms.

· · ·

In the roundhouse, sitting before Hems' fire, with a pot of broth before her, Dehra spilled out her story.

The Forest People sat around her and listened without speaking. Even when she told them of the fever that had swept through the two villages by the Pillar of the Sky, no one said anything, although the women drew their children closer and the men put their arms around their wives. But when she told them that Bahedyr had slain Wahela, and had tried to slay Moloquin himself, a shudder passed through them all.

Dehra spoke of Moloquin's rage on the Pillar of the Sky, and how he had ordered her away, and she leaned toward her mother who sat beside her, and Shateel held her close. The others looked at one another, still gripped by what they had just heard, and Hems gave a sudden shake of his head.

"He should never have left us," Hems said. "He should have stayed here, with us, where he belonged."

One or two of the others nodded, murmuring in agreement, and Ap Min covered her face with her hands. Shateel held her own child in her arms, her face against Dehra's lank hair, and as the others began to move about on their own business, she drew Dehra away down to the stream where they could speak without being watched or overheard.

She bathed her face and hands in the icy water, and watched as Dehra did so also. Dehra was thin even for her, who had always been thin, and her face was drawn and wild in its looks, watchful and angry.

She said, "I have been searching for you since the Bloody Gathering. I thought you were dead."

Shateel laughed. Her hands and face tingled from the cold water. "I am alive, my child, as any soul between Heaven and earth. But what has become of you? Why did you go to the Pillar of the Sky?"

"Looking for you. And to fight against Moloquin! He is evil, Ana, he has drawn such evil on us—"

The girl broke off; she beat the ground with her fists. Shateel put out her hand to her.

"Tell me of my own People."

Dehra wiped her fingers over her face. "Ana-Joba-el is dead."

"Ah."

"And Ladon's son is dead, in the fever."

Shateel looked sharply at her; she saw that Dehra knew Ladon's son only as the headman of Moloquin's People, and she lowered her eyes again. She thought of Ladon's son with an unexpected wrench of the heart. Dehra was staring at her.

"How have you done here, Mother? Have you suffered much?"

"I have suffered nothing," said Shateel.

"But you have been alone here. These People shun you, I have seen it."

"They were told to shun me. They have worn the thing into a habit. I have suffered nothing." Shateel gathered herself up; night was coming, the early winter night, and she had to find some place for her and her daughter to sleep. She remembered the pots she was to fire, and thought of finding food for the evening meal; the commonplaces of life crowded in around her, and yet the center of her mind was struggling with a larger problem, and she got up absent-mindedly to do the immediate tasks.

Dehra was tired; as soon as Kayon accepted them into his hearth for the night, the girl fell asleep. Shateel did the work that was set before her in return for her night's shelter, and in the deepening cold and dark of the night, she went out of the hut and walked away into the forest.

She went up from the meadow a little, away to the clearing above, where the People had their gardens. There she sat down on an old stump. The moon was rising through the trees, and the wind swept cold and sharp among the branches; far away a wolf howled, a quiver of warning passed over her, a foreboding older than she, older even than the People, old as the world itself.

Before her lay the garden, given over now to the winter snow, to the foragings of night creatures. It was a small enough enterprise anyway, this garden. Because of Hems' forge and the riches that poured forth from it, the Forest People received much of their food from other places, other gardens, the labor of unknown hands. Their own soil, dense and hard to work, mattered little to them. Yet once this place had been the heart of the village. Moloquin himself had cut down these trees, and Shateel had cleared away and burned away the brush so the gardens could be planted: the work they had done here remained here, part of them both remained here.

Part of Another remained here. Before Moloquin cut the trees, before he even led his People into this place, Another had lived here. Another had planted and harvested, fit herself into the endless cycle of the turning year and sustained herself by the tilled earth and the summer sun. Ael had been here first.

Since Shateel had been sent away to this place, whenever her heart had sickened with her exile, she had come here and fixed her mind on Ael, the Woman Alone, and Ael had healed up her wounds.

Not her wounds, this time.

She thought of him as Dehra had spoken of him, raging and wild in the place where his soul lived most intensely. Driving away the crows, driving away his People. Driving away Dehra. Was there not something desperate in that? He had known long before that Dehra sought her mother.

She remembered him as he cut down the dead trees, a young man, overflowing with story and ambition, his strength seeming endless, his vigor enough to enliven a whole People. When he came to her wanting her among his women, with what a silly pride she had denied him! She smiled now to think of it—how she had denied him.

She would not deny him again what he needed.

The moon had risen above the trees. Full and round, its face eaten by corruption, its light a vehicle for madness, it rode the night into the dawning. Off to the north, did he rage still? Did he struggle still to keep the crows away—to hold back death? Before her, the garden lay in the wintry grip of death, but the spring would come, and the green life would shoot up through the straw and the dry stalks. She rose and turned her back on this, and turned her face to the west; she turned her face again toward Moloquin.

They brought the great stone down from the Old Camp, and among those who labored at the ropes was Bahedyr.

Moloquin set him at the back of the lines that dragged the stone, where the dust was thickest; the other men were moved up to the front of the line, to give them some relief, but Bahedyr struggled always in the dirtiest and most punishing place in the line, and if he slowed, Moloquin was there, ordering him beaten with ropes. Moloquin himself travelled along in his litter off to one side of the stone, where he could rest his gaze on the sufferings of the man who had betrayed him and slain Wahela. Thus, day by day, the great cracked stone came to the Pillar of the Sky.

Midwinter came. Barakal stood before the West Watcher and saw the sun rise over the stone to the east, and all the People came to the Pillar of the Sky and the men danced, and the women made a feast, and all through Midwinter's Night, with bonfires and feasting, dances and music, they waited for the sun. Moloquin sat at the middle of it, hunched down in his litter, his face turned away.

The People danced and feasted through the night, and when the dawn came, they lay sleeping, their bodies scattered like corpses through the Pillar of the Sky. Moloquin alone watched the sun rise, a white ghost climbing through the fog, her rays creeping over the earth to cast the shadows of the gateways over the ground around him. He sat as he had all through the night, slumped beneath his litter, his head sunk down on his chest.

He heard someone coming toward him, but he expected Barakal, whose life it was to watch the heavens, coming to see the sun rise. Therefore he did not look up until the newcomer stopped before him.

He raised his eyes; he looked long into the face of Shateel, who stood before him.

"What are you doing here?" he said at last.

"You called me," she said calmly. "Didn't you?"

"I called no one," he said.

She shrugged her shoulders. "Perhaps I misunderstood." She was smaller than he remembered, spare, brown from the sun, her face seamed and creased with the wear of her years; her eyes met his without fear or favor. She said, "I heard that Wahela is dead. I came because I am your wife, and it is not good for you to be alone."

He turned his head away. There was something in the gesture of a wounded animal, trying to avoid more blows. Shateel watched him closely, amazed at the change in him. She remembered wondering once if anything would ever surprise him again. Now she wondered if anything would ever again move him.

His great head swayed toward her; he said, "Come with me, Shateel." Heavily he arose from his litter and walked down out of the Pillar of the Sky, down toward his roundhouse, and she followed him.

As he walked, he said, over his shoulder, "Did you bring that daughter of yours?"

"No. She stayed behind, in the Forest Village."

"Good. She is nothing but trouble."

"You have given her nothing but trouble!" She trotted a few steps to catch up with him. They walked in through the village, empty save for the dogs and the goats, all the People being at the Pillar of the Sky. The dogs skulked away from Moloquin as he passed by. Shateel looked around her at the little huts, thinking with surprise how much like the Forest Village it was—as if to be Moloquin's People they had to do everything the same. They went by the great mill and she stared at that. Then they came to the roundhouse.

He walked straight ahead into the roundhouse, but Shateel stopped. There on the threshold of the roundhouse was Bahedyr, staked to the ground, so that any who went in or out had to tread on him, and as Moloquin went in, he stepped full on Bahedyr, and the bound man groaned. He was the color of the dust, and Moloquin paid no more heed to him than to the dust, even when he groaned.

Shateel stepped across him and went into the roundhouse. She followed Moloquin to the center of it, and they sat down together.

"Why have you done that?" she said, and nodded toward the doorway. "Because of Wahela?"

"Wahela is dead," Moloquin told her. He drew forth a basket with a lid and opened it up. "Here, see this."

He reached into the basket and gathered up a handful of ornaments, clinking and jingling, and raised them before her eyes. She gasped. The metal shone like the sun in the light of the sun, shone with a seductive glow, and she put out her hand and touched it, expecting warmth. It was cold and hard like stone. She let the mass of metal slide back into the basket.

She turned her eyes toward Moloquin again. "And why have you done as you do to Bahedyr?"

"I raised him up," Moloquin said. "Now I make him lower than the dogs in the village."

"Your power is great," she said.

"All the People obey me," he said. "They do as I wish of them, they come when I call, and go when I dismiss them. Whatever they do, they bring to me, and I decide who shall have and who shall not have."

"Greater than any other is Opa-Moloquin-on," she said.

"From across the sea men bring me riches," he said. "Even across the sea they know my name and bow their heads to hear it."

"Most great is Opa-Moloquin-on."

"Why do you mock me?" he cried, and wheeled toward her, his fist raised.

"I do not mock you, Moloquin. I hear what you say to me."

He looked long into her face, and she saw in his face something she had never seen before, nor ever expected to see in him: she saw that Moloquin was afraid.

She said, "What torments you, husband?"

"Ah, wife."

He lowered his head, and his shoulders rounded. With his two hands he picked up the lid and set it on the basket, and then suddenly, violently, he thrust the thing away from him.

He said, "I cannot sleep, Shateel. I look around me and see none that I know, only strangers, even my own children are strangers to me, and if they are strangers, then they may be my enemies, and I dare not trust them. If I sleep, they may come and stab me as I lie there. I dare eat only what has been tasted first by another, I go nowhere without many men around me, and yet even those, I fear."

He pressed his fists to his eyes, and he gave his head a shake, his hair tossing.

"Perhaps you were right, Shateel. Perhaps I am an evil man, and a scourge of my People."

"I said not that you are evil, but that you did evil, which is different, Moloquin."

"Perhaps." His hands dropped into his lap. "I know nothing certainly any more. I cannot make sense of it any more, it is too tangled together. All I know is the Pillar of the Sky. That is certain, that is what I must do, and so I do it."

"It is magnificent," she said. "It makes me tremble to see it."

"I hate it," he said. "I hate it and yet I must be there, I ache to go there when I am away, but I hate it, it has eaten up all that I loved, and soon, I know, it will eat me."

She lowered her head. She had seen him, sitting there in his litter, in the center of the Pillar of the Sky, and he had seemed small and frail in the midst of his creation, small and old and frail among the towering stones. She considered what he had told her, the words pouring forth from him like blood from a wound, and she saw where the wound was, and there was no healing for such a wound as this.

She said, "Tell me a story, Moloquin."

"I cannot."

"Ah?"

"I have no more stories, Shateel. The stories came from Karella, and she has deserted me. She has not been with me since I broke the sampo." He shook his head. "I turned away from Ael, and now Karella has turned away from me." He struck with his hand at the basket. "I have nothing left but this, and the Pillar of the Sky."

Then Shateel understood him, and she knew why Bahedyr lay staked to the threshold. She drew closer to her husband, and he leaned toward her; he put his arm around her, and she laid her head on his shoulder, but he turned his head away, even as he held her tight against him, he turned his head away from her, into the darkness.

Barakal did not go into the Pillar of the Sky during the days of midwinter, except to watch the sun rise, which was his inescapable task; he could not bear to be among so many people. But when the celebration was over, and the people gone, he went up to the place, and he slept there at the foot of the Great Gateway all through the afternoon, so that he would be awake when the stars appeared.

The first few nights were overcast. The mist seemed to ooze up out of the land and rise through Heaven in columns and tendrils, and it covered the sky with an opaque veil. But on the fifth night the wind rose a little, coming out of the north, and blew away the fogs.

He sat there through the night, watching as one family of stars after another climbed up over the horizon and whirled away toward the west, and so he was there, watching and ready, when the gateway stars rose, and there between them was a star he had never seen before.

When he saw it he lost his breath, astonished. Fergolin, his master, had told him that new stars came sometimes and always meant some grave trouble for the People, but Barakal had not been ready for this. The star was magnificent, brighter even than the Great Traveller, and it gave off fiery rays of red and green and yellow. It seemed to him that he could see it slowly revolve in its place between the two gateway stars, there at the edge of Heaven, and he knelt down beneath it and spoke to it with his head bowed, telling it of its beauty, and asking to be allowed insight into its message.

He knew at once he should take this news to Moloquin, but the star gripped him; he watched it all the rest of the night, seeing how it stood near the other stars. When the dawn came, and the great star faded with the rest, he struggled to his feet, exhausted.

On slow feet he went down toward Moloquin's Village, to carry his news to the chieftain of the People, but halfway between the Pillar

of the Sky and the roundhouse of his father Barakal stopped. There
before him, on the gradually declining slope, the village was coming
awake in the dawn. Already the dogs ran sniffing and snorting over
the midden heap. The first smoke trailed up into the sky like a
smudge of dirt. He could hear sleepy voices; he saw an uneven train
of people wandering away to the ditch to relieve themselves. All their
smells and sounds, all their untidy comings and goings repulsed him.
His mind was full of the new star, full of its purity and order; against
the perfect order of the sky, this low, disgusting, human confusion
was meaningless, distracting, and degrading. He turned and went
back to the Pillar of the Sky, back where he belonged.

Some few days later the work began again at the Pillar of the Sky.

Half the men set about smoothing the stone; the others began to
dig the hole for it, and Moloquin got some of them also to dig a hole
in the entry, between the two old stones there. He showed more interest in this hole than in the one that would receive the stone, leaning over it, and dropping things into it.

In the midafternoon he sent for Sickle, who was guarding Bahedyr, to bring the prisoner to the Pillar of the Sky. Shateel was there
also by then, and many other people, and they all stood watching as
Bahedyr was dragged into the place of the dead.

He himself was half the way to death. He could barely keep on
his feet; Sickle had to carry him as he walked, one arm under Bahedyr's shoulders, and the one-time hero's head slumped down, his
hair matted and knotted with dust. When he was led forth, all the
other People shrank back from him. There were a few angry cries,
but most of the People turned away, full of pity and fear, until Moloquin said, "Put him in the hole."

Then they all watched. Even Shateel drew closer to see what
Moloquin would do to the man who had betrayed him.

Sickle and another man dragged Bahedyr to the edge of the
hole and pushed him in; as soon as they let go of him, Bahedyr sank
down to the bottom of the hole, and no one could see him. Moloquin
said, "Make him stand up."

The two men standing by the hole hesitated a moment, looking
down past their feet, until Sickle gathered his courage and jumped
down beside Bahedyr. He pulled the condemned man up onto his

feet and held him, and their two heads showed above the ground. Moloquin walked up and down past them, his hands on his hips.

"You and you." He pointed to men near the hole. "Fill the dirt in around him. Sickle, hold him until the dirt holds him."

At that, a gasp went up from the crowd. The two men looked one another in the face and turned and went slowly away for tools. In the hole, Sickle lifted his head, his eyes ringed with white.

Shateel started forward, one hand raised toward her husband, but before she could speak, another spoke. Another came out of the crowd, and shouted, "Moloquin! What evil do you now?"

His head swivelled toward this one; his face showed no surprise, only an implacable purpose. When he saw who had spoken, he turned to Shateel.

"I thought you said she was gone."

Shateel stood where she was, midway between him and Dehra who had come out of the crowd, and stood alone now, her hands made into fists before her, her face dark with rage. Shateel said, "She said she would not come back. Yet perhaps it is best. What you are doing is horrible."

He heard that; he looked from her to Dehra and back to her, and he began to laugh; the sound of his laugh made Shateel turn her head away, her lips pressed together. She went forward, past him, to the edge of the hole, where Bahedyr slumped in the arms of Sickle, his eyes barely open.

Yet he was aware of her. His lips moved a little, and when she crouched by the side of the hole she heard him say, "Help me, Shateel."

She looked into his face, masked with dust; she looked over his shoulder into Sickle's face, and saw another mask there, a look of bland obedience. In Sickle's face she saw a warning. She stood up.

"Moloquin," she said, "for my sake, do not do this."

He stood as he had when Dehra first stepped forward, in the open between Bahedyr's hole and the hole being dug for the stone from the Old Camp; his head was sunk down, his eyes gleaming, his gaze travelling from Bahedyr to Dehra and back again. Shateel went straight to him.

"Do not do it," she said, low. "You bring some evil on us, do not do it!"

As she spoke she put her hand on his chest. He looked down at her for a long while, took her hand and thrust it away. Now the men had come back with their shovels, and were preparing to scoop the dirt into the hole around Bahedyr, to bury him alive, but Moloquin said, "No. Take him back." With a gesture of his arm he waved them all away, and he turned and went into the middle of the Pillar of the Sky, where his litter sat, and he went into the litter and stayed there, all the rest of the day.

Dehra said, "I could not stay there, Ana-el—it is no different there than here."

She and Shateel sat in a corner of the roundhouse yard. A cold rain had begun to fall, lightly at first, and mixed with grains of snow.

Dehra said, "Hems is no other than Moloquin. He told me to carry wood, to haul water, in return for my food and shelter, and when I went to build my own hearth, to make my own place, he sent his children to tear it apart."

Her voice trembled. In her eyes Shateel saw tears of anger, tears of shame. She put out her hand and touched her child's cheek, thinking at the same time, *She is a child no more.*

"So I came back here," Dehra said. "Here at least I can—"

Her voice broke off. She looked away.

"Here you can fight Moloquin," Shateel said mildly.

Dehra nodded, her eyes downcast. Swiftly she brought her burning gaze back to her mother.

"He is the root of it, Ana. If he is destroyed—"

Shateel put her hand over Dehra's mouth. "Don't speak of that."

"What!" Dehra thrust angrily at Shateel's hand. "You are his again, are you? He sent you away, now he lets you come back, and you are so grateful you will be his creature—"

Shateel slapped her. Dehra recoiled, dark with anger, and the two women stared at each other. Shateel said, "You do not understand—"

"I understand," Dehra said. She got to her feet. "You are no more my mother." Stiff-backed, she walked away, out of the roundhouse yard. Shateel lowered her head. The snow fell around her, melting as it fell.

Ael, she thought, are you here now, can you hear me? Her heart was sick with confusion. Behind her was Moloquin, rotten with evil as a corpse full of worms; before her was Dehra, drawn to the evil, thinking herself good for being drawn to the evil. How could she stand between the two of them—between them and their destiny? She pulled her shawl over her head and covered her face from the cold, the snow, and the light.

Moloquin woke, and found himself alone. Beside him the bed was cold where Shateel had lain. He rose and went away through the roundhouse to find her.

Although he dared not tell her, he needed her. In all the terrible things that had happened to him the only good thing was that Shateel had come to him, come to him, at last, of her own wish. Through her eyes he could see himself a whole man again, a man worthy of being loved, or merely of being. Yet he dared not tell her this, for fear of the power it gave her over him. Instead he went through the roundhouse with a thunderous frown on his face, and when he found her outside in the yard, sitting in the new-fallen snow, he berated her like a master scolding a green novice.

"What are you doing here? Are you not my wife? Come inside, be where I am."

She raised her face to him; he saw she was unhappy, and an enveloping fear came over him: if she was unhappy, would she not go? He got hold of her arm and pulled her up onto her feet.

"Come inside. You are my wife! For my sake, at least, show some pride in what you are."

He dragged her inside and made her sit down, and the people of the roundhouse brought them beer and seed-cakes and honey, unmilled grain steeped in broth until the kernels popped open, soft and white. Moloquin kept Shateel close by him, where he could touch her whenever he wished, only by raising his hand; he never took his eyes from her.

"What were you doing out there in the snow? Can you not see it is snowing? Even the dogs and the pigs know to come inside when the snow falls."

She said, "Will you go to the Pillar of the Sky today?"

"I will." He took a cake of seeds and honey and broke it in half, and laid one half on her knee. "If any other comes, it will surprise me. We cannot work in the snow. Eat."

He wanted her to come sit behind him, as Wahela had done, and comfort him with her hands, comb his hair, pick the lice out of his hair, wind the curls around her fingers, but he did not know how to ask for that. Instead he shot words at her.

"Why did that daughter of yours come back? You said she was gone."

"I don't know," Shateel said. "I am very low over it, husband, she ought not to have come. She hates you."

He grunted. "She does not concern me. She is only a stupid girl, what can she do to me?"

"I don't know," Shateel said. "I know nothing of this place, except that I know nothing of it. I will go to the New Village later, if you will let me."

He looked sharply at her; on his tongue the words waited: *will you come back?* His gaze lingered over her face. She had been beautiful once, or at least he remembered her beautiful; now in the lines and sags of her face something else drew him. As he looked on her, she smiled at him, and he thought, *There is nothing in me she does not know.*

That soothed him. He reached out his arms to her and drew her close to him, set her down before him like a child, and stroked her hair. He was awkward at this, his fingers too stiff, too thick and rough with callus, so that the threads of her hair clung to his fingers. She sighed. Trusting and warm, she moved against him, pressing her back to his belly, her head to his shoulder. He put his arms around her and buried his face in her hair.

In the afternoon the snow stopped, and Moloquin went to the Pillar of the Sky. Shateel walked across the slope and down to the New Village, looking for some of the women she had known; she thought if she could talk to them she would understand better the mood of the People, and she could see how the power of the women would work, for or against Moloquin.

The New Village lay on an eastern-trending slope just beyond the Pillar of the Sky from Moloquin's Village. Its two longhouses were lined up side by side, with the roundhouse before their front doors, so that they all shared the same yard. A brush fence surrounded all of this, but outside the fence there were other houses, small and round, with roofs of thatch and sod.

She went into the yard, where a little herd of goats was gathered, protected from the snow; two young women were bringing them armloads of dry grass to eat. Shateel watched them a moment, reluctant to interfere with their work, and looked around her for some place where the women gathered—the sampo, or a loom, or a pot-making wheel.

There was nothing. She guessed that the women took their grain to the great mill in Moloquin's Village; certainly they had no sampo of their own. Nor was there any of the bustle and shared labor of women that she had known from her own village, where the women did everything together. Here, except for the goats, the women feeding them, and two old dogs asleep in the shelter of the fence, the yard was empty.

She thought it was the cold; certainly the cold kept the men inside the roundhouse. She went into the longhouse on her left.

Usually, even in the coldest weather, the longhouses were warm from the fires of the women, warm from the people living under one roof. When she went into this longhouse the cold air struck her face, and she recoiled from the smell of rot and age and abandonment. Shocked, she stopped still on the threshold. This longhouse was almost deserted.

The hearths still lined either side, marked out with rings and low walls of stone, but most of the spaces were empty of belongings and people, and the ashes were cold as the snow. She went slowly down the length of the old building. The roof was breaking and the cold wind blasted in through it, sweeping the whole place, whirling the ashes in their beds. She went by a hearth where someone slept wrapped in a blanket, buried away inside the blanket so well she could not make out if it were a man or a woman, and in a sudden rush of uncontrolled imagination she thought it was a corpse, the corpse of this village, and her skin went rough and she broke into a run to get away from it.

There at the far end of the longhouse was a fire, and she stumbled toward it, toward the warmth, the cheery crackle, and the people gathered around it. But when she reached it, all the people there were men.

They stared up at her, startled at her appearance. She stood at the entrance to the hearth and stared back. There were many of them, all young, shaggy, dirty, and their hearth was dirty, smelling bad of old food, of stale beer, and littered with blankets and bones and pots. She looked around at them, and saw that among them was Sickle, the young man whose duty it had been to guard Bahedyr at the Pillar of the Sky.

She said, "What are you doing here? Where are the women?"

Sickle stood up. He was lean and rough, and for an instant she was afraid of him: she stiffened, hardening herself against him, but he made no move toward her and eventually he sat down again.

He said, "You are Shateel, the old man's wife."

"I am that," she said slowly, amazed. "Is that how you speak of your chief—the *old man?*"

"Opa-Moloquin-on," Sickle said quickly, and glanced at the others around him, and suddenly they were all snickering and giggling, their heads bowed together, sharing their amusement, and with their hands they made elaborate, mocking gestures of respect. Shateel's temper climbed; she fought the urge to scold them into proper humility and docility, but she forced herself to be cold, to see this without passion: this was why she had come here, to see how the People fared, and now she was seeing it.

"Where are the women?" she said.

"In the other longhouse," said Sickle. "The ones who have not gone off with their husbands."

"With their husbands," Shateel said.

Another of the young men wiped his nose between his fingers, rubbed his hand on his thigh, and spat into the fire. "Most of the married women live with their husbands now. They go off outside the village and make their own huts and have their own gardens, and that way the men can see that the women do their work and don't have other men, you see."

Shateel looked around them again, seeing now that many of these young men were boys still, boys from the boys' band, and she realized that they were the bachelors: they should have lived in the roundhouse, with their societies, but now the societies were failing even as the sampo had failed. Swiftly she guessed at the reason: Moloquin belonged to no society. Moloquin lived together with his women, and the men chose to do what he did, they took their wives away from the other women, as Moloquin had done with Wahela.

She turned and swept the longhouse with her eyes. Was it the same roof as the one she had lived under, when she was the wife of Ladon's son? If they moved their villages, the women had been used to taking the old roof. Perhaps this roof had sheltered many longhouses, back through the generations; perhaps this was the first roof ever made over a longhouse, and now it would be the last. Falling in, letting in the cold wind, collapsing into the dead fires. The women were gone. Without the sampo, they had no common center for their lives; separated from each other, isolated from one another, what power did they have? Only to follow their husbands, to obey their husbands.

Standing there, the cold wind roaring past her, she felt the wind sweeping away the whole world around her, leaving her like a star alone in the center of the void. Quickly she went away down the longhouse and out into the real world.

Sickle thought, *Moloquin is just a man. I could do as well as he.*

But when he went to the roundhouse of the chief, or into the Pillar of the Sky, intending to face Moloquin like a man, to stand eye to eye with him and defy his orders, something went soft in his belly. When, face to face, Moloquin told him, *Do this,* Sickle bowed his head and meekly did it.

It was magic, as the women said. It was magic that gave Moloquin his ascendency over them all, the magic in his great bronze axe, in his armbands and belts and collars of metal, the magic in all his accoutrements. Not Moloquin himself.

If another man wore the armbands and the belts and the collars, if another man took the great axe into his hand, then another man— any other man—could rule over the People.

Sickle knew that if he ruled the People he would do no evil. He would rule justly and well. None would wish to harm him, but if one did, then Sickle would not stretch him out on the ground and walk on him, nor dig holes and threaten to bury him. Sickle would be merciful, if he were the chief.

He spoke of this to his friends, the young men who lived with him in the half-deserted longhouse, and they agreed with him. Dehra was right: Moloquin was evil.

He went up to the chieftain's roundhouse in the evening, to guard Bahedyr, which was his duty. As he went he played with the idea that this time he would tell Moloquin face to face to show some mercy for the prisoner—to show some heart: they were of the same People, after all, he and Bahedyr.

He knew if the other men saw him speaking so to Moloquin, they would look on him with awe and respect. He imagined their wide eyes, their amazement at his courage. He saw himself standing before Moloquin, tall and straight, speaking in a clear voice, with words that left no questions behind.

But when he went into the yard, the chieftain was there, just getting down from his litter. The sun had come out after the snow and shone hot and bright on the ornamented litter, the tinkling bronze tassels and the ribbons. Moloquin climbed slowly out of the deep well of the seat. Sickle stood before him, ready to confront him, but as the chieftain left the litter, he seemed to grow taller. He moved slowly, ponderously, every move an emblem of his confidence; when he straightened, his great head wreathed and framed in greying black curls, he seemed to Sickle to stand as tall as the Great Gateway at the Pillar of the Sky, and the young man's voice froze in his throat. When Moloquin's gaze fell on him, he bowed his head to avoid that look, that awful attention.

Moloquin said, "Where is my wife?"

Someone else answered him. Sickle stood with his head bowed, his eyes averted, as the chieftain passed by him; his heart pounded, for fear that even without words between them Moloquin would know his mind. As the heavy footsteps passed him by, as the earth grew still again after Moloquin's passage, he was overcome with relief.

He went into the roundhouse, his face turned away from the other people, lest anyone should see he was afraid of Moloquin.

Dehra was not afraid of him, but Dehra was mad: everyone knew that. Some ancestral demon had taken possession of her. She wandered here and there through the two villages, telling everybody how evil Moloquin was, and the people threw stones at her sometimes, or merely laughed at her, and the children made fun of her to her face. Sickle did not want that for himself. He went into the second circle of the roundhouse, where the grain of the harvest was stored in great baskets, and where Bahedyr lay, bound hand and foot, and staked to the ground.

The prisoner was stirring, but he was not awake: perhaps the same demon who drove Dehra now tormented him. He lay writhing in his bonds, murmuring, "Water. Bring me water." Sickle went off to another part of the roundhouse and brought a little bronze cup of water to him.

He sat there in the dark, holding Bahedyr's head up with one

hand and with the other feeding him water by the sip. Doing this
aroused in him a certain tenderness toward the prisoner. Sickle had
been caring for this man regularly, had kept him alive, giving him
food and water—for what? So that Moloquin could kill him when
Moloquin chose? And make nothing of Sickle's work and Sickle's
power?

Bahedyr drank the water, and his soul came back to him a little:
he whispered, "Ah, in the name of my ancestors, let me die."

"Be still," Sickle said, and laid him down again on the ground.
"Be still. The night is coming, wait until then, be still."

Barakal said, "Watch there. Soon it will rise. The horizon is clear
tonight—it will appear tonight surely."

His voice rang with his excitement. Dehra shifted a little, moving
closer to him; the night was cold and the wind was gathering force
as the stars began to appear. She tipped her head back, looking up
past the looming beams of the gateways, into the center of Heaven,
trying to remember the names of the stars.

He knew them all. Even as she looked, he was leaning back beside her, his arm extended, his finger picking out each little fire as it
blazed alive in the deepening sky. "Vendra," he said, "the Smokehole
of the Sky. When she rides upon the height of the sky, the equinox is
coming. And there, Umulon, Squirrel-Killer, the Damned Man,
whose light is sick and well by turns. You see tonight he is well, and
his light shines bright, but other times you can barely see him, and
when that is so, it means there is sin and error among the People."

"There is sin and error now among the People," she said, and
glared at Umulon who would not confirm her convictions. From the
left, suddenly, there was a loud crack.

"What is that?" she cried, startled.

Barakal put his arm around her. "Have no fear of it. It is a stone
popping. I have heard it often—at first it frightened me, too, but
then one day I was here when the workmen were trimming a stone
with fire and with water, and I heard the stone pop then and knew
what it was that I heard other times."

The pride in his voice annoyed her: he was so pleased with his
own understanding. His arm around her was too tight, a confine;
warm as it was, still a bond.

She said, loudly, "There is sin and error now among the People, why does Umulon not shrink away?"

"Perhaps what you see as sin Umulon does not."

"Bah!" She got up. Better to keep warm by moving up and down here than by submitting to Barakal's embraces. "You know as well as I that Moloquin has—"

"No. No, I do not know that Moloquin has done anything." Barakal thrust at her, sweeping at her with his arm. "You are in my way, Dehra!"

She turned, looking behind her, out through the space between the upright stones. He was sitting so that the gap in the outer ring framed the horizon; he would see his new star rise directly over the hole that waited for the stone from the Old Camp. Across the hole that waited for Bahedyr.

She moved a little, her gaze sharp; the horizon was still pale from the late passage of the day, and no stars appeared above it. She walked away a little, in among the ring of silent stones, and paused and looked up.

In among the stones like this, looking up at the monstrous stones, she wondered at herself. Moloquin had done this: soon Moloquin would raise another stone, and close the ring. Then he would bury Bahedyr, and all his other enemies also, perhaps—she had a sudden vision of a third ring, outside the ring of stones, a ring of people, buried upright, their souls forever bound to this place, guardians of it, forever. She shuddered. It was cold.

"There!" Barakal leapt to his feet and pointed.

She turned, her eyes seeking the horizon. A low cry escaped her lips. The horizon was the color of the inside of a mussel shell. The rough line of the edge of the earth was black against it, but in one notch of this line a new light blazed, so brilliant she thought at first it was a fire lit on the hilltop.

As she watched, it climbed slowly into the sky, and the last earthly veils fell away from it: its radiance shone brighter and fiercer and more beautiful, and she sighed.

"It is magnificent. What is its name?"

Barakal sat there smiling, his legs crossed, his arms loose over his knees. "Her name is Erwenda, the Companion, the Messenger, the Mouth of Truth."

"What truth does she bring, then?"

He shrugged. "She stands in the Gateway of Heaven. Perhaps she has come to greet someone who will soon pass between worlds."

Dehra faced the star again. Even Barakal was unsure what the burning light meant; he loved it, saw no harm in it, but Barakal loved all the stars. Surely there was some harm in it. It glittered as it rode the sky. Shafts of light erupted from it. She saw them suddenly as spears, a shower of malicious beams, raining down on the People.

"I am going," she said, and started away.

"Why? Come sit with me, if you are cold."

"I am tired. I am going." She hurried away, her head bent, her back bent, away from the cruel punishing star, to hide in the shelter of the hut.

Moloquin startled awake, jumping awake all over, sitting up at once in his bed, and looked all around him. Slowly he grew aware that he had been dreaming.

Someone had called his name. He had been dreaming; it was only in the dream.

Not his name. Not Moloquin. Some other name. Or just the word "boy," and him the only boy.

Dreaming.

Beside him Shateel lay sleeping, half-uncovered now, and he put forth his hand and drew the bearskin over her. Suddenly from the deep of his mind, part of the dream came back—a flash of the dream—the forest, the trees towering all around him, and from the distance, someone calling.

Not his name. The words that had called him before he had a name. Before he had a name for her who called him.

He shut his eyes. The dream was gone, even the feeling gone; with a sense of desperate loss he yearned after it, and after her who had called him once, before he had a name; he longed for that moment, that place, where he sat quiet and whole in the center of the forest, all the trees rising tall around him, while she called him.

From another part of the roundhouse came a shout, hoarse and loud and real. Again he pulled the heavy bearskin over his sleeping wife and sat up.

On the far side of the roundhouse someone cried out, "He's gone!"

Moloquin grunted. Here was something he could deal with. He thrust off the cloaking gloom of the dream and got heavily to his feet, took his axe down from the post North Star behind him, and went swiftly toward the voice. He was naked, and the night was cold, but his blood burned enough to keep him warm. He went straight into the back of the roundhouse, where Bahedyr was supposed to be imprisoned.

This part of the roundhouse was utterly dark. He walked by memory, one hand out before him to encounter posts and other obstacles. In the darkness around him were scurrying feet, and voices.

"He's gone, I tell you! Go look there!"

Moloquin filled his lungs; into the darkness he shouted, "Shut the roundhouse door!"

His voice boomed out through the building, and abruptly all other sounds stopped. All through the roundhouse, men froze, hearing him. Then suddenly there was a trampling of many feet as they ran to do his bidding.

"Light a lamp!" Moloquin shouted.

He trudged forward, sliding his feet over the floor, creeping forward into utter darkness. In his right hand he held the axe, ready to strike, and his left hand reached forward into the dark. He sniffed, smelling burned oil from a lamp, smelling stale sweat, smelling the fragrance of the grain stored nearby, and he went toward the smell of the grain, groping his way into the dark, until his foot caught in cloth lying on the floor.

He stooped and felt over the floor. A pile of rags lay there, and some rope. He raised the rope to his nostrils and on it smelled Bahedyr.

"Gone."

Now suddenly the light bloomed, behind him, reaching its long fingers forward among the posts of the roundhouse, casting shadows past him into the tight pack of the stores. He stood up. Bahedyr had escaped somehow, but he was too weak and sick to go far.

"Find him," he shouted, and struck with the axe at the nearest post. "Find him, Sickle—"

He strode back toward the door of the roundhouse. There the men were gathered, murmuring, and at his approach they spread out, facing him. Sickle was not among them.

"Where is he?" Moloquin walked in among the men, thrusting them away from him; he reached the door without finding either his prisoner or the guard, and his temper rose like a fist in his throat. He struck out with the axe again, and the blade bit deep into one of the posts of the door.

"Find him! I will take you all to the Pillar of the Sky if you do not find him—"

They rushed away. He unlatched the door and thrust it open and pounded out to the yard. The cold greeted him like a dash of icy water. He remembered he was naked; he remembered he was a fat old man. With his axe he slashed the air.

"Find him—I will kill you all—"

Through the door behind him came Shateel, wrapped in her cloak and carrying his bearskin coat. He turned his back on her, grateful, and let her put his clothes on him.

"Where is Sickle? He let him go—I'll kill him too—"

Abruptly Sickle was pushing toward him, coming in the gate of the roundhouse fence; after him came a great crowd of men. Moloquin bellowed wordlessly at them. Sickle turned toward him, straining; he was dragging something after him, and Moloquin relaxed.

It was Bahedyr, too nearly dead to walk. Sickle hauled him up before the chief and dropped him there at Moloquin's feet.

"Pagh!" Moloquin raised the axe at arm's length. "I should kill you now, and be done with it."

Bahedyr curled up into a ball at his feet. His face turned up toward his captor; his eyes shone. Moloquin lashed out at him with the axe, holding short, so that the blade passed just over Bahedyr's head.

The tormented man flinched away, and Moloquin laughed.

"What! Don't you long for death, Bahedyr? Don't you want to die? That's the only way you will escape me! Don't shrink back from it, Bahedyr—"

He swung the axe in great sweeping blows at the man cowering before him, each strike missing by a finger's breadth, and as he swung the axe, Moloquin capered in a strange dance, laughing and mocking.

"You cannot escape me alive, Bahedyr—no matter who helps you—" saying that, Moloquin turned his head and looked for Sickle in the crowd—"I alone can free you, Bahedyr—"

In the crowd, Sickle backed away, hiding himself among the others. The others pressed forward to watch: no one had ever seen Moloquin dance before.

"Bring Dehra here," Moloquin shouted; he leapt and struck around Bahedyr, the axe hissing in the air, cutting away the space on all sides of the man who crouched and whimpered in the dust, the blade sometimes grazing his skin or his hair. "Bring Dehra, let her see this, let her see what may become of her next—"

He glared at Shateel, standing in the doorway of the round-house, her hands hidden inside her bearskin cloak. If he frightened her with these threats against her daughter she showed no signs of it. He swung the axe up above Bahedyr, and for a moment, his arms stretched, the axe heavy in his hand, he thought, *End it now,* and his arm quivered with a lust for this power, to drive the axe down and destroy the man before him.

But if he did that, it would all be over. Instead he slashed the air by Bahedyr's dust-caked head, he whirled around again, leaping into the air.

Something else caught his eye. He lowered the axe, his head raised, his gaze on the sky, and a low exclamation left him. He took two steps forward, his eyes on the sky.

"What is that?" He pointed.

They all looked; they all turned together, with a rustle and hiss of their turning bodies, and looked into the sky, up at the great new star that burned there, brighter than the two gateway stars. They gasped, and many went down on their knees, folding their arms over their heads to shield them from the star. Moloquin gave a long howl like an animal.

"Barakal! Barakal—" he whirled around and flung the axe down, stabbing it deep into the ground beside Bahedyr, and with the bearskin flapping around him he ran out the gate in the round-house fence, ran away through the village, toward the Pillar of the Sky.

Sickle said, "He is brainsick. Some demon has taken power over him. He is mad."

Around him the little crowd stirred and murmured, and most turned away from him. Shateel, in the doorway of the roundhouse, watched him as he put out his hand, reaching for the man nearest him, his mouth open to say more about Moloquin. That man pulled roughly away, but others drew nearer; other men leaned toward Sickle, whispering. Agreeing with him. Shateel looked up into the black bowl of the sky, toward the fiery new star, and a shiver passed over her, as if the star had touched her.

Barakal said, "I do not know what it means, Opa-on. Perhaps it means nothing."

"Don't be a fool," Moloquin said. "If you do not understand it, that is your failure, not the star's."

Barakal shrugged. Long and pale, he seemed as unlike one of the People as his star was unlike the rest of the night sky. He said, "The Heavens are perfect in their order. Nothing is left out, nothing is unknown. Talk of meanings is of things that are unknown, things that are missing, and that must be drawn forth from what is known and not missing. In the perfection of Heaven, maybe there are no separate things at all, only an illimitable being."

Moloquin said, "I have no use for such words, Barakal."

He smiled as he said it. Barakal had amused him somehow. Shateel studied the tall young man; what he said had a strange effect on her, slipping by her, leaving no pictures in her mind. What he said had nothing to do with the People. His mind was wholly with the stars, he belonged to the stars, not to the People at all.

Shateel said, "Yet many will think the star means something. And they will say it means whatever it serves them to have others believe."

Moloquin shrugged. He sat in his litter, in the shade, at the center of the Pillar of the Sky, with his wife on one side of him and his son on the other. All around them were the sounds and bustle of the workmen, hammering on stone and dragging up logs and rope to raise stones. They had finished shaping the stone from the Old Camp; all morning they had been dragging it in through the gap in the embankment, and the air was full of dust.

Shateel said, "There is a runner here from my old village."

Moloquin nodded. "Let me see him."

She turned and with her eyes sought out the man who waited between the small gateways, and at her look he came forward. Shateel stepped back. The dust made her nose itch and her throat hurt. She was tired of standing at her husband's shoulder, milling all the world into words. Soon the year would turn, the spring would come, and the earth would soften to the hoe and the pick, to the first probing roots of seedlings. She took some reassurance from that: against the sudden appearance of new stars she could raise up the constancy of the year, the eternal return of the spring.

The runner was kneeling down before Moloquin, spouting words of praise and honor. Shateel laid her hand on her husband's shoulder. Since Bahedyr's betrayal, Moloquin had given the village into the keeping of one of his sons, a younger man even than Barakal. It was in the name of this young chieftain that the runner spoke. Yet when the runner appeared this morning in Moloquin's Village, he had come first to Shateel, to ask her help in delivering his message to Moloquin.

"Opa-Moloquin-on, we have had word from the northern villages that someone is attacking their herds of cattle, and we wish your permission to go and hunt them down."

"*Someone,*" Moloquin said. "Men? A bear? A pack of wolves? And what have you to do with the northern villages? Let them send to me themselves if they have need of me. You have other business. I need stones—I need two great stones from the Turnings-of-the-Year, and you are to get them for me. Tell him that."

The runner knelt down again, and again poured forth a river of words. From the far side of the Pillar of the Sky, suddenly, there was a shout.

Moloquin wheeled around toward the sound; Shateel twisted to see, and Barakal went swiftly over to find out what had happened. Moloquin turned back to the runner.

"Go to my son, bid him tend to what is his to do. Go."

The runner backed away until he nearly hit one of the uprights of the nearest Gateway; with his hand behind him he groped for the way out and was gone. Barakal came up beside Moloquin.

"They are ready to begin raising the stone."

"I will come," said Moloquin.

Shateel said, "Should you not have given more heed to the runner? It is spring—until the gardens are well grown we need the meat from the north. If someone is attacking the herds—"

Moloquin gripped her hand. "I will raise this stone," he said, low. "Raise this one, and close the ring. Then there will be time for all these other matters." He pressed her hand roughly to his face. "Have you no faith in me?"

"Moloquin," she said, and could say no more.

Barakal squatted down beside his father. "She is right. You

should pay some attention to what is going on, Opa-on—the People murmur against you, they will murmur more if there is no meat—"

"Pagh." Moloquin began to get up; he flung back the bearskin robe that covered his knees, reached for his axe, and prepared himself to get up onto his feet. "You make too much of it. They have whined and complained before, they have shrunk away before from the task, but they will do it. My People will not fail me. In small things they speak against me, but when the matter is great, when I need them, when I call them, they will come, they will obey me."

He put out his hand, and Barakal took it and helped his father rise up out of the litter; Moloquin grunted at the effort. He thrust his axe into his belt and swept the bearskin cloak around his shoulders. Shateel watched him go with heavy steps toward the work. His trust in the People moved her; she longed to believe him.

She could not believe him. His People had already failed him. He was alone in his dream, as he had always been alone. Before, he alone had always been enough. She hoped it went on that way. Quietly she followed him across the Pillar of the Sky.

Dehra lived in the hut of the star-watcher Barakal. Sickle waited until he saw Barakal far away from there, and went around to the hut and looked in the door.

She was asleep. She lay curled like a dog on a mat, without even a blanket over her, although the day was cool. Sickle on hands and knees crawled into the hut, but before he could rouse her she sprang awake, leapt up, still crouched below the low roof, and cocked her fist at him.

"Be easy!" Sickle slid backwards away from her, and raised both hands, palms out, to mollify her. She was ferocious: the demon who tenanted her mind would defend her against anything. "Be still, Ana-el, I have come to beg your favor, not to harm you."

"Ana-el," she said slowly, watching him, and wrapped her arms around herself. Her eyes glistened in the semi-darkness. She and the star-watcher were fit for each other: both strangers to everybody but themselves. She said, "What do you want, boy?"

"There is a story—" he cleared his throat. "There is talk, in the villages, that when Moloquin closes the ring—have you any knowledge of this?"

"Of what?" she said. She wiped her eyes with her fingers; sleep still clung to her like a veil of fog.

"That when Moloquin closes the ring the world will end. He is making a gateway, some say, and through it will come all the Over-world—" he gulped; he was babbling now, repeating words that had no real meaning for him, just words he had heard long ago that sounded ominous, to make his effect on her. "Once he makes his gateways, then the world shall be destroyed."

She blinked at him. "Who told you this?"

"Have you not seen the great star?"

"It is Barakal's star. He says there is no evil."

"Dehra—" he drew closer, his hands out, appealing to her. "When he has closed the ring he will kill us all, all his enemies."

"Are you his enemy?"

"I hate him," Sickle said, and was surprised to realize this was true.

She stared at him a moment. Tendrils of her hair hung around her face, her eyes were sunken, she looked suddenly older than any woman he had ever seen. His spine prickled up. What a fool he had been to come here—to think to seduce the demon in her. He slid his feet backwards.

"I have heard you," she said, clearly. She blinked at him. He went out, his hands shaking, wondering what use she would be.

Braced on its cradle of logs, the great stone from the Old Camp tilted up into the air, its foot overhanging the hole where it would stand. All around it the workmen bustled, making ready for the day's labor, and their dust rose in gusts and clouds, billowing on the early morning breeze.

Taller, heavier, moveless, the other stones stood there also, like great beings that watched the world, waiting for their brother. They loomed through the dust like monsters, and their long shadows spread out through the Pillar of the Sky and touched everyone.

Dehra hugged her arms around her, blinking. She hardly remembered what she was doing here. Behind her was the bank, which still gave her some shelter from the sun, and she drew back near to it. Moloquin was not yet here.

Without Moloquin she was lifeless. She thought about him every moment, she dreamt of him at night, a black brooding overhanging half-shaped enemy dappled with stars. During the day she went as close to him as she could, living on the power that surrounded him, hungry for more; sometimes she imagined she was eating him alive, consuming his soul.

She hated him. Her hatred was the purest and most sublime and uplifting feeling she had ever known; she would give it up for no one.

The workmen were coiling rope now, standing beside the great stone rising at its awkward angle; on the far side of the hole they had raised up three poles and bound them together at the top, and while she watched, shivering in the shadow of the bank, they flung their ropes up over the top of the three-legged tree. The coils uncoiled slowly through the dust.

Down the plain, behind her, someone shouted. Dehra got up and went to the opening in the embankment.

Moloquin was coming. Up through the dust and the slanting morning sunlight came a procession of men and women, indistinct in the dust, so that first she saw only the vast collective action of their arms and legs, the rhythmic motion of a single beast. In their beast, swaying above them, came Moloquin's litter, and now as it came nearer she could hear the jingle and clash of the ornaments, see the flash of the sun on the bronze and copper.

She stood up. Coppered with the sun, he approached her step by step, and she awaited him in an ecstasy, a bride for the bride-groom, and she never saw that her mother walked first, ahead of all the others, and passed by her without a word.

With Moloquin came Bahedyr, filthy and unable to walk, and they put him down into the hole in the ground, facing the stone they were about to raise. When this was done, and Moloquin, in his litter, was watching from one side, the work began.

Half the men went to the ropes; the others bent their backs to the levers that would raise the stone, and all waited for Moloquin's shout. Instead, another shouted.

"Wait," Dehra cried, and rushed in among them. "Do not do this—leave it!"

Moloquin stood up. "Take her. She is in the way." He grunted, kicking at the dirt, his black brows drawn down over his nose, his eyes gleaming. "She may harm herself here, take her away."

Dehra rushed at him, her hands raised. "Stop this—you must not do as you do. You will destroy us all! The world will end when you close the ring, Moloquin—"

At that, the people all around them began to mutter and turn to one another, and the whole great mass shifted and stirred in the morning sunlight.

Moloquin straightened. He cast a wide look around him, and with his hands on his hips he faced Dehra.

"She is brainsick. Look at her! Not a rag to cover her. She lives in a hole in the ground, like a dog—"

Dehra flung her arm up, shouting at him, contending with him. "Leave this! Stop it now, I say, in the name of Ael!"

At that Moloquin startled all over, as if she had struck him. His face went black with rage. In two strides he reached the girl; with one hand he seized her, and with the other he whirled up the great axe out of his belt. He thrust her down on the ground before him and he raised the axe at arm's length over his head, and between Dehra and the axe lay nothing but Moloquin's will.

The People screamed; Shateel too screamed; she hurried forward from the crowd and threw herself down over the body of her only child.

"No, Moloquin, no!"

"Get away from her," the chieftain shouted. He still had Dehra by one arm, and now he shifted his weight, the axe moved, ready to sever the arm, to strike beyond Shateel. "She has said that which I cannot forgive or ignore, Shateel—"

"Do not slay her!" Shateel sprang up, her hands out, her face lifted to his; she rose up into the face of his wrath, she laid her white hands on his chest, and spoke into the fury of his temper.

"Do not kill her, Moloquin—she has done wrong, but if you kill her, will she not be with you always, as Ladon is? Drive her away, send her far away, and then she will be alive and cannot torment you. But if you kill her, she will never leave you."

The whole People hushed, to hear this; all looked on Moloquin, waiting. All saw that Shateel's words had changed him. His furious look calmed. He lowered the axe, and with a contemptuous gesture he freed the girl who cowered beneath her mother. Straightening, he seemed tall as one of his great stones.

He said, "So let it be. Take her, now, to the tin mines. Let her work there in the mines until she dies. Take Bahedyr too! Let me be free of them both forever."

He turned away, and among the People many sighed and were grateful, and saw a great wound being healed. Some of the young men went to the hole where Bahedyr slumped, and dragged him up; the women came quietly toward the stones and took Dehra in among them, and drew her away. Moloquin went back to his litter and sat down, and Shateel went with him and stood beside him, her hand on his arm.

Then Moloquin said, "Raise the stone."

They hesitated. The murmur sprang up among them, like the whisper of the grass when the wind played in it, and their eyes were wide and white with fear. What Dehra had said remained with them even though she was gone down, dragged away over the bank. They dreaded the work now.

Moloquin stood up. "Do you deny me? Raise the stone!" He went forward from his litter; he tossed the axe behind him into his bearskins, and went to the stone, and took his place at one of the poles. "Now, come!"

One by one, they came forward. One by one, the men took up their levers and gripped the ropes, and with Moloquin among them they set to the work.

With a yell and a gasp, they flung themselves on the levers, they dragged on the ropes, and the stone lifted slowly up off its supports, creeping higher; at a shout from Moloquin, two men on each side rushed forward to jam another log under the weight. The men stepped back a moment, wiped their burning hands, took a deep breath, and began again.

The stone tipped up into the sun, and it slipped, its foot sliding down a little way into the hole before it. The men drew away again, resting, gathering themselves, and went forward, and leaned their backs into the work. They pried the stone up again, and this time the stone cracked.

The sound was like a thunderclap. The People screamed to hear it, and the workmen fled from it; they darted back in all directions, leaving the stone there hanging above the hole.

One remained. Moloquin remained there, gripping a lever, and he turned and shouted to them: "Come! Come—the stone is finding its place—come!"

They hesitated. Their faces wrung with worry, they hung there like dead leaves in the wind, that had no will of their own. He turned and swept them with his gaze.

"Come! Now, come!"

They heard him; this time they obeyed him. Reluctant, cowering, they crept back to the stone and took their places, and at his shouted order they heaved all their strength against the power of the stone.

Its foot slipped again. With a roar it rushed down into the hole. The stone heaved up off its supports. The ropes popped and lashed the air and the men ran madly to the edge of the hole, to kick and shovel in the dirt, to brace the foot of the stone. The stone swayed, it rocked from side to side, and its head swung across the sky; it leaned hard to one side and was about to fall in spite of them, and then again, it cracked.

The men howled. As one being they fled away from it. Only Moloquin remained with it. He shouted to them. He flung himself against the stone, his arms stretched up, his hands on the stone, striving to hold it upright, and his voice bellowed out.

"Come—come to me—now! Come!"

None moved. Safe outside the ring, they watched the stone sway, they watched Moloquin strive with it, they heard him cry for help, and they left him there alone. He stretched upward, trying to hold the swaying stone, and with a shattering crack the top of it broke.

It fell down through Moloquin's arms; as if he tried to lay it softly down, he sank with it to the ground. For a long time no one moved. All watched Moloquin, slumped down over the stone; all waited for him to get up, to rise again to his feet, and turn and punish them for their failures.

A black shadow swept over them. A great black crow flapped down from the sky, and with a beat of its wings it came to roost on Moloquin's shoulder, and at that they all knew he was dead.

For a moment, still, they waited, thinking he would come back to them. The crying of the wind was the only sound. Then, one by one, they understood. One by one, with a wail or a cry, they turned and fled away. Like waves of the sea, they ran away from the Pillar of the Sky and from Moloquin.

Barakal stood by the North Watcher and saw them go, and in a wild voice he called curses on them. In the confusion of his passions, one thought was clear: they had betrayed Moloquin, and that had caused his death. This was what the star had meant, Erwenda, the Messenger. He turned toward Moloquin, dead at the foot of the broken stone, with Shateel already kneeling beside him.

He nearly went to help her, but instead he looked around him, at the Pillar of the Sky, and in a rush of understanding he saw that now, with Moloquin dead, the circle would never be finished. They had come so close, and now the thing would never be done. He could not bear to look on it. He could not bear to live among these People any more. He turned his back to it all and walked away, out past the West Watcher, over the bank, and into the forest.

There was no mark on Moloquin, no blood, no broken bone. Shateel, bending over him, her hands on him, could find no sign that the stone had killed him.

She thought the People had killed him. When they abandoned him, they killed the heart in him.

Now no one remained but her. Even Barakal had gone. The wails and cries of the People drifted back to her from down the slope; the sound had changed a little. They were rallying, someone was gathering them. Sickle, perhaps, or some other she had no name for.

She wondered what would become of them, without Moloquin; could they find another such among themselves, or could they do without him? She doubted that. Yet their old way was gone, and she had no faith that they could recover it. They would stumble blindly on through the new, half-made world, seeking another Moloquin to take them home.

When Barakal's star rose again, Moloquin would lie at the foot of its light; he would follow its beams to Heaven. She made him ready. She dragged him away from the stone where he had died, hauling him in through the unfinished ring toward the Great Gateway, and there she laid him down on his back. His body was gross and shapeless; she imagined she could already smell it rotting. Overhead, the crows were gathering, their scythe-shaped shadows flashing over the ground around her. She paused once and looked up at the stones, rising around her like the ribs of a great skeleton, and the power of death overwhelmed her, the omnipotence of death. She bowed her head over Moloquin, her grief too superficial to matter against the power of death.

Around the feet of the stones he had raised, she gathered blades of grass, the first green shoots to show themselves in the new spring. She thought of him as a young man, when this place had been only a dream, when he lived in the forest with his people, when he built what other men built. Had he done no more, he would not have been Moloquin, who had called her forth from her selfish and useless and ingrown ways, had called her to a new and higher soul. That lifted her heart, to think of him as he had been—a star in the endless night. She spread the grass over him, telling him good-by, and then she went away and left him for the crows.

A NOTE ON THE TYPE

This book was set in a film version of a typeface called Baskerville. The face itself is a facsimile reproduction of types cast from molds made for John Baskerville (1706–1775) from his designs. Baskerville's original face was one of the forerunners of the type style known as "modern face" to printers—a "modern" of the period A.D. 1800.

Composed by Graphic Composition Inc.,
Athens, Georgia.
Printed and bound by Fairfield Graphics,
Fairfield, Pennsylvania.

Typography and binding design
by Virginia Tan.